This book is dedicated to my READERS. To those who have entered my crazy dream world and breathed life into my adventures and characters. Thank you for your kind words of encouragement, and for your enthusiasm. You make writing such an enjoyable experience, and I hope you'll stick around for more.

And as always…a special thank you to my beta readers, KARLA BOSTIC, KIMBERLY BELDEN, and HEATHER ADAMS. Also to my amazing editor, VICTORIA RAE SCHMITZ, and my publisher, SARAH DAVIS, who have been with me on this awesome journey. Love you ladies!

WHEN
DARKNESS
SURROUNDS,
LOVE
WILL LEAD
THE WAY.

BROKEN WINGS

ONE

"**D**AMN, THOSE STINKING EVIL BASTARDS!" Malachi yelled, pounding his fist on the table. "They just took out one of our cameras."

I could barely make out his booming voice. Everything hit me all at once, spinning out-of-control in a whirlwind. I felt nauseated and overwhelmed. My sweaty palms clasped over my face as I blacked out and fell to the floor with a thud.

"Hey, are you alright?" Dominic asked, kneeling down beside me. "You hit the floor like a ton of bricks."

"Yeah, I just—" I couldn't speak. The sudden rush of tears flowing from my eyes became my answer. It was all too much to bear.

Malachi's eyes were fixed on a small screen which gave him access to see everything going on outside. With six different camera views, he could see all the flashes of Darkling, desperately trying to find a way in.

There had been no sign of the Fallen, but they're smart. They used the Darkling to do their dirty work, and we all knew they were still out there...waiting.

"Hey, it's alright, Emma. Don't worry about the floor. It's fine," Dominic jested. "See?" He tapped the wood with his knuckles. "Not even a dent."

He offered me his hand, pulling me off the floor, before assisting me to one of the couches. "You should really get some sleep."

I sank down into the fluffy beige cushions, and pulled a throw blanket over me.

"He's right, Emma. There's nothing we can do but wait." The voice came from Samuel, my father. Just the thought—my father—seemed so odd.

I quickly wiped my face dry, and glanced at Alaine through the bedroom doorway. Her hands were covered in blood, and she looked weary, still trying to keep Caleb stable and alive.

James was at her side. I could tell they'd worked a lot together in the past because whenever she called for a medical instrument, he immediately handed it over.

My eyes flitted about the room, before they landed on Danyel's door. I didn't see any light in the crack of the doorway, so I assumed he was sleeping.

Sleep. I didn't think I'd know the meaning of that word for a while.

Samuel walked over and joined us in the living room, plopping down on the other couch. As he landed, he winced in pain. He'd broken a few ribs from his recent encounter with the Fallen, but still managed to smile.

His room had now become the operating room.

"I guess I'll be sleeping out here tonight," he said.

"No. Please take the last room. You need it much more than I do," I offered. "Besides, I'm going to stay out here tonight."

He deserved a warm bed, especially with his injuries.

It hit me how little I knew about him. I knew absolutely nothing, besides his name and that he was my birth father. There were so many unanswered questions…seventeen years' worth.

"No. I can't take your room, Emma," he replied.

I knew he was just being polite.

"Suit yourself. I'm already stuck in a comfortable position, so that lonely bed in there will be totally wasted."

"You're too kind, Emma. Even though I know you're doing it on my account."

"I'm not. I swear. I really want to be out here. I like the couch. It's much softer than the bed," I said with a smile.

The real reason I wanted to be in the living room was because I wanted to be close to the door, just in case Kade came back with reinforcements. I had to know he was okay.

"Thank you, Emma. I appreciate it," Samuel said. He slowly rose off of the couch, and gave me a quick kiss on the top of my head.

"You're welcome. Good night."

"Good night, Sweetheart." He shuffled off into the room and snapped the door shut behind him.

My mind drifted to Kade.

Where was he?

Was he safe?

Thoughts of his return melded into memories of my parents. I missed them so much.

Before the full pain began to set in, Malachi spoke. "Don't worry, Emma. Kade will be fine," he said, as if he could read my mind.

"How far is it to Midway?" I asked.

"There is a portal about eighty miles away."

"Portal?" I asked. "Wait. Did you just say *eighty* miles?"

"Yes, on both accounts. There are portals set up around the earth, which transport us to and from Midway, and also the Otherworlds. It's mostly for those who don't have wings."

"Yet! We don't have wings...*yet*," Dominic butted in. He wandered back to the kitchen table with a handful of medical supplies, attempting to tend to his own injuries.

"I thought all angels had wings?"

"Not all. Guardians, don't have wings. Eventually, when we move up in rank, we will earn our wings; but some spend their eternity without them."

"Why wouldn't they give Guardians wings?" I questioned.

"We are sent into the mortal world, and need to blend in, looking as human as possible. Showing our wings to mortals is forbidden, so as not to be tempted, the Guardians aren't given any. However, we are damn good looking, but that can't be helped. It's all part of the total Angelic package," Dominic snickered, followed with chuckles from Malachi and Alexander.

"Sure. Whatever." I rolled my eyes.

comforting, and actually looked...concerned.

I was now shoulder-deep, with arms raised above the thick muck gripping my chest, slowly constricting it. I reached a hand out toward the red eyes, and felt something grasp it...

"Wake up, Emma, wake up! It's Kade. Hurry," a panicked voice yelled.

I sat up, breathless, my heart frantically beating. I was trying to focus, when all the lights clicked on.

Malachi was at the front door, yanking it open. Dominic and Alexander ran to assist him. As soon as the door swung open, Kade fell limp into Malachi's arms, and all I saw was red. Dominic and Alexander pushed around them and ran down the tunnel with their weapons drawn.

"Kade? Kade. Hey man, are you with me?" Malachi questioned, shaking him. He quickly carried him to the couch across from me.

The only answer was a groan, but his eyes remained closed.

"What the hell happened to him?" I gasped, frozen in place. He looked like he was badly injured.

I jumped up off the couch, and knelt at Kade's side, holding his hand in mine. It felt very cold and weak. Then a most horrifying realization hit me like a brick.

There was no heat, no surges, no feeling of euphoria...nothing.

"Oh my God. Something's really wrong with him. He can't die, right? Tell me he can't die!" Hot tears welled in my eyes as I looked at Malachi for answers. I couldn't feel Kade and it scared the hell out of me.

"We cannot die unless our heads are cut off, or our hearts ripped out, or pierced with an immortal blade," Malachi answered.

"But why isn't he responding?" I couldn't tell what kind of injuries he had because he was soaked with blood.

"I don't know. Maybe his injuries are too extensive for him to heal quickly enough. I've never seen an angel in this bad of a condition. Especially, Kade. He's too quick for someone to have beaten the shit out of him like this," he exhaled.

I became even more worried, knowing Malachi was concerned.

Dominic and Alexander came back in and secured the door.

"It's clear. Kade was the only one who made it through," Alexander announced.

"Alaine!" Malachi yelled. Within a few seconds, her face appeared in the doorway.

"Yes?" she responded from the room where Caleb was still under her watchful care.

"We need your help in here, now," he answered.

I heard Alaine quickly giving instructions to James, and then she exited the room.

"What's wrong?" she asked. Her eyes suddenly locked onto Kade's lifeless body. Gasping, she hurried toward us.

I moved out of the way so she could get to him.

Her eyes furrowed as she checked his pulse. "Malachi, help me get his shirt off."

He lifted the upper body, while Alaine tugged the shirt over his head and dropped it on the ground. Kade moaned, but was still unconscious. There were two noticeable puncture wounds in his chest, blood flowing from each of them. He also had a deep gash on his right shoulder.

"Dominic, bring my medical bag. Quickly," Alaine instructed.

In seconds Dominic was at her side, passing her the bag. She quickly opened it and started pulling out supplies. She took a syringe and vial of fluid, and pushed it into Kade's arm, then started to clean out his wounds.

Alexander went into the kitchen to watch the monitors.

"What happened to him?" she asked.

"I don't know. I saw him on the monitor, entering the tunnel, but didn't see what happened before that," Malachi answered.

"Were there any others?"

"None that we know of. He showed up alone."

"Where's his vial?" Alaine asked in an urgent tone.

"He keeps it in his right pocket," Malachi answered, with narrowed eyes.

"Get it and pour some into his mouth, immediately." She continued to clean out one of the deeper wounds on his chest.

"Why? It doesn't work on immortals," he responded, confused.

"I know that. Something's happened to him. I don't understand how, or why, but right now, Kade is…mortal."

"*What*?" The room exploded with gasps and murmurs.

"Look," she said, tilting his head to the side. She pushed the hair back from behind his ear, revealing nothing. His mark was gone. There was nothing, not even a scar.

I'd never really seen Kade's mark, so I didn't know what I was looking for. From what I learned, each angel was born with a special mark, unique to them alone. Their insignia. It was that mark which distinguished them from all others.

The room fell silent.

Could Alaine be right? Was Kade really mortal? And if he was…how?

It was difficult to watch him lying there, quiet and still, beaten and barely hanging on. Just a few hours ago, he was strong, fearless, and full of life—slaying demons and saving my life. He was my hero, my knight-in-shining-armor.

"Just do it Malachi, and hurry," Alaine scolded.

Malachi must have been in shock over her last words. He quickly snapped into motion, reached into Kade's pocket, and pulled out the blue vial. Twisting the top off, he poured half of the contents into Kade's mouth. He coughed a bit, but swallowed. A few seconds later, he groaned, and his eyes slid open. They were red and glazed over, filled with pain.

"Kade," Alaine nudged. His eyes rolled back and closed again.

"We need to get him stabilized so we can get some answers." Alaine looked weak and weary.

"How is our perimeter?" Malachi called to Alexander, who was watching the monitors.

"Fine so far. I don't think they saw where he came in. Right now, I can only see about three Darkling wandering around the outside, and they look completely lost. Freaking idiots. There are no signs of the Fallen, and I'm pretty sure the Darkling won't find the entrance anytime soon. We should be safe, at least until morning."

"The Fallen are definitely out there, waiting. We just need to be ready in case they do find the way in," Malachi answered.

"If they do, I'll alert the rest of you," he chimed, wiggling an air horn in his fingers.

"Yes, don't forget to keep your weapons close," Alaine warned.

I spent the next few hours watching her carefully stitch and bandage Kade's wounds. I didn't move an inch. I just sat still, watching her fingers work like magic. She worked tediously, until her work was finally complete. She definitely knew what she was doing.

"Nothing vital was punctured, so he should be fine after lots of rest," she whispered loudly enough for me to hear.

"Malachi, could you please take Kade into the middle room? Danyel is in there now, but it's closer and will be easier for me to check-up on both Caleb and Kade. I hope Danyel doesn't mind."

"Sure," he answered.

"And please give him one more dose from the vial before you leave." He nodded and carefully lifted Kade.

A few minutes later, Danyel stumbled out of the room carrying an extra blanket and pillow. He looked horrible, like he'd just been awakened from the dead. He must have been out cold, because he didn't move with all the commotion earlier.

His black hair was disheveled and the whites in his eyes were a bright red, but he seemed to be fine with crashing on the couch across from me. He plopped down on his back, threw his hands behind his head, and stared blankly at the ceiling. I wasn't sure if I should try and make conversation, but I wanted to at least give him my gratitude for saving my life earlier.

I waited a few minutes, in complete silence, before I finally built up enough nerve.

"I didn't get a chance yet to say thank you, you know, for saving my life tonight. You didn't have to do what you did. You put yourself in danger for me, and for that...Well, I just wanted to say thank you," I said softly.

A smile grew on his face, and after a minute or so, he flipped over to his side and faced me.

"I did what I had to so you could get free, not for you to come right back into the middle of danger," he sighed.

"I know, but it wasn't really my idea. They were all going in for Caleb, and didn't want to leave me behind. Alaine insisted I go with them. However, it *was* my idea to go in for Caleb alone. I just figured if I could get Lucian's attention on me, they wouldn't be ready for an attack. I realized it was a risk, but we didn't have much of a choice."

"Well, it was a very dangerous decision. Your father and I were ready to die, and you...well, you could have easily been killed. I could see it in Lucian's eyes. The marks on the back of your neck had completely confounded him. It was something he'd probably never seen before; something that has only been talked about. Until now that is."

"Angels only have one mark?"

"Yes, and it's always behind their right ear."

"They are all different?"

"Yes, except for the case of the Nephilim. The Nephilim are given the mark of their pureblood parent, and the mark is on the back of their neck, at the base of the skull. But you have a Nephilim mother, and a Pureblood father, so you were given both marks. I have never seen Alaine's mark, but whatever Lucian saw, brought a bit of fear into his eyes."

That had me baffled. I wondered if Alaine knew who her birth father was.

"Will you tell me the story behind the prophecy?" I questioned.

"Sure." He exhaled. "But there's really not much more to tell you."

I sat up on the couch, eager to hear even a little bit more.

Maybe there was something I'd missed in the past—something I could gain from hearing again. It meant more now that I was being hunted.

Alexander and Malachi were in the kitchen with their eyes glued to the security monitors, and Dominic was passed out at the kitchen table. Alaine was going in between Kade and Caleb's rooms, with James assisting her. Samuel, who had taken my room, must have been sleeping because the light that had been shining under the doorway earlier was now off.

Danyel moved back to staring at the ceiling. He had a distant look in his eyes, a look of rewinding past events, trying to get to the one pertaining to the prophecy. He sucked in a deep breath and began.

"It was hundreds of years ago, when a Demon Seer had a vision. In that vision he saw a child born with a double mark. This child was born of both Pureblood and Nephilim, with a power so great, it superseded those of any other immortal, except the creator. After the child's transformation, it would have to choose a side. Darkness or light. Whichever side it chose, would have the power to rule." He turned and looked at me. "Can you imagine what's running through Lucian's mind right now? He was standing right next to the child with the double mark. The very child who could make him the most powerful being in the Otherworlds, next to God himself."

I sat there in awe and suddenly realized my mouth was gaping wide open, so I snapped it shut.

"That is *so* crazy," I said in a complete zone. I realized I sounded like a child. But pffft. What did they expect? I was only seventeen and recently learned I wasn't completely human. That humanity was actually the smallest part of my genetic makeup.

"The Seer was talking about you, Emma. You are that child in the prophecy. You are one of a kind, and there has never been another born like you. I'm almost certain Lucian has figured out the meaning of your mark. If I'm correct, he will stop at nothing to capture you, and force you to become a slave under his will. He's cruel, evil, and craves power like a drug. He is determined to rule the Underworld. If he cannot get you to conform to his will, then he'll stop at nothing to kill you and everyone you love. His philosophy is, and has always been…if he can't have you, no one will."

Holy hell! That was one *crazy* pill to swallow. I went from being a girl who dreamt of one day kissing a boy, attending prom, and graduating, to being number one on Hell's top wanted list.

My new life would most likely consist of choosing a comfortable pair of running shoes, and learning to shoot a gun, or swing a sword. The only perks of this new life was getting to hang out with gorgeous, kick-ass Guardians, and my birth parents.

"You don't have to worry, Emma. You have a great team of Guardians surrounding you. Midway sent their best to protect you and Alaine, and they will fight, to their last breath, to keep you alive. As for your father and I…well, we have now joined in this particularly complicated crusade. It will be an exciting new journey for the both of us; keeping you alive and safe until your eighteenth birthday." His smiling eyes were comforting.

Danyel was very handsome, and now he had showered and shaved, he looked in his mid-twenties. His long, onyx hair was pulled back into a tight ponytail, and his dark brown eyes almost looked black. The muscles on his arms were defined, as they were on the rest of his tall frame. I wondered how old he really was.

"Thank you," I breathed. There was so much more I wanted to know, more I wanted to ask, but the next question just popped. "So, how did you meet Samuel?"

I still felt a little uncomfortable referring to him as my father, because I'd only found out who he was just a few hours ago. He had saved my life a few times though, which was a *huge* plus.

"Well," he began, "after the Fall, most of us trained to become warriors. There were a few who stuck out and were given rank, and your father was one of them. I was a bit younger than he, and was sent to him. Your father became my partner, best friend, and mentor. He taught me everything I know about fighting and survival.

"Together we were undefeated, and accomplished every task thrown at us. We were, what the mortals would call, bad asses." A large grin grew on his lips. "We were born to fight. It was in our blood, and something we knew we'd do for the rest of our lives. But after the centuries passed by, we began to question our motives and what we were fighting for. It seemed that everything we were fighting for was in vain.

"We fought against angels, who were once our brothers, over

human souls and dominion over the earth. It's been a never-ending war. Although immortals can be killed, it is very difficult to do so. Angels are skilled and train exactly like the Fallen. Once together, then divided...we fought amongst ourselves. It all became tiresome and fruitless. If I could go back, I would have stayed in Heaven, and I know your father feels the same. We were banished for all eternity. Once we chose, we could never go back."

"Never?" I breathed.

"Never," he sadly echoed.

"Well, now that you are assisting the good guys, maybe they'll take that into consideration. Your good deeds should count for something, shouldn't they?"

"Unfortunately, it doesn't work that way. We are outcasts, and have killed hundreds of Heaven's angels. There is no way we could ever make it back."

"Well, I think you should ask. If I ever meet God, I will make it a point to put in a good word for you. It wouldn't hurt to try. If they say no, you can always go rogue, like Lucian."

Danyel laughed out loud.

"Huh? What? I'm up," Dominic blurted. He jumped to his feet from a deep sleep. His eyes were bloodshot, and he was holding his hand out like he had his weapon in it, but it was empty.

Danyel rolled with even more with laughter, and Malachi and Alexander joined him.

"Dom, go back to sleep. Emma and Danyel are just having a conversation," Malachi scolded.

Dominic ambled over to us, grabbed a pillow from the couch,

and tossed it on the floor in the corner of the room. Then, he plopped down on top of it. "Keep the noise down please. Some of us are trying to recover," he slurred, his voice muffled by the pillow. In less than a minute, he was out cold, snoring.

"He's right. We all need our rest so we can heal," Danyel said, rolling onto his back. "Goodnight, Emma. It was a pleasure meeting you again and getting to know you a little better," he said, turning his head to me with a smile.

"Goodnight," I answered.

"Goodnight!" Dominic yelled. We all turned to look at him, but his face was to the wall.

"What the hell, Dom?" Alex blurted. "Just go to sleep!"

Everyone laughed, and then the room fell eerily silent.

The rest of the night was spent tossing and turning. I couldn't help but think about Kade, and what happened to him.

Was it even possible for an angel to become human?

He must have really pissed someone off in the higher authorities, because he didn't even come back with reinforcements. And now, we were on our own, still trapped underground.

All these questions and more bombarded my brain. I laid there, listening to the not-so-wonderful symphony of the Guardian's snoring. I guess snoring wasn't only something mortals did. It was just my luck it was universal.

I laid in the dark for what seemed like hours, while constant questions and thoughts swirled in my mind.

I didn't remember when, but sometime during the night, I finally passed out.

TWO

"WHY THE HELL WOULD YOU do something so freaking stupid?" someone quietly shouted, waking me from slumber.

"I agree. That was a pretty stupid move, bro. I can't believe you did that, and for a girl?"

That was Alexander.

"You don't understand," Kade rebutted.

"Hey now, everyone quiet down. What's done is done, and we can't do anything about it. We just need to figure out our next move," Alaine snapped.

I wiped the sleep from my dry eyes, and pushed up a bit to see what all the commotion was. Everyone, except Caleb and Samuel, was gathered around the kitchen table. Kade was seated at the head, his face buried in his hands. My heart began to beat a little faster, and my stomach twisted happily inside.

Thank God he was alive, despite the fact he looked very weak and pale. Why was he out of bed?

"Why didn't Midway send any backup?" Malachi growled.

"They said our situation wasn't something they could be directly involved with. They weren't given permission, and that came directly from the top. This is something that needs to be settled between the Fallen. Whatever dispute there is between Lucian and Lucifer, must be settled by them.

"Ephraim, the head of Midway, told me our best bet is to go directly to Lucifer himself. His fire for revenge will be rekindled once he learns there is a way to get back at Lucian," Kade explained.

"And how is Lucifer supposed to hear out about our predicament?" Dominic asked.

"That's obvious. Go to Hell, Dom," Danyel interjected.

Dominic stood to his feet and glared at Danyel. "What did you just say to me?"

"I said go to Hell, as in actually go there. We need to make a plea to Lucifer. If we can get him to see what Lucian is doing, then he might want a piece of the action. Lucifer has been waiting for a chance to get back at Lucian, and this just might be it. This *might* be our only hope," Danyel responded.

"I would never send any of my boys into Hell, or risk any of their lives," Alaine said firmly. There was an obvious strain in her voice. "Besides, none but human souls or Fallen are allowed to enter Hell."

"*Exactly,*" Kade exclaimed.

His weak eyes glanced up at Alaine, and she stared sadly back at him. She sighed and nodded slightly, like she understood whatever he was trying to say.

"So, that's why you did it," Dominic said sympathetically, patting Kade on the shoulder. "It was still a dumb move, bro."

"I had to," Kade said in a quieted tone. "I'm her Guardian, and it's my duty to protect her."

"But you're no good to her as a human," Malachi sighed in concern.

"The only way we can get Lucifer to listen to us, is to have Emma speak to him directly. He has a soft spot for the Nephilim, because his only son is one. If Emma can convince him Lucian has vowed to kill every last one, including his son, he might join us. Yes, it's a risk, but it also might work. Emma hasn't transformed yet. She is still human and can enter," Danyel noted.

"No! No way. I will never allow it," Alaine shouted. She stood and pounded her fists on the table. Her big, brown eyes glared at Danyel.

"Alaine, it's the *only* chance we have. Midway said it themselves, they are not getting involved. We cannot fight Lucian on our own, and right now, even though it would be the last thing we'd want to do, going to Lucifer is our only option. If we don't, Lucian will kill every one of us. He must be stopped. I'm only suggesting this because if Emma is the one in the prophecy, we have a fighting chance."

"Never. *You* can go Danyel, but I will not send my daughter into Hell. Lucifer will kill her if he finds out about her, or he'll keep her for himself and do God-knows-what with her. I forbid it, and that's the last I *ever* want spoken about it," Alaine yelled. Tears streamed down her face. "I'm going to check on Caleb," she said, whipping her face. She walked into the room where Caleb was, and shut the door behind her.

"She's right," Kade said. "Emma can't go down there, and whoever does will be going on a suicide mission. But if it means a chance that she'll live, then I'll go and speak to Lucifer myself."

"It won't work, Kade. Lucifer won't speak to you. You've become an insignificant mortal, something he despises. Mortals aren't allowed near him, let alone speak to him. You probably won't even make it past Hell's first level, and there are five total. Each level more deadly than the last," Danyel said sadly.

Just then I snapped myself back into reality. The whole conversation, the one everyone else was having, was revolving around me. Yet, I was sitting in the very next room, in the dark, watching, listening, and letting them decide *my* fate.

They didn't even attempt to wake me, or ask me what I thought about this whole situation. My life was no longer my own. I was one, out of how many other innocents, who were being hunted and killed for selfish, stupid reasons, and all because of one, idiotic Fallen named Lucian.

He'd already killed my mortal parents, and now he was going to kill the rest of the people I loved? No way. I wasn't going to lie around, pretending to sleep, while everyone planned their possible deaths—especially if there was a chance I could save them. Even if it was a small chance, it was still a chance, and worth risking.

I felt a spark from deep within, and my mouth took on a life of its own.

"So, do I get a say in what happens with my life?" I stood up from the couch.

Every head turned and every eye steeled on mine, looking more surprised than anything.

"No, Emma. You're still human and only seventeen, which makes you a minor. So, Alaine has the final say," James answered.

It would be him to give an answer like that. He was the closest to her, and the oldest of the bunch, aside from Samuel and Danyel.

"Well, I don't accept that answer. If we do nothing but sit here, we're as good as dead. They *will* eventually find a way in, and Lucian will kill every last one of us. I agree with Danyel. If we have the slightest chance, we should take it. At least we'll be fighting for something that could possibly save us all," I said, proud of myself for standing up. It was liberating.

There was complete silence. Everyone stayed still, probably letting what I said, sink in. I knew I was right. I just needed them to agree with me. If I stood firm, I knew I could change their minds. They knew all about fighting, and not giving up.

"I'll do it," I said loudly, breaking the silence. "I'll go and speak to Lucifer."

"If you're going, I'm definitely going," Kade said, with a wide smile. His hazel eyes glimmered, telling he was in agreement.

My heart swelled as I looked at his handsome face. I wanted to run to him, wrap my arms around his neck, and hold him. I was so glad to see him back, even though he looked so weak.

"I'll go too," Danyel added. "You'll need someone to guide you."

"And you know that if you are going, Emma, I'll be there to protect you. It is my duty as your father," Samuel said, walking out from the bedroom, drying his wet face.

I suddenly had a *Lord of the Rings* flashback…the moment they all decided to go on the quest with Frodo. Then, a picture of Jeremy and Lia, flashed in my mind. The movie was Jeremy's favorite, and I could picture them jumping at the chance to be my companions on this quest. But thank God they weren't, because there wasn't an athletic bone in either of their bodies and they'd probably both end up dead.

With a large smile on his face Samuel walked up to Danyel and greeted him with a warm hug.

"It's so nice to see you *alive*, dear friend," Danyel said. He patted Samuel on his shoulders, and then pulled him into another bear hug.

This was the first time they'd seen each other since they were captured by Lucian, and it must have been the first time they'd actually had a chance to speak.

"Yes, and you too, friend," Samuel exhaled loudly. "But easy. My ribs are still on the mend."

"Sorry," Danyel apologized, releasing his grip.

"Danyel, thank you for saving my daughter," Samuel said kindly, turning to me with a smile.

"How could I not? When I looked into her eyes, it was as if I were looking into the eyes of my old friend. I could not sit by and allow the fate of her father to become her own." Danyel's brow furrowed, and his eyes saddened. "And what did happen to you Samuel? How did you manage to come back from the dead after all

23

these years?"

"It's a long story my friend, and too much to explain right now. But, it looks as if we will get to spend some time together. I'm sure there will be a chance for us to talk."

"That sounds good," Danyel grinned.

"Well, it looks like we will be together on another mission. At least this time we will have a chance to redeem ourselves," Samuel said. They both laughed.

"You better keep her safe, Samuel," Alaine appeared in her doorway, sobbing. She'd been listening the whole time. "You keep her safe, and bring her back to me. You both better come back to me."

"I will guard her with my life, but I cannot make you any promise greater than that," he breathed, opening his arms to her. She walked into his embrace and wept.

I was surprised to see Alaine give in. And as mind-blowing as it all seemed, we were going on a quest. A quest into the depths of Hell, to save not only myself, but Alaine, the Guardian's, and any other Nephilim whom might have survived.

My fellowship was Kade, Danyel, and Samuel. All had proven themselves, and saved my life on several occasions. Each was a hero.

"We still have a lot to plan, like getting you guys out of here in one piece and making sure the Fallen don't kill you before you get to the portal," Malachi stated. "Plus, Kade will definitely need another day to rest, being that he is mortal now. It wouldn't hurt for Samuel and Danyel to have another day to recover as well."

I still couldn't wrap my head around the fact that Kade was

human, and it scared me. He was now just as fragile as I was.

"Did anyone update Thomas on what's been happening?" Alaine asked.

"No, and there's no way of getting in touch with him now. Those damn demons must have found the box and cut the wires, because there is no service. The last time we talked was last night, before they left and were attacked," Malachi said. "We'd told Thomas they were on their way home with Caleb. He must know something went wrong by now. He knows where we are, so I'm pretty sure he'll try and figure out a plan to get us out."

James butted in. "I hope he stays put. He's one against, who knows how many Darkling and Fallen out there? I wouldn't doubt it if Lucian is watching Alaine's house, or is right outside this bunker, just waiting for us to exit. There's not much Thomas would be able to do anyway. Besides, he can't leave Courtney and the others alone; he's the only Guardian there. We're on our own."

"Well, I'm going to make some breakfast, and then we can discuss our options after." Alaine wiped her tears, and headed into the kitchen.

"I'll help," I said, offering my services. I used to love helping my other mother in the kitchen. It was our time of bonding, since she had work and I had school, which gave us little alone time.

"We'll have pancakes," she said, gathering ingredients and placing them on the counter. The pancake batter was premixed, and all we had to do was add water. Alaine did the frying, and everything was served on paper plates.

After everyone ate their fill, we all sat around the table. The only one not present was Caleb, who was still in the room sleeping from the pain medication.

"I think the only way to get out of here is to just charge out and fight," Malachi spoke first. "Once we clear the field, the four of you can make your escape."

"Well, how far is it to Hell?" I asked. As soon as the words left my lips, they sounded so ridiculous, I laughed out loud. A few seconds later, the whole table was laughing with me, and even Alaine had a smile on her face.

At least we could laugh about it right now. I looked at all of the faces around the table and hoped we could all be together again.

"The closest portal to Hell is in the town of North Pole. It sits in Santa's workshop, directly behind his chair," Malachi said.

I burst into laughter again. "You're kidding me, right? The place where Santa lives and happy Elves sing and make toys?" I answered in a snarky tone.

"Who do you think created Santa? The real man, Nicholas, lived over two-thousand years ago. He was a Christian man, a man of faith, a Bishop, a Saint, and known for his anonymous giving's to children. His story was passed down through the generations, but Lucifer thought it brilliant to take and twist the meaning.

"He used the story as a distraction, to haze the true meaning of Christmas, and replace it with a chubby man in a red suit, who would travel the world in one night, fulfilling worldly desires of children - toys, decorations, twinkly lights, feasts…yadda yadda.

"Christmas has become his ploy. What was once a time for celebration of life and love has now become about getting the biggest and best gifts. Most mortals have become spoiled and ungracious, and fail to appreciate the things right around them. They forget that Christmas is about love, and God's perfect, selfless gift. So, ultimately...Lucifer's ploy is working," Malachi answered.

Alexander blurted, "Yeah, and didn't you know that if you twist the word Santa a bit, you get—"

"Satan," I breathed figuring it out. But even if that wasn't what it was meant for, it seemed like a damn good explanation.

I wasn't expecting that, and it really made me feel bad for all the times I begged for gifts, and wasn't grateful for the ones I received and didn't want.

"Wow," was the only word that crept from my mouth.

"Yep. Through the years, Lucifer's learned to play dirty. Human minds are soft and easy to bend and mold. Most will just follow, never questioning. They are like sheep being led to slaughter.

"Given, there are a few that rise up, and see the truth for what it really is, but they are usually seen as outcasts, preposterous, and maniacal for going against the majority. Mortals are a sad, ignorant race, and Lucifer thrives off of that," James sighed.

"And we're going to him for help?" I questioned, starting to doubt this whole quest. "If he's as cunning as you say he is, then what's to stop him from tricking us?"

"There's no way of really knowing, Emma, and that's the risk we'll be taking. Right now, he's the only one who can stop Lucian. Because there is a huge rift between them, Lucifer might be open to listening. This will be a great chance for him to seek vengeance. Yes, Lucifer is cunning, but more than that, he loves power and revenge.

"Lucian wants to rule over the Fallen, and has always questioned Lucifer's power. He's taken part of the Fallen army with him, and outright defied him. But if I know Lucifer, he'll want to put him in his place. He's planning something, I'm sure of it. I'm a bit surprised it's taken this long," Danyel noted.

If anyone knew about the Fallen and Lucifer, it would be him and Samuel.

"Danyel, I heard you say there were five levels of Hell. I thought there were nine circles," I questioned, remembering a paper I did in school on Dante's Inferno.

"You must be referring to Dante's Inferno," he grinned. "It was a book, written by a man who'd mixed religion with his own private concerns; concerns primarily of his enemies. He was a poet and a writer, in which war, exile, and other fateful events, caused his heart to harden. Ultimately, disgust and bitterness with his enemies, set in motion the outlines of the inferno, and his pages became a place of eternal damnation for all those he despised."

Wow. I was getting re-schooled by the Fallen themselves, and a lot of it was going right over my head. I guess I'd get the hands-on experience of Hell soon enough.

"Well, if there's a chance it will save us, then I'm in," I spoke.

Yeah. I was talking brave now, knowing I'd have the three of them with me, but right now, we were all safe and together. Tomorrow my words and bravery would be tested, if we could even escape this place. I just hoped I wouldn't start screaming and crying when the action hit, proving my mortal chicken-ness.

"Don't worry, Emma. We'll make sure you get the chance,"

Dominic chimed, with a wide smile on his face.

"Yeah! We'll kick ass for you tomorrow!" Alexander added, giving knuckles to Dominic.

Their colliding fists would have shattered any human hand, but after they crashed their knuckles together, they laughed.

Immortals.

At least they were fun.

Samuel turned to Danyel and placed a hand on his shoulder. "When we escape from here, I'll take Emma and you'll take Kade." Danyel nodded, but Kade's brow furrowed.

My heart was breaking inside for him, thinking about how he must be feeling. Probably helpless, and now, hearing he was going to be carried by a Fallen...that must suck.

It all seemed so strange, like a horrible nightmare. Just last night, Kade was carrying *me* as we flew effortlessly through the forest making our escape. I could picture him fighting and killing the Darkling with ease. So strong. So fearless.

I couldn't believe he'd chosen to become mortal just so he could travel with me into Hell. He was thinking about me over himself. Still trying to be my protector. I hoped I could make it up to him one day.

Wait a minute.

My mind started to whirl, and my heart thumped loudly.

Kade was *human*, which meant he was no longer a pureblood.

Did that mean we actually stood a chance of being together, without any law or bond binding us?

"Emma? Emma, did you hear what I said?" Alaine waved a hand in front of me.

I snapped myself from my blissful thought, and instantly felt my face flush with heat.

"I—I'm sorry. My mind was—was somewhere else," I stammered. Thank goodness none of them could read minds. That would have been embarrassing.

"I wanted to know if you would go and keep an eye on Caleb for a bit, while we discuss a few of the details. He should be fine, but he might be waking up soon. If he does, he will be very thirsty. I've put a pitcher of water and a glass on the table next to him."

"Sure," I said, getting up from my seat.

"Thanks, sweetheart," she said with a smile.

"No problem." I had a feeling this was her nice way of sending me out of the room, which most likely meant there were details they didn't want me to know.

I opened the door to Caleb's room, and quietly snapped it shut behind me.

"Emma?" Caleb said in a sleepy voice.

"You're up?" I turned to see his pale face.

His eyes looked like they'd sunken, leaving black rings around them, and his head and arms were wrapped in bandages. Using maximum effort, he tried to sit up, but fell back down again. I rushed over to his side and helped him back up. His lips were cracked and dry.

"Are you thirsty?"

He nodded, his eyes were still heavy.

I grabbed the glass and filled it with water. "Here," I said, handing it to him.

He slowly raised his hand, took the cup, and gulped it all down.

"Do you want some more?" I asked.

"No, thank you," he answered, lying back down. He winced in pain, his eyes clinched tight, and his breath became shallow.

"I'll go get Alaine." I was worried, and just about to turn when he grabbed my arm.

"No. I'm alright," he said. "Please stay."

"Alright. Are you sure you're okay?"

"Yeah, I just laid down a bit too fast. Alaine said I have a few broken ribs, and they hurt like hell if move too fast. Actually, if I move period."

"I know. I had a broken rib once." My thoughts went back to the airport bathroom. It was only a few days ago, but it seemed like forever.

I took a chair from the corner of the room and set it next to his bed.

"Emma, can I ask you a question?"

"Sure," I said, taking in a deep breath. I wasn't sure what was going to come out of his mouth because he was medicated, and some crazy things could come from medicated mouths.

"What are you?"

"Huh?" I shook my head, confused by his question. "What do you mean?"

"I know about Alaine. I know that she's a Nephilim, and the rest of them are Guardians. Alaine explained it all to me a while back because I knew there was something different about them.

"But last night, that old guy, Lucian, seemed confused, and even a little afraid, when he saw your mark. So, what did he see, Emma?

Are you one of them?"

I took in another deep breath and exhaled loudly.

I'd forgotten Caleb was there last night, and actually witnessed everything. I couldn't see Lucian's eyes, because my back was facing him. If Caleb was right, then Lucian must have known something. Maybe he figured out I was the one in the prophecy. If he did, then I would become an even bigger target than before.

"I really don't know," I answered truthfully. "What I do know is that Samuel and Alaine are my birth parents, and I am three-quarters angel. They say there has never been another like me, but no one will know exactly what I will become until I turn eighteen. That's when my transformation happens."

Caleb was frozen, trying to take in what I'd just said. His brow was creased, his eyes were wide, and his mouth was gaping open.

"Alaine is your mother?" he breathed each word slowly.

"Yes." I guess she didn't share that part.

"But how?"

"It's a really long story. One I don't know all the details of, but I do know that Alaine and my mom were half-sisters. I was placed in her care because Samuel and Alaine were afraid for my life.

"There is some stupid law among the immortals stating purebloods can only be with other purebloods. Alaine is only a half-bred, so her relationship with Samuel was forbidden. They were breaking an Immortal Law, and the punishment was death." I shifted in my chair as he seemed to be thinking about all the information I was dropping on him.

"Samuel was supposed to have been killed for it. Everyone

thought he was dead, but he showed up last night, very much alive,"
I added.

"Whoa. So Samuel is one of the Fallen?"

"Yes."

"If Alaine is your mom, then that makes you my sister? I mean legally, because she adopted me and Courtney. Right?"

"That's right," I agreed. This was good. It was much better having him think of me as a sister, than having him being all creepy, and stalking me until I was eighteen.

"You're my sister. That's so cool." He gave a weak smile and closed his eyes.

"Yeah. Cool," I whispered.

His eyes popped open again.

"Well, sis, it looks like your eighteenth birthday will be the party of the century. I won't miss it, and you better make sure I'm on that list," he laughed, and then moaned in pain. He held out his hand to me and I took it.

"Hey, no laughing," I teased. "Don't worry. I'll see to it myself you're on that list. That is, if I survive until then."

His eyes had a bewildered look.

"Never mind. Just get some rest."

I released my grip, but he held on tightly. The medicine was kicking in again, and his eyes were getting heavy. I tightened my grip and as I did, he smiled and closed his eyes. I didn't want to stress him out, and tell him what we were planning. I doubted he'd even believe me if I told him I was going on a quest into Hell to speak to Lucifer. Heck, it even seemed crazy in my own mind.

"Emma?" Caleb breathed, his eyes still shut.

"Yes."

"Thanks for coming and rescuing me from those monsters," he whispered. "I didn't think anyone was going to come for me."

"Of course they would have come for you," I answered.

"But, you did. You came. So, thank you."

"You're welcome."

I smiled and watched his chest rise and fall, and listened to the clock on the wall...tick-tock, tick-tock. Within a few minutes, his fingers loosened, and his hand fell from mine.

THREE

I WASN'T SURE HOW LONG I was supposed to wait in the room, but I started to get antsy and a little irritated.

I could hear their muffled voices, but they were faint and I couldn't really make out what they were saying. I noticed a gap at the bottom of the door, so I laid flat on my stomach and pushed my ear as close to the opening as I could.

"Your orders are to take her directly to the house. It's the only way she'll be safe. There is no way I will put her life in greater risk than it already is. If you all believe that going to Lucifer is our only hope, then you need to decide who will go and speak to him. I'll not decide for you, or be responsible for any of your decisions. But I am responsible for Emma."

That was Alaine. She was trying to change the original plan, which had already been set. I knew she didn't want to lose me or Samuel, but out of her desperation she probably didn't realize she was putting pressure on the rest. Of course they would risk their lives, knowing that this was their only chance to save us.

Danyel spoke next. "Kade, being human, can help us get in. If I'm in possession of his mortal soul, we might have a fighting chance of making it through Hell's first gate. They'll think I'm delivering his soul. But the only way we will be able to get to Lucifer is attempting the five levels, which no one has ever survived. And, just saying...by the slimmest of chances we do survive, Lucifer would *not* see us. We have nothing urgent enough to present them, which would acquire an audience with him. They would never let us pass the last gate, and Lucifer does not take kindly to unwanted visitors."

There was silence for brief moment.

"Like I said before, I am not making any decisions for you, Danyel," Alaine spoke. "I am not asking you to carry this burden, but I *am* asking that Emma and Samuel be kept out of it."

"I understand, Alaine, and I have already made my decision. Even if our chance of entering Hell, and speaking to Lucifer, is as small as a grain of sand in the vast sea, it's still a chance, and I will go," Danyel answered.

"And I will go with Danyel," Kade spoke without hesitation.

My pulse started to race and my stomach twisted.

No way. There was no way they were going to do this alone. Everyone already knew without me, the journey into Hell would be suicide. I was the key. The Nephilim who might be able to get access to him, and let him know that his son, like me, was in danger.

I was amazed at how they were willing to risk everything, knowing full well they didn't have a chance. It wasn't fair.

I was just about to get up and make my entrance when I heard another voice. It was Samuel.

"I agree with Alaine, but only partly. Emma should not take this journey. It's way too great of a risk for her, and for the rest of us. If anything happens to her, hope for the future will be lost. But I will be going. I'll not allow Danyel and Kade go on this quest alone. Both have already risked their lives to save my daughter, and it's not fair they be abandoned to this perilous journey alone, knowing full well it will end in vain."

Samuel.

My father.

He was so brave and compassionate, and I didn't see how he could be one of the Fallen. His heart was too big and too good.

I jumped up from the floor, gripped the door knob, twisted, and swung the door wide open. All heads turned toward me. I glanced at all their faces, and set my eyes on Alaine.

"I just want you to know that I've been listening to your conversation. I know you don't want me to go, but I believe I should have a say. When I was brought into this world, I didn't have a choice. I never asked to be whatever it is that I am. But I'd like to be given a choice now. If fate chooses death for me, then I'll die. But if it isn't my time, I *will* come back to you.

"If Lucifer has a Nephilim son, then I will have the best chance of speaking to him. And if he loves his son as much as you love me, then he should help us. I have to make him see, make him believe, that if he lets Lucian continue, his son will eventually become a victim." I made my stand. "I will go, and I will have the best of

Heaven and Hell to guide and protect me."

My mouth was on autopilot. I'd never spoken before with such devotion or conviction. A few days ago, I would have never risked my life, or put myself in any kind of danger. I could feel the old me slowly starting to fade.

I guess that's what death does. Seeing and experiencing it all around you. It changes you from the inside out. My heart ached whenever the memories of my parents would flash through my mind. I missed them horribly, but I also had to learn to block out the memories because they made me weak. This new life, the one I was thrust into, didn't allow me to be weak.

But there was something else which gave me strength, and it happened the moment I met Kade. His touch held me together during my darkest hours. It helped me gather myself, and pull me to the moment to where I stood right now...strong and determined.

Now, I no longer needed his touch because I could feel a change happening within myself. I was a caterpillar, in the process of wrapping myself in a cocoon. Wrapping up all the sadness, anger, frustration, and horror, only to be transformed and released on my eighteenth birthday.

I wasn't sure what type of butterfly would emerge, but I didn't have time to sit and ponder it. Right now, all I cared about was staying alive. I was still very mortal, and my cocoon was fragile.

If I was going to emerge and be stronger than the angels, as they said, then I was going to start making a hit list. Right now, Lucian was at the top.

I noticed a smile on Samuel's face. He was proud of me. Alaine, on the other hand, didn't look happy at all. She looked heartbroken. Tears streamed from her red, swollen eyes as she slowly walked up to me, and wrapped me in a tight embrace. I hugged her, assuring her everything was going to be okay.

She cradled my face in her hands, kissed my forehead, and then walked into Caleb's room, quietly shutting the door behind her.

Samuel came to me and wrapped an arm around my shoulder.

"It's only because she loves you," he whispered in my ear. "She was heartbroken, not being able to see you grow up, and it took her a long time to deal with the fact she had to send you away. Your mother tried to keep her updated, but it was very infrequent, through little notes or pictures."

I sighed. All of this was news to me, because growing up, the name Alaine had never been mentioned—not even in a whisper.

"I know she cares about me," I breathed. "But this is a decision I had to make. We don't have much of a choice. If I'm the only one who has a chance of getting close to Lucifer, to make him understand, then I'm going to try. I won't sit here in this hellhole and let the demons come in and slaughter us. I'd rather be out there, fighting for something. Besides, I have the best Guardians of *any* world."

He laughed and shook his head.

"Spoken like a true warrior." He placed his hand on the side of my face, and nodded with a smile, then leaned in and kissed me lightly on the top of my head and walked away.

I guess I'd acquired my bravery from my father, and hopefully, I'd be handed down some of his fighting skills too. Sooner would be much better than later. Knowing they would be with me made it easier, but the lingering thought of Kade, no longer an immortal and able to die easily, made my heart ache.

What would happen if he were hurt? In this new world, anything was possible. Death was possible. Samuel and Danyel would have to protect us both. They were warriors, but the mental picture of them last night, beaten and on the brink of death, sent my stomach in knots.

Were we really making the right decision?

My heart said yes. We had one more day in this underground prison, and I'd have to keep reassuring myself this was the right decision. We were doing this to save everyone we loved, and that alone should be more than enough.

I walked back over to the couch and sat down. I was just about to close my eyes and try and black out the world, when I felt a touch on my shoulder.

"Hey, Emma," a voice whispered. I turned around to see Kade. His eyes were tired, but still as beautiful as the first time I saw him. The light which emanated from them had dimmed, but only just a bit. He looked battered, weary, and far from the Kade I was with last night, but he was still handsome and made my heart flutter with a touch.

I scooted over so he could sit next to me.

"What happened to you?" I breathed.

He sat and his leg brushed up against mine. I was sad because I'd become accustomed to the buzz of electricity which flowed between us. But his touch and his closeness still sent butterflies dancing through my stomach. That was something I'd never be able to control around him.

"Last night after we were attacked, I went to Midway for help. I knew you'd be safe down here with the others until I returned. It took hours to get there, and when I finally arrived I was crushed to hear they couldn't offer us assistance. Authority from above denied permission to send any more help than they already had. We were on our own.

"I don't fully understand why we were denied, but one of the leaders pulled me aside. He told me our best chance was to go directly to Lucifer. That if he sees and speaks to you, and you can convince him of Lucian's executions, which are putting his son in grave danger, there might be a chance he will help us.

"I know Lucifer is very protective of his son, and because of Lucian's betrayal, this might be the perfect catalyst to end the war…once and for all. The thing I'm most concerned of is that with Lucifer, everything has a price. I just hope he'll be lenient, knowing his son's life is also at stake."

I blinked. "Okay wait. Lucifer has a Nephilim son, and he wasn't sentenced to death?"

"He's not his real son. He was his brother's son, and his brother *was* executed for disobeying the law. I don't know the whole story, but I'm sure Samuel does. You should ask him about it. It was a pretty big deal in the Underworld."

"Okay. I will ask him when I get a chance. But what I really want to know is what happened to you. Alaine told us last night that you'd become mortal. But how is that even possible? You can't just change from immortal to mortal, can you? I mean, I can tell something has *changed*, and it scared me."

His sad eyes found mine and they spoke loud and clear. He knew exactly what I was talking about, because he probably didn't feel the spark either.

"It's not that I don't have any feelings for you, Kade, because I do. But it's the other, overwhelming feelings that used to happen when you were close, or when we touched. They aren't there anymore."

Kade sighed and closed his eyes.

"I'm so sorry, Emma. It was the only thing I could do to help." He took in a deep breath and exhaled. "I requested for the head of Midway to make me mortal. Every immortal has that choice, and can only make it once. I was assigned to protect you, and if becoming mortal was the only way to keep you safe, then it was an easy decision. A decision *I* consciously made on my own."

"Kade," I whispered. I was overcome with sadness. Tears filled my eyes, knowing he'd chosen me over his immortality.

"Don't cry, Emma," he said shaking his head with a sad grin. He gently touched the side of my cheek, wiping away a tear. "I'm at peace with the decision I made, and I'll still be able to protect you. I'll always protect you."

I looked into his eyes, and they were filled with so much love.

"Thank you," I whispered. My heart wanted to burst.

"Hey don't get all teary eyed for me. I'll be fine. Being mortal isn't so bad. You've been one for the past, what...seventeen years? I think I can manage it," he said with a crooked grin. I wanted to hug him, to kiss him, to tell him how much I loved him.

I had fallen for him. I *was* in love with Kade. Maybe the bonding thing was real, and we were meant to be together forever. All I knew was the feelings I was experiencing deep inside were true. I'd never felt so strong about wanting to be with him, and knew my life would never be the same if he ever left.

He smiled at me and I melted.

"So they can really do that? Change you into a human?" I questioned.

"Yes," he answered.

"Will they be able to change you back when we're done? You know, after we get back from our quest?"

His eyes stared blankly at his hands, and then he slowly shook his head.

"No. Once you change from immortal to mortal, you can never change back."

My last breath caught in my throat, and my heart felt like it had been bashed in and broken. It began to ache with a deep pain and sadness. I could only imagine what Kade was feeling. His whole life, like mine, had completely changed in an instant. He went from immortal to mortal because of me.

My head began to flood with questions, and my heart began to swell with an unknown warmth and admiration for him. I reached over and took his hand in mine, lacing my fingers through his. He squeezed gently.

Yes, there was still a strong connection between us.

"Kade, you didn't have to do this for me. Samuel and Danyel could have taken care of me. They are my Guardians too."

"Yes," he hesitated. I could see a faint glimmer in his eyes as he took in a deep breath and exhaled the truth. "But, *I* am your true Guardian, Emma. I was the one assigned to watch over and protect you, and I was the one given orders directly from above. They sent me to Alaine first, only to wait until the time my mission started.

"I guess they got wind of Lucian's executions, and told me I was to start protecting you right after your sixteenth birthday. My orders were very strict and specific. Someone in the upper hierarchy must really care about you, because I was to keep an extra close eye on you, and protect you at all costs. No other Nephilim has been assigned a Guardian, except for you and Alaine."

I felt my mouth gaping wide as my brain processed his words.

Kade was mine. He was my Guardian, sent to protect me, and only me.

"I didn't know," I breathed. Another thought crossed my mind. Something Courtney had mentioned earlier when she was giving me the tour of the house. She said Kade had been gone for a year, and went away for work. Well, she was right. I was his work.

"That's why I was the one who came to escort you from the hospital. Alaine sent Malachi to assist me. He'd met me the night before, and had also been given orders, along with the Watchers, to assure your utmost safety in reaching Alaine.

"I'm still pissed the damn Darkling attacked you at the airport, and I'll never forgive myself for letting him hurt you. Every time I picture that bastard on top of you, with his hand wrapped around your neck...It'll haunt me for a long time," he sighed. His beautiful hazel eyes swam with a mixture of sadness and relief. Relief, most likely, that he'd finally told me the truth. Now I understood why he made the decision to become mortal.

"Kade, it wasn't your fault. You told me not to go, but I had no idea a Darkling would be waiting for me."

"Still. It was my job to protect you, and I failed. I'm sorry," he breathed.

I squeezed his hand tighter around mine. "You didn't fail. I'm still here, and that Darkling is dead. Mission accomplished," I smiled, trying to make light of the situation.

He smiled, but only slightly.

"So, if you were sent to watch over me after I turned sixteen, then why hadn't we met before?"

"Guardians aren't supposed to be seen. We're supposed to be invisible to those we protect. During the day, I wasn't too worried about you being attacked because the Fallen and Darkling do most of their evil affairs under the cover of the night. But once night came, I kept an extra, watchful eye over you."

Yeah, that info was kind of overwhelming; knowing he had been watching over me for a whole year and I had no clue.

Kade chuckled, probably reading my expression.

"Don't worry. I'm not a creeper or a stalker. I was just doing my job and fulfilling my orders. And just so you know, I never entered your home or your room. I always watched from a distance, and never interfered with your privacy."

I felt embarrassed and heat instantly flushed through my face, probably turning a dark shade of pink. I don't think I would have minded if Kade had stalked me. He'd be the kind of guy any girl would want stalking her, and I already knew he definitely wasn't a creeper. He'd proven himself to be a loyal protector.

"So where'd you hang out, you know, while you were guarding me?" Yes, I was going to pick his brain. He was invisible for a whole year, and probably knew everything there was to know about me, and yet, I practically knew nothing about him.

"Well," he dragged out.

I wasn't going to let him pass on this question. I stared intently at him, putting on the pressure. "I mostly hung out on the rooftop of the three story house across the street—the Taylor's. It gave me a good view of all areas surrounding your house, and was the perfect spot to see any intruders. I was either there, or in a car down the street, but never too far."

The Taylor's? They were a quiet family who traveled a lot, but they were friends with my parents. The thought of them sent a pang of sadness through me.

Wait a minute.

If Kade was guarding me since I was sixteen, and watching me extra close during the night…I wondered if he saw the accident? Was he there the night my parents were killed? Maybe he held the answers I had been longing to hear. What truly happened that night?

My heart raced, thinking about asking him. How would I approach it? I didn't want him to feel bad about keeping it from me. I knew if he was, it was only to protect me. Maybe he didn't know the answer. But I'd never know if I didn't ask.

"Can I ask you a serious question?" My voice was shaky.

I could see a look of bewilderment enter his eyes, but he nodded.

"Sure."

"Were you there the night of the accident? The night my parents died?"

Kade's brows furrowed deeply and then he closed his eyes. I waited patiently for his answer, but it was clear he knew something.

"You were there. Weren't you?" I breathed.

He nodded, then began to speak softly.

"I was following your car from a distance, and remember how dark it was. The road didn't have much light, and there wasn't much traffic. I had a feeling something might happen, so I sped up to get closer.

"You'd just turned seventeen, and it seemed like the perfect time for the Fallen to strike. My instincts were right. I watched one of the Fallen drop down from the sky, and land directly in front of your car. I remember the sound of brakes screeching and echoing through the cold air; smoke bellowed from the tires as your father hit the brakes. He must have panicked and swerved out of the way. It all happened so fast. Too fast. The car veered over the embankment and headed straight for a bunch of trees alongside the road.

"Before the car crashed, I managed to jump through the back window, and keep the impact from crushing and killing you. You were screaming and in so much pain, so I did the only thing I could think of. I put the sleeper on you, and fled as help arrived." His voice was weak, and sadness swam in his eyes. "Emma, I wish I could have saved your parents, but I only had time to save one. You were the one I was sent to protect. I'm so sorry."

He couldn't look at me any longer, and I noticed a tear escape

47

his eye and trail down his cheek. He turned away from me and tried to release his fingers from mine, but I held on tight. I didn't want him to leave.

"They said it was a complete miracle I was alive. The impact should have killed me, but the tiny area right around me wasn't crushed, when it should've been. Now I know the reason why. It was because of you. You saved me," I said, breathless. "Kade, it wasn't your fault. My parents would be grateful you saved my life. *I'm* grateful. I just wish you could have met them. They would have loved you…as I do." Hot tears streamed down my face.

His eyes snapped up to me, and in an instant, I closed the distance between us, burying my face in the warmth and security of his chest. I sobbed as he wrapped his arms around me. I melted into him, wanting him to hold me forever.

He was my hero, my protector, my Guardian. Even though I didn't get the overwhelming rush of euphoria I did when he first touched me, the connection we had was still very, very strong. Just knowing he was my Guardian, and had saved my life, made my heart grow that much fonder for him.

"I'm sorry you gave up your immortality for me."

"I'm not," he returned. I felt the warmth of his breath on the top of my head. He gently raised my chin with his fingers, so my eyes met his, and then softly wiped away the tears.

Time froze as we gazed deeply into each other's eyes. At this moment, he had become my world.

"I wish I could kiss you right now," he whispered.

"Are they watching?" I asked.

He looked over my shoulder.

"Yeah."

"All of them?"

"Mmm-hmm," he hummed. "*All* of them."

"Okay, then. I'll settle for another hug." He laughed as I wrapped my arms around him, and he hugged me back.

"Get some rest, okay? We'll be going through Hell tomorrow."

I caught his pun and laughed.

He stood from the couch, gave me a wink, and then headed off into the kitchen with the others.

FOUR

THE DAY FLEW BY AND before I knew it, night had arrived. If not for the clock on the wall, none of us would have even known the time. Being underground sucked, and I tried hard not to think about it. Whenever I did, I started to feel a bit claustrophobic.

Everyone gathered around the table and discussed the plans for the morning's quest. I stayed out of it and volunteered to tend to Caleb. This time I didn't want to worry about the details. I'd leave those to the others I'd be traveling with.

After a few boring hours of listening to Caleb snore, I ended up back on the couch. My mind was way too wound up, and insomnia would be my enemy. How was I supposed to function, let alone run and dodge demons, when I was exhausted?

Constant thoughts of the crash, the death of my parents, my new life, and Kade swirled through my mind like a tornado.

I tried to shut it all out and think of happier, simpler times, but the darkness was much too overpowering.

"Can't sleep?" A loud whisper called from across the room. My eyes strained into the kitchen area, focusing on a large figure heading toward me.

Dominic.

He ambled to the couch and tapped my feet to get me to make room for him, so I pulled my legs up and he sat.

"No. Too many things wrapped around this sad mind," I replied, tapping my brain.

"I hear you," he responded. "Well, I just wanted to tell you, in case we don't ever meet up again, that you're a pretty cool chick. Very pretty and very cool," he reiterated.

"Thanks. And you're pretty cool yourself. But not pretty. Well, maybe pretty in a guy kinda way," I giggled.

Dominic was very pretty. He had a Greek god-like appearance that would make any girl swoon. He was tall, muscular, had beautiful piercing green eyes, and a way about him that was completely fun, witty, and sarcastic. His happiness was contagious. Without him this whole death adventure definitely wouldn't be as bearable.

"I guess I could take that as a compliment," he smiled widely, "but just don't tell the others you think I'm pretty. That should be kept just between us. I wouldn't want them to start getting jealous. But, you're free to throw around the words handsome or gorgeous as much as you'd like whenever you're referring to me," he said, with a big toothy smile.

"Okay. I'll be sure to remember that," I laughed.

He then cleared his throat and shifted to face me.

"By the way, I've been noticing the way you and Kade look at each other. You have *that look*."

"Oh? And what look would that be?" I questioned, raising my brow.

"You know. That certain look you get when you've found that special someone. Your perfect match."

"Really? You see that in us?"

"Yes, and I just wanted you to know that I like Kade. He's a good guy, and one of my best friends. In all the years I've known him I haven't seen him happier, or smile as much as he has since he met you. And let me tell you…it's been a long time."

"So I've heard," I breathed, knowing he was referring to immortal years. "So what would *you* know about finding a perfect match?"

He sighed and nodded with a slight smile. A sad sort of smile. Then his eyes went blank, like he was reliving a moment in time.

I cleared my throat, breaking him from his momentary trance.

"I'm sorry," he whispered. "I was just remembering someone. It seems like an eternity ago."

My heart sunk as I began to understand.

"Was she your perfect match?"

His green eyes locked on mine. They almost looked like they were glowing neon.

"Yes," he answered, and then his eyes went distant again. "She *was* my perfect match, and she was beautiful. I remember the first time I saw her. My emotions went crazy as soon as she came near. I'd never seen or met her before, but my body was instantly pulled

52

toward her, and my heart felt like it was being tugged to hers by an invisible thread. I knew instantly she was to be mine for all eternity. I'd never felt that way with any other, or ever since.

"To this day when I close my eyes, I can see her face. She had the most beautiful, long, golden hair which sparkled like the sun, and the deepest sapphire eyes that reminded me of the ocean. Every molecule of my being screamed to be near her. When she'd walk by, it felt as if I had been struck by lightning. Her presence weakened and strengthened me." He shook his head, as if shaking the memory free.

"What happened to her?" I asked, overwhelmed by his story. I wanted to know more.

He sighed and closed his eyes.

"She was murdered." His voice was shaky and I suddenly felt horrible. I didn't want to ask him any more questions, but he started speaking before I could tell him it was okay. "She was a Guardian, and a damn good one. One of the very few female Guardians ever sent out on missions. One night, while on her watch, she was attacked by a group of Darkling. She was alone, but fought them as best she could. She managed to take out two, before the third overpowered her. It beat her until she was unconscious, and then the bastard sliced her throat, barely leaving her alive.

"When the news hit me I rushed to her side, but I couldn't feel her life force. I held her in my arms until she took her last breath," his voice cracked on the last words.

"What was her name?"

"Khelsey," he whispered, and then quickly looked away from

me. He wiped his face, and then rubbed his arms. The strong, happy Dominic was broken, and it made my heart ache.

"I'm so sorry," were the only words I could find.

"Oh, it's alright. I'm fine," he said, sucking in a deep breath. He turned and painted his happy face on, but I could still see the pain behind his eyes. "Well, just keep an extra eye on my buddy for me. Now that he's mortal, things will be a lot harder for him. He can probably kick a little ass, but I won't be there to cover his back. Just promise me you'll take good care of him."

"I will," I promised.

"Now, the real reason why I came over here is because I have something for you." He reached over to his other side. "This is a dagger, given and entrusted to me by Michael the Archangel. He told me that one day I would find the person who was meant to have it, and I think I've finally found her. I seriously didn't think it was going to a girl. No offense, Emma, but it's now yours.

"This dagger has brought me amazing good luck, and every demon I've fought with it has fallen and died. It's magical," he said, handing me a medium sized dagger in a sheath. "Here. Take it."

I was speechless as I carefully unsheathed it and held it in my hands. It was very old and very beautiful. I suddenly started to feel a tingling in my hand, and then the dagger started to glow. I gasped and looked to Dominic for an explanation.

"See. I knew this dagger was meant for you. I started to feel it as soon as we met. It's almost like it's been calling for you. I know it sounds strange, but this dagger is much more than it seems. Like I said, it's magic."

"I can't take this from you. You'll be fighting tomorrow and will need it much more than I will. I don't even know to use it or if I could," I said, handing it back to him.

"Believe me, Emma, you will definitely need it much more than I will. It's yours now, and it *will* help you. I have two new blades that were designed just for me. I'll let you in on a little secret. It's not really in the blades, it's all in the technique, baby," he snickered and started flexing his biceps.

The old Dominic was back. The one I was used to seeing.

"Thanks Dominic," I whispered, laughing quietly. I put the blade back in its sheath, then reached over and hugged his neck. He hugged me back.

"Yeah, you better not hug me too long, 'cause my boy Kade might get the wrong impression. I don't want him getting all jealous over us." One of his brows lifted. "We just have to be careful. His new mortal heart is very breakable," he said with a wink and a grin.

"Riiiiight…" I said, rolling my eyes.

"Yep, and you're welcome. Oh, and one more thing before I go. It's Dom…just call me Dom," he said, gently tapping my shoulder.

"Thanks for everything, Dom," I said softly.

He smiled and his white teeth glimmered in the darkness. He pushed off the couch and disappeared back into the kitchen. It was his shift to watch the monitors.

I pulled the dagger back from its sheath and held it in my grasp. It was razor sharp and I dared not touch the blade. The handle was a marble white, and had a large golden symbol engraved into it. It looked a lot like one of the symbols that were imprinted on their necks. Maybe it was Michael the Archangel's symbol? I really didn't know too much about him. I'd heard his name a few times in church, but never really knew his story. I didn't even know what an Archangel was, or what they did. That would be something I'd have to Google later.

I carefully sheathed the blade again and placed it safely under my pillow.

The night and my overactive mind stole precious sleep from me, and before I knew it, I was watching the clock turn 6:00am. Soon after, everyone began stirring.

I should have asked Dom to put the sleeper on me, but I wasn't thinking at the time. I sighed and got up to see if anyone started brewing coffee. It would need to be super strong this morning.

Kade stumbled out of his bedroom looking as just as tired as I felt. I wondered how we'd make it through the day, let alone survive Hell and whatever horrors it would throw at us. Thank God, Samuel and Danyel were joining us. We'd definitely have to rely on them for our safety.

As the morning dragged on, everyone eventually made it to the table and ate breakfast.

"So, what's the plan?" I asked.

"There is no actual plan," Malachi answered. "We have two groups. The first group is just going to charge out there, fight off whatever Fallen are present, and then clear a path so the second group—you guys—can make your escape."

That sounded easy enough.

"It's a good thing the Darkling can't be out during the day," I mentioned.

"Yes, but the Fallen are twice as strong and fast," Alexander added.

"Then I guess it's great you guys are even stronger and faster than they are," I added. All their faces brightened at my remark.

"She's right, you know," Dom muttered. "Except she was actually only talking about me."

"Whatever, dude," Alexander huffed. "We'll see who gets more kills today. I'm on my game. I can feel it."

"You're on, little man," Dom nodded, narrowing his eyes at his new opponent. With a sly grin plastered to his face, he shoved the last piece of toast in his mouth.

"Let's just see if the two of you can survive today. There might be more Fallen than you can handle," Malachi added. His dark sunglasses were donned on his usual smug face.

"Malachi, don't be sour. You can play too, if you want," Alexander teased. Malachi shook his head, and shot him an evil look.

"Alright everyone. Time to get serious," Danyel jumped in. "Today is the reason why you've been sent here. You are Guardians, whose mission is the safety and protection of Alaine and Emma. We all need to make sure Emma gets out of here safely. She is our top priority."

"We will fight to keep her safe, even until death," James answered, with confidence on his face.

"Until death," everyone cheered in unison.

My heart instantly swelled and broke at the same time. I looked at their faces, and realized I'd come to love each and every one of them, even if I'd only known them for a short time. They were fearless. They were beautiful. And they were looking out for my safety.

Even if they were just obeying orders and doing their job, each one had a special place in my heart. But there was one who had a piece of it—my Guardian. The one who gave up his immortality so he could travel with me into the depths of Hell.

I glanced over to Kade, and he had a smile on his handsome face. His eyes were still beautiful, but were now tainted with dark circles around them; the first flaw I'd witnessed since I'd met him. I smiled back at him, glad he would be taking this journey with me.

"The sun will be at its highest point in four hours. That's when we'll make our move," Samuel announced. "Let's get ready."

Everyone agreed with shouts and fist bumps, and left the table in high spirits. That was something I would never understand. How could they be so excited before heading into battle?

"Emma, could I speak to you?" Alaine asked, peeking from Caleb's room.

I nodded and walked toward her. She widened the opening as I entered, and closed it quietly behind us.

"I just wanted to reiterate I don't agree with you leaving, but I know in your heart you have already made your decision. Before you go, I want you to have something from me," she said, carefully removing a necklace from around her neck and placing it on mine.

It was a teardrop shaped pendant on the end of a petite, golden chain. I grasped it in my fingers and as soon as I touched it, it felt warm. It was beautiful. The stone was reddish, with tiny specks of yellow and green through it. It was simple, yet elegant.

"What kind of stone is this?" I asked.

"It's a Bloodstone," she answered. "And, not just any Bloodstone, this is one of the originals."

I looked up to her, puzzled. "I've never heard of a Bloodstone."

She smiled and took the pendant in her fingers.

"The Bloodstones are part of a legend, or at least those who tell of it, think it is. The legend states while Christ hung upon the cross, the blood which flowed from his wounds dripped down onto the earth below, covering the surrounding stones. One of his followers gathered the precious stones, saturated with the crimson blood of his Lord, and carefully hid them away.

"Soon after, things started to happen. The man suddenly fell into an abundance of wealth, and while others around him contracted disease and sickness, he and his family remained healthy and well. He also knew when someone wanted to hurt or steal from him, because the Bloodstone would glow bright red, alerting their closeness. He believed the stones held strong magical powers.

"Rumors began to spread about the magic of the Bloodstones, and many outsiders tried steal them, so he hid them away and told no one of their whereabouts. Not even his wife or his children. The man took the secret to his deathbed. But it's been told, that right before he died, he was visited by an angel. And it was to that angel, he whispered the secret hiding place of the Bloodstones."

"Wow. So how did you get it?" I whispered.

"As you probably know, I was also adopted. Right after birth I was taken from your grandmother, and secretly whisked away to a family who was chosen to raise me. They loved me as much as any parent could love a child, and gave me a happy, fulfilled life. Eventually, they both passed from illness.

"But it was the day before my eighteenth birthday I received this gift. When I returned home from school that afternoon, I found a small box placed atop my pillow. I questioned my parents, but they said they knew nothing about it. My mother had been home all day, and she said there were no visitors. But, someone had gone into my room and placed it there.

"Later, I found a small handwritten letter neatly folded and tucked into the bottom of the box. I read the letter a million times, memorizing every single word. It was from my father. My birth father."

She paused for a brief moment, and stared blankly at the amulet, still rubbing it between her fingers.

I didn't move and remained silent.

"The note read...

My dearest Alaine,

I am so sorry I have never had the pleasure of meeting my beautiful daughter in person. Please know this, I have always kept a watchful eye over you. Now that you will be turning eighteen, I wanted to present you with this gift. It is a small token of my love, on the day before your transformation.

Do not be afraid of your gift, and as much possible,

keep it secret. Human minds will never be able to comprehend it, and their hearts will be envious. One day, I will send someone to explain, but until then, remain steadfast to your own heart and discernments. They will, at most times, steer you in the right direction.

The adornment is a Bloodstone of Christ, one of the rarest and most sacred of all amulets known to both men and angels. This stone will give its wearer protection, power, and health. Wear it always my daughter, for there are many evils that abound in your world.

There is a small mark on the back of your neck, which is the mark of your descent. Keep it hidden, especially from those who ask. Knowledge of this mark could lead to death.

My wish is that fate will one day bring us together, for it has been a weighted burden upon my heart. There are many troubling and perplexing circumstances which have kept the distance between us, but always know this...I love you, and have always loved you, my beautiful Alaine.

Keep safe,

Your Father"

She stopped and then snapped from her trance.

"So, you've never met your real father?" I questioned.

"No," she said sadly.

"Do you know his name?"

"No," she repeated.

"I can't take this from you," I said, unhooking the chain from my neck.

"Yes, you can, Emma. I am giving this to you as a gift, from a mother to her only daughter. This is for your seventeenth birthday. I am no longer in need of it, but you will need it, especially where you are going," she said. She refastened the amulet to my neck, and then took me in her arms and hugged me tightly. I wrapped my arms around her and hugged her back.

"Thank you so much," I whispered.

I opened my eyes and saw Caleb's wide eyes, staring at me. As soon as he noticed me, he quickly snapped his eyes shut again. I couldn't help but giggle. Alaine stepped back and looked at me, befuddled. Giggling at a moment like this didn't seem appropriate.

"I'm sorry. I just...I just thought of something funny."

I didn't want to rat on Caleb. He probably didn't want Alaine to know he was up anyway.

"Well, you better get ready," she said.

"What should I wear?" I asked. What was one supposed to wear for a trip into Hell? I assumed it would have to be something on the cooler side. A fire suit would probably be a great choice, but I knew we didn't have any of those just lying around in an underground bunker.

"Oh yes! I do have something for you to wear. I knew this would be the perfect place to keep it, in case we ever ended up here," she smiled, walking over to the closet. She pushed a bunch of clothes on hangers to one side, and pulled out an outfit draped in white plastic and handed it to me. "This was mine, given to me after my transformation. It was another gift from my mysterious father, but I've only used it once. I do have a feeling it should fit you perfectly."

I gave her a confused look, and she laughed, hugged me again, turned me around, and pushed me out the door. I walked into the last bedroom, since Samuel was out in the kitchen, closed the door, and then carefully peeled the plastic off of the outfit.

I gasped.

This had to be a joke. She couldn't have been serious. This wasn't an outfit! This was a superhero suit that looked like it belonged to cat woman. There was no way I'd be able to fit my body into that small, black leather material. But the longer I stared at it, the more I wanted to try it on...mostly just to humor myself. It was actually kind of cool looking. I ran my fingers down the soft leather, and suddenly felt tingles shoot up through my hand.

I gasped and stepped back.

Maybe it was magic.

I quickly peeled out of my clothes and slipped into it.

Holy hell. It *was* a perfect fit. Too perfect almost. Like whoever made it had measured every part of my body, hugging every curve. It fit like a glove.

I stepped into the bathroom and stood in front of the mirror. At first, I was embarrassed because I'd never worn anything that fit this tight in my life, but the longer I wore it, the more it felt like it was a part of me—another layer of skin. I brushed my fingers across the material down my arm. The inside was super soft, but the outside felt hard to the touch, rock hard. I knocked on it and it was like solid steel. What the heck was this material? It couldn't have been manmade.

I quickly tied my hair up into a tight ponytail, and for a split second, I thought I was looking at Alaine—a younger Alaine. I was in awe at how much I actually looked like her.

I turned around and held up my hair, trying to see the mark on the back of my neck, when there was a knock on my door.

"Emma?"

My heart skipped a beat. It was Kade.

"Come in," I said. Then I remembered I was in this ridiculous outfit, and it was too late to change.

The door opened and he stepped in.

As soon as he saw me, his eyes widened.

"Whoa. You look…"

"I know. Ridiculous. Alaine gave this to me, but I was just about to take it off," I said embarrassed, heading towards the bathroom.

"No. Don't take it off," he said with too much urgency, quickly making his way over to me.

"Why?" I asked, in a coy voice.

"Well, I'm not going to stop you if you really want to take it off," he said, his eyes sliding downward.

"Hey," I said, feeling even more embarrassed.

"Sorry," he grinned. "First of all, you do *not* look ridiculous in that outfit, and before you interrupted me, I was actually going to say that you look…very beautiful."

I felt my face flush with heat. "Thank you."

"I'm just speaking the truth."

"And why shouldn't I take it off?" I questioned, curious.

"Because it's a Vestimentum Angelorum," he stated with a wide, cocky smile. He knew I had no clue what he'd just said.

"A what?"

"A garment of the angels," he laughed. "This is a rare suit. There were only a few ever made. It becomes part of the wearer, acting as an armor and camouflage. When it senses danger, it adjusts to its surroundings, blending in, and in some instances, even making the wearer invisible. But its powers differ from each user.

"Angel's wings are stitched in between the materials, making it nearly impenetrable. It will also adjust to your body's heat. If you become too hot, it will cool you down. Too cold, and it will warm you up. It's the best protection you could have right now, since you won't have me." His eyes dropped to the ground.

"Kade," I whispered, shaking my head. He looked so handsome, and so vulnerable standing there. His hazel eyes were swimming with a sadness that was continually breaking my heart. Dark, disheveled hair framed his flawless, porcelain face, and his black shirt and blue jeans hugged his lean, muscular body. He was perfect, just like the sculpture back at the house.

I sucked in a deep breath. There was no way of telling him how much he meant to me. I'd never opened my heart to any boy. Never shared a kiss, and never shared my heart, or any of my hidden secrets with anyone.

I reached out and touched his arm. He took my hand and

stepped closer. Heat rushed through my entire body, reminding me of the first day I met him. Our eyes met and locked tight on each other, and then he quickly closed the void between us. In an instant, our worlds collided.

He leaned in and the heat of his closeness made me anxious. I closed my eyes, letting my remaining senses take over. The warmth of his lips pressed against my forehead, the tickle of his breath across my cheek, and his soft kisses trailing down the nape of my neck.

My heart and pulse began to race, and a surge of heat and electricity coursed through my veins. This felt like a dream. A dream I never wanted to wake from.

His fingers carefully traced the lines of my face, and then slowly raised my chin so my eyes met his. I became dizzy with his closeness and his sweet scent.

He kissed my cheek, and softly whispered into my ear. "Emma."

"Yes?"

"I want you to know, before we leave this place…that I love you."

"Kade." I was breathless when his lips found mine, and for the first time, desire and passion burned within me. His lips were sweet and gentle. I opened my mouth slightly, and let his tongue enter, eagerly and passionately searching for mine. My body melted into his embrace.

He was intoxicating.

I wrapped my arms around his neck to keep myself from falling, but it was too late. I had already fallen, head-over-heels for him.

His mouth was as hungry for mine, as mine was for his. My fingers wrapped in his hair and pulled him closer. He held me tight in the warmth of his embrace. I'd never felt more safe.

He lifted and carefully carried me over to the bed, his lips never leaving mine. He gently laid me down and pressed his hard body on top of me. I was lost. Lost in him. Lost in the moment. Lost in happiness.

"Kade. Kade? Where the hell are you man?" a voice yelled from the outside area.

Our lips separated.

"Shit," Kade sighed loudly, closing his eyes in disbelief. He shook his head.

It was Malachi.

Damn. His timing was impeccable, like he had some sort of alarm that went off whenever Kade and I were together.

"Where the hell is Kade? Doesn't *anyone* know?" Malachi said, sounding like his normal, annoyed self.

Kade leaned down and gave me one last kiss, which sent my head into a spin. He stood up, and I found the edge of the bed, still feeling the lingering effects of my very first kiss.

"I'm sorry, Emma. I don't know what came over me. It could be the fact that I'm human now, or…it could have been that thing you're wearing," he laughed, gesturing to my suit.

I blushed, shaking my head.

"Are you really sorry?"

He paused for a brief moment, and ran his fingers through his hair. Then his eyes found mine. "Actually, no. I'm not sorry. Not at all."

"Then don't apologize. It would be beyond pathetic to die without being kissed, and I'm glad you were my first."

"Kade?" Malachi called again.

"I guess I'd better get out there before he comes busting down the door."

"Yeah, I guess you should."

"I'll see you soon," he winked.

My heart melted.

"Yes. I'll see you soon."

He opened the door and left, leaving me alone with my head in a whirl.

It was just a kiss, but only the most unbelievable kiss ever. What would have happened if we were left alone? Hey, I was an Angel, but half of my genetic make-up was Fallen. I guess I'd have to keep an extra eye out on myself.

I knew, deep inside, it was fate which brought us together. I felt right, complete, and perfect whenever Kade was around. He made my world a better place. What kind of future would fate allow us to live? Would we be allowed to be together, or would we die trying? Only time would answer that question.

I walked over to the closet and found a bunch of jackets off to the side. There was a black leather trench coat, so I slipped it on. It reached just below my knees, covering most of my upper body. Good. I didn't want the others to see me in this suit.

FIVE

TIME FLEW BY AND BEFORE I knew it, everyone had gathered in the living room, dressed and ready for battle. Samuel, Danyel, Dominic, and Alexander miraculously seemed to be as good as new. Completely healed and no scars. That was crazy. They were so lucky, and I was still amazed by it all. But then again, I was healing almost as fast as they were.

Kade came and stood next to me. He looked tired and weak compared to the rest of them, but still managed a smile when he saw me. As always, it melted my heart.

Thank goodness Alaine had some pretty strong medicine, which seemed to be working its magic, helping him to manage his pain and heal as quickly as a mortal could. She even returned his blue vial, which looked like it had been refilled.

"Hey Emma, you're looking pretty damn hot in that tight leather outfit," Dominic jested.

Oh God. I quickly hugged the coat around me.

I glanced at Kade and he had a grin on his face. "Told you," he whispered.

"Yeah, I have to agree with Dom, which I hardly do," Alex chimed, smiling at me.

All eyes were now looking at me, making me feel like I was naked. My face flushed with heat.

"Hey, hey, hey. Keep those eyes in your heads, boys. That's my daughter you're talking about," Samuel stepped in.

"Watch out. Daddy's gonna take names and kick ass," Malachi laughed, punching Dom on the arm.

"Hey, watch the goods, man. It just healed and it's still tender." He rubbed his muscle.

"Whatever, big baby," Malachi snickered.

Samuel walked over to me, and placed both of his hands on my shoulders. "You're beautiful, Emma. You look so much like your mother," he said softly with a smile. He leaned down and kissed my forehead.

I smiled and he stepped to the other side of me, opposite of Kade.

"Okay. So let's go over this one more time," Samuel spoke. Everyone quieted and looked at him. "Once the cameras show the way is clear, the first team will go out and clear any debris before we exit. Malachi and James will go out first, Danyel and I will follow with Kade and Emma, and Dominic and Alexander will cover our backs. Alaine will be staying back with Caleb. He is still too weak to move.

"Once we're out, we will make our way to the portal. Dominic and Alexander, you will head back to the house and alert Thomas. Then, you all will need to find a way to get Alaine and Caleb back to the house safely. Pray for us. Even if we make it to the portal, it's a deadly journey into Hell, and we'll need all the help we can get."

Everyone stayed silent and nodded in agreement. They all knew what they had to do. It was the same as they'd always done from the beginning. It's what they were born and trained to do. Fight. Even until death.

Samuel walked up to Alaine, wrapped her in his arms, and softly whispered, "Alaine, no matter what happens, I want you to know that I love you. There has not been one day, nor one breath, nor one beat of my heart, in which I have ever doubted that love. If I don't find my way back, please be strong, and rest assure I will do everything in my power to make sure Emma gets back to you safely."

Alaine wrapped her arms around him and wept.

I still had a difficult time wrapping my head around the fact that they were my parents. They were much too beautiful, and didn't look old enough to be my parents.

But what really blew me away was the way they looked at each other. There was something in their eyes that spoke loudly to everyone around them. They were meant to be together, and they knew and felt it. A perfect match. A bond. A love so true and so strong, it withstood years of separation and pain.

How could there be a law that forbade them to be together? Love should have no boundaries, no limits, and no law. Love should be free, and freely given to whomever it wants.

I wondered if I would ever share a love like theirs, and if Kade was the one I'd share it with? I still had time to figure it all out. But right now, at this moment, love wasn't on the top of my list. My number one priority was to stay alive, and help to keep the people around me alive.

Kade's hand reached for mine, and as I took hold of it, we laced our fingers together. I glanced up at him, and he smiled. His eyes were bright, and a little more blue than green today. I wondered if he was thinking the same thing I was.

As we watched Samuel and Alaine share their last kiss and embrace, he gently squeezed my hand and then let go.

"Are you ready?" he whispered.

I nodded.

Alaine walked up to me and wrapped me in her arms.

"I love you, Emma," she sobbed. "Please be safe, and take care of yourself."

Even though I'd only recently learned Alaine was my mother, she was exactly that—my mother.

What she did when I was born was for my own safety, and I came to realize it was done unselfishly. Over the course of these intense few days, she'd proven her love, so I in return, would let her hear the words I knew she wanted to hear from her only daughter.

"I love you, too."

As soon as I spoke those words, she broke down even more, and my heart broke for her. Tears streamed from my eyes, knowing I'd be leaving her, and not knowing if I'd ever see her again. I hugged her tight, one last time, and whispered, "Goodbye."

Samuel took her into his arms again, led her back into the room with Caleb, and returned a few minutes later.

"She'll be fine. It's been a rough few days for her, and she hasn't had much sleep."

I nodded, wiping the tears from my eyes.

"Alright sweetheart, it's like we did coming out of the cave the other night. Just hold on tight, even if I have to let go," he said with a smile.

"Got it," I replied.

Malachi and James were already at the door.

"You guys ready to kill some Fallen ass?" Dominic cheered, raising his blades in the air. He suddenly stopped and looked over to Samuel and Danyel. "Hey, no offense Sam and Dan. I meant the 'other' Fallen…ass…out there," he said, gesturing towards the hallway.

"None taken," Danyel responded.

Samuel just laughed and shook his head.

Malachi opened the door, and started out.

"As soon as we get to the next door, I want you to hop on," Samuel said. I nodded, trying to slow my breathing. In a matter of a few minutes we were at the next door, and Malachi held his hand up for everyone to stop.

"This is it. You all ready?" he asked.

Everyone readied their weapons. Samuel took out a dagger similar to the one Dominic gave me, which was strapped to my waist.

"Ready!" everyone cheered in unison.

I hopped onto Samuel's back and Kade did the same on Danyel's. He looked so uncomfortable, and I tried not to look.

Malachi pushed the numbers on the side of the wall, and my

heart pounded as the door slid open. He and James charged out first, weapons drawn with war cries. But they were met with nothing.

The place was empty.

"It's clear! Go, go, go!" Malachi yelled, waving us to come.

I knew the Darkling couldn't be out in the light, but I had a gut feeling the Fallen weren't too far away.

Watching.

Waiting.

"Emma, whatever happens, just hold on tight," Samuel repeated.

"I will," I breathed. I was anxious knowing that anything could happen, and praying that nothing would.

"Danyel, follow me. We'll stay on the ground and use the cover of trees to stay hidden. We will be easy targets if we fly."

Danyel nodded.

Fly? Did he just say fly? Oh my God. My father could fly, which meant he had wings. I wondered if they were black and beautiful like Lucian's?

I glanced over to Kade who didn't look too happy about being a passenger, so I shot him a smile. He smiled back and gave me a slight nod. I was just about to wish him luck, when Samuel yelled.

"Let's go!"

Before I could think another thought, Samuel took off. I almost fell off from his initial burst forward, but quickly repositioned myself and tightened my grip. I gasped as the cold Alaska wind whipped against my face. Samuel headed for the cover of trees, and in seconds we were there.

He tried to avoid tree branches, but there were way too many. I knew I'd have tons of scratches on all exposed skin; especially since he was traveling like the speed of light. We were going so fast, it made me dizzy. Everything around us was a complete blur, so I kept my eyes closed, and my head down to try and avoid being hit in the face.

It already felt like we were flying, because I didn't feel or hear his feet pounding over the ground. Our journey was silent, and I wondered if Danyel and Kade were anywhere near us. I tried to peek behind us, and to the sides, but I couldn't focus long enough to see a thing. I heard branches cracking ahead of us, and resigned myself to think it was them. At least it made me feel better.

We must have been traveling for a while because my muscles started to ache. I wanted to relax them, but I was afraid if I slacked even the slightest bit, I'd fall.

After what seemed like hours, Samuel started to slow down, and eventually came to a stop. He tried to set me down, but my body was plastered to his. I had been in that position for so long, it took a while for me to release from him. Once down, I stretched my tired and achy muscles, but was thrilled when I glanced up to see Danyel and Kade walking toward us.

"We'll stop here for a short while to stretch and have something to eat. The Fallen are out there, so we cannot linger," Samuel urged, in a hushed tone.

"How much longer will it be before we reach the portal?" I asked.

"We've come about halfway," he said, digging in his pouch. He pulled out a bag that contained pieces of jerky and a flask of water, and handed it to me. I unscrewed the cap of the flask and took a sip.

The water was ice cold, and as soon as it began to run down the back of my dry throat, I instantly felt better. Rejuvenated.

I couldn't help but wonder if my aching, tight muscles could handle another few hours of traveling. They were still weak and trembling from the first half of our journey.

Kade came and took a seat next to me on a downed tree stump. I handed him the bag of jerky and the water.

"How are you holding up?" he asked.

I sighed and shook my head. I didn't want to sound like a wimp, but I was totally feeling like one. "I – I guess I'm fine," I lied. I had a feeling he knew I was lying.

He reached into his pocket and pulled out his blue vial.

"Here," he said handing it to me. I took the vial, placed it to my lips, and took a small sip. A wave of tingles started at my brain, and made its way down my whole body, numbing the pain and instantly relaxing my muscles.

"Whoa," I breathed, getting to my feet, stretching my body out. No aches and no shaky muscles. "That's some pretty powerful stuff."

He chuckled as I handed back the vial, and he took a sip. He closed his eyes letting it work its magic. After a few seconds his eyes popped open and he smiled. "Yeah, I never knew how good this stuff really was until now. It's pretty awesome."

We were deep in the middle of a dense forest filled with spruce and birch trees. I glanced up at the beautiful green canopy provided by the leaves. The birds were chirping, and it seemed so peaceful.

Samuel and Danyel were quietly chatting a few yards away, when there was a loud snapping sound, like a huge tree being broken in two. Kade jumped up, grabbed my arm, and then twisted me, pressing my back against the trunk of a wide birch. He was facing me, our bodies pressed tightly together, so close I could hear his heart beating, and feel the heat radiating from his skin.

"What is it?" I whispered.

"I don't know. It could be a falling tree, but I don't want to take any chances." He glanced around me, and then slowly unsheathed his sword. Samuel and Danyel were nowhere in sight. They had to be near. They'd probably ducked behind some trees too.

My pulse began to race, not only because of Kade's closeness, but because if the Fallen were out there and had been following us, then we were in trouble. *Big trouble.* I had no doubt Kade would try and protect me, but as Dominic said earlier, he didn't have the strength or quickness he had as an immortal. I wish I knew where Samuel and Danyel were. Seeing them would make me feel a whole lot better.

A thunderous noise rattled the ground. Suddenly, a whole tree, about thirty feet long headed toward us. The branches from the tree scratched my face as it flew past, missing us by mere inches.

"Shit! That was too damn close," Kade swore, grabbing my arm and pulling me away behind another bunch of trees. "Are you okay?" he asked, assessing my scratches. His fingers lightly touched the side of my face.

"I'm fine." I said.

He nodded and grabbed hold of my waist and set me down between a large fallen stump wedged between two other trees. Then he grasped his sword tightly and stood behind another tree a few feet away.

"Shhhhh," he said silently, mouthing the words, "Don't move."

I nodded. Then, I suddenly felt heat on my chest. As I glanced down at the Bloodstone amulet—it was glowing bright red. My heart started to hammer.

I slowly rose to my knees, and peeked through the leaves, letting one eye spy. I had to know what was going on. I hated surprises, especially when it was a deadly surprise meant for me. But what my terrified eye spied was worse than I imagined. Three Fallen angels were a few hundred yards away, sniffing the air.

They'd found us.

I couldn't really tell the difference between the good angels and the Fallen; they all looked the same to me. The only way I could tell they were Fallen was by the evil look in their eyes. They were on a mission. A mission of death and destruction. A mission to kill us.

I glanced over to Kade, and knew there was no way he'd be able to take on all three of them on his own.

The Fallen were well over six feet tall, tanned, muscular, and strikingly handsome. They looked like Gladiators. The one in front had long black hair, which hung in front of his face and his dark black eyes. He was holding a long, sharp, golden sword. The other two had long dark-brown hair with dark eyes, each carrying their own swords.

"Danyel," the Fallen in front called out. "Danyel, we know you're out there. We can smell you and the others. If you give up the girl, even though our orders are to kill you, we will let you live."

Yeah right. I'd heard that line too many times, and we all knew the outcome of that scenario. With the Fallen—everyone dies.

There was a brief pause, and I watched as the first one nodded to the others. They quickly disappeared into the thick brush. One to the right, and one to the left. I turned back to Kade, and pointed to the sides of us. He nodded and closed his eyes. I assumed he was listening for any sounds.

I tried not to breathe, but my adrenaline kicked in, making it nearly impossible. Being frozen was easy because fear had already done that.

I glanced at Kade, and couldn't believe how strikingly attractive he looked. His brown hair waved slightly in the wind. His face showed no sign of fear. He was perfection. Keeping my eyes on him made the evil world around me temporarily dissolve.

Branches snapped loudly to the left of me.

As I whipped my head around, I saw one of the Fallen charging at us. His eyes were dark and set unwaveringly on his target—me. His sword was positioned over his head, and he had a look of pure hatred and determination.

"Kade," I gasped, frantically pushing myself backwards toward him.

Kade jumped in front of me and charged straight at the Fallen. A loud clanging of metal against metal pierced the quiet around us. As their swords clashed, sparks rained down like fireworks.

"Kade!" I screamed. My heart frantically beat against the walls of my chest as I watched him fight.

The Fallen kicked him in the gut and knocked him to the ground. He landed hard on his back. The Fallen smirked and charged again, with a look of murderous intent in his eyes.

"Kade!" I cried again, as the angel thrust his sword at his chest.

Kade rolled to the side, letting the blade pierce the earth just inches from him.

My heart stopped.

Kade quickly turned and kicked the Fallen's blade, sending it flying out of his hand. It landed a few feet away from me. He lunged for his weapon, but I jumped forward and pulled it just out of his reach.

The Fallen glared at me, his eyes had gone completely black.

He then lunged forward, but Kade jumped and landed on his back, sending him crashing to the ground. As he pushed up, Kade swung his sword and took off his head, quick and easy.

I was in shock and complete awe. He was still a killing machine, even as a mortal. It was as if he hadn't changed. He was still my Guardian and my hero.

He stared at me with a look of satisfaction; he'd saved me again.

One down. Two to go. Hopefully there weren't any others lingering out there.

The earth suddenly shook around us again. Out of nowhere a body came flying at us, crashing against the tree behind me and falling to the ground with a thud. I leaned forward, and shielded my eyes from the splintering debris.

What the—?

I peeled my eyes open and gasped.

It was Danyel. And he wasn't moving.

Oh God. He better not be dead. Please don't let him be dead!

I nudged him and there was no response.

When I looked up, Kade was gone, but the body of the dead Fallen angel was still on the ground in front of me. His head was a few feet away, facing the opposite direction. Thank goodness. I didn't think seeing his mangled face would be good for me right now.

I quickly unsheathed my dagger and moved a little closer to Danyel. I placed my fingers on his neck, trying to feel for some type of pulse or any sign of life.

I felt a thrum. It was faint, but it was there.

"Danyel," I whispered in his ear, giving him a quick shake. "Danyel!"

He still didn't move.

There was heat on my chest and as I glanced down, the Bloodstone amulet was glowing bright red. I was almost certain now, the red glow meant danger.

The sound of breaking branches was close.

Standing up, I pressed my back against a tree, opposite the direction of the sound. As the footsteps grew louder and louder, the Bloodstone got hotter. It was warning me.

I carefully snuck a glance around the tree, and I saw him. It was the leader. His eyes were steeled on Danyel, and a wicked smile was adorned on his lips.

"Danyel, Danyel," he said sarcastically. "See what happens when you become soft? When you turn traitor?" He walked over and kicked him.

Danyel's body flew up against another tree. I covered my mouth and tried not to make a sound.

The Fallen paused, and started sniffing the air.

I suppressed my will to run because he'd catch me way too easily, so I froze. My pulse raced madly, and my hand gripped the dagger so tightly it hurt.

He stepped around the tree; his body mere inches from mine. I held my breath, and then he turned and stared directly at me.

I was dead.

I shut my eyes tight and awaited the inevitable.

"Where are you, Nephilim?" he growled. "I smell you. I know you're close. Come out and I'll make sure you and your friends live through this."

He then stepped around the tree and out of my sight.

What the hell just happened?

I looked down at my body and almost passed out.

I wasn't there. My hands, my body… they were gone. Completely gone.

I held my hands out in front of me.

Nothing.

I was freaking invisible.

SIX

I T HAD TO BE THE suit. I remembered Kade telling me it was magical—it could blend into its surroundings and even make the wearer invisible. I thought he was exaggerating, but he was telling the truth.

I looked back down at my hands again, and even the dagger I was holding was invisible. The more I focused, the more I could start to see an outline of myself; it was like a thin line tracing my shape, but everything inside of that line was gone. I was invisible. This was *crazy*.

Maybe I should have tried to kill that bastard, but if I missed or just injured him, he'd have known I was there and would have probably killed me. At least he was gone, for now.

Samuel and Kade were still out there, but so were the other two Fallen. I hoped they were okay. I figured if I stayed near Danyel, it would be easier for all of us to find each other.

Danyel moaned and his arm slightly moved. I knelt down beside him and carefully shook his shoulder. As soon as I touched him, he started to disappear.

I quickly let go and he reappeared.

"Danyel," I whispered.

There was no response.

A loud yell echoed through the dense forest, and was soon followed by a noisy clanging. I quickly grabbed Danyel's arm and pulled him behind a fallen log. I covered him as best I could with the dead leaves and branches.

I turned to see who was battling. It was Samuel and the Fallen I'd just encountered.

Danyel started to moan louder. He was slowly coming to.

"Emma. Emma!"

Kade was charging toward me, one hand grasping his sword, the other waving for me to either get down or move.

How could he see me?

I turned around and the last Fallen angel was charging at me, his sword raised above his head, only yards away. I gripped my dagger tightly and held it out in front of me, realizing I was no longer invisible. The Bloodstone was glowing bright red.

The Fallen angel swung at me, and as he did, I dropped to the ground just under his blade. I could feel the wind as it brushed against my face. He turned back and swung again, his blade meeting my arm. Pain radiated, but beyond the pain, I felt compelled to move.

In one fluid movement, I rolled over and jumped to my feet. I was behind the Fallen, and quickly pushed my dagger into the middle of his back. It went in easily, and I could feel the blade exit his chest.

I let go of the handle and stumbled backwards.

He turned to me. His eyes wide with shock. Blood dripped from the sharp metal protruding from his chest. He glanced down at the blade and then back up at me again.

Kade snuck from behind, and with a quick swish of his sword, took his head clean off. It hit the ground with a thud, and rolled to my feet.

I jumped backward and turned away.

Breathe. Just breathe.

Making a big mistake, I looked at my bloodied hands, and then it all set in.

Was I the one bleeding?

I checked my arm where his blade made contact, but the suit was still intact and there were no signs of injury. I knew I'd probably have one killer bruise under there, but at least I still had my arm. With the force he swung his sword, he should have easily taken it off. This suit, and Kade, had saved me again.

I looked at my bloody hands again, and everything became numb. My brain buzzed with the reality I had just helped kill someone. It was strange though, like I was on autopilot and the suit had taken over and assisted me. But the fact still remained, I'd taken a life with these hands. I had pushed a sharp dagger into a living, beating heart.

My world spun like a tornado, and darkness slowly crept over my eyes. The last thing I saw was Kade, rushing to catch me before I hit the ground.

"Emma," Kade whispered in my ear.

We were walking hand in hand down a beautiful forest pathway. It was bright, and the trees were in full bloom, dressed in their entire fall splendor. He turned to me and smiled. His hazel eyes were sparkling in the brightness of the sun, and his touch sent electric waves pulsing through every part of me.

I felt happy. Happier than I'd felt in a very long time. The gaping black void that was left by the death of my parents was filled because he was with me. Holding my hand. Making me want to live again.

As we continued to walk, the sun faded away, and the forest around us became dark and ominous. Kade's hand started to feel cold in mine. It felt different. Not the perfect fit like it usually was. I turned to him and the darkness enveloped us.

"Kade?" I breathed.

His hazel eyes changed to blood-red, glowing in the darkness. I screamed in horror as the fiery eyes locked on mine.

I tried to break loose from the grip, but whoever it was squeezed tighter, holding me still.

"Kade," I cried.

Whoever the red eyes were attached to didn't answer, but squeezed a little tighter.

"Stop. You're hurting me," I shouted.

"Emma. Emma." Kade's voice called.

"Kade! Where are you?"

I opened my eyes and was back, swimming in the warmth of his hazel eyes and his beautiful, familiar face. Samuel and Danyel were standing behind him with worried looks.

We weren't in the forest anymore, but in an enclosed building lit with glow sticks.

"Have a bad dream?" Kade asked, with a grin. He took hold of my hand.

"Yeah. It was actually pretty horrifying," I answered.

"I hope I wasn't the horrifying part," he said with narrowed eyes.

"Yes, Emma. We were getting worried that Kade had put some kind of spell on you, the way you were screaming his name," Danyel chuckled.

Samuel rolled his eyes and shook his head.

I was talking in my sleep. *How embarrassing.*

"I'm glad you came back to us, Emma," Samuel smiled.

"Yes, we're glad to have you back," Danyel chimed.

"I'm glad to see you're back to your normal self, too," I said to Danyel. He grinned widely, and looked as if he was as good as new. "How long was I out?"

"For a while," Samuel answered. "It's been a day and a half."

"What?" I gasped. I was out for a whole day and a half?

"Here Emma, drink this," Kade said, carefully holding the back of my head up, and placing the blue vial to my lips. I took a sip and let the effects of the potion work it's tingly magic throughout my body. After a few minutes I sat up and tried to remember what had happened.

"Where are we?" I questioned.

"We're at the portal," Samuel answered.

"Portal? How'd we get here?"

"We flew," Danyel answered with a smile.

"You flew and I was out for the whole thing?" I sulked.

"Well, I'm sure you'll get another chance, since your father has wings," Danyel laughed.

Kade offered his hand to help me to my feet. I scanned our surroundings. We must have been in the Santa Claus house. It was warm, cozy, and decorated with beautiful and sparkly Christmas things.

I was standing near a pine tree, fully decorated, with wrapped gift boxes placed underneath. On the opposite side of the room sat a plain green chair, with some kind of white, snowflake pattern on it. It had to have been Santa's chair. Behind the chair was a fireplace, but I didn't see any sign of a portal, and was hoping we wouldn't have to climb up the chimney to get to it.

"Emma, are you well enough to travel?" Samuel asked.

I did a quick assessment and felt completely fine.

"Yeah, I'm ready," I said.

"Then we should be going. We need to get to Lucifer as quickly as possible," he said.

I nodded as the acid in my stomach began to bubble.

"Don't worry, Emma. We'll all get through this together," Samuel nodded. He cracked a glow-stick, and walked up to Santa's chair. He then spoke two words.

"Patefacio portal."

I glanced at Kade.

He leaned over and whispered, "It means 'open the portal.'"

I nodded. I guess *that* was the most obvious thing to say.

I started to feel a chill in the air, and Kade took hold of my hand. He didn't say anything but he held it tight, and gave me a slight grin. Behind the green chair, a small red light began to swirl, reminding me of a spinning top.

"Are you sure you're ready?" Samuel asked.

"Ready," we all answered in unison.

"Wait," I exclaimed. "What will happen to us when we get there?"

I had no idea what to expect. Would we be entering a land filled with Darkling and Fallen ready to attack us? If we were, then maybe I wasn't ready.

"Don't worry, Emma," Samuel responded. "We'll have time to discuss everything once we cross."

I nodded and sucked in a deep breath. I was squeezing Kade's hand very tightly, but he didn't say anything. He just turned and smiled, and instantly melted my stress away.

"We'll be okay," he whispered. "I'll be right here with you. Just don't let go, and remember to breathe."

"Okay," I said, taking in another very deep breath and then exhaling.

Samuel stepped forward. He turned back and gave me a wink. "Don't worry, sweetheart. I'll see you on the other side." He then stepped into the red swirling lights, and he was gone.

I felt my heart stop for a brief moment and then Danyel stepped forward. He casually took another step into the lights, and by magic, he was gone too.

This was totally overwhelming. Kade wrapped his arm around my waist and led me up to the light.

"Are you sure this is safe?" my voice trembled.

"It's like taking a step, except your step will land you in a different world. This particular step, will be taking us into Hell," he grinned.

"Great," I murmured. That wasn't the kind of one-stepping I think I'd enjoy.

Saint or sinner, whether I liked it or not, Hell was my next destination. Kade still had a smile on his face and seemed to be fine with it, so I guess I should be too—as long as he was with me. I tightened my hand around his.

"Ready?" he whispered. He leaned over and pressed his lips against mine, taking me by total surprise.

"I am now," I breathed.

He grinned and we stepped forward, crossing the threshold from my mortal world, to the Underworld...where Fallen, Demons, and Lucifer awaited us.

Kade was right. As soon as my foot touched the ground we were in an unfamiliar territory. The ground was a desert wasteland.

Dry. Desolate. Dead.

The air was thick and heavy, and the heat coming out from the ground hurt my lungs. I felt like a fish out of water, trying to gasp for cool, fresh air, but there was none. And, the *smell*. The stench burned my nostrils, and was a hundred times worse than Darkling. I almost couldn't stand it. I wanted to puke.

"Don't worry, Emma. Eventually your senses will adapt and it won't be so bad," Kade said.

"Are you sure?" I said, gagging. My eyes were watering and my skin felt like it was melting.

"Well, not completely sure, but I'm hoping for both of our sakes that it does," he laughed and pinched his nose. *God, he was so adorable.*

I was glad we weren't in the dark, and we could see our surroundings. Steam rose from the larger cracks in the ground, and I started to feel beads of sweat trickle down my brow.

I had no doubt this was Hell.

I could feel my breath quicken, and my muscles tense, then, my body started to cool down; like someone hit a switch and turned on the AC. It felt like an icy blanket was placed over me, and instantly cooled my hot skin. It brought my senses back to life, and I felt I could breathe a bit easier too.

"Whoa, this suit *is* magic." Kade shot me a bewildered look. "It's cold. The inside of this suit just got really cold," I laughed, baffled.

"Do you have room for one more?" he asked.

"You wish," I said, blushing. "Actually, it would totally make you feel better."

"Yes, I'm sure it would. In more ways than one," he winked.

Damn. Even in Hell, he was charming.

I was really beginning to love this super suit. It was awesome. Yes, it had a few blood stains and dirt blemishes, but it was working.

And it seemed the longer I wore the suit, the stronger I felt. Even if it was a false sense of strength, at least it was something. Right now, I'd take anything.

I was now a part of an entirely different world, and being a part of this new world, I needed to rewire my thinking. I'd have to kill, or be killed. I'd have to watch loved ones suffer and die, and yet continue to live.

Kade gently squeezed my hand, bringing me back to reality.

Samuel and Danyel were just ahead of us, quietly discussing our next move.

About a hundred yards away, I noticed a solitary tree sitting in the middle of the vast barren land. It was massive and looked out of place, completely void of life. Its large twisted branches appeared to be charred...stretching, reaching, and trying to escape the constant torture of its habitation.

Torment. It was the one word that came to mind as I observed the tree doomed to spend its eternity here. A perfect depiction of Hell.

"So what's up with that tree?" I asked, curious to see if he knew anything about it.

"That, is the entrance into Hell," Kade answered, with his hand outstretched toward it.

"That *tree* is Hell's gate?" I replied, shocked.

He nodded and grinned.

"I guess I thought the entrance of Hell would have been a bit grander, but I can also see how the nightmarish, Tim Burton tree seems to fit."

Kade laughed, but the longer I stared at it, the more anxious I became.

I seriously hoped this tree wasn't like the trees in the *Wizard of Oz*. The ones that came to life, spoke, and threw things at you. Yes, I did have an overactive imagination, but this was also Hell, and anything was possible. I'd already seen my share of the unbelievable, and knew my world would never be the same.

How many people—human people—actually travel into Hell and live to tell about it?

None.

At least none that I knew of. I never thought this place truly existed, or even gave it a second thought. It was just a place where evil people were sent when they passed.

Samuel's voice broke the insanity swimming around in my head.

"Alright, this is the plan," he announced. "I'll be taking Kade this time. The reason being, I'm supposed to be dead. If anyone notices me, my quest will be over. Emma, Danyel will be taking you. It's our best bet. Lucian's band of Fallen haven't returned to Hell since they left, so Danyel should be safe from anyone recognizing him."

"What are we supposed to be doing?" I asked.

"You should appear to be unconscious, like you've been put into a sleeper, and we will be the ones delivering you into Hell," he said.

"Is that legal? I mean, taking someone into Hell before they die?" I asked.

"There is a code. No one can go to Hell, unless they choose it, or deserve it. Sometimes, those bound for Hell will pray to be taken before death. The Fallen are sent to collect them, then put them to sleep and deliver them." Samuel explained.

I sighed.

"Emma, no one comes to Hell unless their hearts absolutely deserve it. This is where the worst of the mortal race live out their lives. In Hell, they relive the horrors they put others through, over and over, and feel every bit of pain and terror their victims felt," Danyel added.

I nodded. I guess that was justice. I just wanted to get in and out as quickly as possible. I didn't care who was there. The only thing I cared about was making it out alive with Samuel, Danyel, and Kade.

"Emma, Danyel will put the sleeper on you. Kade, you will need to stay awake just in case we need you," Samuel said.

Kade nodded.

"Wait, can't I just fake it? I don't think I'd want to be sleeping if something happens. I'd like to be able to help, and not just be dead weight," I said.

But as soon as the words left my mouth, and I really thought about it, maybe it wouldn't be such a bad idea...to die without knowing.

Samuel smiled. "Alright then. When we make it past the guards, we'll follow Danyel's lead. He knows the best way to maneuver through Hell. Are you sure you can do this awake, Emma?"

"Well, my mom always called me a drama queen. This will be my chance to prove her right," I admitted.

He grinned and nodded in agreement.

So this was it. Our quest was officially starting.

When we were about fifty feet away, Danyel swooped me up into his strong arms, and I rested my head on his muscular chest, letting my limbs fall limp.

"Just try not to move. Our lives depend on it, Drama Queen," Danyel teased. His mouth turned up into a wide smile. His black hair cascaded over his dark brown, almost black eyes. He was very handsome, for an older guy.

He raised his head and began walking, carrying me like I was a bag of feathers in his arms. I couldn't believe this was my father's best friend, and they were centuries old. That's the part I liked about the whole immortal thing. They didn't age quickly.

What would I look like in a few centuries?

I sighed deeply and then glanced over my shoulder to Samuel and Kade. Kade looked like he was dead, perfectly limp and lifeless, and I wondered if I could pull that off.

"We're almost there," Danyel whispered.

That was my warning to play dead. I closed my eyes, took a deep breath and tried to relax. Deep inside I wanted to see the entrance of Hell and what we'd be facing, but even though my inquisitive mind wanted to know…there was no way I'd risk my life to appease that curiosity.

After another minute of walking, Danyel stopped. We were at the tree. The suspense was killing me, but I stayed as still and lifeless as I could.

I listened to the slow and steady beating of his heart, and felt the steady rise and fall of his chest, and it helped to relax me. He was extremely good under pressure.

Danyel started speaking loudly, in a language I didn't understand. It didn't sound like any language I'd ever heard on earth. Maybe it was the language of the angels. Whatever language it was, it was breathtaking.

Boom! Boom! Boom!

Loud footsteps shook the ground beneath us.

"I am Danyel, and this is Vassago," he spoke in a low, authoritative tone.

Vassago? He must have been referring to Samuel.

"We've been sent by Beleth. We bear two human souls for delivery. Murder suicides," Danyel added.

My mind instantly painted a picture of a huge troll-like creature with sharp teeth, while my heart continued beating wildly. Danyel gave me a slight squeeze and I realized I had tensed. He adjusted and I relaxed into him.

Butter. A vision of a block of butter, slowly melting, shrinking, and turning into a liquid began to play through my mind. Why butter? I seriously had no clue, but it helped.

"Marks," a very deep voice growled. It sounded like it belonged to something horrendous. My mind flashed to the Darkling on steroids. Danyel bent slightly to the left to show behind his ear, then straightened back up.

"And you."

He must have been referring to Samuel. There was silence for a few moments, and I began to feel the thump, thump, thumping of my heart, pounding loudly like a drum. But just before I could conjure up any more horrific visions, I heard a word that instantly settled me down.

"Enter." The voice behind the words didn't sound happy at all. But who would be happy guarding the gate of Hell? Not me, that's for sure.

I felt Danyel walking, but dared not open my eyes or move. He didn't say a thing either and I figured if the coast was clear, he'd give me some kind of indication. I tried to listen to our surroundings.

I could hear voices in the distance, but as time went on, I recognized the noises as cries—tormented cries that made my stomach churn. My pulse raced again, the air around us was hot and suffocating. It felt like I was sitting in a car on the hottest summer day, with the sun beating down on us, while all the windows were rolled up. It was torturous.

The places on my body covered with the super suit were somewhat cool, but everything else was in danger of melting off. I didn't know how much longer I could take it. The heat was slowly smothering me, and not being able to move was making me claustrophobic.

Suddenly, I felt a blast of cool air over my face—instant relief. I wondered how, but felt Danyel's chest rise and then fall again with another cooling breeze. His breath was unexplainably sweet, and felt as wonderful as a cool winter's breeze. He breathed life back into me, just in time.

After a few more minutes we stopped, and I heard Danyel's voice whisper in my ear, "Emma, you can open your eyes now."

As soon as my eyes popped open, they burned from the heat. I blinked rapidly, allowing them a moment to adjust.

Samuel and Kade were to the left of us. We had entered the Underworld, an underground cave.

A shiver ran down my spine.

If I had my phone, I would have totally snapped some photos of this journey. It would have made an awesome photo journal. Emma's Descent into Hell. Yeah, come to think of it, I probably wouldn't like flipping through those pages, or taking a trip down this particular memory lane.

I silently vowed to myself that when this was all over, I'd never set foot in another cave. Unless I had to save someone's life, like this time.

I was surprised at how easy it was to get into Hell. But then again, wasn't Hell the easier path to take? And I guess there weren't too many people knocking on the door to get in.

"Hey, how are you holding up?" Kade asked, taking a seat next to me.

"Hot, but alright I guess," I said with a smile. "And, you're looking pretty hot yourself."

He caught my little joke and laughed. "Why, thank you."

I noticed trails of sweat down the side of his face. His hair was damp, and his face was a bit red and flustered. Being mortal, he was probably feeling the same torment I was, except worse, because he didn't have a super suit.

"Don't you have one of these?" I asked him.

"No," he laughed. "Angels don't need those garments. Those suits were created to mimic what angels already have, with the exception of a few magical things only the wearer can summon. There were only a handful created, and the humans, given these suits, were carefully selected. A chosen few. This suit was given to Alaine, and she possesses the gift of invisibility. Because you are her daughter, you were able to pull out the same gift from this suit. The cooling system is something all wearers can enjoy. If you look at Samuel and Danyel, they don't look flustered, and aren't even breaking a sweat. Withstanding the elements is part of being immortal."

"Really? Wow," I breathed, completely astounded.

"Here." He handed me the blue vial. I noticed it was only half full, which wasn't much. "You should take a sip."

"No, I'm fine," I said, pushing it back at him. "You need it more than I do."

"I've already taken mine. Please. It will help to manage the heat," he said, handing it back to me. He was still trying to protect me. Still trying to be my Guardian.

As I reached for the vial, our fingers touched. I missed the shock I'd get whenever he'd touch me, but he still made my heart thrum.

I took a sip of the liquid, and this time it felt like a tall glass of ice water, running down and coating my parched throat. I closed my eyes and let the chill continue to run its course through my veins, cooling every cell. Whatever was in this bottle was miraculous. This liquid could change the world and help a lot of people.

"So what's next?" I questioned.

"Well, that was the easy part," Danyel said. "We haven't even reached the first level yet, and there are five. That's even before we reach the last gate to Lucifer, if we get that far."

I exhaled, and along with my breath went a bit of my hope.

"But we're here, and if we all work together, I believe we can get through this. We will all make sure of your safety, Emma," Samuel said.

"'Til death," Kade and Danyel agreed.

"I don't want you to risk your lives for me. I just want all of us to get out of here together," I said. And that was the truth.

I shook my head as they pulled out their weapons. Danyel had a samurai looking sword strapped to his back. Samuel had a beautiful sword that looked like it belonged to a Knight, and Kade had his own sword, the one he'd already used multiple times to save my life. All razor sharp, all immortal blades.

Samuel took Kade and went up ahead to see if the area was clear. I decided to pull out my dagger and hold it in my hand. If it was out, it would be easier to use.

"Where did you get that?" Danyel asked, taking hold of my wrist so he could observe the blade closer.

"Dom gave it to me."

"This dagger looks like the one which belongs to the Archangel Michael," he whispered mostly to himself.

"It is," I replied. "Dominic said Michael gave it to him."

His eyes narrowed.

"Michael gave Dominic his dagger?" He looked completely baffled. "Angels never give up their weapons, especially when it's as unique as this one. The only reason they would is if they know of a greater purpose for them," he said, still holding my wrist tightly.

Kade and Samuel appeared from around the corner.

"Hide," Samuel urged.

We all ducked into a small side cave and waited as a bunch of loud voices passed. A handful of drunken Fallen passed by, laughing and spurting obscenities.

"Is there an easier way to get down to the lower level without being seen?" I asked.

"Usually, when a member brings a soul into Hell, they take it to a collection area. They do not actually deliver the soul themselves, it's just dropped off. There is no way we would be able to go that way, because that place is riddled with Fallen. We'd be spotted and killed for sure."

"So what's our other option?"

"We travel through the five levels of Hell, and deal with each one of the horrors guarding them."

"Are they worse than the Fallen?" I questioned.

"Let's just say, if we go the first way, we will be met with hundreds of Fallen all at once. If you go through the levels, you will meet whatever was placed there. Each gate has a Guardian, specifically placed by Lucifer, to ensure no one would dare attempt to pass. Each Guardian is worse than the last, and no one has ever survived."

"Until now," Samuel said, patting my shoulder.

"Until now," Danyel said, with a grin.

What had we gotten ourselves into? No survivors? And, I was pretty much worthless when it came to fighting.

But, I did have two Fallen warriors with me, and my kick-ass Guardian.

"Don't worry, Emma," Samuel whispered. "We'll take each

level slowly, and make sure everyone gets through safely."

I nodded, because there wasn't much more I could say. What he said sounded easy enough, but I had a sinking feeling that taking it slow wouldn't matter.

Samuel stood, and the others followed.

"Level one is a few hundred yards away, and we need to get moving. But first, let's go over all the rules. No deviations. No questioning. If any of us should get separated, the remaining ones will continue on with Emma. If one is hurt and cannot continue, the others must leave him behind. If one is killed, the same applies. The only way we retreat is if Emma gets injured and needs to be taken to safety. We have one goal, and that is to get Emma to Lucifer. If she doesn't make it, we fail, and all the others will die. Failing is not an option. Do you understand?" Samuel was dead serious, looking at Danyel and Kade.

"Yes," they agreed, and then hugged each other in the manliest way possible.

The speech was good for them, but totally sucked for me. There was no way I could walk away if I saw any one of them injured, or worse. I could not move on knowing someone was lost. It was not going to happen. Yes, we needed to complete this quest, but no one was going to be left behind. Not on my account.

"Are you ready, Emma?" Danyel asked, holding his hand out to me.

"Yes," I answered, taking hold of it.

"You'll need help walking."

"Walking? Why would I need help walking?"

"You'll see," he returned.

SEVEN

LEVEL 1

OUR DECENT INTO THE DEPTHS of Hell felt like we were slowly being boiled alive.

Hot as Hell.

Now I completely understood the saying, and I quickly understood why Danyel asked for my hand. It was to help guide me through a steep, narrow path, littered with large, sharp stones. A hellish nightmare. On one side of the path was a wall covered in sharp rocks, and on the other was a straight drop, down into a hot lake of lava about a thousand feet below. Above us hung large stalactites, deadly, and ready to fall and pierce any one of us.

The cooling effects of the potion were beginning to wear off, and sweat poured down my face. As we traveled downward, it became even hotter, and the suit was having a hard time adjusting and keeping me cool.

Come on, cool me down. If you don't, I'll die.

Right after I thought it, I could actually feel myself get a little cooler. Whoa. This suit could actually read my thoughts. That was freaky. Cool, but freaky.

How was Kade handling without a suit?

"Once we pass the first gate, the heat won't be as bad. It's hotter here because we are directly exposed to the heat from the lava below, but it'll be a little more bearable once we get into the caves," Danyel said.

We were nearing a large dark cave when he stopped me, and held up his hand. We all paused. My heart beat a thousand times per minute and the Bloodstone glowed bright red.

"What is it?" I whispered.

Danyel sniffed the air.

"We need to be careful. The first Guardian is very near. Probably right beyond the veil of darkness, watching us," he said softly, his eyes locked into the darkness of the cave. I strained to see whatever it was he was talking about, but then I heard it.

The ground quaked all around us, from steps being taken by whatever humongous creature was coming. My breath quickened and my heart thrummed loudly against my chest. I slowly stepped behind Danyel.

Kade came and stood right behind me. I leaned back into him, not only for support, but because knowing he was there, gave me strength. My body was trembling—his was firm and unshaken.

His lips lightly brushed against my ear, and then he softly whispered, "I'll still protect you, no matter what. I won't let anything hurt you."

"Thank you," I whispered back. My heart expanded with his words.

I didn't realize how fast and hard I'd fallen for him. If what Samuel and Alaine had told me was true, then the moment we touched, our hearts were bonded. I wouldn't have believed it if I didn't feel it. I'd never felt like I wanted to be so close to someone before.

His arms wrapped tightly around me, so I closed my eyes and focused on being safe in his strong embrace. His beautiful face was close to mine, and his voice was warm and comforting.

The moment didn't last long. We were in Hell after all.

Danyel whispered and motioned for us to move back.

He and Samuel had taken crouching positions, ready to battle whatever showed itself from the darkness. A terrible growl echoed through the cavern. A growl unlike any I'd ever heard on earth. It sounded evil. Very, very evil.

The closer it got, the more the earth shook, throwing my balance off. I turned and wrapped my arms around Kade's neck and he held me tightly against himself.

"Here it comes," Danyel warned.

"What's coming?" I asked Kade, with my face buried in his chest.

"I don't know," he answered. "This is my first time into Hell too."

I had to look. I had to see what was coming, so I pulled away from Kade and turned around. Two huge, glowing eyes which looked like they were on fire, appeared out of nowhere. Kade quickly stepped in front of me, readying his sword.

"You'll be fine, Emma," Samuel said, attempting to reassure me. "Kade, stay back with her."

"I will," he answered.

As Samuel moved closer to Danyel, Kade grabbed hold of my hand and laced his fingers in mine. I was glad he did, because it connected us. His steadfastness and bravery transferred to me, and I didn't want him to let go. I needed his strength now.

The ground shook again. I tried to peer around Kade, but just when I thought the flaming eyes were shocking, what stepped out of the cave made my knees weak.

It was like no other creature I'd ever seen. It was huge, towering over twenty feet tall. It had a gray monstrous face carved from rock, which ran down its neck. Long pointy horns protruded from its head. But its body was different, and I recognized the fur instantly; a desert sand color, with huge paws and sharp claws. It was a lion. But tucked on its back were long, shiny black wings.

It stepped out and pounced at Danyel, mouth opened and filled with razor-blade teeth. Danyel leapt out of the way.

Something snapped from behind the creature, crashing only inches away from him.

I screamed.

The creature had a tail... and not just any tail, the tail of a freaking scorpion.

It stepped into the dim light and now glared at Samuel, baring its sharp teeth.

"State your business." The deep voice rumbled; fire spewed

from its mouth.

This was not happening.

I could feel myself start to hyperventilate, and I didn't think the super suit would be able to help me.

"We wish to see Lucifer. We have urgent news regarding his son, and a threat placed upon his life by Lucian," Danyel answered with the truth.

"Not possible. Lucifer sees no one, unless he calls for them. If you do not heed my warning, I will feed on your corpses and throw your bones into a pile to rot for all eternity. Leave now and return from whence you came," the creature growled, pointing his sharp claws towards the exit.

Heck yeah. I was ready to leave…like yesterday.

"We will *not* leave," Samuel yelled back. "And if you do not let us pass, we will have to kill you."

The creature began to laugh loudly. So loudly, everything around us began to quake again, sending sharp rocks crashing down around us.

Kade grabbed my arm and pulled me down, bending over to shield me.

"You…kill *me*?" The creature roared with laughter. "Why do you think Lucifer assigned me as Guardian? I'll cook you with a breath, and then eat you. When I'm done, I'll pick my teeth with your bones."

Samuel and Danyel looked at each other for a moment. They looked like they were pondering his advice. Were we going to leave? I seriously couldn't tell. Then, Samuel whispered something into

Danyel's ear, and there was another brief pause. Then, they burst into laughter.

I watched the creature's eyes flame with malice.

"Watcher of the gate," Danyel announced loudly. "You have done your job well, until now. But I'm deeply saddened to announce that you will be relieved of your duties this day, and for the rest of eternity."

Oh God. They were seriously flirting with death. I hoped they knew what they were doing. They were used to fighting in battles together, and hopefully had some kind of a plan. If they didn't, I'd be running toward that exit just as fast as my legs could carry me.

I glanced behind me to see if I could find the easiest route out. It was a nightmarish maze of jagged rocks, and I was shocked we'd even made it this far.

"Hey, don't worry about them," Kade whispered in my ear. His warm breath on my cheek sent tingles through me.

"Are you *seeing* that creature? Look how huge it is, and it breathes fire. They're gonna be toast. Burnt, crunchy toast," I breathed, and then looked into his hazel eyes. He was smiling, like he knew something I didn't. "Am I missing something?"

"Emma, they were trained before the Fall, and have been in battles for centuries. They are two of the best warriors, of Angel and Fallen alike," he whispered.

I stood there staring at him. My father and his best friend were not only centuries old, but two of the greatest warriors that had ever lived. I exhaled and I turned, looking at them with a new admiration. They didn't look old, not even close. Their bodies were fit, tanned, muscular, and glistening with sweat. I shook my head in complete disbelief.

"You insignificant scum. Prepare for death," the creature roared, baring its pointed teeth. Liquid dripped from its mouth and as soon as it hit the ground it burst into flame.

Its eyes burned an even brighter red as I watched it crouch, ready to strike again.

It leapt at Danyel, but Danyel ran and slid under its belly, popping up behind him.

With a quick swish, its scorpion tail whipped over its head and smashed right next to Samuel. Over and over it struck, but Samuel dove and rolled across the sharp rocks, dodging every strike.

I didn't realize I was holding my breath until I exhaled a loud sigh of relief when Samuel was finally out of its reach.

I watched Danyel raise his sword and slice the creature's hind leg. A blood-curdling roar reverberated off the walls, sending even more rocks crashing down around us. Fire spewed from its mouth like a flamethrower, torching everything in its path. I was horrified as I saw the flames heading toward Samuel.

"Samuel!" I shrieked.

He looked at me and grinned, as the most beautiful black wings appeared from his back and wrapped around him. I screamed as his body was engulfed in flames, but Kade put his hand over my mouth.

"He's alright, Emma," he whispered.

My instincts were to run to Samuel, but Kade held me back.

And then the creature fixed its fiery eyes onto me and Kade. We had nowhere to hide.

I watched its chest expand and mouth open—my life flashed before my eyes.

We were going to be burned to death.

I quickly turned and looked into Kade's eyes, hugging him tightly. His eyes were focused on the creature.

I instantly felt a searing heat.

Burning.

Excruciating.

I gritted my teeth and felt Kade lift me. He turned us around, and took the flames directly on his back.

I felt him groan, and watched his face wince in pain. I couldn't watch, and wouldn't allow him to die for me, not like this. I pulled him, trying to turn him away from the flames, but he held me tightly in place. Hot flames engulfed us, but he kept his arms wrapped tightly around me.

"Kade!" I screamed. "Kade move!"

But he didn't move, or say a word. He just kept me steady, away from the flames. The heat was almost unbearable. And then, it stopped and we were covered in darkness.

Samuel had come and shielded us from the scorching heat with his wings.

Another loud scream sent shockwaves over the ground. Danyel had sliced the creature's belly, but now it was pissed.

"Emma, I have to help Danyel. I'll be right back," Samuel said, with a look of concern on his face.

"Okay, but please hurry," I urged. "Kade needs help."

"I will," he said, before taking off in a split second.

Kade's eyes rolled back and he became limp. I tried to hold him up, but he was too heavy, and we both fell to our knees.

"Help!" I screamed, but they were busy battling the creature.

Kade moaned and then slumped over, unconscious. I sat back and placed his head on my lap, and that's when I noticed his back. My stomach lurched and I began to sob. It was the most horrific sight I'd ever seen.

The back of his shirt was gone, completely melted, along with his skin. All I saw was charred flesh, and bones, and blood oozing from the massive wounds. My heart broke, thinking of the pain he was enduring. Thank God he was unconscious right now.

In a flash Samuel was back, standing next to me.

"Emma, when he wakes you'll need to give him the potion from his vial. It will help ease some of the pain," he said, placing his arm around my shoulder.

"Is he going to die?" I sobbed. Just the thought was killing me inside.

"I cannot say. But he'll need that potion as soon as he wakes. Do you understand?"

I nodded, and looked into his deep brown eyes, mesmerized for a moment. I knew there was something familiar about him, the first time we met, and now I knew why. I had his eyes.

"You'll need to be strong now, strong for him, strong for all of us."

"I will be," I breathed.

Samuel leaned forward and kissed my forehead. He started to rise, but paused. "I'm proud of you, Emma. I've always been. I'm sorry I never had the chance to be a father to you, and I do wish things were different," he said with sad eyes. Jumping up, he was gone before I could answer him.

Tears cascaded in waves down my cheeks. I wanted to tell him it was okay. I wanted to tell him that even though he wasn't there for me before, he was now. I wanted him to know that I loved and appreciated him. I hoped he knew.

It wasn't his fault he fell in love with Alaine. And it was absurd to think their love was forbidden, or that their love child, was even more forbidden. At least the good angels sent Guardians to protect us.

Kade moved slightly and moaned in pain, and I didn't know what to do. His eyes suddenly popped open, and he tried to get to his feet.

I grabbed hold of his arm to keep him down.

"Don't move," I sobbed. "Please don't move."

His hazel eyes were bloodshot and riddled with pain. I reached in his pocket and pulled out his blue vial, twisted the cap off, and held it to his lips. "You need to drink this."

He didn't refuse.

When he was done, I noticed there was only enough for a few more doses, and we hadn't even made it past the first level yet.

A wave of doubt crashed over me, drowning my hopes. How was Kade going to survive through the rest of the levels without the potion? I wasn't even sure if he could stand, let alone walk. How were we supposed to go on? There was *no way* I was going to leave him.

"Hey," he said softly, breaking my sudden panic. I knew he was in much more pain than he was allowing me to see.

"Kade, I'm so sorry. You shouldn't have turned around. This suit would have been able to withstand the heat," my voice trembled.

The flesh on his back had completely melted off, his bones were showing, he was bleeding, and yet, he still managed to hide the pain and make me feel like everything was going to be okay.

"I wasn't about to take that chance," he said. His breaths were shallow and his voice was weak.

"How are you feeling?" I asked. That was an extremely stupid question, and I knew it the second it left my lips. He wasn't good. He should be in a hospital, in critical care.

"I've had better days," he laughed, and then winced in pain.

"You can't go on. You need to go back and let Alaine help you," I said. I didn't want him to leave me, but even more than that, I wanted him to get the medical attention he needed.

"No," he said shaking his head.

I knew he'd say no. He was my Guardian and thought it was still his duty to stay and protect me.

"You need to get help, Kade. You're severely burned, and we don't have much potion left. I don't even know if you can walk, and we still have a long, long way to go. There is no way I'll be able to leave you. You have to go back," I pleaded.

"I'm not leaving you, Emma. I'll be fine. Just give the potion a moment to take effect and I'll be able to move."

I knew the potion should have already taken affect. It was instant, but his words showed it was barely taking away his pain.

An ear-piercing scream sent a shiver up my spine. Samuel had just removed the creature's stinger from its tail. It was pretty sliced up, its golden fur was soaked with crimson blood, and one of its horns was missing. There were several deep gashes across its sides.

"If you let us pass, we will let you live," Danyel said, with his sword held to the creature's neck.

"Even if you let me live, Lucifer will kill me for allowing you pass," he growled. "I'd rather die by your sword, than to be tortured forever in Hell."

Danyel looked to Samuel, and Samuel gave him a slight nod.

The creature lowered its head to the ground and closed its eyes. Danyel raised his blade into the air, and in one, quick fluid motion his sword came down, severing the creatures head from its body. It happened so fast that if I blinked, I would have missed it.

Danyel stepped away and wiped his blade. I almost had pity for the creature, until I heard Kade moan. And then, I was glad it was dead. It had gotten what it deserved, and was lucky it didn't have to suffer like Kade.

Danyel and Samuel hurried back to us, and their faces grew with concern as they noticed Kade's back. Samuel knelt next to me, resting his hand on my shoulder, and Danyel stood behind him. His eyes were deeply troubled.

"Kade, have some of my water," Danyel said, bending down to hand him a flask.

Kade drank, and I could see a bit of relief on his face as the ice-cold water touched his lips.

"That needs to be tended to," he said, looking at Samuel, gesturing to his back.

"Is there any potion left?" Samuel asked.

"There is enough for about two more doses," I replied, handing him the vial.

Samuel took it, unscrewed the cap, and then leaned over Kade, pouring most of what was left of the liquid onto his burns. Kade's jaw tightened and the look on his face told me he was in agonizing pain, a pain I wish I could help relieve or take away. I watched, helpless, as his muscle began forming and binding across his back. That should have been me, but because of Kade, and the suit, I barely had any burns. Whatever I did have would probably be healed by morning.

"The potion will help him with the healing process and also take away some of the immediate pain," Samuel said, reading the horrified expression on my face.

I glanced at Kade. His face had relaxed a bit, but his eyes and jaw were clinched tight, and he was taking shallow breaths—which I found myself mimicking.

"Is the potion gone?" I asked.

"No, there is just enough for one more sip," Samuel said. "We have to go. Can you walk, Kade?" Danyel asked, placing a hand on his shoulder.

"What? He can't go anywhere! There is no way. Can't you see his back?" I cried.

Kade's eyes opened. They were weary from pain, but he turned and looked at me. "Don't worry about me, Emma. I'll make it. I'm not sure how long this potion will last, but the sooner we get this over with, the better," he said, with a crooked grin.

How the heck could he do that? How could he act like he wasn't in excruciating pain? It must have been the potion. That was some pretty powerful stuff, but it would eventually wear off and out, and then he'd be in a worse position.

His smile was like a beam of sunshine in the darkness. I wanted to wrap my arms around him, but right now that was just not going to happen.

Samuel and Danyel reached down and each took one of Kade's arms, carefully lifting him to his feet. Once he was up, they slowly let him go. He wobbled a bit, and I held my breath. His weak eyes found mine, and he winked. He actually winked.

I reached for his hand, and he quickly laced his fingers through mine. His hand felt hot, like I had gripped the handle of a red-hot pan, but I dared not let go. Right now, we were each other's strength.

"Let's move," Danyel urged. "Kade, would you like help?"

"No. I'll be fine," he answered.

Danyel and Samuel had their swords ready, and slowly started walking toward the dark tunnel the creature had come out of. I moved forward, but Kade didn't move with me.

"Are you okay?" I asked. I studied his face, which seemed to be growing more and more pale.

"I'm fine. I just wanted to—"

He pulled me until I was against him, and then leaned down and pressed his warm lips against mine. His fingers carefully wrapped around the back of my neck, pulling me deeper into the kiss.

My hands found his face, and I steadied myself, drinking in his warmth and love. His lips were soft and sweet, and his kiss took me to an unknown place. I was no longer in Hell, but floating somewhere else, somewhere beautiful, alone with him. We were lost in a heaven all of our own. I never wanted the moment to end, but he pulled away, leaving me numb and dizzy.

"Thank you," he whispered with a smile. "You give me strength. Much more than that potion."

I couldn't speak. His kiss had sucked all words from my mouth. I smiled at him and he reached and took hold of my hand. My heart felt like it was going to burst from my chest. All I wanted to do was get out of this miserable place.

I knew it was just a matter of time before he would be in torturous pain again, and all I could do was hope and pray we could get through it all before that happened. I needed him, and it seemed he needed me just as much.

"Hey, are you two coming?" Danyel yelled.

I looked at Kade and he nodded. Confident with him by my side, I took in a deep breath and stepped forward.

EIGHT

THE TUNNEL WAS LONG, PITCH black, and at a downward slope. There was a faint glow at the end, a few hundred yards away. Here, a few hundred yards seemed like a thousand miles, especially with the damned treacherous terrain.

Samuel dropped glow sticks about every ten feet to help light our path. I kept a tight hold on Kade, each of us trying to hold the other up from tripping and falling onto the jagged rocks below. With every step, deeper and deeper into Hell, the air was getting thicker. I could barely manage, and began to worry about Kade, who was starting to slow down.

As we finally made our way out from the tunnel I glanced over to him. He caught my eye and I could tell something was very wrong. He was looking much paler, and the dark circles under his eyes had become prominent. He didn't look like he was going to hold out much longer.

"Let's stop for a minute," I said. I knew we needed to, and I wasn't going to let him go any further. Each breath he took was labored.

"I'll be fine," he answered weakly, and then coughed.

He was lying because he was trying to keep me from feeling sorry for him. The heat in this place made my skin feel like it was boiling, and I had on the suit. His burnt flesh was directly open to the scorching heat.

I stopped and held him back.

This wasn't supposed to happen. I couldn't let him suffer like this. I knew he'd follow me all the way into the depths of Hell to protect me, even if it killed him. But I wouldn't allow him to. I couldn't stand by and watch him suffer, let alone watch him die.

"Samuel," I called in an urgent tone. I didn't care if it was louder than it should have been, this was a matter of emergency. I needed them to stop and listen.

Both he and Danyel turned back.

"No, Emma. I'll be fine," Kade pleaded, but I noticed a line of blood trickling down the corner of his mouth. He noticed my eyes, which were wide with horror, and he quickly wiped it away.

My breath caught in my throat.

"You're not fine, Kade. *This* is not fine. We need to get you out of here!" I could feel myself losing it. Seeing him like this was tormenting every part of me.

Samuel quickly made his way back to us.

"What is it, Emma?" he questioned.

"It's Kade. He needs help. You have to help him," I cried.

Samuel took a good look at Kade, and I saw his eyes close.

Kade's grip loosened, and I watched his eyes roll back as he went limp. Samuel reached out and grabbed him under his arms to keep him from falling to the ground.

"Kade!" I screamed. At this moment I didn't care about anything else but him.

"He won't make it any farther," Samuel noted. "He's losing too much blood."

"Blood?" I looked down and noticed a small puddle of blood by his feet, and we'd only been standing there for a few minutes. I wondered how much blood he'd lost while we were walking.

Kade moaned and it made my stomach twist.

"I'm sorry, Emma," he breathed.

"No, Kade. I'm sorry. I'm so sorry," I sobbed. "We need to get him out of here, *now*." My heart was being torn apart, bit by bit. Tears poured down my cheeks.

Samuel paused. His eyes furrowed.

"Don't let him die, Samuel. Please, don't let him die," I pleaded, holding Kade's hand. "Promise me. Just promise me that you won't let him die!"

I couldn't bear to watch him suffer. I wished there was a way he could be turned back into an immortal, that way he would be able to heal. But I knew that wasn't going to happen. Not here, not now.

"Emma. I made a promise to your mother that I would keep you safe. We need to finish this mission, or Kade, along with everyone else, will die."

"So what are you saying? We're going to leave him here to die?"

I yelled, at the brink of hyperventilating. If he was assuming I'd leave Kade, he was out of his mind. It wasn't even an option.

"Danyel!" Samuel called. Danyel was up ahead, sword ready, eyes peeled, making sure that we didn't have any unexpected visitors. His head snapped back and Samuel motioned him to come.

"What are we going to do now?" Danyel asked.

"I want you to take him back," Samuel replied, followed with an exhale.

"What? I'm not leaving you on this mission alone, Samuel." His eyes narrowed.

"You have to. We have no other choice. Kade will die if he stays here any longer and Emma refuses to leave him behind. You'll have to find a way to get him back to Alaine, or at least to the safe house."

"And what about you and Emma?" Danyel asked, glancing over to me.

I sobbed, "Please, Danyel. I won't go any further unless you take him. I can't go on if he dies. He needs help, badly. He needs Alaine."

Danyel paused for a brief moment, considering the situation.

Samuel placed his hand on Danyel's shoulder. "Don't worry, brother. I'll take Emma the rest of the way, and make sure we complete our mission."

Danyel sighed. His eyes told me he was torn between taking Kade to safety, and leaving us in Hell to continue this perilous journey alone. I knew he didn't want to leave Samuel, but he also knew if Kade stayed in this place any longer, he would die.

"Please, Danyel," I begged.

He finally nodded, conceding, and took in a deep breath.

"You already know what will greet you at the next four gates," he said to Samuel.

Samuel nodded.

"Strength and honor, brother. And Godspeed." Danyel said. He hugged Samuel like he'd never see him again.

"Godspeed," Samuel repeated.

That was something I never thought I'd hear coming from the mouths of Fallen angels, but then again, they weren't your average Fallen. They had been around since the beginning, and were starting to doubt their choices and what they were fighting for.

"Emma. If you should reach Lucifer, just remember not to be deceived by him. Keep your head. His tongue is forked, and he will try to seduce and lure you into remaining here. Remember what's real. Think on those you love. Alaine, Samuel, and Kade," he said with a wink. "Just remember who you are. Be confident. Lucifer, and those around him, feed off of your fear, so don't show it. Your father will guide you, and the suit should help. You just have to have faith."

I nodded, yet doubted his words because I wasn't really sure of who or what I really was. The only thing I had going for me was I could heal a lot faster than a human, but I was still mortal.

I felt like Frodo. My fellowship was falling apart, and instead of a Sam, I had Samuel. I knew he'd protect me and take me as far as he could. Would it be enough?

I wiped the tears from my face and stood to my feet. If anyone could do it, we could.

Samuel lifted Kade to Danyel's shoulders so he was lying across them.

"Can you put the sleeper on him so he won't wake up?" I asked Samuel.

"Yes, that's a great idea," he answered. He then placed his mouth near Kade's ear and whispered, "Sleep."

I was glad Kade would be able to sleep through the pain. I touched his limp hand and wished there was something, anything, I could do to help him.

My hope now rested in Danyel. Hopefully he would be able to make it out of this place, and back to Alaine without any trouble.

"Fly safe, brother," Samuel said, stepping in front of Danyel.

They each grabbed hold of the others' right forearm and gripped firmly.

"I'll see you both on the other side," Danyel returned. Samuel nodded, and then Danyel leaned over and kissed my forehead. "You are in the best of hands, Emma. Please, be safe."

"I will," I promised. "Thank you, for taking him."

He nodded, but I knew it was killing him to not be here for us.

Danyel started walking, and as soon as he hit the tunnel, he disappeared in a blur, leaving Samuel and I alone.

Everything rapidly got dark and eerie.

Sadness overwhelmed me. I had assumed Kade was going to be with me throughout this entire journey, but he was gone. Just like that. And almost every ounce of hope went along with him.

Samuel and I still had a ways to go, and if the guards of the next levels were anything like the one we'd just encountered, we were in serious trouble.

I mean, we barely made it past the first level, and already lost half of our team. This suit had better kick in some major super powers other than a dang cooling system. The invisibility thing was pretty awesome, but I needed extra super powers and some kick ass abilities to help Samuel.

Danyel said this suit could help me. But, how? Was there some kind of special power button I didn't know about?

Just in case nothing else worked, I figured I should shoot a quick prayer to God. A God I'd never known, a God I'd never met, and a God I'd only heard of in church, or on special occasions. But he was Kade's God, and once upon a time, Samuel, Danyel, and even Lucifer's. They believed in him, so I guess I should too.

I just wondered if my frail words could even escape this evil place and travel the long distance up to his ears, wherever he was. And even if they did make it to him, would he do anything? Would he help us?

It was worth a shot.

I said a quick prayer, a prayer that simply asked Him to protect Danyel and Kade on their journey, and to give me and Samuel the strength we needed to get out of Hell safely. That was it, followed with an *Amen*. I figured there wasn't much more I could say.

"Are you ready, sweetheart?" Samuel said, holding out his hand to me.

"Yes," I answered, taking hold of it.

"Alright, we are going to be entering the second level soon. I don't want you to be afraid, but I also want you to be aware of some very important details. I need you to keep your eyes on me at all times, and do *not* let them wander," he urged. "Coming up, there will be things you should not look upon, especially because you are not yet dead."

"That sounds completely dreadful," I exhaled. I didn't know if my heart could take much more.

"This next level is filled with soul snatchers, or ghouls. They feed off of the living and suck their souls right from their bodies, so keep your eyes focused on me at all times. If you should ever look away, call for me immediately. And whatever you do, *never* touch them. They will paralyze you with a single touch. Once they taste your essence, they will stop at nothing to steal your body and suck your soul from it, where it will remain with them for all eternity."

Okay, that was definitely not painting a pretty picture in my head right now. I started to envision zombie-like creatures hovering in the air, skin hanging off, mangled faces, and bulging eyes. Shivers ran up and down my spine.

"Emma." He stopped and steadied my head in his hands. "Do you understand what I just explained to you?"

"Yes. Can't you just blindfold me and carry me through?" I asked.

Samuel laughed. "I wish I could, but my arms need to be free to protect us. Just keep focused and keep your eyes forward. They won't even notice you unless you make eye contact with them. It's the eye contact that is the connection."

I sighed and started to doubt myself. I loved to watch scary movies, and tried to cover my eyes during the scary parts, but I always had to peek. I had to see what was coming, and what was going to happen, even if it was scary and they were going to die.

This time I couldn't peek because if I did, those scary soul snatcher ghouls would come and suck my soul and take my body. This confirmed my opinion of the Underworld. I hated Hell…every stinking part of it.

"Let's get going, sweetheart," Samuel said kindly. "We'll do this together."

NINE

LEVEL 2

"TELL ME ABOUT YOUR PARENTS," Samuel asked. "Tell me what they were like. I'd really like to know more about them."

That question threw me, but it took my mind off of everything around us, which I guess was his goal.

All the events that happened over these past few days, really kept me from thinking about them. The parents who raised and loved me as their own. The only ones I'd ever known my whole life. The ones who were ripped away from me in an instant. I missed them. I missed them horribly.

Emotions kept the words down in my throat. I didn't know what to say or where to begin. All I knew, from what I could remember up until the day they died, was that I loved them and they loved me.

"I'm sorry. You don't have to tell me. I was just trying to distract you, and thought that if your mind was on something familiar, or on the ones that you loved, maybe it would help. But, if it will cause you too much pain, let's think about something else," he said.

"No. I want to tell you."

"Good." He smiled and then gestured with his head. "The next gate is coming up."

"Okay," I breathed, and everything inside me started to tremble.

"The Fallen refer to this level as the Gate of Lost Souls," he said, in a ghostly voice.

We started into the dark tunnel, which was the next gate, but there nothing but darkness. I didn't hear any noises or moving around, and for a second, thought this level was going to be easy. As we came out of the tunnel and into an area where there was some light, I kept my eyes on Samuel, who was a few feet in front of me. If I reached out, I could have touched him.

I just started to relax when there was movement from the corner of my eye. I unexpectedly felt heat on my chest, and as I glanced down, the Bloodstone was glowing bright red. Evil was near. I fought the urge to turn my head and look, and it was killing me. Then, I thought I saw a white mist, but I wasn't sure. I kept my eyes glued to Samuel.

Stay focused. Keep your eyes ahead. Don't look. If you look, you die. I had to remind myself over and over again.

"So, tell me about your mother. Her name was Victoria, right? She and Alaine were half-sisters, so she must have been a wonderful person."

The thought of her made me smile, even in the midst of this terror.

"Yes. She was beautiful, and the best mom anyone could have

ever asked for. She was always there for me, and I never questioned her love. She and my dad gave me no clue that I was adopted. I did always wonder about my eye color, because theirs were green and blue, and mine were brown. Now, I know why. I have your eyes."

There was more and more movement on both sides of us. I felt helpless, as if hundreds of evil eyes were glaring at us, watching our every move.

I wanted to look. It was my natural reaction, and it took everything in me to keep from doing so. Things were hovering, and I could see them from the corner of my eyes. Soul Snatchers. It was the fear of what they could do which kept my eyes locked on Samuel.

"And your father, his name was Christian, right? What was he like?" he asked. I paused for a moment. "You're doing fine, Emma. Just keep moving. With every step, we're getting closer."

Yeah, to the next gate of horror.

I took in another deep breath, filled with hot air.

Focus. I tried to focus on Kade. Alaine. The other Guardians. Courtney. Caleb. We were doing this for all of them. To save them. I took in another deep breath.

"My father was really cool. If there was ever an argument between me and my mother, he'd take my side. He was always there for me. Whenever I was sick, he'd always check up on me. If I ever needed anything, he'd run right out and get it. He was a great dad. A really awesome dad." A tear escaped my eye, and trickled down my cheek.

"I saw them once, from a distance. I think it was on your fifth birthday. They had thrown a party for you in their back yard. You were so beautiful, Emma, even at that young age. I could tell they truly loved and adored you.

"Victoria and Christian were Alaine's only choice to be your parents, and she knew you would be safe with them. When Alaine was born, she was secretly whisked away, as you were, so no one knew who her real birth parents were. Well, very few immortals knew, but none in the mortal world. Not even her adopted parents knew. Alaine didn't find out about her mother and half-sister, until she turned eighteen. She sought them out after she went away to college, and found out her mother was dying from cancer. She only lived a few weeks after Alaine met her. It was devastating, but having Victoria in her life made things a little easier.

"When she asked Christian and Victoria if they would take and raise you, they immediately agreed. It killed her to have to give you up. The night you were born she held you in her arms and didn't want to let you go. She was devastated when they took you away. I tried to comfort her, but she closed herself off, not only to me, but to everyone. It took her a very long time to accept that giving you away, and letting you live a normal life, was the best thing for you.

"I'm glad she's had the chance to see you again and spend some time with you, but sad that it had to be this way. I'm sorry for the loss of Victoria and Christian, but it is my hope we return to Alaine safely. She's a remarkable woman with a huge heart, and an abundance of love to give," he said with a smile.

Wow. That was quite a story. I was learning more about Alaine and my parents every day. Things I never knew. Things that were kept from me my entire seventeen years.

Samuel turned back to me. His face was glowing, and his brown eyes gleaming. He was very handsome, my father, and I was glad that I had this time to spend with him. Even if we didn't make it through the five levels, at least I had a chance to put some of the missing pieces of my life together. I could see how much he and Alaine cared for me.

The sounds around us were growing louder and louder. Screams of pain and terror were so loud, it was as if they were right next to me. I wanted to close my eyes and disappear from this nightmare, but I continued to push on.

Samuel reached back and took my hand. His fingers tightened around mine, and as they did I took in another deep breath and refocused.

"Come on, Emma." He was calm but firm. Leading me forward, we moved step by miserable step, across the field of jagged rocks.

We were more than halfway there when I heard a familiar voice calling my name. I paused, but only briefly, trying to decide if my ears were playing tricks on me. There was no way it could have been the voice I thought I was hearing. I wanted to look, but my inner voice was telling me to keep my head straight.

"Emma. I'm here, my sweet Emma. Come to me my darling," the voice sang.

No way.

There was no mistaking that voice. It was my mom, Victoria. I knew her voice well, and the one that was calling me, was undeniably hers.

"Emma," she called.

I couldn't refrain. I had to look. I turned my head, and immediately heard Samuel's voice yelling, pleading. "No, Emma. It's not her!"

He jerked my hand, but it was too late. My eyes had already locked onto my mother. She was floating towards me, as graceful and beautiful as she'd always been. She was dressed in a flowing white gown, her face was flawless and beaming, and her perfect red lips were turned up into a warm smile. Her green eyes were piercing, and her delicate hand was outstretched, beckoning me to come.

I was tingly all over and my head felt like it was lost in a fog. My heart was telling me no, but my mind was telling me to go. I must have been in some sort of trance, but my mind warring within itself. Every cell within me wanted to run into her arms and never let her go, but yet…there was that still small voice, telling me this was not real.

Why would my mother be in Hell? There was no way she could end up in a place like this. My mother was destined for Heaven.

"Come to me, my sweet Emma, and we will be together forever." Her voice was melodic, pushing my better judgment deeper and deeper into a dark, shrouded abyss.

I attempted to shake Samuel's hand free and run to her, but his grip was locked securely around me. He pushed me back, then jumped in front of me and swung his sword at her.

"*No,*" I cried, as his blade passed right through the center of her, causing the apparition to disintegrate into a white haze. The haze instantly began to take shape again, but this time, the reappearing apparition was not my mother.

I gasped and fell backwards. My eyes locked with this grisly creature. They were black and deeply sunken; its face was shriveled, long, and terrifying.

Pain shot through the palms of my hands. I knew they'd been sliced from falling back onto the sharp rocks. Warm liquid dripped from my wounds, but right now that was the least of my worries.

Samuel swung again and again, but his efforts were useless. The creature would dissipate for a few short moments, only to reappear with arms outstretched, eyes locked—heading straight for me.

"Run, Emma," Samuel yelled.

I tried to get up, but was surrounded with dozens of terrifying ghastly creatures. I reached for the dagger, unsheathed it, and grasped it tightly in my bloodied hands. I held on as tightly as I could, hoping it wouldn't slip. I forced myself to stand, and then glanced toward Samuel. He was still swinging away, and trying to make it back to me. "Run, Emma. *Now*. Get to the third gate!"

Gate? It wasn't really a gate. It was just another dark tunnel. But right now, that dark tunnel seemed much safer than the demon creature chasing me, wanting to steal my soul.

These past few days had drastically altered my life. I'd learned never to question those around me. In my new world, I could die if I paused, or questioned. I took off as fast as I could toward the next gate.

It looked about twenty-five yards away. I kept moving.

Twenty yards.

I was still on my feet, but my ankle twisted a few times. Sickening screams echoed on both sides of me. From the corners of my eyes I could see more white figures hovering in my direction.

Keep moving, don't look.

Fifteen yards.

A sharp pain shot through my ankle as it twisted again on an uneven rock jetting out from the ground. I went down hard, throwing my arms out in front of me to catch my fall. They were now doubly sliced to shreds. I should have been impaled by the sharp rocks, had I not been wearing the suit.

I managed to keep the dagger within my grasp, despite the slippery blood oozing from them. I knew the creatures were much too close, and I was out of time. Instead of getting up and running, I quickly rolled to my back to defend myself.

The nearest creature, a few feet away, had its mouth gaping wide, like a python unlocking its jaws, ready to swallow its victim whole.

I thrust my dagger upward, not sure if it would find its mark. As the dagger rose, its hilt began to glow with a blinding light. The light was so bright, it fully illuminated the darkness around me.

The point of the dagger passed through the creature, making it scream a painful cry, and then it shot off into the darkness.

Two more creatures attacked, so I swung the lighted weapon towards them. As soon as the light touched them, they shrieked and writhed in pain. Their withered hands tried to block the blinding light from their hollowed eyes, and they quickly retreated to the cover of darkness.

Samuel came and took hold of my other hand and pulled me up.

"Are you okay?" he asked, with a concerned look on his face.

I held the light over me to do a quick examination. No holes or anything life threatening, except for the blood covering my sliced hands.

"I'm fine."

Holding the dagger up high like a torch, we continued to move forward, listening to the painful screams all around us.

"Where did you say you got that dagger?" Samuel asked.

"Dom gave it to me last night. He told me it belonged to Michael the Archangel."

"I know exactly to whom that dagger belongs. I was there the day it was presented to him, as a gift from the Almighty himself. Only Michael, or those deemed worthy by him, could ever possess this dagger. Let alone be in possession of it for any given length of time.

"To be deemed worthy to possess such a gift is one of the greatest honors ever bestowed. Only a handful has been chosen to possess this magical and ancient relic, and up until now... they were only purebloods," he exhaled and shook his head, as if in complete awe.

He didn't need to speak another word. I could already read his expression very clearly. He was completely baffled. How could I, his seventeen-year-old, non-pureblood daughter be in possession of Michael the Archangel's dagger?

Hell if I knew. I was just as, or even more, baffled, and didn't even know who Michael the Archangel was. It was Dominic who he gave it to last, so Dominic must have been deemed worthy.

But now, the real question was...how did I end up with it?

Was it really calling to me, like Dominic said? Did Michael the Archangel know his dagger would end up in a non-pureblood's hands?

It couldn't have been an accident, so it must have been fate. It had to have been. There was no other reasonable explanation. None I could think of anyway.

Fate. That was such a broad word, one which I didn't fully understand, let alone use in my everyday vocabulary. I was beginning to learn that my life was now completely in fate's hands.

I shook my head.

Way too much information. My brain was already at full capacity.

I glanced at the dagger again. Its white handle was steadily glowing, keeping the creatures away. We were now only steps from the next gate, and I felt almost certain there was something, even more terrifying, waiting for us within the darkness.

Samuel wrapped his arm around me, most likely to keep me from tripping and falling again. I was thankful he did, because I didn't know how much more my injured hands could take.

"Any last words?" I questioned. He turned and looked at me with a raised eyebrow. "I mean, do you want to give me a heads up on what I should or shouldn't be doing when we enter this next gate? I sort of want to be prepared, and this time I won't question your advice."

He chuckled. "The only advice I have for you is to stay on your feet and move as quickly as possible."

"Crap. So what will I be running from this time?"

He paused. "Do you like snakes?"

"Snakes?" I exhaled. A shiver rolled down my spine at the thought of them. "I hate snakes. I'm terrified of them. So, like how many are we talking about?"

"Rough estimate? I'd say somewhere between one and thousands," he answered flatly.

My heart stopped beating, and I felt every ounce of blood drain from my face.

"But don't worry. I'll get you through it. There is one particular serpent I'll need to take care of first. You just keep your distance, and wait for my signal. Once I give you that signal, you will need to run."

"Where will I be running to?"

"To the end of the tunnel, but do *not* go beyond it." I was afraid to ask why. "There are many dangers beyond this cave, and things you definitely don't want to run into. Just stay about ten yards in. Hide yourself, and stay hidden until I come for you."

I nodded.

He sounded so sure. I just hoped he would be able to defeat whatever he was up against, without Danyel's help.

My body began to heat up, and I felt like I was suffocating. I closed my eyes and tried to focus and slow down my breathing. As I did, I felt a coolness wrap around me. I took in a deep refreshing breath.

"Emma, just stay behind me. Remember, when the next creature comes, I'll divert its attention, and will yell when it's safe for you to run," he whispered.

The ground began to shake, and I heard something moving ahead of us. And then, as added warning, the Bloodstone started to warm my chest.

TEN

LEVEL 3

I HELD THE LIGHTED DAGGER down to the ground to see what I'd be running through. The rocks here were different. They weren't sharp, nor did they jet out as much as the places we'd been. They were actually pretty smooth in comparison. But as I looked closer, I could see why. Something had broken off all of the jagged parts. Something humongous, which had probably slithered over them.

"Cover your light," Samuel breathed.

I quickly, but unwillingly, sheathed the dagger before gripping tight to Samuel's arm. It was pitch black and eerily quiet. The air had a heavy putrid smell lingering. The smell of death mixed with something else.

My feet crunched loudly with every step.

I reached down and touched ground. Whatever it was, it was rough.

"What is that?" I asked Samuel.

"I don't think you want to know," he replied.

I bent down and grabbed whatever was under my feet, and lifted it so I could see what it was. I could barely make it out, so I slowly lifted the dagger, just a bit, to reveal it.

Holy crap. I knew exactly what it was.

A loud hissing filled the tunnel. A sound that could only mean one thing. Snake. An exceptionally large snake...and I was holding its dead skin.

A shiver surged down my spine, and I dropped the giant snakeskin. Danyel was right. Each level was worse than the previous.

Out of nowhere, in the far right corner of the tunnel, bright yellow eyes floated toward us in the darkness. But it wasn't the ginormous eyes that had me terror-stricken—it was what was connected to them. I couldn't begin to imagine how much larger the rest of it was.

Samuel readied his sword, and as much as I dreaded to let go of him, I did.

"When I yell, take out your dagger and run. Let the light lead your way, and don't worry about me."

I nodded, swallowing hard.

"Emma? Did you hear what I said?"

I realized he couldn't see me because I was standing behind him.

"Yes," I breathed.

My eyes were glued on the approaching horror. Its devil eyes were targeted on us. From what I knew, snakes either used their tongues to taste their prey, or they had super keen night vision. I was assuming this one had night vision because it never wavered from our direction.

"You know what to do, right?" he asked again.

"Run, but don't run too far. Stay hidden and avoid venomous fangs," I breathed.

"Perfect."

My trembling hand gripped the handle of the dagger. I ran the plan through my mind, and prayed my feet wouldn't stumble, and would take me quickly and safely to my destination.

The serpent appeared in the dimmed light. Samuel started to run in the direction opposite of my escape route, yelling and waving his sword above his head. The serpent's eyes snapped in his direction. Its gargantuan body coiled into a striking position.

Crap, crap, crap.

"Emma, *move*!" Samuel yelled.

I paused, just for a moment, and watched the creature send its first strike at Samuel. It barely missed his arm, but its massive head struck the ground, sending rocks flying through the cave, like bullets from a gun.

I yanked out the dagger, and my heart fell hopelessly to the ground.

Its light was extinguished.

I pounded it, like I'd seen my dad pound a flashlight, trying to get it to work. It didn't help. Time was ticking and I was still in the same place. I needed to move.

I sucked in a deep breath and stumbled into the darkness, keeping the dagger in my hand and my arms out in front, to catch me in case I fell.

"Please light up. Please help me find my way," I begged.

After a few more steps, I felt a tingling and a heat in my palm, and the dagger began to flood my surrounding area with light.

"Oh, thank you. You don't even know how much I love you right now," I whispered, not caring I was talking to an inanimate object.

I willed my feet to move, and quickly made it past Samuel and the serpent. The serpent struck at Samuel again and again. Its loud hissing echoed throughout the tunnel. Pieces of rocks flew all around me, as its long tail whipped back and forth.

Sharp fangs were exposed, dripping with a clear liquid. Snakes had venom, and I suspected this particular one was deadly.

I moved as fast as I could, twisting through the rocky terrain, staying as far away from the serpent as possible. Just as I reached the end of the tunnel, I stopped. I'd reached my destination, and even decided to take a few steps back.

I slowly pushed the dagger out in front of me. A few feet ahead was a drop off. If I'd gone any further, I would have fallen. I held out the dagger even further, but was a bit too far from the edge to see how deep it went down. There was definite movement, and lots of it. I slowly inched my way closer, and against my better judgment, held the dagger out over the drop.

Thousands of snakes slithered in the depths of the pit. I stumbled back, my legs trembled. Samuel. Where was Samuel?

Why did it have to be snakes when I was alone?

I quickly turned back to the darkness of the tunnel and strained to find Samuel, but the darkness had completely enveloped him and the serpent. I could hear the swishing of the serpent's tail, the thrusting of Samuel's sword, and watched sparks fly as it clanged against the walls of the cave. I hated I couldn't see what was happening. At least Samuel had the ability to see clearly in the dark.

Samuel yelled and there was loud swooshing sound. The serpent screamed in pain so loud, I had to cover my ears. Something ricocheted off the ground and shot towards me. A long white object bounced a few feet in front of me. I held out the dagger to see what it was. It was one of the serpent's fangs. That was a close call because it was like a deadly arrow.

The fang was about twelve inches long. One side was jagged, where it had cracked off, and the other had a needle sharp point, wet with venom.

The battle continued, Fallen against serpent, and they started to move closer to me. I quickly tucked the dagger back into its sheath, not that it mattered.

My eyes slowly adjusted to the darkness, and I could barely make out the silhouettes of the serpent and Samuel slowly moving around each other. The serpent's head was flared out, like that of a cobra, ready to strike its prey.

Samuel lunged forward, and pierced its belly. It let out another ear piercing scream, and then returned with a quick strike of its own.

Samuel cried out, but I couldn't tell if he'd gotten hit or bitten. My eyes strained for an answer, and my heart twisted in my chest.

I watched the snake slowly withdraw, but there was no movement from Samuel.

What was I supposed to do?

I quickly unsheathed the dagger, which was still glowing, and headed toward him. I had to help. I had to make sure he was all right.

Out of the darkness, yellow eyes appeared in front of me, feet away. I screamed, almost falling backwards, but regained my balance and readied myself, holding the dagger toward it.

There was no way I'd be able to outrun it. It had total advantage in this hellhole.

I had to stand up against it and fight for my life, even if it meant my life would be taken. The Guardians would have fought until death.

I felt myself crouch, as I'd seen Samuel and Danyel do when they readied themselves for a battle. I was ready. I was going to be strong. For them.

The serpent slithered closer. Its long, forked tongue flicked in and out. One, sharp fang glistened in the dim light; its venom calling my name.

"Sss-weet child," it hissed.

What the—? Did that freaking snake just talk to me?

"I tassste your sssweetnesss. Your esssssence lingersss in the air. Ssso sssweet."

I felt pressure around my ankles. Glancing down, I watched its tail coiling around them, quickly spiraling upwards. I was terrified of being in tight, enclosed spaces, and instantly panicked. The horror of the situation almost got the best of me, but I refused to go down without a fight. Hell if this creature was going to squeeze the life out of me without getting some damage first.

"Let me go!" I shouted, threatening it with my dagger.

"Sssweet child. You won't feel a thing. I promissse."

And then it stopped abruptly. Its pupils became dilated and started to glow bright red. Its head swayed slightly, back and forth, like it was mesmerized. I could feel its grip on me start to loosen.

I'd seen this happen on before, on the Discovery Channel, to cobras when the snake charmers charmed them with movement and music. But there was no movement or music, so what the heck was happening?

I glanced down at my chest as it started to heat. It was the Bloodstone. Its bright red glow was pulsing.

I gasped, looking back into the creature's eyes. They were blank.

The Bloodstone was charming the serpent.

Its body was still wrapped too tight around me, keeping me from getting free. I tried to push out, as hard as I could, but then started to feel it constrict even tighter.

The charm was wearing off.

I watched the serpent's eyes begin to flicker from red to yellow and back again. I didn't have much time.

Adrenaline shot through my veins, so I took a deep breath and started to slash away at all of the parts of the creature constricting me. Its tail began to coil around my waist, squeezing tighter.

The dagger was sharp and had no problem slicing through it, but it was so huge and thick, it barely made a difference. The creature wailed. Its head flared, its eyes were now completely yellow, and very pissed.

As its head cocked back a bit, I quickly dropped my entire

weight to the ground. It struck, its head whizzing right over me. I quickly pushed my dagger upward under its throat and pulled downward toward its stomach, slicing into its flesh. It shrieked and squeezed tighter.

"Ssstupid child," it hissed, getting ready to strike again, "you can't kill me."

"But I can," a voice rang through darkness. I suddenly heard a loud swish, and then watched the serpent's head fall right off from its body.

I winced as blood splattered all over me. Lifting the lighted dagger, I saw Samuel standing there. He looked weary, but managed a smile.

"Samuel," I cried, as tears cascaded from my eyes.

"I told you I'd be fine. Killing serpents is a piece of cake," he chuckled, trying to pull the creature off of me.

"Yeah, sure," I exhaled in relief, attempting to uncoil its tail from my legs.

He walked over, pulled me up, and wrapped his arms around me.

"Look at us. We're a mess, but we've traveled more than halfway. I think we make a pretty great team." He carefully wiped my face with a rag.

"I guess we do," I answered. "But how are you? Did you get bitten?

"No, but he caught me a good one in my jaw, and knocked me out for a bit," he said, rubbing the right side of his face.

"I'm just glad you're still here," I breathed. And it was the truth. I wouldn't know how, or what to do without him.

"So, what do you say we finish this mission and get home?" He held his hand out to me.

"Deal." I shook it.

"I never thought I'd get the chance to meet you face to face, let alone be on a quest with you, traveling into the depths of Hell. But I have to admit, I am very proud of you, Emma, and I want you to know I will be here to protect you until my last breath," he said with deep sincerity in his eyes.

"Thank you," were the only words I could find. But they were sincere.

"I just want you to know I love you. I have always loved you and Alaine."

I nodded. "I know." Tears filled my weary eyes. I didn't know how else to respond, but I could tell my tears had spoken the words I couldn't.

We started to move forward toward the end of the tunnel when I remembered the drop.

"Samuel, we can't go that way. There's a huge pit full of snakes ahead," I said, holding his arm back.

"I know," he said, tightening his belt and tucking his sword away.

A hushed hissing slowly became louder and louder, and there was movement in front of us. Samuel reached in his pack, cracked a light stick, and threw it about twenty yards ahead.

The ground was moving, slithering, and completely covered with snakes.

They'd found a way out of the pit.

There were snakes of every kind, color, and length quickly

slithering towards us. I backed up, but Samuel grabbed my arm and held me in place. We were completely surrounded.

"No sudden movements," he whispered.

"Don't worry. I won't," I said, already frozen in place. A pang of horror shot through my body, knowing I was surrounded by one of the things I feared most.

"Emma," he whispered.

"Yes?"

"I want you to climb onto that rock to your left. Very slowly." I turned my head a bit, and saw a rock to the side of us, about three feet high. It was very uneven and had sharp pieces jetting out all over it.

Great. I was already having a hard enough time trying to stay balanced on solid ground.

"You can do it. Just move very slowly," he coaxed.

I couldn't look at the ground, so I lifted my leg, placed my foot on the rock. I gripped Samuel's hand and took in a deep breath.

"You'll be okay, Emma. Go."

I slowly shifted my weight to the foot on the rock and pushed myself up. My ankle was bent, so I glanced down to find a spot a little more even. I shouldn't have looked because the whole ground around the rock was moving. The snakes had completely surrounded it.

"Up," Samuel said evenly.

I pushed my body away from his grasp and made it onto the rock. Just when I thought I was safe, a piece of the rock cracked, twisting my ankle, sending me falling backward. I hit the ground with a thud, and in seconds was surrounded by dozens of snakes.

I froze. I knew snakes responded to movement, so I stayed as still as possible, trying not to breathe.

"Emma, don't move," Samuel yelled. He didn't have to worry about me. I was a stone.

I watched him attempt to slice the snakes around me, but as fast as he slayed one, a dozen took its place.

There was a sharp pain in my leg, and when I looked down a larger snake had sunk its fangs into my right shin. Then another, and another, struck at my legs and arms. I tried to shake them free, but their jaws were locked on tight.

I felt the bites, but wasn't feeling any side effects of any toxins. Maybe the suit was helping. I needed to get up and the very moment I thought it, Samuel was above me, kicking and pulling the snakes off of me. He reached down for my hand, and in one swift movement, swung me around onto his back.

The snakes were striking at him, but his boots kept their sharp, venomous fangs from his flesh.

I instantly felt pressure on my chest, and then miraculously, two of the most beautiful, silky, black wings appeared on Samuel's back. I gasped, and wrapped my arms around his neck.

"Are you ready to fly?" Samuel called back to me.

"Heck yes," I answered, and wrapped myself tighter around him.

With one flap we were in the air, and my stomach felt weightless. With another flap, we were up about fifty feet off the ground.

"Hold on," Samuel said.

"I am," I answered.

He leaned forward and with another flap, we were soaring above a huge pit of thousands and thousands of slithering snakes. The sight made my skin crawl.

But, I was actually flying on my Father's back, and he had wings. It was the most amazing and exhilarating feeling, and literally took my breath away. Aside from the fact my first flying experience had to be in these disturbing conditions, I was glad to have been given the chance. And with my father. It was a moment beyond description.

In a matter of a minute, we were at the fourth gate. Samuel landed softly on the ground, just before the tunnel, and helped me off.

I had a smile plastered to my face.

"So I take it you liked the flight?" he smiled.

"I think *like* is an understatement."

"Well, hopefully it won't be our last," he said with a saddened smile.

"Why can't we just fly the rest of the way?" I questioned.

"If it were that easy, I would, but they've taken that into account. It was easy to fly over the snakes, because they cannot fly or attack us while we are in the air, but there are other things much worse, which can possibly injure, or even kill us if we take to the air. I won't risk it," he said, "especially when I have my daughter on my back."

I smiled, because I was proud of that fact. Proud to be his daughter.

ELEVEN

LEVEL 4

"SAMUEL, CAN I ASK YOU a question?"

"Sure, but the keepers of this fourth gate will smell our presence soon, so we should get moving. You can ask on the way."

"Okay," I gasped, and completely drew a blank.

We were about ten yards away from the gate. Samuel was being very cautious, moving slowly and deliberately, sniffing the air. He then sat behind a large boulder.

"Ask away," he whispered.

"Shouldn't we be moving?" I asked.

"Yes, but I want you to have my full attention," he said. "Once we enter the cave, we will not get a chance to speak." I swallowed hard and sat down next to him, and pulled out the dagger.

"The symbol on this dagger, is it Michael the Archangel's?" I questioned, lightly tracing it with my finger.

"Yes," he said with an odd look.

The symbol was a small circle, attached to the left side of a V. The right side of the V continued up and then became an upside down triangle, which continued then came to a stop, even with the bottom of the V.

It looked oddly familiar. Like I'd seen it somewhere before. Maybe one of the other Guardians had one that looked similar.

Samuel's symbol was an X with a small diamond in the center. It also had an arrow going through it, from right to left. The left had the point, and the right had a small circle.

I tried to feel for the mark on the back of my neck, but it was smooth. I never looked at my mark, because I was told I had acquired it when I was a child, and had forgotten it was even there. Plus, I never looked at the back of my neck anyway. Who does?

"So, the double mark on the back of my neck is the same as yours and Alaine's?"

"Yes."

"And, Alaine's mark is the same as her fathers?"

He paused, and there was a look of confusion in his eyes.

"Yes," he nodded. "You amaze me, child," he said, shaking his head, laughing. "Just a day ago, you were a scared, sad little girl. Look at you now. You have not only shown strength and fearlessness, but you are also very intelligent."

I smiled.

The Bloodstone around my neck started to heat up, just as a loud growl echoed in the cave behind us. I knew our conversation was over.

"What kind of creature can make a sound like that? Is it a dog?"

"No. It's not a dog. What lives in that cave is called a Grimlock."

"A Grimlock?" I did *not* like the sound of that. It sounded horrifying and...grim.

Another booming growl was followed with large steps, making loose dirt and pebbles dance all around our feet.

Samuel pushed me behind him.

"Emma, don't make any loud noises or run. Grimlocks are blind, but they have an exceptional sense of smell, and impeccable hearing. They'll be able to smell you, and hear every move you make."

"Okay," I breathed, which was nearly impossible to do in our situation. I caught a whiff of something horrible. It was the smell of death. Like rotted, decaying corpses. "Ugh. What's that smell?"

"I guess I should tell you that Grimlocks are carnivores. They'll eat anything...humans, angels, animals, even their own kind," he said in a quieted voice.

"Are you serious?" I gulped.

"Yes. So, stay right behind me. Unsheathe your dagger and be ready to fight if necessary. If you get into trouble, go for the neck, and make sure it's deep enough to kill. You cannot be afraid, Emma. Fear will kill you down here. Do you understand?" he asked. His eyes were boring into mine, making sure I understood.

I steadied my nerves and nodded. I hoped I wouldn't come into contact with whatever that Grimlock creature was, but it was inevitable. I would soon have to face this creature. Just the name alone was pretty scary, and the fact we could feel its footsteps meant it had to be huge.

"Is there only one Grimlock in there?" I asked.

"No," he answered. "The last time I came down here, there were around twenty-five or so. But that was hundreds of years ago. There are probably a lot more now."

"Hundreds of years?" I gasped. Those numbers did some major work on my brain. It was hard to accept my father was centuries old.

"Yes," he said with a small grin. "This gate is the place where Lucifer has assigned the Grimlocks to dwell. He has also allowed a portal to open for them into the human world, a few times a month. During the night, they enter areas ridden with drugs and crime to hunt for food. So, I suggest when we make it through the tunnel, you don't focus on anything around you. Just focus on getting to the next gate as quickly and quietly as possible."

"Are you telling me there might be other humans down here?"

"Yes, but they'd already be dead. Grimlocks always kill their prey before dragging them back to Hell."

Oh God. The thought made my stomach turn and I instantly felt nauseous. That was completely unnerving, and made me want to hurl.

If that Grimlock tried to take a bite out of my flesh, I wouldn't have any problem slicing its neck.

I couldn't believe the thoughts running through my mind. Slicing necks? That totally wasn't me. But I could feel a change inside. Something making me a little stronger. A little braver. It all started the moment I realized who I really was. My father was a warrior, and his blood flowed through my veins. I would do anything to save the ones I loved. Alaine, Kade, Courtney, Caleb, all of those who were falling prey to the evil agendas of Lucian.

From the darkness of the tunnel came a loud swishing sound. It sounded slow and then started to gather momentum, soon sounding like a tornado. I peeked behind the rock, and strained to look into the darkness, but I couldn't see a thing.

Then out of the blue, a huge object shot from the cave, heading directly at us. In a second, Samuel grabbed hold of my arm, and shoved me flat to the ground, landing over me.

Whatever it was, crashed into the wall, sending shards of rocks flying everywhere. I shielded my face with my arms until the debris cleared. When I uncovered my eyes, Samuel was already on his feet, with his sword drawn. I sat up, and noticed a huge weapon lodged in the side of the rock wall. It looked like some type of medieval club with sharp spikes, around ten inches long, set all around it. There was a thick, long rope attached to its handle.

"Stay down, Emma," Samuel instructed. As soon as I dropped back down, the weapon retracted and whizzed right over my face, missing me by inches. My heart was racing, and I couldn't breathe. That was too damn close.

"What the hell is that thing?" I screamed.

"Morning Star," Samuel answered, his eyes fastened into the darkness. "It's what they use to capture their prey."

"What do we do?"

"Just stay put, and stay still."

Again, the loud swishing sound filled the air, and from the darkness, the huge weapon came flying like a bullet, headed straight for Samuel. He dove to dodge the oncoming weapon, but I heard a ripping sound, and then he cried in pain.

"Samuel," I called.

One of the spikes was lodged deep in his right leg. The spike had gone through one side and out the other. He was on his back, and his leg was twisted and bloodied.

"Emma, hurry!" He cringed in pain.

I jumped up and ran over to him.

"What? What do you want me to do?" I cried.

"You need to pull it out," he urged.

"What?" I gasped. I started falling apart, but knew I needed pull myself together. Quickly.

"Emma, you need to pull it out *now,* before that Grimlock retracts his weapon and takes my leg off."

"Holy shit."

I knelt next to him, my hands were trembling. There was blood everywhere. The long spike was embedded deep into his calf and it looked broken.

"Emma, you have to do it. Please," he said in a more relaxed tone, knowing I was panicking.

"Okay, okay," I hyperventilated.

Without thinking I reached down, putting one hand between the club, and the other against his leg, and pushed as hard as I could. It didn't budge. The club felt like it weighed a hundred pounds.

"It's not budging." Tears poured down my face.

"Don't stop, Emma," he said, through clenched teeth.

I sat down on the side of him, securing both of my feet against a few of the spikes on the club, and both my hands on either side of his leg, where the spike had entered. I sucked in a deep breath, and pulled back with all my might. I could feel the bones in his leg giving to my touch; they were shattered in pieces. With one final tug, I set his leg free from the spike.

Instantly, the rope on the Morning Star tensed and was yanked back into the darkness.

That was too close!

I was just about to breathe, when Samuel said, "Emma, you have to get us back behind that rock." He pointed behind us, to a larger rock about ten yards away.

Right now, that rock was as good as ten thousand miles away, but I had to do it. I had to get him to safety. As I started to move, I heard it again. The loud swooshing sound of the Morning Star filled the air.

Adrenaline coursed through my veins. I jumped up, grabbed Samuel under his arms, and yanked as hard as I could. He tried to help by pushing back with his good leg, moving us backward about five feet.

The Morning Star whizzed out of the cave like a heat seeking missile.

I pulled again, moving Samuel a few more feet back, but then dropped to the ground, flat on my back. The weapon of death flew inches overhead, crashing again into the wall behind us. I quickly leaned forward over Samuels face, shielding him from the flying debris. I wasn't sure if I should try and move him again, because I knew soon, whatever was on the other end of this death weapon was going to retract it back.

I waited for a few moments and decided to try. I pulled him again, with all my might. We still had about five feet to go.

"Emma," Samuel said weakly. I looked at his leg, and it was bent, at the calf, blood was pouring onto the ground all around him.

"What do I do, Samuel?" My voice was shaking just as much as I was.

"Just be strong, and remember I love you," he breathed.

"I love you too," I answered. "But, don't you dare leave me. You need to tell me what I need to do." Everything began to spin around me.

"Just pray," he exhaled, and closed his eyes. He must have gone unconscious because I could still see the rise and fall of his chest.

Pray? I already prayed. Did God really need to be reminded that we were in danger? Wasn't he was supposed to know all and see all? I wasn't about to take any chances, so I quickly whispered another prayer hoping it would reach him.

Blood continued to pour from Samuel's leg. He was losing so much of it, and I needed to stop it. I pulled out my dagger and reached over to Samuel, ripping off a piece of his shirt. I then crawled over to his leg, and tied it tightly just above the wound. I'd seen it done in the movies, and hoped it would help slow the bleeding.

There was so much blood. Right now, more than anything, I wished Alaine were here with me. I knew he couldn't die from a wound, but until he healed, he wouldn't be able to move. And if we stayed here, the Grimlocks would eventually find us, kill us, and eat us.

I wasn't going to be a meal for anyone, and neither was Samuel.

There had to be a way out of here. There just had to.

I pulled Samuel as hard as I could. Inch by inch we finally made it to the rock.

The Morning Star was still embedded into the side of the cavern's wall, and all I could think about was when its owner would reclaim it. It had only been a few minutes, but the sooner the better. We were about a foot away from complete safety, and I needed to stand to pull Samuel around behind the safety of the rock. If I could get him behind the rock he would be safe from the danger of any more flying Morning Stars. But pulling him from a seated position was nearly impossible.

Every second felt like a lifetime.

I saw the rope attached to the Morning Star tense. I quickly laid flat on my back, waiting for the weapon to retract.

But something happened.

Something went horribly wrong.

The rope tensed and with a flash it retracted. But as it was ripped from the wall, a piece of it got caught on something and sent the weapon crashing to the ground—directly on top of Samuel.

Everything, from that moment, seemed to move in slow motion.

The huge spikes pierced through Samuel's chest, his eyes opened wide, then his body was torn from my grasp and pulled across the jagged rocks, disappearing into the darkness.

His screams echoed, shattering my heart and soul.

He was gone. In less than a second.

I glanced down and looked at my empty, bloodied hands. Hands that weren't strong enough to hold onto him, or pull him to safety.

Up until this very moment, I'd never felt more helpless, or more alone.

My world was crashing down all around me.

Samuel's cries continued to thunder through the cave, sending jolts of excruciating pain through my heart. He was dying. My father was dying at the hands of that horrible creature.

What the Hell was I still doing here, allowing it to happen?

A small flame awakened in the deepest part of me. A flame that began to burn brighter and brighter, quickly torching every ounce of fear I'd had up until this moment.

I rose to my feet, grasped my dagger tightly, and ran toward the cave.

I would either save him, or I would die trying.

TWELVE

SAMUEL'S CRIES ECHOED OFF THE cave walls and even though I was running as fast as I could, his cries were getting softer and softer, like he was quickly being carried further away.

I finally reached the mouth of the darkened cave, and my nostrils began to burn with an overwhelming stench of rotted flesh. I swallowed down the bile attempting to push its way up my throat.

The dagger started to glow, lighting my path. I was glad it had come to me. It saved me so many times, and gave me a sense of hope. It was my only companion and ally now I was all alone.

I held it down to the ground and noticed mammoth-sized prints that looked almost like those of an elephant.

"Dear God. Please help me," I whispered, as I pushed on into the darkness.

My steps were quick but short, trying to get through the maze of rocks, attempting to see what was ahead of me, and trying to stay on my feet. Then, I finally reached the end of the tunnel.

Outside of it, small fires were spread out about every twenty feet or so. As I got closer, I noticed a few of the fires had spits above them. A few were empty, but there were a few that had...*No.*

I gasped, and closed my eyes hoping the disturbing scene I'd just witnessed would disappear, but when I opened them again, everything was still the same. I was living the nightmare.

There were whole, human bodies on those spits. A few even had limbs missing, torn from the bodies. The surrounding ground was covered with the bones of those who had already been consumed. I quickly became sick, and had to focus and fight the nausea overwhelming me.

I noticed the whole area was empty.

Where were the Grimlocks?

And, where was Samuel?

I needed to get to him before they killed him.

I scanned the area, stepping out of the cover of darkness. I walked a few yards out, and saw them. A few hundred yards away, in the far right corner.

Giants.

That was the only word I would use to describe them. And there were at least fifty or more, all huddled together. To me, from a distance, they resembled the Cyclops. Enormous, hideous creatures that lived only in myths.

They began to growl loudly, and looked as if they were fighting each other.

And then, I heard him. Samuel. I heard his cries again, but they were very weak.

He was dying, and I needed to get him out of there. I needed to save him. I knew exactly where he was. He was directly in the middle of the Grimlocks.

I swallowed my fear, but my pulse and breath quickened at the same time. Heat began to emanate on my chest and glanced down to see the amulet glowing a bright red. I took hold of it, and squeezed, hoping whatever enchantment was on it, would somehow enter me.

Deep inside, I knew I was going to try and save Samuel, but we probably wouldn't make it out alive. It was inevitable. I hadn't transformed yet into the prophesized super angel. I was still mostly human, and weak—easy to kill.

I closed my eyes, focusing on advice my mom would give me whenever I felt defeated. I smiled, hearing it as if she were speaking her words directly into my ear.

The power of one can achieve any goal, if one wants it bad enough.

Then there was another voice.

Are you planning on kicking that entire group of Grimlock ass alone, or would you like some help?

That was definitely not my mother's voice.

I quickly opened my eyes.

"Oh my God," I gasped, and nearly collapsed.

"You shouldn't call me that, Emma," Dom smirked.

Dominic and Malachi stood behind me with their swords drawn.

"Are you real?" I breathed, as tears began to well in my eyes.

"Of course we're real. Are you hallucinating? Did one of those snakes back there bite you?" Dom asked with a raised eyebrow.

"No, I just can't believe you're here," I said, walking over to them. I touched his arm.

It felt real.

Overwhelmed with emotion, I fell into Dom's arms and hugged him tightly, and then turned and hugged Malachi.

"You've got to save Samuel. He's injured, and they're killing him," I sobbed.

"Whoa! Where is he?" Malachi questioned.

I pointed.

"They have him, and he doesn't have much time left," I cried.

"Okay, Malachi. Let's move. I bet I can get through half those Grimlock before you get through two," Dom jested. The mere sound of his bravado brought hope, which had vanished as soon as Samuel was ripped from me.

"Whatever, Dom. Just shut your mouth and move it," Malachi rebutted.

"Emma, stay right here. We've got this," Dom said, with a wink. "We'll be right back."

He took off, but Malachi paused and turned back to me.

"Emma. Kade made it safely to Alaine. I just thought you should know," he said, and then took off toward the Grimlocks.

His words immediately comforted me, but the longer I dwelt on them, the more I began to question. Kade made it to Alaine, but would he live?

I watched as they battled the creatures, and just as I began to relax a bit, the amulet around my neck started to heat up and glow even brighter.

"Ouch," I breathed as it became hot. Why was it heating up?

A sudden movement behind startled me.

I turned and immediately froze. My breath and heart stopped.

I was standing ten feet away from a Grimlock, and it was even more terrifying up close. It leaned forward, sniffing the air.

It had found me.

It was massive. Its arms and legs were huge. Its eyes were milky white and looked possessed, and its skin was the color of a corpse, but it was thick and wrinkly.

Its head snapped forward and blind eyes fixed on mine, like it could see me. I wanted to scream, but my voice had caught in my throat.

Stay or run? That was the question.

I watched as it lifted a massive Morning Star and began to swing it over its head.

As I turned to run, the whole area around me filled with the loud swooshing sound of the Grimlock winding his weapon. I ran as fast as my legs could carry me. In the distance I could see Dominic and Malachi battling the multitude of Grimlocks. They were too far to get to me in time, and too far to hear my cries.

I quickly glanced behind, as the creature sent its weapon flying towards me. I dove out of the way but it was much too fast. The weight of the club whacked me in the back, knocking me to the ground.

I couldn't breathe. Excruciating pain tore through my spine like it was broken in pieces. I couldn't tell if the weapon was embedded in my back, but it felt like it was. I tried to move. Nothing was working.

I was paralyzed.

Half of my face was buried in dirt, rocks, and bones.

I knew the Grimlock was getting closer. Its footsteps rattled the loose debris around me, but there was nothing I could do. I was helpless.

"Help! Help me!" I screamed.

Thoughts of being hung from a spit, and eaten, overwhelmed my mind. I had failed, and now I was going to die.

I closed my eyes, and flashes of my parents, Jeremy, Lia, Kade, Alaine, and Samuel appeared before me. I hoped they would forgive me for not being strong enough. I hoped Dom and Malachi would be able to save Samuel. Maybe they could finish this mission, and find a way to save the others.

The ground stopped shaking, and when I opened my eyes again, the creature was crouched down near my face, sniffing. Its blind eyes were set on my face, inches away. It knew it had hit and incapacitated its target.

"God, please let me die right now. Please," I whispered, sobbing, hoping he would hear and grant me this one wish. The pain had become unbearable, everything became blurry, and then…everything went black.

I was in complete darkness, but two paths lit up before me.

One was covered in sharp, jagged rocks and looked nearly

impossible to cross.

The other was perfect, a straight and narrow path that sparkled and glistened. No obstacles. No stumbling blocks.

I started to take a step down the easy path when someone shouted my name.

"Emma. No!"

I paused and looked around me.

At the end of the jagged path were two familiar hazel eyes, glowing in the shadows, just beyond the light.

"Kade?" I called, but he didn't answer. "Kade is that you?" I knew they were his eyes, but I looked at the land mine of sharp rocks I needed to cross to get to him.

Another voice called to me. "Emma. Come to me, Emma. We are destined to be together." In the shadows at the end of the easy, sparkling path were two glowing, blood-red eyes. I felt drawn to them, with the same feeling I once had with Kade. My insides were compelled to run toward those red eyes, but the beautiful hazel eyes at the end of the jagged path, kept me from taking a step.

I was frozen. Locked in indecision.

The ground around me started to crumble and fall below into a smoldering, flaming lava pit. Waves of intense heat surrounded me.

Two paths.

Simple or near impossible.

Did I really need to think about it?

I made my choice and just as I took a step, the ground below me gave way, sending me falling into a fiery grave.

My eyes slowly peeled open, but everything around me was dark and blurred. It took a moment to focus.

There were voices nearby, whispering and laughing. I noticed the glow of a small fire a few yards away and tried to move. Pain shot through my body, especially when I tried to breathe.

"Emma. You're awake," a voice spoke behind me. Light footsteps crunched on the rocky ground, heading toward me. In the dim light a warm, familiar face came into view.

"Danyel?" I breathed.

"Yes, I'm here," he answered, sitting at my side.

I tried to sit up, but it felt like a thousand knives were pressing into me.

"Don't move. You've broken a few ribs and back bones," he said, holding me down. "Lucky for you, you were wearing this suit. It kept you from getting skewered from those Morning Star spikes. And, thank goodness I showed up when I did because that creature had you by a leg, dragging you off to who knows where."

I was still alive, and had so many questions, but when I opened my mouth, only one word pressed out.

"Samuel?" I needed to know if they had saved him.

He smiled. "He's sleeping just over there. Those damn Grimlock bastards broke both of his wings. They were just about to sever them from his body, but Dominic and Malachi got to him just in time. He also has a broken leg, and lost quite a bit of blood, but he'll live. He's mending pretty quickly, and in another day or two, he'll be as good as new."

I felt nauseous. My pain must have been nothing compared to

his, but I was relieved to hear he was alive.

"And, Kade?" I breathed.

"He's alive, but barely. We made it to Alaine without any major problems. The rest of the Guardians helped get her back to the house with Caleb. Caleb is doing well. Don't worry, Emma. If anyone can save Kade, Alaine can. She has some strong medicine, and I'm sure he'll pull through."

My heart was broken for Kade and Samuel. I shut my eyes, letting the tears that had pooled there, spill out and run down my face.

"Don't cry for them. Samuel and Kade are born fighters. Your father will be good as new in no time. He just needs to rest and heal. And, Kade... well, he's one of the strongest Guardians I've ever known," he said, placing his hand on my head.

"He's not immortal anymore," I sobbed, feeling the pain radiate through my back and chest.

"I know, but that doesn't matter. Once a fighter, always a fighter. I do have faith he'll live," he said, with a glimmer of hope in his eyes. If a Fallen angel could have faith, then I could. "Kade actually woke for a brief moment when we arrived at Alaine's. Do you want to know what his only words to me were?"

"Yes."

"He said, 'Go back to Emma. Protect her.'"

I smiled and nodded as the tears continued to flow.

Kade was still trying to protect me, and that was something I didn't think I'd ever understand. I did know this much...our hearts were connected, and there was a bond formed the moment we touched. I couldn't wait to get back to him. He told me that he loved me, and I was determined to tell him how much I loved him back.

I glanced over to where Samuel was, and could only see a portion of his head, which was turned away from me. Dominic and Malachi were sitting on either side of him, with a small fire in between them. They looked to be in good spirits.

Dom was laughing as usual, and Malachi was nodding. I wondered how badly Samuel was hurt. Broken wings. I just hoped they would heal quickly. As far as Kade was concerned, he'd also given up his wings forever, just for me.

"How long have I been out?" I asked Danyel.

"About a day," he answered.

"A day?" I winced as pain shot through my chest.

"Hey, you need to rest. A day is nothing. Both of you needed it," he said.

"I'm glad Alaine made it back to the house."

"Yes. She's with James, Alexander, and Thomas."

I nodded, emotionally and physically exhausted.

"Hey, you should go back to sleep. It's been a really long few days for all of us, and we still have quite a ways to go. You're not alone anymore. We've taken out all of the Grimlocks, so you're safe here," he said, placing his hand on my forehead. My body was still in excruciating pain, and it hurt to breathe. My head felt like a thousand needles were being pressed into it.

I wanted to fall back asleep and not deal with the pain, and before I could say anything, Danyel leaned over me and whispered in my ear.

"Sleep, sweet Emma."

I felt my pain being sucked away into darkness, and my eyes quickly followed.

"Emma. Emma," a voice in a distance, called out to me. "Emma, time to get up."

I opened my eyes to the most wondrous sight. Samuel, my father, was kneeling beside me. He looked weary, but had a wide smile on his face. Dom and Malachi were standing behind him, peeking over his shoulder. I turned my head and noticed Danyel in the corner gathering his things.

"Damn. With the amount of sleep you've been getting, you should be the fairest maiden in all the land," Dom jested. Malachi punched his shoulder and shook his head in disapproval.

"She is the fairest. Next to her mother, of course," Samuel added.

"Awwww," Dominic sang, and I shook my head.

"How long was I out?" I asked. My voice was very weak and my throat was dry.

Samuel handed me a canteen and answered, "For a while. We don't have watches, so there is no way of really telling time down here. But, I'd say a few days."

"What?" I said, choking on the water.

"Yep," Malachi confirmed. "We figured the longer you slept, the faster you'd heal."

"How are you feeling?" Samuel asked.

I sat up straight and twisted. I couldn't move an inch without pain the last time I was awake, and now I barely had any. Even my head felt clearer and free of pain. I guess I was healing quickly.

"How are *you* feeling?" I asked Samuel.

He grinned and paused for a few seconds. I figured he was weighing his words, trying to be strong for me.

"I'm good," he answered. "But, it will be a while before I'm able to fly again."

"I'm sorry," I said.

"Hey, don't worry about me. In a few more days, I'll be as good as new," he winked. Behind him, Dom nodded with a thumbs-up.

That would be perfect if we had a few days. I wasn't sure how we'd get through the next gate, or even what was waiting for us. Yes, we'd survived the first four levels, but we still had one more to go. And it was worse than this one?

On the upside, we now had reinforcements. Dom, Malachi, and Danyel were with us now. I didn't feel alone anymore, or like the rest of the journey was a Kamikaze mission.

Their presence gave me hope.

"Well, now that we know everyone's fine and healing nicely, we should get a move on. Don't get me wrong. I'm not anxious to move, but I'm also not planning on being in Hell any longer than I have to. This place stinks, and is wreaking havoc on my skin," Dom blurted.

"Pretty boy forgot to pack his lotion? That's too damn bad," Malachi huffed.

"Actually, I don't really need that crap. The heat here is making my skin glisten. See?" He flexed his huge biceps and admired them for a few seconds, and then turned to me with a wink.

I could feel my face flush with heat, because I was actually admiring them as well. Dom was quite the specimen; a picture of perfection. They all were. But, Dom was the one who loved to flaunt it.

"Okay, Dom. I think you've admired yourself enough for a few lifetimes," Samuel laughed.

"I mean, who could ever get tired of looking at these gorgeous guns?" Dom asked.

"*Me*," Malachi, Danyel, and Samuel all said in unison.

"Whatever. You're all just jealous," Dom sputtered, covering his biceps with his sleeves. "They're just jealous of you," he whispered to and kissed his arm.

"Yeah, whatever, big guy. Get your damn stuff, and get ready to move," Malachi huffed and turned around to the rest of us. "Do you guys see the crap I have to put up with daily? Why did God do this to me?"

"Aww, buddy. Come on. You love me, and you know it. Without me, your life would be one huge, dark, grumpy mess." Dominic smiled widely. Malachi shot him a dirty look and walked away.

I giggled, and even Samuel and Danyel had grins on their faces. I loved my Guardians. Now, more than ever, I was glad they were here—my glimmers of hope in the darkness.

I sat up and assessed the damage. My garment was definitely the most awesome super suit in existence. There were no holes or scratches on it anywhere. Any normal threads would have been torn to shreds, and I definitely would have been dead a long time ago. I guess fate had something else in store for me.

For a moment, I'd forgotten the real reason why we were risking our lives.

Lucian.

The thought of him sent a surge of emotions through me, and hate and horror were right at the top. It reminded me why we needed to get through the next gate to speak to Lucifer. It wasn't something I was looking forward to, but if he was the only one who could stop Lucian, then I was more than willing to take the chance.

With a renewed strength, and three more Guardians, I gathered my things and readied myself for the next part of the quest. I had no clue what we were up against, but I had a feeling whatever it was, we'd get through it. I now had four of the most remarkable warriors that had ever lived at my side. One of them was my father. A Fallen angel, choosing to journey into Hell to protect his daughter.

"Are you ready, sweetheart?" Samuel asked.

I nodded.

"Are you?"

"I was born ready," he grinned, his chocolate brown eyes glistened in the light of the fire. He seemed to be fine. It was incredible what a few days of rest could do to a badly injured immortal.

"Are you sure you're okay?" Samuel asked.

"Oh yeah, I'm fine. I was just thinking, and sometimes that's not too good for me," I replied.

"Well, if you ever need to talk, I'll be here for you," he said.

"I know. Thank you."

"And, I'll be here if you ever need a firm, muscular shoulder to cry on," Dom added, tapping his hand on my shoulder. "But if you ever need a softer, fluffier shoulder...Malachi's your guy." His eyes shifted to Malachi, whose face flushed red with anger.

"Dom, I think you need a mini lesson in ass kicking, and I'll be more than happy to give you a hands-on," Malachi snickered. In a nano-second he did a spin, kicking Dom's legs out from under him, and jumped on top of him.

Malachi was big brawny guy. Muscular, but he didn't flaunt it like Dominic. His tanned skin defined his bulging muscles.

"Whoa, big guy. You got me. I totally didn't see that one coming," Dominic admitted, pushing Malachi off to the side. "Touché brother...touché."

A wide smile of accomplishment spread across Malachi's face. He turned and gave me a slight nod. Samuel and Danyel just laughed and shook their heads. I had a feeling they must've been a lot like Dominic and Malachi when they were younger.

Dom jumped up, dusted himself off, then helped Malachi to his feet. They both laughed and gave each other a quick fist bump.

"One day, Emma, you'll be able to kick all of our asses," Dom said, grinning at me.

"Whatever," I said, blushing.

"You just might," Danyel added. "If you are truly the one of whom the prophecy foretold, then your strength and abilities might be greater than any angel, in Heaven or Hell. Which serves as a good reminder why we can't let Lucifer find out about your true origins. He must believe you are a Nephilim—a half breed—just like his son."

"But what if he finds out, or sees the mark like Lucian did?" I questioned. "I mean, if Lucifer is as cunning or as smart as Lucian, he'll find out one way or another. The mark on the back of my neck will make it totally obvious."

"Then we will have to make sure he doesn't," Samuel replied.

I didn't feel like questioning them right now. I knew they wouldn't send me into a lion's den without warning, nor would they let me enter without strict instructions first. We still had one more level to go through before we reached him anyway.

One more chance to try and cheat death.

THIRTEEN

LEVEL 5

THE GUYS GATHERED THEIR WEAPONS and prepared to enter the next gate. We had to travel a few hundred yards down a dark, rocky slope to get there. One gate left. After all we went through, I couldn't imagine anything worse than the gargoyle-lion-scorpion creature, soul-snatching ghouls, snakes, or Grimlocks.

I was just thankful Samuel was still with me, and he was okay. I really thought I was going to lose him, but he looked like he was almost as good as new.

"Everyone stay quiet," Danyel whispered loudly, taking the lead.

Samuel walked over to me, and took me by the hand. "Just stay with me. They will go in first and clear the way. Then we will enter," he said.

"So, what are they expecting to run into at the next gate?" I whispered to Samuel. We ducked down behind a medium-sized boulder.

"Hell Hounds," he answered.

"I bet they aren't the kind of hounds I'd ever want to run into."

"No. No one would want to run into these dogs. They are Lucifer's guard dogs; birthed and bred right here in the fiery pits of Hell. They are invisible to the human eye, and are exceptionally strong, fast, and very ferocious. Their teeth and claws are their weapons, and their skin is thick like a shield. The fur on their backs is as sharp as barbs.

"The hounds are kept right here, rabid and starved, until such time as they are needed. The Fallen sometimes send them to collect souls. They are unleashed into the human world with one goal—to seek out their targets, kill them, and drag them back to Hell. However, most victims cannot be recognized once they're brought down. Once the soul is taken, they become the hound's next meal."

I tried to swallow the huge lump caught in my throat. I was slowly starting to become numb to it all. Not really numb, but more, not surprised. I never knew there were horrors from Hell that entered my world. My mortal world. I thought these stories were all fairytales, but to find out they actually existed, was more than shocking.

He turned to me.

"I'm so sorry, Emma. I'm so used to briefing warriors before going into battle. I shouldn't have given you all of the gory details."

"No, it's okay. I'm fine. But will they be?" I whispered. I pointed to Danyel, Dominic, and Malachi, hunched behind three separate boulders about twenty-five yards ahead of us.

"I'm sure they will. I don't know if Malachi and Dominic have ever come across Hell Hounds before, but I'm certain Danyel will brief them on what they need to do."

"Do they need to take off their heads to kill them?" I asked. That was the most logical explanation and seemed to work for everything else.

"Yes," he said with a confused grin. "That's definitely one way to do it, but it's not as easy as it seems. Hell Hounds come and go, like wisps of fire and wind. As I said before, they are extremely fast, and they also have layers of razor, sharp teeth. Once they latch on to their victim…" he shook his head.

He didn't need to finish the sentence. I knew the ending, and it wasn't a happy one.

I could feel my heart pounding so loudly it echoed in my ears and reverberated through the rest of my body, making it tremble.

"So how many of those Hell Hounds are there?" I questioned.

"Six," he answered.

"Are they big?"

He nodded, and I exhaled, trying to steady my nerves.

I liked dogs, but I already hated these ones. Their description painted a not so pretty picture.

"Hell Hounds, like the Grimlocks, have an exceptional sense of smell and sound, so we'll have to stay back here, and be as quiet as possible."

"Do you think they can take them?" I asked, in an even lower whisper.

"Danyel has worked with the Hell Hounds, about a century or

so ago. He knows exactly how they move, and where their kill spots are. It'll probably be…a bit tricky for the others. But they're warriors, I'm sure they'll be just fine."

I carefully unsheathed the dagger and held it in my grasp. It looked like it was brand new. There wasn't a scratch or any blood on it, and it was as sharp as it had been the first time I held it in my hands. There was something about this dagger, a feeling I couldn't quite put my finger on. Like it was becoming a part of me, like we were meant to be together.

"You have been blessed with such a rare and remarkable acquisition. That dagger does not answer to just anyone, and bad things have happened to those who have tried to possess it by their own means. This weapon will only perform for those it deems worthy. It is truly an extraordinary gift, as you are, my daughter," he whispered, grasping my hand.

"Thank you," I smiled. "So, are you telling me this dagger is alive?"

"In a sense, yes. It has magical powers only the possessor can wield. No one knows exactly what it can do, because each gift is unique to the bearer. As this dagger was a gift from the Almighty himself, you can be sure they are all wondrous."

"Oh," was the only word pushed from my lips. This was all way, way over my head. What other magic could I call out of this thing? Just the mere thought of it was crazy.

"We will get through this, Emma. I've spent too many of these last years in the darkness, being invisible just to stay alive. It's time for me to take a stand and fight. But I want you to know, if anything should happen to me—"

"No." I shook my head. "I've just found you. You can't just suddenly pop into my life and then disappear again."

"I'm not saying it will be intentional. I was merely trying to say *in case* anything should happen to me, I love you. I've loved you from the moment you took your first breath, they placed you in my arms, and I looked into your beautiful brown eyes. From that day, I was smitten, and there hasn't been a day that has gone by where I haven't thought about you. I just wanted you to know."

"I love you too, and that's why I won't allow you to die."

"Alright," he smiled.

I wasn't going to accept any other answer. I mean, I'd just found out he was my real father a few days ago. We'd been through a lot in, and Hell, one short week, and learned so much about each other. I was glad he'd chosen to come with me. I just hoped and prayed we'd make it through this, and our father-daughter relationship would continue.

I soon felt heat on my chest, and glanced down to see the Bloodstone glowing again.

I took in a deep breath. *Here we go.*

Chilling growls echoed all around us. The Hell Hounds knew they had visitors.

Samuel placed his finger to his lips, but he didn't have to worry about me. No sound was going to be leaving my mouth. Not anytime soon.

I closed my eyes and wished this super suit could make me invisible again. I suddenly felt a small tingling all over my body, and when I opened my eyes, I saw Samuel looking in my direction, with a look of bewilderment on his face. I held my hands out in front of me.

I was invisible. No wonder Samuel looked confused.

"Emma?" he questioned. He hadn't seen me invisible before.

"I'm here," I whispered

I reached out and touched his shoulder. And as I touched Samuel, he started to become invisible too.

I pulled my hand back, and he instantly became visible again. I reached out and touched his shoulder again and watched him disappear. In a few seconds, Samuel's outline started to come into focus.

"Samuel, you're invisible. I think whenever I'm invisible, whatever I touch also becomes invisible."

"You have the same gift as Alaine," his voice said softly. "This could definitely work to our advantage. Too bad it couldn't work for the others."

"I know," I sighed.

I wondered if he could see my outline, as I saw his. He probably did, because he was directly facing me.

I peeked back over the rock to check on the others. I wasn't as afraid now, knowing we were, for the time being, invisible to the Hell Hounds. Red-orange eyes, flaming like fire, illuminated the darkness, stalking closer and closer. Danyel was the closest. Dominic and Malachi were a few feet behind.

And then, as if by magic, five more sets of flaming red eyes appeared, spread throughout different areas of the darkness, all headed toward Danyel.

Danyel turned back and nodded to Dom, who turned and nodded to Malachi. They knew they were coming.

I caught a glimpse of one of the creatures. It was about five feet in height, with thick fur as black as the night. Its claws were as long as daggers, its muzzle was folded back, baring razor sharp teeth, and its eyes were filled with hatred and hunger.

My stomach twisted with each step they took. Danyel grip his sword tightly in his hand. I kept reassuring myself he knew what he was doing.

When the first Hell Hound was a few feet away from Danyel, it let out three loud barks. As it did, flames shot from its mouth.

A sudden wave of horror washed over me, drowning me in the memory of what happened to Kade. The searing heat, the look of pain on his face, and his horribly burned flesh.

This creature was not only fast and ferocious, but it also breathed fire. We needed every bit of help we could get with this last level.

I turned to Samuel, "You didn't mention those things breathed fire."

"It's not the kind of fire you think. It's not like the creature that injured Kade. The fire from the Hell Hounds cannot be thrown, but it can still burn if you're close enough."

I sighed, overwhelmed and terrified.

The nearest Hell Hound crouched; its eyes were focused on the rock Danyel was crouched behind.

I almost dropped my hand from Samuel, but he grabbed hold of it. I turned to him for a split second and that's when it happened.

Hell was unleashed.

The creature bounded towards Danyel. He quickly laid flat on his back and thrust his sword upward, scraping the creature's underbelly. It landed in the middle them, acting as if it hadn't been injured.

Malachi turned and gave a quick nod to Dom before jumping from his cover and yelling at the top of his lungs. He waved his sword at the creature, demanding its full attention. The creature snapped its head toward Malachi, and within a second, pounced at him. Malachi dove forward, sliding under it.

At the same moment, Dominic was in the air and landed on the Hell Hound's back as soon as it landed. With both blades raised in his hands, and a quick swish, he took the creature's head off. Its body dropped, its head haphazardly rolled away. Dom stood above the creature, smiling, thick blood dripped from his blades. He was amazing.

"Dom!" Danyel yelled. "I think you've pissed them off."

Turning, he noticed the five remaining Hell Hounds surrounding him. Their howls were loud and piercing. Their eyes burned with even more hatred, and set on the one who killed their own.

Dominic readied his weapons, and Danyel and Malachi stood to join him.

FOURTEEN

WE WATCHING THE DREADFUL EVENTS unfold. I felt Samuel's hand hold me down, and I hadn't realized I was standing.

I felt hopeless, because they were outnumbered and we weren't there to help. Three against five. The odds were not in their favor.

The creatures slowly and methodically made their way around them. Their deadly growls echoed all around us. The flames from their eyes and mouths burned brightly. The Hell Hounds had surrounded them on all sides.

One hound charged at Dominic. It moved so fast, it had almost disappeared. In a flash, it had traveled the full distance to him, leaving a trail of flames behind it.

I watched in horror as Dominic dove out of its path. His first blade swung and missed, but the second sliced through the hound's rear leg. The hound didn't flinch, turning its head and sinking its razor sharp teeth into his arm.

Dom yelled out in pain, as the creature rabidly shook, tearing and ripping his arm to shreds. With his free hand, Dominic managed to lodge one of his weapons into one of its eyes. It yelped in pain, but kept its jaws tightly locked. I could see flame burning brightly from his mouth. Dom's tortured screams turned my stomach.

Danyel and Malachi were busy fighting off the other Hell Hounds. There was no way they'd be able to help Dominic, especially when they were fighting for their own lives.

Dom was helpless, and looked like he was going to lose his arm, or die, if someone didn't help him. Samuel gripped my arm tighter, trying to push me down, but I knew in my heart I had to help him. I felt compelled to run to his aid.

I quickly shook Samuel's grip free, which made him visible again.

"Emma, *no!*" he shouted, reaching out for me. But I was still invisible, and quickly moved away from him and headed toward Dom.

Something inside of me clicked on again. A switch that wouldn't allow me to stand by and watch him die. I was on autopilot. My body was reacting to the situation, and I was determined to help him.

Adrenaline gave me an added boost and had me running towards him. The dagger was still gripped tightly in my hand. I knew I'd have to use it, and this time I was prepared.

I shot a quick glance toward Danyel and Malachi. Danyel had just taken the head off of his hound, and Malachi had just dodged an attack. The jaws of his hound were inches from his face, but it missed.

I exhaled and focused on Dominic. There was blood everywhere, yet he was still fighting hard to release his arm. He appeared to be getting weaker and weaker, trying and failing to release the sword he'd embedded in the creature's eye.

I ran as fast as I could, and lifted my dagger praying it would hit its mark.

As I neared them, I jumped up behind the creature, and thrust my dagger into the back of its neck, pushing it down with all of my might. The sharp blade found its mark and easily went through the creature's thick skin.

The hound yelped in pain and immediately released its grip from Dominic's mangled arm. It looked around and had no idea what just attacked. I gripped the handle of my dagger and pulled it from its neck. Its cries pierced my ears. I raised my dagger again, and thrust it down, from one side of the Hell Hounds neck, straight through to the other, taking its head completely off.

At that moment, I felt strong. Stronger than I'd ever felt before. Total kick ass.

I had just slayed one of those Hell Hounds single handedly and saved my friend. Damn. We just might be able to survive.

Three dead Hell Hounds and three to go.

Dominic was completely baffled at what had just taken place. He had no clue I was there, or that I'd just saved his life.

I reached down and touched his shoulder, and watched his body disappear.

Within seconds I could see his hazy figure. He glanced at me, his eyes became wide, and after a few moments, he grinned.

"Emma?" he asked.

"You need to get out of here."

"Emma, you just slaughtered that Hell Hound's ass," he smiled and shook his head. He then winced in pain, so I released. He took off his shirt and wrapped it tightly around his bloodied appendage. I was glad he did because I didn't think I could take seeing the mutilated flesh and bone hanging from his arm. Within seconds it was soaked and dripping with blood.

I touched him again, making him invisible, and helped him to his feet. I made sure to keep a hand on him as we made our way back to Samuel. My heart dropped as we got closer and I noticed Samuel wasn't there. I quickly glanced behind us, and saw him standing between Danyel and Malachi.

They were all standing back to back, crouched, with their weapons drawn. Three warriors against three beasts.

I helped Dominic take cover behind the boulder, and then let go of him. He was safe for now, but my job wasn't finished. I needed to help my father and my friends.

"Emma," he called out. I stopped and turned back to him, but then realized that he couldn't see me.

"Yeah?" I asked.

"Thank you."

"You're welcome."

"They need you. The Hell Hounds can't see you coming. Just stay away from those teeth. We don't want them turning any part of you into hamburger."

"Deal," I answered, and headed toward the others.

I couldn't explain all of the emotions running through me as I watched my father and friends surrounded by those beasts. They were growling, and snapping their sharp teeth, setting up their next attack.

There was one Hell Hound larger than the others, and the other two kept turning their heads toward it, like they were looking for confirmation on when to strike. It lowered its head, fiery eyes set on Danyel. The other two had marked their targets and were also ready to strike.

I was moving as quickly as possible, about fifteen yards away.

I wished I could call on some super speed.

With a loud growl, the large one shot forward. Samuel was right. They did move like the wind, and were so fast, their movements were blurred.

Samuel, Danyel, and Malachi all dove in opposite directions as the beasts made their attack. It seemed like all had missed, until I heard a bloodcurdling cry.

The larger beast had pinned Danyel. Its sharp claws embedded into his chest, and its face was inches from his.

I gasped in horror.

My heart hammered against my chest as I ran toward him. Holding my dagger tightly in my hand, I was knocked from behind. I flew forward, the dagger thrust from my grasp as I slammed into the sharp rocks.

Malachi's beast had pounced out of nowhere, knocking me down.

"Danyel!" I screamed, glancing over to him. He had lodged his weapon into the creature's side, but it did nothing to stop the attack. Danyel struggled to push it off, and to get out from under its weight, but his efforts were useless.

I shot up, and quickly searched for my dagger. It was lying about five yards away, in the opposite direction of where Danyel was. I ran to grab it and turned back toward them.

The creature's claws were still locked in his chest. Danyel lifted his arm to shield his face, and the creature sunk its teeth into it.

"Danyel!" I screamed.

Danyel turned his head toward me, like he knew I was there.

He smiled, already knowing what I had yet to process.

"Be strong, Emma. Take care of your father," he yelled.

And then… my heart shattered.

The Hell Hound released his arm, and sunk its teeth deep into his throat.

"*No!*" I cried.

His eyes shut tight, and in one quick snap, the Hell Hound tore his head from his body.

I dropped to the ground, numb, as I watched the beast take his head and crush it between its jaws.

Shock and pain.

Not just any pain…excruciating pain radiated through my entire being, crushing and shattering my heart.

Every negative emotion ever known or experienced to man had overcome me. I sat there, completely numb, and watched the vile creature mutilate my father's best friend. My friend.

And then, my feelings began to blaze, like a huge inferno.

Feelings that soon torched and overtook all other feelings inside of me, to the point of overflowing.

Rage.

Hate.

Revenge.

I grasped the dagger in my hand and rose to my feet. The creature had no clue what was coming. I was a few yards away and there was too much blood on his muzzle for him to smell me. I sucked in a deep breath, and charged forward.

Jumping up with all my might, I thrust the dagger deep into its skull. I felt the splintering of bone as the dagger went through.

The hound shrieked in pain, and violently thrashed its head, sending me flying backward.

It growled, and snapped at the air around it, trying to figure out the location of its attacker.

I noticed Danyel's sword, still embedded in its side. My fears were again extinguished by the rage. Lurching forward, I tightly grasped the handle and yanked it out. The creature wailed.

With every last ounce of hate and revenge, I swung Danyel's sword. The blade tore right through the creature's neck, and I watched with utter satisfaction as its head fell and its lifeless body dropped to the ground.

As gratifying as it was to see the creature dead, the fact still remained, Danyel was also dead. His lifeless body was trapped under the weight of the beast.

This time, he wasn't able to heal himself, and would never wake up.

But I had to snap out of it. My job wasn't over.

As I glanced back, Malachi's beast had faced me. Its eyes trained on its slain leader, which was now dead and headless. As it paused, I saw an opportunity and took it. With every ounce of strength I had left, I lifted Danyel's sword. My eyes locked onto my mark, and I swung. In a split second, the next beast's head was severed from its body, and tumbled to the ground.

I had now slain three Hell Hounds.

Malachi stood bewildered, looking around him at the carnage behind me.

One beast remained.

"Malachi," I yelled.

"Emma? Where the hell are you?" he called, looking around in all directions.

"I'm in front of you, invisible. Samuel needs help."

He turned to Samuel.

"Don't worry, Emma. Wherever you are, just stay put. I've got this," Malachi said, then charged to Samuel's aide.

The beast was outnumbered. Samuel and Malachi gave each other another nod, as if they already had some sort of plan figured out. The beast charged at Samuel, snapping its razor sharp teeth, but Samuel side-swept it. At the same time, Malachi flew from above, and took its head off.

It was done.

The Hell Hounds had been defeated.

But the cost was great. We'd lost one of our own in the process. I watched as Samuel glanced over to Danyel. His companion, partner, and best friend since the beginning. Since the Fall.

Danyel didn't have to come back to help us. I knew he came back because of my father, and because Kade had asked him to. I didn't care if he was one of the Fallen. Danyel was a good angel. He was a true friend, and Guardian. I hoped God had seen what he did and would reward him.

I suddenly felt my emotions flood over me as we stood over Danyel. I hated my new life. I hated there was so much death and pain in it.

Why couldn't I have been left alone to live a normal life?

I didn't want to be a hero, or the answer to some crazy prophecy. I was seventeen, dammit. I just wanted to live a normal life. I wanted my parents, and my best friends, and a boyfriend. Just a normal boyfriend, whom I could be with, without any crazy supernatural laws being involved.

I glanced at Samuel, and immediately had to turn away from him.

I couldn't bear to watch the pain in his eyes. As I looked down, I realized I'd become visible. The suit had saved me yet again, but it was useless when I needed to save Danyel.

I walked over to Samuel and hugged him tightly. He wrapped his arms around me while I wept.

"I'm so sorry," I sobbed.

"It's alright, Emma. You don't need to shed any more tears for Danyel. He wanted this. His suffering is now over, and he will be able to rest in peace."

He and Malachi removed Danyel's body from beneath the Hell Hound, and carried it over to where Dominic was.

Malachi had found Kade's flask attached to Danyel's body, and it was filled. I wished it worked on Immortals, because Dom really needed it. At least I knew he was going to live.

Samuel made me take a drink, and as soon as the liquid magic touched my tongue, I instantly stopped shaking. Its effects were fast, and tingled as it made its way through my battered body. It helped stabilize me, and I needed that. I was broken. We all were.

They carefully laid Danyel's body out, and built up a small wall of stones around him. We all gathered around him, and Samuel began to recite some ancient words. They were beautiful, poetic, and melodic, but I didn't understand a word he was saying. He was speaking in another language. The language of the angel's.

As soon as Samuel finished, Danyel's body burst into flame. I didn't question it. I just assumed it was all part of the process of burying a fallen member.

When it was done, per my request, Malachi collected as much of his ashes as possible. I wanted to take Danyel's ashes with us, and refused to leave any part of him in Hell. He didn't belong here. He belonged someplace beautiful and peaceful, so I vowed to carry his ashes with me. After we made it out of here, I would take them someplace beautiful and scatter them.

Four of us remained, and for a while, we sat in a somber silence.

They all seemed to deal with it much better than I did, but I was still human. A girl. They were warriors, and had already dealt with centuries of war and death.

"We'll stay here until Dom heals enough to move without pain," Samuel said.

Malachi nodded in agreement. Dominic was quiet, but his jaw was clenched tight. The wrap he put around his arm was soaked and dripping with blood. He looked pale and his eyes were bright red and glossy. I could tell he was in a lot of pain.

"Can't one of you put him to sleep so he doesn't have to deal with the pain?" I asked.

"No," Dom blurted. "I've never been put under the sleeper. Ever. Believe me. I've seen much worse days."

"Why? Ugh. Men and angels…so damn full of pride," I sighed and shook my head. "I don't understand how you'd choose to suffer, rather than just closing your eyes and sleep."

Dominic paused for a moment, and we waited for a response.

"So, you really think I'm prideful?" he asked.

"Understatement," Malachi said, and everyone laughed.

Dominic winced in pain. "Fine," he gave in. "But what happens in Hell, *stays* in Hell."

A wicked grin crossed Malachi's face.

"And, I don't want him to do it," Dominic blurted, gesturing to Malachi.

"Why? I'd tuck you in all nice and tight," Malachi said, puckering his lips and giving him air kisses.

"Whatever dude. Just stay the hell away from me," he huffed. "Emma, you better make sure—"

"Don't worry, Dom. I've got your back," I assured him. "No one will breathe a word, and I'll keep Mr. Kissy Face away from you."

"Your no fun," Malachi sighed.

I glared at him and rolled my eyes.

Samuel walked over to Dom. "You should get into a comfortable position."

"Wait," Dom answered, and then slid down to lay on his good side. "Okay, do it."

Samuel knelt next to him, and spoke into his ear, "Sleep."

In less than a minute, Dominic was sound asleep and snoring loudly. If he kept it up, we'd all need the sleeper.

"Emma, do you need some help to sleep?" he asked.

"Not right now, but maybe later," I said.

As time slowly ticked, my heart and thoughts were on Danyel. It didn't matter whether my eyes were open or closed, my mind kept replaying the horror of his death. The last look on his face was what killed me the most. He knew he was going to die, and yet, told me to be strong and take care of my father.

I kept watching and reliving the Hell Hound sink his teeth deep into his neck and pull away. It wouldn't stop.

"You haven't eaten in a while, Emma. Here." Samuel offered me some jerky.

"No thanks. I can't eat right now."

Samuel's eyes had a look of concern. A look my mortal father used to give me when he knew I was sick or down about something.

"I understand what you're going through," he said exhaling. "It's been a rough journey for all of us. Danyel was my best friend, but he was tired of it all. Tired of having to be on a side. Tired of fighting. Tired of not knowing what we were fighting for anymore.

"Believe me when I tell you he is finally at peace now. It's something he has been waiting for, and for a very long time."

I nodded, tears spilled from my eyes.

He came and hugged me. "Don't worry, Emma. We'll get through this."

"Do you really think we'll make it past the last gate?" I asked.

"I think we stand a very good chance," he answered. "Especially with Malachi and Dominic with us now. And after watching you today, I'd say you're more than capable of holding your own."

"I don't understand what happened to me. It must have been the suit, the dagger, or a combination of both that helped me. They gave me the strength to do what I needed."

"No," he shook his head. "It was you, Emma. The suit and the dagger only enhance what is already inside of you. You have the power to make a difference. When faced with a deadly decision, you charged forward instead of staying back and watching, and it was that decision which saved Dominic's life.

"If you had paused, even for a moment, there would've been two tragedies, and three of us left. You saved him and saved the rest of us. That's not something that can be taught. It's something you're born with."

I couldn't really grasp the full extent of what he was saying, because I was still unsure of what I could do in my new skin. This new world, this dark world of death and torment...was burying me alive.

Dominic made a sound, and we both turned to him. He looked so peaceful, and was finally free from his pain and suffering. Malachi was turned away from us, and looked like he was sound asleep.

"So what do we do now?" I asked quietly.

"We wait. Once Dom's arm heals, we will be able to plan the next step." He grabbed his small pack and placed it on the ground. He then lay down, and placed his head on it.

"Do you think they'll let us see him?" I asked.

"I have high hopes," he said, yawning.

He must have been exhausted, and we were safe for now. Samuel and Malachi were not under the sleeper, so they would be on full guard.

"You should get some sleep. And, don't worry, we will wake you if anything happens," Samuel whispered.

"I don't think I can. Not after what happened."

"Do you need some help?" he smiled.

I nodded. I did help, especially with the constant horrors playing over and over in my mind.

"Are you comfortable?" he asked.

I tried to lie down in the most comfortable position I could. Samuel leaned over and brushed the hair away, which was stuck on my cheek. "Sleep sweet, my daughter."

My eyes suddenly became heavy, and my brain started tingling and became numb. Soon, my world faded to black.

FIFTEEN

SAMUEL GENTLY NUDGED MY SHOULDER to get up, and when he did, I realized we were still in Hell. I was still in the nightmare. My reality *was* the nightmare, and it wasn't going to go away. I had wished when I opened my eyes, Danyel would still be alive and Kade would be with me as an immortal. But that wasn't going to happen, and I had to deal with it.

"Hey, Emma. Why so glum?" The sound of Dom's voice broke me from my mental state, and put a small smile on my face.

"Just wishing things were different," I answered.

"You know, the answer to your problem is just an attitude change away," he said with a wink. "Just saying."

I thought about his words for a moment, and he was right. If I focused on the positive, then maybe I could drag myself out of this negative tar pit.

Samuel was still alive, Kade was safely with Alaine, and we made it through the five levels of Hell. That had never been done before, and would probably never be done again.

I was thankful that Dom, Malachi, and Danyel came to rescue us when they did. They saved us both. But the thought of Danyel kept breaking my heart. I couldn't allow my thoughts to linger on him for too long, or I'd lose it.

"So how are you feeling?" I asked Dom.

"Better than ever," he said, carefully unwrapping the dry bloodied shirt from his arm. My mouth gaped wide as he revealed it. The once mangled, shredded, bloody skin and bones had completely healed. In its place was pink, baby skin.

The last time I saw his arm, it was barely there! Now it was brand new.

"Amazing what a little rest can do to an immortal, huh?" he chimed.

"Heck yeah. I just hope I'll be able to heal that quickly," I said.

"What are you talking about? You're already healing like us," Malachi said.

I guess he was right. Ever since my seventeenth birthday, it seemed I'd started the change, getting closer to the time of the real transformation. I had eleven more months to survive.

"We need to get moving," Samuel said, opening his pouch. He pulled out some jerky, crackers and a few nuts. "Emma, you have to eat something before we leave."

"I'm not hungry," I said, stretching my tired limbs.

"I know, but you're still mortal. You need to eat, or you'll get weak."

I took the food and forced it down. It didn't taste good at all, but at least it was added fuel to keep me going. He gave me what was left in his canteen, and that was it. We didn't have any left. All we had to do was survive the last leg of this quest, and hopefully we'd all be home soon.

"So do we have a plan?" I asked.

"Yes. You and I will be going to the last gate together, and Malachi and Dominic will be going back to Alaine."

"Wait. Hold up. We aren't leaving you guys," Malachi interrupted. He didn't look too happy with the plan, and I realized Samuel had made this decision on his own.

"Malachi, there is zero chance the Fallen will let you enter those gates. Showing yourself at the gate will start a war we cannot win. You and Dom have done all you can to get us here safely. Your part of the quest is over, and now Emma and I must finish ours," he answered.

"Samuel, I don't think that's a good idea. I think we should wait out here, just to make sure everything is okay," Dom answered.

"Once we get to Lucifer—if we get to him—we will not come back this way, and you will not be able to enter. We will have to make this journey alone."

Without Dom and Malachi, the strongest half of us, Samuel and I were nearly powerless. But I guess we didn't need strength where we were going. Danyel told me I'd have to be smart when dealing with Lucifer, so brains would be needed more than brawn.

"Samuel, you're supposed to be dead. They think they've killed you. Won't it be a huge gamble if you go through there?" Malachi asked.

"It might be, but it was Lucian who saw to my execution. I doubt Lucifer even knew anything about it. He probably has no idea I'm supposed to be dead. For the past century, he hasn't been much into the details of his members. I think I should be fine," he said.

Malachi exhaled loudly and shook his head.

I knew he and Dominic weren't in agreement with what was going on. They thought they were going with us to the end. But Samuel was right, they'd never get past those gates unless they were part of the Fallen, and they knew it.

"Well, we aren't leaving until we make sure you've both entered safely. If we hear anything, we will be kicking down those gates, and kicking some ass as we come through," Dominic noted.

"I agree with Dom. We will make sure you enter safely, and only when we're certain you've made it, then we will leave."

"Well, it won't be long until they find out their undefeatable Guardians of the five levels are dead. Then you'll both be in real danger," Samuel urged.

"Hey, don't worry about us. We can hold our own. Just make sure Emma makes it in and out safely, and that we'll see you both back at the house in one piece."

"Agreed," Samuel said.

We all stood somewhere in the depths of Hell and said our last goodbyes. I walked over to Malachi and gave him a hug.

"Hey, you can do this. I know I seem a bit rough on you, but I know you have what it takes, inside, to survive," he said.

"Thanks, Malachi," I blushed.

Next, I hugged Dom tightly.

"Don't worry, Emma. We'll be seeing each other again. Just remember when we do, don't go getting all emotional and lovey-dovey with me, especially if Kade's watching," he winked.

"Oh my God," I giggled.

"I told you to stop calling me that. It's Dom. Just Dom." He winked.

"Shut up, Dom," Malachi snapped. "Emma, just stay safe. Keep your dagger close to you and don't be scared to use it if you need to."

I loved Dom. Not in a romantic way, but he was the coolest, most fun of all the Guardians. Without Dom, this new world I was thrust into would have sucked. Of course Kade was part of that world, but he was in a category all of his own.

"About Emma's dagger," Samuel added. "Dominic, how did you come into possession of it?"

Dom shrugged his shoulders. "Actually, Michael approached me, asking if I would be its keeper until it found the next. He said it would let me know…that I'd feel when it had chosen its next keeper. Ever since Emma came near it, it started to buzz, almost begging for me to give it to her. I know it sounds strange, but it's true. I don't know what kind of connection Emma has to the dagger, but I've never seen, or heard, of it passed to anyone other than a pureblood," Dominic noted.

"Me either," Samuel agreed.

"Yeah, I thought it was strange for her to be in possession of it for so long and not show signs of ill effects, along with being able to control it." Malachi added.

"Well, as long as it works for her, who cares about the formalities. Right?" Dom said, patting my shoulder.

"I do agree with you Dom...again," Malachi sighed. "And that is just wrong. I really need to get the hell out of Hell and clear my head."

"Dude, I'm just growing on you."

"Yeah, like a damn tumor," Malachi huffed.

We all laughed.

"Well, it's time for us to go our separate ways," Samuel said. He walked up to Dominic and Malachi. "Goodbye my brothers. I wish you a safe passage back to Alaine and the others. Please tell her I love her, and I will do my best to return to her."

"Hell yeah. You'd better return because living with Alaine, if anything happens to you *again*, will be unbearable. I don't think any of us would survive for long. So you better keep yourselves safe and make it back. Deal?" Dom held out his hand to Samuel, and in return he shook it.

"Deal," Samuel answered.

"Wait!" I gasped, picking up the container which held Danyel's ashes. "Please take him out of here."

"Sure," Dominic said, taking the container and placing it in his pocket.

"Thank you."

"You're welcome. But just so you know, I won't be spreading these ashes anywhere. These will be staying in this container until you come back and spread them yourself, wherever it is you wanted them spread," he said.

"Fine," I exhaled.

Dom was giving us both some pretty good incentives, which was good. At least we did have more than a few good things to look forward to when, and if, we did return.

"Please tell Kade I'm okay, and I'll see him soon," I added with a grin.

"Fine," Dominic huffed, rolling his eyes.

"Alright, Emma. Are you ready for the last part of the quest?" Samuel asked.

"As ready as I'll ever be," I breathed. He held his hand out to me and I grasped it. We gave one last glance at Malachi and Dominic before we turned and started toward the last gate.

I was glad when our backs were facing them, because tears had begun to pool in my eyes, daring to spill over. I tried hard to contain them, but a few escaped and trailed down my cheeks. I quickly wiped them away.

Samuel glanced at me, but didn't say a word.

We continued past the corpses of the Hell Hounds, through the last tunnel. It was dark and smelled horrible—typical Hell stuff. When we reached the end, we still had a ways to go before we reached the final gate to Lucifer.

Samuel stopped me five feet before we exited the tunnel.

"Emma, your mark. We need to disguise it," he said.

"Just do whatever you need to. I want to make it out of here alive."

"Alright, but it's going to hurt a bit," he said, pulling out a small knife from his pouch.

Oh dang. This was *really* going to hurt.

"I just have to mask Alaine's mark for the time being. It's her mark that will make them question."

I nodded. "So—," I drew out a breath, "are you planning to cut it off?"

"No," he said kneeling down. "I'm going to burn it, but it will only be temporary. Your mark will come back once it heals. This is just to keep anyone from suspecting you are anything more than a Nephilim."

"Okay," I said. That sounded good enough for me.

He gathered a few things from his pouch and laid them on the ground on top of each other. With a wave of his hand, there was a spark, which quickly became a flame. He held his blade over the fire until it glowed a bright orange. I swallowed hard.

"Are you ready?" he asked.

"Yes," I lied. I turned my back to him, closed my eyes tight, and sucked in a deep breath. As soon as I did, Kade's face flashed in front of me. His smile, his dark-brown disheveled hair, and his glowing, hazel eyes. I suddenly felt horrible I was acting like a baby. Kade had endured the worst burns I'd ever seen, and still managed to be strong.

Samuel placed one hand on my shoulder and paused.

"Is everything okay?" I asked through gritted teeth, waiting for the pain.

"Yes. This is the first time I've seen Alaine's mark," he admitted.

"Is it bad?"

"No."

"Do you know who the mark belongs to?"

"Yes, but this is something I cannot share. It's not my place to," he said.

I sighed, already used to unanswered questions. I just wanted to get this over with.

"I'm ready," I said.

"Alright. Deep breath."

I sucked in as he pressed the hot blade to the back of my neck. I flinched at the searing pain, but didn't move. I bit down hard, and sent my thoughts to Kade. This was nothing compared to what he was enduring.

After a few moments, the heat ended.

"It's done. You're so strong, Emma."

"I don't think so. Not compared to the rest of you. Not compared to Kade," I breathed.

"You're stronger than you think." He softly squeezed my shoulder then released. "Well, that should do it."

"Is it noticeable?" I asked.

"No. They will only be able to see my mark."

"That's good," I sighed.

"Yes. Very good. They can't question what they can't see," he added. "But just remember what Danyel told you. Don't be fooled by Lucifer's words. His words are smooth, yet deceiving. Just remember why we are here."

"So, is Lucifer as scary as everyone paints him to be? Does he have horns and a tail?"

Samuel laughed and shook his head. "Not even close. Lucifer was one of the most beautiful angels in Heaven before the Fall. He was a worshiper. And his voice was like that of a hundred choirs, filling the air with the most beautiful melodies. As time went on, he received more and more praise from the angels around him. His heart began to fill with pride. Pride turned into jealousy, and jealousy into bitterness and hate. It was that which became his downfall and had him expelled from Heaven.

"Because of his gift, he could easily sway others with his words. A third of the angels chose to leave with him. Danyel and I were amongst them. We were part of the Fall."

Samuel's face was saddened. He'd succumbed to the Prince of Darkness' forked tongue, and it worried me. If they couldn't withstand his deceiving words, how was I supposed to?

I smiled at him. "Well, I have you with me now. I'm not worried. Plus, I *really* would like to get out of Hell as soon as possible."

"Good then. Let's do this, and get back to the others."

"Sounds amazing. I stink and I am dying for a shower."

"No dying on my watch," he chuckled.

"I'll try not to," I laughed.

We drew closer. The gate was towering and ominous. It was tall, black, and twisted, with large, sharp barbs covering it. I couldn't see how far it extended because it disappeared into the darkness on each side.

Two large torches were set on either side of the gate's opening, and in front of it stood a tall, hooded creature.

Was that the Grim Reaper? It looked exactly like him. Whatever it was, it was what I had always envisioned standing at the gate of Hell.

SIXTEEN

W E WERE ABOUT TWENTY-FIVE FEET away, and the tall, hooded figure remained frozen. I wondered if it was real, or if it was just a statue.

"What is that?" I whispered to Samuel.

"The last gate keeper."

"Is he real? I haven't seen him move since we exited the cave."

"Yes. He's very real. Let me go in first and talk to him. You stay here, and I'll let you know when, and if, it's safe to come."

"Okay."

"Emma, if anything should happen, Malachi and Dominic are still waiting beyond the tunnel on the other side. I'm not saying it will, but just in case... run back to them."

My heart twisted.

"Just don't let anything happen. Please," I begged. I needed him.

"I'll try," he said, resting his hand on my shoulders. He nodded, and I nodded in return.

I remained in my spot and watched Samuel walk towards the creature. My pulse started to race as different scenarios ran through my head. Would he call me to come, or would I have to run? I watched in anticipation, hoping for one outcome, but ready for the other.

As Samuel moved closer, the creature it raised a large, sharp sickle above its head.

I strained to see if I could make out what was under its long, black cloak, and as the light from the torch illuminated it, I gasped. It was bones. Like…only bones. A skeleton.

What the heck was holding all of its pieces together? It *was* the damn Grim Reaper.

Samuel stopped a few feet in front of it. It towered over him, at least at ten feet tall.

I listened quietly as Samuel spoke.

"It's urgent we speak to Lucifer," he said, in an even, serious voice.

The creature shook his head and pointed behind him. It looked like he was telling him to leave. Right now, that seemed like a pretty damn good idea.

"It's regarding his son. Lucian is planning to murder him, and he needs to be warned."

The creature stood as still as a statue for a few long seconds, then made a motion with his arm. Samuel stepped closer and turned his head, showing him his mark. Samuel spoke to him in a softer tone which I couldn't hear.

I waited. Anxious. What was going on?

A few minutes later the creature stepped forward, unlatched the gate, and swung it open. He then stepped aside.

No way! That was too easy.

We'd fought for our lives through every single gate, and I assumed we would have to do the same to get through this one too.

But no. The scary death creature…a.k.a. the Grim Reaper…was the coolest of them all. He actually gave us a free passage into Hell. I couldn't believe I was excited about it.

Samuel motioned for me to come to him, so without fear I went forward and took hold of his hand. As I walked past the Reaper, I didn't know what to do.

Did I look at it?

Should I *not* make eye contact?

I had to look, and then found myself whispering, "Thank you." As soon as I did I turned away, and felt stupid. Samuel pulled me through the gate, chuckling.

"Was I not supposed to talk to it?"

"Well, I think you were the first, in all of existence, to tell the gate keeper of Hell 'thank you'. I'm not sure he knew what to do with that."

"Well, I was thankful he let us through so easily."

I took a quick glance behind us to see if I could spy Malachi and Dom, but the cave was too dark. They were probably watching us enter the gate, thankful they didn't have to come and fight.

As soon as we were inside, the Reaper slammed the gate shut. The sound of the metal clanging made my insides jump. He then turned and resumed his stance back at the front, and froze.

Samuel quickly led me down a rocky corridor that opened up into a huge cavern, which was almost circular. It was dark, but beautiful. The walls looked like they were made of a black marble. There were carvings of gargoyles inset into the walls; each placed six feet from the next, and continued all the way around.

They were creepy, and looked like they could come to life at any moment and attack us. Their stone eyes were glaring at us, their teeth and claws were razor sharp. I tried not to look at them, because they resembled the creature at the first gate that burned Kade.

There were three different passages around the room. One to our left, one to the right, and one directly in front of us.

"Come, Emma," Samuel said leading me down the tunnel on the left. I wondered if he knew where he was going. He was a Fallen member, so he must.

The corridor was dark, and sporadically lit with torches. The ground was flat and easy to walk on. No more jagged rocks, which I was thankful for. We weaved our way through the tunnel, and went through another series of passages, traveling deeper and deeper. Samuel seemed to know exactly where he was going, so I just followed.

"Why aren't there any Fallen around here? Shouldn't there be a bunch of them guarding this place?"

"Not really. There are only a few Fallen who are allowed this far, because no one has ever survived the five levels to make it here. For centuries, Lucifer has had no need to worry about intruders. We will be reaching Lucifer's dwelling soon, and that area will have guards."

"Do we have a plan?"

"No, but as usual, just leave the talking to me." He winked.

"Sounds like a good plan," I admitted.

There was no way I would ever doubt Samuel. I knew he wouldn't do anything foolish and put our lives in jeopardy. He wanted to get out of here as much as I did.

I didn't know what to expect. I'd heard so many horror stories about the Prince of Darkness, and saw so many movies depicting him as this evil, ugly creature who tortured and killed innocents, and loved to strip souls. He was the ruler of the Fallen and the Underworld. So, why the heck would he want to listen to me?

We could only hope the rift between him and Lucian was deep enough to make him listen. And the fact his son was on a hit list just might make him want to help. If Lucifer was as proud as they said he was, then I'd bet he was waiting for a moment of revenge. This could be the perfect time.

"Can I ask you a question?"

"Sure," Samuel said, stopping and turning to me.

"What is the whole story behind Lucifer and his Nephilim son? Kade told me it was his brother's son. Is that true?"

"Yes," he answered.

"And his brother was executed because of it?"

"Yes, he was. Lucifer's brother raped a mortal woman and she became pregnant. He tried to cover it up and went to Lucifer for help, but somehow word spread to Lucian. When Lucian learned of this, he immediately went to the rest of the Fallen leaders, and had them confront Lucifer's brother with the law. In order for Lucifer to keep headship, he had to hand his brother over to them. He was taken and immediately executed.

"Lucian sent a few Fallen to kill the woman, but she gave birth before they found her. Lucifer had also sent one of his personal guards to collect the child, and bring it to him. There was no law stating the child had to be executed, so Lucifer raised the Nephilim boy as his own.

"Lucifer cannot bear children, as was one of the curses put upon him when he fell. Thus, this child, his brother's son, is his only heir."

"Oh," I breathed. That was something I never expected the devil to do. To take in his brother's son and raise him as his own. "But what if they find out you are my father? You were supposed to be executed. What if they take you from me, or worse?"

He placed his hands on my shoulders. "That's something we will have to deal with when we get there," he said.

"You can't leave me," I pleaded. I could feel hot tears pool in my eyes, and began to wonder if this was all worth it. We'd come so far, and the thought of losing him made me very afraid.

He wrapped his arms around me and pulled me into a hug. "I'm not leaving you. We will get through this somehow. We just have to have faith. Faith is something I lost a long, long time ago, but since you've come back into my life, it's slowly returned to me," he said in a quieted voice. "I do have faith we will make it back. Alive."

I agreed with him and nodded.

"Onward?" he asked.

"Onward," I sniffled.

He took my hand and we continued. Not long after, boisterous laughter echoed through the corridor. I glanced up at Samuel, and he turned and smiled at me. It was reassuring to see he wasn't afraid.

We soon entered a small room with six Fallen angels, who looked drunk, sitting around a circular table. There were platters filled with all kinds of food, and large goblets of drink set in front of them. Behind them were two huge golden doors with hundreds of shimmering gems inset into them, in every color imaginable. I assumed it was the entrance to Lucifer's dwelling.

As we entered the room, Samuel held me back from taking another step further, and then he stepped in front of me. All heads looked and all eyes glared at us, their roaring laughter immediately turned to silence.

One of them stood, and towered about seven feet tall. Huge muscles bulged from his arms and legs. His skin was tanned and slightly dirty, like he'd recently been in battle, or hadn't taken a bath in a while. His hair was long and stringy, and his eyes were raven black.

He stepped toward Samuel and stood about a foot over him. His huge fingers brushed the handle of his sword.

"What do we have here?" his deep voice boomed. He was speaking to Samuel, but glaring at me.

"We are here to see Lucifer," Samuel answered.

The Fallen angel turned back to the others. "He wants to see Lucifer."

There was a moment of silence before they all burst into laughter. I could feel my temperature rise as I watched them make fun of Samuel, but he remained calm and collected.

"Hey, you look familiar. I've fought alongside you many years ago." One of the other Fallen stood from the table and pointed at Samuel, confused.

"I'm sure you have," Samuel confirmed.

"Wait. Aren't you the one who—" he paused and glanced at me, and then back at Samuel.

Oh crap. I had a feeling this wasn't going to be good.

"Yes. You are the one who was supposed to have been executed for mating with a mortal," he yelled, pounding his fist on the table.

All eyes snapped to me.

"Is *that* your abomination?" he growled, throwing his finger at me.

"She is *not* an abomination, you bastard," Samuel growled through gritted teeth.

All eyes in the room went pure black.

"You dare bring your abomination here?" Another stood from the table and reached for his sword.

Samuel took a step back and reached for the handle of his sword but didn't unsheathe it.

"I didn't come here for trouble. I came only to speak to Lucifer."

The huge Fallen angel took a step toward Samuel, while all the others stood and drew their swords. My pulse started to race. There was nothing I could do.

"Samuel?" My voice was shaky.

"Go back, Emma," he said, turning to me. "Now."

"I'm not leaving you," I said.

"Emma, please."

His words pierced my heart. He wanted me to go because he didn't want me to see what was going to happen to him. Six against one. It was going to be a slaughter, but there was no way I was going to leave him. I was prepared to stay and fight alongside him if I needed to.

I grabbed the handle of my dagger and slowly unsheathed it.

"You shouldn't have come here. Now you and your filthy spawn will die," the largest Fallen yelled.

He suddenly raised his sword and charged toward Samuel. Samuel stepped forward and ducked under the Fallen's sword. With a quick flick of his own sword, Samuel sliced right through his wrist. Within seconds the large brute was dismembered. His hand, along with his blade, fell to the ground.

He looked confused, staring at his bloodied stump. He was drunk, and much slower than Samuel. Maybe we did have a chance.

"I don't want to fight you," Samuel urged. "I just need to speak to Lucifer. It's regarding his son."

I suddenly felt lightheaded and dizzy, like I was going to faint. My world started to spin, and a feeling of warmth and euphoria rushed through me.

"And what of his son?" A voice called from behind us.

As turned back, and as soon as I saw him, my world went spiraling into complete confusion.

Red eyes.

Fiery red eyes met mine, the same eyes which recently haunted my dreams.

He stepped into the room and the rest of the Fallen stepped

back. Whoever he was, he was young and very beautiful. He was about the same height as Kade, but his skin was tanned and muscles framed his lean figure in all the right places. His features were dark, as was his ebony hair, which was drawn back.

"Ethon," the largest Fallen spoke, grasping his bloody wrist. "This Fallen has broken the law and committed a crime. He should have been executed for spawning with a human, and that thing standing in front of you is his abomination."

Ethon came and stood next to me, so close, my body reacted. Heat and dizziness coursed through my veins. The air felt like it was alive and buzzing with electricity. I felt magnetized to him.

What the hell was happening to me, and who was this person?

"Azzah, I suggest you pick up your limb and tend to your wound. Let me deal with this," Ethon spoke in an authoritative tone. "The rest of you can resume whatever it was you were doing."

The other five Fallen took their seats at the table, but kept their swords drawn. The large one, who he called Azzah, bent down and picked up his severed hand and sword, and then proceeded out of the corridor with a look of defeat smeared over his face.

"So, what is this business you wish to speak of with my father?" he asked.

My head snapped up to look at him, and he smiled a wide smile. He knew I was surprised to find out who he was, and I felt my face flush with heat.

The person who was haunting my dreams was Lucifer's son.

I quickly turned toward Samuel, who regarded him with a nod.

"Ethon, we've come to ask for help. Lucian is out there wreaking havoc."

"So, what else is new?" He laughed.

"He has sent out a decree for his members to seek out and execute *all* Nephilim. He has succeeded in killing all but three. You, my daughter, and one other," he said glancing at me.

He must have meant Alaine, and then I quickly realized they could never know she was my mother, although Lucian and his crew might have.

"There are only three Nephilim left?" Ethon asked.

"Yes," Samuel answered.

"So, my fellow Nephilim, may I have your name?" he asked.

"Emma," I answered.

"Well, it's a pleasure to meet you, Emma," he said, extending his hand out to me.

As I placed my hand in his, *bam!* Electricity surged through my arm and traveled through my body. It was the exact feeling I felt the first time I touched Kade.

"Shit," I gasped and pulled my hand back.

I felt weak and backed up to Samuel. His hand found my shoulder, steadying me. I turned to him to see if he had answers. His brow was furrowed and his eyes showed deep concern.

This could *not* be happening!

Ethon looked at his hand, confused.

How could this even be possible?

There had to be some kind of explanation. There was no way I could be destined for two completely different people.

But maybe that was it. Maybe that was the answer to the

question. I was part angel and part Fallen. Maybe the good part of me was drawn to Kade, and the Fallen part was drawn to Ethon. Danyel told me, one day I would have to choose a side, but I'd bet he didn't expect this to happen. I don't think anyone did.

Either way, this was all completely wrong. I'd have to sit down and have a long discussion with Alaine and Samuel about this when we got back. *If* we got back.

"Ethon," Samuel said, snapping him from his confusion.

With just one word spoken, I could sense stress in Samuel's voice. He knew exactly what happened between us, and I could tell he didn't like it. What father wouldn't be concerned, especially knowing his daughter had just been zapped by the son of Satan?

Ethon's head lifted, his brow was furrowed.

"Come. I will take you to see my father," he said, stepping around me.

I could hear my heart beat loudly in my ears, and felt his eyes on me, but I dared not look. As soon as he walked past us, I felt my body begin to relax a bit.

The five Fallen remained extra quiet in their seats. Ethon opened the golden doors and motioned for us to enter. Samuel took hold of my hand again and I was glad. I needed him to steady me, and I was glad he was here. We'd already gone through so much together and my love and admiration for him had grown to overflowing. He was my hero. My protector. My father. He was here to make sure I was safe, and now steady.

SEVENTEEN

AS WE PASSED THROUGH THE doorway, there was another long, dark tunnel which led us downward. We followed Ethon in silence, and I noticed him flex and release his hand a few times. I wondered what he was thinking, and if he'd ever experienced those feelings before. Whether he did or not, he didn't utter a word about it.

We soon made our way into another large room, which was like nothing I had expected. It was a huge underground cavern, the kind where you'd probably find large bats living. Jagged rocks lined the ceiling and walls, but the floor was covered in a beautiful black marble, like that of the first room we entered. The air was a little less thick in here. And a lot cooler.

"Father," Ethon called. His voice echoed throughout the cavern.

Wicked growls and barks returned, and instantly reminded me of the Hell Hounds. I backed up, and reached for my dagger, expecting to see fiery eyes appear. But instead, a black two-headed dog bounded towards us. As soon as it saw Ethon, it stopped growling, and huge tongues hung out of each mouth. It jumped up and down, as if it were happy to see him. Both heads kept glancing at us, and then back to Ethon, confused as to who we were.

Before the creature reached us, Ethon stepped in front of us and held his arms up. The dog jumped into his arms, and knocked him to the ground. He laughed and wrestled the beast as it licked his face. Both slobbery tongues completely soaked him.

Gross.

"Dum Dum, get *off*. You big, stupid dog," he said, pushing the two heads away. The dog backed off, and then both sets of eyes were glaring at me and Samuel. Two sets of sharp teeth were bared, and deep growls rumbled through the cavern.

Ethon walked up to the creature and smacked its heads. "Get outta here," he scolded. It yelped and ran away.

"Sorry. I don't know why my father keeps that worthless creature around."

"Well, it—or they—seemed to love you," I giggled.

"Yes, because I'm the only one who gives it attention," he laughed back, attempting to wipe the slobber from his face.

"Ethon?" a low voice called.

We turned as an older gentleman, who had strong resemblances of Ethon, made his way toward us. He was about six feet tall, and very handsome. His hair was salt-and-peppered, clean cut and nicely combed back, with a matching mustache and goatee. He was slim and dressed in an all-black suit, but his eyes...his eyes were a deep crimson red, much darker than Ethon's.

"Father, you have visitors," Ethon said, bowing his head.

So this was Lucifer? The Devil. The one multitudes feared?

He didn't look so bad. But then again, neither did Lucian before he morphed into his terrifying, evil mode.

Lucifer walked up to Ethon and placed his hands on his shoulders, giving him a stern look of...*who are they*? But I also saw a hint of softness in his eyes as he continued to look into Ethon's eyes. That was a plus on our side, and something we could definitely use to our advantage.

"And whom, may I ask, has my son escorted into my forbidden chambers?" There was a definite tone of chiding, hidden behind false humor.

"Father this is—" Ethon started to speak, but Lucifer held up his hand to stop him.

"Can they not speak for themselves?" he questioned.

"Yes, we can," Samuel said with a bow of his head. "My name is Samuel, and this is my daughter Emma."

I didn't know whether to bow, or wave, or just stand there and smile. I mean, he was the leader of the Fallen angels. Samuel never told me how I should address him.

He stared me down, and I stood there, frozen.

I heard a quiet laughter and glanced at Ethon. He quickly turned away with a smirk on his face.

Why was he laughing? Was he laughing at me?

Lucifer glanced at Ethon and cleared his throat.

Ethon's expression suddenly changed from playful to serious, and I fought to keep a grin off my face, which he noticed.

As soon as Lucifer turned from him, he glanced at me and rolled his eyes.

Lucifer turned his gaze to Samuel and slowly paced toward him. I suddenly felt fearful. With each step, my pulse raced faster and faster.

"Samuel?" Lucifer asked.

"Yes."

"Why do you look so familiar to me? Are you not one of my warriors?"

"I am," Samuel answered.

"And your daughter. She is not a pureblood?"

"No. She is a Nephilim. One of the last in the mortal world, which is why we've come to you," Samuel replied.

"Nephilim?" Lucifer paused, and then circled him slowly, and as he came around his crimson eyes set on me. "Well then, I guess the next question should be, why haven't you been executed?"

Lucifer's eyes were locked on me, and it was really beginning to creep me out. I could see a look of concern flash through Samuel's eyes which made me feel even worse.

"Lucian ordered my execution, and those orders were carried out on Montem Mortis. Somehow, I survived," Samuel answered. "But, that is not why we are here. We've come because Lucian has given a command, to execute all Nephilim who still exist. We have word that he has succeeded in killing all but three. Emma, Ethon, and one other. The other is in a safe house in the mortal world, but Midway has made it very clear they will not get involved. Right now,

Lucian has gathered his army, and is seeing to it that every last one is wiped from existence. Once Emma and the other are dead, they will come for Ethon."

A deep laugh echoed throughout the cavern and sent a prickling chill down my spine. I guess Lucifer thought it was funny.

"Midway? Those good for nothing bastards. They never want to dip their hands in the affairs of the wicked. As for Lucian...that deceitful betrayer is no threat to me, and he will never, ever, touch one hair on Ethon's head," Lucifer answered. His voice was dark and evil. "If he sets one foot in my domain, I will rip off his wings, sink my hand into his chest and yank out his black heart. Then I will laugh as he takes his last breath, and watches his heart being crushed in my hands."

"Father, I cannot stay in Hell forever, and when I do travel into the mortal world, Lucian will be there, waiting. How much do you think he would give to have the head of Lucifer's son on a platter, just to prove he is greater than you? I will never be safe until he is dead, and you are the only one strong enough, and smart enough, to kill him."

Was Ethon siding with us? I watched as Lucifer's demeanor changed.

He paused, and for a brief moment I saw a look of compassion as he glanced into Ethon's red eyes. They looked oddly alike, like they could actually be father and son.

There was a long, deep pause and then Lucifer stepped away from Ethon.

"This is what I'll do. I will gather an army together that will take care of Lucian and the rest of his betrayers, however…" he paused again and started to slowly walk back toward us. His eyes again set on me. He came inches from my face, and I remembered what Danyel said. I stood and tried to show no fear, even though my insides were trembling.

"What?" Samuel asked.

"I want this beautiful child in exchange. She will make a perfect mate for my Ethon. Two of a kind, and who knows what kind of power could come from their progenies? The power of two Nephilim. Now that would be something to behold," he said slowly, his eyes still locked onto mine. He raised his hand and his hot fingers traced the lines of my face. "She is very beautiful, Samuel."

"Thank you, Lucifer, but I cannot agree to that exchange," Samuel replied.

"My price is high, Samuel. I will not send my warriors out there for a matter that is really of no concern to me."

"Father. I'm of no concern to you?" Ethon loudly rebutted.

Lucifer closed his eyes.

"Of course you are, son," he answered, and then pointed to me. "But *this* child means nothing."

"Then do it for me. Send your army to defeat Lucian once and for all. This has been long in coming, father. He blatantly betrayed you, and led many of your warriors astray. It is time Lucian is put back in his rightful place. A place of submission to you."

Lucifer crossed his arms over his chest and smiled widely at Ethon. He shook his head and laughed. "You have such a wonderful way with words my son, and remind me so much of myself. I would love nothing more than to see Lucian fall, but I have no time for him, nor his treacherous affairs. I will make sure you are safe Ethon. You will never have to worry about that."

"And, what about Emma?" Ethon questioned.

"What about this girl? You've only just met her, Ethon. You are the Prince of the Underworld, and she is but a mere half breed."

I looked at Ethon for his answer, and he looked back at me with a look I couldn't read.

"If you will not send your army to defeat Lucian, then I will leave with Samuel and Emma, and will try and protect them myself," Ethon said, turning to face his father.

"Why? What makes you want to protect those you know nothing about?"

I wanted to know the same thing. Why was he doing this for us? And then, Ethon walked over to me and took hold of my hand.

Electricity surged through my arm and through my body, filling me with that wonderful feeling of euphoria, confusion, and warmth. I felt a strong pull towards him, and tried to shake his hand free, but he held tight. I gasped and he suddenly let go.

I didn't realize I had shut my eyes, until I opened them and both Lucifer and Samuel were staring back at us with wide looks of bewilderment and concern.

"Because of that father. I don't understand what it is about her, but when I touch her, I feel something I've never experienced before. It's like a current flowing from her to me. It draws me to her like a moth to flame. I feel as if we are connected, somehow."

Ethon *did* experience the exact same feelings, and he was just as

226

confused.

Samuel looked at me and then closed his eyes, shaking his head in disparagement.

But it wasn't my fault. I didn't choose this. I didn't understand what was happening, and it started to make me sick.

This was wrong. Totally and completely wrong.

Lucifer looked at both of us, and a wide, wicked smile grew on his lips.

"That, my son, means you have found your mate. The one you will spend the rest of your life with. I have never, until now, heard of it happening to any other but purebloods. This is odd, but it seems as if you both have the connection." Lucifer walked up to Ethon and stood in front of him.

"You see, once a pureblood has found his mate, a connection and a bond is instantly formed. Their energies begin to pull toward each other like that of a magnet. Once contact is made, it will be nearly impossible for one to be away from the other. It's a magical thing. One which cannot be explained. This miracle only happens once in a lifetime, and if that is what we have just witnessed between you and Emma, then you have been bonded. "

No! I wanted to scream, but kept my mouth shut.

It didn't only happen once in a lifetime. I'd had it happen to me twice in less than a month. Ethon could not possibly be my future mate. If I were meant to be with anyone, it would be Kade. He was the one I felt the connection with first, and now because of me, he was a mortal and barely hanging on to life.

My heart ached as I thought of him, and I fought the urge to curl up into a ball and cry. Cry until I couldn't cry anymore.

But I couldn't let them see I was weak.

Strong arms wrapped securely around me, and I knew they were Samuel's.

"It's okay Emma. It's okay," he reassured.

"So you will help them, father?" Ethon questioned.

"First, I want to see their marks. I want to make sure they are truly father and daughter, and that she is in fact a Nephilim."

Doubt suddenly rushed through me and my heart began to hammer against the walls of my chest. I hoped whatever Samuel did to Alaine's mark worked. If it didn't…well I didn't want to think about what could happen. There were too many horrifying scenarios, and I didn't have time to run them all through my mind.

I could sense Lucifer could be very evil, and after all the horror stories about him, the thought of what he could do had my stomach twisting in knots. I turned back to Samuel, and he smiled and gave me a nod. I guess he seemed to think everything was going to be okay.

Lucifer held out his hand to me, so I walked up to him, and pulled my hair to the side to show him my mark. "What happened here?" he asked, lightly touching the burn. I held my breath.

"She was burned by a certain flame-thrower on our way here," Samuel started to explain. "We've been through a lot to get to you, and cheated death on several occasions."

"That you have. And one day you shall have to humor me, and explain how you made it through my invincible levels of Hell. That will be a story I should like to hear in full, brilliant detail," Lucifer stated, still studying my neck.

"Yes. It was quite an adventure," Samuel answered.

"And my Guardians?" Lucifer questioned.

"Dead," Samuel stated.

"All of them?" he asked, turning to Samuel with a look of amazement.

"Yes. All of them," Samuel said, with a voice of satisfaction.

"And it was…just the two of you?"

"No. There was another, but he fell at the last gate."

"Hmmm. Then, I guess I can call it even. I would have killed the Guardian's anyway for allowing you to get so far. I am curious though, as to the details. It will take me some time to gather new Guardians, but right now I do not have the time, or the patience."

He was still fingering the burned mark on the back of my neck.

What the hell was taking him so long?

Did he see something?

I could feel sweat start to run down my face, and I had to slow my breath.

I glanced up and saw Ethon staring at me, with a look of worry, so I smiled. I smiled as a cover, to show him I was all right, and it worked. He immediately smiled back.

"Father?" he questioned.

Lucifer finally stepped back, so I stood straight letting my hair fall back over the mark. As I stood, the Bloodstone around my neck released itself from the suit, glowing bright red.

"What is this?" Lucifer questioned, curiously reaching for the stone. As soon as his finger touched it, he immediately pulled it back, like it had burned him. "What is this witchcraft which glows around your neck?" he growled, glaring at me.

"It was a gift. A Bloodstone of Christ," Samuel responded quickly.

"How did this half breed come in possession of such a rare relic? And explain to me, Samuel, why a member of the Fallen would allow his daughter to wear such a treacherous object?"

"It was a gift from her Guardian. He gave it to her before he was killed," Samuel answered.

We were in trouble. Deep, deep trouble.

EIGHTEEN

I QUICKLY POSITIONED MY ARM to cover the sheath of the dagger, praying Lucifer wouldn't see it. If he found out I not only had a Bloodstone of Christ, but Michael the Archangel's dagger…there was no way we would make it out of here alive.

"Father, please. They've been through enough to get here to speak to you. If they hadn't come and warned us about Lucian, I could have traveled into the mortal world without a clue, and could've been executed. You would have never known what happened to me, or understood why I never returned."

I was amazed at Ethon's persistence to help save us.

Lucifer looked at his son and exhaled loudly, and then walked away from me. I also quietly exhaled and relaxed a bit, still hiding the dagger as best I could, but trying not to make it too obvious.

"And your mark," he said turning to Samuel. Samuel lifted his hair and showed him the mark behind his right ear.

"Well, she is definitely yours, Samuel. There is no doubt about that."

"Then will you help them?" Ethon questioned. He was really making this so much easier for us. I glanced at him and gave him a smile. He deserved that much.

Lucifer paused. "I will help, but it will still cost something. Nothing is free, and if you've come to me, then you know speaking with me has a price. But, because my son is smitten with your daughter, and there seems to be a bond, I think I can cut you a deal. A soul. A single soul in exchange for my help. And, let me tell you, right now, that is more than a fair price for what you are asking of me."

"A soul?" I questioned. My stomach started to churn. I never expected him to ask for that type of payment. There was no way I would be able to agree to that, unless it was the soul of someone evil. A murderer or molester. I would have no problem handing him over one of those.

But, then he clarified his answer.

"On the day Lucian is defeated, you will have to choose one soul. One soul that will become mine. Because you have come to me, and what I have to do is no easy task, the soul will have to be of one which is close to you, besides your Fallen father. It's a small price really. You get your father, and will be free to live out the rest of your miserable lives in the mortal world."

"Yes. We agree," Samuel said immediately, stepping forward and offering Lucifer his hand.

"No! What do you mean we agree? We can't give away the soul

of anyone close to us! I've already lost too many," I cried.

Tears began to pool in my eyes as I thought about my parents, and now Danyel. Too much death in such a short time, and I wasn't about to offer anyone's life up but my own. Especially to be gifted to Lucifer and have to live in Hell for all of eternity. No way.

Samuel came and stood in front of me, taking both of my hands in his.

"Don't worry, sweetheart. I'll take care of it. This will not be your decision to make. It will be mine," he whispered. "You need to be strong, Emma. You'll just have to trust me."

I did trust him. There was nothing else I could do but trust him.

Who would he choose? There wasn't one single person around me I would be willing to give up and hand over to Lucifer. This place sucked, and I was so ready to leave it and never return.

Samuel stood back up and walked over to Lucifer, offering him his hand.

Lucifer took a small, sharp knife out of his pocket and slit Samuel's palm open. He then took a piece of parchment and rubbed it over the wound, covering it with his crimson blood. Lucifer then held up the paper, and right before my eyes, the blood start to move, forming some type of ancient writing. At the bottom, I saw it clearly. Samuel's mark appeared boldly, in bright red.

Lucifer held the parchment near his lips and blew lightly upon it.

"Thank you, Samuel," he said, as he rolled up the parchment, and tucked it into his jacket pocket. He then held out his hand to Samuel, and they shook.

Lucifer turned back to Ethon.

"Ethon, you will escort them back into the mortal world, and help to protect them until I can assemble the army. I will send a few of my warriors to travel with you as well. This should make for an interesting turn of events for Lucian."

So this was it. We were teaming up with the Devil to defeat another one of his Fallen members.

Holy crap.

I wondered if God knew what was happening. Did he even care? I sighed.

"So, I will be traveling with you," Ethon said, nodding to Samuel.

"It's not necessary, Ethon," Samuel said. "You will be safer here, and besides, Midway has sent a few Guardians of their own."

"Ethon has been fully trained in the ways of the Fallen. He can sense when they are near, and would be the best protection for your daughter. Because of the bond, there is no way they will be able to be away from each other for too long. He will enter the mortal world to be with her anyway."

Samuel paused, glanced over to me, and then nodded. I could tell it wasn't a nod of agreement. It was a nod that told me he was going to go along with whatever was being planned.

Just knowing we would be leaving this place made me happy. Our mission had succeeded and we were soon going to be home with Alaine, Kade, and the others. I suddenly felt a huge load lift from my shoulders

But then…what would the others think about Ethon and a few Fallen in their midst? Fallen they'd probably fought against. Fallen they'd hated for all these centuries. I had a feeling this was not going to be good.

Kade was still in recovery. What would happen when he found out Ethon and I had the same connection? All of these things ran through my mind like a whirlwind, yet I couldn't think about any of it right now. I had to block it out, and would deal with it when I needed to.

Ethon was just another Guardian in my life. Right now, he meant nothing to me. Yes, it was strange I had dreamed of him and his red eyes over the past days, but maybe it was because I was getting closer to him, and it was the weird connection which triggered them. But, dreams weren't going to determine my future, and I wouldn't let them dictate who my mate would be.

"Ethon, I want you to call Azzah and Bane. They will be traveling with you," Lucifer spoke, breaking me from my thoughts.

"Father, Azzah seems to have lost a limb," Ethon chuckled saying the last part. I held back the urge to laugh too.

Lucifer shook his head and sighed. "His head?"

"His hand, actually," Ethon noted.

"Well, as long as he still has his head, his hand will heal soon enough. He and Bane are two of my best, and I want them to escort you."

"You know I don't need escorts. I'm more than capable of protecting myself. Besides, Azzah is such a pain."

"I have no doubt you can protect yourself, but if Lucian should decide to strike early, I want my best warriors there to help you."

"Fine," he huffed. "How will you know when to send the army?"

"I will be sending Ash with you as well. I will assemble my

warriors, and as soon as Ash contacts me, we will come."

Lucifer whistled, and in a few moments we heard a loud caw. A huge black raven came swooping down and landed on his arm. It had crimson eyes, the same as his owner. Lucifer kissed its head. "Take good care of him, Ethon."

"I will," Ethon replied, stepping forward. The large bird hopped onto his shoulder, and then he turned and left the room to get the others.

Great. Azzah. He was definitely going to cause a stir in the house.

"So, what about the wall of protection? If any of the Fallen enter the house, the shield will come down. Right?" I questioned.

Samuel's eyes widened and he seemed to be glaring at me. Did I say something I shouldn't have? Was it the fact the house was covered by protection?

"So it seems you have had some help from above?" Lucifer asked in a snide way.

"Yes. When Midway found out the Nephilim were being slaughtered, they sent a few Guardians to help the last survivors. They put up a dome of protection to cover the house." Samuel's words flowed and there was no hesitation, only sincerity.

Lucifer glanced over to me and then back at Samuel.

"I will make sure Azzah and Bane are on full alert. Be aware they are only going for the protection my son. No one else is of my concern. Not you, or your daughter. Ash will be my eyes. He'll alert me once Lucian is ready to attack. It has been a long time since I've seen or heard the name of that deceiver. This is something I will gladly take care of soon." His eyes seemed to burn brighter, with a deep seeded hatred toward his ex-Fallen partner.

But look who was calling the kettle black. Wasn't the whole Fall because he was just as, or even more, deceitful and treacherous? Whatever. He can keep his hatred and whatever else was buried in his shriveled, black heart. I never expected him to do this for anyone other than himself anyway.

I was surprised he even had an ounce of love left to take in his brother's son and make him his own. Our whole mission was to get to him, and to have him help us defeat Lucian. And it worked. After this, I wanted nothing to do with him.

The door pushed open and Ethon came walking in with Azzah, whose hand was thickly bandaged, and another very large man. He was also huge, darkly tanned, with bulging muscles. He was bald but had black eyes, and a dark mustache and beard. He looked really scary. They all came walking towards us and stopped in front of Lucifer.

"Master," they both breathed, bowing their heads, and kneeling at his feet.

These two men looked like they could kick Lucifer's ass all over Hell and back, but they were bowing at his feet. Weird. There must be a very dark side to Lucifer I had not seen yet. A side that had these two huge brutes cowering at his feet.

"I want you two to escort Ethon, Samuel, and his daughter, Emma, back to the mortal world. Lucian has issued an order of execution on all Nephilim. Keep a watchful eye at all times. He will strike at the most unsuspecting of times, and his goal is to wipe them from existence. These two will be your top priority. I will be assembling the warriors together, and awaiting Ash's details. If you fail, and either of them is injured, you will feel the pain of my wrath for all eternity. Guard them with your life."

"Yes, master," they answered bowing a little lower. A few moments later they stood.

"Ethon," Lucifer spoke.

"Yes, father."

"It is imperative you protect yourself, above all others. Do not put yourself in harm's way."

Ethon didn't say a word, but just bowed his head.

I knew Lucifer was putting up a front, randomly throwing my name onto the *save them* list just to satisfy Ethon, and I was pretty sure his goons already knew the exact reason they were going. It wasn't to protect me. This was about Lucifer's revenge, and keeping Ethon alive.

Well, to Hell with them. I had my own Guardians back home, who I loved and trusted with my life, and had proven themselves. I had no doubt each one would do whatever it took to keep me and Alaine alive.

"Take the portal in my chambers," Lucifer said firmly.

"Yes, master," the goons answered in unison, and then bowed again.

"Thank you, Father. I will see you soon," Ethon said, placing his hand on his father's shoulder, and in turn, Lucifer did the same. They regarded each other with a nod.

No hug. Wow. That sucked. But why should I expect anything more from the Devil?

Ethon glanced at us and gestured to follow him.

I paused, not sure if I should say goodbye to Lucifer or just walk out.

"Bye," I said, and then quickly followed after Ethon. I didn't want to say thank you because he wasn't really doing us a favor, and his part in all of this came with a very high price.

Samuel followed right behind me, and I wasn't sure if he even said goodbye. I really didn't care.

We walked through the huge cavern, which looked way more enchanting than it should have, and stopped in front of a huge set of sparkling silver doors—engraved with large snakes. Two gargoyles sat on either side of the door, glaring at us as we stood there. The hairs on the back of my neck stood on end. As we passed, I swore I saw their eyes following us, but when I turned, they were still frozen. Creatures in their stone prisons.

As we entered Lucifer's chamber, it was something I imagined a King's quarters to look like. It was lavishly decorated in black, gold, silver, and red velvet. It was gorgeous and breathtaking.

This was Hell?

I'd imagined Lucifer forever burning in a lake of fire, but this was plush and expensive. He was actually living in luxury, the totally opposite of what I'd thought. He had it good down here in the depths of the Underworld.

Ethon walked over to a large oversized mirror on the wall. It was about ten foot tall by six foot wide, and framed in the brightest silver I'd ever seen. Ethon waved his hand over the mirror and it began to shimmer, and then started to take on the effect of water.

"Where is our destination?" he asked.

Samuel gave the exact coordinates to Alaine's house.

Ethon began to speak in a different language, and within a few moments the water in the mirror shifted, swirling round and round.

"Samuel, you and Emma should go first since they'll be expecting you. I'd hate to step through and get my head whacked off before I could explain."

"That's fine," Samuel answered, and then turned to me, offering his hand. "Are you ready, sweetheart?"

"Yes," I answered. I was excited we were finally going back home, and getting out of the Underworld. It was a constant nightmare here.

I took in a deep breath and grasped tightly to Samuel's hand.

NINETEEN

WE STEPPED CLOSER TO THE mirror and I started to see the front doors of Alaine's house. They were unmistakable. I'd never seen another set of doors with angels carved into them with such detail or precision. It actually warmed my heart.

Samuel stepped forward pulling me closer, and I remembered what Kade told me. One step will take you from one world into the next.

I squeezed Samuel's hand and took that step.

We landed on the front driveway of Alaine's home. It was daytime, and the sun was shining brightly above us. A few seconds later, Ethon was standing behind us with the huge raven on his shoulder. The huge bird cawed, and he immediately sent it into flight.

After a few more seconds, the two goons appeared. I'd nickname them the goons because that's exactly what they looked like. I definitely wouldn't say it out loud though, because they could easily smash me with a finger, or…at least Azzah could with his stump.

The thought of it made me laugh inside, but hey, at least his hand was reattached and would heal. He was lucky. He totally deserved losing it for trying to kill us.

"Let's go," Samuel said, walking up to the front door.

I suddenly became nervous, and wasn't sure why. My stomach twisted and turned, and although I was glad to have made it back, I was anxious to see Kade.

As we walked up the stairs, Henry opened the front door.

"Oh, for goodness sake. You're home!" he exclaimed in his awesome English accent. His hand covered his heart, and he was gaping at me like he'd just seen a ghost. Stepping forward, he hugged me tightly. "I'm sorry. We were all beginning to worry, and were thinking something horrible had happened to you. It's been such a long time." He peered behind me, and bewilderment flooded his face.

"What are you talking about Henry? We've only been gone a few days," I giggled. He had to be joking, although he didn't look like the type who would make jokes.

"No. You've been away for a little over four months," he answered dead serious.

"What?" I laughed out loud, but when he didn't laugh back, I glanced over to Samuel.

"He's joking right? We haven't been gone that long, have we?" I asked.

He nodded slowly.

"But how?" I questioned.

This had to be a crazy joke. There was no way we were gone for four months. I knew we'd only been gone for a week, maybe two, tops.

Then Samuel explained. "Emma, time here in the mortal world is much different from that in the Otherworlds. Time slows there, and runs at a much faster rate here. Have you heard the term 'a thousand years is like a day'?"

"Yes, but I didn't think it was true," I exhaled.

I was beside myself. We were gone for over four whole months? Now I knew why Henry's face went pale when he saw us. He was genuinely shocked.

But if four months had gone by, then Kade was probably well into his healing. At least I hoped he was.

"Come. Come inside," Henry motioned. "I will immediately alert Alaine of your presence."

We all entered the foyer and made our way into the large front room. I glanced up the stairs, and just as I did Courtney rounded the corner.

She froze, her eyes wide with wonder and confusion. Then her eyes found mine, and they widened even more.

"Emma? Emma," she yelled, bounding down the stairs, heading directly for me. I didn't know what to do, so I held out my arms to welcome her.

She was really excited to see me, and I had no idea why.

She jumped down the last three stairs and ran to me, wrapping her arms around me, practically sending me flying backward.

If Ethon didn't put his hand on my back, pushing me forward, I would have ended up on my backside. But his touch also sent an electric jolt through me. Thankfully he pulled his hand away as soon as I regained my balance.

"Emma, you're alive! Oh my gosh. Caleb and Kade told me the whole story. The story of how brave you were. I was so worried you weren't going to come back. We were all beginning to think you and Samuel had been killed," she said hugging me tightly, and then she pulled back with a scrunched up nose.

"What?" I asked.

"You really need a bath," she whispered.

"Tell me about it," I answered. "Apparently, I haven't had one in four months."

"You haven't bathed since you left?" she gasped.

"Courtney...there are no public showers in Hell," I huffed.

"Oh," she sighed, glancing behind me. "Who are they?"

I turned around and my eyes caught Ethon, smiling.

"This is Ethon," I said, pointing to him.

He bowed his head slightly and held out his hand to Courtney. She giggled and offered him her hand, and he gave it a light kiss.

"Hi Ethon," she said batting her eyes. I watched her face blush. Ethon glanced at me with a smile and gave me a wink.

Oh man, I was in trouble.

"And who are they?" Courtney asked. She looked upward at the two towering goons behind Ethon.

I had to pause, because I almost referred to them as the goons.

"They are with Ethon. Their names are Azzah and Bane, and they've come to help protect us," I said in a nice way.

"Azzah and Bane?" she squeaked, with a twisted face.

"Yep, Azzah and Bane," I repeated, and she giggled again.

"Samuel! Emma!" Alaine's voice carried from down the hall. Her face lit up as soon as she saw us, and tears began to fall in waves down her cheeks. She ran and then wrapped her arms around Samuel in a tight embrace, and then me right after. "Oh thank God. I'd thought I'd lost you both. When Dominic and Malachi came back, they said you had gone past the gate to see Lucifer. It's been over a month since they returned. I started to think maybe you were—," she paused, when she suddenly noticed Ethon and the goons.

"I'm so sorry. Forgive my rudeness. I didn't notice you'd brought guests. And you are?" she asked, holding her hand out behind me.

"I'm Ethon. And they are Azzah and Bane," he replied, taking her hand and giving it a kiss. At least he had manners, and I could tell Alaine was mildly impressed.

"Alaine," Samuel said, clearing his throat. "Ethon is Lucifer's son."

She looked at Ethon with confusion.

"Lucifer's son? And why would Lucifer's son be in our midst?" she answered in the nicest way possible.

"Lucifer sent him back with us to help protect Emma, until he gathers together his warriors. They are here to make sure Lucian does not fulfill his evil deeds," Samuel noted.

"Well, this means our shield of protection is now down, and we

245

have no defense against the Fallen since they are already within our perimeter," she said with a voice of concern.

"We understand your concern, and will take watch over your perimeter ourselves. We will not be in your way, and will make sure everyone is alerted when Lucian is near. I am here to help make sure of Emma's safety."

"And, why would Emma's safety be of any concern to you?" Alaine pushed.

"Because she and I have bonded," he answered.

Whoa!

That was *way* too much information to dump on Alaine all at once. I noticed her eyes widen in bewilderment, and she turned to look at Samuel and then back at me. I just shook my head and shrugged my shoulders. I had nothing to add to that.

"Courtney, maybe our guests are hungry or thirsty. Why don't you escort them back to the kitchen and see if Miss Lilly can whip them up something to eat? And please offer them something to drink, as well," Alaine instructed.

"I'm hungry," a deep voice muttered.

I turned to see Bane raising his hand, and heard a deep sigh come from Ethon.

"Fine, follow me," Courtney exhaled.

Ethon paused and looked at me, as if he was asking for my permission. I nodded, and then he followed after her, with Bane and Azzah in tow. That was odd.

"I'd like to speak to you both in my study," Alaine said wrapping each of her arms around Samuel and me, and leading us back down the hall.

"Where's Kade?" I asked.

"I was wondering when you'd ask me that question," she turned with a grin. "Kade is doing well. It was a bit of a fight in the beginning, but he is starting to heal nicely.

"Krystal Kross, a nurse friend of mine from a burn ward at the city hospital, came to stay with us for a while. The wounds were so extensive, they will still need a few more months of care before they will completely heal. But he'll live." She smiled. "He's on the second floor, in one of the guest rooms. You can go and visit him as soon as we're done."

"Thank you," I said with a lot of happiness in my voice.

She and Samuel smiled. They knew the connection I had with Kade.

"So, before we get to the story behind Ethon, I want to hear what happened. I'm so glad to have you both back."

"It's really a long story," Samuel admitted. He was right. It was a very long story. "How about I give you a completely detailed version later, because I am sure Emma wouldn't want to relive it so soon."

"That will be fine," she replied.

"The short version is, we made it through, but we lost Danyel along the way." He paused and I could tell the realization of his best friend's death was kicking in again.

The thought of Danyel made emotions run wild again, and I soon found tears sliding down my cheeks, remembering the last look on his face before his life was taken. That vision would haunt me for a very long time. Probably for the rest of my life.

"I'm so sorry, Samuel. I knew how close Danyel was to you," Alaine said. She walked over and hugged him. He didn't cry, but I was crying enough for the both of us. "Come here, sweetheart," she said, opening her arms to me.

I found myself automatically wrapping my arms around her. She reminded me so much of my mother, and the thought of her made me cry even harder.

I sobbed and sobbed and couldn't stop. I cried until I couldn't cry anymore, until there were no more tears left to be shed. I cried for what seemed like forever, but she stayed put, holding me, stroking my hair, telling me everything would be all right.

I never really had a chance to mourn my parents like this, and now Danyel had been added to the list. It felt good to release all of the sadness, anger, and confusion. I needed this. I needed to get it out of me. Mourning my life, a life that was forever changed. It would never be the same. It would never be normal.

At times, I even felt Samuel's hand gently pat my back, and that was something my mortal father would do. They weren't too different. They both loved me.

After I cried myself out, we all sat around Alaine's desk.

"So now, tell me about this craziness with Ethon, and him being your mate?" she questioned, with a raised brow.

I paused and had to figure out the best way to explain what I myself didn't understand. But, she waited patiently.

"I don't know. Not really. Well…" I paused, and Samuel and Alaine's eyes were locked on mine. That made me feel awkward, but if I told them the truth, maybe they would be able to make sense of it all.

"You can tell us anything, Emma. We're here to help, not to condemn," Alaine said with a soft smile.

"Well," I continued. "I guess things started happening the night Kade went missing. I started having these weird dreams, and in those dreams were two sets of eyes. One set belonged to Kade, and the other were these blazing red eyes.

"I remember the feeling I had before Kade entered my room at the hospital. It was a feeling that took my breath away and zapped all the air from my lungs. When he touched me, it was like a surge of electricity flooding through me.

"The same thing happened when I first saw Ethon. Before I saw him, I could feel him, and when he touched me, I felt the same electricity."

I looked at both of them for some sort of explanation, but they both looked just as confused as I was.

"Samuel, do you think it's because she is a part of both angel and Fallen? Or could it be when Kade became mortal, the bond was broken and transferred to Ethon?"

"I don't know," he answered. "I honestly don't know the answer to that question, and I doubt we will ever find the reason. Because Emma does have both good and Fallen, that very well could be the reason why she has a connection with each of them. One of darkness and one of light. It's part of the prophecy. Eventually, she will have to make a choice."

"I don't have to make my choice soon, right?" I asked.

"No, sweetheart, you don't," Alaine spoke up. "Not anytime soon, anyway. And, from a mother's point of view, I don't think you and Lucifer's son would make a good match."

"Alaine," Samuel rebutted, in a soft tone. "Ethon is a fine boy. I know Lucifer has some major issues and if I could go back, I would have chosen a different side, but the boy is different. He doesn't have the same wicked heart as Lucifer.

"His mother was a virtuous woman, raped by Lucifer's brother. The boy had no choice who his father would be, and I've heard from other Fallen members, he is nothing like Lucifer. Lucifer may have saved his life, but didn't spend much time with him. Maybe Ethon will be the one who can help to bring change."

Alaine looked nonplussed. Shaking it off, she said, "Well, I don't really care about all of that right now, Samuel. What I do care about, is what's best for our daughter. Right now she's too young, and doesn't need to be burdened with making mate choices."

Samuel laughed. "I agree, Alaine. I was just stating that since a connection has been made with both young men, sooner or later she *will* have to choose. Right now, however, we will have to focus on keeping the suitors separated. I have a feeling, once they find out about each other, there will be no peace in this house."

"Yes. We will definitely need to keep them separated. Ethon agreed to stay outside, so I will give him, and his company, access to the tower," Alaine added.

"That is a great idea," Samuel agreed. He rose to his feet, walked over to Alaine, and wrapped her in a tight embrace. They gently kissed and then faced me. "You should have seen your daughter down there. You would have been very, very proud. She really held her own, and even saved a few of the Guardians. She slayed *three* of the Hell Hounds on her own."

They were both beaming with smiles as they looked at me, and I suddenly felt awkward. I was still donning the black super-suit, the Bloodstone around my neck, and the dagger around my waist. These gifts saved my life. If it weren't for them, I would be dead. But, I also didn't want to start explaining any of that right now. The only thing I wanted to do was see Kade, and then take a *long*, hot bath.

"I think you both should get some rest. Samuel, you can take the first room to the left, on the second floor. Emma, Kade is in the first room on the right."

"Do you think it would be okay if I go see him?" I asked.

"I think he'd be expecting you to, and probably knows you're back by now. He's been so worried about you. Dominic and Malachi have been thoroughly interrogated since their return, giving him word for word descriptions of what happened while they were with you," she laughed. "I know he'll be thrilled to see you."

"I think I'll stop in and see him before I take a bath. He'll probably beg me to leave, since I smell like Hell," I laughed.

"Yes," she said, crinkling her nose. "You both do."

"Well, I guess that's my exit," I said, stepping into their arms for one last hug.

"You go ahead Emma. I'll be right out," Samuel said, still hugging Alaine.

I left the office and walked back down the hall. As soon as my foot hit the first step of the staircase my heart began to race. I was so excited, but also nervous about seeing Kade, especially knowing he'd waited for four months.

I was halfway up the stairs when I heard laughing and felt an overwhelming dizziness, and then that all too familiar electricity shot through my body. I felt compelled to move back down the stairs, but I was too tired to respond. I knew Ethon was the cause.

I glanced down as Courtney bounced around the corner holding two bottles of water.

"Emma. Miss Lilly wanted me to bring these to you and Samuel," she said, with a wide grin.

"Thanks," I replied, waiting for her to deliver them. I was staying put. She had enough energy to run up and down the stairs a hundred times.

As soon as she started up the stairs, Ethon came into view. When his eyes met mine a smile grew on his lips. His red eyes looked almost black in the distance, and his face was glowing. He looked happy.

Ethon was very handsome, and I had to pull my eyes away. The attraction was there. A connection I couldn't control, especially when he was near.

"Hello, Emma," he called. I took in a breath and faced him.

"Hey, Ethon," I answered, giving him a smile.

"So, you'll be staying up there?" he questioned, raising an eyebrow.

"Yes," I answered. "Alaine is making arrangements for you and your friends to stay in the tower. I've heard it's really nice out there."

"That's very kind of her," he said.

Bane and Azzah glared at me. They'd made their way behind

Ethon, and had permanent scowls on their faces.

"Emma, are you going to see Kade now?" Courtney squealed. "He's been waiting for you, and he's been *so* worried."

"Yes, Courtney," I said through gritted teeth, as she got closer.

"Well, he's awake now. I'll go take you to see him," she exclaimed.

Oh God! She was going to throw this whole situation into a complete disaster.

"Who is this Kade?" Ethon asked. His eyes narrowed with concern, and he made his way up a couple steps.

My pulse started to race, and my heart pounded so loudly I could hear it in my ears.

"Kade is Emma's Guardian," Courtney sang in a high, lovey-dovey tone.

Oh hell. Someone must have explained everything to her while I was away.

I heard a door open up behind us, and Ethon's eyes told me exactly who it was.

My heart, my head, my stomach…everything suddenly went into a tail spin.

"I thought your father said your Guardian died? That before he passed, he gave you the Bloodstone amulet?" Ethon asked.

I was speechless, and didn't know what to tell him.

"Emma?" Kade's voice called from behind me. "Emma, is that you?"

My head snapped back to look at him and I instantly became breathless. *Oh God.* I didn't realize how much I missed him until now. He was shirtless; he'd lost weight over the past four months, but his muscles were still defined across his chest and abs. His chocolate hair was disheveled, in the sexiest way possible, and his hazel eyes smiled and beckoned me to come.

I wanted to dash up the stairs to him. I wanted him to wrap me in his arms, carry me away, and make me forget the hell I'd just been through. But I also knew that every other eye in the room was staring and scrutinizing. I could only imagine the expressions on Ethon, Azzah, and Bane's faces. I didn't want to look.

Kade brushed back his hair with his fingers, which made my heart flutter. "Wow. I can't believe you're here," he said, with a smile and gleam in his eyes.

"Yes, we just got back," I said, breathless.

"I was getting worried," he paused, and then glanced at Ethon.

"Well, you look...great," I said. I didn't know what else to say. I couldn't see his back, but he looked like he'd been healing just fine.

Another door opened and soon the voices of Dom and Malachi echoed off the walls.

Dominic rounded the corner first and nearly bumped into Bane. "We have visitors?" he asked, in a snarky voice.

They both stood firm, eyeing each other, but the goons towered at least two feet over him and Malachi.

Dominic's eyes suddenly caught mine. "Emma, you're back! And you're alive!" he yelled.

I nodded. "Yes. I'm alive," I answered.

But by the looks of things, it might not be that much longer.

"So what did you drag in with you?" Malachi asked, in a deep tone. The same tone that scared me the first time I met him.

Bane and Azzah began to growl and glared at them like they wanted to tear them apart.

"I am Ethon, and these are my companions Bane and Azzah," he said, holding out his hand to Malachi. "I'll be here to watch over Emma and protect her until my father arrives."

"Why would she need your protection when she already has us?" Dominic asked, his eyes narrowing on Ethon.

"Because Emma and I have bonded," he paused and glanced up to me with a smile, "and because of that bond, her safety and well-being are now my main priority."

Ho-ly crap. He did *not* just say that. My heart sunk down to the ground, and my face began to burn with heat and confusion. *This cannot be happening right now.*

"What the—?" Dominic snapped. His eyes darted to me for answers.

I couldn't speak. All I could do was shake my head and shoot him a look of bewilderment.

"Oh shit!" Malachi muttered, also shaking his head.

I glanced up to Kade. He was completely confused and hurt, and I felt it.

Everyone else's eyes quickly darted between the three of us.

It was utter chaos, and I felt like I was being suffocated.

Alaine exited the hall and walked up to Ethon, just in time.

"Come, gentlemen. I will personally escort you to the tower. There is a bathroom where you can shower, and we have a small kitchen that is fully stocked with whatever you require," she said, leading them to the front door.

"Goodbye, Emma," Ethon said with a small smile. He turned to follow Alaine out.

I stood there...frozen.

Azzah and Bane gave me evil glares before they turned and left. I was glad they were going to be tucked far away in the tower, but even that wasn't far enough.

With Ethon and the goons gone, I still felt the heat of everyone else's stare on me, boring huge holes right through my soul. I had a lot of explaining to do, and they were waiting for me to give an answer.

Yet, I had none.

This was all too overwhelming.

Yes, our quest was over, but my journey was just beginning. Right now, all I could think about was being with Kade. I wanted to melt into his warm embrace, and get lost in his kiss. I had missed him from the moment he was carried away.

I hoped he would understand. I hoped he would be able to help me figure everything out.

I knew this much...I wasn't going to make any choices. Not today. Not for a while. Right now, I just wanted to be with him, and find some peace again.

I closed my eyes and sucked in a deep breath. Then I turned to Kade, and headed up the stairs toward his beautiful hazel eyes.

The State of Asian Pacific America

TRANSFORMING RACE RELATIONS
A Public Policy Report

Paul M. Ong
Editor

LEAP
Asian Pacific American Public Policy Institute
and
UCLA Asian American Studies Center

2000 | Volume IV

A joint publication of
the LEAP Asian Pacific American Public Policy Institute
and the UCLA Asian American Studies Center

LEAP
Leadership Education for Asian Pacifics, Inc.
327 East Second Street, Suite 226
Los Angeles, CA 90012-4210

UCLA Asian American Studies Center
3230 Campbell Hall, 405 Hilgard Avenue
Los Angeles, CA 90095-1546

ISBN: 0-934052-33-6

Cover design and Layout: Jennifer Woo, The Network Company

Table of Contents

PREFACE

7 | Don T. Nakanishi
J.D. Hokoyama

INTRODUCTION

13 | **Paul M. Ong**
The Asian Pacific American Challenge to Race Relations

PART I. RACIAL IDENTITIES

43 | **Yen Le Espiritu and Michael Omi**
"Who Are You Calling Asian?": Shifting Identity Claims, Racial
Classifications, and the Census

103 | **Taeku Lee**
Racial Attitudes and the Color Line(s) at the Close of the
Twentieth Century

159 | **Robert Lee**
Fu Manchu Lives! Asian Pacific Americans as Permanent Aliens in
American Culture

PART II. RACIAL INTERACTIONS

191 | **Tarry Hum and Michela Zonta**
Residential Patterns of Asian Pacific Americans

243 | **Karen Umemoto**
From Vincent Chin to Joseph Ileto: Asian Pacific Americans
and Hate Crime Policy

279 | **Pauline Agbayani-Siewert**
Asian Pacific Americans and Human Rights/Relations Commissions

PART III. NATIONAL RACE POLICIES

313 | **Paul M. Ong**
The Affirmative Action Divide

363 | **Shamit Saggar**
Asians and Race Relations in Britain

395 | **Christine Inglis**
Asians and Race Relations in Australia

PART IV. NEW POSSIBILITIES

435 | **Leland T. Saito and Edward J.W. Park**
Multiracial Collaborations and Coalitions

475 | **Angela Oh**, *Member, Advisory Board to the President's Initiative on Race*
Reaching Toward our Higher Aspirations: The President's Initiative on Race

495 | **Contributors**

"The State of Asian Pacific America: Transforming Race Relations" is the fourth major public policy research report produced by our two institutions – Leadership Education for Asian Pacifics (LEAP) and the UCLA Asian American Studies Center. We hope this policy study, like others we have already released and those we will publish in the future, will serve to inform public discussions and shape public policy deliberations about the most important and compelling policy issue-areas facing the nation's rapidly growing and diverse Asian Pacific American population.

At the beginning of a new century, it is obvious that race relations remains as one of America's most significant, ongoing national dilemmas. Race continues to influence, in both subtle and overt ways, our access to and mobility within public institutions and private enterprises; what we see and do not see on television or movie theater screens; and what we talk about, debate, and act upon in our great legislative halls, on radio talk shows, and in ballot booths. Although the dynamics and scope of racial inequities, racial prejudice, and racial intolerance and violence changed in quite significant ways during the course of the past century, they continue to stain the American fabric.

Asian Pacific Americans have a major stake in the future of race relations in American society. No longer a small, regionally-based population, the over 11 million Asian Pacific Americans now reside in all fifty states, with large and highly visible communities from New York to Los Angeles, from Houston to Chicago, and from Honolulu to Boston. By 2020, they are projected to reach 20 million, and represent 1 in 20 Americans. Along with their rapid population growth, especially during the closing decades of the 20th century, has been their ever-increasing presence and significance in virtually all aspects of American race relations from public policy discussions over affirmative action to the alleviation of inter-group conflicts in multiracial urban centers.

This policy report is intended to respond to the continuing significance
race in American society by providing the most comprehensive, multidisciplin
empirical analysis of the diverse ways in which Asian Pacific Americans
redefining and indeed transforming contemporary American race relations.
doing so, we are interested in infusing the policy decision-making process w
fresh and accurate information, as well as rigorous analysis and creative pol
perspectives and recommendations. A team of renowned social scientists, his
rians, and public advocates from institutions across the nation, along witl
scholar from England and another from Australia, was assembled to undert.
this path-breaking endeavor with state-of-the-art quantitative and qualitat
research techniques, and oftentimes original data. We are hopeful that the rep
will provide an abundance of meaningful, insightful and hopefully provocat
views on how we should respond to the continuing and new challenges of ↺
racial situation.

Like our other joint policy research activities and publications, this rep
reflects the special strengths and goals of our two institutions. The UCLA As
American Studies Center, established in 1969, is one of four ethnic studies cen
at UCLA, and the largest and most comprehensive program of its kind in
nation. Through its research, teaching, publishing, video productions, library a
archival acquisitions, and community-university collaborations in fields rang
from literature to urban planning, the faculty, staff, and students of the Cen
have sought to advance scholarly and policy understanding of Asian Pac
Americans.

Leadership Education for Asian Pacifics, Inc. (LEAP) is a natior
nonprofit, nonpartisan, community-based organization based in Los Angel
California. Founded in 1982, LEAP's mission is to achieve full participation a
equality for Asian Pacific Americans through leadership, empowerment a
policy. With a wealth of information on Asian Pacific Americans and a natio
reputation as a leading Asian Pacific American organization, LEAP continues
raise the visibility and leadership effectiveness of Asian Pacific Americans.

We would like to pay special tribute to Professor Paul Ong of ↺
Department of Urban Planning and the Asian American Studies Center
UCLA for serving as the principal investigator of this major policy report, as v

the research director of the joint public policy research activities involving
:AP and the UCLA Asian American Studies Center. Professor Ong is the
:ion's foremost scholar addressing the most significant public policy issues
ing the Asian Pacific American population, and we are tremendously grateful
· the leadership, commitment, and vision which he has provided for this and
ıer research endeavors.

We also would like to thank the extraordinary team of researchers who partic-
.ted in this project, as well as the individuals who worked on producing this publi-
ion. Finally, we would like to express our gratitude to the Board of Directors of
:AP and the Faculty Advisory Committee of the UCLA Asian American Studies
nter for their continued support of our joint policy research activities.

on T. Nakanishi, Ph.D.
rector and Professor
CLA Asian American Studies Center

). Hokoyama
esident and Executive Director
·adership Education for Asian Pacifics, Inc. (LEAP)

Acknowledgements

We wish to thank the following individuals and institutions who have provided their generous support to the Asian Pacific American Public Policy Institute and have made this study possible:

The Charles Stewart Mott Foundation provided major funding for this research study. The Levi Strauss Foundation, Fannie Mae Foundation, ARCO Foundation, and Farmers Group, Inc. also contributed significant funds for the project. We wish to thank The Carnegie Corporation of New York, The Ford Foundation, State Farm Companies Foundation, Procter & Gamble Fund, and the GTE Foundation for their continued support of LEAP and the Asian Pacific American Public Policy Institute, and for making this project possible. We also wish to thank American Express and IBM, whose partnership and support of LEAP have contributed to our organization's success.

Many people contributed to the successful completion of this project. We are grateful to the UCLA Lewis Center for Regional Policy Studies for providing space and office support for the project, and to Don Nakanishi and the UCLA Asian American Studies Center for their constant support. We would also like to thank the members of the Center's Faculty Advisory Committee who, along with LEAP Board members and staff, served on the joint executive steering committee: Professors James Lubben, Jerry Kang, Geraldine Padilla, Pauline Agbayani, and David Takeuchi. The editorial assistance of Glenn Omatsu was invaluable for his expertise and professional insight, and Christine Wang provided exemplary guidance on financial matters. Levin Sy was indispensable in offering his technical assistance and project coordination skills. Kylee Williams and Thuong Mong Ha assisted in preparing the manuscript. We are also grateful to Jennifer Woo for the layout and cover design. Finally, each of the authors were supported by research assistants who are acknowledged in their respective chapters.

Finally, the individuals at LEAP deserve special recognition for their dedication to the project at every stage of its development. We wish to thank J.D. Hokoyama and John Y. Tateishi for their continued support of the project. We also wish to thank Melissa Reyes and Melissa Szeto, Program Coordinators, for their technical assistance and administrative support throughout the project. And, finally, we are indebted to Gena Lew, Director of Development, for her skillful management in working with the writers and the project team, and for her perseverance in seeing the final product through to its completion.

The Asian Pacific American Challenge to Race Relations

Paul M. Ong

Introduction

The "race problem" has followed us into a new millennium. W.E.B. DuBois' argument that the "color line" was society's problem of the Twentieth Century is applicable to the Twenty-first Century. At the same time, much has changed. Blatant and state-sanctioned racism has disappeared, yet racial inequality persists. We still face the enormous challenge of achieving racial justice, but the nature of the issues and cast of actors have been transformed. Further progress requires us to formulate strategies and policies that address current realities, including those linked to Asian Pacific Americans (APAs).

This volume examines how Asian Pacific Americans are redefining racial concepts, race relations and race-related policies. Over the last three decades, the APA population doubled every ten years. According to the Bureau of the Census, there were approximately 10.5 million in 1998, and we project that there will be at least 20 million by the year 2020. With this dramatic growth, APA issues should no longer be ignored in policy debates. APAs have taken the initiative to push these concerns onto the national stage. One question is how should this group be included. Unfortunately, responses are often polemical, based on narrow group interests, with some APA organizations and leaders insisting on participation on the same terms as other minority groups and some non-APA organizations and leaders taking the opposite position. The policy question is frequently postulated as whether APAs constitute a disadvantaged minority or a part of the advantaged segment of society. This is, however, not a productive way to frame the discussion.

Difficulties in resolving inconsistencies suggest that the prevailing black-white paradigm of the "race problem" has seriously flaws. The limitations are mostly felt by APAs struggling with group identity and politics, but the problem is more pervasive. New concerns are confounding the national debate. Beneath the polemics is a conundrum because APAs do not fit widely held assumptions about race relations. One major challenge is whether the core of the black-white framework can be preserved by absorbing new ideas such as multiculturalism and diversity. The alternative is a radical transformation, a new approach to race relations. Regardless of how this question is resolved, it must be done without diminishing the moral obligation to remedy racial inequalities.

An informed discussion requires an understanding of the material conditions of APAs, and an assessment of the political debates and processes in disparate policy arenas. The findings from the original research reported in this book uncover common elements of a new framework encompassing all racial groups and their concerns. The book also includes policy essays identifying effective practices and institutional arrangements that enable APAs and non-APAs to work together productively. The ultimate goal of the participants is to redefining the principles that form a collective vision of what this nation ought to be with respect to race. Their contributions are based on reconceptualizing notions of social groupings and relationships, and reformulating public policies.

THE EXISTING FRAMEWORK

The current framework is predicated on a widely accepted concept of race and the forces generating inequalities, and is modeled after the black experience vis-à-vis whites. Racial grouping is a societal, economic and political construction with enormous ramifications at the individual and collective levels. Racial membership is ascriptive, where group assignment imposes liabilities and confers privileges. This grouping takes on a collective self-consciousness when racial solidarity becomes instrumental in protecting and enhancing group status, or in fighting oppression. A racial hierarchy is created and maintained by stereotypes and prejudices that overtly and subtly shape individual behavior, by institutionalized racism that systemically limits opportunities, and by a historical legacy of discrimination that disadvantages subsequent generations. The outcomes are both glaring and deplorable—a disproportionate number of minorities are economically marginalized, politically disenfranchised, residentially segregated, and under-served by basic institutions like public schools.

During the latter half of Twentieth Century, public policy has evolved progressively to encompass strategies to eliminate discriminatory practices within the government, to fight overt employment and housing discrimination in the private sector, to correct *de jure* and *de facto* biased institutional practices, and to establish affirmative action programs to remedy past injustices. These efforts have been accompanied by others to improve race relations, with much of the activities occurring at the local level through human rights/relations agencies and grass-root efforts. In implementing policies, membership in a racial minority has become a pragmatic and convenient operating principle. Over time, this nation has developed classes of protected populations that are entitled to participate in government sponsored programs. The use of a simplistic racial criterion for government action, however, creates a potential conflict with some deeply held values, such as individualism and equal protection. This inherent tension in race-based policies has been exploited by its opponents to attack affirmative action.

The present policy framework faces another difficulty because it does not easily encompass all nonwhites. Obviously, African Americans fully fit the paradigm. This match is based on the fact that African Americans have dominated the Civil Rights Movement, the political force behind race-oriented policies. The black-white experience has defined the popular image of what constitute prejudicial attitudes, discriminatory behavior, biased institutional practices, and racial inequalities. This black-based framework has been stretched to encompass other minorities. This same paradigm fits American Indians, who in many ways are more disadvantaged than African Americans. While Hispanics are not a racial group in a narrow sense of the term, they too have been considered a disadvantaged population covered by race-oriented policies. APAs are more problematic, a group that is disadvantaged in some arenas but not in others. The elasticity of the black-based framework, however, is finite. American Indians, Hispanics and APAs raise issues outside the existing paradigm: sovereignty rights, immigration and nativism, and ethnic rather than racial concerns.

THE CALL FOR A NEW DIRECTION

One indication of the growing complexity of race relations is found in President Clinton's speech that was delivered on June 14, 1997, at commencement at the University of California at San Diego:

> To be sure, there is old, unfinished business between black and white Americans, but the classic American dilemma has now become many dilemmas of race and ethnicity. We see it in the tension between black and Hispanic customers and their Korean or Arab grocers, in a resurgent anti-Semitism even on some college campuses, in a hostility toward new immigrants from Asia to the Middle East to the former communist countries to Latin America and the Caribbean—even those whose hard work and strong families have brought them success in the American way.

Of course, race relations in America have always been more diverse than black-white relations, but the President's remarks correctly identied a pressing need to move beyond the bipolar framework.

The increasing complexity of race relations comes at a time when current strategies have come under political and judicial scrutiny. For example, recent Supreme Court rulings have restricted the use of remedial programs, requiring the government to demonstrate compelling reasons for public action and to develop programs narrowly tailored to remedy specific problems. The passage of California's Proposition 209 (the "California Civil Rights Initiative" to end affirmative action in admissions to public colleges and universities, in public-sector employment, and in public-sector contracting) represents a growing public concern and uneasiness with race-based policies. At the same time, there is unfinished business. Racial inequality and injustice are still too prevalent, and racial tensions and conflicts are on the rise.

While affirmative action has received much attention, the debate is broader. In a search for a new direction, the President has called for a "great and unprecedented conversation about race." The message is that we should not retreat from a commitment to fighting racial injustices. The task, as framed by the President in the area of affirmative action, is to "mend not end," and this task applies equally to other aspects of race relations. The desire for a new perspective is not just one person's opinion. Polls taken prior to the vote on Proposition 209 show that a majority believe that racial discrimination remains a major problem that must be addressed. The debate was, and continues to be, over how far government should go to ensure fairness, to fight discrimination, and to improve inter-group relations. This question cannot be answered by just repeating the justifications from the 1950s and 1960s. A meaningful national dialogue requires incorporating new and emerging race realities.

THE ASIAN PACIFIC AMERICAN CHALLENGE

APAs present a major challenge to the existing framework on multiple fronts. Their experience raises questions about the nexus between being a minority group and being disadvantaged. Although a disproportionate number of APAs live in poverty and some subgroups experience extremely high welfare usage, these phenomena are not rooted in the failure of domestic American institutions. Instead, the problems are linked to the educational limits and political upheavals of the home country of immigrants and in the failures of America's foreign policy. Moreover, this population as a whole is not economically disadvantaged as indicated by median income and earnings, and there is a disproportionately high number of APAs in prestigious and higher paying jobs. While APAs are underrepresented among voters and elected officials, political disenfranchisement is linked to a lack of citizenship, which is being gradually rectified through acculturation and naturalization. While many are under-served by basic institutions like public schools, this problem is due to a lack of appropriate cultural and linguistic facilities than to traditional racism. And while many APAs live in enclaves, residential segregation is lower than for other minorities. For many, the decision to live in a segregated community is driven by a voluntary desire to associate with others of the same ethnicity.

There are also differences regarding how race is played out. APAs are subjected to stereotypes but not just negative ones. In fact, there is a widely held view of this group as a model minority. We can agree that stereotypes, regardless of nature, are undesirable because they reduce all members to a simple caricature, but it is also important to acknowledge that the prejudices against APAs are more benign than those for other minority groups. APAs do suffer from institutionalized practices that limit employment opportunities, but the most widely discussed restriction is a "glass ceiling" to top management position. This is dramatically different than the gross underrepresentation in all desirable jobs experienced by other non-whites. APAs enroll in record numbers at elite universities but are subjected to biased admissions decisions aimed at capping their share. Finally, APAs have suffered from past discrimination—for example, immigration exclusion, restrictions on naturalization and political participation, and mass incarceration—but the historical legacy is not a personal one for most. Only a minority can directly link their family history to these past wrongs; nonetheless, APA history serves as a powerful reminder of the potential for a nation to do evil with respect to race.

APA realities are changing the nature of race politics by inter-jecting ethnicity. Community activists and advocates have promoted pan-Asianism, but this identity is fragile. Subgroups have insisted on maintaining their national identities. This can be seen in the incorpo-ration of ethnic groups (e.g., Chinese, Japanese, Filipinos, Vietnamese, etc.) into the racial categories for the decennial census. APAs are also altering the notion of race as a dichotomous hierarchy. This is most apparent in the uncomfortable role of Korean merchants in the inner-city, in which they are depicted as both exploited and exploiters. In these situations, inter-group conflicts entail interactions between members of minority populations. The notion of race is also being contested by individuals of mixed parentage. Persons who are part-APA comprise a disproportionate share of the multiracial category because APAs have a high rate of out-marriages, and many of these multiracial individuals have been adamant in expressing their combined racial heritage, thus challenging the notion of mutually exclusive racial categories.

The incongruencies discussed above point to severe weaknesses in the current race framework. We are left with plausible claims for including APAs in race-oriented policies and programs and contradictory reasons to doubt these claims. One could argue that APAs constitute an exception to the rule or that their problems should be recast as immigrant issues. Neither, however, is acceptable politically or intellectually. One cannot ignore that many elements of the APA experience are tied to their status as a racial minority, and APAs themselves are not likely to abandon their claim to a place at the table in the debate over race and race-related policies. So far, the contradictory claims have been worked out piecemeal, with *ad hoc* solutions based on situation-specific compromises. These tenuous solutions represent an uncomfortable truce that can only temporarily allay an escalating frustration with the prevailing framework.

THE PROJECT

To assess the APA impact on race relations, this project assembled a multi-disciplinary team of nationally renowned researchers and scholars to examine various issues and topics. Because of a paucity of information in several areas, the project sponsored original research by Pauline Agbayani-Siewert (University of California, Los Angeles), Yen Le Espiritu (University of California, San Diego), Tarry Hum (Queens College and New York University), Taeku Lee (Harvard University), Michael Omi (University of California, Berkeley), Paul M. Ong (University of California, Los Angeles), Edward J.W. Park (University of Southern California and Loyola Marymount University), Leland T. Saito (University of California, San Diego), and Michela Zonta (University of California, Los Angeles). The research has produced empirical studies covering six areas:
- Attitudes on race and race-oriented policies.
- The political construction of racial categories.
- Affirmative action.
- Residential segregation and integration.
- Multiracial collaborations and coalitions.
- APAs and human rights/relations programs.

Each study tackles an important question and offers policy recommendations.

The project also invited five experts to write policy essays. An essay does not require new research, and the contributors used their previous work, experience and knowledge to address major policy questions. The writers were encouraged to take normative stances, arguing what ought to be. Three of the essays examine issues in the

United States, and the other two examine issues in the United Kingdom and Australia. The essayists includes Christine Inglis (University of Sydney), Robert Lee (Brown University), Angela Oh (Advisory Board to the President's Initiative on Race), Shamit Saggar (University of London), and Karen Umemoto (University of Hawai'i at Manoa).

The book is organized into four parts, mixing both case studies and essays when appropriate. Part one examines the way race is constructed within institutions and perceived by individuals. Part two focuses on racial interactions, including the degree of residential contact, race-bias crimes, and the response by human relations agencies. Part three includes chapters analyzing race-related policies in the United States, the United Kingdom and Australia. The final part explores "new possibilities" to guide how APAs should constructively transform race relations in this nation.

Summary of Analytical Studies and Policy Essays

PART I: RACIAL IDENTITIES

This part of the book looks at the concepts of race, focusing on the ways racial classifications, concepts and attitudes are defined, negotiated, debated and constructed. The first chapter is by Yen Espiritu and Michael Omi, "Who Are You Calling Asian?: Shifting Identity Claims and Racial Classification, and the Census," which explores racial terms used in the official count of the population. In 1980 and 1990, Asian American legislators, community leaders, and advocacy groups successfully maintained ethnic breakdowns within the Asian/Pacific Islander "racial" categories. Over the years, other political claims have arisen. Some groups have increasingly questioned the appropriateness of their group being counted as part of the APA category, and multiracial APAs have challenged the notion of mutually exclusive racial categories and demanded new ways to categorize racially mixed people. Espiritu and Omi examine the following questions:

- What types of political claims have APA groups made for inclusion (or exclusion)?
- How do different groups want to be defined and represented?
- What is the slippage between individual conceptions of identity, group collectivities, and state definitions?
- What is the significance of a multiracial category or the allowance of
multiple racial check-offs?
- What is the impact of "moving" certain groups (e.g., Native Hawaiians) out of the APA category?
- What are the differences between federal and state/local classifications of APAs, and what are the policy implications that result from these differences?

To answer the above questions, the authors draw on a range of data sources, including recent census studies and surveys on race and ethnicity questions, selective state and local documents on race/ethnic classifications, and interviews with key APA constituencies (e.g., multiracial Asians, Native Hawaiians, Asian Indians). The analysis starts with a review of how APAs have been an object for racial classification for over a century, with categories changing to accommodate the racism of each decade.

The rest of the chapter takes up four case studies. The first case study is on Asian Indians. The convoluted history of how this group has been classified illustrates how the concept of race is subject to constant revision—driven by shifting demographic trends, changing concepts of race, and claims for political/legal recognition. The second case study focuses on the largely unsuccessful efforts by Filipinos to separate from the APA grouping. A major incentive for requesting the reclassification was possible economic gain derived from affirmative action programs, along with a desire to emphasize the group's unique cultural and racial identity. The third case study examines the successful reclassification of

Native Hawaiians for the upcoming 2000 Census. The creation of a new category was spurred by the claims of Native Hawaiians that the Asian and Pacific Islander category failed to recognize their status as an indigenous population. The final case study documents how multiracial Asians challenged the practice by the Bureau of the Census to assign individuals to a single racial category. The United States has always been a nation of blended racial and ethnic groups, and those of a mixed heritage have demanded the right to be counted as such. As a group with a high rate of interracial marriages, multiracial APAs played a role in changing federal policy to allow individuals to declare more than one race on census forms.

Espiritu and Omi's analysis offers a detailed and nuanced account of current debates regarding the racial/ethnic classification of APAs. The study provides an important window to examine how this group is situated in the broader politics of race in the United States. The ability of APAs to interject ethnicity into the classification scheme disrupts the black/white framing of racial issues. Clearly, racial identity can be reconstructed and negotiated. The authors, however, caution that achieving ethnic recognition is not sufficient. APAs often disappear with respect to official reporting of racial and ethnic statistics, and remain unacknowledged with respect to major policy decisions.

The conceptualization of race and its meaning is not just shaped by official classifications but also by the knowledge, beliefs, and experiences of ordinary individuals. Taeku Lee's chapter, "Racial Attitudes and the Color Line(s) at the Close of the Twentieth Century," examines public attitudes about race relations and APAs within a multiracial context. Because race relations are shaped by notions and values held by individuals, analyzing popular opinion and political preferences is critical to understanding how APAs are situated in American society. The chapter focuses on answering the following questions:

- How commonly do APAs and others experience racial

discrimination?

- What beliefs do different groups hold about discrimination, racial inequality, economic conflict, and the opportunity structure in theUnited States?
- Do APAs' views on these matters align with whites, do they exhibit a multiracial consciousness, or do APAs occupy a distinct "third space" on racial matters?
- Do negative stereotypes and sentiments about APAs exist?
- Are white, black, and Latino views on public policies affecting APAs determined by antagonistic attitudes?

To answer these questions, Lee analyzes several recent media polls that include significant numbers of APA respondents, including those conducted by the *Washington Post* (with the Kaiser Foundation and Harvard University), *Los Angeles Times*, *Asian Week*, and *San Francisco Chronicle*/KRON/KQED. Additional information comes from several academic surveys: the Los Angeles County Social Survey, the Los Angeles Survey of Urban Inequality, and a University of Massachusetts poll.

The analyses offer three major findings. First, there is a clear but complex hierarchy to racial attitudes. Black and white opinions are at the two ends of the racial order with the relative position of APA opinions (along with Latino opinions) shifting with issues. At times, APAs are closer to whites, and at other times they are closer to other minorities. Second, APAs are distinguished by a high level of personal experience with discrimination and a diversity of attitudes varying by ethnicity, region, and length of residence in the United States. Third, opinions by non-APAs are influenced by knowledge of and interactions with APAs. These opinions in turn influence attitudes over government policies that impact the Asian Pacific American community.

Robert Lee provides a historical and contemporary view of how racial identity is externally imposed. In the essay chapter, "Fu Manchu

Lives! The Asian American as Permanent Alien," he argues that APAs have been made into a race of foreigners, the Orientals. This unique racialization is deeply imbedded in American culture, but like other "irrational" constructs, the images are frequently contradictory and subject to change, depending on particular historical circumstances. Despite being sometimes mutable, this ascriptive identity has stubbornly resisted eradication. At one level, APA racialization is based on "color." This is exemplified by the use of the infamous "Yellowface" in the March 1997 cover of *National Review*. That illustration used racist Asian features (buck-toothed, squinty-eyed, stereotyped clothing, etc.) as caricatures of the Clintons and Vice President Al Gore to depict the political corruption associated with illegal campaign contributions. The singling out of Asians through the characterization is in itself telling, but the cover also reveals that the racist image of APAs is tied to both physical and "exotic" cultural features.

For Lee, the designation of yellow as the "color" of the Oriental is a prime example of the social construction of a racial identity. As a group, APAs occupied a particular position within the economy and society. They were feared as unwanted cheap labor, unassimilable heathens, sexual deviants, and more generally, the "Yellow Peril." Equally important, the racial identity is intertwined with the notion that the Oriental is indelibly alien. Besides being based on exotic cultural misconceptions, APAs as aliens is also a political and legal status. Historically, this group had been denied full membership in American society. They were barred from citizenship, from interracial marriage, from owning land, and from bearing witness in trials. The tragic consequences of being permanent aliens reached an apex when 110,000 Japanese Americans, two-thirds of whom were citizens by birth, were incarcerated because they were considered potentially dangerous foreigners. Overt bigotry and anti-Asian hostility have waned since World War II, but the racialization of APAs still continues. In recent decades, two competing and contradictory images prevailed, the "model minority" and the "gook." The emergence of a positive stereotype, nevertheless, does not negate the fact that APAs have not escaped from the imposition of an externally defined identity, one that continues to be predicated on the notion of a race of permanent aliens.

PART II: RACIAL INTERACTIONS

The second part of the book focuses on the ways racial groups interact with each other in several arenas, and explores ways people and institutions address interracial issues. Collectively, these studies capture the diversity and intricacies of inter-group relations.

Tarry Hum and Michela Zonta's chapter, "Residential Patterns of Asian Pacific Americans," examines one of the most visible aspects of racial interaction, the neighborhoods where APAs live. The dramatic growth of the APA population over the last three decades has transformed many urban and suburban neighborhoods throughout this nation, and this transformation has added to the complexity of the relationship between residential choice and race. Race and ethnicity influence housing patterns but certainly not to the extent that prevailed in the past. After a century of housing discrimination sanctioned by state and local governments, the period following WWII provided opportunities for APAs to choose their residential locations. What emerged was a high degree of residential assimilation that mirrored the acculturation of the predominately U.S.-born Asians of this period. Although ethnic communities such as Chinatown continued to exist, APAs in general were no longer an isolated racial group by the late 1960s. During the 1970s, the majority of APAs lived in predominantly non-Asian neighborhoods where they constituted a small minority. The movement toward integration, however, slowed in subsequent years as immigration played a key role in attenuating residential integration. In the 1990s, APA settlement patterns were highly complex and varied with both the reemergence of historic enclaves in the central city and new communities in the suburbs, including "satellite" Chinatowns and "ethnoburbs."

Their study addresses the following questions:

- What is the level of APA residential segregation relative to other minority groups, and how does segregation vary by demographic factors?
- How do factors such as the racial composition of neighborhoods affect residential choice?
- What are the trends and characteristics of old and new ethnic enclaves?

To study the patterns of residential settlement among Asian Pacific Americans, the authors examine the level of housing segregation and integration for the top 30 metropolitan areas with the largest APA populations using 1970, 1980 and 1990 census tract level data. They use the dissimilarity index to measure the spatial distribution of different groups and the degree of contact or interaction between minority and majority group members. They examine how demographic factors across metropolitan areas and over time influence neighborhood-level outcomes. The study uses micro level data (the 1993-1994 Multi-City Survey on Urban Inequality) to provide information on neighborhood preferences, i.e., the reasons why people select their residential locations. The findings provide important insights on APA attitudes and preferences that contribute to locational decisions and patterns of residential integration and segregation. To examine ethnic enclaves, Hum and Zonta examine neighborhoods within the four key metropolitan areas: New York, Los Angeles, San Francisco, and Oakland. This analysis uses both the 1990 Census data and more recent data from the Immigration and Naturalization Service (INS) to elaborate on APA immigrant settlement.

Karen Umemoto's chapter, "From Vincent Chin to Joseph Ileto: Asian Pacific Americans and Hate Crime Policy," examines one of the most unfortunate aspects of interracial interactions: racially motivated violence. Her chapter provides an overview of hate-crime policy, presents data describing the nature and magnitude of the problem for APAs, discusses the challenges that hate crimes and related policy discourse pose for race relations and, finally, discusses recommendations for research, policy and organizing. Her analysis relies on both published and unpublished data.

Hate crimes are extreme manifestations of personal antagonism toward a group of people, including vandalism, threats, assaults and murder. While the victims are individuals, hate crimes are also considered acts against groups and society. The federal government and several states have recognized the uniqueness of these actions as special crimes. When it is demonstrated that a crime is motivated by racial bigotry, the law allows for enhanced penalties. Despite the importance in dealing with hate crime, there are several problems, including the lack of local laws in several states, under-reporting, and inconsistent enforcement. Consequently, the recorded crimes, especially the most visible and heinous ones covered by the media, are only the tip of a larger problem.

Like other minority groups, APAs have long been victims of hate crimes. The beating death of Vincent Chin is the most well-known case of a hate crime against an Asian, but there are hundreds of cases. The number of nationally reported crimes averages close to 500 per year, but this is a severe undercount because many, particularly immigrants, are reluctant to report such crimes. A review of the evidence shows that anti-APA violence is caused by several factors: perceived or real economic competition, prejudice and bigotry, and scapegoating APAs for social ills. Umemoto examines 1994-97 data from Los Angeles, California, one of the most diverse places in the world, to gain additional insights into the nature of hate crimes involving APAs, both as victims and as perpetrators. They were victimized equally by Latinos and whites and less frequently by African Americans. In contrast, the racial group most often victimized by APAs was African American. These findings, however, should be placed in a larger context and complex picture. Members of all races are victims as well as perpetrators, and hate crimes against people of color are perpetrated by whites and people of color. Hate crime is a multiracial phenomenon.

Umemoto concludes with several recommendations: improve reporting, strengthen hate crime legislation, develop law enforcement protocols that are culturally sensitive, support APA and other community organizations addressing hate crimes, build multiracial coalitions and a human relations infrastructure, and conduct research to better understand and address underlying sources of conflict.

How society responds to new racial tensions and conflicts is determined in part by the ability of its institutions to adapt. Pauline Agbayani-Siewert's chapter, "Asian Pacific Americans and Human Rights/Relations Commissions," examines how these agencies respond to the growing presence of APAs. While many of these agencies were initially concerned with systemic problems in housing, schooling and employment, over time, the human rights/relations organizations have taken on a narrowly defined set of activities, including conflict resolution, cultural sensitivity training, leadership training, and providing forums for inter-group discussion. In recent years, HRCs have faced new changes due to declining resources, new developments and understanding of race relations, and new forms of inter-group (especially between minority groups) tension and conflict, many of which involve Asian Pacific Americans. The chapter analyzes the nature and extent of group tensions and conflicts, the responses of human rights/relations organizations, and the effectiveness of conflict-resolution through negotiation and mediation.

The study relies on an organizational analysis of agencies in large and moderate-size urban areas (Los Angeles, San Francisco, Seattle, Chicago, Austin and New York) and a detailed review of conflicts involving APAs. Published materials and news accounts are utilized to determine each agency's structure (e.g., public institution, private institution, public-private collaboration), staff size and composition, membership on its governing body, history and stated mission, mechanisms utilized to carry out its mandates, and sources and funding. Most of the detailed insights come from interviews with key individuals involved with the agencies.

One of the positive findings is that most human relations agencies and APA community members shared a common vision of going beyond ethnic/minorities as separate groups with separate issues and concerns. Achieving this vision will require meaningful APA participation in both the agencies and city government.

PART III: NATIONAL RACE POLICIES

Nowhere is the national debate over race-based policies more heated than over affirmative action. Paul M. Ong's chapter, "The Affirmative-Action Divide," examines the APA position in this divisive ideological battle. Over time, affirmative action has emerged as the contested boundary defining how aggressive government ought to be in correcting racial inequality. The battle has been waged within governmental agencies, in the courts, and more recently on ballots. APAs are materially and ideologically on both sides of the political divide, with some adamantly supporting and others vehemently opposing the policy. To understand how APAs are aligned, the chapter focuses on the following questions:

- What is the status of APAs relative to whites and other minorities in education, employment, and business?
- How does socioeconomic standing affect APA participation in

affirmative action programs?
- What is the political position of APAs on affirmative action in particular, and race-based policies in general?

The analysis relies on Current Population Survey data, EEOC (Equal Employment Opportunity Commission) data and reports, and annual reports on minority-business programs. The chapter also relies on opinion polls, secondary material, and unpublished sources.

The statistical evidence reveals a mixed picture of high achievement in education, partial parity in employment, and sub-performance in business. The diversity in outcomes points to a multi-faceted racial structure rather than a simple dichotomous racial hierarchy. Variations in socioeconomic status translate into differences in APA participation in affirmative action programs. They bear some of the cost of affirmative action in education, make some selective gains through employment programs for targeted occupations, and are fully incorporated into contract set-aside programs for minorities. Because of this spread, APAs have taken competing political positions in pursuit of both self-interest and broader principles. Some have argued that "preferential treatment" for other minorities hurt APAs, but others have defended the policy as necessary for increasing APA presence in public-sector employment and contracting. Despite this heterogeneity, a majority of APAs believe that some type of race-oriented policy is needed to address racial inequality.

The next two chapters offer different views on how Asians have influenced national discussions on policies related to race in the United Kingdom (U.K.) and Australia. The term Asians is used because the two nations do not have an official term equivalent to the Asian/Pacific Islander (A/PI) category used in the United States. This is not surprising since the A/PI category is a socially constructed concept anchored to circumstances in the United States. Interestingly, all three nations have a large white majority, a dominant culture with a common

English root, and an APA/Asian population that constitutes an estimated 4 to 5 percent of total population. Despite these similarities, there are significant differences, such as in the size of the black population, the ethnic composition of the Asian population, and the way race is discussed within the policy arena.

Shamit Saggar provides a British perspective. His chapter "Asians and Race Relations in Britain," starts with a review of the historic context of post-war immigration and recent statistics on the components of multiracial Britain. The next section focuses on Asian participation in employment, education and mainstream politics. The final section explores the Asian public policy agenda. The study relies on both published census data, voting information, and opinion surveys.

Saggar notes that immigration has been the driving force behind the emergence of a multiracial and multicultural society. The inflow started during the 1950s with the recruitment of migrants to fill labor shortages, followed by chain migration through family reunification starting in the 1970s, and finally by the in-migration of politically displaced refugees. Most immigrants came from the former British colonial empire, that is, from areas with nonwhite populations. Asians comprise the single largest racial group among all immigrants, with South Asians being the majority of Asian immigrants. As a consequence of this movement, the relative number of nonwhites has increased dramatically. By the early 1990s, Asians and blacks comprised 5 percent of the total population. Asians account for approximately two-thirds of the nonwhites, making them the largest racial group. The initial growth of the minority population interjected race into policy discussions. The first wave of immigrants led to a racialization of the "immigration question," but that divisive debate eventually waned. During the 1960s, Britain pursued an integration policy to address discrimination and promote cross-cultural awareness. This approach appears to have had some success because compared with the situation in other European countries, ethnic minorities in the U.K. are better integrated. This is not to say that race has disappeared from the policy arena, but race does not have the same potency as in the United States. One indicator of the difference is the fact that there are few supporters of race-based policies in the U.K., even among its minority population.

It would be too simplistic to attribute the current moderate view on race-based policy to the effectiveness of the integration policy. After all, the United States pursued a similar policy during the 1960s but without the same results. The difference may be due to a lack of a domestic legacy of slavery and an absence of a black dominance of minority politics in Britain. Instead, Asians have a substantial influence on race relations, and that influence is shaped by the group's material status. This group is overrepresented at the bottom end of the occupational distribution, but is also roughly at parity with whites at the top end of the spectrum. There are, however, ethnic differences in this class structure, with Indians faring considerably better than other South Asians. Despite this ethnic difference, youths from all Asian groups have high access to education, with enrollment rates well above that for whites (and blacks). A common thread among Asians, then, is a heavy reliance on education for inter-generational mobility. Asians also have an impressively high level of participation in electoral politics (above that for other groups), and while the number of elected Asians is below parity, there is an upward trajectory. Within politics, there is another common thread among Asians, a strong preference for the Labour Party, which tends to have a progressive policy agenda.

Despite the commonalities, Saggar concludes that there is an "absence of convincing evidence to demonstrate high and enduring levels of ethnic-based political consciousness among this group." Their high level of economic, social and political incorporation mitigates against the formation of a reactive racial identity based on opposition against being marginalized. Moreover, internal ethnic and class divisions are barriers against pan-ethnic politics. The consequence is a moderation of the use of race by Asians. At the same time, there is still a unique "Asian dimension" to a number of policy questions, which is shifting away from immigrant concerns as the number of British-born Asians increases.

Christine Inglis provides another perspective from halfway around the world in the chapter "Asians and Race Relations in Australia." The chapter starts with a review of the history of Asian immigration, which parallels the history in this country. Inglis then turns her attention to the impacts of the most recent wave of immigration, which commenced in the 1970s. She uses census and other data to examine both the composition of immigrant population and its implications. Finally, she explores the policies and politics affecting Asians.

Asian immigration to Australia dates back to the 1850s when Chinese migrated in search of economic opportunities in Victoria's gold fields. They were soon met by racially-motivated hostility and violence, and by anti-Asian laws. The antipathy took on moral overtones with the popular press depicting the Chinese as opium-smoking degenerates and destroyers of white women. Anti-Asian racism slowed but did not entirely stop immigration from Asia. The Chinese were later joined by smaller numbers of other Asians, particularly from India and Japan. By the end of century, even that small flow came under attack. The campaign to erect the "Great White Walls" culminated in the Immigration Restriction Act at the beginning of the 20th century, which put into place the White Australia Policy. Despite some limited exemptions for Asian immigration, the policy led to a gradual decline of the Asian population. A reversal started in the post-World War II period, when the country gradually relaxed its restrictions. The major break with the White Australia Policy came in 1973, when Australia enacted a non-discriminatory immigration policy.

The renewal of substantial Asian immigration has had a major demographic impact. Asians comprised less than one percent of the total population after World War II but over two percent of the population by 1986. A decade later, Asians (immigrants and their children) made up over 5 percent of the Australian population. The Asian population is ethnically diverse, with South East Asians comprising over a half of all Asians, Far East Asians comprising another third, and South Asians comprising the final sixth. The economic character of the Asian population has been shaped by the 1973 immigration policy. Although many entered through family reunions and as refugees, a substantial number took advantage of the openings for highly skilled professionals and wealthy business entrepreneurs. Asians with advanced degrees from Australia and other English-speaking countries have been incorporated into the middle-class. On the other hand, those with an education from non-English-speaking countries have had difficulties translating their credentials into comparable employment. There is also a significant number of marginalized refugees with very limited education and marketable skills.

Australia does not have an explicit race-based policy, at least not in the same way as in the United States. Instead, Australia has pursed a policy of multiculturalism, which was institutionalized in the late 1970s. Since the late 1980s, the policy has emphasized the promotion of diversity and the reduction of social disadvantage. According to Inglis, this strategy "has been remarkably successful in ensuring the incorporation of diverse groups into a previously very homogenous society in an equitable and surprisingly non-contentious manner." All is not perfect, however. Many Asians still experience discrimination, a sizable minority of whites has negative feeling about Asians, and racist politics erupts periodically. However, as Inglis points out, the current hostility is not a replay of the anti-Asian movement of the 19th century. Considerable gains and rights have been won, and additional progress can come by strengthening multiculturalism.

The comparison of the three countries reveals that the role of race in national politics and policy is contingent on historical and contemporary factors. All three nations have a history of racism and anti-Asian hostilities, and have attempted to eliminate institutional forms of racism in the post-World War II era. Each nation, however, has taken a different path. Race remains central to politics and policy in the United States but not in the United Kingdom and Australia. A part of this is due to the size and composition of the minority population. In the United States, where African Americans constitute the largest minority group, black activism and white resistance have shaped race relations. The growing presence of APAs (and Latinos) is transforming this situation, but the transformation has been difficult and so far incomplete. In the United Kingdom, Asians have emerged as the majority among nonwhites, which effectively precludes a simple black-white framework to race. Asian concerns have moved the political discourse away from a purely race-oriented one, although race cannot be totally ignored. Australia appears to have gone the furthest in dismantling the centrality of race, replacing it with a policy of multiculturalism. Australia is also the country where Asians are the overwhelming majority of the nonwhite population.

The APA/Asian experience in all three countries points to two common phenomena. First, class plays a key role structuring the APA/Asian influence. A significant proportion of the APA/Asian population is comprised of the highly-educated who are incorporated into the middle-class. Their class interests moderate minority politics. Second, the APA/Asian experience reveal the importance of immigration and foreign affairs. In the new global order, even domestic race-related politics has become intertwined with international politics. Again, how that nexus is played out varies from one country to another. The diversity, however, can be a blessing. The United Kingdom and Australia can offer alternative models of what is possible.

Part IV: New Possibilities

The chapters in the previous sections of this book examine the issues and problems associated with the APA impact on race relations. This final section examines what ought to be done to improve race relations. Responding to new racial realities requires not only transforming existing institutions such as human relations agencies, but it also requires developing new ones. Leland Saito and Edward Park's chapter, "Multiracial Collaborations and Coalitions," examines multiracial coalitions in cities across the United States. The efforts are part and parcel of the "New Urban Race Relations," which is embedded in a globalization of the economy and a demographic transition created by an influx of Asian and Latino immigrants. As Saito and Parks note, recent immigrants bring new multiracial complexities that are not easily absorbed into the existing political process and structure. This eventually moves racial politics gradually from "the simplicity of white over black discrimination to the more nuanced and complex dynamics of 'post-Civil Rights' politics."

To understand the new urban politics, Saito and Park focus on grassroots efforts that provide "lessons" on what may or may not facilitate cooperation among diverse racial groups. The analysis includes four case studies of multiracial relations: the mayoral campaign of African-American Lee Brown in Houston; redistricting in New York City involving Chinatown; high school violence in the San Gabriel Valley of Los Angeles County; and the campaign to support union jobs in Los Angeles. These case studies cover a range of ethnic and racial groups, class positions, and issues, situated in different regional and political contexts. The major research questions are:

- How, and under what circumstances, do such formations emerge?
- Can the participants successfully articulate a common agenda, and if so, how?

- How do they address potentially divisive questions?
- What are the limitations of such efforts?

The study utilizes in-depth interviews, which provide information about the history, issues, goals, participants, methods of collaboration, and community context. The interviews are supplemented by archival research and other historical data.

Their analysis produces four major findings. First, racial coalitions emerge when groups are able to set aside short-term objectives to address more fundamental issues such as making public institutions more accountable and fighting for a living wage. Second, successful coalition building resists narrow race-based politics, while clearly recognizing the importance of race in society. APAs must be willing to transcend their own interests when addressing the broader problem of racial inequality, and other groups must be willing to make room for APAs. Third, building alliances requires establishing and sustaining relations among individuals and organizations. A track record of working together, constructing networks, and engendering trust lays the foundation as new concerns emerge. Fourth, ethnic-specific organizations are not necessarily a source of divisiveness but are potential vehicles for community mobilization, leadership training, and resource building. They can promote communication and negotiation among various community groups.

To respond effectively to the new race relations, grassroots strategies must be complemented by national strategies. Angela Oh, who served on President Clinton's Advisory Board to the President's Initiative on Race, offers some constructive suggestions in the book's concluding chapter, "Reaching Toward Our Highest Aspirations: The President's Initiative on Race." The Initiative, launched in June 1997, was designed to rekindle America's desire to solve this nation's race problem. The process started with an effort to promote a constructive dialogue on race relations, and the Advisory Committee, along with a professional staff for the President's Initiative on Race (PIR), played a key role in conducting town-hall meetings throughout the country. One of the most difficult tasks was moving beyond a black-white discourse. Some argued that the spotlight should remain on African Americans because slavery and its legacy have determined so much of this nation's history and continue to shape inter-group relations. This resistance to change, however, varies by regions, with the West and Southwest being much more open to including APA and Latino experiences. This inclusion adds an ethnic flavor to the dialogue and interjects immigrant issues into the discussions. Acknowledging the new racial complexity, however, is not tantamount to ignoring the uniqueness or importance of the black experience. Despite the reluctance by some to expand the race-relations framework, many of the activities of the PIR proved to be inclusive.

One would be naive to assume that the Initiative can solve the race problem, and it is more realistic to see the effort as a start. Angela Oh argues that the dialogue and related activities should be integral to "the inter-generational work that requires all of us to take a step into the future." This will require courageous leadership that supports open and frank discussions, and an educational system that teaches the next generation to fully understand and appreciate America's racial history, the current problems of racial injustice, and the potential for a better society. Progressive social change to promote racial justice will require a "politics of possibility," and constructive innovations to solve racial conflicts are most likely to emerge in areas undergoing the most rapid change in race relations. APAs can and must play a major role in generating new possibilities.

Part I

Racial Identities

"Who Are You Calling Asian?": Shifting Identity Claims, Racial Classification, and the Census

Yen Le Espiritu
and Michael Omi[1]

Introduction

Tiger Woods may be popularly regarded as a "black" golfer, but Woods himself writes that he is "Asian" on forms requesting racial and ethnic data. "Actually," Woods says, "I am 90 percent Oriental, more Thai than anything."[2] How Woods classifies himself reveals the inherent slipperiness of racial identity, and the gap between popular under-standings of racial belonging and state definitions of race and ethnicity. Nowhere are these issues as evident as in the contested framing of racial categories for the U.S. Census.

This chapter describes how Asian Pacific Americans (APAs) have been affected by, and in turn have shaped, census classification. Through an examination of specific cases, we illustrate how racial categories have been significantly transformed by the advancement of APA political claims. A shifting consciousness regarding group "sameness" or "distinctiveness" has mobilized APAs to lobby for the creation of new categories, for the expansion of existing ones, or for the relocation of groups from one category to another. The cases illustrate how specific forms of classification are the result of dynamic and complex negotiations between state interests, panethnic demands, and ethnic-specific challenges. As such, APA census categories both reflect and help create group identities, influence the formation of public policy, and shape the popular discourse about race in the U.S.

Racial Classification and the Census

The census is regarded by much of the population as a bureaucratic routine—a form of national accounting that provides a collective portrait of who we are as a people. Part of that picture involves dividing and clustering the population into meaningful and significant groups. Among others, the census establishes categories based on nativity, citizenship status, age, household income, and marital status. None of these categories, however, has been subject to such intense scrutiny, vigorous debate, and political controversy as that of race and ethnicity. The census has increasingly become the site where competing political claims for group recognition by race and ethnicity are advanced, and where classifications are established in response to statistical needs, administrative record keeping practices, and legal requirements. At stake is not only the "appropriate" classification of groups, but also the political and policy implications that flow from these definitions.

Sociologist William Petersen notes that, "Over the history of the American census, enumerations have helped create groups, moved persons from one group to another by revised definition, and through new procedures changed the size of groups" (Peterson 1983, 188). Contemporary national censuses have had to confront the demise of biological notions of race and its attendant impact on state classifications. For most of the modern period, race was considered something objective and fixed, much like one's age or nativity status. The concept of race is now widely regarded as a social construct, and census categories are seen as an important force in the generation and reproduction of collective identities (Omi 1997, Goldberg 1997).

In the wake of the civil rights movement, new record keeping practices needed to be developed to monitor discriminatory trends and enforce equal opportunity laws. In 1977, the Office of Management and Budget issued Directive 15, which defines the federal standards for racial and ethnic classification:

This Directive provides standard classifications for record keeping, collection, and presentation of data on race and ethnicity in Federal program administrative reporting and statistical activities. These classifications should not be interpreted as being scientific or anthropological in nature, nor should they be viewed as determinants of eligibility for participation in any Federal program. (OMB Directive 15)

Originally conceived to provide consistent categories for use by federal agencies, OMB Directive 15 has inordinately shaped the very discourse of race in the United States. Its categories have become the *de facto* standard for state and local agencies, the private and nonprofit sectors, and the research community. Social scientists and policy analysts use Directive 15 categories since data is organized under these rubrics.

Given the importance of racial data for monitoring and redressing the nation's racial inequalities, some demographers and statisticians hope that we can have racial and ethnic categories that are conceptually valid, exclusive and exhaustive, measurable, and reliable over time. However, as this chapter will illustrate, racial/ethnic categories have proven to be fundamentally unstable. Official racial categories have changed nine times in the past ten U.S. censuses. In the planning of the 2000 Census, the Census Bureau once again faced increasing public demand for revising or expanding the racial categories. This demand is driven in part by demographic shifts—the entrance of "new" immigrant groups since 1965 and increasing ethnic heterogeneity among preexisting categories. It is also fueled by the "increasing recognition of the fluidity and accompanying ambiguity of racial and ethnic identities for many people" (Edmonston and Schultze 1995, 141). There is, for example, frequently a gap between state definitions and individual/group self-identities. Immigrant groups who come from societies organized around different concepts of race and ethnicity often have difficulty navigating and situating themselves within U.S. categories (Omi 1997). Another concern is the temporal effect of evolving racial and ethnic labels. New labels come into vogue, old groups dissolve through assimilation, and new groups emerge as a result of changes in civil status or patterns of immigration.[3]

Our discussion of APA census classification takes place at a time when the very use of racial categories is being challenged from a number of political positions. For over a year, the American Anthropology Association debated the appropriateness of any form of racial classification (American Anthropology Association 1997a, 1997b, 1998a, 1998b, 1998c, 1998d). The Association concluded that there was no scientific basis for the concept of "race" and urged that the term not be used in scholarly practice. Political conservatives, in arguing for "color-blind" social policies, have also denounced the use of racial categories. Such race thinking, they argue, runs counter to the move to "get beyond race" and to judge individuals by "the content of their characters."[4] Liberal voices have also expressed their dissatisfaction with racial categories, contending that to classify groups along racial line is to reify race. Sociologist Orlando Patterson, for example, questions why the Census Bureau needs an "Asian" category, arguing that such an umbrella category would only reinforce "the notion of race as a separate, meaningful entity" (Patterson 1997). The on going challenge to the practice of racial classification and record keeping has important social policy implications, for it can potentially affect the government's ability to monitor trends and discern forms of racial inequality.

In this chapter, we address the complexity of classifying APAs— a diverse and changing population. When and under what conditions should APAs be classified as an aggregate? When do we need to disaggregate the category? And when do we need to advocate for new categories? In so doing, we hope to address the larger question of the relationship between racial classification, individual identity, and the efforts by the state and various populations to address racial inequalities. We first turn to a consideration of how APAs have been historically classified by census definitions and practices.

Historical Continuities and Contradictions

The U.S. federal government has been collecting racial data since the eighteenth century. From the very beginning of census taking in this country, a basic differentiation was established between nonwhites and whites. As Peterson (1983, 190) notes:

> Those of European origin have been specified as the "foreign stock" if they or one or both of their parents were born abroad, but from the third generation on, whites of any nationality disappear statistically into the native population. For nonwhites, however, a separate category has been maintained, irrespective of how many generations lived in this country.

Extending this point, we would argue that such a distinction was explicitly linked to the political dynamic of racist inclusion and exclusion. Until the passage of civil rights legislation in the 1960s, census categories were utilized to politically disenfranchise and discriminate against groups defined as nonwhite. From prohibitions on naturalization rights to the setting of quotas for the 1924 National Origins Immigration Act, census categories were evoked and strategically employed to circumscribe the political, economic, and social rights of particular groups (Anderson 1988).

As nonwhites, Asians in the United States have always been counted separately in the "Race" or "Color" question. As indicated in Table 1, Asians first appeared in the census schedules in 1870 when "Chinese" was included in the "Color" question. After the passage of the Chinese Exclusion Act in 1882, Japanese were recruited as substitute

TABLE 1. ASIAN/PACIFIC ISLANDER CATEGORIES IN THE U.S. CENSUS: 1870 TO 1990

Year	Chinese	Japanese	Other Asian or Pacific Islander	Other
1870	Chinese			
1880	Chinese			
1890	Chinese	Japanese		
1900	Chinese	Japanese		
1910	Chinese	Japanese		Other + write in
1920	Chinese	Japanese		Other + write in
1930	Chinese	Japanese	Filipino, Hindu, Korean	Other race, spell out in full
1940	Chinese	Japanese	Filipino, Hindu, Korean	Other race, spell out in full
1950	Chinese	Japanese	Filipino	Other race, spell out
960	Chinese	Japanese	Filipino, Hawaiian, part Hawaiian, etc.	
1970	Chinese	Japanese	Filipino, Hawaiian, Korean	Other (print race)
1980	Chinese	Japanese	Filipino, Hawaiian, Korean, Vietnamese, Asian Indian, Samoan, Guamanian	Other (specify)
1990	Chinese	Japanese	Filipino, Hawaiian, Korean, Vietnamese, Asian Indian, Samoan, Guamanian, Other Asian or Pacific Islander	Other race

Source: Edmonston and Schultze (1995: table 7.1).

workers. The Japanese category thus appeared for the first time in the 1890 Census. In the Twentieth Century, the "race" question continued to be a combination of color, tribal status, and Asian national origin. Reflecting increased immigration from different Asian countries, the 1930 and 1940 Censuses added Filipinos, Koreans, and Hindu to the "Color or Race" question. However, presumably because of their small numbers, Koreans were dropped from the "Color or Race" question in the 1950 and 1960 Censuses. As we will discuss below, the classification of Asian Indians in the United States has been most fluid, beginning with "Hindu" in 1930 then changing to "white" after World War II and then to "Asian Indian" in 1980. Pacific Islanders were added to the census schedules in 1960 with the introduction of the categories "Hawaiian" and "Part Hawaiian."

Civil rights legislation beginning in 1964 has stimulated vested interest in the racial and ethnic classification and enumeration of the Census. At the time of the 1960 Census, the race question had become discredited and would have been excluded in 1970 had it not been for the passage of civil rights and equal opportunities laws, which made it necessary for the census to continue to compile racial statistics (Kaplan 1979, 4). Civil rights legislation requires federal authorities to look for patterns of discrimination as evidenced by the under-representation of disadvantaged minorities; and where such under-representation is found, affirmative action by the responsible party must be undertaken to correct it. Disadvantaged minorities are defined as those who have been histori-cally subject to racial discrimination and economic oppression in the United States. Congress also used census population statistics to ensure equal access to the electoral process. Until census data began to provide comprehensive data on an underlying population including its disadvan-taged minorities in a specific geographic area, it was very difficult to demonstrate patterns of discrimination practiced by businesses, schools and political institutions against disadvantaged minorities. Thus, census statistics became absolutely critical for the enforcement of every civil rights law passed since the 1964 Civil Rights Act. Not surprisingly, because the census tabulations of racial and ethnic groups had the potential to form the benchmark for many legal tests of minority under-representation, the accuracy, adequacy, and precision of census statistics became an explosive political controversy, as well as an important site for the political activity of racial and ethnic political interest groups. The passage of civil rights legislation thus marked an important shift in the use of racial and ethnic data—from a tool to identify populations who were excluded from citizenship to one that is used to ensure the inclusion of groups (Lott 1998, 31).

Responding to political pressure from racial and ethnic interest groups seeking to acquire not just substantive but legally authoritative data on their populations, the U.S. government undertook the standard-ization of the collection and presentation of data on race and ethnicity. In 1977, the Office of Management and Budget (OMB) Statistical Directive 15 required all federal agencies to use five standard categories in program administrative reporting and statistical activities: American Indian or Alaskan Native, Asian or Pacific Islander, Black, White, and Hispanic. Directive 15 defines an Asian or Pacific Islander in relation to geographical origin and ancestry as "a person having origins in any of the original peoples of the Far East, Southeast Asia, the Indian subcontinent, or the Pacific Islands."[5] From a civil rights perspective, this directive is significant because it formalized and institutionalized the collection and representation of presumably compatible, nonduplicated, exchangeable ethnic and racial data by all federal agencies. This policy has resulted in a wealth of data previously unobtainable on the disparities between white and nonwhite populations, especially in the areas of voting rights, public accommodations and services, education, employment and housing (Lott 1998). The directive has also shaped the very discourse of race in the United States, becoming the de facto standard for state and local agencies, the private and nonprofit sectors, and the research community. Directive 15 has also influenced group identity and community-formation patterns. For example, new organizations have emerged representing the interests of "Asian and Pacific Islanders" or "Hispanics" in a variety of forms from service providers to professional caucuses.

Although Directive 15 allowed the collection of additional detailed race and ethnicity categories, it required that such groups be reaggregated into the five basic racial/ethnic categories. To satisfy the new federal guidelines on the collection of racial statistics, the Census Bureau proposed to do away with the individual Asian Pacific racial codes in favor of one summary category "Asian or Pacific Islander" in the 1980 Census and again in the 1990 Census. According to the Bureau, this single classification would provide a 100 percent count of the total APA population, as required by the OMB. Both times, APA legislators, community leaders, and advocacy groups united to fight the Census Bureau's proposal to lump all APAs together and recommended instead separate categories for the various APA populations. Citing the huge influx of recent immigrants from Asia and the Pacific Rim, APA community representatives argued successfully that new immigrants, particularly limited or non-English speakers, would not relate to the racial category "Asian or Pacific Islander" and that these newcomers have unique health, education, and welfare concerns that need to be separately identified (Espiritu 1992, 118-130). Mounting pressures from APA constituencies and unfavorable pre-census test results, which demonstrated a great deal of confusion about the summary category of "Asian or Pacific Islander," ultimately forced the Census Bureau to not only retain the separate categories for APA groups from the 1970 Census, but to add Asian Indian, Vietnamese, Samoan, and Guamanian. In the 1990 Census, an "Other API" category was added.

Although APAs have been most effective in lobbying for representation on the census forms, it is important to note the limitations of these successes (Lott 1998, 91). Most importantly, despite these victories, data on APAs continue to be difficult to obtain. Many federal agencies do not solicit, record, or report data on APAs separately, claiming that it is difficult and costly to obtain data on such small populations. For instance, in the Census Bureau's survey of minority-owned businesses, data on APAs is combined and reported with data on American Indians and Alaskan Natives (House Committee on Government Reform and Oversight: Subcommittee on Government Management, Information, and Technology Hearings 1997, 670-671). Even when APAs are included in the collection of data, they often fail to appear in the actual reporting of data.

In recent years, the continuing utility of Directive 15—and of racial and ethnic categories—has been questioned. When Directive 15 was implemented in the 1970s, racial and ethnic minorities were a stable and small proportion of the American population. Moreover, African Americans were the only sizable minority group in the United States, comprising approximately 90 percent of the nonwhite U.S. population (Payson 1996, 1257). Since then, the United States has witnessed a substantial influx of immigrants from Asia, Africa, and Latin America and the emergence of a new generation of multiracial families and children. As the United States becomes more heterogeneous, public pressure has increased for revising and expanding race and ethnicity classifications in the census as well as for increasing recognition of the fluidity and multiplicity of individuals' self-identification (Edmonston and Schultze 1995, 141). In the following section, we will discuss how APAs have negotiated, contested, and made use of these official racial and ethnic categories.

Negotiating and Contesting Racial/Ethnic Categories

APAs are a diverse and changing population—a multicultural, multilingual, and multiethnic people who have different socioeconomic profiles, immigration histories, and political outlooks. Despite these differences, APAs have at times come together as a panethnic group to lobby for recognition, to assert political claims, and to argue for increased resources (Espiritu 1992). Because the APA category is a social and political construct, it is inherently unstable. Within the broad and imprecise pan-Asian boundary, subgroup identifications remain important, leaving room for shifting levels of solidarity and mobilization, backsliding, or dropping out of the pan-Asian framework altogether. In recent years, APA groups have lobbied for both inclusion into and exclusion from the APA category. In this section, we examine how the issues of racial classification have been negotiated and resolved among APAs, between APAs and other minorities, and between APAs and the federal and state governments.

ASIAN INDIANS

Racial terms used in census enumeration schedules are subject to constant revision—driven by shifting demographic trends, changing concepts of race, and claims for political/legal recognition. The convoluted history of how Asian Indians have been classified in the census provides a compelling illustration of some of these factors. In 1930, Asian Indians first appeared in the census schedules when "Hindu" was added to the "Color" question. The term "Hindu" or "Hindoo" in the popular parlance of the era was constructed as a racial classification, and not as an indicator of religious affiliation. Ironically, only a small portion of the initial wave of Asian Indian immigrants was Hindu. In fact, a third of the Asian Indian population was Muslim, and the clear majority was Sikh (Takaki 1989, 295). "Hindu" was omitted as a category in the

1950 Census. Despite the abolition of the Hindu category, enumerators were instructed in 1950 and 1960 to write in "Hindu" for the race of persons they regarded as Asian Indians (Colker 1996, 236).

The question of how to racially "situate" Asian Indians has historically been the focus of intense legal battles, primarily centered on securing naturalization rights. Between 1909 and 1923, court decisions on whether Asian Indians were "white by law" were contradictory and relied on different principles to arrive at their judgments (Haney López 1996). The courts found Asian Indians to be "white persons" in 1910, 1913, 1919, and 1920, but not in 1909, 1917, or after 1923 (Haney López 1996, 67). The deliberations of these legal cases are interesting because they reveal the tensions and contradictions between science, popular consciousness, and the law. At the turn of the century, leading anthropologists considered dark-skinned people from western and southern Asia, such as Syrians and Asian Indians, as "Caucasians." At times, the courts agreed with this classification and its meaning for the extension of legal and political rights. At other times, the court decisions reflected the acknowledgment of a disjuncture, from a legal standpoint, between "scientific" evidence and "common knowledge" as rooted in popular conceptions of race.

This disjuncture is clearly revealed in the Supreme Court decision in *United States v. Thind* (1923). Bhagat Singh Thind, born in India and a graduate of Punjab University, had immigrated to the United States in 1913. He was petitioning to become a naturalized citizen based on his racial classification as "Caucasian." The Court found that although Thind was "Caucasian," he was not "white" by commonly understood notions of "whiteness," and therefore ruled that Thind was ineligible for naturalization. "It may be true," the court declared, "that the blond Scandinavian and the brown Hindu have a common ancestor in the dim reaches of antiquity, but the average man knows perfectly well that there are unmistakable and profound differences between them today" (*Thind* 1923, 209).

The *Thind* decision had an enormous impact on immigration and naturalization policies and practices. In the immediate wake of the decision, the federal government attempted to deprive naturalized Asian Indians of their citizenship. The result was the denaturalization of at least 65 people between 1923 and 1927, including one man, Vaisho Das Bgai, who committed suicide after being divested of his citizenship (Haney López 1996, 91). Within weeks after the decision, California's Attorney General began proceedings to revoke Asian Indian land purchases under the restrictive terms of the state's Alien Land Law (Takaki 1989, 300). Finally, Asian Indian status as "aliens ineligible for citizenship" made them subject to the 1924 Immigration Act that denied admissions quotas for such persons. In 1946, Asian Indian immigrants, along with Filipinos, were finally granted naturalization rights.

In 1950, the "Hindu" category was removed from the census "Race" question; Asian Indians were then relegated to the category "Other" and subsequently classified as "white/Caucasian." Because Asian Indians defy the logic of U.S. established racial categories, it has continued to be difficult to situate or identify them by their "race" or "color." In 1978, a National Opinion Research Center (NORC) survey asked, "Would you classify most people from India as being white, black, or something else?" Twenty-three percent of respondents described Asian Indians as "brown," 15 percent as "black," and 11 percent as "white." What is striking is that 38 percent of respondents classified them as "other," while 13 percent said they could not classify them at all (cited in Xenos et. al. 1989, 3). This ambiguity and confusion extends to Asian Indians themselves. In the 1980 Census, many people who identified themselves as Asian Indian by ancestry also considered themselves to be white by race (Xenos et. al. 1989, 1).

In the mid-1970s, to challenge the "invisibility" of Asian Indians, leaders affiliated with the Association of Indians in America (AIA) lobbied for an Asian Indian category under the larger APA category.

The desire to obtain an accurate count provided the initial impetus for petitioning for a new category. Dr. Manornjan Dutta, an economist at Rutgers and former president of the AIA was the first to serve on the Census Advisory Committee and the principal actor behind the call for an Asian Indian category. He explained that it was important for Asian Indians to be "counted":

> I have said this in many meetings from San Francisco to Boston: "When you left India, you promised your mom and dad that you would be counted. You will not remain uncounted." The first place to be counted is in the census of the country where you pay taxes. (Dutta interview 1999).

Dr. Jilen Shah, a physician and former president of the AIA who served on the 1990 Census Advisory Committee, underscored the need to clarify the racial status of Asian Indians:

> Prior to the 1980 Census, nobody knew how many Indians there were in the country. When the questionnaire came, we didn't know how to fill out the form. A lot of people were filling it out that we were black. Some were saying we were Hispanic. We just did not know (Shah interview 1999).

Dr. Narendra Kukkar, an endocrinologist and AIA member who actively petitioned for the category, notes the slippage that existed between census categories, popular conceptions of race, and individual/group self-identity:

> We were listed on the official reports as Caucasians and we knew that we didn't look like Caucasians....We didn't act like Caucasians. We didn't speak like Caucasians. Our names were not like Caucasians...Anthropologically they felt that we were Caucasian...our plea to [the Census Bureau] was that we didn't fit into the category (Kukkar interview 1999).

The move for a separate category provoked debates within the broader Asian Indian community regarding its policy implications. Was the category meant to insure a more accurate count or to make claims to "minority status"? The debates primarily circulated in professional circles. The issue became framed, as it has in other instances, as one of individual merit and socioeconomic mobility versus group demands for recognition and collective empowerment. Many Asian Indians, subscribing to the former perspective, opposed the idea of a separate category:

> There were many Indians that resented the idea that one should become a minority and claim a minority status...They would say, "What do you mean? You are undermining my own ability and my own education. You are trying to tell that I have to be a minority to get this? I'm getting this because I am capable of this" (Kukkar interview 1999).

On the other hand, the proponents of the Asian Indian category felt that the category would assist the next generation who may face some difficult obstacles with respect to access to higher education because of "the name factor, the color factor, and the pronunciation factor" (Kukkar interview 1999).

In the end, however, the group that would substantially benefit from the creation of the category was small businesspeople:

> The fortunate part, which at that point none of us had realized, was that when the new wave of immigrants started arriving many of them were small businessmen and contractors. Minority businessmen have received most of the benefits of this minority status. They were eligible to get loans at a preferred rate from the federal government and from the state governments...That was totally unforeseen. In terms of benefits to kids who wanted to get into Harvard or Yale or UCLA...that did not even materialize. (Kukkar interview 1999)

In 1977, the OMB agreed to reclassify immigrants from India and their descendants from "white/Caucasian" to "Asian Indian." They were officially listed on the 1980 Census as "Asian Indian" and were one of the subgroups under the "Asian or Pacific Islander" category under Directive 15. The term "Asian Indian" itself apparently emerged in response to comments from the American Indians who wanted to avoid confusion between the two groups. As Dutta recalls, "[American Indians] suggested that Indians should take a prefix or suffix otherwise Columbus' mistake would persist. I said I preferred Asian Indian" (Dutta interview 1999).

The inclusion of Asian Indians under the APA classification has been contested by both Asian Indians and other APAs. Contending that they are *racially* different from other Asians, some Asian Indians have questioned the potential alliance with other APAs and argued that Indians run the risk of being ignored and marginalized in pan-Asian organizations (Misir 1996; Shankar and Srikanth 1998). On the other hand, some APAs have challenged the validity of Asian Indian claims to minority status as an APA group. For example, in San Francisco, Chinese American architects and engineers protested the inclusion of Asian Indians under the city's minority business enterprise law (Chung 1991). Citing a Supreme Court ruling which requires cities to narrowly define which groups had suffered discrimination to justify specific affirmative action programs, Chinese Americans argued before the Board of Supervisors that Asian Indians should not be considered "Asian." Obviously, at stake were economic benefits accruing to designated "minority" businesses.

The 1980 Census data-which indicated that the Asian Indian population was one of the most highly educated and had one of the highest incomes in the country-also challenged Asian Indian claim to minority status. As Kukkar stated, "They say, 'You guys do so well. You're so highly educated. What do you mean you want minority status?'" (Kukkar interview 1999). Asian Indian leaders have had to counter the claims of being another "model minority" by demonstrating the existence of class cleavages and significant differences in life chances within the population. They have also emphasized discrepancies between educational attainment and income when compared to whites, and the phenomenon of the "glass ceiling" with respect to job mobility among professionals.

The case of Asian Indians illustrates the inherent fluidity of racial categories and how they are shaped by political interpretation and contestation. Labeled "Hindu" when the majority were Sikh, declared "Caucasian" but not "white" by the Supreme Court in 1923, and recognized as "Asian Indian" and "Asian American" in 1977, the category still remains open to further interrogation and change. As the number of South Asians has increased in recent years, questions regarding the relationship between Asian Indians and other South Asian groups have surfaced. In many academic and community-based settings, the term "Asian Indian" is being replaced with the term "South Asian" in an effort to decenter India and encompass groups from Bangladesh, Bhutan, Nepal, Pakistan, and Sri Lanka, among others. "South Asian" was entertained as a possible term in the mid-1970s, but it was argued at the time that the majority of South Asians were Indian, so the term should reflect that. In addition, Dutta notes that, "[Indian] immigrants from several Caribbean and Latin American countries whose forebears immigrated from India also contacted me and preferred the term Asian Indian" (Dutta interview 1999). How other South Asian groups negotiate their location within the "Asian Indian" category is still an open question.

FILIPINOS

As indicated by the Asian Indian case study, the state's effort to classify racial and ethnic groups is imprecise at best, thus leaving room for ethnic groups discontented with their classification to challenge the validity of racial/ethnic categories. Whereas some Asian Indian leaders have lobbied to be reclassified from the "white/Caucasian" category to a subgroup under the APA category, Filipinos have at times fought to be removed from the APA grouping. However, in both cases, a major incentive for requesting the reclassification was possible economic gain derived from civil rights affirmative action programs. Other motives included a desire to emphasize the group's unique cultural and racial identity and to assert their significance in U.S. racial schema.

Large-scale immigration of Filipino agricultural workers to the U.S. mainland coincided with their influx to Hawaii. The 1920s was a decade of dramatic increase in their numbers, with some forty-five thousand Filipinos migrating to the Pacific Coast. The 1921 and 1924 Immigration Acts which barred Asian immigration and restricted European immigration, prompted West Coast farmers and canneries to turn to Filipinos to fill the labor shortage created by the exclusion of the Chinese, Japanese, Koreans, and South Asians. Filipinos were the favored source of labor at that time due to their unusual legal status, for until the passage of the Tydings-McDuffie Act in 1934, Filipinos could migrate freely to the United States, protected by their colonial status as U.S. nationals. Due to the influx of Filipinos during the 1920s, Filipinos first appeared in the census schedules in 1930. The 1930 Census indicates that Filipinos were scattered across the nation; however, the majority concentrated in California (Espiritu 1995).

The precise racial classification of Filipinos was contested almost from the beginning. In 1905, California's lawmakers passed a bill to prohibit marriages between whites and "Mongolians." Because it was unclear whether Filipinos were Mongolians or not, some county clerks issued marriage licenses to Filipino-white couples, while others did not. In 1931, a Los Angeles county superior court judge decided that Filipino-white marriages did not violate the state antimiscegenation law because, in his view, Filipinos were not Mongolians. In 1933, the majority opinion handed down by the appellate court, based on an exhaustive reading of the works of nineteenth-century ethnologists, declared that Filipinos were Malays, and not Mongolians, and therefore could marry whites. Undaunted by their failure in the courts, anti-Filipino forces, portraying the largely single Filipino men as sexual threats to white women, successfully lobbied the state legislature to expand the existing antimiscegenation laws to unambiguously include Filipino-white marriages (Chan 1991, 60-61).

The racial status of Filipinos vis-à-vis other APAs came up again during the Asian American movement of the late 1960s and early 1970s. In the summer of 1968, more than one hundred students of diverse Asian backgrounds attended an "Are You Yellow?" conference at UCLA to discuss issues of Yellow Power, identity, and the war in Vietnam (Ling 1989, 53). In 1970, a new pan-Asian organization in northern California called itself the "Yellow Seed" because "Yellow [is] the common bond between Asian-Americans and Seed symbolize[s] growth as an individual and as an alliance" (Masada 1970). However, Filipino Americans rejected the "yellow" references, claiming that they were brown, not yellow (Rabaya 1971, 110; Ignacio 1976, 84). At the first Asian American national conference in San Francisco in 1972, Filipino Americans made it clear to the conferees that they were "Brown" Asians by separating themselves from the larger Asian American body and organizing their own "Brown" Asian caucus (Ignacio 1976, 139-141). Calling attention to their "braiding of cultures"-of Asian, Spanish, American, African, and Pacific Island cultures-Filipinos have also differentiated themselves culturally from other Asians. Maria Root (1997, ix) described Filipino cultural heritage in the following way: "Not dominated by Confucian philosophy, oral in tradition, coming from societies that have matri-archal structures and bilateral kinship systems, intersected and invaded by seafarers, traders, military, missionaries, and colonizers, Filipinos in America are seldom accurately situated in history or culture and are therefore often misinterpreted."

In addition to the perceived cultural and racial gap, Filipino Americans also claimed that they had a different socioeconomic profile from other APA groups and thus should be separated from the APA rubric. As indicated above, Directive 15 collapsed all Asian Pacific groups into the one summary category of Asian or Pacific Islander. As a result, federal agencies collect civil rights compliance data using the inclusive Asian or Pacific Islander category. However, aggregate data can be misleading, masking the economic diversity of the APA groups and ignoring the needs of high-risk groups. In the early 1980s, Filipinos in California began to clamor to be separated from the APA category, claiming that their socioeconomic status was lower than that of other APAs, namely the Chinese and Japanese. For example, in 1979, college-educated Japanese Americans on the average earned $23,000 and Chinese Americans $21,000. The same year, similarly educated Filipinos averaged just over $16,000. Moreover, compared to Chinese and Japanese Americans, Filipino Americans "appear to be more of a working-class ethnic group, with greater occupational concentrations in semi-skilled jobs" (Nee and Sanders 1985, 82-85; Cabezas, Shinagawa, and Kawaguchi 1986-87). Because of their relatively disadvantaged position in the labor market, Filipino Americans have a potentially strong claim for inclusion in affirmative action programs. However, they feared that, when lumped together with other APA groups who are stereotyped as the "model minority," their claim on the state could be diluted due to the relatively high economic level of the APA aggregate.

Filipino Americans also fare less well in secondary and higher education than other APAs: Filipinos have a significantly higher high school dropout and non-completion rate than other APA groups; fewer Filipinos graduate from colleges; and fewer still enroll in graduate school (Okamura and Agbayani 1997). Although Filipino educational profiles differ from those of other APA groups, only seven percent of all public schools, mainly in the West, used "Filipino" as a separate racial/ethnic category in addition to the five federal categories of Directive 15 (U.S. Department of Education 1996). Classified as APA, Filipinos have been presumed not to be an underrepresented minority and in higher education, in 1986, were removed from affirmative action recruitment and admissions programs in the University of California system (Almirol 1988, 6). In subsequent years, Filipino American admissions and enrollment at UC Berkeley and UCLA declined. For example, in fall 1996, at UCLA, only 26 percent of Filipino applicants were admitted-the lowest admission percentage of any ethnic/racial group. Similarly, UC Berkeley records indicated that the acceptance rate of Filipinos (16 percent) for fall 1996 was 16 percent-the lowest in recent years and also the lowest of all ethnic/racial groups and well below the overall admission rate of 25 to 30 percent. In contrast, during this same period, APA representation in the UC system and in higher education in general showed unprecedented gains (Okamura and Agbayani 1997). Because Filipino American experiences and status in higher education have not been comparable to those of other APA groups, lumping them together with the latter could only mask their specific academic needs and concerns. The post-1965 influx of immigrants from the Philippines has substantially increased the number of Filipinos in the United States. According to the 1990 Census, Filipinos now total more than 1.4 million, comprising the second largest immigrant group as well as the second largest APA group in the United States, and the largest APA group in California. Their increasing numerical strength has fortified their contention that they no longer need to coalesce with other APA groups. Some Filipino American community advocates have claimed that the pan-Asian grouping allows the more established groups to dominate the resources meant for all APAs; newer and less powerful groups are simply used as window displays. As a Filipino American aide explained:

There is a sense of feeling that Japanese and Chinese have gotten a piece of the pie and that Filipinos are not getting enough of the pie. The issues being addressed have always been Japanese and Chinese issues. Filipinos believe in coalition building with other Asian Americans. They understand its strength. At the same time, they don't feel that the coalition is benefiting them (Tony Ricasa interview, 1989).

A 1988 editorial in the Sacramento-based *Philippine News* argued that Filipino Americans should be separated from the Asian Pacific classification because "the Japanese and Chinese...dominate every outreach funding meant for Asian and Pacific Islanders combined" and that "[they] are only using the numerical strength of the Filipinos to attract larger funding for the Asian and Pacific Islanders" (Jacaban 1988a).

In 1988, Filipino Americans were successful in lobbying for the passage of California Senate Bill 1813, which requires state personnel surveys or statistical tabulations to classify persons of Filipino ancestry as Filipino rather than as Asian or Hispanic. With this bill, Filipino Americans can potentially reap affirmative action benefits independent of the APA grouping because these outreach programs or funds "shall include equitable allocations based on the percentages of Filipinos in local governments in the State of California." The numerical strength of Filipino Americans was indeed a factor in the passage of California Senate Bill 1813. In a letter to State Assemblyman Peter Chacon, United States Congressman Jim Bates (1988) urged the passage of the bill stating that "there are more Filipinos in California than Japanese or Chinese and they are the fastest growing ethnic group in the state. The Filipinos should be separately categorized and given separate funding for outreach programs to serve their own people." The sponsor of the bill, Melecio Jacaban, also made use of the politics of numbers. In a memo to the bill committee, he wrote:

> As you are all aware of, the Filipinos are the third largest
> ethnic group in the state...We estimate that there are
> about 850,000 Filipinos in California at this writing.
> And out of that number, there are approximately half a
> million Filipino American registered voters. This is
> quite a sizeable number of voters, and they could prove
> to be the margin of election victory for some of the legis-
> lators who have a heavy Filipino population in their
> district (Jacaban 1988b).

In a telephone interview that took place soon after the bill was
passed, Melecio Jacaban argued that since affirmative action laws are
based on numbers, Filipino Americans should be receiving a larger share
than the Japanese and Chinese Americans:

> If numbers count, then why should the Filipinos take a
> back seat? Because there are more Filipinos than
> Chinese or Japanese, we are the ones who should be
> dominating the outreach programs for Asian Pacific
> groups. We should be getting the directorship and the
> funding (Jacaban interview 1989).

After the passage of California Senate Bill 1813, California has
devised more detailed categories than those specified by OMB's
Directive 15. As the following examples indicate, the Filipino category
was separated from the Asian and the Pacific Islander categories:

> *California State Employee racial/ethnic categories:*
> White, Black/African American, Hispanic, Asian,
> Filipino, American Indian, Pacific Islander, and Other

> *California Department of Education racial/ethnic categories:*
> American Indian/Alaskan, Asian, Pacific Islander,
> Filipino, Hispanic, Black, White

These more detailed categories indicate that state government racial/ethnic categories can differ from those specified by the federal government. However, it is important to note that in areas where there is Federal-State partnership and cooperation, the racial/ethnic data would be reaggregated into the five standard racial/ethnic categories before they are transmitted to the Federal government. For instance, the racial statistics of Filipino students in California's public universities are reaggregated into the APA category when they are reported to the National Center on Educational Statistics. In other words, even when Filipinos lobbied successfully at the state level for a "Filipino" category distinct from an "Asian American" or "Pacific Islander" category, the federal mandate meant continued Filipino inclusion in the APA category at the national level.

Native Hawaiians and Pacific Islanders

One recent dramatic change to OMB Directive 15 is the disaggregation of the existing "Asian or Pacific Islander" category into the separate categories of "Asian" and "Native Hawaiian or Other Pacific Islander." The creation of the latter category was spurred by the claims of Native Hawaiians that they were ill served by inclusion in the Asian and Pacific Islander category. The "Hawaiian" and "Part Hawaiian" categories first appeared on census schedules in 1960. In 1970, Part Hawaiian was deleted, and in 1980 Guamanian and Samoan were added. Under OMB Directive 15, these subgroups were aggregated into the Asian or Pacific Islander category.

The 1990 Census reported 211,014 Hawaiians, or slightly less than 0.01 percent of the total U.S. population. The population was highly concentrated with almost two-thirds (138,742) residing in the State of Hawaii. The second highest concentration was California with more than one-sixth (34,447) of all Hawaiians. While Native Hawaiians comprised only 2.9 percent of the total Asian and Pacific Islander population, they constituted about 59 percent of the total Pacific Islander population. Data from the 1990 Census illustrated deepening differences in the demographic profile between Asian and Pacific Islander groups (Lott 1998, 95-96). One trend was the decreasing proportion of the Pacific Islander population. Between 1980 and 1990, Pacific Islanders decreased from 7 percent of the total APA population to 5 percent. There were 365,000 Pacific Islanders in 1990 compared to 6.9 million Asians. Differences in nativity status were dramatic. In 1990, only 13 percent of Pacific Islanders were foreign-born, compared to 66 percent of Asians. Socioeconomic indicators also suggested two distinct groups. With respect to education, only 11 percent of Pacific Islanders 25 years and older had a bachelor's degree compared to about 40 percent for Asians. Median household income was $41,583 for Asians and $33,955 for Pacific Islanders (Federal Register 1997b, 92).

Beginning in the early 1990s, Senator Daniel K. Akaka (D-HI) initiated a discussion and subsequent lobbying effort to move Native Hawaiians out of the Asian and Pacific Islander category. Senator Akaka's office had been receiving phone calls from students and alumni of Kamehameha High School complaining of the difficulty of convincing mainland colleges and universities to consider Native Hawaiian admissions and scholarship decisions separate from those of Asian Americans (Kiaaina interview 1999). Native Hawaiian students cited unique social hurdles and economic difficulties in pursuing higher education. College and university administrators countered that in line with OMB Directive 15, Native Hawaiians would be considered as part of the APA category and not be guaranteed any form of "special" consideration.

In March 1993, Senator Akaka contacted then OMB Director Leon Panetta and proposed to reclassify Native Hawaiians in the same category as American Indians and Alaskan Natives. Akaka did not advocate for the creation of a separate category for Native Hawaiians in the belief that many federal agencies would not support the creation of any new categories under Directive 15. His move was to argue for a reconstituted indigenous category that would be called "Native Americans." Akaka believed that Native Hawaiian interests would be best served in this expanded category. He stated: "Like the varying cultures among the hundreds of American Indian tribes and Alaskan Native groups, Native Hawaiians have a unique political and historical relationship with the United States" (House Committee on Post Office and Civil Service: Subcommittee on Census, Statistics and Postal Personnel Hearings 1994, 200). The move to classify Native Hawaiians as Native Americans called attention to the indigenous status of the population and to the past wrongs exacted on Hawaii's native people by the United States.

In 1993 testimony before the Congressional Subcommittee on Census, Statistics and Postal Personnel, Senator Akaka contrasted the indigenous status of Hawaiians to the immigrant status of other APA groups and argued against their classification as Asian or Pacific Islander in Federal record keeping practices:

> As a result, there is the misperception that Native Hawaiians, who number well over 200,000, somehow "immigrated" to the United States like other Asian or Pacific Island groups. This leads to the erroneous impression that Native Hawaiians, the original inhabitants of the Hawaiian Island, no longer exist. We exist, Mr. Chairman. The fact that I am sitting before you today is proof that we exist. And I want to make it clear that Native Hawaiians are Native Americans. While we are culturally Polynesian, we are descendants of the aboriginal people who occupied and exercised sovereignty in the area that now constitutes the State of Hawaii (House Committee Hearings 1994, 200).

Akaka received strong support for his proposal to expand the definition of "American Indian or Alaskan Native" to include Native Hawaiians. In an earlier statement before the Subcommittee, Henry Der of the National Coalition for an Accurate Count of Asians and Pacific Islanders pointed out that some federal statutes already recognized and classified Hawaiians as Native Americans. For example, under Title VI, FTA Circular C4702 defines "Native Americans" as a category that "includes persons who are American Indians, Eskimos, Aleuts, or Native Hawaiians" (House Committee Hearings 1994, 99). The U.S. Commission on Civil Rights also supported Akaka's proposal. Then Chairperson Arthur A. Fletcher stated before the Subcommittee that Native Hawaiians are the indigenous, aboriginal people of Hawaii and that they should be included under the category of American Indian or Alaskan native. Fletcher (p. 259) drew out the implications of this reclassification:

> The Congress should promptly enact legislation enabling Native Hawaiians to develop a political relationship with the Federal Government comparable to that enjoyed by other native peoples in the Nation. Such legislation would encourage the realization of sovereignty and self-determination for Native Hawaiians, a goal that this Advisory Committee strongly endorses.

The proposal to relocate Native Hawaiians to the American Indian or Alaskan Native category subsequently received support from the entire Hawaii Congressional delegation, then Governor John Waihee, and a range of Native Hawaiian organizations.

On the other hand, groups representing American Indians vigorously opposed the proposed reclassification. Some feared that such reclassification would reduce data consistency over time for American Indians, without improving the data available for Native Hawaiians (Edmonston et. al. 1996, 31). They argued that minor changes in terminology and formatting would yield better data for Hawaiians. The

Results of the 1996 Race and Ethnic Targeted Test by the Bureau of the Census (1997, 1-22) found that use of the term "Native Hawaiian" in place of "Hawaiian," combined with listing this category immediately as the first of the APA groups, increased reporting of Hawaiians in the Asian and Pacific Islander targeted sample. This conclusion supported the additional, more minor request by Akaka and others to shift the terminology from Hawaiian to Native Hawaiian.

The more contested issue was over the political legal status of Native Hawaiians. Some Native American representatives feared that Native Hawaiians, when reclassified as Native Americans, would be granted special tribal status akin to the government-to-government relationship, which exists between federally recognized Indian tribes and Alaskan Natives and the federal government. Testifying before the House Subcommittee on the federal measures of race and ethnicity and their implications for the 2000 Census, Senator Akaka sought to allay these concerns: "My proposal...does not, and I repeat does not affect...the political status of Native Hawaiians. That is something that we, as Native Hawaiians, will resolve through the legislative process" (House Committee Hearings 1997, 262). Representative Akaka (House Committee Hearings 1997, 270) submitted an analysis done by Roger Walke of the Congressional Research Service as documentation. This analysis noted that the proposed move of Native Hawaiian to the American Indian and Alaskan Native category might not be as significant as it might seem at first glance. This was because the majority of federal spending on Indian programs was not based on a *racial* classification, but on a government-to-government relationship between the United States and federally recognized tribes. In his analysis, Walke (House Committee Hearings 1997, 272) made a distinction between a racial group and a *genealogical* one based on a chain of kinship relations: "A federally-recognized Indian tribe, no matter what its apparent racial makeup, is assumed to be a genealogical grouping whose kinship ties, to whatever degree of consanguinity required by tribal (or federal) laws, can be adequately demonstrated." Because of this, Walke argued that a shift in racial classification for Native Hawaiians would not imply either "tribal existence" or recognition of a government-to-government relationship. It is interesting to note that while the proposed change was over the 2000 *race* question, the *racial* logic of moving Native Hawaiians into the American Indian and Alaskan Native category never surfaced. Instead, debates swirled around the issues of unique federal status, territorial assignment, and the aggregate profile shifts that a change in classification would precipitate. This case study clearly illustrates that the concept of race is not a biological but a social and political construction.

Towards the end of the hearings, Sally Katzen of the OMB reported that the OMB-appointed Interagency Committee had recommended that the term "Hawaiian" be changed to "Native Hawaiian" but that Hawaiians should continue to be classified in the Asian or Pacific Islander category (House Committee Hearings 1997, 600, 131-132).[6] Principle findings in favor of this classification included: geographically, Hawaiians should be classified with other Pacific Islanders; time series and other analyses would not have to account for the change in classification. More importantly, the report asserted that the reclassification of Hawaiians into the same category as American Indians would confuse the question of special legal status. It would also have a major impact on the social and economic profile of the category since Hawaiians would comprise 9.7 percent of the total population of a combined American Indian, Alaska Native, and Hawaiian category (Federal Register 1997b). Again, it is noteworthy that the OMB recommendations on the 2000 race question were not about race per se, but about geography, special legal status, and record keeping needs.

Advocates of the proposed change in classification were "flabbergasted" when it appeared that OMB would decide that Native Hawaiians would remain in the Asian and Pacific Islander category (Kiaaina interview 1999). Many felt it was a political decision that was not determined by the actual merits of the case. Advocates organized a grassroots campaign to challenge the maintenance of the existing framework of classification. Over 7,000 cards were sent to OMB requesting the change (Federal Register 1997a, 6). Representatives of major Hawaiian service organizations, including Alu Like, the Office of Hawaiian Affairs, and the Department of Hawaiian Homelands meet with Clyde Tucker (Bureau of Labor Statistics) and Nancy Gordon (Census Bureau liaison to OMB) to exchange information and express their concerns.

In a September 8, 1997 letter to Katherine K. Wallman of OMB, three Congress members strongly opposed the recommendation that Native Hawaiians continue to be classified in the Asian and Pacific Islander category. Among other points, they refuted the "geographical basis" for classification and stressed the indigenous status of Native Hawaiians (Abercrombie et. al. 1997, 3):

> While Hawaii is geographically a Pacific island, the circumstances of Native Hawaiians...must be differentiated from other Pacific Islanders...Native Hawaiians are a dispossessed people (see P.L. 103-150, legislation offering a U.S. apology to Native Hawaiians for American complicity in the 1893 overthrow of the Kingdom of Hawaii). This accords them a special status compared to other Pacific island groups in their relationship with the United States.

Placing the issue within an international context, the letter quotes Article 8 of the U.N. Draft Declaration on the Rights of Indigenous Peoples, stating that "Indigenous peoples have the collective and individual right to maintain and develop their distinct identities and characteristics, including the right to identify themselves as indigenous and to be recognized as such (Abercrombie et. al. 1997, 2)." The Congress members urged that the country needed to adhere to this principle and respond to the concerns of its indigenous peoples.

On September 7, 1997, Senator Daniel K. Inouye (D-HI) wrote to Franklin D. Raines, Director of the OMB in response to the Interagency Committee's recommendation.[7] Inouye argued that "if it is the pre-existing sovereign status of the native people of the United States which is the underlying rationale for the American Indian/Alaska Native category, that rationale applies with equal force to Native Hawaiians, and thus is not a credible basis upon which to exclude Native Hawaiians" (Inouye 1997, 3). He concluded that the adoption of recommendations for changes in classification and data gathering would constitute "the single most important instrument in our ability as a nation to ensure that Native Hawaiians are afforded the same rights and opportunities as other Americans" (Inouye 1997, 5).

It was speculated that the OMB staff was faced with two political concerns emanating from the White House. First, the White House did not want to upset American Indians in light of then recent Congressional battles regarding contested amendments to the Department of Interior appropriations bill. Second, the White House wanted to allay the concerns of the Hawaiian delegation with respect to the neglect of Native Hawaiian issues (Kiaaina interview 1999). Faced with competing demands, OMB's Sally Katzen proposed a compromise at a meeting with the Hawaiian delegation that completely surprised Native Hawaiian advocates: Why not put Hawaiians and Pacific Islanders together into a separate category? Her proposal had the political asset of avoiding further conflict with American Indians and satisfying Native Hawaiians, whose statistical numbers had been swamped by other groups in the Asian and Pacific Islander category. The sudden and unexpected prominence in negotiations of a major change in racial and ethnic categories acts as strong evidence supporting the notion of race as a socially and politically constructed concept.

While a version of this proposal was entertained earlier in the Report from the Interagency Committee (Federal Register 1997b, 92-94), the concerns were that it might become difficult to obtain adequate sample data from such a small group. Only a few agencies, such as the Department of Education in its assessment of reading proficiency collect data separately. Substantial costs might be incurred by federal agencies if they had to collect data separately. In addition, it was feared that splitting the Asian and Pacific Islander category would have an impact in those areas (such as Hawaii) where APA populations have significantly inter-married. Individuals with both Asian and Pacific Islander ancestry who would currently respond to a single category, would now have to choose between two categories or declare themselves as "other race" or "multiracial" (Federal Register 1997b, 92-94).

The proposal became official on October 30, 1997. OMB decided to break apart the Asian and Pacific Islander category into two categories:

Asian. A person having origins in any of the original peoples of the Far East, Southeast Asia, or the Indian subcontinent including, for example, Cambodia, China, India, Japan, Korea, Malaysia, Pakistan, the Philippine Islands, Thailand, and Vietnam.

Native Hawaiian or Other Pacific Islander. A person having origins in any of the original peoples of Hawaii, Guam, Samoa, or other Pacific Islands. [8]

In announcing the reclassification, OMB acknowledged the significant efforts waged by Native Hawaiians for changing existing racial categories:

> The Native Hawaiians presented compelling arguments that the standards must facilitate the production of data to describe their social and economic situation and to monitor discrimination against Native Hawaiians in housing, education, employment, and other areas...By creating separate categories, the data on Native

Hawaiians and other Pacific Islander groups will no longer be overwhelmed by the aggregate data of the much larger Asian groups (Federal Register 1997a, 9).

In the wake of the OMB decision, concerns still remain. The National Asian Pacific American Legal Consortium (NAPALC) wrote to Katherine Wallman on April 14, 1999 to express their concerns regarding the recently released Draft Provisional Guidance on the Implementation of the 1997 Standards for the Collection of Federal Data on Race and Ethnicity (1999). The Consortium feared that data on Native Hawaiians and Other Pacific Islanders would be lost due to data quality and confidentiality reasons because they are expected to total less than 0.2 percent of the populations. The Consortium urged that information be provided to the fullest extent possible adding that if significant data is not provided for the Native Hawaiian and Pacific Islander groups, then the goal of creating a separate category is thwarted (NAPALC 1999, 7).

Advocates remain fearful that the Census Bureau might resist implementing the changes in the new directive (Kiaaina interview 1999). For example, the Census Bureau did not create a separate committee for the Native Hawaiian and Other Pacific Islander category within the structure of the Census Advisory Committee. In addition, formatting changes to the census forms did not adequately reflect the changes in classification. It is clear that Native Hawaiian and Pacific Islander advocacy groups will have to vigilantly monitor the implementation of the directive and data collecting efforts.

This case study illustrates that for smaller and more economically impoverished groups such as Native Hawaiians, the inclusion in a panethnic category can mask their specific needs and interests. It also illustrates the power of a small group—in this case, Native Hawaiians—to successfully make claims based on its historic grievances against the

Asked of all persons on Short and Long Forms

Is this person Spanish/Hispanic/Latino?

Mark the "**No**" box if not Spanish/Hispanic/Latino.

☐ No, not Spanish/Hispanic/Latino.

☐ Yes, Mexican, Mexican Am., Chicano

☐ Yes, Puerto Rican

☐ Yes, Cuban

☐ Yes, other Spanish/Hispanic/Latino [*Print group*]

What is this person's race?

Mark one or more races to indicate what this person considers him/herself to be.

White

Black, African Am, or Negro

American Indian or Alaskan Native

[*Print name of enrolled or principal tribe*]

☐ Asian Indian	☐ Native Hawaiian
☐ Chinese	☐ Guamanian or
☐ Filipino	☐ Chamorro
☐ Japanese	☐ Samoan
☐ Vietnamese	☐ Other Pacific Islander - *Print race*
☐ Korean	[*Print name of other Asian and/or Pacific Islander race*]
☐ Other Asian- *Print race*	

☐ Some other race

[*Print name of other race*]

Asked of a sample of persons on Long Form only

What is this person's ancestry or ethnic origin?

[*Print ancestry or ethnic origin*]

(For example: Italian, Jamaican, African Am., Cambodian, Cape Verdean, Norwegian, Dominican, French Canadian, Haitian, Korean, Lebanese, Polish, Nigerian, Mexican, Taiwanese, Ukrainian, and so on.)

Source: Census 2000 Questionnaire "Informational Copy" Form D-61B

United States. Native Hawaiian advocates, lobbying to gain more access to college/university admissions and scholarship awards, ended up *changing* federal classifications: the separation of the Asian and Pacific Islander category *and* the expansion of the minimum set for data on race from four to five groups. The crucial role played by APA legislators supporting the Native Hawaiian effort also reinforces Espiritu's conclusion on the important role ethnic representation plays in political struggles over the census (Espiritu 1992, 131). Finally, the case called attention to the fact that the fight for "appropriate" racial categories is not only waged between interested groups and the state but also between interested groups themselves—in this case, between Native Hawaiians and Native Americans.

MULTIRACIALS

Like the case study of Native Hawaiians, this case study documents how multiracial Asians have challenged the existing racial classification and substantially modified the ways individuals classify themselves on census forms. As a new millennium looms, the United States is set to become more a nation of blended races and ethnic groups than it has ever been. By 2050, demographers calculate that the percentage of the U.S. population that claims multiple ancestries will likely triple, from the current 7 percent to 21 percent (Puente and Kasindorf 1999). APA multiracials will comprise a significant proportion of this increase. In an analysis of multiracial households in the United States, Chew, Eggebeen, and Uhlenberg (1989) report that a significant number of these households comprise a person of some Asian ancestry through marriage, birth, and/or adoption. It is estimated that in the post-civil rights era, approximately half of U.S.-born Chinese and Japanese Americans are married to whites (Jacobs and Labov 1995). A 1990 California survey found that 25 percent of Asian-ancestry children in the state were the product of both Asian and European-descent parents

(Federal Register 1995). The Japanese American community has the highest rate of interracial marriage and of multiracial children. According to the 1990 Census, there were 39 percent more Japanese/white births than monoracial Japanese American births that year (U.S. Bureau of the Census 1992).

The state—as represented by the Census Bureau—has routinely distorted or disregarded the reality of interracial families and multiracial individuals. Through the categories it uses to count and classify ethnic and racial groups, the census has often legitimated the hypodescent rule, bolstered the claim of white racial purity, and imposed an arbitrary monoracial identity on individuals of mixed parentage. As an example, the 1920 Census stipulated that "any mixture of White and some other race was to be reported according to the race of the person who was not White" (U.S. Bureau of the Census 1979, 52). In the post-civil rights period, OMB's Directive 15 provides that "[t]he category which most closely reflects the individual's recognition in his community should be used for purposes of reporting on persons who are of mixed racial and/or ethnic origins." The presumption of monoracial identification is evident from the language of this provision, "which takes as given that a mixed-race person will be identified monoracially by 'his community'" (Payson 1996, 1257).

In an attempt to assert their multiracial heritage, some multiracial persons have ignored census instructions to "[f]ill ONE circle for the race that the person considers himself/herself to be" by marking two or more boxes. However, since the census scanners are designed to read only one marked box, such a person ended up as monoracial based on whichever box was marked more firmly (Payson 1996, 1261). In the 1990 Census, nearly 10 million persons marked the "Other" race category, making it one of the fastest growing racial categories. Although the bulk of the growth came from a shift in racial identity among Hispanics,[9] the growth can also be explained in part by the increase in the number of multiracials who used the "Other" category to write in "multiracial," "biracial," "mixed-race" or other alternatives to the monoracial categories (McKenney and Cresce 1992). However, the Census Bureau routinely reassigned such persons to one of the OMB's distinct racial categories based on the first race listed or the race of the nearest neighbor who gave the same response in the Hispanic category (Payson 1996, 1270). As legal theorist Kenneth E. Payson, the child of a Japanese mother and a white father, laments (Payson 1996, 1234):

> While I am able to explain that I am of both Asian and European descent to curious people on the street, I am not able to do so with respect to federal agencies. Were I to describe myself as a mixed-race to a federal agency, my race would be reassigned to one of the distinct racial categories outlined in the Office of Management and Budget (OMB) Statistical Policy Directive Number 15.

Among several APA groups, the high reporting of "European" as a first ancestry may reflect personal attempts to report on multiracial identities (Edmonston and Schultz 1995, 150).

Since the 1980s, multiracial advocacy groups[10] have consistently challenged the notion of mutually exclusive racial categories embodied in the "single-race checkoff" policy. In June 1993, the Association of MultiEthnic Americans (AMEA), the first nationwide group of its kind in the United States, testified before the Census Subcommittee of the U.S. House of Representatives and proposed that the Census Bureau add a multiracial category to the 2000 Census (House Committee Hearings 1994). Under the vigorous leadership of Executive Director Susan Graham, Project RACE (Reclassify All Children Equally) also actively lobbied for the multiracial category. Whereas Project RACE framed the multiracial category as a "self-esteem" issue, APA organizations such as the Asian and Pacific Islander American Health Forum and Hapa Issues Forum viewed it as an opportunity to generate more accurate data on their communities and to educate the larger public about race (Guillermo interview 1999; Mayeda interview 1999). As Greg Mayeda, co-founder Hapa Issues Forum, stated:

> Hapa Issues Forum was more interested in changing people's perceptions about race, generally speaking, and the census was one avenue. We kind of got thrown into the census debate. We were never motivated by a touchy feely good thing, feeling validated by the government. There was something that was clearly wrong and inefficient [about the old census categories], and we were willing to work on it. If anything, we were trying to make society conform to our reality rather than the other way around (Mayeda interview 1999).

The public education sector has been the source of much of the public pressure for a review of the current OMB race and ethnicity classifications, as parents of multiracial children became increasingly concerned about the (mis)classification of their children in public schools. In a survey of U.S. public schools, only about 5 percent of the schools used a general multiracial category; the others employed the standard racial/ethnic categories as specified by OMB's Directive 15 (U.S. Department of Education 1996, iv). From the perspective of the multiracial/ethnic families, forcing a multiracial/ethnic child to favor one parent over the other offends the child's personal dignity and interferes with his/her development of self-esteem. It also constitutes an unwarranted intrusion by the government into the families' fundamental right of privacy. As Graham, executive director of Project RACE, stated:

> The reality is that multiracial children who wish to embrace all of their heritage should be allowed to do so. They should not be put in the position of denying one of their parents to satisfy an arbitrary government requirement (House Committee Hearings 1997, 286-87).

Sociologist Reginald Daniel, who has done extensive research on multiracial issues and is himself a multiracial, likened the "single-race checkoff" policy to "psychological oppression," stating that the most consistent grievance expressed by multiracials centers "around not being able to indicate their identity accurately on official forms that request information on race/ethnicity" (p. 395). The growth and activism of the multiracial movement—along with increasing skepticism of the continuing utility of Directive 15—forced the federal government, in its preparation for the 2000 census, to launch a comprehensive review of the race and ethnicity categories.

Among Asian Pacific Americans, the interests of the panethnic APA group and those of multiracial Asians diverged and even collided over how best to classify and count multiracials in the 2000 Census. Denouncing the government's past attempts to wedge mixed-raced Americans into one rigid racial category, multiracial advocacy groups and their supporters favored adding a mixed-race category under which multiracial people could check all the boxes that applied. It is important to note that proponents of the multiracial category did not challenge the continuation of current categories but instead requested an expansion of categories (Lott 1998, 98). However, following the stance of most civil rights groups, many APA organizations lobbied against the inclusion of a multiracial category, arguing that it could substantially change the APA count and thus cause the community to lose hard-won gains in civil rights, education, and electoral arenas (Nash 1997, 23). For example, while multiracial Asians consider the meaning and importance of the racial/ethnic categories to be highly personal matters, NAPALC opposed the multiracial category because:

> the issue of whether to add multiracial to the existing racial categories is more than a personal issue. The data is being collected for use as a basis for important research, policy development, and resource allocation.

The data is also extremely important to monitor and fight discrimination, both institutional and otherwise (House Committee Hearings 1997, 414).

The Consortium then concluded that "adding a multiracial category would undermine the effectiveness of civil rights enforcement agencies because of the inconsistent counts and the uncertainties it introduces in being able to analyze trends" (House Committee Hearings 1997, 418). In another opposing statement, the National Coalition for an Accurate Count of Asians and Pacific Islanders questioned the appropriateness of including a multiracial category alongside racial minority categories that are protected under civil rights and other federal programs:

Like individuals of single race group, persons of biracial or multiracial backgrounds seek acknowledgment and identification through the race question. Because existing federal civil rights laws and programs are premised largely on exclusive membership in a racial group, it becomes difficult to ascertain the salience of biraciality or multiraciality in relationship to the specific provisions and intended benefits of these Federal laws and programs...What can be stated about common experiences shared by biracial or multiracial persons?...biracial or multiracial persons have the burden to document what distinct experiences or disadvantagement, in contrast to persons of protected single race backgrounds, they have had because of their biraciality or multiraciality before the decision to establish a multiracial or biracial category would be appropriate (*Hearings* 1994, 96).

The arguments in opposition to the multiracial category essentially deny the possibility or the appropriateness of multiple affiliations and pose the interests of multiracials—the right to claim their full heritage—in opposition to the civil rights needs of APAs-the possible loss of political clout and economic benefits that are tied to numbers. For their part, multiracial Asians have charged that APA community leaders claim multiracial Asians because "it is politically propitious and advantageous" (Houston 1991, 56) but that APA organizations have largely ignored or marginalized multiracial concerns. They point to the fact that even today, few Asian American Studies programs in the country incorporate multiracial issues into their curricula; and few APA organizations have multiracial representatives in their leadership circles. Finally, some APA leaders call attention to the political importance of self-identification. As Tessie Guillermo, director of the Asian and Pacific Islander American Health Forum, stated, "I think the civil rights community has to remember that self-identification is a civil liberty" (Guillermo interview 1999).

Confirming the concerns of APA civil rights organizations, the preliminary survey findings suggest that the provision of multiracial options may well lead to declines in the proportions reporting as Asian and Pacific Islanders. In May 1995, the OMB-established Interagency Committee asked the Bureau of Labor Statistics to design a supplement to its Current Population Survey that would obtain data on the effect of having a multiracial category among the list of races. This survey found that about 1.5 percent of the population reported as multiracial and that the inclusion of a multiracial category decreased the proportion of Asian and Pacific Islanders from 3.83 to 3.25 percent (U.S. Department of Labor 1995). Similarly, the National Content Survey (NCS), conducted by the Census Bureau in 1996, found that when the multiracial category was included, about 1 percent of the respondents reported as multiracial. Of those identifying as multiracial in that sample, 30 percent partially identified themselves as Asian and Pacific Islander (House Committee Hearings 1997, 416). While the study found that the inclusion of a multiracial category had no statistically significant effect on the percentages of larger race groups, it indicated that the proportions reporting as APA declined, from 4 percent to 2.7 percent-a possible decline of at least 3,250,000 APAs. (U.S. Bureau of the Census 1996, 26; House Committee Hearings 1997, 416). Finally, the results of the 1996 Race and Ethnic Targeted Test further confirms that the inclusion of a multiracial category and the provision of instructions to "mark all that apply." while not statistically significant, nevertheless reduced reporting of Asians and Pacific Islanders in the targeted samples (House Committee Hearings 1997, 416).

In December 1996, citing the NCS results, the Census Advisory Committee on the Asian and Pacific Islander Populations recommended that the "OMB Directive 15 should not be revised to include the multiracial category" (Census Advisory Committee 1996). In May 1997, the Asian and Pacific Islander Census Advisory Committee, along with the Census Advisory Committees on the African American, American Indian, and Alaska Native, and Hispanic populations, jointly recommended that the "Census Bureau does not add a multiracial category in Census 2000 form, and that no separate instructions be added for multiple responses in the race question" (Census Advisory Committees 1997).

After four years of heated debate, the OMB's Interagency Committee for the Review of the Racial and Ethnic Standards rejected the proposal to create a separate multiracial category. Instead, in July 1997, the 30-agency task force recommended that Directive 15 be amended to permit multiracial Americans to "mark one or more" racial category when identifying themselves for the census and other government programs. Critics of the inclusion of a multiracial category were generally supportive of the "check one or more" proposal because they perceived it to be less likely to reduce the total count of their respective groups (Fiore 1997). The Interagency Committee rejected the creation of a new multiracial category because committee members feared that the category would generate yet another population group and add to racial tension and fragmentation. The Association of MultiEthnic Americans disagreed with the Committee's reasoning:

We disagree that a multiracial/ethnic classification would create a new population group. The population groups to which they refer already exist and are growing rapidly. We also take issue with the opinion that a multiracial/ethnic classifier would add to racial tension and fragment our population. The essence of the multiracial/ethnic population is one of racial/ethnic unity. As we have stated before, our community is specially situated to confront racial and interethnic issues because of the special experiences and understanding we acquire in the intimacy of our families and our personalities. Of all populations, ours has the unique potential to become the stable core around which the ethnic pluralism of the United States can be united (House Committee Hearings 1997, 573-74).

However, the Association of MultiEthnic Americans and allied organizations and individuals regard the Interagency Committee's recommendations as necessary and even revolutionary. They believe that, if implemented appropriately, the proposed changes to OMB Directive 15 will meet their most fundamental concern: the acknowledgement by the state that multiracial/ethnic people do exist and have a right to be counted as such.

The controversy then shifted to the tabulation of multiple racial responses. The 1997 standards require that at a minimum, the total number of persons identifying with more than one race must be reported. Beside this provision, it is still undecided as to how federal agencies will tabulate the new racial information, particularly what they will do with the overlap. In a 1998 joint report to the Census Bureau, the four Census Advisory Committees on the race and ethnic populations made the following recommendations:

1) That the OMB prepare two sets of data tabulations: one set would be the "full distribution" that preserves all of the multiple responses; and a second set that would collapse the multiple

combinations back to the OMB standard six racial categories and would be used for redistricting, affirmative action, voting rights, distribution of funds for government programs, and other mandates to reduce racial inequality.

2) That the following approach be used to collapse the combination responses back to the OMB standard six groups: individuals who check both a nonwhite majority group and white would be classified as a member of the specific racial minority.

At the time of their report to the Census Bureau (June 1998), the four committees had yet to reach a consensus on how individuals who check off two or more racial minorities would be classified. For its part, the Asian and Pacific Islander Advisory Committee had recommended assigning the multiple minority individual to the smallest minority. The Committee further proposed that whenever the response is a Black and Asian racial combination, it should be reassigned to Black or Asian depending upon whether the respondent lives in or near a Black or Asian community; otherwise, the response should be assigned equally randomly to Black and Asian. In all, the recommendations of the Census Advisory Committees represented a compromise, designed to recognize the concerns of multiracial individuals and organizations as well as to protect the rights and interests of historically underrepresented groups. In contrast, the Association of MultiEthnic Americans (AMEA) vigorously opposes the reassignment of multiracial individuals to monoracial categories. Ramona Douglass, AMEA president since 1994, argues that such reassignment would defeat the purpose of the multiple responses and expects that AMEA will pursue litigation if reassignment of any kind occurs (Douglass interview 1999).

In August 1999, for the purpose of redistricting data, the Department of Justice selected the "full distribution approach"—or the "PL 63 Matrix" approach[11]—to tabulate the "more than one race" census responses. Multiracial advocacy organizations praised this decision since the full distribution approach reports multiple responses in the most expansive and detailed way possible-with no reassignment of multiple responses to monoracial categories. Under this, people would be placed in a racial category that matches the combination of races they list. In all, the various combinations would give the United States 63 officially recognized races. However, for non-redistricting issues, as of this writing, no decision has been made on how to allocate the multiple check-off responses. It is expected that the decision will be put off until the 2000 Census data comes out and studies are done on it.

Conclusion

The decennial national census has increasingly become *the* site of demands for political recognition. Until very recently, census categories were created and strategically employed to politically disenfranchise and discriminate against groups of color (Anderson 1988). In the wake of the civil rights movement, by contrast, state definitions of race and ethnicity have been increasingly used to monitor discriminatory trends and for the enforcement of equal opportunity laws. Given this, the census has become the focus of intense debates over the recognition and definition of groups. Groups realize the political value of racial categorization, along with the strategic deployment of "numbers," in highlighting inequalities, arguing for resources, lobbying for particular forms of redistricting, and other policy debates. Strategic APA political actors, aware that hundreds of millions of dollars-not to mention political fortunes-are dispersed based on data gathered from responses to the racial and ethnic questions, actively seek to influence the content of the race item on the decennial census. Over the past several decades, APAs have been quite successful in challenging and expanding existing racial and ethnic categories to address specific concerns and interests. Census numbers are also extremely important to APAs because relative to other groups like African Americans, so little data is generated elsewhere on their population. The absence of census data on APAs means that they are generally not sufficiently counted and acknowledged in social science and policy discussions of broad racial trends.

Asian Pacific American campaigns for recognition have not been waged solely to secure state-sponsored benefits but also to advance distinctive forms of identity claims. Some multiracial organizations have argued for the creation of a separate multiracial category as an issue of "self-esteem"—not as an issue of seeking underrepresented status. Other groups, such as Native Hawaiians, may be responding to both historical oppression and contemporary forms of inequality by asserting specific identities that question their current classification. What is interesting is how the census becomes the site of distinctive identity claims, how they are handled through the existing framework of state definitions, and how classification correspondingly shapes particular policies.

While APA accomplishments and gains regarding census classification are impressive given their small political base, the overall impact of these achievements on the quality of APA lives has been limited. Part of the problem is the generation and publication of quality data. In the Native Hawaiian and Other Pacific Islander case, for example, NAPALC fears that data would be lost due to data quality and confidentiality reasons since the category constitutes less than 0.2 percent of the population. The Consortium has urged that data be collected and provided to the fullest extent possible. If significant data cannot be gathered in a timely fashion for Native Hawaiian and Other Pacific Islander groups, then the goal of creating a separate category may fail to address the initial concerns that generated it (NAPALC 1999).

The collection and dissemination of data is an important, but insufficient step towards addressing APA social, economic, and political concerns. Data is always subject to multiple interpretations, and distinct policy options can emerge from a common set of trend lines and observed disparities by race (along with other axes of stratification). One issue centers on the tabulation of results. APA political actors have been concerned with the tabulation procedures for the multiracial count in Census 2000. At issue is not only the different numbers generated by distinct tabulation procedures, but the meaning of these counts for the established relationship of collecting and reporting race data to enforce civil rights laws.

Another important concern is to assess the impact of this data on specific policy initiatives to improve APA life chances. Our sense has been that while APA categories are used for administrative reporting and record keeping, the data generated has neither been widely disseminated nor sufficiently analyzed. Thus the generation of categories and data obtained under these rubrics has not translated into substantive policy outcomes. The Census Bureau has decided that untabulated census data from the 2000 Census will be made available via the internet for public access. How this data will be used in policy discussions will remain unclear for several years after the census.

We recommend and urge that APAs be more attentive to the publication and use of the data collected on APAs. They need to strategically utilize the data on APAs in the advancement of specific policy proposals. APAs also need to actively follow up on what federal agencies do, or fail to do, with APA data. In pursuing these actions, the focus extends beyond the process of simply adding up and demonstrating the "numbers" to make claims, but to deal with the complex social issues that lurk behind them.

One hopeful sign is the recent Executive Order (June 7, 1999) issued by President Bill Clinton to "improve the quality of life of Asian

Americans and Pacific Islanders through increased participation in Federal programs where they may be undeserved (e.g., health, human services, education, housing, labor, transportation, and economic and community development)." Relevant to the issues addressed in our chapter are Section 2a and Section 5a which call for the collection of data related to Asian American and Pacific Islanders, and Section 2c and Section 5c which call for ways to "foster research and data on Asian Americans and Pacific Islanders, including research and data on public health." The Executive Order establishes the President's Advisory Commission on Asian Americans and Pacific Islanders in the Department of Health and Human Services. It is important that this Commission advise the President with respect to the issues considered here, and underscores the importance of quality data as a policymaking resource.

Racial and ethnic classification is an eminently political process, subject to change under specific historical contexts. One might interpret our selective case studies as a challenge to the appropriateness and utility of the APA category. We caution against such a reading. APAs continue to be "lumped by race" in employment practices, cultural representations, and as victims of anti-Asian violence. Aggregate data is necessary for discerning broad trends and to comply with existing laws and practices. For example, the Equal Employment Opportunity Commission collects compliance data using the inclusive APA category. Similarly, the Voting Rights Act and the redistricting process require data on the collective group, not on the individual subgroups. In fact, no federal legislation requires the Census Bureau to provide 100 percent data for the Asian Pacific subgroups, but only for the APAs as a whole (Espiritu 1992, 132).

That said, a delicate balancing act between the needs/interests of the larger category and that of the individual subgroups needs to be maintained. Summary statistics (regarding educational attainment, income, and housing trends) mask the heterogeneity within the category.

Different numbers need to be invoked in different policy contexts. A wide gap in subgroup profiles can lead, as in the case of Native Hawaiians, to a radical reconsideration of the category itself.

So who makes the call with respect to balancing competing demands and making political claims to state institutions? Thomas P. Kim suggests that there are several different "groups" of APA political elites involved in census politicking (Kim correspondence, 1999). There are elected legislators like Senator Akaka, lobbying organizations like NAPALC, insider/appointees like Acting Assistant Attorney General for the Civil Rights Division Bill Lann Lee, and the APA members on the Census Advisory Committee. A loose collection of political consultants and elected officials also emerges around census and redistricting debates, reflecting an interest in consolidating particular voting blocs for future electoral campaigns.

On the issue of political empowerment, it may well be that only groups with sufficient political capital can effectively lobby for change. Other groups may be marginalized, and not sufficiently "connected" to present their concerns to appropriate bodies. For example, other Pacific Islander groups did not appear to have been consulted by OMB officials regarding the creation of the Native Hawaiian or Pacific Islander category. They were simply relocated as a consequence of balancing competing demands between those groups that had voice in the political process. A question for continual study is who gets to speak and what specific interests do they represent. APAs must be attentive to the organization of political actions in the politics of racial and ethnic classification.

We are at an important juncture with respect to racial and ethnic classification and data. Under the guise of "colorblind" policies and practices, conservatives are urging the abandonment of racial and ethnic classification-specifically their use in record keeping procedures and in establishing eligibility requirements for various programs. For instance, former Speaker of the House Newt Gingrich tied his support of a multiracial category to efforts to end affirmative action. Scholarly works in anthropology, genetics, and other fields have rejected biologically based notions of race, rendering any form of classification as suspect. While race is no longer seen as a biological "fact," the reality of race as a social concept persists.

The notion that race is a social concept is amply illustrated by the history of the Census. Classifications utilized since the first census was taken reveal the inherent fluidity of racial categories, and how demographic changes, shifts in collective attitudes, panethnic coalitions, and individual identity formation constantly shape and re-shape the processes of classification. APAs have been subject to specific forms of classification from "above"—by federal, state, and local policies and practices—and have challenged such classification from "below"—through grassroots mobilization, political elites, and organized lobbying groups—to advance their own distinctive political claims for recognition.

APAs have often been rendered "invisible" by the broader emphasis on black/white relations. As a consequence, policy debates regarding health, immigration, labor, housing, and economic and community development, among other areas, have not taken into account nor discerned the impact of different policy initiatives on APA communities. Debates over census classification need to be situated in this context. Demands for specific categories are driven by the issue of appropriate "representation," and the perception of unique issues and concerns not addressed, or disguised, by a particular group's current location.

The goal of establishing racial and ethnic categories that are conceptually valid, measurable, exclusive and exhaustive, and reliable over time is an illusory one. That said, we do not argue for abandoning the use of racial and ethnic categories. Without some form of classification, we cannot monitor and track invidious forms of racial inequality and discrimination. The current debate on police profiling of black motorists illustrates this issue. To get at the "reality" and scope of this problem, one needs to engage in racial record keeping that employs specific categories. However "unscientific" and imprecise these categories may be, some form of racial/ethnic classification is needed to discern trends and discriminatory patterns.

The determination of these categories is a policy issue. Categories are the result of processes of intense negotiation between state institutions and different groups advancing claims for recognition. As we have seen, the OMB has had to weigh different claims, assess their merits, and consider their impact on different federal agencies and their practices.

This process is not exclusively confined to the dealings between the state and a particular group. In the Native Hawaiian case, American Indians voiced their concern and dismay over the proposed relocation of Native Hawaiians to their "racial" category under Directive 15. The point is that different groups often contest the boundaries of state definitions in ways that bring them into conflict with each other. In so doing, the broader dynamics of racialization in the United States are revealed.

Outcomes with respect to census classification are never easy to predict, and no clear, coherent principles exist to guide and frame the decision-making. The process, despite claims to the contrary, is inherently political. Specific forms of classification are the result of dynamic and complex negotiations between state interests, panethnic demands, and ethnic-specific challenges. APA census categories both reflect and help create group identities, influence the formation of public policy, and shape the popular discourse about race in the U.S.

Endnotes

[1] Both authors made equal contributions to this chapter, and alphabetical order determined the order of names. We are truly grateful to Paul Ong for his helpful comments, support, and prodding throughout the project. We are also greatly indebted to Thomas Kim for his invaluable assistance in all phases of the research process, and Monali Sheth for her interview work on the section on Asian Indians. We would like to thank our numerous respondents for generously giving of their time and expert insights. Lastly, we want to acknowledge each other's help and support. In an often competitive and isolating academic environment, it is truly a pleasure to engage in a collective project with a kindred spirit.

[2] "Earning his Stripes," Newsmaker Column, *Asian Week*, October 11, 1997, 9. On a 1997 Oprah Winfrey show, Woods complicated his identity further by declaring himself "Cablinasian"-an amalgamation of Caucasian, Black, Indian, and Asian.

[3] In the past several years, for example, the Census has studied whether to maintain the term "Guamanian" or use the term "Chamorro." The 1997 RAETT study observed the following trend: "Recently, 'Chamorro' has become more preferable to some, much like 'African American' has in the Black population...Younger and more educated respondents preferred 'Chamorro' and older respondents preferred 'Guamanian' (RAETT 1997, 2-15)." The final compromise was to use both terms in the check-off category.

[4] Newt Gingrich, prior to his resignation from Congress, used the issue of a multiracial category to illustrate the indeterminacy of all racial categories, and to advocate for their abolition in government data collection: "America is too big and too diverse to categorize each and every one of us into four rigid racial categories...It is time for the government to stop perpetuating racial divisiveness" (Federal Measures of Race and Ethnicity and the Implications for the 2000 Census 1997, 662). Some have done just that. In 1998, then-California Governor Pete Wilson ordered state agencies to stop tracking data on women and minority-owned businesses in the state's $4 billion public contracting system.

[5] See Directive No. 15, Race and Ethnic Standards for Federal Statistics and Administrative Reporting, 43 Fed. Reg. 19, 260, 19269 (1978).

[6] The Interagency Commission for the Review of the Racial and Ethnic Standards was established by the OMB in March 1994. Its members come from more than 30 federal agencies that represent the many and diverse Federal needs for data on race and ethnicity, including statutory requirements for such data (Federal Register July, 9, 1997, 20).

[7] Inouye had special credibility on this issue. Not only did he represent Hawaiian constituencies, but he had served on the Senate Committee for Indian Affairs for 19 years, including 8 years as its Chair.

[8] The Native Hawaiian or Other Pacific Islander category includes the following Pacific Islander groups reported in the 1990 Census: Carolinian, Fijian, Cesarean, Melanesian, Micronesian, Northern Mariana Islander, Plain, Papua New Guanine, Ponapean (Pohnpelan), Polynesian, Solomon Islander, Tahitian, Tarawa Islander, Tokelauan, Tongan, Trukese (Chuukese), and Yapese.

[9] Between 1980 and 1990, many Hispanics abandoned the white racial category in favor of the "other" racial category.

[10] Initially, multiracial advocacy groups were organized by parents in interracial unions who advocated on behalf of their mixed-race children. However, the people who are currently challenging the monoracial paradigm and resisting monoracial labels are predominantly the offspring of interracial couples (Payson 1996, 1233, n. 16).

[11] For the sole purpose of the 2000 Census, OMB has granted an exception to the Census Bureau to use a category called "Some Other Race." Thus, there are 63 mutually exclusive and exhaustive categories of race, including six categories for those who marked only one race and 57 for those who marked more than one race. (See Draft Provisional Guidance on the Implementation of the 1997 Standards For the Collection of Federal Data on Race and Ethnicity (1999).

References

Abercrombie, Hon. N., Akaka, Hon. D.K., and Mink, Hon. P.T. (1997, September). Letter to Katherine Wallman, Chief Statistician at the Office of Information and Regulatory Affairs,Office of Management and Budget.

Almirol, E.B. (1988). "Exclusion and Institutional Barriers in the University System: The Filipino Experience." In G. Okihiro, S. Hune, A. Hansen, and J. Liu (Eds.), *Reflections on Shattered Windows: Promises and Prospects for Asian American Studies.* Pullman, WA: Washington State University.

Anderson, M. (1988). *The American Census: A Social History.* New Haven, CT: Yale University Press.

American Anthropology Association. (1997a, October). *Anthropology Newsletter*, 38(7). Washington, DC: Author.

_____. (1997b, December). *Anthropology Newsletter*, 38(9). Washington, DC: Author.

_____. (1998a, February). *Anthropology Newsletter*, 39(2). Washington, DC: Author.

_____. (1998b, March). *Anthropology Newsletter*, 39(3). Washington, DC: Author.

_____. (1998c, May). *Anthropology Newsletter*, 39(5). Washington, DC: Author.

_____. (1998d, September). *Anthropology Newsletter*, 39(6). Washington, DC: Author.

Bates, J. (1988, April 5). Letter to Assemblyman Peter Chacon, 79th District, CA.

Cabezas, A., Shinagawa, L., and Kawaguchi, G. (1986-87). "New Inquiries into the Labor Force: Pilipino Americans in California." *Amerasia Journal*, 13(1):1-21.

Census Advisory Committee on the Asian and Pacific Islander Populations. (1996). *Minutes and Report of Committee Recommendation, December 5-6, 1996.* Washington, DC: Government Printing Office.

Census Advisory Committees on the African American, American Indian and Alaska Native, Asian and Pacific Islander, and Hispanic Populations. (1997). *Minutes and Report of Committee Recommendations, May 22-23, 1997.* Washington, DC: Government Printing Office.

_____. (1998). *Minutes and Report of Committee Recommendations, June 4-5, 1998.* Washington, DC: Government Printing Office.

Chan, S. (1991). *Asian Americans: An Interpretive History.* Boston, MA: Twayne.

Chung, L.A. (1991, June 25). "S.F. Includes Asian Indians in Minority Law." *San Francisco Chronicle.*

Colker, R. (1996). *Hybrid: Bisexuals, Multiracials, and Other Misfits under American Law.* New York, NY: New York University Press.

Edmonston, B., Goldstein, J., and Lott, J.T. (1996). *Spotlight on Heterogeneity: The Federal Standards for Racial and Ethnic Classification.* Summary of a Workshop. Washington, DC: National Academy Press.

Edmonston, B. and Schultze, C. (1995). *Modernizing the U.S. Census.* Washington, DC: National Academy Press.

Eggebeen, D., Chew, K. and Uhlenburg, P. (1989). "American Children of Multiracial Households." *Sociological Perspectives*, 32: 65-85.

Espiritu, Y.L. (1992). *Asian American Panethnicity: Bridging Institutions and Identities.* Philadelphia, PA: Temple University Press.

_____. (1995). *Filipino American Lives.* Philadelphia, PA: Temple University Press.

Federal Register. (1978). Directive No. 15, Race and Ethnic Standards for Federal Statistics and Administrative Reporting, 43 Fed. Reg. 19,260, 19269.

_____. (1995, August 28). "Standards for the Classification of Federal Data on Race and Ethnicity."
http://www.whitehouse.gov/WH/EOP/OMB/html/fedreg/race-ethnicity.html

_____. (1997a, October 30). "Revisions to the Standards for the Classification of Federal Data on Race and Ethnicity."
http://www.whitehouse.gov/WH/EOP/OMB/html/fedreg/Ombdir15.html

_____. (1997b, July 9) "Recommendations from the Interagency Committee for the Review of the Racial and Ethnic Standards to the Office of Management and Budget Concerning Changes to the Standards for the Classification of Federal Data on Race and Ethnicity."
http://www.whitehouse.gov/WH/EOP/OMB/html/fedreg/Directive_15.html

Fiore, F. (1997, October 30). "Multiple Race Choices to be Allowed on 2000 Census." *Los Angeles Times*.

Goldberg, D.T. (1997). *Racial Subjects: Writing on Race in America*. New York, NY and London, UK: Routledge.

Haney-Lopez, I.F. (1996). *White By Law: The Legal Construction of Race*. New York, NY: New York University Press.

House of Representatives, Committee on Government Reform and Oversight: Subcommittee on Government Management, Information, and Technology. (1997, March 23, April 22, and July 25). *Hearings on the Federal Measures of Race and Ethnicity and the Implications for the   2000 Census*. 105th Congress, 1st Session, Serial No. 105-57.

House of Representatives, Committee on Post Office and Civil Service: Subcommittee on Census, Statistics and Postal Personnel. (1993, April 14, June 30, July 29, November 3). *Hearings on the Review of Federal Measurements of Race and Ethnicity*. 103rd Congress, 1st Session, Serial No. 103-7.

Houston, V.H. (1991). "The Past Meets the Future: A Cultural Essay." *Amerasia Journal*, 17(1): 53-56.

Ignacio, L.F. (1976). *Asian American and Pacific Islanders (Is There Such an Ethnic Group?)* San Jose, CA: Pilipino Development Associates.

Inouye, Hon. D.K. (1997, September 7). Letter to Franklin D. Raines, Director of the Office of Management and Budget.

Jacaban, M.H. (1988a, February 24). "SB 1813 Gives Filipinos Full Benefits of Affirmative Action Law." *Philippine News*.

_____. (1988b). Memo to the Committee on Senate Bill 1813. San Fernando Valley Office of Senator Alan Robbins.

Jacobs, J., and Labov, T. (1995, August 21). "Sex Differences in Intermarriage: Asian Exceptionalism Reconsidered." Paper presented at the American Sociological Association Meeting, Washington, DC.

Kaplan, D.L. (1979). "Politics and the Census." *Asian and Pacific Census Forum*, 6(2): 1+.

Kim, T.P. (1999, June 30). Correspondence.

Ling, S.H. (1989). "The Mountain Movers: Asian American Women's Movement in Los Angeles." *Amerasia Journal*, 15(1): 51-67.

Lott, J.T. (1998). *Asian Americans: From Racial Category to Multiple Identities*. Walnut Creek, CA: AltaMira Press.

Masada, S. (1970, October 9). "Stockton's Yellow Seed." *Pacific Citizen*.

McKenney, N.R. and Cresce, A.R. (1992, April). "Measurement of Ethnicity in the United States: Experiences of the U.S. Census Bureau." Paper presented at the joint Canada-United States Conference on Measurement of Ethnicity, Ottawa, Canada.

Misir, D.N. (1996). "The Murder of Navroze Mody: Race, Violence, and the Search for Order." *Amerasia Journal*, 22(2): 55-76.

Nash, P.T. (1997). "Will the Census Go Multiracial?" *Amerasia Journal*, 23(1): 17-27.

National Asian Pacific American Legal Consortium. (1999, April 14). Letter to Katherine Waldman.

Nee, V. and Sanders, J. (1985). "The Road to Parity: Determinants of the Socioeconomic Achievements of Asian Americans." *Ethnic and Racial Studies*, 8(1): 75-93.

Office of Management and Budget. (1999, October 6). "Draft Provisional Guidance on the Implementation of the 1997 Standards For the Collection of Federal Data on Race and ethnicity." Prepared by the Tabulation Working Group of the Interagency Committee for the Review of Standards for Data on Race and Ethnicity.
http://www.whitehouse.gov/OMB/inforeg/race.pdf

Okamura, J.Y. and Agbayani, A.R. (1997). "Pamantasan: Filipino American Higher Education." In M.P.P. Root (Ed.), *Filipino Americans: Transformation and Identity* Thousand Oaks, CA: Sage.

Omi, M. (1997). "Racial Identity and the State: Contesting the Federal Standards for Classification." In P. Wong (Ed.), *Race, Ethnicity, and Nationality in the United States: Toward the Twenty-First Century*. Boulder, CO: Westview Press.

Patterson, O. (1997, July 11). "The Race Trap." *New York Times*, 146: A21(N), A27(L)

Payson, K.E. (1996). "Check One Box: Reconsidering Directive No. 15 and the Classification of Mixed-Race People." *California Law Review*, 84: 1233-1291.

Peterson, W. (1983). "Politics and the Measurement of Ethnicity." In W. Alonso and P. Starr (Eds.), *The Politics of Numbers*. New York, NY: Russell Sage Foundation.

Puente, M. and Kasindorf, M. (1999, September 7). "Blended Races Making True Melting Pot." *USA Today*.

Rabaya, V. (1971). "I Am Curious (Yellow?)." In A. Tachiki, E. Wong, and F. Odo (Eds.), *Roots: An Asian American Reader*. Los Angeles, CA: UCLA Asian American Studies Center.

Root, M.P.P. (1997). "Introduction." In M.P.P. Root (Ed.), *Filipino Americans: Transformation and Identity*. Thousand Oaks, CA: Russell Sage Foundation.

Shankar, L.D. and Srikanth, R. (1998). "Introduction: Closing the Gap? South Asians Challenge Asian American Studies." In L.D.

Shankar and R. Srikanth (Eds.), *A Part, Yet Apart: South Asians in Asian America*. Philadelphia, PA: Temple University Press.

Takaki, R. (1989). *Strangers From a Different Shore: A History of Asian Americans*. Boston, MA: Little, Brown and Company.

United States v. Bhagat Singh Thind, 261 United States 204, (1923).

U.S. Bureau of the Census. (1979). *Twenty Censuses: Population and Housing Questions, 1790-1980*. Washington, DC: Government Printing Office.

_____. (1992). *Marital Status and Living Arrangements: March 1992.* Current Population Reports, Population Characteristics, Series P20-468. Washington, DC: Government Printing Office.

_____. (1996). *Results of the 1996 Race and Ethnic Targeted Test.* Population Division Working Paper No. 18. Washington, DC: Government Printing Office.

U.S. Department of Education. (1996). *Racial and Ethnic Classifications Used by* Public Schools. National Center for Education Statistics, 96-092. Washington, DC: Government Printing Office.

U.S. Department of Labor (1995). *A CPS Supplement for Testing Methods of* Collecting Racial and Ethnic Information: May 1995. Bureau of Labor Statistics.

Xenos, P., Barringer, H., and Levin, M.J. (1989, July). "Asian Indians in the United States: A 1980 Census Profile." Papers of the East-West Population Institute, 111.

Interviews

Douglass, Ramona. (1999, August 5).
Dutta, Dr. Manoranjan. (1999, April 15).
Guillermo, Tessie. (1999, September 10).
Jacaban, Melecio H. (1989, June 23).
Kiaaina, Esther. (1999, April 26).
Kukkar, Dr. Narendra. (1999, April 9).
Mayeda, Greg. (1999, September 16).
Ricasa, Tony. (1989, October 31).
Shah, Dr. Jiten. (1999, April 6).

Racial Attitudes and the Color Line(s) at the Close of the Twentieth Century[1]

Taeku Lee

If we remember nothing else about W.E.B. DuBois today, we remember his sober proclamation some 100 years ago that "the problem of the Twentieth Century is the problem of the color line." This diagnosis is so well remembered because we sit on the edge of one century—a century Max Lerner dubbed "The American Century"—prepared to embark upon the next, and the problem of that next century most assuredly promises to remain that of the color line. Yet, the boundaries of this color line can no longer be drawn simply in black and white. Rather, the defining boundaries of race relations at the end of the Twentieth Century are multichromatic intersectional, heterogeneous, and constantly shifting.

This chapter examines the contours and cleavages in public attitudes about race relations and Asian Pacific Americans in an explicitly multiracial context of blacks, whites, Latinos, and Asians (APAs).[2] The focus on racial attitudes is vital because race relations are shaped not only by the material conditions of different racial and ethnic groups and the policies that governments enact, but also by the knowledge, beliefs, and experiences of ordinary individuals. As such, an analysis of what unites and divides popular opinion and political preferences on racial matters is critical to understanding how race relations are structured and what kinds of race relations are possible.

The analytic framework is expressly comparative: across racial and ethnic groups, across different constituent Asian Pacific American ethnic groups, and across national and local contexts. The substantive and interpretive focus foregrounds the racial position of APAs in seeking to answer the following questions. How commonly do APAs and others experience racial discrimination? What beliefs do different groups hold about discrimination, racial inequality, economic conflict, and the opportunity structure in the United States? Do APAs' views on these matters align with whites, do they exhibit a multiracial consciousness, or do APAs occupy a distinct "third space" on racial matters? Do negative stereotypes and sentiments about APAs exist, and are whites', blacks', and Latinas' views on public policies affecting APAs significantly determined by such antagonistic attitudes?

The analyses show, first, the simultaneous order and discontinuity that characterizes the public's views on Asian Pacific Americans and race relations. There is a clear hierarchy to racial attitudes. The discontinuity arises in the hybrid forms this hierarchy takes. By some measures the hierarchy divides whites from nonwhites. By other measures, the hierarchy splits blacks from nonblacks. By still others, whites and APAs together are differentiated from blacks and Latinos. And sometimes racial attitudes are lexically ordered from whites to APAs to Latinos to African Americans *seriatim*. The racial order, then (other permutations notwithstanding), locates blacks and whites at the antipodes of public opinion with Latinos and APAs shifting contingently in the interstices.

The other prominent result in the forthcoming pages is the specificity and shifting position of Asian Pacific Americans within this multiracial configuration. APAs themselves are distinguished by the pervasively high level of personal experience with discrimination and a rich diversity of attitudes and experiences that cuts across ethnic groups, geographic region, region length of residence in the United States, among other things. For non-APAs, opinions about APAs are strongly influenced by knowledge of and interactions with APAs, beliefs about APAs' economic threat and acculturation, and anti-Asian stereotypes and sentiments. These dynamics of racial attitudes specific to APAs, importantly, carry over to preferences over government policies that impact the Asian Pacific American community. As such, public opinion among and about APAs captures the unique, but unstable and vulnerable, position APAs face at the close of the Twentieth Century.

Surveying Racial Attitudes Beyond Black and White

A persistent feature of the study of racial attitudes is the predominance of a black-white paradigm. Until as recently as the 1980s—this paradigm has largely been the study of what white Americans think about African Americans.[3] More recently, survey researchers have increasingly recognized the interdependency of public opinion across different racial and ethnic groups. Accordingly, there has been a significant rise in data and research on racial attitudes in a more inclusive, multiracial context. The last few decades have also seen surveys that attempt to understand the dynamics of public opinion indigenous to specific communities of color.[4] Yet even today, the most prominent contemporary works in the field restrict their analysis to debates over blacks' and whites' opinions.[5] And until recently, few surveys included sufficiently large samples of whites, blacks, Latinos, and Asians together, with even fewer polls that examined exclusively the opinions of Asian Pacific Americans.[6]

This chapter takes advantage of several recent media polls that place racial attitudes in an explicitly multiracial, multiethnic context. Specifically, it draws from two surveys of the four largest racial/ethnic groups in the U.S. (a 1995 *Washington Post*/Kaiser Foundation/Harvard University poll and a 1993 *Los Angeles Times* poll) and four *LA Times* ethnic-specific polls of Southern Californians of Chinese, Filipino, Korean, and Vietnamese descent.[7] Where appropriate, the discussion will also draw from several other recent academic surveys and media polls as well: the 1992 Los Angeles County Social Survey, the 1993-94 Los Angeles Survey of Urban Inequality, a 1996 *Asian Week* poll, a 1998 *San Francisco Chronicle*/KRON/KQED poll, and a 1998 University of Massachusetts poll.[8]

Several prefatory, precautionary remarks on these data bear mention. First, although the *Post* poll offers significant insights into racial attitudes in a national context, five of the six primary data sets used draw only from residents of Southern California. And while racial attitudes and politics in California often presage those of the nation writ large, the two contexts are clearly distinct. Moreover, although the polls of Chinese, Filipinos, Koreans, and Vietnamese reflect a broad diversity of Asian Pacific American ethnicities, by no means do they capture the full diversity of the Asian Pacific American community.[9]

Along these lines, although the chapter primarily looks at race and ethnicity in terms of the four most commonly aggregated groups— whites, blacks, Latinos, and Asian Pacific Americans—the reality of racial attitudes and racial politics is (to paraphrase Lisa Lowe) heterogeneous, hybrid, and multiple.[10] Data from the ethnic-specific *LA Times* polls, for example, reveal a remarkable diversity and differentiation in the opinions Chinese, Filipino, Korean, and Vietnamese Americans hold and in the company they keep. Thus, while the ensuing pages liberally refer to racial and ethnic groups in global, homogenizing terms, the analyses and interpretation should be read with the complexity of actual experiences and opinions—especially for putatively "pan-ethnic" groups like Asian Pacific Americans and Latinos—firmly in mind.

Too, there are nuances to polling predominantly immigrant communities of color that limit what we can infer from these data. Three specific such caveats are the sampling of respondents, the wording and sequence of questions, and the language in which interviews are conducted. In addition to the chronic worry of "randomly" sampled survey respondents, communities that are disproportionately immigrant, impoverished, or otherwise marginalized like APAs, Latinos, and African Americans are especially difficult to sample without bias. Strategies to circumvent these problems, further, often fall shy of their mark. The *LA Times* poll's decision, for example, to select their pool of potential respondents by identifying "Asian"-sounding surnames risks missing many APAs with non-standard surnames and errantly sampling many non-APAs with "Asian"-sounding surnames.

The survey data on APAs are also susceptible to subtleties in the text and language of the interviews. The *LA Times* polls, for instance, contain questions that are worded and ordered in ways that may reinforce stereotypical views of Asian Pacific Americans—e.g., as perpetual foreigners or as a homogeneous, monolithic ethnic bloc. Further, data from surveys such as the *Post* poll that interview Asian Pacific Americans exclusively in English may miss the full diversity of opinion. U.S. Census Bureau data show that 73 percent of APAs speak a language other than English at home, and this figure is even higher for APAs in the Los Angeles region. Consistent with this, between 50 to 90 percent of respondents in the ethnic-specific *LA Times* polls—which gave a choice of languages to be interviewed in—opt for a non-English language of interview. And the evidence from these polls suggests that APAs interviewed in the languages of their countries of origin give substantively different answers than APAs interviewed in English.[11]

Such caveats warn us against accepting the results of poll data on APAs too enthusiastically or uncritically. That said, survey data on APAs and race relations remain singularly rare and abundantly illuminating. While we know plenty about what political elites have to say on racial matters, the voices of ordinary APAs remain obscure. As APAs rapidly emerge into the political limelight and as that limelight rapidly casts racist and nativist shadows back at Asian Pacific Americans—witnessed by the recent maelstrom of controversy around campaign finance and military espionage—a clearer understanding of how rank-and-file APAs negotiate these treacherous racial currents is increasingly urgent. These data, then, warts and all, offer a unique vantage point into race relations and racial attitudes among and about APAs.[12]

Interracial Interaction

How often and in what settings do APAs interact with each other and with others? Do APAs remain socially insular, do they assimilate and integrate seamlessly with the majority white population of the U.S., or do they forge multiracial, pan-ethnic ties across communities of color? In this section, we take a rough hew at these questions in three contexts: racial intermarriage, close personal friendships, and residential integration.

The results show a rich heterogeneity in the company that Asian Pacific American ethnicities keep. This diversity is evident not only across racial and ethnic groups, but across regions of the United States and types of interracial contact as well. The results also demonstrate the extent to which interracial interaction in the U.S. is strongly shaped by a racial ordering that places whites as the most socially desirable and African Americans as the least socially desirable. Accordingly, by most measures Asian Pacific American ethnics tend to either keep with their own ethnic group or cross-over to interact with whites. Moreover, attitudes toward racial intermarriage and neighborhood composition strongly evince such a hierarchy of racial preferences. At the same time, the levels of friendship ties across multiracial and panethnic boundaries are quite high. And intimate interracial relations (and respondents' tolerance to them) increase with time in the United States.

Evidence of interracial interactions is often accepted with the uncritically positive expectation that direct social contact will give the lie to stereotypes and prejudices and harmonize race relations as a consequence. Indeed, we shall see that direct experience with APAs does diminish racial resentment towards APAs later in this chapter. Yet it is imperative to keep in mind that close contact can sometimes worsen, not improve, race relations.[13] Moreover, actual levels of interracial interactions may differ considerably from desired levels of such contact;

individuals cannot always freely choose the company they keep. There is a long and fully documented history in the United States of socially, economically, and politically segregating racial minorities by law, institutional practices, social custom, and—as we shall see—by the preferences and prejudices of private individuals as well.

Figure 1. Attitudes on Racial Intermarriage

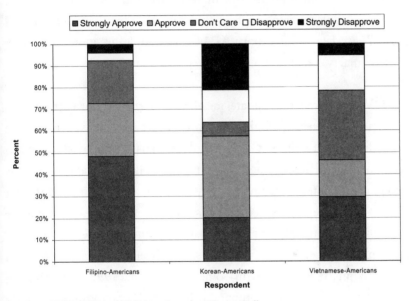

Source: 1992, 1994, 1996 *Los Angeles Times* Poll

RACIAL INTERMARRIAGE

Chinese-, Filipino-, and Korean-Americans in the ethnic-specific *LA Times* polls are overwhelmingly—from 90 percent of Filipinos to 98 percent of Koreans—wedded to partners within their own ethnic group. At least at first blush, these numbers seem to reinforce popular beliefs that Asians choose to socially isolate themselves. Of course, there are a myriad reasons why particular marital unions occur ranging from legal codes, population growth and immigration flows, and residential and geographical settlement patterns at the macro-level to familial pressure, cultural norms, social distance, racial prejudice, and simple partner preferences at the individual-level.

Moreover, the intermarriage rates from the *LA Times* poll data differ quite a bit from more exhaustive demographic studies that use U.S. Census Bureau data. For example, 1990 Census data show that fully 15 percent of married APAs formed ties outside their ethnic group.[14] As with close friendships, length of residence and the rapid influx of Asian immigrants explain much of this difference between Census data and *LA Times* data. Native-born APAs, for example, are more than twice as likely marry outside their racial/ethnic group than foreign-born APAs.[15]

When asked to evaluate racial intermarriages normatively, the Asian Pacific American ethnic groups in Figure 1 manifest a markedly greater diversity of opinion.[16] Filipino Americans appear most favorable among the Asian Pacific American ethnicities polled, with about three in four approving interracial unions. By contrast, only about one in two Korean- and Vietnamese-Americans appear tolerant of exogamy. Interestingly, the modal view for Vietnamese is indifference to intermarriage while well over a third of Koreans actively oppose such bonds.

To put these figures in some context, the 1992 Los Angeles County Social Survey finds comparably high levels of opposition to racial intermarriage among whites, Latinos, and Asian Pacific Americans generally.[17] Notably, the greatest opposition is to intermarriage to African Americans followed by intermarriage to Latinos and Asian Pacific Americans. Opposition to intermarriage to white Americans is minimal. Perhaps ironically, African Americans are the least resistant to exogamy across all possible interracial partners, while whites are the most resistant to every possible interracial partnership. This hierarchical pattern of responses—from whites at one end to blacks at the other—is one we will see again across a broad range of racial attitudes in the coming pages.

Another kindred tie across racial and ethnic boundaries is the bond of friendship. The *LA Times'* ethnic-specific polls asks Chinese-, Filipino-, Korean-, and Vietnamese-Americans who their "close personal friends" are—blacks, whites, Latinos, members of other Asian Pacific American ethnic groups, or of their own ethnic in-group.

Figure 2 shows that Chinese and Filipinos form a large number and a broad heterogeneity of friendships. Although three in four Chinese and Filipinos surveyed report friendship ties within their in-group, about 40 percent or more also report intimate acquaintances with blacks, whites, Latinos, and other APAs. Vietnamese and Koreans, by contrast, appear considerably more socially isolated. Vietnamese respondents almost exclusively build friendships with other Vietnamese. Koreans exhibit a modestly greater frequency of friendship ties across racial lines, most commonly with whites.[18]

Clearly many plausible reasons might explain this interethnic variation. One such possibility worth noting is the relatively longer history in the U.S. for Chinese and Filipinos.[19] Among respondents to the *Times* polls, almost 15 percent of Chinese and 12 percent of Filipinos are U.S. born, while less than 1 percent of Koreans and less than 2 percent of Vietnamese were born in the U.S..[20] These cross-generational differences in friendship ties and racial intermarriage bear mention because they sustain (albeit indirectly) sociological studies which show that immigrant communities of color become more racialized and politi-cized with their length of tenure in the United States.[21]

Accordingly, U.S.-born Chinese and Filipino respondents are significantly more likely to hold close acquaintances outside their ethnic group than their foreign-born counterparts. Second-generation Chinese-Americans, for instance, are more likely to form close ties with blacks, whites, Latinos, and other APAs as they are with other Chinese Americans.[22] Focusing on pan-ethnic ties, more than half the Chinese-

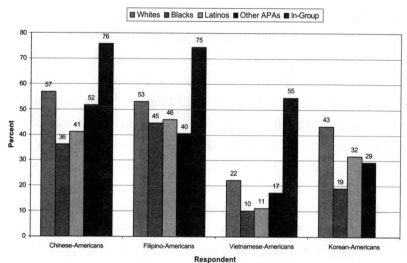

Figure 2. Close Friendships, by Race/Ethnicity of Acquaintance

Source: 1992, 1994, 1996, 1997 *Los Angeles Times* polls

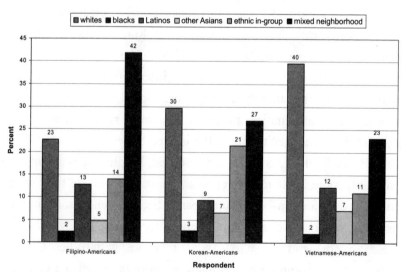

Figure 3. Racial/Ethnic Composition of Majority of Neighbors

Source: 1992, 1994, 1996 *Los Angeles Times* polls

Americans and fully 40 percent of Filipino-Americans report close friendships with Asian Pacific Americans outside their ethnic in-group.

NEIGHBORHOOD COMPOSITION

A third aspect of racial interactions that the ethnic-specific *Los Angeles Times* polls speak to are the spatial contexts that either bring diverse groups together or keep them apart. Existing residential settlement patterns show that while Asians are geographically concentrated and tend to live in urban areas, they do not face the kind of "hypersegregation" that typifies black Americans. Some studies even suggest that multiethnic cities like Los Angeles may actually engender relatively stable integrated neighborhoods over the long term.[23] Our data illuminate two dimensions of spatial context for APAs: the degree of segregation in APAs' residences and the attachment APAs hold to an ethnic center of community life.

Once again there is both commonality and diversity across different Asian Pacific American ethnicities. Filipino, Korean, and Vietnamese respondents are more likely to live either in racially-mixed neighborhoods or in majority-white communities (See Figure 3). That said, Filipinos are much more likely to live in racially integrated communities than any other racial/ethnic composition, Vietnamese are more likely to live in majority-white communities than any other composition, and Koreans were fairly even split between the two. In all respondent groups, a moderate proportion live in a majority ethnic in-group or majority Latino neighborhoods. Very few respondents live in neighborhoods that are either majority African American or majority Asian Pacific American outside their ethnic in-group.

As with interracial partnerships, we cannot assume a direct correspondence between residential settlement patterns and preferences over where to live and with whom to live. These results are consistent with the perceived social desirability of white neighbors and the perceived social undesirability of African American neighbors in other surveys. The 1992 LA County Social Survey, for example, shows that between one-third and one-half of whites, Asians, and Latinos oppose moving into a majority-black neighborhood. By contrast, fewer than 10 percent of all nonwhites oppose a move to a majority-white neighborhood. Partiality for majority-Asian and majority-Latino neighbors falls between these opposites. More generally, the 1993-94 LA Study of Urban Inequality shows that African Americans, Latinos, and Asian Pacific Americans most prefer racially mixed communities, while Anglos favor either all-white or only marginally integrated neighborhoods. Importantly, these preferences for certain neighbors and not others is conspicuously shaped by ethnocentrism and racial prejudice.[24]

This general in-group bias over residential space is bolstered in the *LA Times* polls by strong identification with ethnically concentrated sites like Los Angeles' Chinatown, the San Gabriel Valley, Los Angeles' Koreatown, or Orange County's Little Saigon. About 40 percent of Chinese respondents identify Chinatown as a "most" or a "very" important center of business, cultural, and social activity in their daily lives and almost two-thirds identify the San Gabriel Valley similarly. Well over 80 percent of Korean- and Vietnamese-Americans either identified Koreatown or Little Saigon as a "very" or "most" important center of life or in fact lived in these neighborhoods. As with the tendency to forge close friendships, this preference is notably more visible among the newer immigrant groups.

Racial Discrimination

The overview of interracial contact—from marriage partners to next-door neighbors—tells us a fair bit about the diversity and fluidity of social arrangements that characterize everyday life for Asian Pacific Americans. This finding is an important reminder that APAs' experiences and opinions cannot be tidily summarized into a small number of uniformly applicable, enduring attributes. We have also seen that the type and intensity of interracial intimacy individuals engage in closely parallels their expressed preferences (or perceived constraints) over marital partners, friends, and neighbors. This finding is an important reminder that race relations are not always freely formed, but quite often operate within a field of binding constraints set by personal preferences and prejudices.

In this section, then, we turn more directly to personal experiences of being discriminated against and perceptions about racial discrimination. The results show that a significant proportion of Americans—black, white, Latino, and Asian—report first-hand experience with discrimination. Notably, contrary to popular beliefs of an overachieving, thriving Asian Pacific American "model minority," the levels of perceived discrimination reported by APAs is quite extensive. In fact, these levels are more comparable to those reported by African Americans and Latinos than they are to whites.

These results capture the hybridity of racial attitudes in a multiracial context. On the one hand, there is a distinct architecture to racial attitudes which situates blacks and whites at the antipodes of social desirability, lived racism, and material well-being, with Latinos and Asians in between. Yet, this racial ordering is neither uniform nor universal. Nor does it map tidily onto statistical realities of the material conditions facing each racial/ethnic group in the United States. In fact, public perceptions about personally experienced discrimination or the racism that other groups face vary substantially by race, region, historical period, and the particular issue at hand. Conspicuously, very few Americans (APAs themselves included) view Asian Pacific Americans as facing a significant level of discrimination.

This leaves us with a disjuncture—between high levels of discrimination reported by APAs and the general perception that APAs do not face high levels of discrimination—that frames the analysis for the remainder of this chapter. Specifically, this disjuncture suggests a more complex, multi-dimensional basis to racial attitudes than is reflected in simple percentages. Here the existing research on racial attitudes points to four "usual suspects": beliefs about social stratification and racial inequality, perceptions of tangible conflict and competition between groups, normative judgments about a group's mores and motivations, and (either explicit or symbolic) racial resentment of out-groups.[25] We consider these in turn. Ultimately, these dimensions yield important insights into how the public thinks about APAs and the public policies affecting the Asian Pacific American community.

PERSONAL EXPERIENCE OF DISCRIMINATION

From the Kerner Commission's infamous indictment of "two societies; one black, one white—separate and unequal" some thirty years ago to the more recent aftermath of the O.J. Simpson trial, we have come to accept a profound divide in the lived realities of racial groups in the United States as a common fact. This divergence is manifest in our survey data on personal experiences with discrimination. Figure 4 compares the national *Post* poll to the regional *LA Times* and *San Francisco Chronicle* polls on this question.[26]

The first finding of note in Figure 4 is the regional specificity of discrimination and perceptions of discrimination. In the national *Post* poll, experience with racism divides fairly clearly between whites and nonwhites. Only 1 in 6 whites report being discriminated against during the last ten years, while over a third of Latinos, 40 percent of Asians, and half of African Americans report such an experience.[27] This pattern recurs when the *Post* poll asks respondents if they are concerned about discrimination in the future. Almost 70 percent of white respondents were either "not very" or "not at all" affected by the prospect of being discriminated against in the future. By contrast over 80 percent of African Americans, and well over 60 percent of Latinos and APAs were either "somewhat" or "very" concerned about facing such experiences in the future.

The landscape of racism in California is quite different. All racial and ethnic groups—in the Bay Area and Southern California—report the same or higher levels of discrimination than their counterparts in the nation writ large. The most precipitous rise occurs, moreover, with whites. In the *San Francisco Chronicle* poll the proportion of whites who report discrimination increases to 28 percent, although a perceptible division between the experiences of whites and nonwhites lingers. In the *Los Angeles Times* poll this is no longer true. Fully half the white respondents report personally experiencing discrimination, a rate higher than that of Latinos.[28]

Figure 4 is also conspicuous for the consistently high levels reported by Asian Pacific Americans. In both the *Post* and the *LA Times* polls, APAs rank second only to African Americans in experiencing discrimination. In the ethnic-specific *LA Times* polls, the prevalence of discrimination remains high, although perhaps at rates closer to that in the *Washington Post* and *San Francisco Chronicle* polls: 57 percent of Chinese, 46 percent of Filipinos and Koreans, and 41 percent of Vietnamese respondents report such incidents.[29] Even with a 1998 University of Massachusetts poll that asks this question over a very narrow time horizon—restricted to experiences within the last three months of the survey—fully 25 percent of Asian Pacific Americans reported being discriminated against.[30]

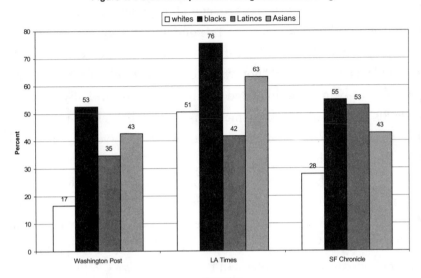

Figure 4. Personal Experience being Discriminated Against

Source: 1995 *Washington Post*, 1993 *LA Times*,
and 1998 *San Francisco Chronicle* polls

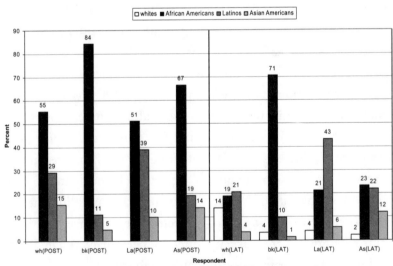

Figure 5. Which Group Experiences the Most Discrimination?

Source: 1995 *Washington Post*, 1993 *LA Times*

Although Asian Pacific Americans report experiencing widespread discrimination, this pervasive experience is seldom perceived by others. One of the *Washington Post* poll items asks which racial/ethnic group in the U.S. faces the greatest discrimination. Figure 5 shows that across all respondent groups African Americans are most often identified. Although about 40 percent of Latinos identify themselves as facing the greatest racial animus, Latinos are only a distant second for white, African American, and Asian Pacific American respondents. Notably, although we have seen that somewhere between 40 and 60 percent of Asian Pacific Americans report personally experiencing discrimination, fewer than 15 percent of any respondent group—Asian Pacific Americans included—identify APAs as facing the greatest discrimination.[31]

The *LA Times* poll's version of this question, however, shows that at least in Southern California, the relatively linear hierarchy of racial attitudes does not always hold. More than 70 percent of African Americans unambiguously rank blacks as more discriminated against than any other group. Yet, less than a quarter of respondents in any other group identify blacks as the most discriminated group in Southern California. Close to half of Latinos view themselves as the most discriminated group, while whites and Asians split fairly evenly between viewing blacks and Latinos as the most discriminated group.[32] Fewer than 5 percent of whites, blacks, and Latinos see APAs as the most discriminated group.

Of course, the wording of this question forces a choice between racial minorities, all of whom may face significant levels of racism. In particular, the gap between reported discrimination by APAs and perceptions of discrimination may simply reflect reasonable differences in perceptions of the intensity of discrimination faced by different groups. Here the *San Francisco Chronicle* poll offers a nice comparison (results not shown). It simply asks whether different groups face "a lot" of prejudice in the Bay Area. The familiar ordering is replicated regardless of respondent race and ethnicity: every respondent group rates African Americans most often as subjected to significant discrimination, followed in order by Latinos, Asians, and whites. Notably, the percentage of respondents who now identify Asian Pacific Americans as frequent victims of discrimination now ranges from 12 percent (whites) to 27 percent (Latinos), although these rates still fall far below the percentages of APAs who actually report experiencing discrimination.

GROUP ASSESSMENTS AND RACIAL INEQUALITY

There remains, then, a significant gap between the levels of discrimination that APAs experience and public perceptions of those experiences. Part of this gap is likely rooted in beliefs about the opportunity structure in the United States and the differential access of blacks, Latinos, whites, and Asians within that structure. When polled about the relative disadvantages facing different racial/ethnic groups—absent any explicit reference to discrimination as the cause of such disadvantages—the American public exhibits a remarkable consensus in opinion. The *Washington Post* poll asks respondents whether or not nonwhites have the same opportunities to lead a middle-class life as whites. Figure 6 shows that all respondent groups perceive blacks and Latinos to be significantly more disadvantaged than APAs vis-à-vis the opportunities and privileges available to whites.[33]

The *LA Times* poll's variation on this theme asks respondents whether different groups face adversity in their efforts to obtain "adequate housing and education, and job opportunities and social acceptance by whites." Keeping the difference in question wording in mind, here again respondents clearly distinguish the barriers facing blacks and Latinos from those facing whites and Asians.[34] More than 40 percent of respondents in all groups identify African Americans and Latinos as facing substantial adversity, while fewer than 20 percent (and usually less than 10 percent) by contrast identify either whites or APAs.[35]

Question wording notwithstanding, few respondents—black, white, brown, or yellow—view Asian Pacific Americans as facing significant barriers to a decent life. In the multiracial *LA Times* poll, only about one in ten Asian Pacific Americans themselves see APAs as facing substantial adversity in meeting basic social and material needs. This rather sanguine view about their own upward mobility is true across specific Asian Pacific American ethnic groups as well. In the ethnic-specific *LA Times* polls, between 87 and 96 percent of the Chinese, Filipino, and Vietnamese respondents rated the conditions they face as good or better than good. No more than 2 percent in any respondent group view conditions as "very bad."[36]

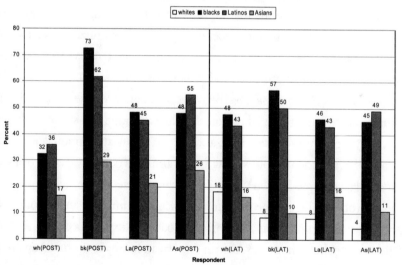

Figure 6. Perceived Barriers to Equal Opportunity
(Data: 1995 *Washington Post*, 1993 *Los Angeles Times*)

Source: 1995 *Washington Post*, 1993 *Los Angeles Times*

This result persists even when potential barriers to equal opportunity are explicitly offered to respondents. When asked to identify the "primary thing holding Asians back in Southern California," the most common response among whites and African Americans is that APAs face no barriers at all (See Figure 7). And where barriers are acknowledged, respondents most commonly point the finger back at attributes internal to the Asian Pacific American community itself—namely, cultural differences, voluntary isolation, and language problems. Conspicuously, only between 10 and 15 percent in any respondent group identify racism as an obstacle for APAs, and APAs stand alone in characterizing lack of political power as an obstacle in substantial numbers.

This general tendency to view a group as facing no significant barriers or to place the burden of hardships facing a group on their own attributes is important because it can be pernicious. Previous studies show that "attributional" explanations of racial inequality that "blame the victim" also engender negative views toward the group in question and legitimate policy positions that are unsympathetic to that groups' plight. By contrast, more "situational" perspectives that recognize the structural, environmental impediments to equal opportunity tend to induce more positive, sympathetic attitudes and policy positions.[37]

In the *Washington Post* poll, respondents are offered a series of situational and attributional reasons for the economic and social problems faced by nonwhites in the U.S. today.[38] Among attributional explanations, all respondent groups view poor family structure (and, to a lesser extent, lack of motivation) as a significant cause of the economic and social problems facing the African American community. All respondent groups view language as a significant barrier for Latinos and Asians. And while beliefs about the African American family or Latinas' desire to speak English may not amount to overt racism, they do signify more symbolic, or "laissez-faire" modes of justifying racially antagonistic views.[39]

In fact, at least in Southern California, Asian Pacific Americans are not only viewed as facing no substantial barriers to opportunity, but they are also considered as too successful and too enthusiastic in their pursuit of material success. Here the *LA Times* poll asks whether any group "is getting more economic power than is good for Southern California" and whether any group "is working harder than the others to succeed in Southern California." Perhaps unsurprisingly, given their relative economic well-being vis-à-vis Latinos and African Americans, whites and Asians are most commonly perceived economically powerful (See Figure 8). What may be more surprising is that white, African American, and Latino respondents are more likely to choose APAs than whites on this question. Whites in particular are discernibly shy about citing themselves as wielding too much economic power.[40]

Consistent with prior research on racial attitudes, these perceptions of economic competition and group threat are key to beliefs about discrimination and (as we shall see) preferences over policy matters. Thus, contrary to classic assimilation theory, economic mobility does not foster greater social acceptance. Instead, the view that APAs are too economically powerful is statistically linked to other negative evaluations of APAs such as the belief that APAs are the most prejudiced group in Southern California. This is true even when we control statistically for other plausible alternative explanations like sociodemographic background, political partisanship and ideology, interracial experiences.[41]

When asked if any group works especially hard to succeed, Asian Pacific Americans are singled out by all respondent groups. From prior research, we know that the belief that a particular group lacks the will to succeed acts as a negative stereotype that gives rise to racial resentment and opposition to racially egalitarian policies. One might logically conclude, then, that if APAs are seen to work especially hard to succeed, that belief ought to generate positive, sympathetic attitudes toward APAs and the policies that affect APAs.

This logic turns out to be only partially sound in general and mostly unsound vis-à-vis Asian Pacific Americans. Specifically, the belief

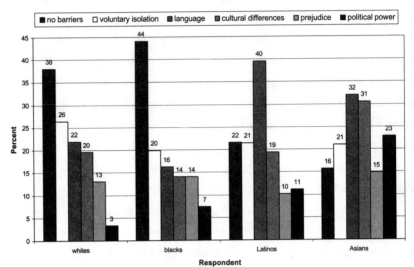

Figure 7. Primary Barriers Holding Back APAs

Source: 1993 *Los Angeles Times* poll

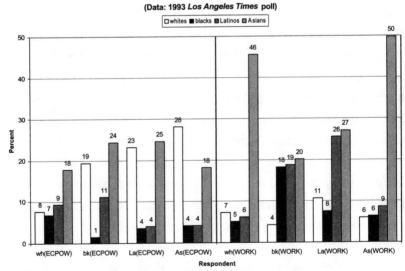

Figure 8. Who Holds Too Much Economic Power, Works Hardest to Succeed?
(Data: 1993 *Los Angeles Times* poll)

Source: 1993 *Los Angeles Times* poll

that a group works harder than others to succeed is positively related to the belief that that group endures extreme discrimination, controlling again for sociodemographic and political factors and one's personal experiences with discrimination.[42] This relationship, interestingly, holds uniformly only when the work ethic of African Americans or Latinos is concerned. When asked about the work ethic of Asians or whites, the relationship holds only within in-groups. That is, only Asian Pacific Americans make the link between their perceived motivation to succeed and the belief that they are widely discrimination against.

Anti-Asian Sentiments and Stereotypes

Thus, while negative stereotypes about blacks' or Latinos' work ethic may vindicate unsympathetic or even hostile attitudes, the converse does not generally hold. We know from prior research that inequality in the United States is consoled ideologically in the public mind vis-à-vis notions of equal opportunity and economic individualism.[43] By this reasoning, racial disparities result from unjust inequalities of opportunity or defects of individual or group character. One implication of these results in this chapter is that such core principles do not apply uniformly to all social groups. In the case of Asian Pacific Americans, few respondents perceive significant barriers to equal opportunity and even fewer perceive an insufficient will to succeed. Yet, Asian Pacific Americans do face significant adversity and injustice—whether measured by the survey-based reports of discriminatory experiences that we have seen or by some other evidentiary basis like statistics on hate crimes, oral histories, government documents, or highly profiled public trials of APAs.[44]

There are at least two explanations for this gap between lived racism for APAs and the public's opinion about APAs. For one thing, the site of anti-Asian discrimination within the U.S. opportunity structure may differ in important respects from other racial minorities. For another, the substance of anti-Asian discrimination may differ from other racial minorities. On the first point, discrimination often hits APAs in formal, institutional contexts as relatively successful individuals hit the proverbial "glass ceiling."[45] Larry Bobo and Susan Suh find that Asian Pacific Americans most likely to report discrimination in the workplace are the highly educated, the highly paid, and the white-collar employees.[46] Thus, APAs may face real discrimination, but people (including APAs themselves) may not view encumbrances at the upper echelons of professional life (cf. a decent standard of life) as a significant barrier to equal opportunity.

On the second point, the paradox between the apparent absence of negative stereotypes about APAs and the visible presence of discrimination experienced by APAs is intelligible if the substantive form of anti-Asian discrimination is distinct and not adequately captured by existing measures of discrimination. In fact, the substantive forms of discrimination *should* be distinct if the prevailing constructivist view of race and racism is correct. Racial formations occur around essentialist stereotypes that differentiate one "race" from another. Thus, we should not expect that epigenetic stereotypes about intelligence, motivation, family, criminality—which in the United States have evolved largely from the history of black-white relations—will necessarily apply to APAs. As Michael Omi and Howard Winant put it, racial hegemony at the end of the Twentieth Century is demonstrably "messy."[47]

Plainly put, survey questions designed to measure racial resentment toward one group will be inadequate and invalid as measures of racial resentment toward another group. Even today, opinion polls that assess the prevalence of negative stereotypes towards African Americans, Latinos, and Asian Pacific Americans generally do so with a common set of questions applied unvaryingly to these distinct racial/ethnic groups. In this last section on racial attitudes, then, we consider whether evidence of negative sentiments and stereotypes unique to APAs can be found using survey data and, if so, how such anti-Asian attitudes are constituted. Here the *Los Angeles Times* poll includes a unique set of questions on popular beliefs and prejudices about Asian Pacific Americans.[48] Specifically, the *Times* polls include four items that measure distinct stereotypes of APAs and three items that measure anti-Asian sentiments.

The first three stereotype measures are specific to historical and contemporary stereotypes of Asian Pacific Americans: (1) that APAs are homogeneous—respondents are asked whether or not APA ethnic groups "tend to have the same mentality"; (2) that APAs are perpetual foreigners—respondents are asked whether "APAs have more in common with Asians who live in Asia or ... more in common with other types of Americans"; (3) that APAs are inscrutable—respondents are asked about the accuracy of portrayals of APAs as "people who are particularly puzzling and mysterious."[49] The remaining measure asks respondents whether or not APAs use a disproportionate amount of government services. This item is not unique to Asian Pacific Americans as it considers the general view that racial minorities and immigrant groups depend on and freely abuse government benefits.[50]

The three measures of anti-Asian sentiments ask respondents: (1) whether they have a negative or positive impression of Japan; (2) whether or not "a substantial increase" of APAs moving into the respondent's neighborhood would upset the respondent; (3) whether or not such an increase in the number of APAs would upset the respondent's neighbors. This last measure is an important check against respondents who might in fact oppose a large influx of Asian Pacific American neighbors, but feel socially constrained to express a more "politically correct," racially tolerant position. In fact, Figure 9 shows that whites, blacks, and Latinos are between two to four times as likely to claim that an influx of Asian Pacific Americans would upset unnamed neighbors than they are to report personal discomfort.

More generally, Figure 9 shows that the belief in distinctly

Figure 9. Anti-Asian Stereotypes and Sentiments

Figure 9. Anti-Asian Stereotypes and Sentiments

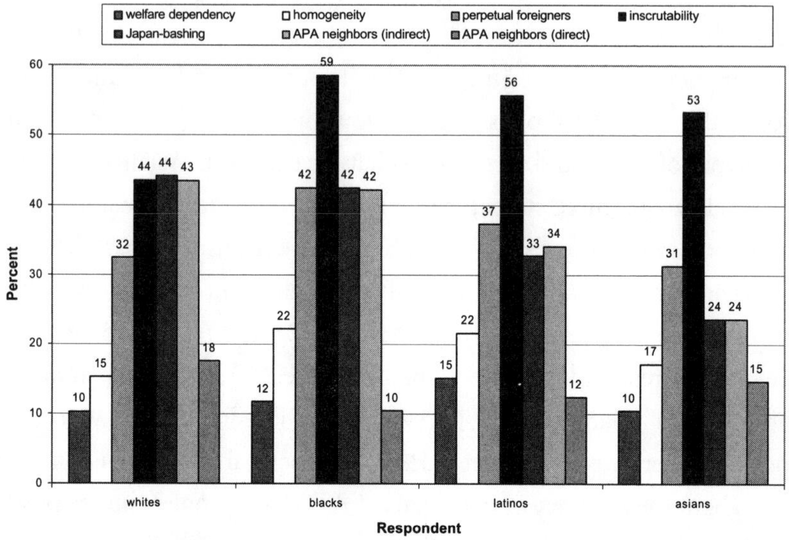

Source: 1993 *Los Angeles Times* poll

anti-Asian attitudes is quite high. The distribution of responses in Figure 9 is also impressive for the extent to which all respondent groups either accept or reject particular sentiments and stereotypes altogether. Hence, across all respondent groups there is widespread acceptance of the stereotype of APAs as inscrutable and as perpetual foreigners and feelings of hostility towards Asian neighbors and towards Japan. Similarly, there is only modest support across all respondent groups for the stereotype of Asian Pacific Americans as welfare dependents or as dispositionally homogeneous group. In fact, these seven items can be cumulated into a statistically powerful and meaningful "anti-Asian" attitude scale. In such a global measure, notably, African Americans exhibit the greatest tendency to stereotype APAs, followed by Latinos, whites, and Asian Pacific Americans themselves.

Figure 9 is also revealing for what, at first blush, appears to be a surprisingly high rate of anti-Asian attitudes among APAs themselves. For example, more than half the APAs polled agree that APAs are "particularly puzzling and mysterious" and almost a third agree that APAs are more Asian than they are American. These high levels may suggest that some items—the stereotype questions in particular—are not really *negative* stereotypes. After all, beliefs about Asian Pacific American homogeneity or inscrutability may be neutral generalizations. Alternatively, these results might suggest the prevalence of "internal racism"; the stereotype items may indeed be pernicious, but APAs may still accept them as true.

It is important to note in this context that the tendency of racial minorities to adhere to seemingly negative stereotypes of themselves is not exclusive to Asian Pacific Americans. The 1991 National Race Survey shows with respect to black-white opinion that African Americans actually appear to be more prone than white Americans to adopt negative stereotypes of themselves.[51] These negative views clearly do not, however, influence race attitudes and support for racial policies in the same way for blacks as they do for whites. As we shall see quite vividly, then, a third possibility is that stereotypes can operate differently for the in-groups to whom the generalizations refer than they do for out-groups.

This is true of the sentiments and stereotypes in Figure 9. The additive scale of the seven items noted above, for instance, enjoys reasonable statistical properties only for whites, blacks, and Latinos. For Asian Pacific Americans, such a scale is much less coherent. More convincingly, when we turn to multivariate accounts of how anti-Asian attitudes are formed, a meaningful narrative emerges for blacks, whites, and Latinos, but not APAs.[52]

TABLE 1. DETERMINANTS OF ANTI-ASIAN STEREOTYPES AND SENTIMENTS[53]

	Whites	Blacks	Latinos
Social Divisions	older, less educated, urban more anti-Asian	no effects (Native borns) possibly more anti-Asian	 no effects
Political Divisions	conservatives more anti-Asian	no effects	no effects
Information Sources and knowledge of APAs	less knowledgeable, informed by personal experience, believes media bias is pro-Asian more anti-Asian	less knowledgeable, believes media bias is pro-Asian more anti-Asian	less knowledgeable, informed by media more anti-Asian
Personal Experience	hear anti-Asian slurs often more anti-Asian more friendly APA contacts less anti-Asian	more APA neighbors more anti-Asian	hear anti-Asian slurs (more APA neighbors, possibly) more anti-Asian
View of Acculturation	multiculturalist view less anti-Asian	 no effects	assimilationist more anti-Asian Multiculturalist less anti-Asian
Group Conflict	perceived negative impact, economic threat more anti-Asian	perceived negative impact, economic threat, APA racism more anti-Asian	perceived negative impact more anti-Asian

Source: 1993 Los Angeles Times poll.

Table 1 summarizes results from such a multivariate account of anti-Asian stereotypes and sentiments. Anti-Asian attitudes here are the previously mentioned additive scale from Figure 9. Variations on this anti-Asian scale are theorized to be the result of the following dimensions of racial attitudes: (1) enduring social cleavages (age, education, family income, gender, urbanicity, and nativity); (2) political partisanship and ideology; (3) knowledge and informational sources on APAs; (4) personal contacts with APAs; (5) views on acculturation (assimilationist and multiculturalist); (6) group threat and competition (whether APAs are the most prejudiced group, whether APAs control too much economic clout, and the positive impact Asians have on Southern California). Each cell shows the influence of the particular variables in that cell on anti-Asian stereotypes and sentiments, *controlling for* (statistically) the independent effect of all the remaining dimensions above on anti-Asian stereotypes and sentiments.

The first observation is that, statistically speaking, this set of variables sheds no significant light on the conditions in which Asian Pacific Americans themselves affirm such stereotypes and sentiments. There are no meaningful effects on any of the dimensions examined. Cumulatively, the set of dimensions explains just about none of the variation in the anti-Asian attitude scale and the results are excluded from Table 1 as a result.

But these dimensions tell us a great deal about where whites, African Americans, and Latinos stand. To highlight the main points, Table 1 shows the consistent and compelling influence of experience, information, and group evaluations on anti-Asian attitudes. Consistent with our earlier discussion of Figure 8, APAs are significantly more likely to be viewed in stereotypical and antagonistic terms when they are seen as too economically powerful or as having a generally negative impact on life in Southern California. Moreover, whites and Latinos who view APAs as inadequately integrated into "American culture" are more likely to hold anti-Asian attitudes.

These group-based and normatively-based influences on racial resentment ought to be familiar to opinion researchers. Assessments about groups and the cherished values they affirm or violate powerfully shape anti-black attitudes.[54] Moreover, Table 1 shows that (especially for whites) age and education make a difference; older and less educated respondents tend to hold more prejudiced and hostile views of APAs. And Table 1 shows that spatial contexts are a battleground for conflict with APAs: Latinos and African Americans who live in neighborhoods with large numbers of APAs are significantly more likely to hold anti-Asian attitudes.

On the more hopeful side, experience with APAs, knowledge of APAs, and information about APAs create a critical counterbalance. White Americans who get their information about APAs from direct personal experience and who have close social ties with APAs are much likelier to reject negative stereotypes and sentiments about APAs. In addition, whites and Latinos who report hearing anti-Asian slurs often take a more negative view of Asian Pacific Americans themselves.[55] For whites, blacks, and possibly Latinos as well, the more one knows about Asian Pacific American history and current events, the more sympathetic one's position toward Asian Pacific Americans. The informational basis of blacks' and whites' attitudes is strongly influenced by what they think about media coverage on Asian Pacific Americans. Respondents who believe that media coverage belies an anti-Asian bias take a more positive view towards APAs.

These results are equally revealing for which factors turn out not to matter. With only a few exceptions—notably, the tendency for older, less educated, more conservative, and urban whites to be more anti-Asian—demographic, socioeconomic, and political influences appear to have little influence on attitudes about Asian Pacific Americans. These are precisely the factors that usually enjoy the most explanatory power in opinion research, and their relatively tepid effects here manifest the fluid, emergent nature of mass opinion about Asian Pacific Americans.

Let me be clear that about what is claimed in this section. The results here do not imply a claim about the equivalence (or even comparability) of anti-Asian discrimination with discrimination against other racial minorities. To compare anti-Asian stereotypes with anti-black stereotypes, for example, being viewed as inscrutable, exotic, or alike is not the same as being seen as mentally inferior, morally dissolute, or criminally predisposed. The primary claim is that discrimination takes multiple forms, and that those forms are specific to the group in question. Thus the measures of anti-Asian discrimination ought to differ from those that examine discrimination against blacks, Latinas, Jews, American Indians, Arab Americans, among others. As we shall see in the concluding section of this chapter, however, negative stereotypes and sentiments about minorities are comparable across racial/ethnic groups in question in one key respect: they play a central role in justifying policy positions that are hostile to the political interests of that racial/ethnic group.

Racial Attitudes and Policy Preferences

We have traversed the polymorphic and paradoxical terrain of racial attitudes in a multiracial, multiethnic context. In large measure, whether these dynamics bear on race relations and how they affect the lives of Asian Pacific Americans depends critically on their political significance. In short, much depends on how racial attitudes (and attitudes about APAs in particular) influence citizens' policy preferences and political activism.

In this final section, we explicitly consider how blacks, whites, Latinos, and Asians form their positions on policies affecting the Asian Pacific American community. This focus on policies that directly impact APAs—as opposed to a broader set of racial policies or public policies writ large—is decidedly narrow, to be sure. That said, there is already a substantial literature on broader public policy preferences, political participation, and voting behavior within a multiracial context.[56] Furthermore, the 1993 *Los Angeles Times'* multiracial survey affords a unique opportunity to examine the diverse policy issues with important consequences for APAs.[57] Lastly, the focus on a narrower and targeted set of policy questions enjoins a more direct test of whether or not the stereotypes and sentiments about APAs in the previous section are, as claimed, negative and antagonistic. Are policy positions on issues affecting predominantly immigrant communities of color guided by the conventional determinants of political opinion (e.g., partisanship and ideology), do they take on the dimensions of racial politics, or are they shaped by factors specific to the immigrant experience?

An ever-growing number of public policy questions—from hate crimes and domestic violence to affirmative action, immigration, and welfare reform to campaign finance reform and the decennial Census—acutely affect the interests of the Asian Pacific American community. An analysis of how whites, blacks, Latinos, and Asians form their preferences on such policy matters will thus be crucial if we are to properly understand the increasingly multiracial dimensions of politics in the U.S. On a more prescriptive note, such an analysis may also shed insights into whether multiracial political coalitions are feasible (or even desirable) and how public support might be mobilized in response to racially-motivated political campaigns or policy debates such as California's Propositions 187, 209, and 227.

Turning to the analysis, then, the *LA Times* poll asks its respondents four policy questions that impact upon the Asian Pacific American community: (1) whether the United States should legislate a moratorium on legal immigration; (2) whether Chinese "boat people" seeking asylum should be returned to China without a hearing; (3) whether reparations to Japanese-Americans imprisoned in World War Two internment camps are merited; and (4) whether admissions to the University of California system ought to welcome the disproportionate number of qualified Asian Pacific American applicants or match the demographic composition of the racial/ethnic groups in California.[58]

Figure 10 shows that the distribution of responses to these questions are highly issue-specific and highly group-specific. While a sizeable proportion of whites, blacks, and (to a lesser degree) Latinos support drastic measures to address both legal and illegal immigration to the U.S., an equally sizeable proportion of Latinos, whites, and (to a lesser degree) blacks support monetary reparations to Japanese-

Americans. Across respondent groups African Americans most consistently appear to adopt policy preferences that are opposed to those of APAs.

While a vast simplification, positions on each issue can loosely be considered sympathetic or antagonistic to Asian Pacific American political interests, where the political interests of APAs are defined by the discernible policy positions taken by a majority of Asian Pacific American

Figure 10. Anti-Asian Policy Preferences

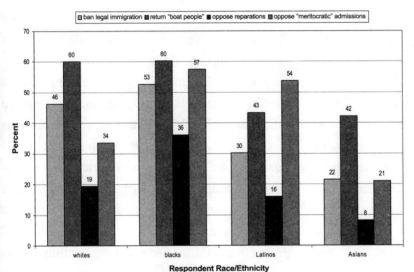

Source: 1993 *Los Angeles Times* poll

respondents.[59] As the results show, a majority of Asian Pacific American respondents oppose a moratorium on immigration, oppose returning Chinese seeking asylum without a hearing, support reparations to Japanese Americans interned during World War II, and support a "meritocratic" University of California admissions policy. What's more, APAs take the strongest position on each of these issues across all respondent groups.

In the remaining analysis, this oversimplified view—of "pro-Asian" or "anti-Asian" policy positions—will be used to make some general claims about how policy preferences on such issues are formed. As with the measures of negative stereotypes and sentiments, responses to the four policy items can be cumulated into a statistically coherent "anti-Asian" policy scale. In this case, restrictive views on immigration, opposition to reparations, and support for a demographically representative admissions policy are taken as "anti-Asian."[60]

As Figure 10 implies, African Americans appear to be the most anti-Asian on such a scale of policy preferences, followed by whites, Latinos, and APAs themselves. The multivariate account of variations in this cumulative policy scale is similar to that for anti-Asian attitudes. Positions on these four issues are examined as a function of social divisions, political loyalties, personal experience with APAs and with discrimination, assimilationist or multiculturalist views of immigrant acculturation, realistic group conflicts, and knowledge and information about Asian Pacific Americans. The one new variable is the extent to which direct negative stereotypes and sentiments (the anti-Asian scale) affects policy preferences on issues affecting Asian Pacific Americans.

The results are summarized in Table 2.[61] For whites, anti-Asian stereotypes and sentiments are the single strongest influence on anti-Asian policy preferences. Anti-Asian attitudes also strongly shape the policy preferences of Latinos and African Americans, but they no longer predominate over other factors. In particular, the belief that APAs are too economically dominant (among blacks and Latinos) and self-identification as a political conservative (for Latinos) is at least equally decisive in shaping anti-Asian policy positions.

Once again, there are important countervailing forces that incline non-Asians toward more pro-Asian policy positions. Where people get their information from and how knowledgeable they are about Asian Pacific Americans—controlling for anti-Asian stereotypes and sentiments—are decisive factors. Whites who get their information on APAs through personal experience are significantly less likely to present an anti-Asian policy profile; for African Americans, it is knowledge that matters the most; and for Latinos, it is media information on APAs. Additionally, whites and blacks (and possibly Latinos as well) who affirm an interest in learning Asian Pacific American history and traditions are decidedly more sympathetic.

Interestingly, personal experience appears to matter in distinct ways for each of the groups involved. For whites, as we have seen, it is the information drawn from direct personal experience that engenders more sympathetic policy positions. Latinos take a more sympathetic position if they report close social contact (either as friends or in a professional relationship) with Asian Pacific Americans. And for African Americans, having personally experienced discrimination leads to anti-Asian policy positions.

In addition, enduring social divisions appear to command considerable leverage over policy preferences, although with few regularities across racial/ethnic groups. Consistent with other research, older and less educated respondents often exhibit greater opposition to racially liberal policies. Notably, simply being born in the United States is the second strongest factor in whites' anti-Asian policy positions.[62]

As with the determinants of anti-Asian sentiments and stereotypes seen in Table 1, the influences on black, Latino, and white opinion on these questions are as telling for what does not appear to matter as they are for what does matter. Ironically, although these are matters of public policy, conventional political factors exhibit a tenuous hold over public opinion. When political determinants do matter, moreover, they appear to be ideological in origin, not partisan. There is a clear implication here

TABLE 2. DETERMINANTS OF ANTI-ASIAN POLICY PREFERENCES[63]

	Whites	Blacks	Latinos	Asians
Social Divisions	older, native born	young, poor, female (possibly less educated)	older, less educated	older, less educated
	more anti-Asian	more anti-Asian	more anti-Asian	more anti-Asian
Political Divisions Divisions	conservatives		conservatives	conservatives more anti-Asian Democrats
	more anti-Asian	no effects	more anti-Asian	less anti-Asian
Information Sources and knowledge of APAs	knowledgeable, informed by personal experience or media	knowledgeable		
	less anti-Asian	less anti-Asian	no effects	no effects
Personal Experience		experienced discrimination	clos contact w/APAs	experienced discrimination close contact w/APAs
	no effects	more anti-Asian	less anti-Asian	less anti-Asian
View of Acculturation	multiculturalist	multiculturalist less anti-Asian assimilationist	possibly Multiculturalist	
	less anti-Asian	more anti-Asian	less anti-Asian	no effects
Group Conflict	APA economic threat	APA economic threat	APA economic threat	APA economic threat
	more anti-Asian	more anti-Asian	more anti-Asian	more anti-Asian
anti-Asian stereotypes an sentiments	high	high	high	high
	anti-Asian	anti-Asian	anti-Asian	anti-Asian

Source: 1993 *Los Angeles Times* poll.

that political parties do not play their usual role in informing and influencing policy positions when the policies are those that primarily affect Asian Pacific Americans.[64] Whether this is the result of a lack of clarity or concern among partisan elites or apathy and ambivalence among its rank-and-file is an open matter beyond the scope of this chapter.

Importantly, Asian Pacific Americans themselves are the singular exception. Partisanship and ideology stand out as the two strongest influences on APAs' policy positions. Democrats are significantly more "pro-Asian"; conservatives are significantly more "anti-Asian." Table 2 also shows that APAs who are younger, more educated, have personally experienced discrimination, and have close social contact with other APAs are more likely to adopt policy positions consistent with the political interests of APAs.[65]

Taken together, the dynamics of Asian Pacific American mass opinion over policy matters appears prominently less mystifying and more intelligible than many public commentators on Asian Pacific American politics would have us believe. APAs who are more personally invested—whether vis-à-vis partisan and ideological loyalties or vis-à-vis personal experiences and sociodemographic location—have much more to say about these policy matters than those who do not. This not only fits comfortably with the dynamics of democratic politics in the U.S. as we generally know it, but it also suggests that the political identity of APAs into the Twenty-First Century (be it pan-ethnic, multiracial, or mainstream) will depend ultimately on factors like political socialization, demographic change, immigrant experiences, and pan-ethnic and inter-racial ties.

Conclusion

In these pages, we have surveyed racial attitudes among and about Asian Pacific Americans. There is a discernible topography whose centrifugal narrative force remains the enduring and evolving history of black-white relations in the United States. The lived realities of African Americans and white Americans remain worlds apart, as do public perceptions about those realities. Yet, these pages also vividly demonstrate the varied, shifting, and contradictory contours and cleavages of this racial landscape, especially for APAs and Latinos.

In particular, much of the analysis in this chapter has focused on the radical disjuncture between the levels of discrimination that APAs experience and the public's perceptions (Asian Pacific Americans included) of the unfettered opportunities open to APAs. This disjuncture, more pointedly, leaves APAs mired between the reality of racial inequality and the ideology of equal opportunity and economic individualism. To make the point simply, for African Americans the disjuncture between personal experiences and public perceptions is more modest in part because the racial inequalities facing African Americans are usually either seen by liberals to result from systemic injustices in the U.S. opportunity structure or seen by conservatives to stem from moral and motivational inadequacies internal to the African American community.[66] APAs, by contrast, are seen to face few systemic barriers and seen to manifest the values and initiative of a "model minority" by both sides of the political aisle.

The conjoint set of public beliefs described in this chapter—that a significant proportion of APAs report anti-Asian discrimination but that most of the American public views APAs as facing few barriers to success, controlling too much economic power, working too hard to succeed, and characterizeable by negative stereotypes and sentiments— thus leaves APAs in the ironic, vulnerable position where their successes are exploited for rhetorical leverage against less-advantaged minorities, their hardships go unrecognized, and their position in the U.S. racial hierarchy is open to scapegoating and racial resentment. Indeed, these results affirm critics who decry the stereotyping of Asian Pacific

Americans as a "model minority and describe well what Claire Kim calls the "racial triangulation" of Asian Pacific Americans—"the processes of relative valorization and civic ostracism, linked together by essentialist readings of Asian/Asian Pacific American 'culture'"(1999, 36)."[67] The results call into question whether popular images of the "Asian Pacific American" work ethic, family values, and economic achievements act unambiguously as a positive conception of APAs. Put bluntly, public beliefs about racial and ethnic groups in a multiracial context are necessarily comparative and interdependent. Characteristics generously conferred upon one racial (model) minority are characteristics meanspiritedly deferred from other racial minorities.

In fact, the structurally contingent and evolving position of APAs in public opinion confounds the already uncertain future of Asian Pacific American politics——among other things, whether an entity such as an "Asian Pacific American politics" can or does exist, and, if so, what form it takes. As we embark into a new century, APAs already comprise about 10 percent of California's population and are poised to comprise the same tenth of the entire United States population sometime around the year 2050. Yet, as Paul Ong and Don Nakanishi have judiciously noted, "[w]hether Asian Pacific Americans become a major new political force in the American electoral system is nearly impossible to predict with any precision" (1996, 293).

To be sure, there is no consensus among scholars of Asian Pacific American politics. Those who have observed the "third space" between black and white that APAs occupy spin at least three fortunes for the future: (1) that the position of APAs exposes the deep incoherence and ambiguity of the very notion of "Asian Americans"; (2) that the position reveals the disquieting vulnerability of a "middleman minority"; (3) or that the position represents a politically strategic opportunity to be a swing vote (or, by Elaine Kim's account, to at least celebrate the irony and creatively exploit the "interstitiality" of Asian Pacific American identity).[68]

This author would gladly report that the empirical results herein confirmed a reading of contingency as opportunity rather than contingency as incoherence or vulnerability. No such unequivocally sanguine reading avails. What this chapter does suggest are morsels of understanding and potential pathways to avoid vulnerability and incoherence. More concretely, we now have a better understanding of what anti-Asian racial resentment looks like, how prevalent it is, what some of its underlying roots are, and what consequences such negative attitudes hold for public policies that impact upon the Asian Pacific American community.

Endnotes

[1] Many thanks are due to Albert Hahn, Charles Jung, Darlene Martin, and Lisa Sanbonmatsu for their expert research assistance; to participants of the Kennedy School of Government's Politics Research Group and participants at a meeting of project contributors at UCLA for their sage advice in the project's formative stages; to John Brehm, Zoltan Hajnal, Claire Kim, Shirley Lee, Doug Suh, and Paul Ong for their insights on early versions of this chapter. Any shortcomings, oversights, and incongruities, however, are mine, all mine.

[2] I use both "African Americans" and "blacks" interchangeably, and adopt the term "Latinos" to refer to U.S. residents of Hispanic descent. The terms "whites" and "Anglos" are used to identify non-Hispanic whites. I use "APA" as shorthand for "Asian Pacific American" and the term "APAs" is used interchangeably with "Asians." No privileged claims are implied for the designations I use over alternatives like "Asian Americans," "Asian Pacific Islanders" or "Asian Pacific Islander Americans."

[3] This tradition owes much to the influence of Gunnar Myrdal's An American Dilemma (1944), which argued persuasively in its time that racial injustice exists as a result of white racism. Smith (1987) argues that the resulting presumption was that the appropriate solutions to racial injustices lie exclusively in an understanding of whites' racial attitudes.

[4] The 1984 and 1988 National Black Election Study (see Tate, 1993 and Dawson, 1994), the 1993-94 National Black Politics Study (see Dawson, 1999), and the 1989 Latino National Political Survey (see de la Garza et al., 1992) are especially pioneering in this regard.

[5] See, for example, Carmines and Stimson (1989), Hochschild (1995), Kinder and Sanders (1996), Schuman, Steeh, Bobo, and Krysan (1998), and Sniderman and Piazza (1993).

[6] Most of these studies have come from three multiethnic surveys: a 1984 survey from the Institute of Governmental Studies at University of California at Berkeley (Cain, Kiewiet, and Uhlaner, 1989; Uhlaner, Cain, and Kiewiet, 1989; Lien, 1994); the 1992 Los Angeles County Social Survey (Bobo et al., 1994; Bobo and Hutchings, 1996; Bobo and Zubrinsky, 1996); the 1993-94 Los Angeles Survey of Urban Inequality (Bobo and Suh, 1995; Zubrinsky and Bobo, 1996).

[7] The two surveys will often hereafter be referred to as the Post poll and the Times poll.

[8] The Asian Week poll sampled 807 registered voters with Asian Pacific American surnames from California (n=596) and four "control" states-Massachusetts (n=57), Ohio (n=53), Pennsylvania (n=45), and Washington (n=56). Respondents were drawn from voter registration rolls and the survey was conducted by Meta Information Services. The San Francisco Chronicle/KRON/KQED poll sampled 1,000 Bay Area

residents. The sampling design included at least 100 African Americans, Latinos, and APAs and the survey was conducted by Baldassare Associates. The University of Massachusetts McCormack Institute poll sampled 729 respondents (381 whites, 127 African Americans, 107 Latinos, and 114 APAs) and was designed in collaboration with the Institute for Asian American Studies, the Gaston Institute, and the Trotter Institute all at the University of Massachusetts Boston.

[9] Surveys that focus on the perspectives of Japanese Americans, Indian Americans, and Pacific Islanders are notably missing. A 1996 India Abroad Center for Political Awareness poll does survey the political opinions of Indian Americans, but with only a limited battery of questions (see Chopra, Kuntamukkula, and Reeves, 1996).

[10] See Lowe (1996).

[11] On the language segregation of Angelenos, see Lopez (1996); on the effect of survey sampling and question wording on interviews of APAs, see Lee (1998); on "language-of-interview" effects, see Lee (1999).

[12] To be fair as well, the LA Times polls go well beyond most other surveys of Asian Pacific American opinion. In addition to making the costly investment in interviewing respondents in non-English languages, the LA Times polls also consulted with key leaders and academics within each Asian Pacific American community.

[13] In a classic observation on the "contact hypothesis," Gordon Allport some forty years ago cautions that "It has sometimes been held that merely by assembling people without regard for race, color, religion, or national origin, we can thereby destroy stereotypes and develop friendly attitudes. The case is not so simple" (1954). Studies of racial and ethnic conflict (see Olzak, 1992 and Green, 1998), for example show that rapid changes in a neighborhood racial/ethnic composition-and the corresponding increase in inter-racial contact-is a critical incitement to race riots, hate crimes, and other forms of racial violence.

[14] These numbers are from Lee and Fernandez (1998); see also Shinagawa and Pang (1996).

[15] They also find that exogamy rates were significantly higher in the previous 1980 Census at 25 percent. One other finding of note in Lee and Fernandez is that of the intermarriages, the proportion of marriages to across different Asian Pacific American ethnicities ("panethnic" unions) nearly doubled from 11 percent to 21 percent between 1980 and 1990.

[16] There is no question on attitudes toward racial intermarriage for Chinese respondents to the Times poll.

[17] See Bobo et al., (1994).

[18] The Los Angeles Times survey of Korean Americans does not ask about friendships with other Korean Americans.

[19] See, e.g., Takaki (1989) and Chan (1991).

[20] Data from the 1990 Census show well over two-thirds of every Asian Pacific American ethnic group are foreign-born, except Japanese Americans (35 percent) and Pacific Islander Americans (26 percent). The corresponding percent immigrant for Chinese, Filipinos, Koreans, and Vietnamese are 70, 68, 82, and 82, respectively (Jiobu, 1996).

[21] See, for example, Cho (1999), Kibria (1997), and Portes and Rumbaut (1996).

[22] This generational, historical explanation of differences also speaks to interethnic differences in forming multiracial acquaintances: more recently immigrated Koreans and Vietnamese also appear to make proportionately fewer social contacts with blacks and Latinos than do Chinese and Filipinos.

[23] See Clark (1996), Frey and Farley (1993), and Massey and Denton (1993).

[24] See Bobo et al., (1994), Bobo and Zubrinsky (1997), Farley et al., (1994), Zubrinsky and Bobo (1996). Zubrinsky and Bobo find that, consistent with Massey and Denton's assessment of "American Apartheid," African Americans face the greatest resistance by other groups and are consensually viewed as facing the greatest discrimination in housing markets.

[25] This research ranges from Bobo (1983) and Bobo and Hutchings (1996) from the "realistic group conflict" perspective; Sniderman and Piazza (1993) from the "principled objection" perspective; Bobo (1991) and Kluegel and Smith (1986) on social stratification; Kinder and Sears (1981) and Kinder and Sanders (1996) from the "symbolic racism" and "racial resentment" perspectives; and Bobo's (1997) "laissez-faire" racism perspective.

[26] In addition to self-reports of discrimination, the 1993 LA Times poll also asks about two specific kinds of racially discriminatory acts: hate crimes and anti-Asian speech. Across respondent groups, between 12 to 18 percent report being victim to a hate crime; one in three Latinos and one in four APAs report frequently hearing such anti-Asian slurs. Exposure to such an anti-Asian discursive environment is somewhat lower for whites (15 percent of respondents) and African Americans (18 percent of respondents).

[27] When asked if a family member or a close friend had experienced discrimination, the pattern across the four groups remained about the same, with an increased percentage reporting second hand knowledge of discrimination.

[28] An important difference between the two surveys, however, is that the Times poll does not identify the discrimination as exclusively racial or ethnic in nature. Thus, whites who perceive or experience discrimination on the basis of age, gender, sexual orientation,

or some other criterion could well respond affirmatively to this question.

[29] Part of this discrepancy between the 1993 Los Angeles Times poll of Asians writ large and their ethnic-specific polls is quite possibly due to the absence of two other sizeable Asian Pacific American ethnic communities in Southern California-namely, Japanese Americans and Asian Indians.

[30] See Watanabe and Hardy-Fanta (1998). By comparison 33 percent of African Americans and 31 percent of Latinos report such experiences. Moreover, well over a half of these individuals (60 percent of African Americans, 52 percent of Latinos, and 57 percent of APAs) report that the discrimination occurs "very" of "fairly" often.

[31] Whites are not included as one of the choices in the Post poll.

[32] The LA Times poll also describes the tangible tensions that intersect the interstices of the black-white divide. While whites and Asians identify themselves as less discriminated against than blacks or Latinos, both groups view themselves as subject to greater racism than the other. Conversely put, almost no whites view APAs as most discriminated against, and almost no APAs view whites similarly. In terms of identifying offending parties, nearly 20 percent of African Americans name APAs as the most prejudiced group in Southern California; nearly the same proportion of Latinos name African Americans similarly. And while whites often identify themselves as the most prejudiced group, the greatest number of them consider African Americans to be most prejudiced.

[33] The most notable deviation from this consensus is the relative reluctance of whites to view any group as facing substantially different opportunities than they do.

' While the Washington Post poll does not have an identical question, it does ask respondents whether or not nonwhites have the same opportunities to lead a middle or upper class life. To this question, there is a qualitative difference in how all respondent groups perceive the opportunities available to blacks and Latinos from those available to APAs. African Americans are most likely to view both blacks and Latinos as facing less opportunity than whites, followed by Asians and Latinos. Whites are least likely to view any group as facing less opportunity than they do. Respondent perceptions on barriers to a middle class or an upper class life do not differ but for one group: Asians. APAs (by a considerable margin) and blacks and Latinos (by a more modest margin) view Asians as more likely to face barriers to an upper class life than a middle class life.

[35] This rift in the perceived opportunities facing blacks, Latinos, and Asians is not always so sheer, however. In yet another variant, the University of Massachusetts poll asks whether or not different communities of color are "still a long way from having the same chance in life than white people have." Here blacks and Latinos are still viewed as having greater hardships than APAs, but the gap is significantly narrower (especially for

Latinos and APAs).

[36] This question was not asked of Korean-Americans, but one point of comparison might be a question that asks respondents how Korean-Americans are faring relative to blacks and Latinos. Here 68 percent view Koreans as doing better, and only 7 percent view Koreans as doing worse than African Americans or Latinos.

[37] See, e.g., Gilens, (1996), Iyengar (1991), and Reeves (1997).

[38] Four of these reasons-family dissolution, lack of intelligence, language problems, and lack of motivation-describe "attributional" views that place the blame on the individual or group affected themselves; the remaining reasons-the lack of education, lack of jobs, whites' resistance to equal opportunity, and discrimination generally-describe more "situational" views that identify root environmental and structural causes of racial inequality.

[39] By contrast, African Americans, Latinos, and, to a lesser extent, APAs-each of whom faces greater disadvantages than whites by many objective measures of inequality-also opt for situational explanations more commonly than do whites. There is in fact the familiar, discernible rank order in respondents' partiality to situational explanations, from African Americans to Latinos, APAs, and last, white Americans. More generally, responses to attributional explanations are roughly formed around perceived characteristics of the target group in question while responses to situational explanations are roughly formed around the conditions facing each respondent group.

[40] Whites rank a close second for African American and Latino respondents, and APAs rank whites as too economically powerful. While a sizeable proportion of Asian Pacific American respondents rank Asians as too economically powerful, very few whites rank whites as being too economically strong. Blacks are least likely to be cited for having an excess of economic resources by any group.

[41] Regression results are available upon request from the author. This relationship between the perceived economic power of a group and the perceived prejudice of that group holds as well for whites and, to a lesser extent, for Latinos and African Americans.

[42] Put conversely, if a group is not viewed as working hard to succeed, that group-actual material hardships or racism notwithstanding-is less likely to be viewed as enduring significant discrimination.

[43] See Hochschild (1995), McCloskey and Zaller (1984), and Verba and Orren (1985).

[44] Data from the US Commission on Civil Rights (1992) and the National Asian Pacific American Legal Consortium (1997), for example, find record increases in anti-Asian violence into the mid-1990s. Too, the much vaunted economic success of APAs comes into question once economic statistics are disaggregated by Asian Pacific American

ethnic group, by the number of workers per household, by regional variation in household income, by the skills-mismatches in employment, inter alia (see Ong and Hee, 1994; Tuan, 1998). On the history of exclusion and discrimination against APAs, see Chan (1991), Hing (1993), and Takaki (1989). On the more recent controversy involving APAs and campaign contributions in the 1996 presidential campaign, see Lee (1998), Wang (1998), and Wu and Nicholson (1997).

[45] I don't mean to imply that APAs face no discrimination or disadvantages at the lower socioeconomic strata. This is especially true of specific Asian Pacific American ethnic groups. To take the example of foreign-born Vietnamese Americans, more than a third fail to attain a high school equivalency, the median household income is equivalent to that of native-born African Americans (and more than $13,000 per year below that of whites). See Cheng and Yang (1998) and Ong and Hee (1994).

[46] Data from the Post poll sustain this finding: only 26 percent of APAs believe that Asians are given less opportunity than whites to achieve the material trappings of middle class life, but fully 38 percent believe that Asians face greater barriers to an upper class life. While of a lesser order of magnitude, African Americans and Latinos also share this belief that APAs face a glass ceiling. Whites remain remarkably constant, nonetheless, in their assessment of relative parity between APAs and whites to achieve either a middle or upper class life.

[47] Omi and Winant (1994, p. 75). See also Lowe (1996).

[48] Regrettably, no other poll, including the Washington Post, includes comparable measures of anti-Asian attitudes.

[49] See, e.g., Chan (1991), Lowe (1996), and Tuan (1998).

[50] See, e.g., Gilens (1996) and Kinder and Sanders (1996).

[51] See Sniderman and Piazza, 1993.

[52] The mean scores on this seven point scale are 1.86 for whites, 2.13 for African Americans, 1.97 for Latinos, and 1.62 for APAs. The reliability of the scale is ($=.44$ for whites, ($=.35$ for African Americans, ($=.37$ for Latinos, and ($=.27$ for APAs.

[53] Regression results are available on request from the author. Sample size for whites on this question is 341 whites, 71 African Americans, 78 Latino/as. Because of the limited sample sizes of nonwhites in the survey, parameter estimates are considered statistically significant when there is less than a 10 percent chance that they are the result of random variation. For whites, the criterion remains the more conventionally used 5 percent benchmark. The adjusted R-squared ("fit") statistics for whites, blacks, and Latinos are 0.26, 0.41, and 0.18, respectively. The adjusted R-squared statistic for Asian Pacific American respondents is -0.013.

[54] See, e.g., Kinder and Sanders (1996), Sniderman and Piazza (1993), Schuman, Steeh, Bobo, and Krysan (1998).

[55] The significance of whether or not one reports hearing anti-Asian slurs is likely to admit multiple interpretations. Most obviously, it may tell us something about contextual effects-the discursive environment (workplace, community of residence, family) and social networks in which individuals are situated. It may also, however, indirectly measure how commonly the respondent herself uses anti-Asian slurs. Note that this survey item permits the respondent to be ambiguous about whether or not she adheres to or condones such anti-Asian speech.

[56] See, e.g., on racial policy preferences, Bobo (1994), Bobo and Zubrinsky (1997), Zubrinsky and Bobo (1996), and Conway and Lien (1997). On voting behavior and political participation, see Alvarez and Butterfield (1997, 1998), Cain and Tam (1998), Lien (1997, 1998-99), Nakanishi (1991), and Ong and Nakanishi (1996).

[57] Pei-te Lien (1997) has also examined some of the policy questions contained in this LA Times poll, albeit subsumed within the question of whether or not political participation makes a difference in policy positions.

[58] The Washington Post poll does not allow us to view policy preferences as intimately as the LA Times poll and are therefore not presented here. In particular, it lacks any items on racial prejudice (whether specific to APAs or more general across racial minorities) and the questions on situational and attributional explanations of inequality were asked of only a small sub-sample of the pool of respondents.

[59] Of course, the "sympathetic" or "antagonistic" nature of particular policy positions can (and perhaps ought to) be justified and defined on more normative, argumentative grounds.

[60] The resulting scale ranges from 0 to 4; the average scores on this scale are 2.44 for African Americans, 2.08 for whites, 1.89 for Latinos, and 1.45 for APAs. The alpha-reliability scores for these scales are 0.48 for whites, 0.38 for African Americans, 0.47 for Latinos, and a meager 0.29 for APAs. Separate results for each policy issue are available from the author on request.

[61] Analyses of the policy items separately are similar to those in the cumulative index, but with important differences. Results on these separate analyses are available from the author upon request.

[62] Regression results are available on request from the author. Of course, nativity per se does not cause one to adopt policy positions antagonistic to APAs. Rather, it is factors associated with nativity that are somehow not captured in the other variables that likely explains its significance.

[63] Sample size for whites on this question is 343 whites, 83 African Americans, 110 Latino/as, and 128 Asian Pacific Americans. Because of the limited sample sizes of nonwhites in the survey, parameter estimates are considered statistically significant when there is less than a 10 percent chance that they are the result of random variation. For whites, the criterion remains the more conventionally used 5 percent benchmark. The adjusted R-squared ("fit") statistics for whites, blacks, Latinos, and Asians are 0.24, 0.42, 0.26, and 0.17, respectively.

[64] The prevailing view in contemporary opinion research is that political elites (vis-á-vis the formative influence of political parties and liberal-conservative ideology) play a dominant, defining role shaping the political opinions of ordinary individuals. See, e.g., Zaller (1992) and Carmines and Stimson (1989); c.f., Lee (forthcoming).

[65] Asian Pacific American respondents who agree with "anti-Asian" stereotypes and sentiments are statistically more likely to adopt more anti-Asian policy positions, although when the policies are disaggregated, this relationship seems isolated to policy positions over college admissions.

[66] As we have seen, however, the disjuncture is not always modest for African Americans: in the Los Angeles Times multiracial poll, for example, whites are notably unwilling to view African Americans as the most discriminated group in Southern California, despite the fact that African Americans report the highest levels of discrimination and almost unanimously view themselves as the most discriminated group.

[67] On the model minority myth, see Cheng and Yang (1996) and Takaki (1989).

[68] See, e.g., Espiritu (1992), C. Kim (1999), E. Kim (1997), Lee (1998), Lien (1998), Lowe (1996), Nakanishi (1991), Omi (1993), Ong, Bonacich, and Cheng (1994), Tam (1995), Tuan (1998).

References

Allport, G. (1954). *The Nature of Prejudice*. Cambridge, MA: Addison Wesley.

Alvarez R.M. and Butterfield, T. (1997). The Resurgence of Nativism in California? The Case of Proposition 187 and Illegal Immigration. Unpublished manuscript. California Institute of Technology.

Alvarez R.M. and Butterfield, T. (1998). The Revolution Against Affirmative Action in California: Politics, Economics, and Proposition 209. Unpublished manuscript. California Institute of Technology.

Blumer, H. (1958). "Race Prejudice As a Sense of Group Position." *The Pacific Sociological Review*, 1:3-7.

Bobo, L. (1983). "Whites' Opposition to Busing: Symbolic Racism or Realistic Group Conflict?" *Journal of Personality and Social Psychology*, 45:1196-1210.

_____. (1991). "Social Responsibility, Individualism, and Redistributive Policies." *Sociological Forum*, 6:71-92.

_____. (1997). "Racial Attitudes and Relations at the Close of the 20th Century: the Color Line, the Dilemma, and the Dream." In J. Higham (Ed.), *Civil Rights and Social Wrongs*. University Park, PA: Pennsylvania State Univ. Press.

Bobo, L. et al. (1994). "Public Opinion Before and After a Spring of Discontent." In M. Baldassare (Ed.), *The Los Angeles Riots*. Boulder, CO: Westview Press.

Bobo, L. and Suh, S. (1995). "Surveying Racial Discrimination: Analyses from a Multiethnic Labor Market." Russell Sage Foundation Working Paper #75.

Bobo, L. and Hutchings, V. (1996). "Perceptions of Racial Group Competition." *American Sociological Review*, 61(6): 951-971.

Bobo, L. and Zubrinsky, C. (1997). "Attitudes Toward Residential Integration: Perceived Status Differences, Mere In-Group Preference, or Racial Prejudice?" *Social Forces*, 74(3): 883-909.

Brehm, J. (1993). The Phantom Respondents: Opinion Surveys and *Political Representation*. Ann Arbor, MI: University of Michigan Press.

Cain, B., Kiewiet, R., and Uhlaner, C. (1991). "The Acquisition of Partisanship by Latinos and Asian Americans." *American Journal of Political Science*, 35:390-422.

Cain, B. and Tam, W. (1998). "Asian Americans and Immigration: An Exploration of Attitudes and Initiative Vote Patterns." Presented at the Woodrow Wilson Center Conference on Asian Americans and Politics, Washington, DC.

Carmines, E.G. and Stimson, J.A. (1989). *Issue Evolution: Race and the Transformation of American Politics.* Princeton, NJ: Princeton University Press.

Chan, S. (1991). *Asian Americans: An Interpretive History.* Boston, MA: Twayne Publishers.

Cheng, L. and Yang, P.Q. (1996). "Asians: The "Model Minority" Deconstructed." In R. Waldinger and M. Bozorgmehr (Eds.), Ethnic Los Angeles. New York, NY: Russell Sage Foundation.

Cho, W.K.T. (1999). "Naturalization, Socialization, Participation: Immigrants and (Non-) Voting." *Journal of Politics*, 61(4): 1140-1155.

Chopra, A., Kuntamukkala, A., and Reeves, K. (1997). "1996 Survey on the Public Policy Concerns of the Indian-American Community." *Asian American Policy Review*, 7 (Spring): 115-131.

Clark, W.A.V. (1996). "Residential Patterns: Avoidance, Assimilation, and Succession." In R. Waldinger and M. Bozorgmehr (Eds.), *Ethnic Los Angeles.* New York, NY: Russell Sage Foundation.

Conway, M.M. and Lien, P. (1997). "Predicting Support for Affirmative Action Among Four Racial/Ethnic Groups." Presented at the 1997 Annual Meeting of the American Political Science Association, Washington, DC.

Council of Economic Advisers. (1998). *Changing America: Indicators of Social and Economic Well-Being by Race and Hispanic Origin.* Washington, DC: U.S. Government Printing Office.

Dawson, M.C. (1994). *Behind the Mule: Race, Class, and African-American Politics.* Princeton, NJ: Princeton University Press.

_____. (forthcoming). Black Visions: *The Roots of Contemporary African American Ideologies.* Chicago, IL: University of Chicago Press.

de la Garza, R.O. et al. (1992). *Latino Voices: Mexican, Puerto Rican, and Cuban Perspectives on American Politics*. Boulder, CO: Westview Press.

Espiritu, Y.L. (1992). *Asian American Panethnicity*. Philadelphia, PA: Temple University Press.

Espiritu, Y.L. and Ong, P.M. (1994). "Class Constraints on Racial Solidarity Among Asian Americans." In P.M. Ong, E. Bonacich, and L. Cheng (Eds.), *The New Asian Immigration in Los Angeles and Global Restructuring*. Philadelphia, PA: Temple University Press.

Farley, R., et al. (1994). "Stereotypes and Segregation: Neighborhoods in the Detroit Area." *American Journal of Sociology*, 90(3): 750-80.

Frey, W. and Farley, R. (1993). Latino, Asian, and Black Segregation in Multiethnic Metro-areas: Findings from the 1990 Census." Research Report 93-278. Ann Arbor, MI: Population Studies Center.

Gilens, M. (1996). "'Race Coding' and White Opposition to Welfare." *American Political Science Review*, 90(3): 593-604.

Green, D., Strolovitch, D., and Wong, J. (1998). "Defended Neighborhoods, Integration, and Racially Motivated Crime." *American Journal of Sociology*, 104(2): 372-403.

Hing, B.O. (1993). *Making and Remaking Asian America Through Immigration Policy*, 1850-1990. Stanford, CA: Stanford University Press.

Hochschild, J.L. (1995). *Facing up to the American Dream: Race, Class, and the Soul of the Nation*. Princeton, NJ: Princeton University Press.

Hochschild, J.L. and Rogers, R. (forthcoming). "Race Relations in a Diversifying Nation." In J. Jackson, (Ed.), *New Directions: African Americans in a Diversifying Nation*. Washington, D.C.: National Planning Association.

Horton, J. (1995). *The Politics of Diversity: Immigrants, Resistance, and Change in Monterey Park, CA*. Philadelphia, PA: Temple University Press.

Hurtado, A. (1994). "Does Similarity Breed Respect? Interviewer Evaluations of Mexican-Descent Respondents in a Bilingual Survey." *Public Opinion Quarterly*, 58:77-95.

Iyengar, S. (1991). *Is Anyone Responsible?* Chicago, IL: University of Chicago Press.

Jiobu, R.M. (1988). *Ethnicity and Assimilation*. Albany, NY: SUNY Press.

_____. (1996). "Recent Asian Pacific Immigrants: The Demographic Background." In B.O. Hing and R. Lee (Eds.), *The State of Asian Pacific America: Reframing the Immigration Debate*. Los Angeles, CA: LEAP and UCLA.

Kibria, N. (1994). *Family Tightrope: The Changing Lives of Vietnamese Americans.* Princeton, NJ: Princeton University Press.

_____. (1997). "The Construction of 'Asian American': Reflections on Intermarriage and Ethnic Identity among Second Generation Chinese and Korean Americans." Ethnic and Racial Studies, 20(3): 523-544.

Kim, C. (1999). "The Racial Triangulation of Asian Americans." *Politics and Society,* 27(1): 105-138.

Kim, E. (1997). "Korean Americans in U.S. Race Relations: Some Considerations." *Amerasia Journal,* 23 (2):69-78.

Kinder, D.R. and Sears, D.O. (1981). "Prejudice and Politics: Symbolic Racism Versus Racial Threats to the Good Life." *Journal of Personality and Social Psychology,* 40: 414-31.

Kinder, D.R. and Sanders, L.M. (1996). *Divided by Color.* Chicago, IL: University of Chicago Press.

Kluegel, J.R. and Smith, E.R. (1986). *Beliefs about Inequality: Americans' Views of What is and What Ought to Be.* New York, NY: Aldine de Gruyter.

Lee, S. and Fernandez, M. (1998). "Trends in Asian American Racial/Ethnic Intermarriage: A Comparison of the 1980 and 1990 Census Data." *Sociological Perspectives,* 41(2): 323-42.

Lee, T. (1998a). "The Backdoor and the Backlash: Campaign Finance and the Politicization of Chinese-Americans." Politics Research Group Working Paper Series. Cambridge, MA: Kennedy School of Government, Harvard University.

_____. (1998b). "Survey or Surveillance? Campaign Finance and Polling the Political Opinions of Chinese-Americans." Presented at the 1998 Annual Meeting of the Association of Asian American Studies, Honolulu, Hawaii.

_____. (forthcoming). *Two Nations, Separate Grooves: Black Insurgency and the Activation of Public Views on Race in the United States from 1948 to the mid 1960s.* Chicago, IL: University of Chicago Press.

Lien, P. (1994). "Ethnicity and Political Participation: A Comparison between Asian and Mexican Americans." *Political Behavior*, 16:237-264.

_____. (1997a). *The Political Participation of Asian Americans.* New York, NY: Garland Press.

_____. (1997b). "Does Under-Participation Matter: An Examination of Policy Opinions Among Asian Americans." *Asian American Policy Review*, 7 (Spring): 38-54.

_____. (1998-99). "Sociopolitical Context, Ethnic Identity, and Political Participation: Continuity and Change among Asian Americans in Southern California." *National Asian Pacific American Political Almanac* (8th edition).Los Angeles, CA: UCLA Asian American Studies Center.

Lopez, D.E. (1996). "Language: Diversity and Assimilation." In R. Waldinger and M. Bozorgmehr (Eds.), *Ethnic Los Angeles.* New York, NY: Russell Sage Foundation.

Lowe, L. (1996). *Immigrant Acts.* Durham, NC: Duke University Press.

Massey, D. and Denton, N. (1993). *American Apartheid.* Cambridge, MA: Harvard University Press.

McCloskey, H. and Zaller, J. (1984). *The American Ethos.* Cambridge, MA: Harvard University Press.

Myrdal, G. (1944). *An American Dilemma.* New York, NY: Harper and Row.

Nakanishi, D.T. (1991). "The Next Swing Vote? Asian Pacific Americans and California Politics." In B.O. Jackson and M.Preston (Eds.), *Racial and Ethnic Politics in California*, pp. 25-54. Berkeley: Institute of Governmental Studies Press.

National Asian Pacific American Legal Consortium. (1997). *1996 Audit of Violence against Asian Pacific Americans.* Washington, DC: NAPALC.

Okihiro, G.Y. (1994). *Margins and Mainstreams: Asians in American History and Culture.* Seattle, WA: University of Washington Press.

Omi, M. (1993). "Out of the Melting Pot and Into the Fire: Race Relations Policy." In P.M. Ong (Ed.), *The State of Asian Pacific America: Economic Diversity, Issues, and Policies.* Los Angeles, CA: LEAP and UCLA Asian American Studies Center.

Omi, M. and Winant, H. (1994). *Racial Formation in the United States* (2nd edition). New York, NY: Routledge.

Ong, P. and Hee, S.J. (1994). "Economic Diversity." In P. M. Ong (Ed.), *The State of Asian Pacific America: Economic Diversity, Issues, and Policies.* Los Angeles, CA: LEAP and UCLA Asian American Studies Center.

Ong, P.M. and Nakanishi, D.T. (1996). "Becoming Citizens, Becoming Voters: The Naturalization and Political Participation of Asian Pacific Immigrants." In B.O. Hing and R. Lee (Eds.), *The State of Asian Pacficic America: Reframing the Immigration Debate.* Los Angeles, CA: LEAP and UCLA Asian American Studies Center.

Ong, P.M. and Valenzuela, A. Jr. (1996). "The Labor Market: Immigrant Effects and Racial Disparities." In R. Waldinger and M. Bozorgmehr (Eds.), *Ethnic Los Angeles.* New York: Russell Sage Foundation.

Portes, A. and Bach, R.L. (1985). *Latin Journey: Cuban and Mexican Immigrants in the United States.* Berkeley, CA: University of California Press.

Portes, A. and Rumbaut, R.G. (1996). *Immigrant America* (2nd edition). Berkeley, CA: University of California Press.

Reeves, K. (1997). *Voting Hopes or Fears? White Voters, Black Candidates, and Racial Politics in America..* Oxford University Press.

Saito, L. (1998). *Race and Politics: Asian Americans, Latinos, and Whites in a Los Angeles Suburb.* Urbana, IL: University of Illinois Press.

Saito, L. and Horton, J. (1994). "The New Chinese Immigration and the Rise of Asian American Politics in Monterey Park, California." In P. M. Ong, E. Bonacich, and L. Cheng (Eds.), *The New Asian Immigration in Los Angeles and Global Restructuring.* Philadelphia, PA: Temple University Press.

Schuman, H., Steeh, C., Bobo, L, and Krysan, M. (1998). *Racial Attitudes in America* (revised edition). Cambridge, MA: Harvard University Press.

Shinagawa, L.H. (1996). "The Impact of Immigration on the Demography of Asian Pacific Americans." In B.O. Hing and R. Lee (Eds.), *The State of Asian Pacific America: Reframing the Immigration Debate.* Los Angeles, CA: LEAP and UCLA Asian American Studies Center.

Shinagawa, L.H. and Pang, G.Y. (1996). "Asian American Panethnicity and Intermarriage." *Amerasia Journal*, 22(2):127-152.

Smith, A.W. (1987). "Problems and Progress in the Measurement of Black Public Opinion." *American Behavioral Scientist*, 30:441-455.

Sniderman, P. and Piazza, T. (1993). *The Scar of Race.* Cambridge, MA: Harvard University Press.

Takaki, R. (1989). *Strangers from a Different Shore: A History of Asian Americans* New York, NY: Penguin Books.

Tam, W.K. (1995). "Asians—A Monolithic Voting Bloc?" *Political Behavior*, 17(2): 223-249.

Tate, K. (1993). *From Protest to Politics: The New Black Voters in American Elections.* New York: Russell Sage Foundation and Harvard University Press.

Tuan, M. (1998). *Forever Foreigners or Honorary Whites?* New Brunswick, NJ:Rutgers University Press.

Uhlaner, C.J., Cain, B.E. and Kiewiet, D.R. (1989). "Political Participation of Ethnic Minorities in the 1980s." *Political Behavior*, 11:195-221.

U.S. Commission on Civil Rights. (1992). *Civil Rights Issues Facing Asian Americans.* Washington, DC: Government Printing Office.

Verba, S. and Orren, G. (1985). *Equality in America.* Cambridge, MA: Harvard University Press.

Wang, L.L. (1998). "Race, Class, Citizenship, and Extraterritoriality: Asian Americans and the 1996 Campaign Finance Scandal." *Amerasia Journal*, 24(1): 1-21.

Watanabe, P. and Hardy-Fanta, C. (1998). "Conflict and Convergence: Race, Public

Opinion and Political Behavior in Massachusetts." An Occasional Paper. Boston, MA: Institute for Asian American Studies, University of Massachusetts Boston.

Wu, F. and Nicholson, M. (1997). "Have You No Decency? Racial Aspects of Media Coverage on the John Huang Matter." *Asian American Policy Review*, 7 (Spring): 1-37.

Zaller, J. (1992). *The Nature and Origins of Mass Opinion*. Cambridge, UK: Cambridge University Press.

Zhou, M. and Bankston III, C.L. (1998). *Growing Up American: How Vietnamese Children Adapt to Life in the United States*. New York: Russell Sage.

Zubrinsky, C.L. and Bobo, L. (1996). "Prismatic Metropolis: Race and Residential Segregation in the City of the Angels." *Social Science Research*, 25(4):335-74.

Fu Manchu Lives!
Asian Pacific Americans as
Permanent Aliens in American Culture

Robert G. Lee

....

Asians in America, immigrant and native-born, have been made into a race of aliens, Orientals. The Oriental is a mode of representation which constructs the alien as a racial category. Deeply imbedded in American culture, the images that constitute the Oriental at any given moment are frequently contradictory, sometimes mutable, but always stubbornly resistant to eradication. It is the common, if not universal, experience of all Asian Pacific Americans to be asked by other Americans: "Where do you come from?" The question is never completely innocent; it is always freighted with the assumption "you aren't from here." The assumption that Asians are indelibly alien is occasionally revealed in a way that provokes more embarrassment than anger, but all too often, the assumption has devastating consequences.

Recently Dr. Wen Ho Lee, a senior scientist at the Los Alamos Nuclear Laboratory was publicly accused of spying for the People's Republic of China. The accusation was leaked to the press on the eve of the presidential impeachment trial, and not surprisingly the critics of the Clinton administration were quick to howl for blood. Pundits routinely compared Wen Ho Lee to Julius and Ethel Rosenberg who had been electrocuted in 1953 for passing atomic bomb secrets to the Soviet Union and claimed his crimes were no less heinous.

Wen Ho Lee is less a Rosenberg than he is a Dreyfus. Lee was publicly accused of committing a crime for which there is no evidence of having occurred. Although the government surmised that China had knowledge of classified information regarding U.S. missile technology, three years of investigation produced no evidence that any such information had come into Chinese hands through Wen Ho Lee; indeed a subsequent careful reading of the Chinese documents which led to these suspicions in the first instance reveals that whatever classified information that China may possess came from a source other than Los Alamos since it replicates errors introduced after the data left Los Alamos.

Were consequences not so tragic for Wen Ho Lee, and the implications so ominous for Asian Pacific Americans, the present case might easily be fodder for satire. Indeed, both the hysterical rhetoric surrounding the case and the investigation itself bear the tell-tale signs of Dr. Fu Manchu, the pulp fiction villain created by Arthur Sarsfield Ward who, as Sax Rohmer, wrote thirteen novels, four short stories and a novelette about the Yellow Peril incarnate. Rohmer's Fu Manchu was a Western-educated sophisticate, whose brilliance is at the service of an evil Asian empire bent on the conquest of the white world. The novels enjoyed massive popularity in the United States, and Fu Manchu was the first universally recognized Oriental, the archetype of villainy and the first celebrity Asian. In the forty years that spanned Fu Manchu's career in evil, millions read the books, listened to stories about him on the radio, watched him on film and television and followed his heinous crimes in the comics.[1]

The principle reason for suspecting Lee was that he was Asian Pacific American, an Oriental, and therefore predisposed to the role of a brilliant yet treacherous mole. Admitting that FBI targeted Chinese Americans, the Bureau's "China expert" claimed that Chinese espionage techniques were so sophisticated that Chinese American scientists were being exploited by the Chinese intelligence gatherers without their knowledge. Indeed, Chinese spying was so inscrutable that it could occur without anyone knowing about it. The last time that America had been warned of such Oriental inscrutability was during the Second World War, when General John Dewitt justified the incarceration of 110,000 Americans of Japanese descent by insisting that the fact that no acts of espionage or sabotage on the part of Japanese Americans had occurred proved beyond doubt that such acts were likely to occur. The General assured Americans that while German and Italian Americans might be vouchsafe as individuals, no such individual scrutiny could certify the loyalty of Japanese Americans who were "of an alien race."

Yellowface—Marking The Oriental

In March 1997 the cover of *National Review* featured President William Jefferson Clinton, First Lady Hillary Rodham Clinton and Vice President Al Gore, all in Yellowface. The President, portrayed as a Chinese houseboy, buck-toothed, squinty-eyed and pigtailed, wearing a straw coolie hat, serves coffee. The First Lady, similarly bucktoothed and squinty-eyed, outfitted as a Maoist Red Guard, brandishes a "Little Red Book," while the Vice President, robed as Buddhist priest, beatifically proffers a begging bowl already stuffed with money.

By using the Yellowface cartoon to illustrate a story about alleged political corruption, the editors of *National Review* subtly shifted the focus to race and revived a tradition of racial grotesque that had illustrated broadsides, editorials, and diatribes against Asians in America since the mid-nineteenth century. The cover illustrates a story which attempts to summarize allegations that the Clinton administration had solicited campaign donations from Asian contributors in exchange for policy favors. These allegations focused exclusively on Asian and Asian Pacific American contributors and ignored the much larger illegal campaign contributions of non-Asians.[2] Not surprisingly, the *National Review* was silent on the broader questions: the impact of multinational corporations on American politics and the baleful influence of big money on big politics. By focusing only on the Asian and Asian Pacific American campaign contributions, the *National Review* made its view clear that it was not corporate money, or even foreign money generally, but specifically Asian money which polluted the American political process. In the eyes of the *National Review* editors, the nation's First Family (with Al Gore as potential heir) had been so polluted by Asian money that they had literally turned yellow.

Here and elsewhere, Yellowface marks the Asian body as unmistakably Oriental; it sharply defines the Oriental in a racial opposition to whiteness. Yellowface exaggerates racial features which have been designated Oriental such as slanted eyes, overbite, and mustard yellow skin color. Only the racialized Oriental is yellow; Asians are not. Asia is not a biological fact, but a geographic designation, from Malaysia to Mongolia, and Asians come in the broadest range of skin color and hue. Because the great pretension of race is to claim that common ancestry is its organizing principle, it is concerned with the physical, the biological, and the reproductive. But race is not a category of nature; it is an ideology through which unequal distributions of wealth and power are naturalized, that is to say, justified in the language of biology and genealogy. Biology is salient to race only, insofar, as certain sorts of physical characteristics, such a skin color or hue, eye color or shape, shape of the nose, color or texture of the hair, shape of the overbite, etc. are socially designated as markers of racial difference.

Race is a mode of marking cultural meaning onto the body. The designation of yellow as the color of the Oriental is a prime example of this social construction. In 1922, the US Supreme Court denied Takao Ozawa, an immigrant from Japan, the right to become a naturalized citizen. The Court recognized the fact that some Asians, including Mr. Ozawa, were of a more pale hue than many European immigrants who America had already accepted into the nation as white. Race, the court concluded, was not a matter of the actual color of his skin but, rather of Ozawa's blood or ancestry. Ozawa, being of Japanese blood, could not claim to be white, no matter how white his skin might be.[3]

What is the racial meaning of Yellowface? Yellowface marks the Oriental as indelibly alien. As a racialized alien, the Oriental represents a present danger of pollution. An analysis of the Oriental as a racial category must begin with the concept of the alien as a polluting body. The cultural anthropologist, Mary Douglas, argues that fears of pollution arise when things are out of place. Soil, she observes, is fertile earth when on the ground with tomatoes growing in it; it is polluting dirt when on the kitchen table. Pollutants are those objects, or persons, which are perceived to be out of place. They create a sense of disorder and anomaly in the symbolic structure of society. Douglas observes that pollution is not a conscious act, mere presence in the wrong place, the inadvertent crossing of a boundary, may constitute pollution.[4] Aliens, outsiders who are inside, disrupt the internal structure of a social formation; their very presence provokes anxiety.

Alieness is both a formal political or legal status, and an informal, but no less powerful, cultural status. The two categories are related but not congruent. Alien legal status and the procedures by which it can be shed often depend on the cultural definitions of difference. In 1923, a year after the Ozawa case, the Supreme Court stripped Bhagat Singh Thind, an Indian immigrant who was already an American through naturalization, of his U.S. citizenship.[5] In Ozawa , the court had ruled that neither skin color nor cultural assimilation counted in the matter of race. In Thind, despite the contemporary scientific evidence presented that Bhagat Thind, a Hindu of high caste was a descendent of Aryans and therefore Caucasian, the Court ruled that nevertheless he was not white and could no longer be a citizen. The court held that race was not a scientific category but a social one. Chief Justice Sutherland cited the existence of a "common understanding" of racial difference which color, culture or science could not surmount. The important thing about race, the Supreme Court held, was not what social or physical scientists at the time may have had to say about it, but rather how it was "popularly" defined; that is to say, race is a product of ideology.

Asian immigrants were finally granted the right to become naturalized citizens in 1952. Even so, well after the legal status of alien has been shed, no matter what their citizenship, how long they may have resided in the United States or how assimilated they are, the "common understanding" that Asians are an alien presence in America is still the prevailing assumption in American culture.   In 1996, the immediate response of the Democratic National Committee to allegations that it had accepted illegal campaign donations from foreigners was to call Asian Pacific Americans with "foreign sounding" surnames who had contributed to the party's coffers and demand that they verify their citizenship or permanent resident status. The question "Where are you from?" took on an ominous and threatening tone.

One such donor, Dr. Suzanne Ahn, a prominent Houston physician and civic leader, reported to the U.S. Commission on Civil Rights that DNC auditors threatened to turn her name over to the news media as "uncooperative" if she did not release personal financial information to them. Ahn concluded that she had been investigated by the DNC, the FBI and the news media simply because she had contributed to the DNC and was Asian Pacific American. The assumption that Asian Pacific Americans are really foreigners in disguise is by no means limited to the Democratic Party officials.   When Matthew Fong, a fourth generation Californian, ran as a Republican candidate for State Treasurer, he was asked by news reporters whether his loyalties were divided between the U.S. and China.[6]

Orientals

The Supreme Court's reliance on "common understanding" is, of course, a legal fiction.   It gives popular convention. The common sense of "real" Americans is in the power to define race. The "common understanding" of the Oriental as racialized alien therefore originates in the realm of popular culture where struggles over who is or who can become, a "real" American take place and where the categories, representations, distinctions, and markers of race are defined.

The creation of the Oriental as a permanent alien in American culture was critical to the construction of an American nationality which identifies itself as white. The Oriental is not simply a distorted reflection of Asian Pacific American realities, but rather is a representation of racial difference produced and deployed in cultural crises in American society. These crises come in the wake of economic change as the social relations of production transform social life and culture.[7] As a part of the process of constructing the national identity, racial images and stereotypes are ideologically active, imbedded in the discourses of race, gender, class and sexuality and thus contradictory and unstable. The Oriental therefore appears in various guises throughout American popular culture and no single image represents the totality of the representation. Instead it is necessary to understand the Oriental as a discursive field within American racial ideology, out of which a wide array of specific images are constructed, reproduced and transmitted through pictures, songs, paraphernalia, books and movies.

Six dominant images, the Pollutant, the Coolie, the Deviant, the Yellow Peril, the Model Minority and the Gook, figure the Oriental as an alien body and a threat to the American national family. Each of these dominant images is paradigmatic and forms a field from which emerge a wide array of specific images. Each of these representations has been constructed in a specific historical moment marked by a shift in class relations accompanied by a set of cultural crises. It is in these crises that American nationality is periodically redefined in terms of class, gender, sexuality and race. It is in this context that the question, "where are you from?" takes its real meaning.

Before Asian Pacific America

The origins of the Oriental predates Asian immigration to the

United States and, indeed, the United States itself. Images of Asia as the source both of immense wealth and of barbarian invasion are deeply imbedded in the European historical imagination from the time of Alexander the Great. It is not necessary to examine here the originary moments of this encounter to examine the role that the images of the Oriental have played in shaping American national identity.

Although scores of Chinese had settled in the United States, mainly on the Eastern seaboard, in the decades before the California Gold Rush, these early settlers, scattered among the waves of European immigrants coming to the United States, were viewed primarily as curiosities embodying the exotic difference of Asia. Before the arrival of Chinese immigrants in substantial numbers in mid-nineteenth century California, the representation of China had enjoyed a long career in American popular culture. In 1784 Peale's Museum in Philadelphia opened a display of Chinese curiosities among its collections of objects from Africa and India.[8]

The opening of Peale's Chinese collection occurred in the same year that the New York clipper *Empress of China* docked in Canton, opening the fabled China Market to American merchants. By 1805 Peale's, which had been renamed the Philadelphia Museum, had introduced life size figures in "life group" dioramas as a way of displaying its Chinese collections. Chinese artifacts were displayed on life-sized wax models side by side with the models of Native Americans and other "exotic" peoples.

Public interest in such displays inspired Nathan Dunn to open the Chinese Museum in conjunction with Peale's Philadelphia Museum in 1838. Peale, a Quaker, had also been a merchant in Canton for many years. Peale particularly wanted to use his collection of memorabilia to refute negative portrayals of the Chinese as barbaric heathens which were being circulated by frustrated Christian missionaries, and instead promote a positive image of the Chinese as potential trading partners. In the

Chinese Museum, well over a thousand Chinese items were on display, but the central attraction were the eleven dioramas or "life groups." These groups of life-size clay figures dressed in Chinese costumes represented the hierarchy of Chinese society—high and low ranking mandarins, literati, ladies of rank, actors, teachers of the main Chinese religions, itinerant craftsmen, a man being carried in his sedan chair, visitors to a wealthy residence, and farmers. The Chinese museum was a huge attraction; an estimated one hundred thousand people visited it between its opening in December of 1838 and the summer of 1841, when the collection was moved to London.

While the museum diorama situated China as a distant exotic object (simultaneously desirable and repulsive in its difference) in the geographic imagery of a emerging middle-class eager to expand its commercial horizons, the immigration of "ordinary" Chinese people to the United States had an altogether different significance. The arrival of thousands of Chinese settlers in California undermined the definition of Oriental difference, which relied on distance. This earlier construction of cultural difference as distant and exotic was displaced (but not completely replaced) by a construction of racial difference as present and threatening. Once thousands of Chinese settled in the United States, they could no longer be imagined as simply foreign, made strange by their distance. The Chinese, who made up the largest single immigrant nationality in mid-century California, constituted alien presence which the fantastics of an exotic China could not contain.

In the eyes of white settlers from the East, Chinese settlers from the West disrupted the mythic narrative of Westward expansion. In the popular imagination, California was a Free Soil Eden, a place where small producers, artisans, farmers, and craftsmen, might have a second chance to build a white republic, unstained by chattel slavery or proletarian labor.[9] In this prelapsarian imaginary, the Chinese were identified both with the moral chaos of the Gold Rush and portrayed as the harbingers of industrial wage slavery. As the national debate over slavery, abolition and statehood came to a boiling point in the late 1860s, the ideal of establishing California as both free and racially pure demanded the removal, or at least exclusion, of both Chinese and African Americans.

"California as It was and Is" was published in 1855 by John A. Stone the prolific writer of such popular songs as "Sweet Betsy From Pike." The song's refrain imagined a golden pastoral era in California

> I remember, I remember when the Yuba used to pay,
> With nothing but a rocker, five hundred dollars a day.
> We used to think 'twould always last, and would, with perfect ease,
> If only Uncle Sam had stopped the coming of Chinese...

and laid the blame for its passing era squarely on the arrival of immigrants from China. In the pastoral image of "California as It was and Is," the Chinese immigrant represents the entering wedge of disruptive capitalism. After the arrival of the Chinese, independent placer mining on the Yuba collapsed and the song complains, "we're compelled to pay a tax which people say is gambled off . . . And certain ones are trying to give our mineral lands away, to build a railroad from the States, to San Francisco Bay."

Scores of popular songs published between 1855 and 1882 portrayed the Chinese immigrant as an agent of economic decline and social disorder for free white workingmen and their families. Thousands had flocked to the Sierra Nevada foothills after the Sutter's Mill gold strike. For the many men who lacked experience, skills or capital, prospecting for gold was the more alluring alternative to becoming wage workers in the rapid industrializing Northeast or to farming on the prairie. For such men, prospecting for gold represented a return to the small producer economy. They imagined California as a small producer economy, free of slavery, free of the cash nexus of capitalism, and free of the Chinese, "when the Yuba used to pay, with nothing but a pan and pick, five hundred dollars, in a day."

The representation of the Chinese immigrant as a polluting racial Other relied on a trope of insurmountable cultural difference. Unlike the popular characterization of free blacks as fraudulent citizens because they were supposed to lack culture, the Chinese were seen as having an excess of culture. This excess had led them into a state of degradation and cultural degeneration. Excess and degeneration, of course, carried with them connotations of disease, contagion, and pollution. In a culture dominated by virtuous republicanism, which held self-control in a highest esteem, excess was also closely identified with moral sloth.

Mary Douglas has observed that when external boundaries of the social system are perceived to be threatened, attention is paid to the orifices of the body and the bodily functions of ingestion, digestion, and excretion as symbols of entry and exit into and out of the social system. The construction of Chinese racial difference in mid-nineteenth century cultural productions such as the minstrel show, focused on three such natural symbolic systems, each closely related to such boundary crises: language, food, and hair.[10]

In the refrain to "The Heathen Chinee," sung by the famous minstrel performer Luke Schoolcraft, nonsense words combined with pidgin construct the Yellowface singer of the song as childlike and naturally incomprehensible.

> Hi! hi! hi! Ching! ching! ching!
> Chow, chow, wellie good, me likie him.
> Makie plentie sing song, savie by and bye.
> China man a willie man, laugh hi! hi!

Minstrel songs also paid great attention to Chinese foodways; indeed it is uncommon not to find some reference to Chinese eating habits in a minstrel song. Food habits, customs, and rules are central symbolic structures through which societies articulate identity; you are, symbolically at least, what you eat. While the eating of wild animals might endow the young frontiersman with savage strength, the Chinese are identified with eating dogs and cats, animals that are domesticated but not raised for food. Typical of these images are these stanzas from Luke Schoolcraft's, "Heathen Chinee."

> Lady she am vellie good, make plenty chow chow
> She live way up top side house,
> Take a little pussy cat and a little bow bow
> Boil em in a pot of stew wit a little mouse
> Hi! hi! hi!
> Some say pig meat make good chow chow
> Too much largie, no muchie small
> Up sky, down sky, down come chow chow
> Down come a pussy cat, bow bow and all
> Hi! hi! hi!

The Chinese are also identified as eating mice and rats, animals considered filthy and disease-carrying and therefore dangerous and polluting. In the last stanza of Billy Rice's "Chinese Ball," the visitor recounts an imagined Chinese supper.

> For supper we had red-eyed cats
> And boot-legs stuffed with fleas.
> We had fish boiled in castor oil,
> Fried clams and elephant knees,
> We had sauer-kraut and pickled meuse,
> and oysters on the half-shell.
> We had Japanese tea in the key of G,
> which made us feel quite well.

A third focus of minstrel attention was the braided plait of hair or queue worn by Chinese men. While nineteenth century Chinese wore the queue as a required sign of loyalty to the Qing dynasty, in California the Chinaman's queue was a public site of ambiguity and transgression and thus became a principal target for the victimization of the Chinese by every bigot, old and young. Bret Harte reported in a letter to the *Springfield Republican* March 30, 1867,

> Even legislation only tolerated [the Chinese], and while they were busy in developing the resources of the state, taxed them roundly for the gracious privilege. Regularly every year they were driven out of the mining camps, except when the enlightened Caucasian found it more convenient to rob them—a proceeding which the old statutes in regard to the inadmissibility of their evidence in the courts rendered quite safe and honorable. They furnished innocent amusement to the honest miner, when gambling, horse racing or debauchery palled on his civilized taste, and their Chinese tails, particularly when tied together, cut off or pulled out, were more enjoyable than the Arabian nights entertainments. Nature seemed to have furnished them with that peculiar appendage for the benefit of the Anglo-Saxon.

The cutting of the Chinaman's pigtail allowed white men in the mid and late nineteenth century to reenact, at least at a symbolic level, an earlier savage eighteenth century American ritual—scalping. Indeed, the cutting of queues in conjunction with the collection of taxes is reminiscent of the taking of Indian scalps for bounty, a popular practice among English colonists on the Old Frontier. The taking of scalps enabled white working-men to relive an imagined earlier pre-industrial past. It enabled them to reenact their economic anxiety and social frustration in the symbolic castration and disempowerment of a potentially dangerous pollutant. While the display of cut-off queues was not a common public practice, the similarity between scalp-taking and the taking of the queue was not limited to the level of the symbolic. Hundreds of Chinamen were murdered before, during, and after their queues were removed.

The Coolie

Although they had come to America as free, albeit highly proletarianized, workers, Chinese immigrants found themselves segregated into a racially defined state of subordination as coolie labor. The
image of the Chinese immigrant worker as a coolie was a product of the
racialized and gendered process of working class formation in the
1870s and 1880s. In the 1850s, the principally American-born
migrants who fled the Eastern seaboard to California in the face of
proletarianization sought desperately to reconstruct a precapitalist
social order on the free labor of small producers. By 1870 such a vision
was problematic. As factory production boomed and as the internal
structure of the industrial workplace became progressively less strati-
fied, the small-producer ethic, which was the basis of Free Labor ideology, was stretched to its ideological limits. Even as ever more skilled
workers became machine tenders working in ever larger factories, Free
Labor maintained a craft consciousness based on a nostalgic reconstruction of a precapitalist White Republic.

In the 1870s, California's fragmented working class coalesced
around the demand to remove the Chinese from the White Mechanics'
Republic by barring them from entering the territory and by driving
them from the workplace. The great majority of those who harangued,
sang, marched, and rioted against the Chinese in the 1870s were themselves new to California. While their anti-Chinese movement scape-
goated Chinese Californians for immediate economic problems, it
could draw on a dense set of symbols already in play in the ideological
imagination of the state. Prior to the Civil War, separated by boundaries of race, from black chattel slavery and Chinese proletarian labor,
the ideology of Free Labor held out the hope to the white workingman
of the 1850s and 1860s that the downward mobility into wage labor
might be only temporary and that the permanent racial status of white-

ness might provide a new center for an imagined organic community of farmers and artisans.

As mechanization threatened to reduce factory work to the lowest common denominator of unskilled labor and craft guilds resisted by striking, manufacturers turned to immigrants as a reserve army of labor. The use of Irish and Italian as well as Chinese immigrants as strikebreakers became commonplace in the 1870s. After Emancipation, anxiety brought about by the absence of slavery as a racially defined category of labor only heightened when cultural differences of language, religion, and folkways exploded on the factory floor or in city life. In the post-emancipation reconfiguration of an industrial working class, white workers responded by invoking whiteness as a broadly inclusive racial category able to encompass broad cultural or ethnic differences among a growing myriad of European immigrants. Although differences attributed to national origin had not yet collapsed into the term "ethnicity," at this moment they were accorded a status different from race and the distinction between ethnicity and race became critically important.

The Chinese coolie was portrayed as unfree and servile, a threat to the white workingman's family, which was the principle symbol of an emergent working class identity which fused class consciousness with national and racial identity. In March of 1876, hoping to influence the California state constitutional convention, *The Marin Journal* printed the following broadside in the form of a resolve against the Chinese residents of California. The broadside listed several charges that had been leveled against the Chinese presence in California "on behalf of the workingmen of the state and their families."

> That he is a slave, reduced to the lowest terms of beggarly economy, and is no fit competitor for an American freeman. That he herds in scores, in small dens, where

a white man and wife could hardly breathe, and has
none of the wants of a civilized white man.
That he has neither wife nor child, nor expects to have any.
That his sister is a prostitute from instinct, religion,
education, and interest, and degrading to all around her.
That American men, women and children cannot be
what free people should be, and compete with such
degraded creatures in the labor market. That wherever
they are numerous, as in San Francisco, by a secret
machinery of their own, they defy the law, keep up the
manners and customs of China, and utterly disregard
all the laws of health, decency and morality.
That they are driving the white population from the
state, reducing laboring men to despair, laboring
women to prostitution, and boys and girls to hoodlums
and convicts.
That the health, wealth, prosperity and happiness of our
State demand their expulsion from our shores.

Subscription to these demands defined the working-class movement in terms of its own craft elite, and simultaneously met the demand
of European immigrant workers, who by 1870 made up a majority of
industrial labor, for inclusion as part of an ethnically diverse working class
which would be racially defined as white.

The myth of the Chinese coolie laborer racially unfit for membership into the brotherhood of workingmen allowed white American
workers, both native-born and immigrant, to racialize a stratum of wage
work which it equated with wage slavery, while reserving for whites a
privileged semi-artisanal status within the wage labor system. The Coolie
representation not only allowed the nascent labor movement long dominated by its skilled trades to exclude Chinese from the working class; it

also enabled the skilled trades to ignore the needs of common labor which it racialized as "coolie labor" or "nigger work."[11]

Irish immigrants who themselves were in the process of consolidating their own claim to Americanness and a white racial identity led the popular anti-Chinese movement. Among the songs praising the Irish immigrant Denis Kearny as the leader of the white workingman, "Denis Kearny The White Working Man's Hero" displays a range of Irish names and places Kearny squarely in the context of Irish immigration, and explicitly links Irishness and whiteness in a war against the Chinese.

> You have heard of Moriarty, Mulcahey and Malone,
> Also of McNamara, O'Malley and Muldoon;
> But I will sing of Kearny, an anti-Chinaman,
> He's down upon Mongolians, and all their dirty clan.
> So give three cheers for Kearny,
> For he's a solid man;
> He'll raise a grand big army
> and drive out the Chinaman.
> Last week we held a meeting, down forenest the City Hall
> The bold undaunted Kearny was first to get the call.
> Said he, my fellow laborers, if you'll be lead by me
> We'll make Capital respect us
> and drive out the cursed Chinee

Kearny's well-known anti-Chinese posture enables him to rally a working class defined by ethnically inclusive but racially exclusive whiteness, not only against the Chinese, but against capitalists as well. In the final stanza, Kearny, the Irish immigrant politician, stands as hero to labor, racially defined in terms of the "white workingman."

> Now goodnight, my fellow-laborers, I have to go away,
> I'd like to stop and talk to you, but believe me I can't stay
> So join me in the chorus now, and let your motto be,

God Bless the poor white workingman
and the devil take the Chinee.

The Deviant

The Oriental as Deviant is a figure of forbidden desire in the person of the Chinese household servant. Nowhere was the capitalist transformation in mid and late nineteenth century America so powerfully felt as within the family. Structures and meanings of kinship changed as extended households were downsized into nuclear families. Gender roles were redefined as women and men both left (or were forced from) hearth, farm, and workshop into the factory.

By 1870, cities populated by a new working class, by free people of color, and by immigrants created new possibilities for encounters across class, racial, and sexual boundaries unimaginable a decade or two earlier. By contrast, in the middle decades of the nineteenth century, the transformation of the pre-capitalist household into the nuclear family established polarized middle-class gender roles and sexual behavior. The Cult of Domesticity established an increasingly binary and naturalized code of gender and sexuality in an attempt to restore order to sexual behavior. Victorian moralists regarded sexual passion in women as unnatural, deviant and a marker of degraded lower-class status. Chastity and moral order formed the ideal in which Victorian middle-class women were to fulfill the true nature of their sex. The unbridled sexual energy of men, celebrated in the myth of the Western hero, was to be sublimated to the psychic demands of the marketplace or brought into the service of class reproduction within the privatized family. Sexuality was harnessed to reproduction; the pleasure of the erotic, especially the autoerotic and homoerotic, was to be strictly suppressed.

The Cult of Domesticity, only partially successful as an ideology of sexual repression, succeeded in constructing the bourgeois family as a private sphere of chastity and piety. It established a reproductive hetero-sexual regime over the erotic. On the other hand, a public sphere of sexualized activity also flourished. Prostitution in various forms, from the informal exchange of sexual favors for gifts and meals to the exchange of cash, grew to be commonplace in mid-century American cities. In his 1858 study of prostitution in New York, the social reformer, William Sanger, found that fully one quarter of his male respondents had visited prostitutes.

In the transition from the male-bonded world of Gold Rush California to the settled California of the 1870s under the discipline of Victorian domesticity, the Chinese represented a "third sex," that is to say, an alternative or imagined sexuality that was potentially subversive and disruptive to the emergent heterosexual orthodoxy. The Oriental in America could be imagined as an erotic threat to domestic tranquillity for two related reasons. First, during the later decades of the nineteenth century, over ten thousand Chinese women were brought, for the most part forcibly, to the United States as prostitutes. The Chinese prostitute embodied the carnal, available, and mute, but proletarianized, sexuality that mirrored the exoticized female long displayed in the Western literary tradition of Orientalism. Unless it could be contained by race boundaries, this image of female sexuality, uninhibited albeit coerced, threatened to undermine the Victorian image of the passionless true woman embodied in the middle-class homemaker as the moral center of the chaste and obedient social order. Second, thousands of Chinese immigrant men, displaced from earlier employment in manufacturing, agriculture, or mining, entered the new middle-class family as household servants. This entry into the domestic sphere not only displaced female labor (more often than not female Irish immigrant workers) but, by opening up possibilities for relations of intimacy and desire across race and class, threatened to disrupt the patriarchal relations of the family. The

Chinese as a "third" sex represents the possibility of alternative desire in a period during which middle-class gender roles and sexual behavior were being codified and naturalized into a rigid heterosexual cult of domesticity. The representation of Oriental as Deviant justified a taboo against intimacy through which racial and class stability could be preserved.

Unlike the unalloyed hostility toward Chinese immigrants on the part of organized white labor, the attitude of middle-class whites towards the Chinese during the late nineteenth century was ambivalent. On the one hand, the Chinese were highly desired and often considered indispensable as domestic labor; on the other, they represented a threat of racial pollution within the household. The construction of a representation of the Oriental which was both seductively childlike and threateningly sexual allowed for both sympathy and repulsion.

The Yellow Peril

By the turn of the century, Asian immigrants were represented as the Yellow Peril, a threat to nation, race and family. The acquisition of territories and colonies brought with it a renewed threat of "Asiatic" immigration, an invasion of "yellow men" and "little brown brothers." At the moment when the United States prepared to pick up "the White Man's Burden" in the Caribbean and the Pacific, "Asiatic immigration" was said to pose "the greatest threat to Western civilization and the white race."[12]

Domestically, the triumph of corporatism, the homogenization or de-skilling of industrial labor, urbanization, and immigration had all contributed to massive changes in both middle and working class families. These changes resulted in the construction of a culture of consumption which was reflected in new gender roles and new sexual attitudes and behavior among both men and women of both classes. In the aftermath of the First World War and the Bolshevik Revolution, these domestic social and cultural transformations were accompanied by deep anxieties about racial suicide and class struggle.[13]

The Yellow Peril, embodied in the Oriental immigrant, threatened to undermine what Lothrop Stoddard, a popular advocate of eugenics and racial geopolitics, called the "inner dikes" of the white race through its subversion of the family. While Sax Rohmer's Fu Manchu was making Chinatown the headquarters for Oriental evil on a global scale, two of the first American feature films, Cecil B. De Mille's *The Cheat* and D.W. Griffith's *Broken Blossoms* confirmed visually to white audiences the subtle and intimate dangers of Chinatown as home to the Yellow Peril in their midst. These movies allowed Americans to "see for themselves" what writers could only describe about the Oriental, Chinatown, and the Yellow Peril. Even Asians who might appear assimilated even upper class, such as the wealthy playboy Tori played by Sessue Hayakawa in *The Cheat*, were, beneath their surfaces, cruel and brutal. Even the wispy and pure of heart Cheng Huan played in Yellowface by Paul Muni in *Broken Blossoms* could transform a white girl into a prostitute, because his intentions were ultimately irrelevant; his very presence induced moral decay in everyone with whom he came into intimate contact.

The Cheat and *Broken Blossoms* followed Fu Manchu in consolidating "The Oriental" as a trope of racial difference beyond the Chinese. Distinctions between Hisuru Tori, the Japanese (or in a later version of the film, Araku, the Burmese), and Cheng Huan, called the Yellowman, and the myriad of Malays, Dacoits, Thugees, and Tibetan princesses that inhabited Fu Manchu's netherworld were collapsed into a single racial trope of a pan-Asian Orient. In a wide angle shot of an opium den deep in Griffith's London Chinatown, a white woman dressed in the masculine mode identified with the New Woman of the Jazz Age reclines among a motley crew of "Orientals" who could have come directly out of a Fu novel. In the scene, "Chinese, Malays, and Indians" and colored men of all sorts mix here easily and scandalously with white women. The audience can imagine that orphan Lucy's missing mother is not dead at all, but has simply abandoned the family. She may be this "new woman" lost, at the level of the visual at least, to the opium den.

This shot visually confirms the reports Americans had read about Chinatowns as sinks of iniquity since the very establishment of Chinese settlements in the 1870s. Even sympathetic travel narratives from journalists such as Charles Nordhoff in *California for Travellers and Settlers* and Mrs. Frank Leslie's travel accounts in *Leslie's Weekly Magazine* reported in detail on the dark side of the Chinese quarters. In 1880, the virulently anti-Chinese San Francisco Public Health Committee issued a report declaring San Francisco's Chinatown a "public nuisance." In the early years of the twentieth century, journalist Louis Beck in New York Chinatown, the Progressive urban social reformers Helen Campbell and Colonel Thomas Knox in *Lights and Shadows of New York*, and Jacob Riis in *How the Other Half Lives* all described in lurid detail the moral corruption of New York's Chinatown.

Both *The Cheat* and *Broken Blossoms* portrayed the Asian male immigrant as undermining national strength by seducing the white woman and subverting the already weakened white family. In both the DeMille and Griffith films, Asian immigrant men are not redeemed either by their social assimilation (*The Cheat*) or by sympathetic and noble behavior (*Broken Blossoms*) because their race renders them irredeemable. In both cases, the irreducible difference of race is revealed through the Asian man's (unrealized) desire for sexual relations with a white woman. In the critical scene of thwarted desire in each film, the white heroine "instinctively" draws away, much as the Supreme Court would later say that the great majority of "our people" will "instinctively reject assimilation" [with Asians].

The Model Minority

The representation of Asian Pacific Americans as a Model Minority, although popularly identified with the late 1960s and 1970s, originated in the racial logic of cold war liberalism of the 1950s. The image of Asian Pacific Americans as a successful case of ethnic assimilation helped to contain three specters that haunted Cold War America: the red menace of communism, the black menace of racial integration, and the white menace of homosexuality. In place of radical critiques which called for structural changes in American political economy, the Model Minority mythology substituted a narrative of national modernization and ethnic assimilation through heterosexuality, familialism and consumption.

The Second World War was a contradictory experience for Asian Pacific America; on the one hand, state sponsored anti-Asian racism reached its apex with the mass incarceration of Japanese Americans, at the same time anti-Nazi ideology and the demands of new political alliances in Asia resulted in the abrogation of racially defined prohibitions against Chinese, and later Indian and Filipino immigration. By 1952, in the midst of the Korean War, the bar against Japanese immigration was lifted and the right to naturalization was extended to all Asian immigrants. The changes in official attitudes towards Asian immigration and Asian Pacific Americans reflected a cold war imperative. After the division of Europe into opposing, but relatively stable blocs, the conflict between the United States and the Soviet Union was to be carried out in what was to be called the Third World. This required a new set of political alliances with post-colonial nationalist regimes, which were often wary of racial segregation and discrimination in the United States. In order to counter Soviet suggestions to the Third World that United States held the same white supremacist attitudes as their former European colonial masters, the federal government began to intervene on the side of domestic racial civil rights. In key landmark cases dismantling segregation, a key rationale put forward by the federal government was that the appearance of racial discrimination had a negative impact of the struggle against Communism.

It was in the context of this policy of ethnic liberalism, that the heretofore unassimilable Oriental became Asian Pacific American. The narrative of Asian immigrants as morally unfit for citizenship gave way to a narrative of the Asian immigrant experience as model of the successful assimilation of a minority which had overcome its racial disadvantage. As the United States assumed the mantle of empire in the Pacific, interracial relations between white men and Asian women were celebrated on the stage and screen in *South Pacific* and *Sayonara*. Indeed, in both of those productions of James Michener's stories, it is the openness of America to these relationships that is the measure of America's claim to be the rightful leader of the Free World.

America's celebration in the new assimilabilty of Asian immigrants was not limited to the stage or silver screen. Magazines such as *Life, The Saturday Evening Post*, and *Redbook* ran scores of stories about the integration of Japanese warbrides into white American families. The narrative of the Warbride became the narrative of Asian assimilation into American society. In the face of anxieties about the American family in an era of bomb shelters and Kinsey reports, The Warbride was not only a symbol of Pax Americana, but also restored patriarchy to its rightful place in the national family.

The Gook

Since the 1970s, the Model Minority image has coexisted with and reinforced a representation of the Asian Pacific American as the Gook. The shift in the U.S. economy from large-scale industrial production to flexible accumulation and the global realignment of capital and labor have brought about new crises of class, race and national identity. In the context of these contemporary crises, the "intact" and "traditional" Asian Pacific American family is promoted as a model of productivity, savings and mobility, not just for African America or Latino families but now for all American families, including those of the white middle-class. Simultaneously, however, in post-Vietnam and post-liberal American popular culture, the Asian Pacific American is represented as the invisible enemy and the embodiment of inauthentic racial and national identities, the Gook.

The Vietnam War is replayed throughout American popular culture as the narrative of America's decline in the post-industrial era. The received wisdom of the Vietnam War narrative is that America's defeat in Southeast Asia was brought about by a faceless and invisible Asian enemy aided and abetted by an American counter-culture. The rapid growth of the Asian Pacific American population and its apparent success render the Model Minority, like the now mythic Viet Cong, everywhere invisible and powerful. In these narratives, for example in the movie *The Year of the Dragon*, or on the television series *Magnum P.I.*, the war in Vietnam is replayed on American soil but with different results.

In more contemporary narratives of American decline, Asian Pacific Americans are represented as the agents of foreign or multinational capital. Asian Pacific American success is seen as camouflage for subversion. The Model Minority is revealed to be a simulacrum, a copy for which no original exists, and thus a false model of the American family. The Model Minority resembles the Replicants in the science fiction film *Blade Runner*, perfectly efficient but inauthentically human, whose difference is invisible to all but the highly trained eye, the perfect Gook.

In the 1990s, Asian Pacific Americans figure in the narrative of American decline as a harbinger of an invasion of Asian capitalism. The films *Rising Sun*, *Menace to Society* and *Falling Down* all tell a story of the impact of globalized capital on American society. In these films, all set in Los Angeles, the American urban landscape is portrayed as an economic and social desert laid waste by the invasion of Asian capital. Much the same way that Chinese immigrants in the middle of the nineteenth century were represented as the polluting harbingers of industrial capitalism, today's Asian immigrant, whether corporate executive or neighborhood shopkeeper, is portrayed as the embodiment of global capitalism.

Conclusion

The racist humor of portraying Bill and Hillary Clinton and Al Gore in Yellowface works only because The First Family is presumptively white, an enduring, if anachronistic, symbol of America as a White Nation in the popular imagination. Yellowface transforms the First Family, historically and symbolically white, into the Oriental family; Bill, Hillary and Al have, through the pollution of Asian money, become alien, Yellow and Oriental.

The reappearance of the Yellowface grotesque on the front pages of a national magazine was deeply unsettling, particularly to those Asian Pacific Americans who had bought into the myth of the Model Minority. Since the mid-1960s the national media had popularized an image of Asian Pacific Americans as the perfectly assimilated and presumptively accepted ethnic minority in the United States. Among many Asian Pacific Americans, the emergence of the Model Minority image led to a popular preoccupation with "good" stereotypes vs. "bad" stereotypes. However, this preoccupation with "positive" and "negative" stereotypes legitimates and reinforces the racial discourse of the Oriental which produces and reproduces both the Coolie and the Model Minority. We need to understand the Oriental as a complex field of racial representation which contains multiple, contradictory images and stereotypes. It is precisely the complexity, the density and ambiguity of the multiple images contained within it, that gives the Oriental its ideological power, its ability to be imbedded within the broadest web of social concerns, race, gender, class, and its power to survive, mutate and reproduce. Only a critical analysis of these images as agents in a complex racial ideology can lead us to a sharper understanding of race as a social practice and provide us a tool for dismantling it.

Endnotes

[1] William F. Wu, *Yellow Peril: Chinese Americans in American Fiction, 1850-1940* (Hamden, CT: Archon Books, 1982).

[2] These included Simon Fierman who had been fined $6 million (the largest such fine ever levied) and Thomas Kramer, a German national who had been fined $323,000, by the Federal Election Commission for illegal campaign contributions. See "Petition of the National Asian Pacific American Legal Consortium et. al. to the United States Commission on Civil Rights," September 10, 1997 reprinted at http://www2.ari.net.oca.org.complaint.html.

[3] Takao Ozawa v. United States, 260 U.S. 178 (1922).

[4] Mary Douglas, Purity and Danger An Analysis of the Concepts of Pollution and Taboo, (London, UK and New York, NY: Ark Paperbacks, 1966), 54.

[5] *Takao Ozawa v. United States*, 260 U.S. 178 (1922) and United States v. *Bhagat Singh Thind* 261 U.S. 204 (1923). For an analysis of these cases see Philip Tajitsu Nash in Hyung Chan Kim (Ed.), Asian Americans and the Supreme Court, (Hamden, CT: Greenwood Press, 1993); Jeffrey Lesser, "Always Outsiders: Asians, Naturalization and the Supreme Court: 1970-1944." *Amerasia Journal* (1985): 83-100.

[6] See Petition of the National Asian Pacific American Legal Consortium et. al. to the United States Commission on Civil Rights.

[7] Of the many and varied periodizations of American economic history, the one I have found most useful for this study is the analysis of changes in the labor market and the social structure of accumulation by Gordon, Edwards and Reich. See David M. Gordon, Richard Edwards, Michael Reich, *Segmented Work, Divided Workers: The Historical Transformation of Labor in the United States* (New York, NY: Cambridge University Press, 1982). Gordon and his colleagues examine the relationship between long cycles economic activity and the social structure of accumulation. They outline three periods in the development of American capitalism with regard to labor: the period of initial proletarianization from 1820s to the 1890s; the period of homogenization from the 1870s to the onset of WWII during which the labor markets became more competitive and jobs in the capitalist sector of the economy were transformed into the common denominator of semi-skilled labor; the period of segmentation from the 1920s to the present, during which political and economic forces have produced qualitative differences in the organization of work and three distinct labor markets, a secondary labor market and a primary labor market divided into independent and subordinate sectors. Gordon and his colleagues link these broad periods to long swings (on the order of twenty-five years) in global economic activity, each associated with a distinct social structure of accumulation, the institutional environment in which capital accumulation takes place. For a periodization shaped by both economy and culture see Herbert Gutman, *Work, Culture, and Society in Industrializing America: Essays in American Working-Class and Social History* (New York, NY:

Knopf, 1976), 1-78.

[8] Charlotte Elizabeth Smith, "West Meets East: Exhibitions of Chinese Material Culture in Nineteenth-Century America," Masters thesis (University of Delaware, 1987), 7.

[9] See David Roedinger, *The Wages of Whiteness: Race and the Making of the American Working Class* (London, UK and New York, NY: Verso, 1991).

[10] Mary Douglas observes that boundary crises most often focus attention on bodily orifices as symbolic entry and exit points into the social system. Douglas, Purity and Danger, 44.

[11] Alexander Saxton, *The Indispensable Enemy: Labor and the Anti-Chinese Movement in California* (Berkeley, CA: University of California Press, 1971).

[12] Lothrop Stoddard, *The Rising Tide of Color Against White World-Supremacy* (New York, NY: Charles Scribner's Sons, 1920).

[13] See for example, T. J. Lears, *No Place of Grace: Antimodernism and the Transformation of American Culture* 1880-1920. (New York, NY: Pantheon Books, 1981).

Part II

Racial Interactions

Residential Patterns
of Asian Pacific Americans

Tarry Hum
and Michela Zonta

Introduction

Residentially segregated neighborhoods are among the most visible manifestations of the perniciousness and persistence of racial discrimination. The significance of residential patterns is tied to very basic and fundamental human needs in forming social relationships and building community. Neighborhoods are also important sites for services and resources including education, employment, and civic institutions that shape individual opportunities and life chances. For these reasons— at once economic and psychological—residential choices and patterns represent a critical terrain where social relations, racial attitudes, and market forces coalesce. Much research on residential patterns, in particular, the persistence of racial segregation has focused on the social and geographic distance between blacks and whites (Massey and Denton 1993). The demographic landscape of many major metropolitan areas, however, has moved beyond this racial duality. New immigration is a vital engine of sociodemographic growth, without which many cities would experience dramatic declines in population numbers, and subsequent repercussions on the local economy and labor force (James, Romine, Zwanzig 1998; Muller 1993). For the past three decades, Asian immigration has been a key catalyst for urban growth and diversification.

The landmark Immigration and Nationality Act of 1965 eliminated restrictive quotas based on national origin and facilitated an influx of Asians contributing to the demographic transformation of many urban and suburban neighborhoods throughout this nation. While race still influences Asian Pacific American (APA) settlement patterns, it is certainly not to the extent that had prevailed in the past. After a century of racial segregation sanctioned by state and local governments, the period following WWII provided opportunities for APAs to exercise greater residential choice.[1] The movement toward full residential integration; however, has slowed in the past decade or so, and APA settlement patterns are increasingly complex and varied. On the aggregate, APAs remain the least residentially segregated among racial groups; however, the influx of new and diverse immigrants has helped to facilitate the reemergence of historic and new enclaves in both central cities and suburbs.

This study documents how racial attitudes, new immigration, and increasing ethnic and class diversification have shaped the formation of APA communities. A brief historic overview discusses the impact of immigration and housing policies. To study contemporary APA settlement patterns, we use a variety of data resources including the 1970, 1980, and 1990 Census, 1992-1996 Immigration and Naturalization Services records, and the 1993-1994 Multi-City Survey on Urban Inequality (MCSUI).[2] We select the top 30 metropolitan areas with the largest APA populations in 1990 and construct dissimilarity indices to measure the spatial distribution of different racial groups.[3] We study how residential patterns as measured by the dissimilarity index change over time and vary across metropolitan areas, and we identify the factors contributing to inter—metropolitan and interethnic variations. In addition, we document how racial group differences in attitudes relate to individual preferences and choices in housing and neighborhood locations.

Finally, we conduct a detailed analysis of APA residential patterns in four metropolitan areas with a large and growing APA population: Los Angeles, New York, San Francisco, and Oakland. Since APA population growth is driven by immigration, we will look at new immigration in the 1990s to examine whether traditional enclave communities continue to be central settlement sites. We conclude with a brief discussion of two related observations on the significance of APA residential patterns. One observation is that while the aggregate profile of APA residential patterns indicates a high level of integration and residential choice, significant disparity in the housing and neighborhood conditions of APAs persists. A second observation is that the process of residential integration has not been free of conflict, with race continuing to be a salient factor in shaping the homes and communities of all Americans.

Patterns of Asian Pacific American Settlement and Segregation

The early history of APA communities has been one of exclusion and ghettoization. Early APA settlements were the products of successive waves of immigrants from China, Japan, and the Philippines who served as an indispensable labor source for the agricultural and industrial development of the West. These spatially concentrated communities, comprised largely of farmers and laborers, became the targets of racial oppression, forced relocation, and anti-Asian violence. Acquiescing to nativist movements and organized labor, Congress passed laws severely restricting Asian immigration and naturalization in the mid-to-late 1800s that remained part of the U.S. legal codes until the 1950s. State and local laws barred land and business ownership, as well as inter-racial marriages, which further constrained social and economic choices for APAs. The California Alien Land Laws of 1913 prohibited "aliens ineligible for citizenship" from purchasing or leasing land for longer than three years. These laws were not repealed until 1956. Restrictive covenants, threats of violence, and landlord discrimination were additional tools employed to effectively segregate APAs (Chan 1991; Hing 1993).

Societal hostility and discriminatory practices circumscribed life for APAs in the United States and fostered a reliance on co-ethnic resources and strategies as a means for survival (Chan 1991). For the Chinese, collective survival strategies and legal restrictions led to the formation of some of the earliest racial ghettos in this country (Ong 1984; Wong 1982). Well before zoning was legitimately used to separate incompatible activities, cities in California innovated the application of land-use laws as a means to segregate and control the Chinese (Kayden and Haar 1989). Largely "bachelor societies" due to the dominance of male laborers, the sociopolitical organization of the early Chinatowns were centered on traditional associations based on regional, dialect, and kinship ties (Wong 1982; Chan 1991; Kwong 1987; Hing 1993). In contrast, Japanese immigrants were allowed to bring their wives and, as a result, they were able to sustain a family-centered community life. In part, the ability to maintain families reduced the need to establish concentrated enclave communities (Kitano and Kitano 1998). Although the 1913 California Alien Land Laws may have prompted the establishment of Japantown in San Francisco and Los Angeles (Hing 1993), Japantown, as an urban enclave, never achieved a level of concentration and centrality comparable to that of Chinatown. Moreover, the forced relocation to internment camps during World War II "essentially ended the Japantown phenomenon" (Hing 1993, 59), as the four-year internment period resulted in lost property, disruption of community life, and the dismantling of many established Japanese communities (Langberg and Farley 1985). This represented the removal of urban minority neighborhoods at an unprecedented scale, many times more destructive than the impacts of urban renewal decades later.

With the implementation of the 1882 Chinese Exclusion Act followed by the Gentlemen's Agreement in 1907, employers turned to another cheap labor source, Filipinos. Filipinos were exempt from immigration restrictions due to their status as U.S. nationals, an outcome of U.S. colonization. The first major influx of Filipino immigrants occurred in the 1920s and was largely a migration of male laborers seeking work in the agricultural and cannery industries in Hawaii, California, and the Pacific Northwest. Due to the seasonal nature of agricultural work, Filipino workers migrated back and forth between California and the Pacific Northwest's farming regions and cities, notably Los Angeles, San Francisco, and Seattle. Similar to early rural Chinatowns, "Little Manila" formed in cities near farming regions such as Stockton, California (Melendy 1976). These early communities served as a refuge during the off-seasons providing information about employment prospects, social supports, and recreational activities (Melendy 1976).

The alliance between China and the United States during World War II created the political necessity to repeal the 1882 Chinese Exclusion Act over 60 years after its enactment, and in 1943 a yearly quota of 105 Chinese was established.[4] The 1946 War Brides Act also provided a mechanism promoting Asian immigration as the wives of U.S. servicemen stationed in Japan, South Korea, the Philippines, and South Vietnam were allowed to join their spouses in the United States. The influx of women countered the gender imbalance particularly acute in the Chinese community and as a result, family formation became a more common event.

After World War II, the residential mobility of APAs improved considerably as a result of changes in housing and immigration legislation as well as in racial attitudes. In 1948, restrictive covenants were declared unenforceable in the case of *Shelley v. Kraemer* thus ending the practice of racist deed restrictions in the sale or leasing of property (Massey and Denton 1993). Stemming from the civil rights movement, the 1968 Fair Housing Act banned discrimination in the rental and sale of housing, and served as a critical catalyst and tool to desegregate residential markets and monitor the key institutions which shape housing consumption patterns, namely banks and realtors. During this period, the 1965 Immigration Act eliminated discriminatory national origins quotas and facilitated a renewed and diverse immigrant flow of which APAs comprised a significant share.[5] The growing APA population further diversified as the 1980 Refugee Act resettled thousands of Southeast Asian refugees from Vietnam, Cambodia, and Laos during the late 1970s and early 1980s. A mandate of this federal policy was to disperse Southeast Asian refugees throughout the country in order to facilitate their economic and social incorporation into American society.[6]

Contemporary Asian immigration represents a rich heterogeneity in national origins, ethnicity, education and skill levels, language, cultural practices, political experiences and orientations. Historic immigrant groups including Chinese and Filipinos are joined by growing numbers of Koreans, South Asians, Vietnamese, Cambodians, Thai, and others. This diversity in human, social, and financial capital promotes varied and complex strategies for incorporation and adaptation to urban life in the United States. For more fortunate new immigrants, along with many U.S.-born and raised APAs, high levels of educational attainment and household income, coupled with less white resistance have enabled them to integrate into non-APA neighborhoods. For other newcomers, migration networks tend to concentrate these immigrants in cities and neighborhoods where families and friends reside. The effect of this settlement pattern have simultaneously revitalized historic enclaves and expanded their geographic boundaries, and established new "satellite" communities (Lin 1998; Zhou 1992; Massey and Denton 1987, 1991; Boyd 1988). This duality of integration and continued ethnic isolation are explored in detail in later sections.

Present Levels of Segregation and Integration

Although APAs constitute a relatively small share of the total population in most metropolitan areas,[7] their rapid and dramatic growth in the past decades has doubled and, in some cases, tripled or quadrupled their numbers. In 1990, APAs made up 20.5 and 17.5 percent of San Francisco and San Jose's total population, respectively (Table 1; see appendix for all tables). Other West Coast metropolitan areas where APAs comprise a sizable share of the total population range from 10.8 percent in Los Angeles to 8 percent in San Diego. The New York metropolitan area represents the largest concentration of APAs east of California with over 550,000 comprising 6.5 percent of the total population in 1990.

Recent population projections indicate that in 1998, APAs numbered well over 1.2 million in Los Angles County, an increase of 24 percent since 1990. According to these census projections, APAs at 111,111 now comprise a full 17 percent of the population of Queens, New York. Overall, APAs are highly concentrated in several West Coast metropolitan areas and the New York metropolitan region on the East Coast, in other words, the historic places of arrival for early immigrants. This pattern of APA settlement is also characterized by notable ethnic group concentrations (Barringer 1995). Chinese, Koreans, and South Asians[8] are concentrated in the Northeast, whereas Filipinos, Japanese, Cambodians, Vietnamese, Hmongs and Indonesians show a higher concentration in the West (Fong 1998).

One common measure of the level of segregation (and conversely, the level of integration) is the dissimilarity index, which ranges from 0 to 1. The higher the value of the dissimilarity index, the greater the level of segregation. The results in Table 2 for thirty U.S. metropolitan with the highest number of APAs show that APAs are the least residentially segregated minority group. However, there is considerable inter-metropolitan variation in the APA dissimilarity indices. For example, in 1970, the index ranged from 0.25 for San Jose to 0.56 for Chicago. The relative ranking changed over time and in 1990, Stockton had the highest dissimilarity index (0.58) while Portland experienced the lowest level of segregation (0.33). The areas with relatively high levels of segregation in 1990 include historic APA destinations (Los Angeles, San Francisco and New York) as well as fairly recent destinations for new Southeast Asian groups (Fresno and Stockton).[9] Interestingly, with the exception of Anaheim-Santa Ana, the metropolitan areas with the lowest segregation levels are found outside of California. Many of them such as Bergen-Passaic, NJ, Newark, NJ, Nassau-Suffolk, NY, and Washington DC have more than doubled their APA population during the 1990s.

While dissimilarity indices show a decline in African Americans' residential segregation in the last two decades,[10] during the same period, the segregation measures for both APAs and Latinos have increased indicating declining contact with whites. This pattern of increasing spatial isolation is largely attributable to the influx of new immigrants and subsequent population growth. For Latinos, the average dissimilarity index increased from 0.41 in 1970 to 0.48 in 1990, while for APAs, the index increased from 0.41 to 0.44. For both groups, however, segregation scores remain considerably below those of African Americans.

Interestingly, this trend in segregation measures varies across different metropolitan areas. As Table 2 shows, sixteen out of the thirty metropolitan areas present an increase in the index of dissimilarity between APAs and whites from 1970 to 1990, while it has declined in the other metropolitan areas. Some of the increase can be explained by the recent status of new groups who tend to concentrate in specific neighborhoods within metropolitan areas. This most likely occurs in areas with sharply increased immigration levels among the new APA groups—Vietnamese, Cambodians, and Laotians. Such groups tend to have a low socioeconomic status and are generally less able to afford to live in integrated neighborhoods. As Table 3 illustrates, the areas showing the greatest increases in APA segregation scores during both decades are in California, and include primary destinations for new immigrant groups from Southeast Asia. In particular, Fresno represents a major pole of attraction for Hmongs, whereas in Stockton, Cambodians and Laotians are the largest APA group.

In addition to regional differences in segregation measures and trends, dissimilarity indices also vary based on ethnic groups indicating important differences in the level of spatial isolation among APAs. While Japanese Americans experience fairly low levels of segregation, the dissimilarity indices for Southeast Asians and Chinese are high indicating that these ethnic groups experience greater social isolation. The dissimilarity indices for APA ethnic groups in the four most concentrated APA populations outside of Hawaii—Los Angeles, New York, San Francisco, and Oakland—indicate general patterns of variation in the level of segregation experienced by different APA ethnic groups (Table 4; see appendix for all tables). In Los Angeles, Chinese and Southeast Asians experience a fairly high level of segregation. A comparable level of segregation is experienced by Filipinos and Southeast Asians in San Francisco, while the only APA ethnic group that experiences a notable level of segregation in Oakland are Southeast Asians. In contrast, many APA ethnic groups—Chinese, South Asians, Koreans, and Southeast Asians—in New York experience fairly high levels of segregation. Clearly, ethnicity remains an important variable in mediating settlement patterns and the level of residential segregation experienced by APAs.

In summary, while the aggregate level dissimilarity index for APAs at .44 indicates that APAs are the least segregated minority group, we find that there is significant variation when we disaggregate these segregation measures based on region and ethnicity. Moreover, we find that APA segregation has increased in the past two decades on both the aggregate or national level and, notably, in several major metropolitan areas including New York, Houston, San Francisco, and San Diego. A factor shaping APA segregation patterns is the dramatic influx of new immigrants in several metropolitan regions. Multivariate models confirm that the arrival of new immigrants in metropolitan areas is related to the changing levels of APA segregation in the past decade. As expected, the increasing numbers may create a critical mass for enclave formations and/or elicit reactions such as out-migration and suburbanization of non-Hispanic whites. In contrast, linguistic isolation and poverty do not seem to be highly correlated with segregation, since in many cases metropolitan areas with high levels of APA poverty and linguistic isolation do not experience high levels of segregation.

Asian Pacific American Residential Integration

Given the history of segregation, the contemporary patterns of integration for a significant number of APAs poses an important question as to why this is the case. As the previous section reveals, APAs are more integrated with whites than any other minority group despite the increase in APA segregation levels during the 1980s. The research on residential segregation points to a multifaceted explanation invoking both involuntary and voluntary forces (Lieberson and Carter 1982). Aggregate residential patterns stem from the combination of several individual-level processes and structural conditions (Bobo and Zubrinsky 1996; Massey 1985; Schelling 1978). An individual's choice of housing location, for instance, may well be influenced by cost and affordability, location, proximity to work and to good quality schools, stage in the life cycle, as well as by an individual's willingness to reside in a neighborhood of a particular racial/ethnic, socioeconomic, or cultural composition. Moreover, the state of the housing market and the urban economy, the history and scale of immigration, and the physical stock of the city bear much of the explanatory weight for residential segregation (Massey 1985). Last but not least, private and public discrimination in the housing market has played a major role in the perpetuation of racial segregation in U.S. metropolitan areas, especially in the case of African Americans (Massey and Denton 1993).

Scholars have generally employed the assimilation model to explain APA integration[11] as well as the difference-in-preference approach. The assimilation model argues that a group's spatial assimilation is an outcome of the social attainment process. According to this perspective, as members of minority groups earn higher incomes and acquire higher educational levels, they attempt to leave behind less successful members of their groups and tend to convert these status achievements into improved residential outcomes by purchasing residence in neighborhoods with greater prestige, more amenities, better schools, and higher-value homes. Moreover, for minority members, economic and social advancement is associated with greater proximity and similarity to white Americans—the historical and current dominant group in American society. Therefore, the process of upward mobility may include the dispersion of minority group members from an ethnic enclave to areas inhabited predominantly by majority group members. Since rising socioeconomic status and acculturation reduce the social distance between minority members and native-born whites, resistance and out-migration by the latter become unlikely when minority members enter a white neighborhood. This process ultimately results in higher residential integration between minority and majority group members (Alba and Logan 1991; Logan and Alba 1993).

Previous research has found that, consistent with the assimilation model, APAs are not only less segregated than other minority groups, but also that their degree of segregation declines significantly with increasing socioeconomic status, especially in metropolitan areas with the largest APA populations (Massey 1985; Denton and Massey 1988; Massey and Fischer 1999). Studies have also found that suburbanization of APAs in a metropolitan area—which is strongly associated with each group's average income level—constitutes a key step in the process of spatial assimilation, since in most metropolitan regions, suburban areas have higher socioeconomic status than central cities, and suburban residence is typically associated with higher probabilities of contact with white Americans (Massey and Denton 1987; Massey and Denton 1988; Alba and Logan 1991; Zhou and Logan 1991). Asian Pacific Americans have been found to be indeed the most suburbanized of the three major minority groups (Massey and Denton 1988a). In suburbs, APAs have been able to achieve access to relatively advantaged resources and experience segregation levels comparable to those experienced by Euro-American ethnic groups (Logan and Alba 1993; Massey and Fischer 1999).

Recent national socioeconomic trends corroborate the spatial assimilation hypothesis in explaining APAs' low segregation levels compared to those of other minority groups. Indeed, APAs have featured a socioeconomic status comparable to that of whites.[12] On the aggregate, APAs have been distinguished from other groups by their unusual human capital investment and, like whites, they have been likely to fill the jobs that are most highly rewarded. As of 1990, APAs represented the most advantaged minority group along such dimensions as school enrollment, educational attainment, employment, occupational achievement, and earnings (Farley 1997). As Figure 1 illustrates, during the 1990s, APAs had the highest median household income among the racial groups. Further, while their income was relatively similar to that of non-Hispanic whites, they clearly continued to be economically advantaged with respect to blacks and Latinos. In 1998, the median household income of APAs was about $46,600 compared to $28,300 for Latinos of any race and $25,400 for blacks (U.S. Census Bureau 1999). Moreover, in recent years, APAs have continued to show high levels of educational attainment. In 1996, the proportion of APAs with a college education was almost twice that of the non-Hispanic white population (42 percent and 26 percent, respectively). Further, APAs were more than 1½ times as likely to have a bachelor's degree than non-Hispanic whites. As these figures suggest, APAs are advantaged compared to other groups in terms of the economic resources that make residential mobility possible. Their higher purchasing power may help them relocate in areas characterized by a high socioeconomic status and by a significant presence of whites, thus increasing the probability of spatial integration with the majority group.

Economic factors and elements of the urban structure, however, do not act alone in generating and maintaining ethnic and racial integration in cities, but often act in association with interethnic attitudes and preferences (Schelling 1978; Clark 1986, 1992; Bobo and Zubrinsky 1996). According to the preferences approach, minor variations in nonrandom neighborhood racial group composition preferences lead in the aggregate to distinct residential patterns. Not all groups show the same preferences or willingness to accept other-race neighbors, and when areas "tip" beyond tolerance levels for diversity, residential segregation eventually occurs. Experimental data on racial attitudes and neighborhood composition preferences have shown a clear upward trend in the acceptance of integration (Schuman, Steeh, and Bobo 1985). Nevertheless, there is considerable variation along the racial/ethnic spectrum. In general, despite being the least likely to object to residential integration, blacks continue to confront the most resistance from other groups. Whites, on the other hand, stand out as the most desirable neighbors, and yet are the most likely to object to interracial residential contact (Clark 1992; Zubrinsky and Bobo 1996; Bobo and Zubrinsky 1996).

In the following discussion, we adopt the difference-in-preference perspective in order to provide a further plausible explanation of why APAs are the least segregated among the three minority groups. We assume that higher levels of integration with whites depend in part upon the willingness of APAs to enter largely white areas. Further, we assume that whites' acceptance of residential integration with APAs also plays a key role in maintaining lower levels of APA segregation relative to those of Latinos and African Americans.

Our analysis is based on data from the 1993-94 Multi-City Study of Urban Inequality. To examine group differences in residential preferences, the survey used the showcard procedure originally designed for use in the Detroit Area Study (Farley et al. 1978) and presented white, black, Latino and APA respondents[13] with a series of hypothetical neighborhood types that varied in degrees of racial/ethnic integration. Like black and Latino respondents, APA respondents were asked to consider attractive levels of integration with other groups – in this case with whites, blacks, and Latinos.[14] Consistent with previous research (Clark 1992; Bobo and Zubrinsky 1996; Zubrinsky and Bobo 1996), our results show that the majority of APA respondents express a clear preference for an all-APA neighborhood, although the attractiveness of the different neighborhoods depends on the race of potential neighbors. Whites stand out as the most desirable neighbors, whereas Latinos are the least desirable neighbors, followed by blacks. Forty-one percent of APAs prefer an all-APA neighborhood when blacks are the target group, and 49 percent prefer an all-APA neighborhood when Latinos are the target group compared to 15 percent of APA respondents who prefer this type of situation when whites are the target group. Sixty percent of APAs rate a nearly half APA neighborhood as the most attractive when whites are the target group. Further, APAs are the least likely to find predominantly out-group neighborhoods attractive. Neighborhoods with only two APA houses or none are unattractive to all APAs with non-white neighbors (Table 5; see appendix).

Another set of questions inquired about the willingness to move into a neighborhood with varying degrees of integration with whites, blacks, and Latinos. Again, whites appear to be the most desirable neighbors. Virtually all respondents express the willingness to move into a neighborhood, which is roughly half-white and half-APA, and 89 percent are willing to move into a majority white neighborhood.[15] By contrast, only 68 percent and 73 percent express the willingness to move into a majority black or Latino neighborhood, respectively. These percentages drop to 0 percent and 1 percent, respectively, when APA respondents are asked whether they would be willing to pioneer in a 100 percent black or Latino neighborhood (Table 6; see appendix).

Table 7 illustrates white respondents' willingness to move into neighborhoods with varying degrees of integration with minority group members. Clearly, as the proportion of non-whites increases, willingness to move decreases. However, willingness to move into majority white neighborhoods depends very much on the race of the target group. As expected, whites seem to favor APAs as potential neighbors, whereas the percentages of whites willing to pioneer in a majority black or Latino neighborhood decrease at a faster rate. While over half of white respondents would move into a 100 percent APA neighborhood, only 31 percent and 45 percent would pioneer in a 100 percent black or Latino neighborhood, respectively. Moreover, while a full 95 percent of white respondents would move into a nearly half APA neighborhood, their percentage drops to 75 percent and 86 percent, respectively, when blacks and Latinos are the target group. Again, our results are consistent with previous research on the degree of comfort with racial neighborhood change (Clark 1992; Schuman and Bobo 1988; Zubrinsky and Bobo 1996).

As the analysis suggests, preferences for neighborhoods with varying degrees of integration with different racial/ethnic groups are race-specific. Both APAs and whites show a relatively strong pattern of avoidance of African American and Latino neighbors, whereas they are significantly more likely to feel comfortable with substantial integration when their potential neighbors are either white or APA. Therefore, it seems plausible to attribute a significant part of APAs' high integration with whites both to APAs' strong preference for white neighbors and to whites' high levels of acceptance of APA neighbors.

Continued Importance of Ethnic Enclaves

Despite a relative low level of housing segregation, APA residential patterns include the revitalization and expansion of enclaves, defined as concentrated ethnic residential neighborhoods (Portes 1995; Waldinger 1987). This observation complicates a simple and "straight-line" trajectory of APA residential integration (Gans 1992; Marcuse 1997). As noted, one of the impacts of new Asian immigration is the revitalization, expansion, and formation of ethnic enclaves. The revitalization of historic enclaves is evident in the post-1965 development of Chinatowns (Kwong 1987; Zhou 1992; Lin 1998). Notable examples include New York's Manhattan Chinatown, which has extended into neighboring historic immigrant enclaves such as the Lower East Side and Little Italy, while San Francisco's Chinatown has spilled into North Beach. In addition, APA immigrants have established and consolidated new "satellite" communities and diversified the "crabgrass frontier" as many increasingly opt for homeownership in surrounding suburban communities.

The revitalization of historic enclaves, namely Chinatowns, has been accompanied by the establishment of new ethnic enclaves. Koreans have established Koreatown in Los Angeles, while Indochinese refugees have established several ethnic enclaves in Southern California, including "Little Saigon" in Westminster and "Little Phnom Penh" in Long Beach. In contrast, Filipinos and South Asians have not established concentrated "territorial" enclaves comparable to a Chinatown or Koreatown. Socioeconomic qualities including higher educational attainment and occupational positions, English language proficiency, and subgroup religious and regional differences mitigate the need to establish an enclave among South Asians and Filipinos (Sheth 1995). While residential enclaves may not characterize the South Asian experience, economic enclaves have formed in many metropolitan areas such as Queens, New York where a section of Jackson Heights is referred to as Little India due to the agglomeration of South Asian-owned retail shops (Kasinitz, Bazzi, Doane 1998).[16]

One of the unique features of many newer enclaves is their location within the region. Although Koreatown is an inner-city neighborhood, others are not. The saturation of historic enclaves has prompted immigrants to "leapfrog" traditional "ports of entry" neighborhoods and settle in new communities (Lin 1998; Zhou 1992; Massey and Denton 1987). The "Asianization" of central city neighborhoods is also accompanied by immigrant homeownership in surrounding areas (Pitkin et al. 1997), the formation of new "satellite" enclaves (Lin 1998; Chen 1992; Smith 1995) and suburban enclaves or "ethnoburbs" (Fong 1994; Li 1999). Few Asian enclaves, however, continue to reproduce the homogeneity and insularity of historic enclaves. Racial exclusion is no longer the key dynamic driving enclave residence, rather the agglomeration of immigrant-owned businesses and ethnic labor markets offers opportunity structures for new immigrants, which are not available in the mainstream society (Zhou 1992; Portes and Rumbart 1990; Li 1999). Typically, immigrants with resources will avoid the dense urban conditions of enclaves and choose to settle in surrounding suburbs.[17] The high rate of APA suburbanization has facilitated the formation of "ethnoburbs" (Li 1999). A common view is that these suburban APA communities are "Chinatown No More,"[18] and notable examples include Monterey Park in Los Angeles, Flushing and Elmhurst in Queens, New York, and Sunset and Richmond in San Francisco (Chen 1992; Fong 1994; Sanjek 1998).

The noncontiguous development of APA enclaves creates different types of community networks. Some civic leaders claim that historic enclaves and their satellites constitute a "community of interest" since they are settled by immigrants with similar socioeconomic characteristics as historic enclave residents. This can be seen among the community organizations which have branch offices in satellite neighborhoods illustrating a shared institutional infrastructure and social service needs. For example, the main offices of New York's Chinese American Planning Council, Asian Americans for Equality, Chinese Staff and Workers Association, and UNITE Worker Centers are located in

Manhattan Chinatown, while branch offices are located in neighborhoods in other boroughs. Similar patterns can also be seen in Los Angeles as the more established institutions in the older urban core reach out beyond their traditional geographic boundaries.

More recently, the high rates of APA suburbanization and the declining influx of immigrants, especially from Japan, have brought increasing attention to the importance of "symbolic" communities centered on cultural institutions and small businesses that serve an ethnic niche market. For example, Bay Area civic leaders are preparing plans to establish a Filipinotown in Oakland's waterfront that will offer restaurants, senior housing, and a cultural center (Wong 1995). There is strong interest among Bay Area Filipinos to create a visible spatial community that will generate a political presence as well as celebrate Filipino cultural heritage and practices. The development plans include senior housing to accommodate those who may need easy access to the conveniences of ethnic services and products. The declining influx of immigrants may also facilitate the transition of enclave communities into "symbolic" communities. As barriers to residential mobility have declined and the numbers of new immigrants are diminishing, the settlement of Japanese Americans is marked by a high degree of spatial assimilation and suburbanization. As a result, traditional enclaves such as Japantown in San Francisco and Little Tokyo in Los Angeles have evolved into a symbolic community serving as cultural centers and home to a largely elderly population.

To provide a better understanding of APA enclaves, we focus on four metropolitan areas—Los Angeles, San Francisco, Oakland, and New York, which contain the largest numbers of APAs outside of Hawaii. We define an enclave as neighborhoods (zip code areas) with a significant number of APAs rather than restricting the definition to only those neighborhoods with a dominant or majority APA population. This approach, moreover, allows us to capture neighborhoods that are undergoing an initial stage of ethnic transition, and neighborhoods that have a significant APA influence. The definition for an enclave is not standardized across the four metropolitan areas but rather was constructed to reflect the relative share of APAs in the total metropolitan population. In other words, since APAs comprise 21 percent of San Francisco's population, the definition of a highly concentrated APA neighborhood (i.e., an enclave) is an area with 41 percent or more APAs compared to 16 percent or more for New York, where APAs constitute only 7 percent of the region's total population. This classification takes into consideration the specific demographic context of each metropolitan area, and allows us to compare the neighborhood qualities of enclaves, and contrast high and low APA concentrated neighborhoods with respect to such social indicators as poverty level, homeownership, linguistic isolation, and proportion foreign-born.[19] Based on our definition, we find that enclaves continue to be important residential communities as approximately one-third of the APA population in New York (34 percent), Los Angeles (38 percent), and San Francisco (38 percent) resides in a high concentration APA neighborhood (Table 8; see appendix). In comparison, only one in five APAs (21 percent) in Oakland similarly reside in an enclave neighborhood.

Enclave neighborhoods are especially important in facilitating the socioeconomic incorporation of immigrants faced with language and skill barriers (Portes 1995; Portes and Rumbaut 1990). The concentration of linguistically isolated and poor APAs affirms this central function of enclave neighborhoods. Moreover, it is consistent with the demography of enclave communities that a larger share of the foreign-born reside in concentrated neighborhoods relative to other neighborhood types, with only a small share of homeownership indicating a concentration of rental housing and a denser environment.

The enclaves in the four metropolitan areas are diverse to the degree that their generalization as insular and ghetto-like is no longer the sole definition of enclave neighborhoods. In our four metropolitan areas, the neighborhoods with the highest concentration of APAs are the Chinatowns with the Chinese being the dominant ethnic group (Tables 9 and 10; see appendix). These Chinatowns have high rates of poverty and linguistic isolation as well as minimal levels of APA homeownership. Asian enclaves also include other ethnic-specific neighborhoods such as Koreatown and Filipinotown in downtown Los Angeles, a Southeast Asian enclave in Long Beach, CA and Filipino enclaves in Oakland's Hercules and Union City, and Daly City in the San Francisco area. Other enclave neighborhoods are multiethnic, that is, pan-Asian in demographic composition. Finally, Asian enclaves are also located in suburban settings with several which are quite affluent indicated by high levels of median household income and APA homeownership.

New York has eight neighborhoods with relatively high concentrations of APAs,[20] including Manhattan Chinatown and the Queens neighborhoods of Flushing, Elmhurst, Woodside, Sunnyside, and Jackson Heights. Unlike historic Manhattan Chinatown, which is ethnically homogenous with the Chinese comprising 95 percent of the APA population, Asian enclaves in Queens reflect the ethnic diversity of post-1965 immigration.[21] For example, Koreans comprise approximately one-third of the APAs who reside in Flushing, Woodside, and Sunnyside. South Asians are also prominent in Queens and comprise the largest APA ethnic group in Jackson Heights. In addition to Asian enclaves in Queens and Manhattan, concentrated APA neighborhoods are emerging in Brooklyn with the largest in Sunset Park. Since Chinese residents comprise more than three-quarters of the APA population in Sunset Park, its designation as New York's third "satellite" Chinatown seems apt (Oser 1996; Aloff 1997; Matthews 1997). While the rates of poverty and linguistic isolation of APAs residing in enclave neighborhoods outside Manhattan Chinatown indicate a less impoverished condition, the differences in our socioeconomic indicators are not so great suggesting that generally, APAs in New York who reside in concentrated neighborhoods, i.e., enclaves, are generally of more modest means.

In contrast to New York, Asian enclaves in Los Angeles encompass a broader socioeconomic profile as well as location. Los Angeles is distinguished by the growth of suburban enclaves (Li 1999). In addition to the cluster of enclaves around downtown Los Angeles—Chinatown, Koreatown, and Filipinotown—enclaves have been established throughout the region, including the San Gabriel Valley, the South Bay, and the "eastern county district."

In the San Gabriel Valley, Monterey Park has been referred to as a "suburban" Chinatown (Fong 1994), and more recently, as an "ethnoburb" (Li 1999). Monterey Park is the only U.S. city outside of Hawaii with an APA majority population and its social, economic and political transformation is the focus of much recent scholarship (Horton 1995, Saito 1999, Fong 1994, Li 1999). More than one-half of Monterey Park's population is APA with close to two-thirds who are Chinese. The surrounding cities of Alhambra and San Gabriel also have large APA populations of which the Chinese comprise the largest ethnic group followed by Japanese and Southeast Asians. In contrast to the downtown enclaves, Koreans have a minimal presence in the San Gabriel Valley. The Alhambra and San Gabriel enclaves comprised largely of Chinese and Southeast Asians are distinguished by high rates of poverty and linguistic isolation comparable to Los Angeles' downtown enclaves.

The dominant ethnic group in the South Bay enclaves is Japanese followed by Filipinos, and Koreans. This cluster of concentrated APA neighborhoods includes the historic enclave communities of Gardena, Torrance, and Carson. They are distinguished by low levels of APA poverty and linguistic isolation, and high rates of APA homeownership. Additionally, the South Bay enclaves includes two in the Long Beach area—one is largely comprised of Filipinos and exhibits similar qualities to South Bay enclaves, while the second is an

Southeast Asian enclave and has a poverty rate of 44 percent indicating an extreme level of economic impoverishment.

The southeast cities of Diamond Bar, Walnut, Rowland Heights, and Hacienda Heights and neighboring Cerritos and West Covina represent fairly wealthy Asian enclaves as indicated by the low levels of APA poverty, high median household incomes, and APA homeownership. Half of these enclaves are also distinguished by its multiethnic composition—no one APA ethnic group is a majority. Rosemead, however, stands out among the southeast cities with poverty and linguistic isolation levels comparable to Asian enclaves in downtown Los Angeles and Alhambra in the San Gabriel Valley. It is also notable that the APA population in Rosemead is largely comprised of Chinese and Southeast Asians and displays the same correlation between high levels of economic impoverishment and the concentration of Chinese and South Asians as other enclaves throughout Los Angeles County. Finally, Cerritos and West Covina are noteworthy since APAs comprise 39 percent and 29 percent of the total population, respectively. Filipinos make up over one-half of West Covina's APA population while Cerritos is multiethnic, and both share the socioeconomic qualities of fairly affluent Asian enclaves in the southeast section of Los Angeles County.

The areas in the Oakland metropolitan area with a high concentration of APAs are in the cities of Hercules, Fremont, Union City, Oakland, and Berkeley.[22] Hercules and Union City represent Filipino enclaves and some community leaders speculate that if Filipino Americans continue their rate of growth, these enclaves will soon replace San Francisco's Daly City as the hub of the Filipino American population in the Bay Area (Wong 1995). The APA population in Fremont is multiethnic comprised of sizable shares of Chinese, Filipino, and a South Asians. Common to these three enclaves are low rates of APA linguistic isolation and poverty. These indicators are further reinforced by high median household incomes and APA homeownership rates. In contrast, the enclaves in Oakland and Berkeley are characterized by socioeconomic hardship. Located in the northern section of Alameda County, the APA population in these enclaves is largely Chinese. Approximately one-third of the APA population in the Oakland enclave is Southeast Asian and is also distinguished by a high rate of poverty and linguistic isolation. In addition to Chinese, Koreans also make up a sizable share of the APA population in Berkeley's highly concentrated APA neighborhood where linguistic isolation is low but the APA poverty is among the highest at 34 percent.

Of the four metropolitan areas in our study, the San Francisco area clearly stands out with the most numerous densely concentrated APA neighborhoods. APAs constitute the majority racial group in seven San Francisco areas. In addition to Chinatown, enclaves are found in the neighborhoods of Sunset, Richmond, and North Beach. With the exception of Daly City, which is referred to as "Little Manila," densely concentrated APA neighborhoods are overwhelmingly Chinese with Filipinos as the second largest ethnic group. Among these neighborhoods, linguistic isolation is correlated with high poverty and is common in the central city enclaves of Chinatown and North Beach.

The profiles show there are important variations in the ethnic composition and socioeconomic characteristics among APA enclaves. They are no longer necessarily poor homogenous communities. Although many are impoverished communities—in particular, Chinese and Southeast Asian enclaves—there are notable examples of affluent and multiethnic enclave neighborhoods. We further examine this bifurcated pattern of neighborhoods by examining in-migration into enclave neighborhoods, focusing on immigrants in the 1992-1996 INS (Immigration and Naturalization Service) data set. During this period, Los Angeles, New York, San Francisco, and Oakland remained key ports of entry. Overall, New York's historic position as an immigrant capital is affirmed in the 1990s as it received the largest number of new immigrants followed by Los Angeles (Table 11; see appendix). Although San Francisco and

Oakland received more modest numbers, more than one in two newcomers during this period are from Asian countries. In fact, Asian countries were among four of the top five sending countries to San Francisco and Oakland. Immigration to New York and Los Angeles is significantly more diverse as APAs constitute approximately one-quarter (23 percent) to one-third (35 percent) respectively, of new immigrants.

While the Chinese comprised the largest ethnic group among APA newcomers to our four metropolitan areas during the 1990s, Asian immigration is, nevertheless, quite diverse. Asian immigration to Los Angeles includes sizable shares of Filipinos, Koreans, and Southeast Asians. Asian immigration to Oakland is similarly ethnically diverse, while in New York South Asians comprise the second largest ethnic group after the Chinese. San Francisco stands apart in that Asian immigration is largely comprised of Chinese and Filipinos. There are notable regional patterns with respect to the national origins of Chinese immigrants suggesting important differences in social background and resources. More than one-third (35 percent) of Chinese immigrants to Los Angeles are Taiwanese and 14 percent are from Hong Kong. Chinese immigration to New York, on the other hand, is dominated by immigrants from the People's Republic of China with less than one-fifth (17 percent) from Taiwan or Hong Kong.

Based on our three level categorization of APA concentrated neighborhoods, we find that overall, new immigrants are only slightly more likely to settle in a highly concentrated APA neighborhood relative to a moderate or low APA concentration neighborhood (Table 12; see appendix). New APA immigrants to Oakland are least likely to settle in an enclave neighborhood. On the other hand, 40 percent of new APA immigrants to Los Angeles settled in a highly concentrated APA neighborhood which may be an outcome of the multiple and diverse clusters of APA communities in the Los Angeles-Long Beach PMSA.[23] Comparable shares of new APA immigrants to New York (36 percent) and San Francisco (38 percent) settled in a highly concentrated APA community.

"Chain" migratory patterns to well-established ethnic enclave neighborhoods continue to influence immigrant settlement patterns, particularly those of historic immigrant groups such as the Chinese. A comparison of the settlement patterns of new immigrants during the 1990s indicates that those ethnic groups with a sizable presence in highly concentrated APA neighborhoods also receive a large share of new co-ethnic immigrants (Table 12). Well over one in two Chinese immigrants to Los Angeles settled in a highly concentrated APA neighborhood. A similar finding applies to New York and San Francisco where close to one-half of Chinese immigrants settled in an Asian enclave neigh-borhood. The centrality of historic and satellite Chinatowns in Los Angeles, New York, and San Francisco is especially notable in the settlement patterns of new Chinese immigrants.

There are notable regional variations in settlement patterns among APA immigrants in our four metropolitan areas which may reflect historic trends in ethnicity and community formations. For example, Filipino immigrants are more likely to settle in a highly concentrated APA neighborhood if their destination is Los Angeles, San Francisco, or Oakland rather than New York, which does not have a historic Filipinotown or contemporary residential concentration of Filipinos. In fact, close to 60 percent of Filipino immigrants to New York settled in a low concentrated APA neighborhood. Japanese immigrants are also more likely to settle in a highly concentrated APA neighborhood if their destination is Los Angeles or San Francisco where historic Japanese enclaves continue to thrive. While Southeast Asians comprise 15 percent of APA immigrants to Los Angeles and Oakland, more than two-fifths of Southeast Asians settling in Los Angeles will reside in an Asian enclave compared to a significantly smaller share of Southeast Asians who settle in a concentrated APA neighborhood in Oakland. This regional difference may be accounted for by the notable presence of a large Southeast Asian enclave in Long Beach. The residential patterns of Korean immigrants also affirm the importance of existing enclave neighborhoods in shaping the settlement patterns of new immigrants. Similar to the Chinese in New York, the 1990 Census finds that Koreans also tend to reside in highly concentrated APA neighborhoods. Subsequently, close to one-half of new Korean immigrants to New York settled in an Asian enclave neighborhood. Interestingly, South Asians are the least likely ethnic group to settle in a concentrated APA neighborhood across all four metropolitan areas.

Finally, the literature also proposes that ethnic enclaves are the destination of low-skill immigrants most in need of the informal networks and resources of ethnic-based institutions, while newcomers with greater human and financial capital settle where APAs are fewer but homeownership and quality of neighborhood life are much improved. By looking at the data on occupational status prior to migration to the United States, we note a difference among the various occupational categories in the propensity to settle in highly concentrated APA neighborhood (Table 13; see appendix). Overall, approximately one in two (48 percent) APA immigrants who held a laborer or farm, forestry, and fishing related occupation settled in an Asian enclave, compared to 29 percent of those who held a professional, executive or managerial position. Even in Oakland where the majority of new APA immigrants settle in moderate or low concentrated APA neighborhoods, those who were employed in low-skill jobs were more likely to settle in a high concentrated APA neighborhood. In New York, San Francisco, and Los Angeles, immigrants who held low-skill employment as farmers or laborers were significantly more likely to settle in a highly concentrated APA neighborhood compared to their professional counterparts. A notable exception in this bifurcated pattern is Los Angeles where 42 percent of new immigrants who held professional positions settled in a highly concentrated APA neighborhood. The establishment of affluent Asian enclaves in Los Angeles may explain why professionals, executives, and managers are just as likely as those with low-skill occupations to settle in a highly concentrated APA neighborhood although they are unlikely to be settling in the same enclaves.[24]

Conclusion

Our study on APA residential patterns is cause for both optimism and caution. The post-WWII trend towards residential integration is a key spatial trajectory of APAs. Their spatial assimilation is evident in the relatively low segregation measures in a majority of U.S. metropolitan areas. The high tolerance for APA neighbors among non-Hispanic whites suggests continued movement towards assimilation. The influx of new immigrants has transformed the local landscape of many communities across the nation. Their residential incorporation has served as a catalyst in revitalizing central city neighborhoods including revitalizing historic enclaves, establishing new ethnic concentrations, and diversifying suburban neighborhoods. Increasingly, multiracial and multiethnic neighborhoods are becoming an integral part of the social fabric of major metropolitan areas (Nyden, Lukehart, Maly, Peterman 1998). The continuing influx of new immigrants to moderate and low concentration APA neighborhoods will certainly further this trend towards a diverse urban demography.

An area of concern, however, is that the resulting sociodemographic transitions in the housing and economic marketplace of local neighborhoods have not always brought welcome reactions. Where APAs constitute a numerical minority such that they pose no visible impacts on neighborhood change, their presence typically does not generate much reaction; however with a growing critical mass, long-time residents resent the "Asianization" of their neighborhood, and racial conflicts often bearing anti-immigrant tones become more overt and frequent (Smith 1992). Moreover, as neighborhoods are increasingly ethnically and racially diverse, conflict often erupts between minority groups (Johnson and Oliver 1989). In our four case study metropolitan areas, the influx of APAs in neighborhoods has generated conflict centered on the "externalities" of economic growth such as traffic congestion and commercial signage, and increasing interracial competition for housing and public education.

A second area of concern is the growing disparity in APA neighborhood and housing conditions. Our profile suggests a broad range in the residential conditions of APAs as indicated by the varying levels of poverty, linguistic isolation, median household incomes, and homeownership rates. The socioeconomic bifurcation of APAs is evident in the residential patterns profiled in this chapter which indicates both the prevalence of affluent suburban communities and central city immigrant enclaves characterized by housing density and substandard conditions (Schill, Friedman, Rosenbaum 1998). Moreover, the significance of these spatial disparities pertains not only to daily-lived conditions, but also addresses the long-term effects of neighborhood structures, institutions, and networks in mediating opportunities for economic and residential mobility (Galster, Metzger, Waite 1999). Hence, while the residential patterns of APAs indicate a high level of spatial assimilation, the continuing influx of new immigrants underscores the need for renewed policy and programmatic strategies and resources to address persistent disparities in community formations and housing conditions.

Endnotes

[1] Although this period represents significant efforts to remedy institutionalized discrimination in the housing market, attitudinal changes and practices were much slower to change. For example, Acting Assistant Attorney General Bill Lann Lee often retells the story of his father returning to New York City as a WWII veteran and experiencing difficulty in renting an apartment due to racial discrimination (Lee 1999).

[2] MCSUI is a large, multifaceted research project designed to explore inequality in the metropolitan areas of Detroit, Atlanta, Los Angeles, and Boston and asks respondents about their general perceptions of various neighborhoods, their personal preferences, and evaluation of the desirability of neighborhoods based on the racial composition of neighbors.

[3] A dissimilarity index measures "the proportion of minority members that would have to change their area of residence to achieve an even distribution, with the number of minority members moving being expressed as a portion of the number that would have to move under conditions of maximum segregation" (Massey and Denton 1988, 284). The dissimilarity index ranges from 0.0 indicating that no minorities would have to move to 1.0 indicating maximum segregation, i.e., that all minorities would have to move.

[4] A provision which exempted Chinese wives of U.S. citizens from this annual quota of 105 was passed three years later (Hing 1993).

[5] In 1996, over one-third (36 percent) of all new immigrants to the U.S. came from an Asian country.

[6] The Refugee Act of 1980 created the Office of Refugee Resettlement in the U.S. Department of Health and Human Services to resettle and assist refugees achieve self-sufficiency. Based on partnerships with state and local governments, the guideline for resettlement states that "a refugee is not initially placed or resettled in an area highly impacted (as determined under regulations prescribed the Director after consultation with (state and local) agencies and governments) by the presence of refugees or comparable populations unless the refugee has a spouse, parent, sibling, son or daughter residing in that area."

[7] Honolulu was excluded from the list.

[8] South Asians are defined as Asian Indians, Pakistanis, Sri Lankans, and Bangladeshis.

[9] It is important to note that for some metropolitan areas, the dissimilarity index for APAs may be inflated due to random effects stemming from the small number of APAs relative to the number of tracts, particularly in large metropolitan areas such as Detroit, Boston, and Dallas.

[10] Over the past two decades, the average segregation scores of African Americans have

declined from 0.78 in 1970 to 0.68 in 1990. Declines in Black residential segregation are consistent with other trends emanating from the civil rights movement including the growth of the Black middle class, changes in racial attitudes, and an increase in Black suburbanization. African Americans, however, continue to be the most spatially isolated of the three minority groups.

[11] Past studies on residential proximity to whites generally offer support for the assimilation model, with the exception of black patterns. As a matter of fact, while residential outcomes are positively related to socioeconomic status for APAs and Latinos, the relationship between social mobility and residential integration is weaker for blacks and Puerto Ricans, suggesting that some external factors-such as discrimination in the housing market-may be impeding the spatial assimilation process for these groups (Alba and Logan 1993; Gross and Massey 1991; Massey and Denton, 1985.)

[12] Note, however, that APAs consist of many distinct groups that differ in socioeconomic characteristics.

[13] There were a total of 8,916 respondents, of whom 2,965 were white, and 3,167 were black. Data for Latinos and APAs were collected only in two of the cities in the MCSUI - Los Angeles and Boston. In such cities, 1,695 of the respondents were Latino, and 1,089 were APA of Korean, Japanese, or Chinese descent.

[14] APA respondents were asked to imagine that they have been looking for a house and have found a nice one that they can afford. They were told that the house could be located in several different types of neighborhoods, and shown a series of five cards. Each card depicts 15 houses with varying degrees of integration with either whites, blacks and Latinos. The respondent's home is represented by the house in the middle of the card.

[15] A majority white neighborhood is defined here as 87 percent white.

[16] South Asian economic centers have also formed in Flushing, New York, and in the cities of Edison and Iselin in New Jersey (Sheth 1995). In Pacific Palisades, New Jersey, community residents have responded negatively to the agglomeration of Korean shops and have amended their city ordinances to require that stores close at 9 p.m. setting off a protest among Korean Americans (New York Times, 24 November 1999).

[17] See David W. Chen, "Asian Middle Class Alters a Rural Enclave," (*New York Times*, 27 December 1999).

[18] *Chinatown No More* is the title of a 1992 book on Flushing, Queens by Hsiang-shui Chen.

[19] The percentage of APAs in the total PMSA population served as the cutoff for the low concentration category. For example, the low concentration category for New York

is 0-7 percent, Los Angeles is 0-11 percent, San Francisco is 0-21 percent and Oakland is 0-13 percent. The bottom range of the high concentration category is approximately twice the APA population percentage while the moderate concentration category captured the range between the low and high concentration categories.

[20] New York City is comprised of five boroughs or counties-Bronx, New York (Manhattan), Queens, Kings (Brooklyn), and Richmond (Staten Island). The New York PMSA includes the five counties of New York City in addition to the surrounding suburban counties of Westchester, Putnam, and Rockland.

[21] See a recent article on Woodside, Queens, "From a Babel of Tongues, a Neighborhood," (*New York Times*, 26 December 1999).

[22] Highly concentrated APA zip codes in Oakland are defined as comprising 26 percent APAs or more.

[23] Highly concentrated APA zip codes in Los Angeles are defined as comprising 23 percent APAs or more.

[24] Approximately 30 percent of new Asian immigrants who settled in a high concentrated APA neighborhood and had previously worked as a laborer or farm worker settled in a downtown LA enclave (defined as zip codes 90004, 90005, 90012, 90014, 90020, 90026, 90031) compared to 11 percent of those who had held a professional, managerial or executive position prior to migration.

Appendix

MSA	Population	APA	%	Population	APA	%	Population	APA	%		
Anaheim–Santa Ana, CA PMSA	1,420,386	24,545	1.7	1,932,709	86,893	4.5	2,410,556	250,136	10.4	254	188
Bergen-Passaic, NJ PMSA	1,068,687	6,621	0.6	1,292,970	25,125	1.9	1,278,440	65,679	5.1	279	161
Boston, MA PMSA	2,753,700	21,792	0.8	2,763,357	37,035	1.3	2,870,669	94,285	3.3	70	155
Chicago, IL PMSA	6,978,947	66,462	1.0	7,103,624	141,349	2.0	6,069,974	229,475	3.8	113	62
Dallas, TX PMSA	1,555,950	7,278	0.5	2,974,805	24,551	0.8	2,553,362	66,097	2.6	237	169
Houston, TX PMSA	1,985,031	11,949	0.6	2,905,353	51,294	1.8	3,301,937	124,723	3.8	329	143
Jersey City, NJ PMSA	608,894	5,805	1.0	556,972	16,167	2.9	553,099	36,658	6.6	179	127
Los Angeles-Long Beach, CA PMSA	7,032,075	238,223	3.4	7,477,503	434,850	5.8	8,863,164	955,329	10.8	83	120
Minneapolis-St. Paul, MN-WI MSA	1,813,647	7,908	0.4	2,113,533	19,689	0.9	2,464,124	64,944	2.6	149	230
Nassau-Suffolk, NY PMSA	2,116,222	8,156	0.4	2,605,813	24,769	1.0	2,609,212	61,099	2.3	204	147
New York, NY PMSA	8,777,683	173,437	2.0	8,247,961	267,007	3.2	8,546,846	553,987	6.5	54	107
Oakland, CA PMSA	1,495,500	59,247	4.0	1,761,759	120,382	6.8	2,082,914	270,136	13.0	103	124
Philadelphia, PA-NJ PMSA	4,817,914	25,099	0.5	4,716,818	45,382	1.0	4,856,881	103,234	2.1	81	127
Riverside-San Bernardino, CA PMSA	1,143,146	17,288	1.5	1,558,182	24,139	1.5	2,588,793	100,232	3.9	40	315
Sacramento, CA MSA	800,592	30,910	3.9	1,014,002	45,474	4.5	1,481,102	114,820	7.8	47	152
San Diego, CA MSA	1,357,854	38,145	2.8	1,861,846	89,861	4.8	2,498,016	198,675	8.0	136	121
San Francisco, CA PMSA	1,416,474	127,501	9.0	1,488,871	215,307	14.5	1,603,678	329,499	20.5	69	53
San Jose, CA PMSA	1,064,714	38,678	3.6	1,295,071	99,935	7.7	1,497,577	261,574	17.5	158	162
Seattle, WA PMSA	1,421,869	33,785	2.4	1,607,469	63,633	4.0	1,972,961	135,468	6.9	88	113
Washington, DC-MD-VA MSA	2,861,123	29,175	1.0	3,060,922	82,148	2.7	3,923,574	201,502	5.1	182	145
Stockton, CA MSA	249,081	8,832	3.5	347,342	19,888	5.7	480,628	59,789	12.4	125	201
Detroit, MI PMSA	4,199,931	17,445	0.4	4,353,413	33,270	0.8	4,382,299	56,122	1.3	91	69
Fresno, CA MSA	413,053	17,944	4.3	514,621	14,777	2.9	667,490	57,278	8.6	-18	288
Middlesex-Somerset-Hunterdon, NJ PMSA	574,528	2,684	0.5	886,383	16,221	1.8	1,019,835	56,830	5.6	504	250
Newark, NJ PMSA	1,855,230	13,193	0.7	1,762,840	24,813	1.4	1,824,321	52,309	2.9	88	111
Atlanta, GA MSA	1,390,164	2,496	0.2	2,029,710	11,751	0.6	2,833,511	49,965	1.8	371	325
Vallejo-Fairfield-Napa, CA	249,081	8,832	3.5	334,402	20,168	6.0	451,186	47,189	10.5	128	134
Portland, OR PMSA	1,009,129	10,977	1.1	1,242,594	23,971	1.9	1,239,842	45,196	3.6	118	89
Baltimore, MD MSA	2,070,670	8,798	0.4	2,174,023	21,675	1.0	2,382,172	41,870	1.8	146	93
Denver, CO PMSA	1,227,529	12,425	1.0	1,620,902	20,483	1.3	1,622,980	36,687	2.3	65	79

Source: U.S. Census 1970, 1980, 1990
Note: 1980 APA includes: Japanese, Chinese, Filipino, Korean, Asian Indian, Vietnamese, Hawaiian, Guamanian, Samoan. Other not included.
1970 APA includes: total other races including American Indians.

TABLE 2. RESIDENTIAL DISSIMILARITY OF ASIAN PACIFIC AMERICANS, BLACKS, AND LATINOS FROM WHITES IN THE 30 U.S. METROPOLITAN AREAS, 1970-1990

MSA	1970 APA	1970 Blacks	1970 Latinos	1980 APA	1980 Blacks	1980 Latinos	1990 APA	1990 Blacks	1990 Latinos	% Pop. Change 70-80	% Pop. Change 80-90
Anaheim-Santa Ana	0.27	0.84	0.32	0.29	0.50	0.43	0.36	0.44	0.54	254	188
Bergen-Passaic	0.40	0.79	N/A	0.37	0.78	0.79	0.39	0.79	0.61	279	161
Boston	0.50	0.81	0.49	0.51	0.78	0.57	0.46	0.72	0.59	70	155
Chicago	0.56	0.92	0.58	0.46	0.88	0.64	0.47	0.87	0.65	113	62
Dallas	0.44	0.87	0.43	0.43	0.79	0.49	0.47	0.68	0.54	237	169
Houston	0.43	0.78	0.45	0.45	0.75	0.49	0.50	0.71	0.53	329	143
Jersey City	0.39	0.73	N/A	0.47	0.74	0.45	0.44	0.69	0.45	179	127
Los Angeles-Long Beach	0.53	0.91	0.47	0.47	0.81	0.57	0.48	0.74	0.63	83	120
Minneapolis-St. Paul	0.45	0.86	0.49	0.43	0.70	0.43	0.42	0.62	0.35	149	230
Nassau-Suffolk	0.42	0.74	0.29	0.40	0.77	0.36	0.37	0.80	0.45	204	147
New York	0.46	0.71	N/A	0.47	0.77	0.69	0.52	0.83	0.68	54	107
Oakland	0.38	0.79	N/A	0.38	0.74	0.49	0.41	0.69	0.41	103	124
Philadelphia	0.49	0.80	0.54	0.47	0.79	0.63	0.47	0.81	0.65	81	127
Riverside-San Bernardino	0.32	0.69	0.37	0.33	0.53	0.38	0.38	0.49	0.39	40	315
Sacramento	0.48	0.69	N/A	0.44	0.56	0.37	0.50	0.58	0.38	47	152
San Diego	0.41	0.83	0.35	0.46	0.64	0.42	0.50	0.61	0.48	136	121
San Francisco	0.48	0.74	N/A	0.48	0.66	0.56	0.51	0.66	0.51	69	53
San Jose	0.25	0.61	0.40	0.32	0.50	0.46	0.41	0.47	0.50	158	162
Seattle	0.47	0.82	0.30	0.40	0.68	0.22	0.40	0.59	0.25	88	113
Washington	0.37	0.81	0.32	0.31	0.70	0.32	0.35	0.67	0.43	182	145
Stockton	0.30	0.63	N/A	0.42	0.64	0.38	0.58	0.65	0.39	125	201
Detroit	0.46	0.88	0.48	0.48	0.88	0.45	0.48	0.89	0.42	91	69
Fresno	0.35	0.78	0.41	0.27	0.62	0.47	0.50	0.58	0.51	-18	288
Middlesex-Som.-Hunt.	0.34	0.65	N/A	0.42	0.60	0.76	0.41	0.61	0.52	504	250
Newark	0.47	0.79	N/A	0.35	0.80	0.74	0.35	0.84	0.67	88	111
Atlanta	0.45	0.82	0.36	0.39	0.77	0.31	0.45	0.71	0.39	371	325
Vallejo-Fairfield-Napa	0.30	0.63	N/A	0.43	0.52	0.33	0.48	0.51	0.27	128	134
Portland	0.33	0.84	0.32	0.33	0.68	0.26	0.33	0.68	0.31	118	89
Baltimore	0.47	0.82	0.44	0.44	0.74	0.38	0.42	0.75	0.35	146	93
Denver	0.36	0.88	0.47	0.34	0.69	0.48	0.34	0.66	0.48	65	79

Source: Compiled by authors from U.S. Census data

Transforming Race Relations

TABLE 3. METROPOLITAN AREAS PRESENTING MAJOR VARIATIONS IN
DISSIMILARITY INDEXES OF ASIAN PACIFIC AMERICANS, 1970-1990

	1970-1980	1980-1990
Biggest Increase		
#1	Vallejo-Fairfield-Napa (.13)	Fresno (.23)
#2	Stockton (.12)	Stockton (.16)
Biggest Decrease		
#1	Newark (-.12)	Boston (-.05)
#2	Chicago (-.098)	Nassau-Suffolk (-.03)

Source: Compiled by authors from U.S. Census data

TABLE 4. PERCENTAGE DISTRIBUTION OF ASIAN PACIFIC AMERICANS BY ETHNICITY AND SEGREGATION MEASURES IN STUDY AREAS, 1990

	Los Angeles PMSA	San Francisco PMSA	Oakland PMSA	New York PMSA
Total APA	955,329	329,499	270,136	553,987
	%	%	%	%
Chinese	26	51	34	45
Filipino	23	26	29	9
Japanese	14	7	8	5
Asian Indian	4	2	7	18
Korean	15	3	5	14
Vietnamese	6	4	6	2
Cambodian	3	1	2	0
Hmong	0	0	0	0
Laotian	0	0	2	0
Thai	2	0	0	1
Other Asian	3	2	2	6
Pacific Islander	3	3	4	0
Dissimilarity Index	0.48	0.51	0.41	0.52
Exposure Index				
Interaction	0.59	0.54	0.68	0.67
Isolation	0.4	0.46	0.32	0.33
Concentration Index				
Delta	0.74	0.84	0.69	0.78
Absolute	0.91	0.93	0.85	0.96

TABLE 5. ATTRACTIVENESS OF NEIGHBORHOODS WITH VARYING DEGREES OF INTEGRATION WITH WHITES, BLACKS, AND LATINOS, ASIAN PACIFIC AMERICAN RESPONDENTS (N=1,067)

| | If remainder of neighbors are: | | | |
	Whites	Blacks	Latinos	Total
100% APA Neighborhood	15%	41%	49%	37%
67% APA Neighborhood	12	39	44	34
46.7% APA Neighborhood	60	20	7	25
13% APA Neighborhood	7	0	0	2
0% APA Neighborhood	6	0	0	2
N	249	471	347	1,067

Source: 1993-1994 Multi-City Survey on Urban Inequality

TABLE 6. WILLINGNESS TO MOVE INTO NEIGHBORHOODS WITH VARYING DEGREES OF INTEGRATION WITH WHITES, BLACKS, AND LATINOS, ASIAN PACIFIC AMERICAN RESPONDENTS (N=658)

| | If remainder of neighbors are: | | | |
	Whites	Blacks	Latinos	Total
100% APA Neighborhood	62%	74%	92%	78%
67% APA Neighborhood	96	99	99	98
46.7% APA Neighborhood	100	91	92	93
13% APA Neighborhood	89	68	73	73
0% APA Neighborhood	36	0	1	6
N	102	353	203	658

Source: 1993-1994 Multi-City Survey on Urban Inequality

TABLE 7. WILLINGNESS TO MOVE INTO NEIGHBORHOODS WITH VARYING DEGREES OF INTEGRATION WITH BLACKS, LATINOS, AND ASIANS, WHITE RESPONDENTS (N=2,705)

| | If remainder of neighbors are: | | | |
	Blacks	Latinos	APAs	Total
100% White Neighborhood	96%	96%	97%	96%
67% White Neighborhood	90	94	97	92
46.7% White Neighborhood	75	86	95	80
13% White Neighborhood	48	66	75	56
0% White Neighborhood	31	45	56	38
N	1,727	444	534	2,705

Source: 1993-1994 Multi-City Survey on Urban Inequality

TABLE 8. Distribution of Asian Pacific American Population by Neighborhood Concentrations

	APAs 1990	Linguistically Isolated APAs, 1990	Non-Linguistically Isolated APAs, 1990	APAs in Poverty 1990	Foreign Born 1990	Homeownership 1990	New Asian Immigrants 1992-1996
Los Angeles	**11%** 957,788	**26%** 250,123	**44%** 422,637	**13%** 124,836	**32%** 2,906,407	**16%** 1,463,315	**100%** 136,204
High [23% and up]	38%	47%	37%	44%	43%	12%	40%
Moderate [12 - 22%]	32%	31%	35%	33%	37%	23%	31%
Low [0 - 11%]	31%	22%	28%	23%	29%	65%	29%
San Francisco	**21%** 330,820	**27%** 88,187	**47%** 153,859	**10%** 33,628	**27%** 442,718	**19%** 312,236	**100%** 49,552
High [41% and up]	38%	44%	38%	39%	44%	15%	38%
Moderate [22 - 40%]	31%	34%	32%	32%	38%	15%	35%
Low [0 - 21%]	31%	22%	30%	28%	20%	70%	27%
Oakland	**13%** 270,136	**20%** 54,546	**41%** 110,925	**11%** 29,240	**16%** 337,435	**22%** 458,376	**100%** 42,726
High [26% and up]	21%	24%	21%	26%	33%	6%	21%
Moderate [14 - 25%]	41%	45%	42%	41%	21%	28%	43%
Low [0 - 13%]	38%	31%	36%	33%	12%	66%	36%
New York	**7%** 553,693	**31%** 171,391	**38%** 207,940	**15%** 83,611	**27%** 2,285,295	**13%** 1,082,791	**100%** 140,432
High [16% and up]	34%	45%	33%	40%	43%	6%	36%
Moderate [8 - 15%]	30%	28%	31%	26%	37%	22%	29%
Low [0 - 7%]	35%	28%	35%	34%	29%	71%	35%

Source: U.S. Census 1990

TABLE 9. CHARACTERISTICS OF ASIAN ENCLAVES IN THE METROPOLITAN AREAS OF SAN FRANCISCO, OAKLAND, AND NEW YORK

Metropolitan Area	Total Population	Percent APAs	Top Two Asian Ethnic Groups	APA Poverty Rate	Linguistic Isolation	Median HH Income	APA Homeownership
San Francisco							
94108 Chinatown	14,230	62%	Chinese (88%) SE Asian/Filipino (4%)	22%	62%	$21,597	8%
94133 North Beach	27,331	61%	Chinese (95%) Filipino (2%)	19%	53%	$28,891	17%
94121 Outer Richmond	40,559	47%	Chinese (70%) Japanese (9%)	12%	33%	$36,673	54%
94015 Daly City	57,539	46%	Filipino (58%) Chinese (27%)	6%	16%	$43,557	64%
94116 Parkside	39,424	43%	Chinese (76%) Filipino (9%)	7%	29%	$42,686	76%
94134 San Francisco	34,603	43%	Chinese (55%) Filipino (36%)	7%	36%	$32,924	74%
94122 Outer Sunset	52,828	41%	Chinese (74%) Filipino (10%)	9%	31%	$36,581	62%
Oakland							
94547 Hercules	16,502	43%	Filipino (60%) Chinese (26%)	2%	12%	$55,619	94%
94555 Fremont	29,312	38%	Filipino (36%) Chinese (32%)	3%	16%	$58,900	86%
94606 Oakland	38,497	38%	Chinese (56%) Southeast Asian (31%)	29%	57%	$22,385	29%
94587 Union City	52,881	34%	Filipino (55%) Chinese (16%)	5%	17%	$47,245	76%
94704 Berkeley	23,487	27%	Chinese (48%) Korean (12%)	34%	9%	$17,930	7%
New York							
Manhattan							
10013 Chinatown-Tribeca	22,115	45%	Chinese (96%) ------	24%	63%	$28,836	6%
10002 Chinatown-Lower East Side	84,206	42%	Chinese (96%) ------	25%	59%	$17,378	4%
10038 Chinatown-South St.Seaport	13,815	32%	Chinese (97%) ------	22%	49%	$22,912	10%
10012 Soho-Chinatown	25,801	19%	Chinese (85%) ------	27%	54%	$32,649	10%
Queens							
11355 Flushing	69,756	38%	Chinese (43%) Korean (28%)	14%	37%	$30,978	32%
11354 Flushing	51,513	28%	Korean (47%) Chinese (37%)	16%	46%	$30,146	29%
11373 Elmhurst	88,039	37%	Chinese (36%) Korean (27%)	15%	37%	$31,230	29%
11377 Woodside	76,519	23%	Korean (31%) Chinese (29%)	16%	36%	$29,490	28%
11104 Sunnyside	26,059	20%	Korean (40%) Chinese (27%)	21%	45%	$27,503	17%
11432 Jackson Heights	53,127	19%	Asian Indian (37%) Filipino (26%)	7%	13%	$35,224	49%
11364 Oakland Gardens	32,093	16%	Chinese (44%) Korean (36%)	8%	34%	$45,695	77%
Brooklyn							
11220 Sunset Park	76,875	18%	Chinese (76%) South Asian (9%)	20%	47%	$25,244	30%

Source: U.S. Census 1990

TABLE 10. CHARACTERISTICS OF ASIAN ENCLAVES IN LOS ANGELES COUNTY

Los Angeles County	Total Population	Percent APAs	Top Two Asian Ethnic Groups		APA Poverty Rate	Linguistic Isolation	Median HH Income	APA Homeownership
Los Angeles								
90020	35,016	40%	Korean (61%)	Filipino (22%)	22%	48%	$21,666	7%
90012	28,487	40%	Chinese (74%)	Southeast Asian (14%)	26%	67%	$16,334	12%
90031	40,111	28%	Chinese (79%)	Southeast Asian (13%)	34%	62%	$22,439	31%
90004	64,141	26%	Korean (48%)	Filipino (34%)	14%	39%	$24,009	20%
90005	35,606	25%	Korean (68%)	Filipino (15%)	17%	50%	$18,724	11%
90026	75,214	24%	Filipino (46%)	Chinese (23%)	18%	31%	$24,997	31%
90014	2,825	23%	Korean (69%)	Chinese (15%)	24%	72%	$7,076	3%
South Bay/Long Beach								
90247 Gardena	41,923	36%	Japanese (56%)	Korean (18%)	6%	27%	$31,863	45%
90248 Gardena	9,624	34%	Japanese (73%)	Korean (10%)	7%	18%	$39,063	76%
90745 Carson	50,116	35%	Filipino (67%)	Korean (6%)	6%	10%	$41,916	74%
90504 Torrance	30,278	31%	Japanese (54%)	Chinese (15%)	7%	26%	$45,811	67%
90503 Torrance	40,330	23%	Japanese (37%)	Korean (25%)	7%	36%	$47,559	52%
90810 Long Beach	36,713	28%	Filipino (70%)	Southeast Asian (9%)	8%	15%	$30,625	59%
90813 Long Beach	58,022	23%	Southeast Asian (80%)	Filipino (7%)	44%	49%	$18,110	
7% **San Gabriel Valley**								
91754 Monterey Park	62,201	57%	Chinese (63%)	Japanese (17%)	18%	40%	$32,508	56%
91801 Alhambra	51,003	39%	Chinese (70%)	Southeast Asian (10%)	22%	46%	$30,753	39%
91803 Alhambra	30,372	38%	Chinese (66%)	Southeast Asian (14%)	16%	43%	$32,343	49%
91776 San Gabriel	34,957	34%	Chinese (66%)	Southeast Asian (14%)	23%	47%	$29,909	43%
91775 San Gabriel	21,299	23%	Chinese (52%)	Japanese (22%)	8%	36%	$45,068	71%
Southeast Cities								
91789 Walnut	42,339	35%	Chinese (32%)	Filipino (30%)	5%	28%	$61,686	95%
91770 Rosemead	59,961	34%	Chinese (58%)	Southeast Asian (22%)	22%	50%	$30,560	58%
91748 Rowland Heights	40,645	30%	Chinese (38%)	Filipino (25%)	10%	25%	$45,635	77%
91745 Hacienda Height	51,987	27%	Chinese (58%)	Korean (14%)	9%	32%	$51,604	81%
91765 Diamond Bar	42,027	24%	Chinese (29%)	Filipino (22%)	8%	26%	$59,544	91%
91108 San Marino	13,067	32%	Chinese (79%)	Japanese (11%)	6%	28%	$100,536	91%
91007 Arcadia	5,745	24%	Chinese (65%)	Korean (14%)	8%	38%	$42,144	67%

TABLE 11. New Immigration to the Four Study Areas, 1992-1996

	Los Angeles	San Francisco	Oakland	New York
Total New Immigrants	384,603	91,382	70,976	613,984
Region of Birth				
Asia	35%	54%	60%	23%
Europe	14	21	9	24
North America	21	6	11	1
Caribbean	0.7	0.4	0.6	31
Central America	15	8	4	3
South America	3	3	2	12
Middle East	8	4	7	3
Africa	2	2	4	4
Pacific Islands	0.5	2	2	0.1
Top Five Sending Countries	Mexico (20%)	People's Rep. Of China (18%)	Philippines (18%)	Dominican Republic (19%)
	Philippines (10%)	Philippines (16%)	People's Rep. Of China (12%)	People's Rep. Of China (9%)
	El Salvador (9%)	Hong Kong (6%)	Mexico (10%)	Jamaica (5%)
	People's Rep. Of China (5%)	Ukraine (5%)	Vietnam (8%)	Guyana (5%)
	Iran (5%)	Vietnam (5%)	India (8%)	Ecuador (3%)

Source: INS 1992-1996

TABLE 12. DISTRIBUTION OF ASIAN ETHNIC POPULATION AND NEW IMMIGRANTS BY NEIGHBORHOOD CONCENTRATIONS, 1990

Ethnic Groups	Los Angeles				New York				San Francisco				Oakland			
	High	Moderate	Low	Total	High	Moderate	Low	Total	High	Moderate	Low	Total	High	Moderate	Low	Total
Chinese																
1990 Population	53%	28%	20%	249366 [26%]	43%	30%	27%	248949 [45%]	48%	27%	24%	168509 [51%]	21%	44%	35%	90703 [34%]
New Immigrants	56%	28%	17%	40492 [30%]	49%	25%	26%	63129 [45%]	48%	28%	25%	23589 [48%]	18%	48%	34%	13522 [32%]
Filipino																
1990 Population	31%	34%	34%	223815 [23%]	25%	27%	48%	51332 [9%]	30%	43%	27%	86445 [26%]	25%	39%	35%	79048 [29%]
New Immigrants	30%	35%	35%	37084 [27%]	18%	24%	58%	18323 [13%]	30%	46%	25%	14670 [30%]	22%	42%	36%	12475 [29%]
Japanese																
1990 Population	33%	33%	34%	132682 [14%]	9%	32%	59%	27461 [5%]	19%	20%	62%	24048 [7%]	9%	38%	52%	22341 [8%]
New Immigrants	28%	33%	39%	4912 [4%]	6%	25%	68%	3691 [3%]	18%	24%	58%	1271 [3%]	8%	29%	64%	664 [2%]
Korean																
1990 Population	36%	36%	28%	143377 [15%]	46%	25%	29%	76029 [14%]	30%	29%	41%	10502 [3%]	15%	41%	44%	13742 [5%]
New Immigrants	37%	35%	28%	15100 [11%]	47%	24%	29%	7959 [6%]	24%	30%	46%	877 [2%]	14%	36%	51%	1036 [2%]
South Asian																
1990 Population	23%	31%	45%	42341 [4%]	24%	36%	39%	98951 [18%]	17%	24%	59%	7716 [2%]	23%	43%	34%	19936 [7%]
New Immigrants	20%	30%	50%	10297 [8%]	26%	40%	35%	40036 [29%]	14%	29%	57%	2189 [4%]	22%	41%	37%	6643 [16%]
Southeast Asian																
1990 Population	39%	33%	28%	94882 [10%]	18%	22%	60%	12146 [2%]	27%	38%	35%	14781 [4%]	26%	41%	34%	26761 [10%]
New Immigrants	42%	27%	31%	20619 [15%]	19%	26%	55%	3043 [2%]	24%	55%	21%	4275 [9%]	26%	44%	30%	6527 [15%]

TABLE 13. DISTRIBUTION OF ASIAN IMMIGRANTS BY OCCUPATIONAL CATEGORY AND NEIGHBORHOOD CONCENTRATIONS, 1992-1996

Occupational Category	Los Angeles			New York			San Francisco			Oakland		
	Total	High	Low	Total	High	Low	Total	High	Low	Total	High	Low
Professional, Executive, Managerial	19,680	42%	28%	13,928	29%	40%	6,535	35%	38%	5,813	19%	38%
Health Professional	4,016	34%	32%	7,110	16%	60%	1,094	35%	29%	851	19%	40%
Administrative, Clerical	7,040	41%	28%	5,190	35%	34%	2,569	41%	28%	1,813	19%	39%
Sales/Services	9,028	38%	32%	12,208	45%	32%	3,523	36%	26%	2,525	19%	38%
Precision Craft	3,169	38%	31%	2,449	44%	29%	1,271	40%	19%	938	20%	32%
Farm, Forest, Fishery	2,450	44%	26%	5,569	48%	23%	2,606	51%	14%	1,256	28%	25%
Laborers	4,070	49%	24%	4,753	48%	25%	2,563	45%	17%	1,442	23%	31%
Unemployed/Retired	29,082	41%	28%	19,838	36%	35%	7,586	36%	26%	7,119	23%	35%

Source: INS 1992-1996

Residential Patterns of Asian Pacific Americans (235)

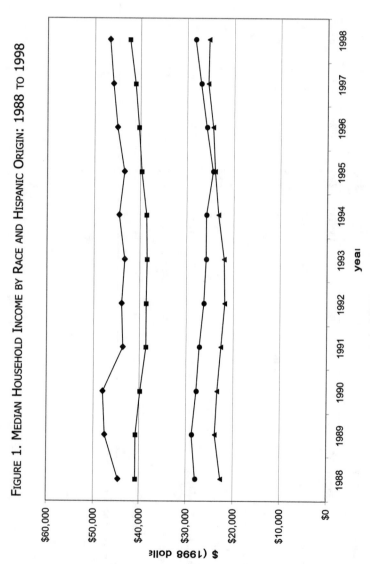

FIGURE 1. MEDIAN HOUSEHOLD INCOME BY RACE AND HISPANIC ORIGIN: 1988 TO 1998

Source: U.S. Census Bureau, Current Population Survey, March 1988-99

Transforming Race Relations

References

Alba, R. and Logan, J. (1991). "Variations on Two Themes: Racial and Ethnic Patterns in the Attainment of Suburban Residence." *Demography*, 28: 431-53.

_____. (1993). "Minority Proximity to Whites in the Suburbs: An Individual-Level Analysis of Segregation." *American Journal of Sociology*, 98: 1388-1427.

Alba, R., Logan, J. and Leung, S.J. (1994). "Asian Immigrants in American Suburbs: An Analysis of the Greater New York Metropolitan Area." *Research in Community Sociology*, 4: 43-67.

Alba, R., Denton, N.A., Leung, S.J. and Logan J.R. (1995). "Neighborhood Change under Conditions of Mass Immigration: The New York City Region, 1970-1990." *International* Migration Review, 29(3): 625-655.

Aloff, M. (1997, February 7). "Where China and Brooklyn Overlap." *New York Times*.

Barringer, H. Gardener, R.W. and Levin, M.J. (1995). *Asians and Pacific Islanders in the United States*. New York, NY: Russell Sage Foundation.

Bobo, L. and Zubrinsky, C.L. (1996). "Attitudes on Residential Integration: Perceived Status Differences, Mere In-Group Preference, or Racial Prejudice?" *Social Forces*, 74(3): 883-909.

Boyd, M. (1988). "Family and Personal Networks in International Migration: Recent Developments and New Agendas." *International Migration Review*, 23(3): 638-670.

Chan, S. (1991). *Asian American: An Interpretive History*. Boston, MA: Twayne.

Chen, H. (1992). *Chinatown No More: Taiwan Immigrants in Contemporary New York*. Ithaca, NY: Cornell University Press.

Clark, W.A.V. (1986). "Residential Segregation in American Cities: A Review and Interpretation." *Population Research and Policy Review*, 5: 95-127.

_____. (1992). "Residential Preferences and Residential Choices in a Multiethnic Context." *Demography*, 29(3): 451-66.

Denton, N.A. and Massey, D.S. (1988). "Residential Segregation of Blacks, Hispanics, and Asians by Socioeconomic Status and Generation." *Social Science Quarterly*, 69(4): 797-817.

_____. (1991). "Patterns of Neighborhood Transition in a Multiethnic World: U.S. Metropolitan Areas, 1970-1980." *Demography*, 28: 41-63.

Farley, R. (1997). "Racial Trends and Differences in the United States 30 Years After the Civil Rights Decade." *Social Science Research*, 26: 235-262.

Farley, R., Howard S., Suzanne B., Colasanto, D. and Hatchett, S. (1978). "'Chocolate City, Vanilla Suburbs': Will the Trend Toward Racially Separate Communities Continue?" *Social Science Research*, 7: 319-344.

Frey, W.H. and Farley, R. (1993). "Latino, Asian, and Black Segregation in Multi-Ethnic Metro Areas: Findings from the 1990 Census." PSC Research Report No. 93-278, University of Michigan, Population Studies Center.

Fong, T.P. (1994). *The First Suburban Chinatown: The Remaking of Monterey Park, California*. Philadelphia, PA: Temple University Press.

_____. (1998). *The Contemporary Asian American Experience*. Upper Saddle River, NJ: Prentice Hall, Inc.

Galster, G.C., Metzger, K. and Waite, R. (1999). "Neighborhood Opportunity Structures and Immigrants' Socioeconomic Advancement." *Journal of Housing Research*, 10(1): 95-127.

Gans, H. (1992). "Second-Generation Decline: Scenarios for the Economic and Ethnic Futures of the Post-1965 American Immigrants." *Ethnic and Racial Studies*, 15(2): 173-192.

Hing, B.O. (1993). *Making and Remaking Asian America through Immigration Policy, 1850-1990*. Stanford, CA: Stanford University Press.

Horton, J. (1995). *The Politics of Diversity: Immigration, Resistance, and Change in Monterey Park, California*. Philadelphia, PA: Temple University Press.

James, F.J., Romine, J.A. and Zwanzig, P.E. (1998). "The Effects of Immigration on Urban Communities." *Cityscape: A Journal of Policy Development and Research*, 3(3): 171-192.

Johnson, J.H. and Oliver, M. (1989). "Interethnic Minority Conflict in Urban America: The Effects of Economic and Social Dislocations." *Urban Geography*, 10: 449-463.

Kasinitz, P., Bazzi, M. and Doane, R. (1998). "Jackson Heights, New York." *Cityscape: A Journal of Policy Development and Research*, 4(2): 161-177.

Kayden, J. and Haar, C. (1989). *Zoning and the American Dream.* Chicago, IL: Planners Press.

Kitano, H. and Kitano, K. (1998). "The Japanese-American Family." In C.H. Mindel, R.W. Habenstein and R. Wright, Jr. (Eds.), *Ethnic Families in America.* Upper Saddle River, NJ: Simon & Schuster.

Kwong, P. (1987). *The New Chinatown.* New York, NY: Hill and Wang. Langberg, M. and Farley, R. (1985). "Residential Segregation of Asian Americans in 1980." *Sociology and Social Research*, 69: 51-61.

Lee, B.L. (1999). "An Issue of Public Importance: The Justice Department's Enforcement of the Fair Housing Act." *Cityscape: A Journal of Policy Development and Research*, 4(3): 35-56.

Li, W. (1999). "The Emergence and Manifestation of the Chinese Ethnoburb in Los Angeles' San Gabriel Valley." *Journal of Asian American Studies*, 2 (1): 1-28.

Lieberson, S. and Carter, D.K. (1982). A Model for Inferring the Voluntary and Involuntary Causes of Residential Segregation, *Demography*, 19(4): 511-26.

Lin, J. (1995). "Polarized Development and Urban Change in New York's Chinatown." *Urban Affairs Review*, 30 (3): 332-354.

_____. (1998). *Reconstructing Chinatown: Ethnic Enclave, Global Change.* Minneapolis, MN: University of Minnesota Press.

Logan, J. and Alba, R. (1993). "Locational Returns to Human Capital: Minority Access to Suburban Community Resources." *Demography*, 30: 243-68.

_____. (1995, October). "Who Lives in Affluent Suburbs? Racial Differences in Eleven Metropolitan Regions." *Sociological Focus*, 28(4): 353-364.

Marcuse, P. (1997, November). "The Enclave, the Citadel, and the Ghetto: What has Changed in the Post-Fordist City." *Urban Affairs Review*, 33(2): 228-264.

Massey, D.S. (1985). "Ethnic Residential Segregation: A Theoretical Synthesis and Empirical Review." *Sociology and Social Research*, 69: 315-50.

Massey, D.S., and Denton, N.A. (1985). "Spatial Assimilation as a Socioeconomic Outcome." *American Sociological Review*, 50: 802-25.

_____. (1987, December). "Trends in the Residential Segregation of Blacks, Hispanics, and Asians: 1970-1980." *American Sociological Review*, Vol. 52: 802-825.

_____. (1988a). "Suburbanization and Segregation in U.S. Metropolitan Areas." *American Journal of Sociology*, 94(3): 592-626.

_____. (1988b). "The Dimensions of Residential Segregation." *Social Forces*, 67: 281-315.

_____. (1993). *American Apartheid*. Cambridge, MA: Harvard University Press.

Massey, D.S. and Fischer, M.J. (1999). "Does Rising Income Bring Integration? New Results for Blacks, Hispanics, and Asians in 1990." *Social Science Research*, 28: 316-26.

Massey, D.S. and Gross, A.B. (1991). "Explaining Trends in Racial Segregation, 1970-1980." *Urban Affairs Quarterly*, 27(1): 13-35.

Matthews, J. (1997, May 7). "The 3 Chinatowns." *The Sun*.

Melendy, B.H. (1976). "Filipinos in the United States." *Counterpoint: Perspectives on Asian America*. Los Angeles, CA: UCLA Asian American Studies Center.

Muller, T. (1993). *Immigrants and the American City*. New York, NY: New York University Press.

Nyden, P., Maly, M. and Lukehart, J. (1997). "The Emergence of Stable Racially and Ethnically Diverse Urban Communities: A Case Study of Nine U.S. Cities." *Housing Policy Debate*, 8(2): 491-534.

Ong, P.M. (1984). "Chinese Unemployment and Ethnic Labor Markets." *Amerasia Journal*, 11(1): 35-54.

Ong, P.M., Lawrence, J.R. and Davidson, K. (1992). "Pluralism and Residential Patterns in Los Angeles." Unpublished paper, UCLA Department of Urban Planning.

Oser, A.S. (1996, December 1). "Immigrants Again Renew Sunset Park." *New York Times*.

Pitkin, J.R., Myers, D., Simmons, P.A. and Megbolugbe, I.F. (1997). *Immigration and Housing in the United States: Trends and Prospects*. Report of Early Findings from the Fannie Mae Foundation Immigration Research Project.

Portes, A. (1995). "Economic Sociology and the Sociology of Immigration: A Conceptual Overview." In A. Portes (Ed.), *The Economic Sociology of Immigration: Essays on Networks*, Ethnicity, and Entrepreneurship. New York, NY: Russell Sage Foundation.

Portes, A. and Rumbaut, R. (1990). *Immigrant America: A Portrait*. Berkeley, CA: University of California Press.

Rosenbaum, E. (1991). "Racial/Ethnic Differences in Home Ownership and Housing Quality." *Social Problems*, 43(4): 403-26.

Saito, L. (1998). *Race and Politics: Asian Americans, Latinos, and Whites in a Los Angeles Suburb*. Urbana, IL: University of Illinois Press.

Sanjek, R. (1998). *The Future of Us All: Race and Neighborhood Politics in New York City*. Ithaca, NY: Cornell University Press.

Schelling, T.C. (1978). *Micromotives and Macrobehavior*. New York, NY: W.W. Norton & Company.

Schill, M.H., Friedman, S., and Rosenbaum, E. (1998). "The Housing Conditions of Immigrants in New York City." *Journal of Housing Research*, 9(12): 201-235.

Schuman, H., Steeh, C. and Bobo, L. (1985). *Racial Attitudes in America: Trends and Interpretations*, Cambridge, MA: Harvard University Press.

Schuman, H. and Bobo, L. (1988). "Survey-Based Experiments on White Racial Attitudes Toward Residential Integration." *American Journal of Sociology*, 94(2): 273-299.

Sheth, M. (1995). "Asian Indian Americans," in P.G. Min (Ed.), *Asian Americans: Contemporary Trends and Issues*. Beverly Hills, CA: Sage Publications.

Smith, C. (1995). "Asian New York: The Geography and Politics of Diversity." *International Migration Review, 29(1): 59-84*.

Sung, B.L. (1976). "Chinese American Manpower and Employment." Report to Manpower Administration, U.S. Department of Labor.

U.S. Census Bureau. (1998). *Current Population Reports, P23-194, Population Profile of the* United States: 1997. Washington, DC: Government Printing Office.

_____. (1999). *Current Population Reports, P60-206, Money Income in the United States:* 1998. Washington, DC: Government Printing Office.

Waldinger, R. (1989). "Immigration and Urban Change." *Annual Review of Sociology,* 15:211-232.

Wong, B. (1982). *Chinatown: Economic Adaptation and Ethnic Identity of the Chinese.* New York, NY: Holt, Rinehart and Winston.

Wong, W. (1995, November 12). "The Number of Filipino-Americans is Growing in West County and Vallejo, and that Should Translate into More Clout." *West County Times/Contra* Costa Newspapers.

Zhou, M. (1992). *Chinatown: The Socioeconomic Potential of an Urban Enclave.* Philadelphia, PA: Temple University Press.

Zhou, M. and Logan, J. (1991) "In and Out of Chinatown: Residential Mobility and Segregation of New York's Chinese." *Social Forces,* 70: 387-407.

Zubrinsky, C.L. and Bobo, L. (1996). "Prismatic Metropolis: Race and Residential Segregation in the City of the Angels." *Social Science Research,* 25: 335-74.

From Vincent Chin to Joseph Ileto: Asian Pacific Americans and Hate Crime Policy

Karen Umemoto

Over the Fourth of July weekend in 1999, Benjamin Nathaniel Smith, a sympathizer of the white supremacist World Church of the Creator, began an interstate shooting rampage, killing two people and wounding eight others. His victims included an African American coach, six Orthodox Jews and several Asian Pacific Americans (APAs). One APA victim was killed. His name was Won Joon Yoon, a 26-year-old Korean doctoral student at Indiana University. At the end of the two-day rampage that began in a Chicago suburb and ended in southern Illinois, Smith took his own life.

Later that month, memorial vigils were held in Chicago, Los Angeles and elsewhere. More than 2,700 people attended the memorial service and candlelight vigil at the campus opera house in Bloomington, Indiana. At the memorial vigil in Los Angeles, one speaker poignantly asked if it must take a multiracial mass shooting to bring such a mixed audience together. This vigil was held at the First African Methodist Episcopal Church in the heart of South Central. Almost half the audience was comprised of APAs, mainly Korean Americans. The rest of the attendees were divided almost equally between African Americans and Jews, with Latinos and others also in attendance. The program began with the music of the gospel choir. It ended with a Korean prayer ceremony. The crowd of over 200 was one of the largest recent gatherings of Korean Americans, Jews and African Americans coming together in solidarity around the common cause of justice. In the backdrop of historic tensions between members of these communities, this unified demonstration of support was quite significant.

One month later, on August 10, 1999, Buford O. Furrow, Jr., an avowed white supremacist, shot and killed 39-year-old Joseph "Jojo"

Ileto, a postal carrier, following a shooting rampage at a Jewish community center in Los Angeles County's San Fernando Valley where he left five wounded. One of Ileto's sisters shared the acronym that her brother has come to represent. She explained that "Joseph" stands for: Join Our Support; Education, Prevent Hate. "Ileto" stands for: Instill Love, Equality and Tolerance to Others.[1] Following the tragic incident, Filipino communities across the nation from New York to Seattle organized protest rallies, vigils and marches. They joined other APA, African American, Latino, Jewish and other communities in statements and demonstrations against violence and hatred.

In the most hopeful scenario, these demonstrations of solidarity may be a sign of a turn in race relations, with unity overcoming instances of conflict. But will it? What are the challenges that must be overcome? And what does the issue of hate crimes portend for the future of race relations in this country? In the following sections, I will give a brief overview of hate crime policy, present data describing the nature and magnitude of the problem for APAs, discuss the challenges that hate crimes and related policy discourse pose for race relations and, finally, discuss recommendations for research, policy and organizing. In the discussion of the implications of policy and policy discourse on race relations, I argue that the reframing of the problem from racial violence to the more specific problem of hate crime presents both challenges and opportunities for multiracial coalition building. I argue that if we are to build meaningful and effective coalitions to combat hate violence, we must reframe the issue into the broader context of racial violence, inequity and, what Eric Yamamoto has termed "interracial justice."

The Meaning of Hate Crimes for Asian Pacific Americans

Hate crimes are the most extreme manifestation of personally felt antagonism toward a category of people. Hate incidents include any criminal act, from vandalism or threat to assault and murder, directed against a victim based on their real or perceived group identity, such as race, religion, sexual orientation, gender or disability. While there are controversies over the definition of a hate crime, which will be discussed later, there is one undisputed fact: the impacts of hate crimes are not only felt by the victims themselves, but are felt by whole groups of people against whom the crimes were directed. APAs have long been victims of hate crimes along with racial, ethnic and religious minorities and others that have faced a history of discrimination and marginalization.

The term "hate crime" is relatively new. It became a legal term upon the passage of the first piece of hate crime legislation in 1990, the Hate Crime Statistics Act. Before this time, APA communities used the term "anti-Asian violence" to define the broader problem.

Perhaps the most significant event that crystallized the current movement against anti-Asian violence was the brutal murder of twenty-seven-year-old Vincent Chin in 1982. Chin, a Chinese American engineer, was killed by a frustrated, unemployed autoworker and his stepson, in the era of industrial downsizing and Japan-bashing. Vincent Chin was celebrating his coming marriage with friends at a topless bar in Detroit when Ronald Ebens and Michael Nitz engaged Chin and his friends in a brawl. After leaving the bar, Ebens and Nitz searched for Chin and his friends. They eventually found Chin and ran him down on the street and, with a baseball bat, bashed him in the skull. Chin died four days later. The case became a *cause celebre* for the APA community and launched a national campaign against anti-Asian violence, giving birth to numerous civil rights organizations that continued long after publicity about the case faded. The case and events leading up to it were documented in a moving film by Renee Tajima and Christine Choy, entitled *Who Killed Vincent Chin?*

But the tragedy of Vincent Chin is only one in a long history of racial violence that has marked the colonial history of the United States. Native Americans bore the brunt of racial violence during the period of westward expansion, resulting in their genocide and forced removal. Much of this took place under government supervision. In the spring and summer of 1838, for example, more than 15,000 Cherokee were removed by the U.S. Army and held in concentration camps and later forced to travel nearly 1,000 miles in the harsh winter months. The trek left 4,000 dead along what was later called The Trail of Tears. African Americans were victims of racial violence from the time of their enslavement and long after the signing of the Emancipation Proclamation. In 1923, for example, an estimated eight to over twenty African Americans were killed during a massacre in the Florida town of Rosewood. White residents burned down the town after a white woman claimed that an African American man attacked her. Survivors and descendants of the victims were awarded 2 million dollars, the first case in which the U.S. government paid compensation in a case of mass racial violence. Chicanos, Mexicanos and other people of color also share this history. And APA communities have certainly not been immune to racial violence. In 1885, for example, over two dozen Chinese mine workers were killed and several hundred driven away in the Rock Springs Massacre as white miners rioted and looted the Chinatown section of the small Wyoming town of Rock Springs. In 1934, Japanese American farmers were targets of a series of bombings during a "yellow peril" anti-alien campaign known as the Salt River Valley incident. These are but a few of hundreds of incidents that reflect a vital aspect of race relations during those periods. Many of these and other events are chronicled by Michael and Judy Ann Newton's (1991) *Racial and Religious Violence in America: A Chronology.*[2]

The stories of resistance against this violence also span this history. Long-time civil rights organizations have utilized the courts, the press, legislative and administrative channels to fight racial violence and create reforms. The movement in support of hate crime legislation during the 1980s and 1990s demanded greater government intervention in acts of violence against historically oppressed groups. This movement emerged in the face of criminal attacks motivated by hatred, especially against racial and religious groups, but also against gays and lesbians. Many criminal acts had gone unpunished, and many feared that the lack of punishment sent a signal that it was the policy of this nation to condone hate-motivated violence. In the case of Vincent Chin, for example, Wayne Circuit Court Judge Charles Kaufman sentenced the killers to three years of probation and fined them $3,780 each, explaining that they were "not the kind of people you send to prison." (Altschiller 1999) APA communities and civil rights organizations, expectedly, expressed outrage at the lenient sentence.

The Chin case became one of several focal points for pan-Asian unity during this period (Espiritu 1992). Within the APA community, many existing organizations such as the west coast Asian Pacific Student Union (APSU), Chinese for Affirmative Action, Japanese American Citizens League and the Organization of Chinese Americans protested the decision and conducted widespread education about the problem of anti-Asian violence. It was also a catalyst for the formation of new organizations such as the American Citizens for Justice in Detroit, Asian Americans for Justice in San Francisco, the Southern California Justice for Vincent Chin Committee, and the Committee Against Anti-Asian Violence (CAAAV) in New York City (Espiritu 1992).

The 1990s saw continued organizing efforts. In 1992, twelve Asian Pacific American organizations joined together to form the National Network Against Anti-Asian Violence to monitor and track cases and also to strengthen their collective organizing efforts. Organizations, such as the Asian American Legal Defense and Education Fund in New York City, Asian Pacific American Legal Center of Southern California and the Asian Law Caucus in the San Francisco Bay area, established outreach and education programs to inform APA communities about the problem of hate crime. Some provided resources to assist victims. In 1993, the Washington, DC headquartered National Asian Pacific American Legal Consortium (NAPALC) began to issue an annual *Audit of Violence Against Asian Pacific Americans*. Groups such as the Committee Against Anti-Asian Violence also published regular newsletters publicizing various cases and support activities surrounding these cases.

With each hate crime against an Asian Pacific American, individuals and groups have joined in coalition with others to address the problem of racial violence. After the murder of Joseph Ileto, the National Federation of Filipino American Associations (NaFFAA) and the Filipino Civil Rights Advocates (FilCRA) joined other APA organizations to support the Ileto family, call for the prosecution of Furrow to the fullest extent of the law, and passage of stronger federal hate crime legislation.[3] Despite the passage of important legislation and organizational sophistication among advocacy organizations, however, hate crimes remain as serious a problem for APAs as it does for the nation.

Hate Crime Policy: Reframing an Old Problem

Hate crime policy has been developed at various levels of government, including Congress, the U.S. Supreme Court, state legislatures and local law enforcement agencies. At the federal level, there are four major legislative acts that address hate crimes.[4] The Hate Crime Statistics Act (28 U.S. Code 534), enacted in 1990, requires the U.S. Department of Justice to collect data from law enforcement agencies throughout the country on crimes that "manifest prejudice based on race, religion, sexual orientation, or ethnicity" and to publish an annual summary of findings. In 1994, the act was expanded to include bias crimes based on "disability." The category of gender is still not included as a bias category in federal law.

The 1994 Violent Crime Control and Law Enforcement Act

(Public Law 103-322) included a provision requiring the U.S. Sentencing Commission to provide sentencing enhancements of no less than three offense levels for crimes that are determined beyond a reasonable doubt to be hate crimes. This act included bias motives based not only on the categories identified in the Hate Crime Statistics Act, but also on national origin and gender. Gender-bias crime victims were given some relief in Title IV of the 1994 Violent Crime Control and Law Enforcement Act which provided training for police and prosecutors, support for domestic violence and rape crisis centers, and provisions for punitive and compensatory damage awards. Finally, the Church Arsons Prevention Act (18 U.S. Code 247) enacted in 1996 broadened criminal prosecutions for attacks against churches and established a loan guarantee program for church rebuilding. Many federal agencies became involved in the implementation of these laws, including the Department of Justice, Department of Education and the Department of Housing and Urban Development.

Since these laws were enacted, several U.S. Supreme Court cases tested the constitutionality of these statutes on the basis of the First Amendment. The outcome of a 1993 U.S. Supreme Court case, *Wisconsin v. Mitchell*, effectively made clear the distinction between an individual's bigoted ideas and hate acts, ruling that hate penalty enhancements do not violate the first amendment when bias motivation is connected with a specific criminal act. Upon this decision, many states upheld or enacted hate crime legislation. State statutes include the prohibition of specific types of bias-motivated acts, the provision of compensation to victims of hate crimes, the training of law enforcement personnel on identifying and responding to hate crimes and the collection of hate crime statistics. Many of these statutes have altered the policies and practices of local law enforcement and criminal justice agencies, many of which have established special units to investigate and prosecute hate crimes. One of the most commonly used policy tools is the enhancement of penalties. Penalties are enhanced by adding years to a sentence, limiting parole, or elevating a misdemeanor to a felony.

Hate crime policies continue to stir controversy. Opponents of hate crime legislation argue that a crime should not be given special consideration based on motive. Not only is motive difficult to discern, but opponents argue that it would be wrong to say that a crime against one person is more serious than a crime against his or her neighbor.[5] But advocates argue that hate crimes are unlike other types of crime. First of all, they tend to be more brutal than other types of crimes as they are committed with the passion of hatred (Jenness and Broad 1997; Herek and Berrill 1992; Levin and McDevitt 1993). More importantly, they not only affect those who are direct victims of crime, but instill fear in the whole category of people against which the hatred was directed. Hate crimes, therefore, constitute a threat to the stability of democratic governance. Not only do hate crimes challenge the moral foundations of tolerance and respect for differences, but advocates also see hate crimes as an attack on our identity as a nation of diverse peoples. Hate crimes scholars like Jack Levin and Jack McDevitt have described these crimes as "acts of domestic terrorism." Frederick Lawrence (1999, p. 8) put it this way, "If bias crimes are not punished more harshly than parallel crimes, the message expressed by the criminal justice system is that racial harmony and equality are not among the highest values held by our society."

A number of high-profile cases emerged in the midst of a campaign initiated by President Clinton under the banner of his "Initiative on Race." In line with this initiative, he convened a White House Conference on Hate Crimes on November 12, 1997, while announcing new law enforcement and prevention initiatives. In 1999, the Hate Crimes Prevention Act was introduced that would allow for greater federal involvement in hate crimes. Though the bill failed to pass, the issue of hate crimes remained on the national agenda. The broad publicity that these hate crimes received, coupled with the political attention given to the issue by prominent officials, has made room for needed national discourse on the issue.

Hate Crimes and Asian Pacific Americans

While the Vincent Chin case is probably the most well-known hate crime case against an Asian Pacific American, there are hundreds of cases in which APAs have fallen victim to hate crimes. These are just a few of the more widely publicized cases since the beating death of Chin in 1982:

- In September 1987, a gang called the Dot Busters in Jersey City beat to death Navrose Mody, an Asian Indian American.

- On July 29, 1989, two brothers beat to death Ming Hai "Jim" Loo in Raleigh, North Carolina. The brothers mistook the 24-year-old Chinese American man as a Vietnamese against whom they harbored resentment after their brother served in the Vietnam War and never returned.

- On December 7, 1993, Colin Ferguson, a Jamaican immigrant, murdered six people and left 19 others injured on the Long Island Railroad in New York. Among the murdered were two Asian Americans, Mi Kyung Kim and Marita Theresa Magtoto.

- On January 29, 1996, two white racist skinheads, including Gunner Lindberg, attacked Thien Minh Ly, a 24-year-old Vietnamese American, on a tennis court in Tustin, California. They kicked, stomped, and stabbed Ly more than a dozen times. Lindberg was the first person in California to receive the death sentence for a murder motivated by racial hate.

- On September 20, 1996, Richard Machado sent threatening email messages to 60 Asian American students at the University of California at Irvine. In his email message, he stated, "I personally will make it my life career to find and kill every one of you personally."

- On April 5, 1999, Douglas Vitaioli shot to death Naoki Kamijima of Crystal City, Illinois after he had gone from store to store asking the ethnicity of the owners.

The detailed stories of each of these cases are filled with horror and tragedy. And there are many others that have not received much attention or have gone unreported.

Underreporting of hate crimes among APAs is a serious problem. There are several reasons for underreporting. First of all, many APAs are immigrants to this country. Immigrants or those who are undocumented are suspected of underreporting all types of crime, including hate crime. Hate crime laws are relatively new and may be reported even less often, especially in less severe cases such as crimes against property. Secondly, law enforcement agencies have only begun to record hate crimes as such since the passage of the 1990 Hate Crime Statistics Act. There were no official or systematic reports on hate crimes before that time. Even after the passage of the federal legislation, there are many obstacles to obtaining accurate reports, as will be discussed further.

The first published report on anti-Asian violence was a report by the Japanese American Citizens League in 1983. A subsequent report was published as a set of proceedings based on a conference entitled, "Break the Silence," sponsored by the Japanese American Citizens League, the Asian Law Caucus, and the Chinese for Affirmative Action in San Francisco in 1985. They noted the increase in hate violence against APAs using 1981 data as baseline information. The rationale for this was that 1981 marked the year when the monetary amount of trade across the Pacific exceeded that across the Atlantic. It was during this period that resentments against APAs were fanned by political pundits who pointed to foreign trade with Asia as the reason for economic woes in the United States. The U.S. Commission on Civil Rights also conducted hearings and published reports on civil rights issues concerning APAs. Their 1992 report, *Civil Rights Issues Facing Asian Americans in the 1990's*, underscored the problem of anti-Asian violence.

As previously mentioned, the National Asian Pacific American Legal Consortium (NAPALC) began to publish an annual *Audit of Violence Against Asian Pacific Americans* in 1993. Up to now, this has been the only national compilation of information on hate crimes against APAs in addition to statistics compiled by the FBI under the Hate Crimes Statistics Act. NAPALC mainly collects information from victims, community organizations and from media sources. Some of the contributing organizations include Asian Pacific American bar associations, Bay Area Hate Crimes Investigators Association, Klanwatch of the Southern Poverty Law Center, National Korean American Service and Education Center, and the Los Angeles County Human Relations Commission. The data they collect not only include hate crimes but also hate incidents that may not be categorized as criminal activity.

According to their figures, there had been a steady rise in the number of anti-Asian incidents from 1993 through 1996 followed by a slight decrease in 1997. Incidents increased from 155 in 1993 to 534 in 1996 with a decrease to 481 incidents in 1997. These numbers are charted in Table 1.

TABLE 1: REPORTED ANTI-ASIAN INCIDENTS BY YEAR, 1993 –1997

Year	Incidents	% Change
1993	155	—
1994	452	192
1995	458	1
1996	534	17
1997	481	-10

Source: NAPALC, *Audit of Violence Against Asian Pacific Americans, 1997.*

Of the 481 reported incidents in 1997 collected by NAPALC, the ethnicity of the victim was unknown in all but 68 cases. Among the 68 cases in which the ethnicity was known, the largest victim group was Chinese (36 percent), followed by Vietnamese (24 percent), Korean (16 percent), Japanese (12 percent) and Filipino (7 percent). South Asian, Thai and Cambodian victims comprised a total of 5 percent.

The most recent count of anti-Asian incidents by NAPALC was higher than the number of hate crimes against APAs as reported to the FBI. According to the most recent FBI hate crime report for 1997, there were 8,049 hate crimes reported in the U.S.[6] 4,710 (69 percent) were race or ethnicity-bias crimes. Of those, 347 (7 percent) were anti-Asian. APAs were also among the hate crime perpetrators, though in a much lower proportions. APAs were perpetrators in 46 (.8 percent) of the 5,898 race-bias offenses, along with six (.4 percent) of the 1,483 religion-bias offenses, five (.3 percent) of the 1,375 sexual orientation-bias, and 27 (.2 percent) of the 1,083 ethnicity-bias offenses.[7]

As with hate crime data generally, it is difficult to make strong conclusions about trends. Many advocacy organizations argue that hate crimes have indeed increased during the eighties and most of the nineties. Others have attributed the increase in hate crimes within jurisdictions primarily to improvements in reporting. As citizens learn to report hate crimes and law enforcement personnel are trained to identify them, the data may reflect an increase in hate crime rates. Conversely, some hate crime scholars and government officials have attributed decreases in national rates to an increase in the number of jurisdictions that underreport such incidents (Balboni and Bennett 1999). National figures show a decrease in the rate of hate crime perpetration over this same time period while the number of reporting agencies have increased. Among reporting jurisdictions are whole states such as Alabama, Arkansas and Mississippi that submit reports, but report zero hate crimes. Many Asian Pacific American advocates have argued that hate crimes are severely underreported among Asian newcomers who are often unaware of hate crime policy, distrustful of law-enforcement or fearful of retaliatory consequences. Immigrants and other vulnerable populations, including women, may very well experience a much higher rate of victimization than official statistics reflect. It is also difficult to discern patterns among the various Asian Pacific American ethnic groups since many law-enforcement agencies do not include information concerning ethnicity.

Hate Crimes in Los Angeles

Data from Los Angeles, California, one of the most diverse places in the world, provide additional insights into the nature of hate crimes involving APAs, as well as other groups. The hate crime rate in Los Angeles is higher than the national rate according to official law enforcement statistics.[8] According to hate crime data collected from various law enforcement agencies by the Los Angeles County Commission on Human Relations, the number of hate crimes peaked in 1996 with 995 reported incidents. Nearly three-fourths of all hate crimes were racially motivated as opposed to gender, sexual orientation, disability or religion biased.

One of the most disturbing trends among racially motivated crimes is the changing face of hate (see Figure 1). Among the cases where the racial identity of the perpetrator is known, there was an increase in a

Figure 1.
Number of Victims by Race
Race-bias Hate Crimes in
Los Angeles County, 1994-1997

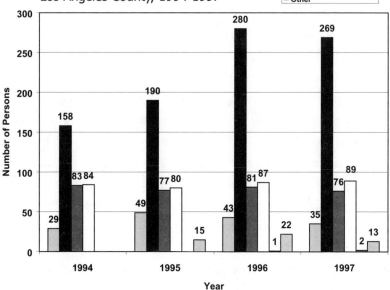

Number of Perpetrators by Race
Race-bias Hate Crimes, 1994-1997

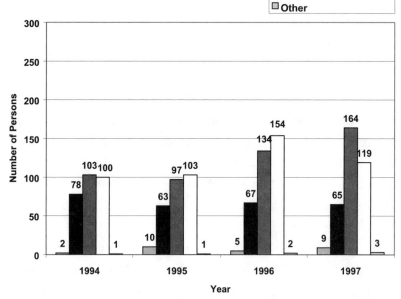

Figure 2. Percentage of Hate
Crime Victims,
Perpetrators and
Population by Race,
Los Angeles County,
1994-1997

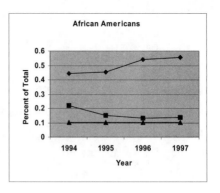

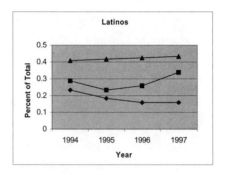

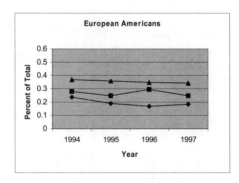

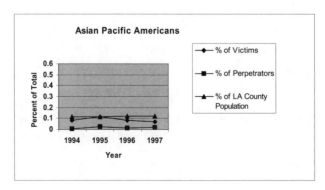

number of white perpetrators from 100 in 1994 to 119 in 1997 (19 percent). But the most dramatic increase was among Latino perpetrators. They numbered 103 in 1994, but steadily rose to 164 by 1997—an increase of almost 60 percent. Concurrently, the racial group that experienced the greatest increase in victimization was African American. These trends in the racial characteristics of victims and perpetrators can be seen in comparison to the population proportion of each respective racial group. Figure 2 shows the percentage of victims, perpetrators and population over the four-year time span.

A matrix of reported victims and perpetrators between 1994-1997 shows the racial distribution of victims and perpetrators by pairs (see Table 2). Of the 1,837 race-bias incidents that were reported during this time, the racial identity of the victim and perpetrator were recorded in 1,166 cases. APAs were reported to be victimized equally by Latino and European American perpetrators and less often by African Americans. In contrast, the racial group most often victimized by APAs during this same period was African American.

TABLE 2. RACE-BIAS HATE CRIME VICTIMS AND PERPETRATORS BY PAIRS, LOS ANGELES COUNTY, 1994-1997

| | Race of Victim | | | | |
	African American	Latino	APA	European American	Total Perpetrators
African American	—	133	12	116	261
Latino	349	—	35	67	451
APA	14	5	—	4	23
European American	306	90	35	—	431
Total Victims	669	228	82	187	1166

Race of Perpetrator (left axis label)

Note: This table includes 1,166 race-bias crimes in which both victim and perpetrator race were reported. There was a total of 1,837 reported race-bias crimes during this time period.

African Americans were victimized more often by Latino suspects than they were by European Americans and much less frequently by APAs. Latinos were reportedly victimized more often by African Americans than members of other groups. And European Americans were victimized more often by African American perpetrators than by members of other racial groups.

Before reaching any strong conclusions from these figures, we must be aware of the serious limitations of the data. Though all the law enforcement and agency reports collected were screened by the Los Angeles County Human Relations Commission using Los Angeles County District Attorney's definition of hate crimes, there are several problems that may skew the data. One is inconsistency among law enforcement agencies in the classification and definition of a hate crime. Law enforcement agencies also vary in the amount of training given to officers in reporting hate crimes. There are also problems of underreporting, especially among immigrant populations, of which a large proportion are Latino and Asian. Also, 37 percent of all race-bias hate crimes for that period had no record of the racial identity of the perpetrator. Many of these involved crimes against property, such as vandalism, in which the perpetrators may have been of one racial group in disproportionate numbers. Also, not all of the 88 cities in the County report hate crime data nor do they all report the data consistently. These irregularities may skew that data, and we should limit the degree to which we make any strong conclusions from them.

The figures do, however, present three indisputable facts. First, members of all racial groups who are victims are also perpetrators. Second, not only is there white-perpetrated hate crime against people of color, but there is also a substantial number of hate crimes perpetrated by people of color against other groups, including whites as well as other non-white groups. And third, there has been a dramatic rise in the number of hate crimes reported by African American victims in which the suspect was Latino as well as white.

Causes of Hate Crimes Against Asian Pacific Americans

The lack of consistently reliable data over time makes it difficult to identify those factors that lead to an increase or decrease in hate crimes directed against APAs. However, we can infer various causes from the literature on hate crimes as well as on racial conflict. These explanations can be categorized in the following ways: a) perceived or real economic competition in overlapping niches; b) ideologically or culturally based prejudice or bigotry; c) popular portrayal of a group as responsible for social ills or as a threat to one's own well-being; or d) exclusionary forms of social mobilization based on racially or ethnically defined boundaries.

Asian Pacific Americans have been victims of ideologically and materially motivated attacks, sources that are usually intertwined. In fact, similar sources of conflict can be seen consistently throughout history. The Rock Springs Massacre of 1885 resulted from anti-Chinese sentiment over their role as cheap labor. Chinese were used by industrialists as strike breakers in the mines and on the railroads. This fed a growing resentment among white workers who felt their livelihood threatened. Organized political movements seeking to end Chinese immigration to the U.S. fed newspapers with degrading depictions of Chinese as subhuman, leading to the passage the Chinese Exclusion Act of 1882. Racial group competition in a racially charged political environment, led to the exclusion of further Chinese immigration, and provided fertile soil for the outbreak of racial violence. Similar sentiments arose against the Japanese who were brought to replace Chinese labor, leading to exclusionary legislation such as the 1913 (California) Alien Land Law prohibiting Japanese immigrants from purchasing agricultural land as well as the Immigration Act of 1924 ending further Japanese immigration to the United States. Turn of the century political movements were well equipped with the demeaning and degrading caricatures of Asian newcomers as heathen, womanizing, slant-eyed threats to the livelihood and way of life of Western pioneers. Vehement anti-Asian sentiment was fanned by politicians for political purposes but took its most physically brutal form in mob attacks on communities and individuals.

While the social norms for many Americans have changed and some degree of political appropriateness has been established to temper acts of mass violence or hatred, many populations continue to feel the effects of this age-old problem. Returning to the case of Vincent Chin once again, we see that his perpetrators were recently laid-off as autoworkers during the height of ferment against Japanese auto-makers. The U.S. auto industry was among those that initiated and supported the "buy American" anti-imports campaign. Detroit, where the killing took place, was the capitol of the auto industry and the hotbed of anti-Japanese sentiment. Vincent Chin, though Chinese American, was categorized in the minds of his perpetrators as responsible for the plight of the unemployed autoworkers. Chin suffered the brunt of this resentment based on economic competition, prejudice and scapegoating. We can find similar threads in other stories of hate crimes against APAs today.

One source of resentment against APAs is what Leland Saito (1998) calls "Asian flack." He describes this problem as resentment against all APAs based on the conspicuous wealth of a small minority of the population. In his case study of APAs, Latinos and whites in the San Gabriel Valley, he documents sources of resentment and arenas of cooperation between these groups. Among the sources of resentment against Asian residents was a perception that most were wealthy and thus able to gain undue control over the economic life and political institutions of the region. One manifestation of the tensions was the perpetration of hate crimes against APAs, particularly immigrants, by Latino and white residents. Nor were APAs faultless in this scenario, as many held their own prejudices against other groups and were not necessarily sensitive concerning the impacts of the rapid Asian immigrant population growth on other long-time residents of the region.

In this way, hate crimes are one barometer of general race relations. As mentioned in the beginning of this chapter, hate crimes represent the most severe form of racial antagonism—that which manifests itself in the form of criminal activity directed against an individual as a surrogate for a whole group. Cities in which hate crimes occur repeatedly are often cities experiencing ongoing racial conflicts or tensions, including those that may not take the form of criminal activity. It is not uncommon that when hate crimes hit the radar screen in a particular city, racial tensions have been festering for some time. For example, hate crimes may first emerge in the form of student fights on school grounds, but only after a series of racial conflicts over school board elections or personnel controversies in which racially defined interests were contested.

There are, of course, exceptions in which the repeated occurrence of hate crimes in a city is less reflective of the tenor of race relations and more indicative of the existence of a small, aberrant group of hate crime perpetrators in a more harmonious social climate. This is an important reminder of the danger of the ecological fallacy in the study of hate crimes. It would be erroneous to think that all individuals who live or work in areas where hate crimes occur exhibit the same characteristics as those involved in hate crimes. In fact, we may often find residents in affected areas who actively promote tolerance and cross-cultural under-standing because they have witnessed hate crimes in their community.[9]

Limitations of Current Policy

Just as hate crimes occur within a social context, solutions are only effective to the extent they address the social context. This is, of course, in addition to dealing with individual perpetrators and assisting victims. We face many challenges in all three areas, social context, perpetrators and victims. Hate crime policies, to date, focus primarily on the latter two areas.

Hate crime legislation is no doubt critical to protecting the ideals of respect and tolerance for difference. It is an important step towards lessening the number of physical attacks and verbal threats against historically marginalized or oppressed groups. It also sends a moral message that abuse against an individual based purely on their identification as a member of a particular group is not an action that society condones. In light of the numerous hate-motivated mass attacks, such as in Littleton, Colorado and Los Angeles, California, not only is the legislation important for hortatory purposes, but also additional resources and powers must be granted by legislation to address this problem. Enhancements to sentences, victim assistance and resources for enforcement agencies as provided by current legislation are vitally important. At the same time, there are many shortcomings of current policy and policy discourse.

LACK OF STATE HATE CRIME LEGISLATION

Not all states have hate crime legislation. As of this writing, eight states have no hate crime laws at all, including the states of New York and Hawai'i, which have the second and third largest APA populations respectively in the nation. Combined, these two states are home to approximately one-fifth of the APA population in the U.S. In addition, not all states protect against all types of bias motivated crimes. For example, 21 states exclude sexual orientation as a bias motive from their hate crime laws (Lawrence 1999).

LACK OF ACCURATE REPORTING

There are two types of problems in reporting which make it difficult to monitor the level of hate crime victimization and perpetration among APAs. One is the lack of reporting and the second is the lack of ethnic information in hate crime reports. As mentioned earlier, the lack of reporting results from the underreporting of crimes among APA victims as well as the problems of data collection among law enforcement agencies. In terms of the latter, only six out of every 10 police agencies voluntarily report bias crimes to the FBI. What is more disturbing, however, is that four out of five police agencies claim that they have no hate crimes (Fritz 1999). Whole states have submitted reports claiming they have no hate crimes statewide. In 1997, for example, Alabama, Arkansas and Mississippi reported tallies from their law enforcement jurisdictions totaling zero hate crimes in each of those states.

Some reasons for the lack of police reporting have to do with procedural problems such as the additional paperwork required to report hate crime. There is also unevenness in personnel training so that not all police officers know how to identify a hate crime. But there are more serious problems that contribute to the lack of reporting. One is the fear among local politicians of having one's city named the "hate crime capitol" of the region. This can affect future economic investment into the city as well as future in- and out-migration of residents based on this image. A second problem is political complicity with the activities of hate perpetrators. In some cities, hate crimes go unanswered because officials may share similar biases with hate crime perpetrators and, in effect, condone their actions by not pursuing suspects or enforcing criminal law. This reporting problem is similar to that of domestic violence in earlier years. As Jack McDevitt, director of the Center for Criminal Justice Policy Research at Northeastern University, stated in reference to the enforcement of hate crime for gay-bashing, "You've got to get them over their bias that it's OK, which a lot of them believe." (Fritz 1999) For APAs, especially those who may live in isolated areas or areas where there is some level of political hostility against them, the lack of reporting and enforcement can leave them more vulnerable to hate crime victimization.

ENFORCEMENT PROBLEMS

Even when hate crimes are reported, there is a low rate of prosecution and conviction. Hate crimes in general have low conviction rates, approximately 15 percent. Part of this is due to the difficulty in finding the suspect who sprayed racial epithets on someone's garage door in the middle of the night. But it is also due to the fact that hate crime victims, like victims of many other types of crime, fear retaliation by suspects and refuse to testify. Since bias crimes are motivated by hatred, not only do victims fear personal retaliation, but retaliation against friends, family and other members of the target group. In the case of organized hate groups or gangs, not only do victims fear retaliation by suspects themselves, but also from members of the suspect's group. Unless the police have a very good relationship with the victim or the victim's community where victims feel they can entrust their safety to law enforcement officers, it is often difficult to gain cooperation from victims or witnesses in hate crime cases. For Asian Pacific American immigrants who may be new to the country or unfamiliar with their local law enforcement agencies, these challenges are multiplied.

Since hate crime legislation is relatively new and there are variations in the laws across states, not all law enforcement agencies have adequate expertise to investigate and prepare a hate crime court case. No only must one prove guilt of committing the crime, but must also prove that bias is a motive in the commission of that crime. Unevenness in expertise between police investigators and prosecutors can also lead to failed cases.

Dangers in Policy Discourse:
From Racial Violence to Hate Crime

The first stage of any policy-making process entails defining the problem. How one defines the problem limits the range of policy solutions that lawmakers consider in addressing the problem. Within the APA community, the term "anti-Asian violence" became the common term in the 1980s to describe the problem. But as policy debates concerning this problem centered on the issue of "hate crimes," the issue of racial violence was defined in the policy vernacular of criminal justice. On one hand, the specificity of the term hate crime helps to identify an institutional and legislative "home" for any policy development and implementation; the problem is defined in terms of criminal law and placed under the jurisdiction of law enforcement and justice agencies. This, however, narrows the scope of the problem as originally defined by APA and other communities.

The original definition encompassed a wide range of issues, ranging from hate crimes to police brutality. In fact, many of the issues championed by groups such as the Committee Against Anti-Asian Violence (CAAAV) included cases of police abuse. In 1996, for example, CAAAV published a report entitled, *Police Violence in New York City's Asian American Communities* (1986-1995). This report was dedicated to Vuthikrai Thienvanich (1946-1987) and Yong Xin Huang (1978-1995). Vuthikrai Thienvanich was a 41-year-old Thai janitor who was shot five times in the chest, abdomen and extremities by Transit Authority police in Brooklyn, New York. Yong Xin Huang was a 16-year-old teen who was playing with a BB gun with friends and was shot in the back of the head at point-blank range by a New York Police Department officer. Neither officer involved was indicted. According to this report, 25 percent of all cases addressed by CAAAV involved law enforcement officers as active or passive accomplices to civilian offenders of anti-Asian violence. They define law enforcement "accomplice" broadly, ranging from passive (an officer who responds insensitively to a hate crime victim) to active (an officer who acts as or assists the perpetrator of anti-Asian violence).

Changing the problem definition from "anti-Asian violence" to "hate crime" and moving the problem of police abuse and racism under the problem of "police community relations" created a separation between civilian hate violence and police misconduct within policy debates and policies themselves. This presents the danger of narrowing the original problem definition and thereby limiting the parameters of policy solutions away from addressing the greater problem of racial violence, whether the perpetrators are civilians or law enforcement officers. There remains no equivalent set of policies to directly address bias-related abuses among law enforcement officers. This is particularly important given the continued occurrence of police misconduct cases in large metropolitan cities like New York and Los Angeles, home to large concentrations of people of color, including APAs.

The narrowing of the problem to an issue of criminal justice also shifts attention away from the political, social, economic, historical and cultural factors that generate racial or ethnic conflicts. By placing the policy discourse so squarely in the domain of criminal justice, the selection of policy tools becomes limited to those available to law enforcement agencies, mediators and human relations agencies. Left outside of policy discourse is a whole range of inequities and unresolved social grievances that may be associated with hate crimes. The question of how we are to resolve conflicts in a multiracial civil society remains out of the scope of enforcement-centered policy deliberations. While hate crime policy is an important element in addressing the criminal manifestation of racial conflicts and antagonism, it is important not to be bound by the parameters of analysis surrounding current discourse. We need to think about racial violence not only as a criminal problem, but as an overarching social problem. Solutions must not be limited to criminal punishment and victim assistance, but to the resolution of the sources of conflict, including a range of justice acts, from atonement and reparations to mediation and institutional reform.

Challenges Hate Crimes Pose for Race Relations Today

White supremacy, bigotry and homophobia have indeed been the culprit in most of the high profile cases that have received national media attention over the past decade. In 1989, Yusuf Hawkins was shot and killed after he and three other African American teenagers walked into the predominantly white, working class neighborhood of Bensonhurst in Brooklyn, New York. The spring 1995 bombing of a federal office building in Oklahoma City turned national attention to the growing problem of organized hate groups in the U.S. More recently, in summer 1998, James Byrd Jr., an African American man, was dragged from a pickup truck for nearly three miles, with body parts and his mangled torso strewn along the road. In fall 1998, University of Wyoming student Matthew Shepherd was brutally and fatally beaten because he was gay. The following year brought more mass shootings, including a massacre of 12 students and a teacher on the grounds of a Colorado high school in April and a shooting spree at a Los Angeles Jewish day-care center in August 1999.

The vast majority of the publicity surrounding hate crimes focuses on white perpetrators of race-bias crimes. There may be some statistical explanation to this. Among bias incidents that were racially motivated, there was a total of 5,898 offenses nationally in 1997 according to the FBI. The racial background of the suspect was known in 3,982 of those cases. White suspects comprised 73 percent of the total number of race-bias hate crimes suspects in which the racial background was known. Of the race-bias incidents in which the race of both the victim and suspects were known, 59 percent involved white perpetrators and black victims. In other words, publicity may have focused on white perpetrated hate crimes because they make up the majority of suspects in race-bias as well as all bias-motivated hate crimes.[10]

But the focus on white perpetrated hate crime overshadows another type of race-bias hate crime, interminority group crime. Focusing on white supremacists keeps the issue in less controversial political waters, especially when many of the victims in these publicized cases are also white.

The enemy is bigotry and the target "problem" populations are organized white supremacist groups and the psychologically unstable followers of their propaganda. The solution that follows this journalistic analysis is stricter law enforcement and a crackdown on hate groups. Indeed, this has been the policy alternative that receives greatest legislative support. But scholars have long noted two facts that run counter to much of the analyses found in the popular press. First, individuals who are *not* members of hate groups commit the most hate crimes. In fact, the majority of perpetrators have no prior history of criminal activity or psychological problems. Second, hate crimes tend to occur where there is a general culture of hate. Political leaders may promote this culture in their efforts to mobilize a constituency. Moreover, popular culture such as music, media and the arts may also contribute to the culture of hate. While a law enforcement crackdown on white supremacist organizations is extremely important, we must not lose sight of the problem in its entirety.

While the Vincent Chin case and the anti-Asian violence movement was a major source of pan-Asian solidarity and coalition building, the interracial and interethnic character of hate crimes in contemporary America carries with it the potential for conflict and division. Asian Pacific American community organizations in the U.S. enter policy debates under these circumstances that have implications for race relations more generally. In the continental U.S., Asian Pacific American populations are concentrated in metropolitan areas where there is a diversity of racial and ethnic groups. While APAs are victims of hate crimes by those with white supremacist views, they are also victimized by other people of color. Likewise, APAs are also perpetrators of hate crimes against all other groups, including other APAs of different ethnic backgrounds. The problem is not as simple or clear-cut as in the case of Vincent Chin. We are victims as well as perpetrators. White supremacy is not the only source of the problem. And when it comes to interminority hate crimes, issues of past oppression, economic disparity and ethnic politics enter the fray. The contained problem of white supremacy is complicated by the multiracial character and entangled social problems of the modern metropolis.

In many ways, the hate crime issue reveals, in the most extreme sense, the challenges before us in addressing the problem of race relations. Indeed, hate crime perpetrators terrorize whole communities, but they do even more. They often create deep chasms between whole groups despite the fact that perpetrators may represent a minority perspective within a community. At the same time, there is a strong basis to build coalitions in opposition to hate crimes. It is safe to assume that the vast majority of people on simply a moral basis would oppose random acts of violence against individuals. Moral beliefs aside, anyone can become a victim of a hate crime, since perpetrators are seeking a category of people rather than a particular individual. In this sense, it is in everyone's interest to prevent hate crimes.

But, building coalitions is complicated by the multiracial character of many urban hate crimes. Take, for example, the case of Kingman Quon, 23, a student at California State Polytechnic University in Pomona. Quon pled guilty to seven misdemeanor counts and was sentenced of two years in federal prison after e-mailing racially charged threats to dozens of Latinos around the nation. On one hand, this incident fueled racial tensions. On the other hand, it was an opportunity for APA and Latino communities to join together against this type of activity. But unless racial communities to which the perpetrator belongs join those of victim groups, hate crimes can lead to greater social division. There is, then, an urgent need for political leadership, community organizing, and coalition building to insure that the issue of hate crimes becomes a focal point for unity, as opposed to greater division.

The Need for Self-Reflective Race Relations Discourse

The multiracial character of hate crimes in diverse metropolitan cities poses a serious challenge for race relations and coalition building. One of the most important challenges is the ability to create public space for dialogue in which members speaking from the position of racial identities can be self-reflective and critical of actions by members of their racial group. Currently, those who do this risk being accused of "selling out their people" or becoming the spotlight of media sensationalism.

A case in point was a summer 1999 talk show on Black Entertainment Television cable network hosted by Travis Smiley entitled "BET Live." The topic was race relations between African Americans and APAs. Two of the guests were Asian Pacific American and one was African American, all active in civil rights organizations and generally advocates of coalition building across racial divides. The host presented a variety of examples where APAs and African Americans have come into conflict or may potentially conflict in the future. Tensions in public housing, public schools and in electoral campaigns were among the topics discussed. The strategy of the Asian Pacific American guests was to tie the problem of intergroup conflict to the institutional structures that produce inequality and perpetuate injustice. The effect was to "depersonalize" the problem and refocus attention to political and economic solutions.

On one hand, this approach is quite prudent. The lack of jobs and competition for housing and resources often leads to conflict along racial cleavages. Many activists argue, and history supports the contention, that meaningful multiracial coalitions are built when groups come together in joint work on common concerns and find effective ways to reach their mutual goals. Focusing on "what we have in common" and "what we can work on together" points forward rather than backward. This is important if we are to move beyond finger-pointing to arm-linking.

At the same time, one of the issues that the guest representing

African American concerns raised repeatedly was the issue of respect. He was critical of those APAs who treated African Americans with disrespect. But instead of addressing that issue squarely, the Asian Pacific American guests repeatedly brought the focus back to structural problems, presumably leaving the other guest and viewers dissatisfied. I can understand the predicament facing the Asian Pacific American guests. If they had spent any substantial amount of time focusing on the problem of bigotry or cultural styles among APAs, those admissions could have preempted any forward-looking discussion on broader structural problems. In fact, statements such as, "yes, there are Asians who hold prejudiced views towards blacks," would probably get reproduced dozens of times through various media. Nothing else may have been reported about the interview. This could further inflame race relations in the reproduction and recontextualization of such statements.

The inability to have self-reflective and self-critical public discourse prevents us from actually getting to those larger institutional issues. It is important for people to hear acknowledgement of their concerns. The issue of bigotry among APAs is very real, as is bigotry against APAs that exists among members of other racial groups. Self-critical discourse is necessary in order to build trust and understanding upon which coalitions can stand. In addition to asking the question "what we do have in common?," we must also be able to ask "how are we contributing to the problem?" Of course, these questions need to be put into the context that creates a "safe" and constructive environment for discussion. In regards to the issue of hate crimes, self-reflective and self-critical discourse is a necessity. Hate crime perpetrators come in all orientations and colors.

There are opportunities to build multiracial coalitions around the issue of hate crimes. I will outline some policy recommendations below. Building coalitions around such a reform agenda, however, will involve much more than a discussion about policy. Key to building effective coalitions is broadening the discourse so that the social, economic and political sources of racial conflict and injustice can be addressed. Otherwise, controversy over hate crimes may degenerate to a discussion of "whodunnit." Not that identifying the perpetrator of a hate crime is not important, but long-term solutions may need to involve a fuller reconciliation of conflict among racial groups.

To the extent that hate crimes are reflective of larger intergroup conflicts involving notions of justice, the practice of intergroup conflict resolution or group reconciliation is critical. Eric Yamamoto (1999) argues for a particular type of resolution that he calls "interracial justice." He argues that a meaningful resolution of conflict is not simply a legal resolution between litigants, but a social process through which parties in conflict reach a mutual agreement based on the concept of interracial justice. This idea rests upon the acknowledgement of the historical and contemporary ways in which racial groups harm one another along with affirmative efforts to redress justice grievances. Conflicts between individuals are always understood in historical context and intergroup relations. Yamamoto writes, "without historicizing contemporary intergroup power relations and grounding them in concrete particulars, racial groups facing real-life intergroup grievances and claims of injustice are likely to assume the understandings of 'others' based on social constructed racial meanings often of stereotypical quality" (p. 122). He outlines four dimensions of interracial justice along which grievances or past injustices may be resolved. He refers to these as the four "R's": a) *recognition* of emotions, constraints, related justice grievances, and disabling perceptions faced by racial group members; b) *responsibility* of racial group members as the subordinated as well as the subordinating group in interracial power relationships; c) *reconstruction* or acts of healing the social and psychological wounds resulting from past injustices; and d) *reparation* in the form of material changes in the structure of the relationship. We may find that long-term solutions to the problem of hate crime against APAs lie in processes of group reconciliation such as these.

Recommendations for Policy, Research and Organizing

Some predict that hate crimes will only worsen in the future while prevention will become more difficult. Petrosino (1999), for example, suggests that the prevention and control of hate crimes will become more difficult given the accessibility of weapons of mass destruction, a growing acceptance of extremist ideology and an increase in religious zealotry among hate crime perpetrators. In addition, the dissemination of hate ideology over the Internet will continue to foster the creation of virtual communities of hate groups that span the globe. Public policies can provide important tools to lessen hate crimes and address their underlying causes.

There are policy reforms, future research and organizing that can benefit Asian Pacific American communities and all others in the prevention and intervention of hate crimes. I outline six major areas: a) improve reporting by Asian Pacific American victims and law enforcement agencies; b) pass or strengthen hate crime legislation at the state and federal levels; c) develop comprehensive law enforcement protocols responsive to the cultural and social circumstances within Asian Pacific American and other communities; d) support Asian Pacific American and other community organizations addressing the hate crimes problem; e) build multiracial coalitions and a human relations infrastructure; and f) conduct research to better understand and address underlying sources of conflict associated with hate crimes.

A) IMPROVE REPORTING BY ASIAN PACIFIC AMERICAN VICTIMS AND LAW ENFORCEMENT AGENCIES

Law enforcement agencies can establish systems, training programs, and job duties so that hate crimes and hate incidents are accurately reported. Public and private agencies can also conduct education to communities so victims can recognize incidents and be encouraged to report them. A critical component to victim reporting is community and law enforcement protection from retaliatory action by perpetrators.

B) PASS OR STRENGTHEN HATE CRIME LEGISLATION AT THE STATE AND FEDERAL LEVELS
Adopt hate crime statutes in states that have weak or no hate crime legislation. Strengthen federal laws to include gender as a bias category and expand federal powers to prosecute hate crimes. Support increased resources to the Community Relations Service of the Department of Justice to assist communities affected by hate crimes and related conflict.

C) DEVELOP A LAW ENFORCEMENT PROTOCOL THAT IS RESPONSIVE TO THE CULTURAL AND SOCIAL CIRCUMSTANCES WITHIN ASIAN PACIFIC AMERICAN AND OTHER COMMUNITIES
Since hate crimes, especially race-bias hate crimes, can be associated with larger community tensions, it is important for law enforcement officers to work with residents, school and human relations personnel, mediators, youth works, community leaders and others to develop more comprehensive community strategies that are culturally and socially appropriate.

D) SUPPORT ASIAN PACIFIC AMERICAN AND OTHER COMMUNITY ORGANIZATIONS ADDRESSING THE HATE CRIMES PROBLEM
Support community organizations in their efforts to document hate crimes among APAs, to provide assistance to victims, to mediate community conflicts, to advocate for effective hate crime policies, and to organize coalitions against hate crimes.

E) BUILD MULTIRACIAL COALITIONS AND HUMAN RELATIONS INFRASTRUCTURE
Multiracial and otherwise diverse coalitions play important roles in demonstrating public opposition to hate activity and in reconciling conflicts between groups. They are an important component of a broader human relations infrastructure—institutional structures based on partnerships between residents, government agencies, human rela-

tions organizations and the private sector equipped with leadership skills, networks and necessary resources to promote tolerance and respond effectively to the outbreak of hate crimes and intergroup conflicts.

F) CONDUCT POLICY-ORIENTED RESEARCH TO BETTER UNDERSTAND AND ADDRESS HATE CRIMES AND ITS UNDERLYING CAUSES

Further research is needed to inform effective policy-making on various types of bias crimes against APAs and others. Areas of further research include: the causes of hate crime perpetration, impact on victims, organization of hate groups, effects of legal sanctions, and methods of prevention, intervention and prediction.

Crimes motivated by hatred against random individuals affect our security, disposition and identity as a nation of diverse peoples. For those who envision a society that lives up to the ideals of equal justice, cultural pluralism and democracy, the issues of hate crime and racial violence are an important part of the work at hand.

Endnotes

[1] Guillermo, E. (1999, October). "What Joseph Ileto Stands For." *Filipinas*.

[2] See also Petrosino, C. (1999). "Connecting the Past to the Future: Hate Crime in America," *Journal of Contemporary Criminal Justice*, 15(1):22-47.

[3] (1999, September). "APAs Unite Nationally to Condemn Hate Crimes, Mourn Death of Ileto," *Pacific Citizen*, 129(10): 3-9, 8.

[4] For a detailed history and legal discussion of hate crime law, see Lawrence (1999).

[5] For a critique of hate crime laws, see also Jacobs and Potter (1998).

[6] According to the Federal Bureau of Investigation's *Hate Crime Statistics, 1997*, there were 11,211 participating law enforcement agencies in 48 states and the District of Columbia. Hawai'i and New Hampshire did not participate in the 1997 report.

[7] Federal Bureau of Investigation, Uniform Crime Reports, 1998. Hate Crime Statistics: 1997. Statistics from Tables 1 and 5.

[8] It is difficult to accurately estimate the rate of hate crime for reasons mentioned elsewhere in the article. Understanding these limitations, official statistics do indicate a higher rate for Los Angeles. According to law enforcement statistics, there were 53 hate crimes per one million persons in Los Angeles as compared to 32 nationally in 1997. Also, the reported rate for the nation overall may be lower than the actual rate, since a number of states report no hate crimes when they may, in fact, occur.

[9] It would also be erroneous to use hate crime data as the only source of data to understand race relations or racial conflict. A study of hate crimes would not capture non-criminal acts nor would they always flag conflicts dispersed over large areas. Well-publicized conflict between Korean merchants and African American residence in South Central Los Angeles do not always involve criminal threats or criminal acts. It is also important to note that hate crime perpetrators vary in their degree of racial prejudice. Jacobs and Potter (1998), for example, argue that not all hate crimes labeled as such accurately represent the extent of the offender's prejudice. Hate crime data can overstate the extent of the hate crime problem depending on the degree to which prejudice was the primary motive of the crime.

[10] In 1997, out of 8,049 bias motivated criminal incidents reported to the FBI by 11,211 law enforcement agencies across the country, the majority (almost 60 percent) were motivated by racial bias. Of the 9,861 total offenses for all bias-motivated crimes that year, the race of the suspect was known in 60 percent of those offenses. And of those offenses for which the race of the suspect was known, whites comprised 75 percent of all suspects.

References

Altschiller, D. (1999). *Hate Crimes: A Reference Handbook*. Santa Barbara, CA: ABC-CLIO, Inc.

Balboni, J. and Bennett, S. (1999). "Improving the Quality and Accuracy of Hate Crime Reporting Nationally." Presented at the Annual Meeting of the American Society of Criminology, Toronto, Canada.

Espiritu, Y.L. (1992). *Asian American Panethnicity: Bridging Institutions and Identities*. Philadelphia, PA: Temple University Press.

Fritz, M. (1999, August 23). "Hate Crimes Hard To Track As Some Areas Report None." *Los Angeles Times*.

Guillermo, E. (1999, October). "What Joseph Ileto Stands For." *Filipinas*.

Herek, G. M. and Berrill, K. T. (1992). *Hate Crimes: Confronting Violence Against Lesbians and Gay Men*. Newbury Park, CA: Sage Publications.

Jacobs, J. B. and Potter, K. (1998). *Hate Crimes: Criminal Law and Identity Politics*. New York, NY: Oxford University Press.

Jenness, V. and Broad, K. (1997). *Hate Crimes: New Social Movements and the Politics of Violence*. New York, NY: Aldine de Gruyter.

Lawrence, F. M. (1999). *Punishing Hate: Bias Crimes Under American Law*. Cambridge, MA: Harvard University Press.

Levin, J. and McDevitt, J. (1993). *Hate Crimes: The Rising Tide of Bigotry and Bloodshed*. New York, NY: Plenum Press.

Newton, M. and Newton, J. A. (1991). *Racial and Religious Violence in America: A Chronology*. New York, NY: Garland Publishing.

Petrosino, C. (1999). "Connecting the Past to the Future: Hate Crime in America." *Journal of Contemporary Criminal Justice*, 15(1):22-47.

Saito, L. T. (1998). *Race and Politics: Asian Americans, Latinos, and Whites in a Los Angeles Suburb*. Urbana and Chicago, IL: University of Illinois Press.

U.S. Commission on Civil Rights (1992). *Civil Rights Issues Facing Asian Aericans in the 1990's*. Washington, DC Government Printing Office.

Yamamoto, E. K. (1999). *Interracial Justice: Conflict & Reconciliation in Post-Civil Rights America*. New York, NY: New York University Press.

Asian Pacific Americans and Human Rights/Relations Commissions

Pauline Agbayani-Siewert

Introduction

Human Rights/Relations Commissions represent one of the oldest institutionalized efforts to improve inter-group relations. Although early efforts can be traced to at least the early 1940s in the form of ad hoc committees appointed by mayors and other elected officials to resolve racial tension and conflicts, the number of human rights/relations organizations grew rapidly in the 1960s and early 1970s largely in response to urban riots in Black communities. However, there are serious limitations. While many agencies have been concerned about basic problems in housing, schooling and employment, the authority to address these problems often resides in other organizations. Over time, human rights/relations organizations took on a more narrowly defined set of activities, including conflict resolution, cultural sensitivity training, leadership training, and providing forums for inter-group discussion.

The commissions have also changed with broader changes in society. The initial focus on race relations has shifted to include a more diverse population and issues such as gender, sexual orientation, religion, and physical disabilities. In recent years, commissions faced new changes due to declining resources, new developments in race relations, and new forms of inter-group tension and conflict (especially between minority groups), many of which involve Asian Pacific Americans (APAs). This chapter is concerned with understanding how commissions can respond to the growing complexity of race relations in general and with APAs specifically.

To gain insights into these issues, the analysis draws on existing literature for Human Relations/Rights Commissions (HRCs) such as published material, news media accounts, and organizational reports and interviews with key individuals associated with each HRC. Existing documentation was used to examine the agency's structure (e.g., whether it is an independent department or operates like a commission), size and composition of the staff and any governing body, decision-making process, particular history and stated mission, mandates and the available mechanisms/resources to carry out its mandate(s), and sources and amount of funding. The purpose of this analysis is to gain an understanding of the organization and how its day-to-day operations are structured to respond to APA race relations. Interviews with HRC executive directors, commissioners, staff, and key individuals from the Asian Pacific American community were conducted on site at seven HRCs representing various regions of the country including Austin, Texas, Chicago, Los Angeles City, Los Angeles County, New York, San Francisco, and Seattle. The interviews were used to expand and elaborate on information gained from the review of agency and news documentation and to provide detailed insights and opinions regarding the organization's response to Asian Pacific American issues and race relations.

The first section of this chapter will present information on HRCs based on case study interviews conducted for this study. The second section will delineate the scope of the problem and key policy questions/issues relevant to Asian Pacific Americans. Specifically, the following research objectives are addressed: 1) The nature and extent of group tension and conflicts involving APAs, 2) the responses of HRCs to APA-related issues, 3) the effectiveness of conflict-resolution through negotiation and mediation, and 4) the roles of APAs on commissions and staff. For APAs who are either staff or board members, the research will also examine the following questions: 1) In their role, have they had the opportunity to provide meaningful input that redefines the mission, operation and priorities of their agency? 2) Have they had access through their agency to key leaders and decision-makers? 3) What are their opinions on the state of race relations, the most pressing immediate problems, and a vision of what America should be?

HRC: History, Mission, and Structure

HISTORY OF HUMAN RELATIONS/RIGHTS COMMISSIONS

The United States has an extensive history of racial conflict and oppression. Racism against APAs in this country reaches back to 160 years when the first sizable number of Chinese immigrants came to work on Hawaii's sugar plantations (Takaki, 1989). The underlying causes and manifestations of and responses to racism can be linked to an ever-changing social, political, economic, and socio-demographic context. The formation of human relations agencies is a reflection of this context.

Within a context of wartime politics and racial oppression, violence began to erupt against minorities, leading to the creation of the first HRCs. During the 1940s, World War II spurred strong racial tensions in the United States, especially in large urban areas such as Chicago, Los Angeles, and New York, where diverse and growing populations resided. The war brought about severe labor shortages in the West and North, attracting poor Black and Mexican Americans who began a significant migration to urban areas in search of jobs in the booming war industry. This mass migration created housing problems and competition for resources, resulting in racial tensions within the working class and often antagonistic responses from the police and justice system. Wartime politics and propaganda further contributed to rising racial tensions. The federal government mounted extensive campaigns to encourage patriotism and spur the defense efforts. Those who jarred cultural norms became vulnerable to abuse (Valdez, 1978). The Zoot Suit Riots erupted in Los Angeles between young Mexican American males and a few Filipino immigrants with Caucasian servicemen on June

3, 1943. At a 13-week trial involving Mexican American youths, newspapers and radio commentators took on a prejudicial tone and accentuated the negative portrayal of these youths as gang members. Compounded by wartime sentiments against Japan, anti-minority sentiment increased. Japanese Americans were forced from their homes on the West Coast into internment camps due to growing hysteria and racial prejudice (Los Angeles County HRC, 1996). It has been suggested that the true source of the violence directed at Mexican Americans by the servicemen involved in the Zoot Suit Riots was subconscious fear of Japanese American residents who had been interned (Greene, 1994). In view of increasing racial tensions, a group of concerned citizens met and recommended to the Los Angeles Board of Supervisors that a governmental agency was needed to confront the issue of intergroup relations. In response, the Joint Committee for Interracial Progress was created to "seek out the causes of racial tension and devise all means possible to eliminate them" (Los Angeles County Commission on Human Relations, 1969). Shifting its focus to include other issues, the Committee stated that the problems which existed between different groups were not only based on race, but included religious and nationality tensions.

Within Black communities, the U.S. involvement in a war against the Nazis and their overt racist ideology brought to the forefront racial inequality in the United States and within its armed forces. Some Black Americans debated whether or not this was a "Black man's war." In this highly charged racial climate, a major riot in Harlem erupted during 1943. A Black American soldier was shot in the shoulder by a New York policeman while attempting to resist his girlfriend's arrest. Rumors quickly spread throughout the Black community that a White police officer shot a Black soldier in the back, in front of his mother.

The 1960s were an era of civil rights movements. Ongoing racism and structural barriers to housing, education and employment contributed to urban poverty in communities of color and gave impetus for the massive mobilization of the civil rights movement. The lack of serious institutional response to this movement resulted in violent urban uprisings. The number of human relation organizations grew dramatically in the 1960s and early 1970s, largely in response to racial tensions. The Los Angeles City HRC was created soon after the Watts Riot. Not all cities waited until violence erupted locally before establishing a municipal HRC. In Chicago, Seattle, and San Francisco, the formation of human relations commissions was not a reaction to urban riots, although local demonstrations and racial tensions prompted a somewhat more proactive response to suppress potential violence. The San Francisco HRC was established after massive protests and demonstrations on "Auto Row" by Black Americans who could purchase automobiles but were barred from employment to sell or service them. In Seattle, community members and the city officials recognized a need for a human relations commission to alleviate tensions that were intensifying between the city and minority groups concerning housing. Although initially many Seattle citizens believed that the city did not have race problems, repeated local demonstrations against housing discrimination, along with a series of racial crises in public high schools, and the death of Martin Luther King, Jr. culminated in the formation of the HRC (City of Seattle HRC Report, 1968). Racial riots in nearby Detroit and conflicts locally provided an impetus for the formation of the Chicago HRC. Following the lead of the creation of a State Department of Civil Rights in Texas, Austin established a local HRC.

Early HRC efforts to resolve racial tension and conflicts generally began in the form of ad hoc committees appointed by mayors and other elected officials largely in reaction to racial tensions. The methods of resolution were generally preventive through education with minimal focus on addressing larger structural issues. Early HRCs were generally characterized by a paradigm structured towards resolving conflicts between minorities and other groups. The paradigm was largely based on conflict resolution between Blacks and Whites. The legacy of this early paradigm is still present in many of the HRCs today.

CONTEMPORARY MISSION

Mission statements describe the nature of the organization, values and beliefs which guide activities and the direction it wants to go. A mission statement has several functions: it serves as a communication tool, educates the public about activities and programs that can be expected from the organization, provides a planning and evaluation tool, and provides a target to which long-range goals can be directed. The early HRC mission statements were strikingly similar. All of the mission statements convey an explicit or implicit goal and vision to eliminate or reduce discrimination and/or improve the quality of people's lives. Here is a sampling of these missions: eliminate discrimination (Seattle), enhance the quality of life and economic well-being of citizens (Austin, Texas), build effective communities where each person is valued and included (Los Angeles County), create a city free of racism and violence (Los Angeles City), create a bias-free city (Chicago) promote human rights for all (San Francisco), and prohibit discrimination (New York). Implicit in the mission statements is the assumption that social problems occur because of cultural and social heterogeneity in their respective cities.

Mission statements are closely tied to the authority granted to the HRC by city ordinances and state and federal anti-discrimination laws. The responsibility to enforce city, state or federal anti-discrimination laws is referred to in mission statements by HRCs with direct or indirect enforcement powers. HRCs without powers of enforcement generally refer to human relations and the quality of life. Regardless of the agency's responsibilities, the vision appears to be one of equality. With the exception of Seattle, the mission statements make no reference to the development of anti-discrimination policies that address structural barriers or social conditions. The mission statements tend to implicitly communicate a preventive response to discrimination through education and/or a reactive response through enforcement after discrimination has occurred.

The formal mission statements do not always reveal the direction and activities of an agency. Two HRC executive directors described HRC mission statements as "fuzzy, vague and outdated" and not reflective of an agency's actual programs and activities (Interviews 3 & 5). HRCs began in response to conflict and violence between minorities and other groups but have now expanded their mission to include almost anyone who can be discriminated against. New York's mission statement explicitly lists the categories to be protected: race, creed, color, age, national origin, alienage or citizenship status, gender, sexual orientation, disability, lawful occupation, arrest or conviction, marital and family status, and retaliation (NYC Commission on Human Rights, Annual Report, 1996). Chicago adds parental status, discharge status and source of income (1997 Adjudication Report: Discrimination in Chicago). The mission statements do not tend to single out one protected group as more important than another. Although APAs as a racial group may be one of many groups, they may also fit into several categories such as alienage, immigrant, creed, gender, sexual orientation and others. Discrimination specifically directed against APAs may at times be difficult to identify depending on the interpretation and context in which the discrimination takes place.

ORGANIZATIONAL STRUCTURE

The HRCs in the study are City and/or County agencies and show some similarities and differences in their structures and in how the Executive Director and Commissioners are appointed, and the agency's place in the hierarchy of government affairs. Disparities in organizational structure are heavily influenced by historical factors and politics. Local HRCs are generally differentiated from State Human Rights Commissions by their powers of enforcement. State commissions have the power to investigate and legally enforce sanctions against proven discrimination cases, while the majority of HRCs may investigate but use powers of persuasion to obtain a resolution. The New York and Seattle HRCs are unique exceptions, with legal authority to investigate and prosecute. Local HRC activity is confined to a particular geographical area such as a city or county, while State HRCs service areas covers the entire state in which it is located.

All local HRCs exist within the hierarchy of city and/or county government. All HRCs are under the authority of city government and ultimately answer to mayors and city councils. Placement in the government hierarchy showed little consistency among the seven HRCs: county department (Los Angeles County), city department (Los Angeles City), city and county agency (San Francisco), city agency (Chicago, New York, and Seattle), and a sub-division within the Department of Human Resources (Austin, Texas). City agencies, such as New York and Seattle, have more extensive powers and independence than departmental and city HRCs.

There are some similarities in the organizational structures within the HRCs. All agencies have an executive director or chair and one or more commissions or advisory commissions headed by a president or chair. Chicago has eight advisory boards representing selected members of identified protected groups specifically, women, immigrant/refugee, gay and lesbians and Asian, Arab, and African American affairs. The Seattle Office for Civil Rights (SOCR) consists of three specialized advisory commissions: Human Rights, Women's Rights, and Sexual Minorities. They are concerned with discrimination in housing and employment against all protected groups including ethnic/racial minorities and overlap with some of the issues relevant to sexual minorities and women. The City of Chicago's Commission is comprised of eight Advisory Committees; African, Arab, Asian, Immigrant/Refugee, Latino, Veterans, and Women's Affairs. Los Angeles City and County, New York, San Francisco and Texas are comprised of one commission.

Commission appointments appear to be highly political. Commissioners are appointed by mayors, city councils, and county boards of supervisors depending on the place of the HRCs in the governmental structure. The Seattle commissioners are appointed by the mayor and city council who, in turn, appoint one to two commissioners. Length of appointment and number of commissioners vary from one agency to another and range from three to four years with an average of 15 members per commission. Criteria for appointment does not seem to be readily available. Except for being representatives of the communities or groups which the HRCs serve, appointments are entirely in the hands of political officials. Since commissioners are not compensated except for reimbursable items related to fulfilling their function as commissioners, motivations to serve may range from altruism to political exposure. The majority of commissions serve in an advisory capacity to the mayor and other city officials who appoint them. Some commissions are charged with monitoring the HRCs programs, approving commission policies and/or agency budget requests. Commissioners may possibly advocate and support the agenda of their "appointers" rather than the needs of the agency (Interview 3). Moreover, without formal criteria regarding qualifications, commission members may not possess the experience or knowledge of race relations and politics necessary to support the direction of the agency. There does not appear to be any one pattern that characterizes how HRCs decide on the composition of the commissions. Seattle and Chicago's specialized commissions (e.g., women, gay and lesbians and ethnic affairs) generally include individuals who are members of the communities they represent. Other HRC appointments appear to be based on a mix of rationales including current concerns to the HRC and their respective city and/or city demographics.

The daily activities of the agency are run by a salaried executive director or chair who holds the highest administrative position. With the exception of one HRC, the appointment of executive directors are subject to the same politics as the commissions. The majority of the executive directors appear to be highly qualified for their positions with previous experience in race relations and city government. Of the seven interviewed HRCs, all had an executive director who was a member of an ethnic/racial group and/or was a woman.

The size and composition of staff vary according to the budget, mission, and programs. Staff sizes range from 15 to 133, not counting commissioners. HRCs that focus on race relations have the smallest staff, while those with enforcement powers, both legal and compliance, have the largest staff. The ethnic composition of the staff vary. The majority of HRCs are ethnically and racially diverse. The demographics of the HRC catchment area does appear to have some influence on the race and ethnicity of the staff. In addition, it appears that staff working in intervention programs are selected to represent those groups who are perceived as requiring attention or being at-risk for possible conflict. Most HRC executive directors who were interviewed and had small staff sizes were able to cite the job positions and ethnicity/race of all of the agency's staff. On the other hand, one administrator of a large urban HRC stated that the ethnic composition of staff was unknown. It was further explained that the ethnic/racial composition of the HRC was an outcome of the civil service system that seeks to be impartial. Applicants for staff positions must take and pass the civil service exam, and the agency then hires from the "top of the list." The administrator went on to add that all ethnic groups complain about low representation on the HRC staff and gave the example of an Italian man who complained there were not enough Italians represented on staff.

PROGRAMS

City and state politics generally mandate the type of enforcement authority that an agency possesses. This is reflected in the types of programs and activities an HRC develops and provides. Based on powers of authority, HRC programs are characterized by the amount of resources (time, staff, and funding) invested in a particular set of activities. The characteristics of the various HRC programs can be grouped into one of three models. Overlap does occur because HRCs will engage in varying degrees in more than one program activity. However, HRC program activities generally tend to emphasize one type of program over another.

The first program model is the "traditional prevention/ intervention" model. These programs are comprised of "process oriented" "human relation" activities that exist along a continuum from proactive prevention to crisis intervention (Interviews 3, 5 & 6). The Los Angeles County HRC employs a "triage approach" of proactive prevention, intervention and suppression programs. Without the legal authority to enforce, this model relies heavily on powers of persuasion. Programs are reminiscent of those that existed when HRCs were first established. These programs do not provide direct services to individuals and instead work with groups and communities. This model relies on establishing formal and informal networks with community groups and organizations. Prevention programs can take many forms including education in the schools, research, the dissemination of brochures and flyers that inform community members of the rights of protected citizens, speakers at community events, annual multicultural celebrations and dinners to honor selected members from the community for their work in combating discrimination. Workshops are offered by some HRCs to train police officers, educate employers and landlords on the rights of protected citizens, provide limited English speaking immigrants with information on how to file for public benefits, and creation of an HIV prison project.

The purpose of an educational component is to empower individuals to exercise their rights and prevent discrimination. Identifying potential risk areas for the emergence of conflict is also seen by some HRCs as a proactive response. However, more intervention programs are implemented after incidences of violence have already emerged. These programs are viewed as proactive attempts to contain large-scale violence. During the proactive intervention phase, risk areas are identified (e.g., reports of hate crimes in a particular geographical location that the HRC serves), and a team of field workers is sent in to coordinate resources to address the problem. The Los Angeles County Human Relations Commission builds existing infrastructure within a community in an effort to provide services. The team of field workers pulls together public and private resources such as law enforcement, community-based organizations (e.g., churches, ethnic/racial and gay and lesbian organizations), schools, and private businesses and corporations. These groups form a mutual assistance consortium to deliver services. This approach is partly the result of limited resources and an attempt to involve all factions in the community to address the problem. When conflict emerges, the community is empowered and the infrastructure is in place for resolution and intervention. A final intervention strategy is suppression. Suppression is employed when conflict has erupted into violence. The consortium of organizations established earlier is put into action. Process-oriented resolution strategies and dialogues are employed to contain the violence. However, some communities do not have an existing infrastructure, and the HRC must assist in creating one.

The second program model is one of "legal investigation and resolution through compliance." HRCs under this model have the power to legally investigate complaints of discrimination and seek resolution. They do not, however, have the authority to legally prosecute. Authority to investigate charges of discrimination is derived from the creation of new civil right laws passed during the 1980s through municipal codes and state legislation (e.g., articles of the Housing and Urban Development legislation). However, enforcement does not include the power to prosecute or impose civil penalties. The Austin, Chicago and San Francisco HRCs are characteristic of this model. This model depends on the formal collaboration of community organizations and agencies. If an investigation finds that discrimination has occurred, resolution then depends on the voluntary participation of the individual, business, or organization charged with discrimination and the individual who filed the complaint. Among the three HRCs in this model, there is some variation in specific procedures during the process of investigation and resolution of complaints. However, all lack legal authority to prosecute. For example, using field representatives and/or lawyers, the San Francisco HRC may investigate a charge of employment discrimination and convene a mediation hearing. The executive director will evaluate investigative and hearing reports, then issue a finding towards resolution (e.g., monetary fine and wages). The individual or organization charged with discrimination reviews the report and is given an opportunity to appeal the recommended resolution. Prior to the appeal stage, the investigation process does not necessarily require the participation or cooperation of the accused. However, both the complainant and the accused must agree to have it go forward to a hearing officer. If the complaint has been determined to be valid and the alleged violator refuses to participate or comply with the recommendations, a referral is made to an appropriate city department or organization with enforcement powers. Programs with investigative powers intervene after an act of discrimination has occurred. Intervention generally occurs on a case-by-case basis. HRCs in this model expend some resources and staff time in prevention and education programs. For example, the San Francisco HRC expends about 20 percent of its resources on prevention and education in such areas as outreach and workshops to inform citizens, businesses, and landlords on civil rights laws.

The third type of program is the "legal enforcement and resolution" model. Nationally, this model is uncommon with only two HRCs having powers to prosecute, New York and Seattle (Interview 6). Not only do these agencies have the power to legally investigate discrimination complaints, they also possess the ability to prosecute and impose civil penalties such as back pay, rent refunds, training, and reinstatement of employment or damages for pain and suffering.

Both New York and Seattle provide an array of outreach and educational programs outside of investigation and legal enforcement. The New York's HRC also has a Community Relations Bureau that includes a crisis intervention component.

Although most of the HRCs believe that the source of conflict is generally other factors than race, they provide programs to prevent discrimination through educating members in the community or intervene after it has occurred through report or conflict. Most of the HRCs have no formalized structure to respond in a proactive manner to the social policies that impact the populations they serve although most attempt to advocate for public policy reform. One interviewee explained that "policy is reactive to social conditions" (e.g., civil rights movement). The Seattle HRC, however, has a policy analysis division which examines the potential impact of new and proposed legislation on the populations it serves. The agency responds by advocating for or against a policy based on how it will affect protected groups.

FUNDING

The main source of HRC funding comes from the city and county, with some federal funds. Federal funds are tied to enforcing anti-discrimination legislation in housing (HUD), employment (EEOP) and hate crimes. The amount of funding granted to an agency appears to be related to the type of programs the HRC provides. HRCs with legal authority to investigate complaints have larger budgets than programs which provide only prevention and intervention services. HRCs that investigate and prosecute generally have larger budgets than the other two types of program models. Geographical or demographic considerations do not seem to be related to an agency's funding. For example, the densely populated New York City HRC has an extensive budget of approximately seven million dollars per year, while the similarly populated Los Angeles County, with a greater geographical dispersion, receives approximately one million dollars per year from the County. It also does not appear that the number of reported discrimination and hate crimes is a consideration for budget allocation. Los Angeles County has experienced a continued growth in hate crimes throughout the last decade (Los Angeles County Commission on Human Relations, 1997). To increase their budget, Los Angeles County relies on fund-raising activities from private agencies and corporations. Agencies may also take on projects that are considered important but of low priority to their overall mission in an effort to increase their funding. For example, Los Angeles County contracted with the INS to produce a manual on the management of day labor at hiring sites. Most HRCs were dissatisfied with the amount of their allocated budget. One city HRC described their budget as "pathetic" when compared to the money allocated to the city fire and police departments (Interview 5). One HRC was not only scaled back in funding, but lost their departmental status when the city experienced a recession. One individual conveyed that current budget allocations have made it difficult and sometimes impossible to carry out the agency's mission (Interview 3), while another voiced concern about the inability to focus on programs believed to be of importance. For example, one HRC wanted to move beyond investigative functions and increase resources in prevention programs (Interview 17). The majority of explanations given for low budgets were attributed to past or present politics, for example, a long-standing former mayor who only tolerated the agency and had no interest in its significance and had failed to understand the implications of the city's socio-demographics (Interview 16). Funding was also explained as an outcome of the agency's organizational structure. Loyalties may be balanced more towards elected politicians who appoint commissioners than the agency and its mission. For example, since mayors or other political officials control the budget and appoint commissioners, there may be a reduced incentive for commissioners to advocate for a budget increase (Interview 3). One executive director was clearly satisfied with the funding and support received by the agency. The executive director conveyed strong support from a relatively new mayor and city administration plus significant increases in funding to carry out mandates and achieve goals (Interview 8). The mayor was described as sharing the agency's mission and vision and as one who viewed the agency as an integral part of city government.

EVALUATION OF AGENCY EFFECTIVENESS

How an agency evaluates its effectiveness and the types of tangible outcomes that are used to measure success is tied to its mission, mandates and programs. The direct effects of prevention activities on discrimination are difficult to measure, thus most of the HRCs focused on outcomes such as the number of multicultural festivals, community presentations, workshops, and media events (e.g., television broadcasts) held during a given year. Reporting the number of accomplished activities does not directly address whether the agency has achieved its mission to reduce or eliminate hate crimes, discrimination and bias, and improve interpersonal relations or the quality of people's lives. One agency counts the number of calls that come in from the community after a presentation or media event as an indicator of successful education and outreach efforts. Surveys are used by one HRC to evaluate client satisfaction of prevention (e.g., workshops) and intervention programs. For example, one HRC surveys both parties of a discrimination dispute about their experiences with the investigation and resolution process.

The effects of intervention programs are somewhat less elusive and provide more tangible measures of effectiveness than prevention programs. Measures can include a reduction in hate crimes and complaints of discrimination, the number of complaints processed and brought to resolution, and community organization efforts. As a tangible indicator of effectiveness, one agency calculated the amount of time it takes for a case to move from a complaint to some type of resolution. Investment in computerized programs to track complaints of discrimination appears to be a new trend. One HRC representative argued that the "conventional methods" of disparity studies comparing minority and non-minorities is unreliable because businesses and public organizations do not necessarily keep accurate records in housing and employment (Interview 8). Instead, the tangible outcome used to evaluate effectiveness is whether the agency has carried out its mandates and met its goals, which can be determined by an agency's record of accomplishments such as a decrease in complaints and the enforcement of affirmative action contracts with public and private businesses.

APA ISSUES AND PARTICIPATION IN THE HRC

ASIAN PACIFIC AMERICANS AND RACE RELATIONS

The way APA concerns are addressed by HRCs is heavily influenced by a public perception that APAs are not generally a target of hate crimes. Relatively low rates of reported APA hate crimes to HRCs support this view, especially when compared to Blacks, Jews, and non-White Hispanics. For example, in Los Angeles County where one of the nation's largest APA population resides, three hate crimes against APAs were reported in the 1997 annual report, while two were reported in Chicago involving Middle Easterners and none in Austin, Texas (Chicago Report, Los Angeles County Report, 1997, Interviews 2, 6, 7 & 10). When cases of violence are reported in the media, they are often presented as an isolated event such as the beating death of Vincent Chin in Detroit in 1988 during massive lay-offs in the automotive industry. Although Vincent Chin was Chinese, racism appeared to take a back seat to explanations of auto industry competition with Japan. Similarly, when a Filipino American postal worker was the only fatality of the perpetrator who committed the violent attack on the Jewish children's day camp during the summer of 1999 in Los Angles, relatively minimal media attention was focused on him or his family.

Discounting acts of violence may further support a perception that APAs do not experience hate crimes. How hate crimes are defined by HRCs has significant implications for agency response and policy. The legal definition of a hate crime varies slightly from state to state but generally is defined as any criminal or attempted act which is motivated by the actual or perceived victim's race, ethnicity, religion, sexual orientation, gender, or disability status (Hate Crime in Los Angeles County, 1997). Racial epithets are not necessarily considered a hate crime unless there is a threat of violence and not otherwise protected by free speech laws (City of Chicago Commission on Human Relations, 1997). Graffiti is a hate crime only when it is directed at a specific group. Vandalism, on the other hand, is considered to be a hate crime directed at houses of worship or institutions, in the absence of evidence to the contrary. One of the primary determinants of a hate crime is the motivating factor behind the act. Motivation can be established by admission from the perpetrator, verbal or written threats, symbols (e.g., Nazi swastika) or a pattern of incidents. Without evidence that the aggression or attack was motivated by racism, a hate crime cannot be determined. For example, during 1999 one large urban area experienced approximately twenty arson carport fires destroying structures and automobiles within a period of a few months. All of the victims were APAs. Although reports of the carport fires were covered in the media, no mention was made to APAs as targets or victims. This information was instead reported to the

County Board of Supervisors and subsequently referred to the County Fire Department Chief who headed an arson investigation. No investigation of possible racism was initiated. It was explained during an interview with an administrator at the local HRC that no actual evidence that a hate crime targeted at APAs had occurred (Interviewee 3). There was a lack of evidence that the perpetrator who was not apprehended had a bias, hatred or prejudice towards APAs. No symbols or verbal and written threats existed that were directed towards APAs. In other words, racism as a motivation could not be established. The acts did not fit the classification of vandalism because they were not directed towards any specific organization or house of worship. One interviewed individual at the local HRC stated that some city officials believed that although all victims of the fires were APAs, no evidence to the contrary existed that the fires were not random acts of arson (Interviewee 3). Thus, incidences such as these will not make their way into the annual hate crime report, and APAs will again show a relatively low rate of hate crimes. This situation is reminiscent of what happened during WWII when returning Japanese Americans were reintegrated into the community. The HRCs chose to promote resettlement quietly to avoid public controversy. Similarly, the movement of immigrant Vietnamese into California was also done quietly to avoid public controversy. This (social response of quietly resolving) fits well with Asian Pacific American's under-reporting of hate crimes and image as a model minority.

Most HRCs acknowledged that the low rates of APA discrimination and hate crime reports may be a consequence of under-reporting. The most common explanation given for under-reporting was Asian cultural values and beliefs. For example, the traditional APA cultural practice of keeping personal problems and difficulties within the family and not publicly airing them to avoid shame was cited by three of the HRCs (Interviewees 6, 8 & 9). Other explanations were language barriers and, for Southeast Asians, fear of any government institution or official. Cultural explanations make an assumption that all APAs adhere to traditional cultural values and beliefs and also imply that the only APA groups who under-report are immigrants. Conversely, one APA interviewee believes that the under-reporting of incidences is partly an outcome of inadequate publicity and community outreach and the political marginalization of APAs (Interview 4).

Although not all of the HRCs have the power of enforcement, all of the agencies conveyed the importance of protecting immigrants and other groups (e.g., ethnic/racial minorities, disabled, gays and lesbians, and women) from discrimination in housing and employment. However, when giving case examples of APA discrimination and/or tension, interviewees almost always described incidences involving Asian immigrants. Urban areas have undergone significant demographic changes since the 1965 immigration law. The Asian Pacific American population has grown from small numbers of primarily Chinese and Japanese to a more dispersed and diverse population. HRC interviewees tended to agree that as the APA population increases, so does tension and conflict as groups begin to compete for resources in housing and employment. Race is viewed as a secondary factor in the rising tensions and conflicts. For example, in one large urban area, a "destabilization" of neighborhoods has occurred as immigrants buy or rent housing (Interviewee 4). One HRC staff member stated that "while one or two Asian families residing in a neighborhood does not pose a problem, more families begin to set off conflicts." It was also stated that White ethnics resist the influx of "outsiders" (i.e., Asian Pacific Americans). This perception of conflict and violence tied to APA population growth and the concomitant competition over resources was supported by the description by an HRC official regarding the violence in Texas between White and Vietnamese fisherman during the late 1970's. "In and of themselves" Vietnamese were not seen as a problem until their numbers grew and they began to be perceived as a serious economic threat to White shrimpers (Interview 6). The mounting tension and subsequent violence culminated when White shrimpers contacted the Ku Klux Klan (KKK) to assist them in removing Vietnamese from the Gulf Waters. The KKK responded by intimidating Vietnamese families and individuals, burning shrimp boats, firing shots at them, and threatening to kill them. The KKK obtained a boat mounted with a cannon and threatened to shoot at any Vietnamese fishing boat that came into the Gulf waters. The response was to file a lawsuit against the KKK and pass legislation dismantling and prohibiting KKK paramilitary training camps throughout the state.

Much of the conflict involving APAs has taken on a decidedly anti-immigration tone (Interviews 4, 8, 9, 13 & 14). Anti-immigration sentiment has made its way into formal legislation such as California's English-only initiatives, the end of bilingual education in the Los Angeles school districts (Interview 8), and welfare reform policies (Interview 14). HRCs are generally not structured to significantly effect these policies. One interviewee stated that policy is reactive to social conditions, that "policy is in front" and HRCs "do not take a leadership role here" (Interview 3). Moreover, social policies do not meet HRC definitions of discrimination, hate crimes or violence, but definitely reflect a climate of intolerance and exclusion towards Asian Pacific Americans and other immigrant groups.

Multiracial conflict between APAs and other minority groups has gained national attention. One APA commissioner stated Asian Pacific Americans are viewed as a model minority except when it comes to their involvement in interracial conflict (Interview 11). The most notable cases have been between Blacks and Korean merchants. Most Whites are "perplexed by it all," and their response has been to avoid any involvement (Interview 5). Both Asian and non-Asians described the source of conflict as primarily about competition over resources with race as a secondary factor. How conflict is defined has a significant impact for response. One interviewee described the conflict between Blacks and

Koreans as part of a historical continuum (Interview 5). In the Black community there has always been a merchant class of "outsiders." Prior to the Koreans it was Jewish and Chinese. Blacks have always complained that they have been cheated, over-charged, and seldom hired. Resources are taken from the community without any investment back into the Black community. Faces and race may change, but these perceptions remain the same. On the other hand, the Black community does not realize the problems faced by small business owners. For example, small businesses do not have the same access to low-cost bulk and discount purchasing as the large supermarket corporations who are able to pass on savings to their customers. Furthermore, both groups seem to lack an understanding of each others' cultural values, beliefs, and behaviors. He states that much was learned after the riots. Koreans have taken a more active role in the community where they own their businesses and have hired Blacks. "The number of incidences have come down and both groups have become sensitized" to one another (Interview 4). However, he notes that underlying tensions remain and that Blacks continue to experience a threat of displacement as more Asians continue to move into the community. Although the conflict was primarily defined as one involving competition over resources, the resolution strategy was primarily one of improving relationships by opening dialogue and mediation and educating the two groups about one another. This method of response appears to be typical of HRCs with mandates and programs that are principally focused on human relationships through education.

APA involvement in multiracial conflict extends beyond the Korean and Black incidences. To further complicate the multiracial nature of conflict, intra-group conflict among APA ethnic groups and with other protected groups has emerged. Youth gang violence between APAs, Blacks and non-White Hispanics has been on the rise during the last two decades. Chinese, Filipino, and Southeast Asian gangs not only have had aggressive and violent confrontations with other minority gangs, ut with one another. Although youth gang membership is based on race, n the APA community confrontations are generally defined as delin- quent criminal behavior and not hate crimes. Two HRC interviewees partly attribute youth gang violence to a structure of race relations tied to an emphasis on ethnic and racial differences that create divisive polarities Interview 3 & 4).

Cultural celebrations are described as "culturally cumbersome" and should not be used as a predominant strategy to improve race relations (Interviewer 3). For example, instead of improving race relations, cultural celebrations have generally led to violence between Black and Brown youth in the high and middle schools and housing projects. An alternative strategy would be to focus on "common experi- ences" such as history and their place in society. Two HRCs have moved to prevention programs which de-emphasize differences and instead emphasize common issues and experiences that transcend race. Most recently, one of the local HRCs supported the removal of cultural celebrations from several of the city's high schools.

To further complicate the multiracial nature of conflict, there is a growing concern regarding complaints of conflict between APAs and other protected groups. In New York, conflicts between Pakistani and Bangladeshi taxi cab drivers and other protected groups (e.g., women and the disabled) have been reported. It is not clear if the conflict is based on religious anti-Muslim or anti-Sikh sentiment or racism, or if it is a case of sexism and discrimination against disabled people (Interview 4). The older paradigm of Black and White conflict does little to advance our understanding (Interview 3).

There seems to exist a perception that non-immigrant APAs are not in need of as much protection as immigrants and other protected groups. As one HRC administrator stated, "Chinese Americans are successful at being given political and economic access" (Interviewee 8). With the exception of two interviewees, issues of discrimination among non-immigrant APAs did not emerge. However, outside of the ethnic enclaves the glass ceiling effect in employment, the under-representation of APA's in institutions of higher learning, the attempts at some universities to place an admission cap on selected Asian Pacific American groups, the glaring absence of APA representation in the media, and the under-representation of appointed and elected APA officials in municipal, state and federal levels of government were generally ignored. APAs are not immune to similar biases and discrimination in housing that immigrants experience. Two APA interviewees described cases of discrimination and bias in purchasing or renting homes in traditionally White suburban neighborhoods (Interview 4 & 14).

Perceptions of Asian Pacific Americans as having "made it" contribute to the minimal attention focused on institutional racism and discrimination. Several of the interviewed HRCs seem to support a contention that non-immigrant APAs are doing quite well without them. Almost all of the HRCs gave at least one model minority explanation that demonstrated stereotypes about APAs. One top-ranking HRC administrator stated that Asian Pacific Americans are largely successful and have done very well in education and economics and that their "children do very well in school" (Interviewee 6). Reflecting a stereotype of APAs choosing to keep to themselves, this same administrator stated that with the exception of the local Chamber of Commerce, there was a lack of interest on the part of Asian Pacific Americans to participate in mainstream organizations or the local governments.

The issue is a lack of inclusion in government, institutions and communities in which Asian Pacific Americans reside. Unlike the more blatant behavioral acts of racial discrimination and hate crimes, institutional racism is subtle. Concerned largely with enforcement, conflict resolution and/or prevention and education, HRCs are not structured to address these more subtle forms of discrimination. Glass ceilings are contained within an institutional infrastructure that does not spill out of those boundaries into street violence and hate crimes (Interview 3). Institutional discrimination and racism is not easy to detect and even more difficult to prove.

APA Participation and Role in the HRC

The role and participation of APAs within HRCs was somewhat mixed. While one HRC had a special Commission on Asian American Affairs, other agencies had no substantive or institutionalized approach to specifically include APAs. The exceptions were the responses to conflict between African Americans and Koreans and issues concerned with all immigrants. Asian immigrants are generally not differentiated from other protected immigrant groups. Overall, it appears as if Asian Pacific Americans have minimal participation within the formal structure of human relation commissions. Several APA and non-APA commission members acknowledged that Asian Pacific Americans as a group have no role in their agency (Interviews 2, 4, 6 &7).

APAs have been able to participate at the commission level, but there are still problems. One HRC reported that there were no Asian Pacific Americans on the commission, but the problem may be more extensive because the available information is incomplete. (One administrator did not know the ethnicity or race of commission members and would "get back" with that information.) At three HRCs dealing with recent tension between Blacks and Koreans, Koreans were appointed to two commissions, while the third HRC did not appoint a Korean. The HRC with no Asian Pacific American commissioners explained that Asian Pacific Americans in that city did not file discrimination complaints and have not indicated an interest in becoming involved with the organization. Considering that there are numerous ethnic groups that comprise the category of Asian Pacific Islander, none are represented on the commission. (This is not a problem unique to APAs, but is also a problem for the ethnically diverse Latino population.)

APAs have been present among the HRC executive directors. In general, the composition of this key position is somewhat diversified. At the time of the study, there were two White women, one male and one female Asian Pacific American, and two male and one female African Americans. Glaringly missing are Hispanics. The Asian Pacific American executive directors are located in areas with one of the highest concentrations of Asian Pacific Americans in this country. All of the interviewed HRCs were asked who was the first Asian Pacific American to serve as an executive director at their HRC. Two of the agencies reported former Asian Pacific American executive directors. Seattle reported one Asian Pacific American male almost thirty years ago, and San Francisco cited two former Asian Pacific American Directors during the last two decades. Asian Pacific Americans comprise a significant population size in both of these cities. Three HRC administrators did not know if there had been a past executive director of Asian ancestry. When considering that HRCs have been in existence for fifty years or more, the appointment of Asian Pacific Americans as executive directors appears to be relatively recent.

As stated earlier, the composition of the HRC staffs are influenced by a number of factors, including the civil service hiring process. The available information indicates that one HRC had no Asian Pacific Americans on their staff. Those HRCs that could report on the ethnicity of staff persons revealed a cross representation of Asian, Latinos, Jews, and African Americans. In these HRCs the number of staff in a particular racial/ethnic category may be related to the ethnicity of the executive director. For example, at one HRC where the executive director was Asian Pacific American, about 38 percent of the staff were Asian Pacific American while about 2 percent were African American. At another HRC where the executive director was African American about 33 percent of the staff were African American, while about 1 percent were Asian Pacific American. Both HRCs served a remarkably similar area with similar demographic distributions of ethnic/racial minorities.

City politics have an important influence on the role of APAs. Politics can enhance and support the role of APAs, or ignore them, or create a negative hostile environment. Mayors have considerable power and authority in influencing an agency's mission, organizational structure, funding, direction and policies and can play a significant role in the appointment of commission members. According to one commission member, "electoral politics is where race relations get played out" (Interview 4). Mayors have the power and authority to direct more initiatives to community outreach and address hate crimes through conferences and public hearings to gather testimony about incidences of discrimination (Interview 18). Current outreach efforts to the APA community generally include flyers and literature distributed at various community events, media and publicity, and appearances by commission members at cultural festivals. Mayors can also appoint Asian Pacific Americans to fairly high level senior and advisory positions as part of the administration's "inner circle." This inclusion of Asian Pacific Americans provides access to key policy-makers. The lack of APAs in government severely limits access to the key decision makers, who without this access have minimal influence on the mission, mandates, programs, and policies of the HRC (Interview 18). This commission member further noted that the commission is supposed to be the "eyes and the ears" of the community, informing the mayor of the racial climate in the city. However, the commission does not serve this function in the current administration. Commission members at three HRCs described past and current mayors as people who don't care, as only tolerating the HRC, as unaware of race relations, and as ignorant of the impact of rapidly changing demographics on race relations (Interviews 3, 4 & 5).

In addition to city politics, characteristics and perceptions of the APA community also appear to shape the APA role within HRCs. Interviews with those in HRCs where Asian Pacific Americans have little or no role revealed that the APA population in their catchment area was very small or that no complaints based on race or national origin are filed (Interviews 2, 6, 7, 9, 11 & 17), implying that population size relative to other groups and the number of complaints filed are equated with an APA role.

The myth of APAs as a model minority was evident during the interviews as reflected in explanations for the lack of APA presence in the HRC. One APA interviewee stated that overall, Asian Pacific Americans have benefited more than any other group from civil rights legislation (Interview 8). Others pointed to the political and economic success achieved by some APA groups. It was noted by several HRCs that other minority groups "still had a way to go," such as Arabs, East Africans, Eastern Europeans, Ethiopians, and Latinos whose populations are rapidly increasing in large urban areas. Discrimination against immigrants as a group was described as problematic by the majority of HRCs. "The new focus" appears to be "on new immigrant groups" (Interview 8). Low rates of complaints were interpreted as an indicator that overall APAs do not have as great a need for HRC services as other groups.

One interpretation of low APA participation in HRCs is that it is due to choice. One interviewee noted that there was a general lack of interest for the APA community to become involved (Interview 6). At this particular HRC, an Asian Pacific American has never been appointed or hired as executive director, commissioner, or staff member. In addition, Asian Pacific Americans were described as being more interested in their own organizations and economic organizations within the community, such as the Chamber of Commerce. Two agencies noted that Asian Pacific Americans are more cohesive than other groups. However, interviews from the APA community dispute the claim of cohesiveness and advocate for stronger coalitions between APA ethnic groups (Interviews 13 & 14).

The perception of APAs as model minorities who are doing quite well affects the perception of HRCs. One interviewee from the APA community stated that HRCs have not yet recognized Asian Pacific Americans in their efforts (Interview 13). With the exception of one, all of the HRCs stated that Asian Pacific Americans were an important part of the HRC missions and programs. However, in the actual organizational structure and day-to-day activities of HRCs, APAs appear to have minimal participation and possess little power.

One APA commission member stated that APAs have been and are in the position to assume the role of an "objective party" in conflicts involving race (Interview 3). APAs occupy the position that Edna Bonachich refers to as the "middleman minority"(Interview 3). For example, Judge Lance Ito who presided in the O.J. Simpson trial was not necessarily acceptable, but not unacceptable to African Americans or Whites. The commission member notes that being an "objective party" in conflicts is a delicate and complicated role. APAs must manage a public and ethnic identify, and remain conscious of different audiences. One implication of the "middleman" role is that APAs are in a position to assist in establishing relations and coalitions among disparate populations.

HRC VISION FOR THE FUTURE

Almost all of the HRCs and APA community members shared a similar vision about race relations of going beyond looking at ethnic/minorities as separate groups with separate issues and concerns. The increase of multiracial conflict and discrimination between ethnic/racial populations with other protected groups and the inclusion of other new groups (e.g., women, disabled, elderly, gays and lesbians, transgender people, veterans) require HRCs to view race relations differently. One executive director calls for a move from a "tribal orientation" to a structure that is inclusive of everyone (Interview 11).

One ethnic minority HRC administrator stated that there need
to be a move away from the ethnocentric politics of race — race relations
are no longer based on a Black/White paradigm nor on a minority versus
White paradigm (Interview 5). To focus on just one group not only
becomes ethnocentric, but further divides groups as one becomes more
powerful than another. A common and consistent theme is to focus on
similarities and what the different groups have in common and share. A
message of common interests seeks to unify groups. This administrator
delivers the message that division has outlived its usefulness. In presen
tations he "downplays ethnicity, blends lines" and delivers a "gentle
presentation." Common interests gain the cooperation and participation
of the community. The executive director refers to this as "interest
politics" instead of racial politics. He defines multiculturalism as "recog
nizing each culture" within a context of interest politics. He further notes
that Whites have been staying away from the tension among minority
groups. He states that "most Whites are perplexed by it all." To present
a unified group to address issues and concerns, the White community
needs to be brought in as part of the dialogue. This executive director
delivers the message that division has outlived its usefulness.

One APA executive director stated that HRCs are currently tied
to a structure that creates polarities. The executive director argues that
racial and ethnic categories should not be a predominant strategy used by
HRCs to address problems of racism and discrimination. Moreover,
ethnic and racial categories are political and foster stereotypes. An alter
native view is to deconstruct categories. If inclusion is the goal, then
hypothetically everyone must be included. Categories are social
constructs and as such create ambiguity about who does or doesn't
belong. The executive director states that "we are lacking a theoretical
model" on how to include all groups." He argues that the current
strategy is to reduce conflict between the polarized groups — right now
everyone wants to "make nice." Instead of celebrating cultural diversity

or managing conflict, the sources of conflict need to be directly addressed, worked through, and resolved.

It is a fine line between respecting each group individually, while trying to find common interests and politics. Common interests that transcend race include economic issues, equity for all races, crack houses, education, gang infestation, prostitution, and community needs. The vision of common agendas that seek to unify diverse groups has already begun to be integrated into programs. For example, field workers involved in prevention and intervention work seek out issues that are shared by the majority of members in a particular community in an effort to unite people in a common cause that is not race focused. One HRC has implemented an outreach campaign named "We All Belong" to symbolize its vision of multicultural inclusion.

The new vision ties discrimination and conflict to existing social factors that create economic and structural barriers. One APA executive director stated a coalition of economic equity made of all oppressed groups is needed. The HRC can tap into community coalitions and coalitions can tap into other subgroups. To form a unified front to combat these problems, problems are re-conceptualized from issues of race to social factors that affect all members within a community. The implication is that splintered competing groups cannot garner the power needed to address social issues unless they join together.

Both Asian Pacific American community leaders and APA HRC members support the new vision. However, in order to participate in this united front, APAs must have a voice and significant role in HRCs and city government. With equal participation, APAs can unite with others to influence HRC mission, mandates, programs, organizational structure, and policies.

References

City of Chicago Commission on Human Relations. (1997). *1997 Hate Crime Report.* Chicago, Illinois: Author.

City of Chicago Commission on Human Relations. (1997). *1997 Adjudication Report.* Discrimination in Chicago: Housing, Employment, Credit Bonding, and Public Accommodation. Chicago, Illinois: Author.

Greene, R. (1994, August 29) "Spotlight on Ron Wakabayashi: Los Angeles County Relations Human Relations Commission, Executive Director." *Civic Center New Source.*

Los Angeles County Commission on Human Relations. (1997). *Hate Crime in Los Angeles County in 1997: A Report to the Los Angeles County Board of Supervisors.* Los Angles, CA: Author.

Los Angeles County Commission on Human Relations. *A Chronology of Most Important Events.* Los Angles, CA: Author.

Los Angeles County Commission on Human Relations. (1996). *A 25 Year History. 1944-1969.* Los Angles, CA: Author.

New York City Commission on Human Rights. (1996). *Annual Report.* New York NY: Author.

City of Seattle Human Rights Commission. (1968). *Report covering the period from August 1, 1966 to December 31, 1968.* Seattle, WA: Author.

Takaki, R. (1989). *Strangers from a Different Shore: A History of Asian Americans.* New York, NY: Penguin Books.

Valdez, Luis. (1978, August. 13). "Once again, meet the Zoot Suiters." *Los Angeles Times.*

Part III

National Race Policies

The Affirmative Action Divide[1]

Introduction

Over the last decade affirmative action has emerged as the defining wedge issue on race,[2] and Asian Pacific Americans (APAs) occupy a unique position in this heated political debate. APAs are materially and ideologically on both sides of the political divide, with some adamantly supporting and others vehemently opposing the policy. Understanding the APA position is important for several reasons. Their socioeconomic diversity poses troubling questions regarding the underlying purpose and coverage of race-based programs. Just as the other chapters in this book demonstrate, APAs do not fit easily into the prevailing black-white conceptualization of race, specifically in this case into remedial policies predicated largely on the black experience. APAs remain significantly disadvantaged in some arenas, thus have a plausible claim for inclusion in group-based programs, but they are not disadvantaged in other arenas.

The socioeconomic status of APAs points to complex hierarchy rather than a simple dichotomous order. The simplicity of a black-white paradigm lies in the absolute and interlocking of the group ordering across disparate arenas, from education to work to capital accumulation. The inequality is so pervasive, glaring and systematic that it is self-evident. In a simple bipolar structure, policies to correct racial inequality are simpler to design and implement, although still controversial with the disputes revolving around the specific causes and solutions. The status of APAs moves us away from this duality to a more nuanced paradigm with APAs occupying a middle position between blacks and whites. Even this ordinal depiction fails to capture the complexity. The material

The Affirmative Action Divide (313)

standing of APAs varies significantly from one dimension to another so that the juxtaposition is not fixed. This inconsistency undermines the validity of the prevailing notion about racism. Rectifying the logical flaw is a necessary step to reconceptualizing race.

The presence of APAs has also complicated the political debate. In a few geographic locations, APAs are sufficiently large enough to affect ballot outcomes; consequently, they are courted by proponents and opponents for votes. (For examples, see the chapter by Saito and Park in this book.) The importance of APAs, however, extends well beyond narrow electoral politics. The ideological position held by APAs is important symbolically. The affirmative action debate is about the extent of society's obligation to address racial inequality and about the mechanisms that ought to be used. As a minority group with a long history of racial victimization, but also one that has overcome many (albeit not all) racial barriers, the position taken by APAs is powerful fodder for political polemics. Coming to grips with the APA political position, however, is not easy due to the heterogeneity of the population.

This chapter examines the unique position of APAs, starting in Part I with an overview of the evolution of affirmative action, an important and divisive policy emerging from the civil rights movement. Affirmative action is the contested boundary defining how aggressive government ought to be to redress racial inequality. Unlike the strong public and judicial support for anti-discrimination laws, support for race-based strategies to attenuate group disparity is ambiguous and conditional. The heated debate revolves around programs governing the internal operation of the public sector: government hiring and contracting, and admission to state-supported schools. The next section, Part II, examines the material positions of APAs in the three major arenas: education, employment, and business. The statistical evidence reveals a mixed picture of high achievement and under representation. The variation in socioeconomic status translates to differences in the lature of APA participation in the major affirmative action programs, vhich is discussed in Part III. The available information shows that APAs bear the cost and reap the benefits. Because of this spread, APAs iave taken varying political positions within the affirmative action debate n pursuit of both self-interest and broader principles. The chapter oncludes with a discussion on the challenges posed by APAs for affirnative action.

PART I: THE EVOLUTION OF AFFIRMATIVE ACTION

Affirmative action must be understood as a part of a political movement by blacks and their allies to fight racism and promote socioeconomic justice. The decades leading up to this policy were ones of iistorical changes. Starting with the integration of the military during World War II, the civil rights movement went on to transform other parts f society, with much of the gains coming in the 1960s. State supported egregation in public schools ended with the 1954 *Brown v. Board of Education* ruling. President Kennedy used executive power in 1961 to equire federal contractors to end any discriminatory employment oractices and to establish the Equal Employment Opportunity Commission (EEOC). Congress enacted the Civil Rights Act of 1964 to orohibit discrimination by privately owned facilities open to the public, by ederally-funded programs, and by both private and public employers. The 1965 Voting Rights Act added force behind the drive to protect the ights of minorities to participate in elections.

Presidents played key roles in setting the pace.[3] Despite ampaign promises and inspiring public pronouncements, President Kennedy moved slowly and cautiously, shying away from fully utilizing his discretionary powers and delaying politically risky legislation. Lyndon B. Johnson's view evolved over his career, initially siding with egregationists as a Congressman, then accepting the necessity of addressing civil rights issues as Senate Majority Leader, and later pressing for legislation as Vice President. As President, he pushed his "Great Society" agenda to attack racial inequality. President Nixon proved enigmatic for initially supporting and then opposing key elements in the civil rights agenda, and his contradictory actions may be best understood as calculated political actions to weaken enemies and garner support.

The enactment of these laws was facilitated by a robust and growing economy, which minimized inter-group conflicts over resources. Paying for the cost of social change from an expanding economic pie enabled this nation to avoid the difficulty of reallocating in a zero-sum game. Even with a favorable economy, the civil rights movement faced obstacles. Some white males who were vested in the old racial order fought to preserve the status quo, thus preserving their power and privileges. Opposition, however, was not just limited to overt racists. Most Americans found racial discrimination and prejudice objectionable, but were reluctant to accept the demands of the civil rights movement.[4] The majority felt that the civil rights movement was "moving too fast."

Despite only conditional support from whites, or because of it, the demand for change escalated as the social movement behind the civil rights movement evolved. The initial struggles focused on integrating schools and public facilities, and voter registration drives in the South. Later, the efforts moved north. Despite measurable economic gains, particularly by better-educated minorities, black expectations rose faster than actual progress and fueled frustration. A growing impatience over slow progress, persistent and pervasive poverty, and the lack of economic opportunity gave rise to devastating urban unrest between 1964 to 1968. Black protest shifted the demands from political rights and integration to economic rights, and the cutting edge of the movement moved from established nonviolent organizations to more militant ones espousing black nationalism and group rights.

Affirmative action evolved as a pragmatic and politically motivated strategy to combat racial (and later gender) inequality. During the early stage of the civil rights movement, the dominant strategy centered on ending blatant racism. When the term "affirmative action" was introduced into policy in President Kennedy's 1961 Executive Order 10952, the proposed remedy was strictly anti-discrimination in nature, promoting hiring and terms of employment "without regard to race, creed, color or national origin." President Johnson's 1965 Executive Order 11246 expanded the notion, requiring federal contractors to develop plans to increase the number of underrepresented minority workers. This expansion transformed the goal from equal opportunity to equal results, that is, to ensure "not just equality as a right and a theory, but equality as a fact and as a result."[6] Even after the Democrats lost the White House, affirmative action continued to gain teeth. The 1970 "Philadelphia Plan" devised during the Nixon administration required federal contractors to establish hiring timetables and goals. Underutilization was defined as a lack of parity, when a firm employed a labor force that did not mirror the racial and gender composition of the larger labor force. Some private firms and universities also adopted this parity approach, but its application was most pronounced in the public sector, in government hiring and procurement and admission to state colleges and universities.

The adoption of affirmative action, as a policy, pushed the envelope of what the government ought to do to address racial inequality. Anti-discrimination laws were designed to protect people against individual acts of discrimination, and their enforcement was predicated on responding after the fact. Unfortunately, this approach failed to address systemic and institutionalized factors that disadvantaged minorities as a group. In other words, racial inequality was maintained and reproduced through forces and structures beyond individual acts of discrimination. For many blacks and their supporters, attacking this

problem required a radically different strategy operating at the grou
level. Programs, such as those associated with the "War on Poverty,
targeted disadvantaged populations by channeling resources to impove
ished neighborhoods, which were highly correlated with rac
Affirmative action took an explicit approach by embracing race-consciou
tactics, including the minority groups protected by voting rights and ant
discrimination laws.

Most affirmative action programs were not strictly a quot
system, but the policy had certainly emerged as a race-based program.
required a redistribution of opportunities, although this often occurred a
the margins. Such a reallocation was justified because the existing syster
of racial privileges was inherently unfair to the oppressed. Nonetheles
affirmative action required some segments to forego some opportunitie
not a simple process even if the privileges were unwarranted. Thi
shifting of opportunities, with real and perceived winners and loser
proved to be an extremely controversial policy, raising opposition fror
white males and also from former supporters of the civil right
movement.[7]

Opponents of affirmative action seized on the policy's race-base
nature to challenge its constitutionality, arguing that granting speci
status to any racial group violates the "due process of law" protected b
the Fourteenth Amendment, and anti-discrimination clause of Title VI
of the Civil Rights Act of 1964. Starting in 1970, affirmative actio
programs came under attack in the courts.[8] The first major setback cam
in 1978 in *Regents of the University of California v. Bakke*. In this case, th
Supreme Court decided that the medical school at the University o
California at Davis, through its affirmative action program, violated Titl
VI of the 1965 Civil Rights Act and the Fourteenth Amendment when i
denied admission to Allan Bakke. The Court, however, left open th
door for the use of race as one flexible factor in the admissions process
with Justice Powell arguing that the state has a legitimate interest i

promoting diversity in the student body. In the 1980s, the Court upheld the voluntary use of affirmative action programs, but it also ruled against preferential protection for minorities in layoffs and imposed a greater burden of proof to justify affirmative action.[9] Further restrictions came in the early 1990s in cases involving contract set-aside programs for minorities. Although the Supreme Court earlier had sanctioned the use of race-conscious contracting programs to remedy past societal discrimination, the Court started imposing the burden of "strict scrutiny" first on local and state governments and later on the federal government. By moving from intermediate to strict scrutiny, the Court imposed a higher standard before affirmative action can be justified. The government must demonstrate that past governmental action contributed to the specific inequality in question, that there is a compelling government interest, and that the program is narrowly tailored to solve only the problem in question. In the 1996 *Hopwood v. Texas*, the Court of Appeals for the Fifth Circuit placed similar limits on admissions programs in higher education, restricting the use of race only when it is necessary to remedy past discrimination by the school itself. Moreover, the court stated that promoting diversity is no longer a compelling state interest, thus making it more difficult to correct any racial imbalance in higher education. While the courts have not outlawed all forms of affirmative action, its application has been severely restricted.[10]

Affirmative action also came under attack from the executive branch. Presidential power proved to be a double-edged sword. Its use had been instrumental in establishing several civil rights policies, programs and agencies, but this approach exposed such actions to changing political winds. This was evident when President Reagan ushered in a neo-conservative era based on an ideology of smaller government, devolution, and supply-side economics.[11] Through selective appointments, Republican administrations placed individuals opposed to affirmative action in the Civil Rights Division in the Department of

Justice and the Department of Education, the U.S. Commission on Civil Rights, and the Equal Employment Opportunity Commission. These appointees in turn weakened affirmative action (and the enforcement of anti-discrimination employment and housing laws). A common theme was to move civil rights away from race-conscious policies to "color-blind" ones. The new mantra was that the government should never use race (or gender) for any public programs, even ones to remedy past discrimination. As anti-affirmative action efforts at the federal level waned with the Democrats recapturing the White House in 1992, the debate shifted to other arenas. In California, for example, Republican Governor Pete Wilson and his appointees on the Board of Regents of the University of California pushed through two resolutions in 1995 directing the university to end the use of race, religion, sex, color, ethnicity, or national origins in its admission process, contracting and employment.

Opponents of affirmative action have made direct appeal to the voting public through referendums, some successful and others not. In 1996, the voters in California passed Proposition 209, the "California Civil Rights Initiative," whose practical implication is to prohibit the state and local jurisdictions from using most affirmative action programs.[12] One year later, the voters in the City of Houston defeated Proposition A, which would have ended affirmative action.[13] In 1998, voters in Washington State passed Initiative 200, forcing the state and its local jurisdictions to stop using affirmative action.[14] Similar initiative and legislative efforts are being pursued in other states, including Colorado, Ohio, Michigan, Missouri, New Jersey, and Texas.[15] Some backers, such as those in Florida, have attempted to soften the impact of abandoning affirmative action with class-based programs designed to assist individuals from disadvantaged neighborhoods and schools, but those are not perfect substitutes.[16]

Despite the victories by opponents of race-conscious policies, the public has no decisive position. A reason for the mixed results on initiatives is that voters are neither totally for nor totally against affirmative action. Race-based policies create a conundrum over how far this nation ought to go to address racial inequality. Most people accept the fact that racial discrimination has not been eliminated, and many believe that something should be done.[17] At the same time, a growing number find that affirmative action goes too far by forcing white men to bear a burden to remedy a societal problem not of their making. In other words, there is support for anti-discrimination policies, but resistance to giving unjustified preferential treatment.[18] This does not mean that the government should not take an active role in eliminating racial inequality. A large majority support "increase recruitment" and a "sincere effort to hire" fully qualified blacks.[19] There is then a nuance in the support and opposition to affirmative action, and how people vote depends on how the debate is worded. This can be seen in a survey of Houston voters prior to the 1997 election.[20] A large majority would support a proposition stating "The city of Houston shall not discriminate against, or grant preferential treatment to, any individual or group on the basis of race, sex, ethnicity, or national origin in the operation of public employment and public contracting." On the other hand, less than a majority would support a proposition stating "Shall the Charter of the City of Houston be amended to end the use of affirmative action for women and minorities in the operation of City of Houston employment and contracting, including ending the current program and any similar programs in the future?" In the end, a majority of the voters opposed Proposition A, which stated "Shall the Charter of the City of Houston be amended to end the use of affirmative action?" If Houston's Proposition A had been worded differently, the outcome could have been different.

The debate over affirmative action has cooled, due in part to a robust economy that has eliminated fears of a zero-sum game, but the future of this policy is very much in the air. Race-based programs to correct racial

inequality are not illegal, but the courts have severely limited their application. Political support has waned but not vanished. President Clinton has
declared that affirmative action should be "mended, not ended," but this
task does not appear to be a priority. The discussion on affirmative action in
the report from the Advisory Board to the President's Initiative on Race is
largely descriptive and noncommittal.[21] What we have currently is not a
coherent policy, and perhaps there never was such a creature.

Part II: The Socioeconomic Status of Asian Pacific Americans

To understand how APAs are situated within affirmative action
programs, it is important to first establish the overall material position of APAs
in three arenas: education, the labor market, and business. Material position
refers to measurable outcomes that define the relative standing of APAs in the
racial hierarchy discussed earlier. This section provides a broad assessment,
saving the discussion on the status of APAs within the public sector to the next
section, Part III. The data indicate that APAs fare better than other minority
groups, and in some areas better than whites.[22] This is not the same, however,
as an absence of problems. In education, APAs are above parity relative to
whites by traditional measures but suffer from restrictive quotas. In
employment, APAs are near parity but encounter barriers to selected occupations, particularly to management positions. APA businesses are below parity,
experiencing difficulties competing in size and return. It is this dramatic
variation in relative standing of APAs across the three arenas that adds to the
complexity of the racial hierarchy.

The one area where APAs have experienced a high level of
achievement is in education. This phenomenon starts early, as seen in the top
panel of Table 1, which reports the racial/ethnic distribution of Californian
schools ranked by performance on standardized tests.[23] The data clearly show
that African Americans and Hispanics are disproportionately overrepresented

in poorly performing elementary schools, and disproportionately underrepresented in highly ranked schools. The opposite is true for APAs. While APAs

TABLE 1. RACIAL/ETHNIC COMPOSITION OF CALIFORNIA SCHOOLS, 1998

Rank	%APA	%Black	%White	Hispanic
Elementary Schools				
Top 10%	17.0	3.1	67.8	9.0
75-90%	11.5	5.2	60.8	17.9
50-75%	7.8	8.5	48.0	30.4
25-50%	6.4	12.0	25.7	51.2
10-25%	4.9	11.9	8.5	72.2
Bottom 10%	3.7	11.1	5.2	78.4
High Schools				
Top 10%	17.8	2.8	67.8	9.0
75-90%	9.7	3.5	67.4	15.3
50-75%	9.0	5.4	57.4	22.6
25-50%	8.6	9.2	40.0	36.8
10-25%	8.5	10.4	17.2	58.9
Bottom 10%	3.6	14.4	20.1	57.1

Source: Compiled by author from data from California Department of Education

comprise 8 percent of all elementary students, they comprise 17 percent of those in schools in the top 10 percent but only 4 percent in schools in the bottom 10 percent. A similar pattern is apparent at the high-school level. African Americans and Hispanics are concentrated in the worst schools, while APAs and whites are disproportionately enrolled in the best schools.

There are also racial differences in high-school dropout and completion rates as documented in Table 2.[24] Dropout rates were estimated from school enrollment status for those without high-school degrees and between the ages 16 to 19. African American and Hispanic youths are disproportionately more likely not to dropout relative to whites, while APAs are disproportionately more likely to be enrolled although the white-APA difference is small. A large number of recent immigrants contributes to the high rate for Hispanics. To minimize this bias, a second set of estimates is made by excluding those who immigrated

TABLE 2. DROP-OUT STATISTICS BY RACE/ETHNICITY

	%APA	%Black	%White	%Hispanic
All				
Not in School, 16-19	6%	15%	10%	26%
W/o HS Degree, 20-24	7%	18%	8%	37%
Excluding Teenage Immigrants				
Not in School, 16-19	5%	15%	10%	21%
W/o HS Degree, 20-24	7%	18%	8%	30%

Source: Compiled by author from 1997, 1998 and 1999 CPS

after the age of thirteen. Even among this restricted population, the dropout rate for Hispanics is the highest among the four racial groups. Of course, some of the dropouts may eventually earn a high school degree or GED. An alternative measure of high school dropout is the percent of young adults (20 to 24) without a high school degree. The statistics for this measure also show a parallel racial hierarchy, with blacks and Hispanics faring far worse than whites and APAs. The pattern also holds after excluding those who immigrated after the age of thirteen.

Along with a high rate of completing high school, APAs are better qualified to compete for entry into institutions of higher learning. This can be seen in the SAT scores, which are widely used by colleges and universities to evaluate applicants. APAs do not perform as well as whites in the verbal section (1998 average score of 498 out of 800 versus 526), but they more than make up the difference on math (562 versus 528).[25] One of the reasons for the lower APA verbal score is that only 28 percent of the APA test-takers speak English as their sole language, compared to 94 percent of white test-takers.[26] In other words, a disproportionate number of APAs do not have English as a first language. One can argue that SAT scores are not perfect predictors of performance as undergraduates and that the test is culturally biased, but colleges and universities do use the results in admissions. To the extent that these scores are weighted, APAs are competitive by this criterion. The relative competitiveness of APAs can also be seen in the 1996 data from the California Postsecondary Education Commission, which calculates the proportion of high-school graduates fulfilling the minimum criteria for admission to the University of California.[27] The APA rate for 1996 (30 percent) is several times higher than that for African Americans (3 percent) and Hispanics (4 percent). More surprisingly, the APA rate is more than twice as high as the rate for white students (13 percent).

Several factors account for the educational achievements of APAs. Culture values and parental beliefs in the centrality of education for success in this country provide a power push for children to succeed. APA achievement is also the product of lower residential segregation of APAs than other minorities, which is discussed in the chapter by Hum and Zonta in this book. The College Board reports that 37 percent of APA students taking the college entrance examine are in suburbs, which is equal to whites and higher than blacks (22 percent) and Hispanics (25 percent).[28] This translates into APAs being more likely to reside in better school districts and neighborhoods with the better schools. (At the same time, APAs are more likely to be in large cities than whites, 37 percent versus 14 percent.) This spatial correlation may be influenced by self-selection, where the quality of education becomes relatively more important for APAs in deciding residential location. This can be seen in the disproportionate number of APAs moving to two of the best school districts in the Los Angeles metropolitan area, Cerritos and San Marino.

The accomplishments of APAs at the high school level carry over to the college and university level. The rate of school enrollment for college-age students (between 20 and 24 years old) varies considerably by race: 36 percent for whites, 30 percent for blacks, 22 percent for Hispanics, and 55 percent for APAs. (If the population excludes immigrants who entered the country after the age of 13, then the enrollment rate for Hispanics is slightly higher, 25 percent.) APAs are not only attending colleges and universities at a disproportionately higher rate, but they also have a strong presence in the elite universities. This can be seen in Table 3, which lists the distribution of the undergraduate

TABLE 3. 1998 FALL ENROLLMENT
IN ELITE UNIVERSITIES BY RACE/ETHNICITY

	APAs	Whites	Hispanics	Blacks
Private				
Harvard	19%	46%	8%	9%
MIT	28%	46%	10%	6%
Stanford	22%	49%	11%	8%
Yale	17%	57%	6%	7%
Public				
Berkeley	39%	30%	11%	5%
UCLA	38%	34%	16%	6%
Michigan	11%	71%	4%	9%
Virginia	10%	71%	2%	10%

Source: Compiled by author from university web pages

student body by ethnicity. The reported percentage for each ethnic group is based on "domestic" students, which does not include foreign students of that ethnicity.[29]   Among the top private universities listed, APAs comprise 17 percent to 28 percent of the student population. The range for the top public universities is wider, from 10 percent to 39 percent, with the higher percentage in schools located in states with large concentrations of APAs.   By any reasonable measures, APAs have had remarkable success in accessing higher education.

Despite the educational achievements of APA students, there are problems. There are still significant segments of APA youths who are struggling because they have a limited command of the English language.[30] This partly accounts for lower APA scores on the verbal parts of standardized tests relative to whites. The push for academic success comes with an emotional cost. The parental pressure to succeed creates tremendous anxiety among APA youths and contributes to intergenerational conflicts.   Moreover, access to the elite institutions of higher education is not an unqualified success. Since the 1980s, many prestigious colleges and universities have been accused of reacting to the "overrepresentation" of APAs by establishing ceilings, a maximum quota, on APA admission.[31]   Audits of some elite schools discovered that the admissions rate for APA applicants were lower than that for white applicants, and among those admitted, APAs had stronger academic qualifications than other groups. One statistical study found that with similar qualifications, APAs had a lower probability of being admitted.[32] A lower admissions rate, by itself, is not *prima facie* evidence of discrimination. In some cases, admission processes used non-racial criteria beyond those based on standard academic performance, and these had a disproportionate impact on some groups. For example, private universities gave extra preferences to sons and daughters of alumni, who happened to be predominantly white. One could argue that this policy merely reproduced the racial inequality of previous generations, but the universities countered that they have legitimate and non-racial reasons for these preferences. In other cases, the evidence pointed to a biased admission process and prejudicial admission officers.[33] Many schools that had such a potential problem have corrected both intended and unattended biases, but APA suspicion has not entirely disappeared. We will return to the quota issue in the next section of this chapter when the discussion focuses on public education.

In the labor market, APAs have an advantage because of high educational attainment, but do not always receive the same remuneration or occupational status as whites. Table 4 reports the educational attainment of those in the prime-working age category, 25 to 64 years old. Among the four reported racial groups, APAs have the highest proportion with four or more years of higher education. The relative difference is even greater for the category that includes advanced degrees (master's, professional degrees, and doctorates). The odds of an APA holding an advanced degree are more than one-and-half times greater than for whites, and four to five times greater than for African Americans and Hispanics. These higher APA rates of educational attainment are the product of two factors. The first is the phenomenon discussed above, that APAs who are educated in the United States (both native-born and

TABLE 4. EDUCATION ATTAINMENT FOR PERSONS 25-64
YEAR OLD BY RACE/ETHNICITY

	NH White	Blacks	Hispanic	APA
Less Than HS	9%	18%	42%	13%
High School	34%	38%	28%	22%
Some College	27%	28%	19%	21%
Bachelor's	20%	11%	8%	29%
Advanced Degree	10%	4%	3%	16%

Source: Compiled by author from 1997-1999 March Current Population survey

immigrants who come here as children or students) tend to complete more years of education. The second factor is that immigration laws since 1965 have favored those with higher education, particularly those in the professional, scientific, medical, and engineering fields. Moreover, the highly-educated immigrant who initially entered through occupational preferences became a sponsor for highly-educated relatives for slots reserved for family reunification, thus adding to the supply of highly-educated immigrants.[34]

Despite the high level of education, APAs have not been fully able to translate their credentials into commensurate earnings and occupational status. Table 5 contains basic statistics for full-time (35 or more hours per week) and year-round (50 or more weeks per year) workers between the ages 25 and 64. Roughly three-quarters of the labor force for each racial group work full-time and year-round (77 percent for whites, 76 percent for blacks, 74 percent for Hispanics, and 77 percent for APAs).[35] Despite the higher education attainment reported earlier, APAs lag behind whites in remuneration. In terms of annual earnings, the median for APAs is slightly lower than for white males ($33,200 versus $32,000). Another measure indicates that APAs are doing marginally better, 23 percent of whites are among the top one-fifth of all earners compared to 24 percent for APAs. However, this is surprisingly close given the considerably higher levels of education for APAs. Another way of viewing the statistics is to consider what is required to win a place in the top tier: 61 percent of whites in this earnings group have at least a bachelors degree, while 80 percent of APAs do. Much of the difference is among those with advanced degrees, 26 percent for whites and 40 percent for APAs.

The disparity in earnings is associated with the problems faced by APA immigrants, and highly-educated male immigrants in particular.[36] Among males with at least a bachelor's degree, recent APA immigrants earn about 22 percent less than U.S.-born whites, after accounting for differences in age and educational credentials. Assimilation as proxied by long-term residency in this country helps, but even established APA immigrants earn 7 percent less than U.S.-born whites. U.S.-born APA males, on the other hand, earn roughly the same amount as U.S.-born white males. Among females (that is, within gender analysis), the earnings show a different inter-group pattern. Recent APA immigrants earn 10 percent less than U.S.-born whites, and established APA immigrants reach parity with U.S.-born whites. Interestingly, U.S.-born APA females earn 7 percent more than U.S.-born white females. On the

TABLE 5. EMPLOYMENT OUTCOMES BY RACE/ETHNICITY FULL-TIME, YEAR-ROUND WORKERS

	White	Black	Hispanic	APA
Median Earnings	$33,200	$25,400	$22,000	$32,000
In the Top 20%	23%	10%	9%	24%
In Management	19%	11%	9%	15%
In Professions	18%	12%	7%	24%

Source: Compiled by author from 1997-1999 March Current Population Survey

other hand, it is important to note that this "advantage" is far from closing the gender gap, for white females earn 27 percent less than white males. U.S.-born APA females close some of that gap, but their earnings are much closer to that of U.S.-born white females than to U.S.-born white males. In other words, the gender gap remains a dominant factor.

Some of the labor-market disadvantages experienced by APA male and female workers can be attributed to a "glass ceiling," a barrier preventing many from moving into higher management positions.[37] Although qualified and competent for higher management positions, many APAs are stereotyped as non-assertive, inarticulate, and too technical. The glass ceiling is certainly a major concern within the APA community. A majority of the respondents to a survey of APAs by *Asian Week* agreed with the statement "There exists a 'glass ceiling' such that many Asian Americans are unfairly prevented from reaching upper management positions in many companies."[38]

The lower probability of being a manager is centered around the highly-educated immigrant population.[39] Among males with at least a bachelor's degree, recent APA immigrants have only half the odds of being in management compared with U.S.-born whites, after accounting for difference in age and credentials. Assimilation has no effect because established APA immigrants face the same low odds. The analysis shows that U.S.-born APA males have lower odds of moving into management than U.S.-born whites, but the estimate is not statistically significant because of the small sample size. Among highly- educated females, recent APA immigrants have only about half the chance as U.S.-born whites to being in management, controlling for other factors. Assimilation closes much, but not the entire gap. The odds for established APA immigrants approach that of U.S.-born whites, with the remaining difference being statistically insignificant. There is essentially no difference between U.S.-born whites and U.S.-born APA females. While APA females may be able to close the racial gap within their own gender, they still face the glass ceiling encountered by U.S.-born white females.

By limiting access to managerial position, the glass ceiling has a trickle down effect on other occupations. An analysis of highly educated workers of both genders shows that U.S.-born APAs, established immigrants, and recent immigrants have the same odds of being a professional as U.S.-born whites. APA males, regardless of sub-group, have higher odds of being in this occupational layer, indicating that overrepresentation in the professions absorbs the underrepresentation in management. In other words, there appears to be a glass ceiling that keeps them from moving from the professions into management. For females, this phenomenon is not present, a finding that points to the additional complexity imposed by a gender-related glass ceiling.

The lack of parity is most apparent for APAs in the business world. While APAs, and immigrants in particular, have a reputation of being entrepreneurs, the self-employment rate (including family members working for no pay) for APAs is no higher than that for whites, and this is true even when comparing APA immigrants with white immigrants. Table 6 provides two sets of self-employment rates for the economically active population between the ages of 25 and 64. The first estimate is based on whether the person reported his or her main class of employment as self-employed. According to this measure, APAs and whites have the same rate. The second set of estimates includes both the self-employed and those working for others, but also receiving some income from self-employment. The latter captures people who operate a business on the side. While the second estimate for whites is slightly higher than for APAs, for practical purpose, the levels of self-employment are identical. On the other hand, the economic returns to self-employment are not identical. The data for those working year-round indicate that median total earnings for APAs is lower than that for

TABLE 6. SELF-EMPLOYMENT OUTCOMES BY RACE/ETHNICITY

	White	Black	Hispanic	APA
Self-employment (1)	13%	5%	7%	13%
Self-employment (2)	16%	6%	8%	15%
Median Earnings	$32,300	$24,900	$21,800	$30,400
With at least a BS degree	36%	27%	14%	51%

Source: Compiled by author from 1997-1999 March Current Population Survey

whites.[40]   The economic disparity is even greater since self-employed APAs have more years of schooling than whites.

Data from the most recent survey of the characteristics of business owners (1992) show a similar picture.[41] By two measures, APAs are doing well. Among minorities, APAs accounted for 31 percent of all firms and received 48 percent of all revenues. While APAs were faring better than blacks and Hispanics, APAs were not overrepresented among all owners. APAs owned 3.5 percent of all businesses and received 2.9 percent of all revenues, which are slightly lower than the APA share of the total population (4 percent in 1998). The picture is even less rosy when compared with white owners. Average (mean) revenue for APA firms was only 64 percent of that for white firms. The average APA firm had fewer employees and paid lower wages per worker than white firms. Only 14 percent of white owners worked 60 or more hours a week, but 21

TABLE 7. BUSINESS CHARACTERISTICS BY RACE/ETHNICITY, 1992

Group	Revenues Per Firm	Employees Per Firm	Payroll Per Employee
All businesses	$192,700	1.6	$19,100
All minorities	$102,800	1.0	$15,200
Hispanics	$94,400	0.9	$15,600
Blacks	$51,900	0.6	$13,900
APAs	$159,100	1.4	$15,500
White Females	$114.600	1.1	$17,000
White Males	$249,800	2.0	$20,300

Source: Compiled by author from Bureau of the Census data on business owners

percent of APA owners did. APAs had smaller markets, with 42 percent serving a neighborhood market compared to only 26 percent for whites. Moreover, 31 percent of APA firms serve a minority-dominated clientele, about four times the level for whites. These facts, along with those presented above, show that APAs in business still lag far behind whites.

The above analysis of the socioeconomic status of APAs demonstrates the complex position of APAs in this nation's racial structure. The unique material position of APAs poses three challenges to a bipolar racial model. The first is that the relative standing of APAs varies across socioeconomic dimensions. The achievements (vis-à-vis whites and other minorities) in one arena are not replicated in other arenas. This can be seen in the extreme variation in the simplistic APA-white parity indices for education, employment and business. The second challenge is that the nature of the disadvantages faced by APAs is not absolute (lower achievements than whites), but relative to what they could achieve if given the same opportunities as whites. For example, APAs are close to parity with whites in the labor market, but would fare even better if they could fully translate educational credentials into employment outcomes. The final challenge is that many of the barriers faced by APAs are not race-based, or at least not in the way racism has been commonly understood. These obstacles are associated with the immigrant experience, where cultural differences and slow acculturation prevent full incorporation. For some, this observation explains away the inequality; however, the explanation does not answer whether the criteria are economically appropriate or based on unwarranted prejudices. Some evidence points to a racializing of the foreign-born, thus blurring the line between racial processes and immigrant processes. Race, after all, is in part a social construction, and this nation has a long history of racializing APA immigrants.

Clearly, APAs cannot be simply forced into a dichotomous

paradigm by defining them as equivalent to other disadvantage minorities or as identical to the advantaged white population. Moreover, the relative standing of APAs varies across arenas, precluding the possibility of collapsing outcomes into a single, consistent measure of racial inequality. These facts force us to reconsider race relations as a multi-group and multi-dimensional hierarchy. The complexity introduced by the material position of APAs presents both a theoretical and a policy challenge.

PART III: THE AFFIRMATIVE ACTION – ASIAN PACIFIC AMERICAN NEXUS

This section examines the link between APAs and affirmative action programs in three areas at the center of the political debate: public schools, government employment, and government contracting. Unfortunately, there is a paucity of systematic, consistent and detailed data across all three sectors; nonetheless, the available information provides intriguing insights. The variation in material position discussed in Part II maps into a similar variation within race-based programs. The diversity in socioeconomic outcomes discussed above is accompanied by a parallel diversity in the nexus between APAs and affirmative action. They both benefit from and bear the cost of the policy. In the field of education, where APAs have been successful, the issue is whether APAs should forego a disproportionate share of privileges in publicly supported schools. In the labor market, where APAs have had conditional success, the issue is which occupational niche is appropriate for APA participation. Finally, in the world of business, where APAs trail whites, APAs are more likely to be unconditionally included in affirmative action.

Given the high levels of academic achievement, it is not surprising that APAs have been largely excluded from affirmative action in public education.[42] Of course, there have been exceptions, most notably when the University of California had included Filipinos. It was felt that Filipinos constituted a highly disadvantaged population, uniquely different from the other two major APA groups at that time (Japanese and Chinese), but Filipinos were dropped from the program in the mid-1980's. Although there have been other efforts to include high-poverty APA ethnic groups, it is difficult to make a case because a relatively higher number of students from these groups goes onto colleges and universities compared to blacks and Hispanics. Not being included as a target population, however, is not the same as having no relationship to affirmative action.

The prevailing relationship between APAs and race-based admissions programs is both controversial and troubling. A part of that relationship is indirect and equivalent to that for whites. The number of admission slots available to those not included in affirmative action (whites and APAs) is tied inversely to the degree that special admission procedures are successful in increasing admissions from targeted populations. Clearly, the policy and program alter the racial distribution, but in practice, the changes are at the margin and small in relative size. Moreover, in situations where past discrimination and institutionalized racism unfairly disadvantages the targeted groups, the reallocation achieves a greater social goal of promoting racial equality. Ideally, the opportunities foregone by whites and APAs are the unearned privileges, that is, the opportunities that would not have been available to these two groups in the absence of systemic and institutional racism. For those opposed to affirmative action, this shifting of admission slots smacks of unconstitutional reverse discrimination. To increase the moral legitimacy of this objection, some conservatives have argued that racial preferences hurt, not only whites, but also APAs. This appeal, however, has not won over the majority of APAs. According to one survey, a majority of APAs are willing to accept "giving preferences to underrepresented minorities in college admissions and scholarships."[43]

The situation is more explosive when restrictive quotas enters the picture, that is, when APAs suffer a double burden, one from any reallocation generated by affirmative action and the other from an enrollment cap to limit "overrepresentation." It is important to note that latter practice, to the degree it exists, reallocates some admission slots from APAs to whites. Unlike affirmative action, restrictive quotas do not correct any past discrimination or institutional racism directed at whites. The one plausible argument is promoting diversity that mirrors the population, but it is doubtful that diversity in the abstract and devoid of the other race-related issues is sufficient to impose restrictive quotas.[44]

As discussed earlier, imposing caps on APA admissions has been an issue in institutes of higher learning, and much of the controversy of the 1980s centered around the practices at the two flagship campuses of the University of California, Los Angeles and Berkeley. Both campuses had lower admission rates for APA applicants than for other major groups, precipitating protest from APA activists and parents. When asked about access to the University of California, an overwhelming majority believed APA applicants should be admitted at a rate commensurate with their achievements.[45] While private universities used a policy of providing "legacy" preference to children of alumni (who happen to be predominantly white) to explain and justify lower admission rates for APA applicants relative to white applicants, the public universities had no such rationale. The concerns were sufficiently strong that the federal government launched an investigation, and the conflict was eventually resolved explicitly at Berkeley and tacitly at UCLA. The controversy in the public universities has subsided, but what remains unresolved is the problematic link between restrictive quotas and affirmative action. That issue reemerged in a different arena, in the public schools of San Francisco.

In the City by the Bay, the link between race-based efforts to correct past discrimination and glaring racial inequality was explicitly tied to restrictive quotas.[46] Although the caps did not explicitly single out any one group, Chinese students eventually were affected by its implementation. Like in other urban school districts, blacks were highly segregated into low performing schools within the San Francisco Unified School District. The local NAACP won a lawsuit in 1971 to desegregate the district and a consent decree in 1983 to strengthen the efforts, with the state providing millions of dollars to implement an integration plan.[47] To produce a more balanced enrollment, the decree required each school to have students from at least four of the nine named groups (American Indian, black, Chinese, Filipino, Japanese, Korean, Spanish-surnamed, other white and other non-white). Furthermore, the agreement established caps on the number for any one group, a maximum of 45 percent on most schools and 40 percent on magnet schools, and these restrictions proved to be lightning rods.

At the heart of the eventual controversy is Lowell High School, the oldest high school west of the Mississippi, the most selective school within the district and one of the most prestigious high schools in the nation.[48] Its alumni include two Nobel Prize winners, a co-founder of Hewlett Packard, a former governor, a U.S. Supreme Court Justice, and a former president of Yale University. Since the 1960s, Lowell operated as a system-wide academic school with competitive admission. Throughout the 1980s and 1990s, Lowell won state and national honors for its academic excellence. Lowell itself was the target of a 1971 discrimination suit against SFUSD for operating a city-wide academic high school that had a disproportionate low number of minorities, but the district won the right to maintain such a program. Lowell, however, was subject to the 1983 consent decree. Despite the desegregation effort, non-APA minorities continued to be underrepresented. During the mid-1990s, blacks comprised about 18 percent of the students in the district but only 5 percent of Lowell's students, and the comparable statistics for Latinos are 20 percent district wide and only 10 percent for Lowell.[49] Whites were above parity (16 percent of Lowell while only 13 percent of the district) but not affected by the 40-percent ceiling. Only one group was affected by the enrollment limit. In the mid-1990s, Chinese comprised slightly over 40 percent of Lowell's student body. To keep within the maximum, the admission criterion for Chinese was raised above other groups.[50] Both the restriction and the higher admission standards were not well received by many Chinese parents, eventually leading to a lawsuit against the district to end what was termed discriminatory quotas. In 1999, the court ruled in favor of the plaintiffs, forcing the district to abandon the cap for Lowell and to develop "race-neutral" criteria to maintain diversity.[51]

While the immediate outcome of the lawsuit is discernible, the motivation for the actions taken by the complainants and the long-term implications are much more difficult to pinpoint. Conservatives, such as Governor Pete Wilson and UC Regent Ward Connerly who were major supporters of Proposition 209, seized on the efforts by the Chinese against the restrictive quotas. They used those efforts to attack affirmative action, accusing the policy as the source of the "perverse" cap on Chinese enrollment and on a system of merit. Some supporters of the suit, however, took exception to this interpretation, stating that they are against discrimination against Chinese, but are for affirmative action. On the other hand, other supporters stated that they are against the use of race under any condition. The reaction from the left was harsh, with some activists chastising the Chinese for allowing themselves to be used by conservatives. In the end, the left argued, the ruling would eventually come back to hurt APAs because it weakens society's ability to redress racism. These varying interpretations point to a division within the Chinese public itself as evident in a 1998 CAVEC (Chinese American Voter Education Committee) survey of Chinese surname voters in San Francisco. When asked about their opinions on admission quotas for Lowell High School, 45 percent of the immigrant respondents thought it was a "bad idea," 32 percent thought it was a "good idea," while 23 percent expressed no opinion. The opposition is not surprising, but there is a surprising level of support from one-third of those interviewed. The long-term implication of the Lowell case is not known, but this controversy underscores the difficulty in decoupling APA concerns about restrictive quotas from affirmative action.

The issues in the area of employment are far less controversial. Two types of affirmative-action programs are relevant: direct government hiring and indirect hiring by firms with government contracts. The indirect hiring is not the focus of this chapter, but the effects are worth noting. Firms with federal contractors are under an obligation to develop and implement recruitment and hiring plans when minorities are underrepresented in their labor force, and this obligation also applies to many firms with state and local contracts. Existing econometric analysis, which controls for observable firm characteristics, finds that this requirement has a statistically measurable impact. African Americans have benefited, with their share of employment increasing by a tenth more in the federal contracts.[52] Interestingly, the governmental requirement has the same impact on APAs, with federal contracting increasing their share by a tenth. While the magnitude of the impacts is small, the findings indicate that affirmative action does open up employment opportunities.

An analysis of direct hiring by the public sector reveals several potential problems for APAs. Table 8 reports the number of full-time workers based on EEOC (Equal Employment Opportunity Commission) data for firms with at least 100 employees, and for state and local governments, and based on the data from the U.S. Office of Personnel Management for federal employment.[53] The top panel shows that APAs are equally represented in both the federal government and the private sector, but are underrepresented in state and local government employment. It is unclear why the latter exists. It may be due to state and local governments being less committed to recruiting and hiring APAs. Moreover, there could be a spatial mismatch between where public sector jobs are located and where APAs reside. Many state capitals are in cities with relatively few APAs.

Another problem is an unequal distribution of APAs across occupations within the public sector.[54] Particularly troubling is the data indicating a glass ceiling in government employment.[55] The underrepresentation is apparent whether the APA share of all employees or the APA share of employees in professional occupations is used as the benchmark. A parity index using the former provides a conservative estimate, while a

TABLE 8. EMPLOYMENT BY RACE/ETHNICITY, 1997

	White	Black	Hispanic	APA
All Occupations				
Private Sector	71%	15%	10%	4%
Federal Executive Branch	71%	16%	6%	4%
States	73%	18%	6%	2%
Local Gov.	68%	20%	9%	2%
Officials/Manager				
Private Sector	88%	6%	4%	3%
Federal Executive Branch	76%	14%	6%	3%
States	87%	8%	3%	1%
Local Gov.	82%	11%	5%	2%
Professional				
Private Sector	84%	6%	3%	7%
Federal Executive Branch	79%	8%	4%	8%
States	78%	14%	5%	3%
Local Gov.	73%	15%	6%	6%

Source: Compiled by author from data from the U.S. Equal Employment Opportunity Commission and U.S. Office of Personnel Management

parity index using the latter partially accounts for the higher educational level of APAs.[56] The ratio ranges from about .5 to .3 depending on which benchmark and which level of government. Moreover, state-specific data for combined state and local government employment indicate that the problem is present in regions with a significant presence of APAs: .4 to .6 for California, .5 to .9 for Florida, .3 to .8 for Illinois, .3 to .6 for Massachusetts, .2 to .6 for New Jersey, .4 to .8 for New York, .4 to .7 for Texas, and .5 to .6 for Washington. While a low index is not conclusive evidence of a glass ceiling, it does suggest that APAs are having difficulties moving into management.

Underrepresentation is not limited to management. There are other occupational niches, and one of the most glaring is protective services. The statistics in Table 9 show that APAs comprise only 1 percent of state and local employees in protective services, compared to 2.5 percent of the all state and local employees, a ratio of .4. The lower the index, the greater the underrepresentation. The ratio is even lower in the public sector, where APA professionals outnumber the APA managers by three-to-one. The ratio is particularly low for firefighters, but even for

TABLE 9. EMPLOYMENT IN PROTECTIVE SERVICES
BY RACE/ETHNICITY, FULL TIME STATE
AND LOCAL EMPLOYMENT, 1997

	White	Black	Hispanic	APA
All Occupations	70.6%	18.7%	7.5%	2.5%
Protective Services	72.7%	17.7%	8.0%	1.0%
Police	72.7%	16.1%	9.0%	1.7%
Firefighters	73.2%	11.1%	6.8%	0.8%
Corrections	66.5%	23.9%	7.7%	1.2%

Source: Compiled by author from data from the U.S. Equal Employment Opportunity Commission and U.S. Office of Personnel Management

police officers, APAs are below parity. The problem is present in the regions with a significant presence of APAs, as indicated by the parity ratio: .4 for California, .4 for Florida, .2 for Illinois, .4 for Massachusetts, .2 for New Jersey, .2 for New York, .3 for Texas, and .6 for Washington.

The underrepresentation in occupational niches has been addressed through selective action, often through court-imposed orders. This is illustrated by the effort to address the small number of Chinese in San Francisco's fire department.[57] (In that city, the Chinese have comprised an overwhelming majority of the APA population.) During the mid-1960s when community leaders first raised the issue of under-representation, only 6 Chinese (and 1 black) were among approximately 1,600 firefighters, and that number remained essentially the same for a decade. Under a 1974 court order to address this problem, the department was expected to increase the number of APA firefighters to nearly 200.

The one area where APAs have been unambiguously included is in government contracting, particularly when federal funds are involved. This inclusion is based on the fact that APA firms are less likely to receive government contracts. The standard measure is the disparity index, which is a group's relative share of government contracts divided by that group's share of all businesses. For example, if group A has 10 percent of government contracts but comprises 20 percent of all businesses, then the disparity index is .50, indicating that this group is receiving only half of its "fair" share of government business. An analysis of public contracting in California reveals that APA firms are consistently under-utilized by local governments.[58] Even in San Francisco, where APAs are the largest minority group, the disparity index for APA firms is (.19). The problem is not unique to California. After reviewing a large number of disparity studies from throughout the nation, the Urban Institute finds that median value for APA-owned businesses is (.19), which is lower than that for women-owned businesses (.26), Hispanic-owned businesses

(.36), and black-owned businesses (.41).[59] The low disparity index, along with the problems discussed earlier, has been the basis for including APA in government set-aside programs.[60] This inclusion has continued after a review of federal contract set-aside, which is a part of President Clinton's "mend it, not end it" approach to affirmative action.[61] The inclusion of APAs poses an interesting question of what is the appropriate or desirable goal.

APAs have taken advantage of this inclusion through participation in programs to promote minority (and women) contracting. At the national level, APA participation can be seen in the federal government's major effort to help minority firms, the 8(a) Program operated by the Small Business Administration.[62] For the decade spanning the late 1980s to the late 1990s, APAs increased their participation in both absolute and relative terms, as shown in Table 10. By the end of the twentieth century,

TABLE 10. PARTICIPANTS IN SBA'S 8(A) PROGRAM BY RACE/ETHNICITY

	88-91 FY	92-95 FY	96-99 FY
Race			
APAs	13%	19%	23%
Blacks	46%	46%	44%
Latinos	25%	25%	25%
All Others	16%	10%	8%
N =	14,234	20,756	23,461

Source: Unpublished data provided by SBA

they made up nearly a quarter of all 8(a) firms. APAs are also participants at the state and local level. This can be seen in California's certification program for minority (and women) businesses, which is required to qualify for set-aside contracts. Both state and local agencies use the certification to determine eligibility. APA firms accounted for 29 percent of the state's certified minority businesses.[63] Although data are not readily available for other states, a review of the certification programs in the largest states show that APAs are among the listed groups eligible for enrollment. Inclusion is driven by the fact that states are required to follow federal guidelines on these matters as a condition for receiving federal funds.

Beyond the active participation of APA entrepreneurs in minority set-aside programs, there is strong support within the APA communities for these programs. This can be seen in a survey conducted in Houston prior to the Proposition A vote. When asked if city government should set aside contracts for minority businesses, only a small minority of non-Hispanic whites (37 percent) approved, but a large majority of blacks (71 percent) approved. The percentage for APA approval falls between these two extremes, 61 percent, which is similar to that for Hispanics, 63 percent.[64] Not all APAs, however, support this type of affirmative action. Edward Chen was a plaintiff in a suit to overturn the results of the election, where a majority voted against the anti-affirmative action initiative.[65]

Taken together, the information for the three areas shows that APAs have taken disparate positions on affirmative action. Not surprisingly, there are systematic and predictable differences across the three areas, but even within a given arena, there are conflicting opinions. These cross currents reveal that APAs are influenced by both self-interest and larger ideological beliefs. APAs face the same dilemma facing this nation as a whole on what ought to be done to redress racial inequality. As mentioned earlier, there are difficult tradeoffs, and most are willing to accept race-based solutions under certain conditions. There are additional complexities in the APA population.

The one event we can gauge where most APAs stand on affirmative action as an overarching policy is the vote on the single most important initiative so far, California's 1996 Proposition 209, the so-called "California Civil Rights Initiative".[66] The result from a statewide exit poll conducted by the *Los Angeles Times* shows considerable racial variation.[67] The strongest support came from whites (63 percent for), and strong opposition came from blacks (74 percent against). What is surprising is that three-quarters of Hispanics (76 percent) also were against the proposition. [68] The poll also found that a majority of APAs (61 percent) voted against the proposition; however, the estimate is based on a small number of responses. Two more specialized exit polls in neighborhoods with high concentrations of APAs also found that a majority, and in fact a large majority, of APAs voted against the proposition. In Southern California, 76 percent of APAs voted against 209, and this opposition crossed party lines (78 percent of APA Democrats and 73 percent of APA Republicans).[69] In the San Francisco Bay Area, a similar percentage of APAs voted against 209 (80 percent), and again the opposition crossed party lines (86 percent of APA Democrats and 63 percent of APA Republicans).[70]

Analyzing one election, however, is not sufficient to discern the dominant APA political position. The APA population is very heterogeneous, and competing factors come into play. The extreme economic and ethnic diversity of this population is very well documented.[71] The APA population is also diverse in its politics, as indicated by party registration data.[72] The emergence of naturalized immigrants as a majority of APA voters further complicates the picture.[73] Many of these new voters are still in the process of formulating opinions on domestic issues such as affirmative action. Their attitudes are fluid as continued exposure to American society shapes and reshapes their opinions. The APA political position remains elusive and is up for grabs.

Part IV: Conclusion - What Next?

This nation is at a crucial juncture in addressing racial inequality, with affirmative action as the primary battleground. In a larger political and historical context, the heated and nasty debate marks a dramatic reversal in the search for a solution. The civil rights movement of the 1950s and 1960s transformed the state from one either supporting or turning a blind eye to racism to one attacking racial injustice, at least in its most blatant forms. Legislation was passed to protect voting rights, proscribe housing and employment discrimination, integrate schools and other public facilities, and fight inner-city poverty. One can cynically point out that the elected officials had to be pressured into enacting these laws, that programs were efforts to prevent escalating social unrest, and that implementation was half-hearted. Such a dismissive view, however, too easily denies the hard-earned victories, the progressive policies and programs. The accomplishments should not be judged by a failure to achieve utopia, but gains made in the face of resistance. At the close of the twentieth century, racial politics in America has taken a turn against race-based policies. Those opposed to the civil rights agenda have found an effective weapon by hijacking the principle of fairness to attack the most controversial policy, affirmative action. This counter insurgence has mobilized the mainstream by arguing that the policy is contrary to civil rights principles and constitutional protections. Of course, the idea that race-based laws and programs violate the rights of some (particularly white males) by giving "unfair" preferences to others (primarily minorities) is not new. That assertion has been at the heart of numerous court cases. What is different is an acceptance of this argument by many mainstream politicians and a significant share of the voting public. The battle, however, is far from over.

APAs occupy a unique position in the political debate because they occupy an ambiguous position within the racial structure. Their presence complicates issues regarding the application of and fundamental justification for affirmative action. On the other hand, resolving these complications can help reformulate a sounder policy. APA concerns cannot be easily pushed aside or folded into a simple black and white framework. Their educational and economic successes preclude them from being classified simply as another disadvantaged minority equivalent to blacks. At the same time, the APA population cannot be simply lumped in with the dominant white population. The social construction of this population as a racial minority is rooted in a long history of anti-Asian racism and reproduced by contemporary anti-Asian prejudices. Some may want to ignore APAs by asserting that they are a small population. This was true for most of the century, but less so today. APAs now constitute about 4 percent of the population, and will constitute about 6 percent within a generation. While it is important to note that APAs cannot be dismissed numerically, it is at least as important to note that the impact of APAs on race-related policies has not rested on population size. Historically, this group profoundly shaped race relations through the laws enacted against them and the legislative and court victories won by them. Within the contemporary battle over affirmative action, APAs make two important contributions.

The first is in the realm of symbolic politics. There are those who point to APAs as a minority group that has experienced historical discrimination, but nonetheless have been able to overcome obstacles without governmental intervention. This "model minority myth" is used to shift the responsibility of closing the racial gap from the larger society to minorities. If one group can do it, so can the others. Some want APAs to go beyond being a passive model to being spokespersons against affirmative action to fight reverse discrimination against APAs. This political strategy rests too much on appealing to self-interest and fails to recognize that many APAs accept the necessity to collectively address racial inequality. As the chapter by Taeku Lee shows, the majority of APAs believes that blacks, and Hispanics to a lesser degree, suffer from discrimination. This translates into support for some race-based policies. In a 1995 national survey, a majority of APA respondents agreed with the following statement: "White Americans have benefited from past and present discrimination against African Americans, so they should be willing to make up for these wrongs." [74] According to a 1996 survey sponsored by Asian Week, slightly more than half of the respondents supported affirmative action and a third opposed it. [75] This shows that many APAs are driven by a broader sense of this country's obligation.

On the other hand, proponents of race-based programs believe that APAs can take an equally powerful stance. Liberals want APAs to be a role model in accepting the sacrifices needed to achieve racial justice. An example of this is the statement by several law professors who support affirmative action. They argue that "APAs can play an extraordinarily powerful role in the debate because they can declare their support for the programs even when they are not directly benefited by them... I am willing to share this burden to help us get beyond racism, to reach a fairer society. I am willing to go beyond my self-interest in order to strive for a community of justice." [76] This call for noble and principled action has great moral appeal, but it minimizes APAs' legitimate self-interest in the affirmative-action debate. Indeed, within our society where the pursuit of self-interest is the norm, acknowledging the special needs of APAs can move the debate forward, if for no other reason than to challenge prevailing ideas.

There are three challenges. The first questions the notions of the primacy of race. APAs are a racial minority, but they are not automatically included in affirmative action programs. As we have seen, inclusion into any particular program (covering higher education, public employment, or government contracting) is predicated on whether APAs are demonstrably disadvantaged. This practice shows that affirmative action as an institution is flexible and reasonable in situating APAs. The policy is not, as opponents suggest, blindly wedded to a simplistic application of race. Unfortunately, the treatment of APAs has been ad hoc rather than based on a well-articulated principle. Such a principle does not preclude a single race from being included in all affirmative action programs when the evidence justifies such a decision, but this result is the product of applying the principle rather than an *a priori* categorization. Even if the final outcome of starting with this principle may not differ much from what currently exists, the exercise is politically important because it provides the justification that many voters want before they support affirmative action.

The second challenge centers on the types of race-related problems that government should correct. Affirmative action was developed to counter the racism experienced by African Americans in the 1960s; however, the problems confronting other minorities are not of the same nature. This chapter has documented that the disadvantaged faced by APAs are different, with many of the problems rooted in the immigrant experience. Hispanics and Native Americans also face hardships that are generated by disparate historical and contemporary forces. While socioeconomic injustice is a necessary common denominator for governmental action, programs should be tailored to address the underlying race-specific causes.

The final challenge is to debate openly the sacrifices that must be made to achieve racial justice. Proponents of affirmative action are uncomfortable with such a discussion because it shifts the discussion away from the disadvantaged and potentially legitimizes the claim that whites must give up some opportunities. Yet, as we have seen, this point has been and will be an unavoidable element in the debate. An enlightened and socially productive debate requires that both sides engage the issues rather than having one side frame the issue through polemics. For better or worse, APAs are a part of the debate on the cost of affirmative action, as well as the broader debate on race-based policies.

Endnotes

[1] I am grateful for the assistance provided by Issac Elnecave and Elena Sovhos. Taeku Lee graciously provided tabulations from several opinion polls.

[2] See for example: Steven M. Cahn (Ed.), *The Affirmative Action Debate* (New York, NY: Routledge, 1995); George E. Curry (Ed.), *The Affirmative Action Debate* (Reading, MA: Addison Wesley Publishing Company, Inc., 1996); Nicolaus Mills (Ed.), *Debating Affirmative Action: Race, Gender, Ethnicity, and the Politics of Inclusion* (New York, NY: Dell Publishing Group, Inc., 1994); Carol M. Swain, *Race Versus Class, The New Affirmative Action Debate* (Lanham, MD: University Press of America, 1996).

[3] Hugh Davis Graham, *The Civil Rights Era: Origins and Development of National Policy 1960-1972.* (New York, NY: Oxford University Press, 1990); James W. Riddlesperger, Jr. and Donald W. Jackson, *Presidential Leadership and Civil Rights Policy* (Westport, CT: Greenwood Press, 1995); John David Skrentny, *The Ironies of Affirmative Action: Politics, Culture and Justice in America* (Chicago, IL: The University of Chicago Press, 1996); Mark Stern, *Calculating Visions: Kennedy, Johnson, and Civil Rights* (New Brunswick, NJ: Rutgers University Press, 1992).

[4] Tom Smith, "Intergroup Relations in Contemporary America: An Overview of Survey Research," in Wayne Winborne and Renae Cohen (Eds.), *Intergroup Relations in the United States: Research Perspectives* (Bloomsburg, PA: Hadden Craftsmen, Inc. for the National Conference for Community and Justice,1998) 69-155; and Seymour Martin Lipset and William Schneider, "The Bakke Case: How Would It Be Decided at the Bar of Public Opinion?" *Public Opinion* 2(April 1978) : 38-44.

[5] United States. Kerner Commission. *Report of the National Advisory Commission on Civil Disorders* (New York, NY: Bantam Books, 1968).

[6] This was a part of his famous 1965 speech at Howard University, where he argued for affirmative action: "You do not take a person who had been hobbled by chains, liberate him, bring him up to the starting gate of a race and then say, 'You are free to compete with all the others,' and still justly believe you have been completely fair. . . . It is not enough to open the gates of opportunity. All of our Citizens must have the ability to walk through those gates. . . . Men and women of all races are born with the same range of abilities. But ability is not just the product of birth. Ability is stretched or stunted by the family you live with, . . . the neighborhood . . . the school . . . and the poverty or richness of your surroundings. It is the product of a hundred unseen forces playing upon the infant, the child and the man." (Stephanopoulos and Edley, *Affirmative Action Review*, p. 115).

[7] George Lipsitz, *The Possessive Investment in Whiteness, How White People Profit from Identity Politics* (Philadelphia, PA: Temple University Press, 1998); Murray Friedman and Peter Binzen. *What Went Wrong?: The Creation and Collapse of the Black-Jewish Alliance* (New York, NY: The Free Press, 1995).

[8] Most of the early rulings reaffirmed the legality of anti-discriminatory laws in employment. The Supreme Court ruled that firms could not use employment tests that are not job related and have a disparate impact on protected groups, and that employers must have some legitimate nondiscriminatory business reason for rejecting minority applicants. *Griggs v. Duke Power Co.* (1971), *McDonnell Douglas v. Green* (1973), *Albermarle Paper Co. v. Moody* (1975), and *Washington v. Davis* (1976).

[9] *United Steelworkers of America, AFL-CIO-CLC v. Weber* (1979), *Firefighters Local Union No. 1794 v. Stotts* (1984), *Wygant v. Jackson Board of Education* (1986), and *Johnson v. Transportation Agency of Santa Clara County* (1987).

[10] The progressively greater restrictions are correlated with an ideological realignment of the Court. From 1969 to 1991, the Republican presidents appointed a new Chief Justice as well as nine additions to the Supreme Court.

[11] See Norman C. Amaker, "The Reagan Civil Rights Legacy," in Eric J. Schmertz, Natalie Datlof, and Alexej Ugrinsky (Eds.), *Ronald Reagan's America, Volume I* (Westport, CT: Greenwood Press, 1997); Robert R. Detlefsen, "Affirmative Action and Business Deregulation: On the Reagan Administration's Failure to Revise Executive Order No. 11246," and Charles M. Lamb and Jim Twombly, "Decentralizing Fair Housing Enforcement During the Reagan Presidency," in James W. Riddlesperger, Jr. and Donald W. Jackson (Eds.), *Presidential Leadership and Civil Rights Policy* (Westport, CT: Greenwood Press, 1995) 39-70 and 127-148; Peter Gottschalk, "Retrenchment in Antipoverty Programs in the United States: Lessons for the Future," and R. Kent Weaver, "Social Policy in the Reagan Era," in B.B. Kymlicka and Jean V. Matthews (Eds.), The Reagan Revolutions? (Chicago, IL: The Dorsey Press, 1988), 131-145 and 146-165; Raymond Wolters, Right Turn: William Bradford Reynolds, *the Reagan Administration, and Black Civil Rights* (New Brunswick, NJ: Transaction Publishers, 1996).

[12] The specific language of Proposition 209 prohibits the state and local government from supporting programs that "discriminate against, or grant preferential treatment to, any individual or group on the basis of race, sex, color, ethnicity, or national origin in the operation of public employment, public education, or public contracting." For a discussion on the development of Proposition 209, see Lydia Chavez, *The Color Bind: California's Battle to End Affirmative Action* (Berkeley, CA: University of California Press, 1998).

[13] "Shall the Charter of the City of Houston be amended to end the use of affirmative action?"

[14] "The state shall not discriminate against, or grant preferential treatment to, any individual or group on the basis of race, sex, color, ethnicity, or national origin in the operation of public employment, public education, or public contracting." Election

result taken from http://www.metrokc.gov/elections/98nov/respage1.htm

[15] American Civil Rights Coalition, "Connerly Welcomes John Carlson To Washington State Civil Rights Initiative," Oct. 9, 1997, www.acrc1.org/pr100997.html

[16] Franklin Foer, "Brother Jeb's Move to End Affirmative Action, Florida's Bush Says Class Rank Works Better," *U.S. News and World Report*, 22 November 1999: 31; William March, "Affirmative Action Battle Roars Back to Life," *The Tampa Tribune*, 16 November 1999: http://tampatrib.com/fr111613.htm. For a discussion on the limits of class-based programs, see Cecilia A. Conrad, "Affirmative Action and Admission to the University of California," in Paul M. Ong (Ed.), *Impacts of Affirmative Action: Policies and Consequences in California* (Walnut Creek, CA: AltaMira Press, 1999) 171-196.

[17] Tom Smith, "Intergroup Relations in Contemporary America: An Overview of Survey Research," in Wayne Winborne and Renae Cohen (Eds.) *Intergroup Relations in the United States: Research Perspectives* (Bloomsburg, PA: Hadden Craftsmen, Inc. for the National Conference for Community and Justice, 1998) 151.

[18] Lawrence Bobo and Ryan Smith. "Anti-Poverty Policy, Affirmative Action, and Racial Attitudes," in S. Danzinger, G. Sandefur, and D.Weinberg (Eds.) *Confronting Poverty: Prescriptions for Change* (New York, NY: Russell Sage Foundation, and Cambridge, MA: Harvard University Press, 1994) 365-395; Dan Morain, "The Times Poll: 60% of State's Voters Say They Back Prop. 209." Los Angeles Times, 19 September 1996: A1.

[19] Tom Smith, "Intergroup Relations in Contemporary America: An Overview of Survey Research," in Wayne Winborne and Renae Cohen (Eds.) *Intergroup Relations in the United States: Research Perspectives* (Bloomsburg, PA: Hadden Craftsmen, Inc. for the National Conference for Community and Justice, 1998) 144.

[20] University of Houston Center for Public Policy and Rice University's Baker Institute for Public Policy, cited in Julie Mason, *Houston Chronicle*, 2 October 1997.

[21] The President's Initiative on Race Advisory Board. *One America in the 21st Century: The President's Initiative on Race* (Washington, DC: U.S. Government Printing Office, 1998) 99-102.

[22] For this chapter, the term whites refers to the non-Hispanic (NH) white population. The broader white category includes a significant number of Hispanics who identify themselves as whites on race-questions. However, Hispanic whites occupy a socioeconomic position that is very different than that for non-Hispanic whites; consequently, statistics for all whites differ from those for just NH whites. For the purpose of this chapter, NH whites are used as a benchmark to determine the relative standing of minority groups. For convenience, the chapter uses the terms whites and NH whites interchangeably. This chapter does not include Native Americans because the sample size is too small in many of the data sets; nonetheless, it is important to acknowledge that

this group is extremely disadvantaged.

[23] Data are the 1998 results for the fourth and eleventh grades for the Stanford 9 test as reported by the California Department of Education's STAR data server at http://star.cde.ca.gov/. The test data are merged with data on the racial/ethnic composition for each school from the same source. The ranking of elementary schools is based on a combined score using results reading, math, language and spelling. The eleventh grade ranking is based on scores for reading, math, science and social science tests. We use the percent of the student body that scored at or above the 75th percentile. The composite score may not accurately represent the true performance level of California students; California elementary students may truly be performing at less than the national average or perhaps the benchmark level is improperly set. Nevertheless, the data does provide a useful way to rank the relative performance of elementary schools. The original 11th grade study used results from reading, math, science and social science tests.

[24] The statistics for Tables 2, 3, and 4, come from a tabulation by the author of the March Current Population Survey (CPS). The CPS is a national monthly survey of about 60,000 households, and is used to collect information on labor market conditions particularly the unemployment rate. The March survey, which produces the Annual Demographic Profile, contains extensive information on current (contemporaneous) status along with work experiences and earnings for the previous year. Since 1989, the CPS has included APAs as a separate racial category. The surveys for 1997, 1998, and 1999 were pooled to derive a reasonable sample of APAs. The size of the sample varies according to the needs of a particular analysis. For example, the sample used to calculate wages for the foreign-born, prime-working-age population includes about 3,600 APAs. The actual number of unique individuals is slightly more than two-thirds of the sample size because the CPS retains a proportion of the March sample over a two-year period. Income data are adjusted to 1998 dollars, and the reported statistics on earnings and hourly wages are the weighted average for the three years (1996, 1997, and 1998). Statistics on the labor market status (e.g., labor force participation rates) are for the survey week.

[25] Table 3: Ten-year trends in average SAT scores by racial/ethnic groups http://www.collegeboard.org/press/senior98/html/satt3.html

[26] SAT Chart 13: Within racial/ethnic groups, first language is related to SAT Verbal scores.

[27] "What Are the Eligibility Rates of 1996 Public High School Graduates for the University of California?" (http://www.collegeboard.org/press/senior98/html/satt3.htm)

28 SAT Chart 9: Percentages of racial/ethnic groups in large cities and suburbs, class of 1998, http://www.collegeboard.org/press/senior98/html/satc9.html

[29] www.holyoke.harvard.edu/factbook/98-99/; web.mit.edu/facts/enrollment.html; www.stanford.edu/home/standord/facts/undergraduate; www.yale.edu/oir/factsheet; osr.berkeley.edu/public.student.data/publications/ug/ugf98.html; www.apb.ucla.edu/apb.html; www.umich.edu/-oapainfo/tables/enr_race.html

[30] For a discussion of this issue and a summary of the literature on APA students, see Paul M. Ong and Linda C. Wing, "The Social Contract to Educate All Children," in Bill O. Hing and Ronald Lee (Eds.), *Reframing the Immigration Debate* (Los Angeles, CA: LEAP Asian Pacific American Public Policy Institute and UCLA Asian American Studies Center, 1996) 223-265.

[31] Don T. Nakanishi, "A Quota on Excellence? The Asian American Admissions Debate," *Change Magazine*, Nov/Dec. 1989: 39-47; Ling-Chi Wang, "Trends in Admissions for Asian Americans in Colleges and Universities: Higher Education Policy," in *The State of Asian Pacific America: Policy Issues to the Year 2020* (Los Angeles, CA: LEAP Asian Pacific American Public Policy Institute and UCLA Asian American Studies Center, 1993) 49-59; Dana Y. Takagi, *The Retreat from Race: Asian-American Admissions and Racial Politics* (New Brunswick, NJ: Rutgers University Press, 1992).

[32] Thomas J. Kane, "Racial and Ethnic Preferences in College Admissions," in C. Jencks and M. Phillips (Eds.), *The Black-White Test Score Gap* (Washington, DC: Brookings, 1998) 431-456.

[33] It is difficult to document many acts of prejudices because they are not conducted openly; nonetheless, there is certainly indirect evidence. This includes stories passed along by those privy to these closed discussions where APAs are not present. The author has received information from white colleagues who were disturbed by discussions among white administrators about their concerns about and desire to minimize the overrepresentation of APAs.

[34] For the new chain migration, see John Liu, Paul M. Ong, and Carolyn Rosenstein, "Dual-Chain Migration: Post-1965 Filipino Immigration to the United States," *International Migration Review*, 25(3): 487-513. For discussion on recent immigration policy, see Paul M. Ong and John Liu, "U.S. Immigration Policies and Asian Migration," in Paul M. Ong, Edna Bonacich, and Lucie Cheng (Eds.), *The New Asian Immigration in Los Angeles and Global Restructuring* (Philadelphia, PA: Temple University Press, 1994) 45-72. This selective migration has not only produced a highly-educated APA immigrant population, but also a highly-educated NH white immigrant population.

[35] This does not take into account those outside of the labor market because they have become discouraged workers. This is a particular problem among black males.

[36] Multivariate methods are used to estimate the independent sources of the earnings

inequality. Linear regressions are used, with the log of total wages and salaries as the dependent variable. The independent (causal) factors include type of credential (bachelor's, master's, professional, and doctoral degrees), nativity (U.S.-born and foreign- born), age and race (APA and white). The sample is restricted to those between the ages of 24 and 64, working full-time (35 or more hours a week) and year-round (50 or more weeks a year), holding at least a bachelor's degree, and classified as an employee (i.e., not self-employed). Moreover, immigrants are divided into recent and established immigrants (those in the country approximately less than 12 years and those in the country approximately 12 years or more). For the analysis, the earnings of U.S.-born white males is the ultimate benchmark. The impact of the independent variables is calculated using the exponential function on the estimated coefficients.

[37] See United States Commission on Civil Rights, *Civil Rights Issues Facing Asian Americans in the 1990s* (Washington, DC: GPO, February 1992) 131-135; Federal Glass Ceiling Commission, *Good For Business: Making Full Use of the Nation's Human Capital* (Washington, DC: GPO, 1995).

[38] "APA Agenda: Asian Americans on the Issues," *Asian Week*, 23-29 August 1996: 14-17. The *Asian Week* survey of 807 APA registered voters was conducted by Meta Information Services between June 25th and July 2nd, 1996. The sample included persons with APA surnames in California, Massachusetts, Ohio, Pennsylvania, and Washington.

[39] To estimate the effects of ethnicity and nativity, logit regressions with the same college/university educated sample are used in the analysis of the probability of being in management for APAs and whites working full-time and year-round and between the ages of 24 and 64.

[40] Total earnings include wages and salaries, self-employment income, and farm income. Wages and salaries are included because many of the firms are incorporated with the owners paid a salary.

[41] U.S. Bureau of the Census, *1992 Economic Census, Characteristics of Business Owners* (Washington, DC, 1997); U.S. Bureau of the Census, *1992 Economic Census, Women-Owned Businesses* (Washington, DC, 1996); U.S. Bureau of the Census, *1992 Economic Census, Survey of Minority-Owned Enterprises* (Washington, DC, 1996); and www.census.gov/Press-Release/cb96-127.html. Some of the statistics for APAs includes a small number of American Indian firms.

[42] Even more interesting is the potential impact of alternative schemes to increase disadvantaged groups. For example, giving preference based on class rather than race (that is, giving greater weight to those from low-income families) would increase the admission rate for APAs but not for other racial minorities. This not only shows the inadequacy of class-based program to replace race-based programs in promoting admis-

sions for underrepresented minorities, but also reveals the unique position of the APA population, which has a disproportionate number of poor families despite a high average income for the total population. Cecilia A. Conrad, "Affirmative Action and Admission to the University of California," in Paul M. Ong (Ed.), Impacts of Affirmative Action: Policies and Consequences in California (Walnut Creak, CA: AltaMira Press, 1999) 171-196.

[43] "APA Agenda: Asian Americans on the Issues," Asian Week, 23-29 August 1996: 14-17. For that specific item, 54 percent of the respondent supported the statement, 34 percent opposed, and 12 percent had no opinion.

[44] Jerry Kang, "Negative Action Against Asian Americans: The Internal Instability of Dworkin's Defense of Affirmative Action," Harvard Civil Rights-Civil Liberties Law Review, 31(1): Winter 1996.

[45] See the results form the Los Angeles Times Poll #318. Respondents were given this question: "As you may know, Asians make up about 10 percent of California's population but they comprise about 28 percent of the students in the University of California system. Which of these statements comes closer to your view about that: 'If Asians are better qualified, more of them should be admitted to college than others.' or 'Despite qualifications, the racial makeup in colleges should generally mirror the population as a whole.'" 65 percent of APAs selected the first statement, compared to 42 percent of blacks, 37 percent of Latinos, and 58 percent whites.

[46] Julian Guthrie, "School Desegregation Teetering in San Francisco," San Francisco Examiner, 16 February 1999; Andrew Quinn, "SF schools agree to drop race-based admissions," Reuters 17 February 1999; Alethea Yip, "New Support in School Desegregation Case 'We Want To Emphasize That This Case Is About Ending Discrimination And Not At All About Ending Affirmative Action," Asian Week, 5-11 September 1997: http://www.asianweek.com/090597/schoolnews.html; Jeff Chang, "On the Wrong Side: Chinese Americans Win Anti-Diversity Settlement-and Lose in the End," Color Lines, Summer 1999:

www.arc.org/C_Lines/CLArchive/story2_2_04.html; Bryant Tan, "Battle over district's consent decree goes to court," 22 November 1996: www.thelowell.org/breaking/news/nov22-districtDecree.html

[47] David L. Kirp, "Race, Politics, and the Courts: School Desegregation in San Francisco," Harvard Education Review, 46 (November 1997): 572-611; Nanette Asimov, "District's Long Struggle with Desegregation," San Francisco Chronicle, 19 June 1995: A9.

[48] San Francisco Unified School District, Lowell on Line, "Distinguished Alumni," www.sfusd.k12.ca.us/schwww/sch697/about/alumni/; "Lowell History, The Oldest

Public High School West of the Mississippi,"

www.sfusd.k12.ca.us/schwww/sch697/about/history/page2.html

⁴⁹ Enrollment data taken from the DataQuest web site maintained by the California Department of Education, http://data1.cde.ca.gov/dataquest/.

50 Nanette Asimov and Tara Shioya, "A Test for the Best Public School," *San Francisco Chronicle*, 21 June 1995: A1 and A5.

⁵¹ In 1996, SFUSD modified the admission process for Lowell: "The new admissions policy prescribes that 80 percent of the freshmen are to be admitted under one cut-off score computed strictly according to their composite score, which is based on their middle school GPA and CTBS percentile ranking. The remaining 20 percent of the freshmen are selected from a pool of 'value-added' applicants who are given extra points if they produce evidence that meets additional criteria, e.g., took honors courses in middle school, lived in public housing, were eligible for the federal lunch program, participated in extra-curricular activities, had parents who did not graduate from high school, etc." www.sfusd.k12.ca.us/schwww/sch697/about/policy/admissions.html. This new process, however, did not directly address the issue of a cap on enrollment. The use of race has remained unresolved. Ryan Kim, "Foe Blasts School's New Admission Plan," San Francisco Chronicle, 25 November 1999: A1 and A9.

⁵² William M. Rodgers. "Federal-Contractor Status and Minority Employment: A Case Study of California, 1979-1994," in Paul M. Ong (Ed.), *Impacts of Affirmative Action: Policies and Consequences in California* (Walnut Creek, CA: AltaMira Press, 1999) 103-120.

⁵³ United States Equal Employment Opportunity Commission, (Washington DC: GPO, 1997); United States Equal Employment Opportunity Commission, *Job Patterns for Minorities and Women in Private Industry, 1997* (Washington DC: GPO, 1997); United States Equal Employment Opportunity Commission, *1997 State and Local Government Information Survey, Aggregate for National Employment Summary* (Washington DC: 1997) Data Compiled by EEOC Staff; United States Office of Personnel Management, *Federal Civilian Workforce Statistics: Race/National Origin: Employment and Average Salary by White-Collar Occupational Category* (Washington DC: GPO, 1998) 44.

⁵⁴ The literature indicates that APAs in the public sector earn less and hold lower positions than whites after controlling for personal characteristics. A summary can be found in M.V. Lee Badgett, "The Impact of Affirmative Action on Public-Sector Employment," in Paul M. Ong (Ed.), *Impacts of Affirmative Action: Policies and Consequences in California* (Walnut Creek, CA: AltaMira Press, 1999) 83-102. Her own analysis shows that in 1990 APAs in government, and male APAs in particular, are less likely to hold a managerial or professional job than whites; however, the gap is even

greater in the private sector.

[55] The precise occupational definitions in Table 8 are not the same as the CPS-based definitions used in the analysis in the previous section of this chapter, which is based on the Current Population Survey. Nonetheless, the relative distributions are similar. For example, both the EEOC and CPS data show that APAs in the private sector are only half as likely to be in a management position as in a professional occupation.

[56] Because APAs are better educated, one would expect a proportionately higher share of the management position, but the detail data are not available to estimate what the share should be. However, the multivariate analysis in the previous section indicates that APAs have reach parity with whites in the professional categories, after accounting for age, educational credentials, and nativity. In other words, the observed APA share of professional jobs is in line with what we expect after taking into account background characteristics. Given that management is also a high-status occupation, we would expect APA share of management position to be roughly equal to that in the professions. In other words, if APAs hold 7 percent of professional jobs, then we would expect APAs to hold 7 percent of management jobs given their higher education. The lower the index, the greater the under representation.

[57] "Proposal to Better Integrate Fire Department," *San Francisco Chronicle*, 19 May 1965: 3; Jerry Kang, "Negative Action Against Asian Americans: The Internal Instability of Dworkin's Defense of Affirmative Action," *Harvard Civil Rights-Civil Liberties Law Review*, 31(1): Winter 1996, 21.

[58] Tom Larson, "Affirmative Action Programs for Minority and Women-Owned Businesses, in Paul M. Ong (Ed.), *Impacts of Affirmative Action: Policies and Consequences in California* (Walnut Creek, CA: AltaMira Press, 1999) 133-169.

[59] Maria E. Enchautegui, Michael Fix, Pamela Loprest, Sarah C. von der Lippe, and Douglas Wissoker, *Do Minority-Owned Businesses Get a Fair Share of Government Contracts?* (Washington, DC: The Urban Institute, 1997).

[60] The extremely low parity index for APAs is due in part to the higher level of entre-preneurship of APAs compared to other minority groups. If the population is used as the numerator to construct a parity index, then the results would show that APAs fare better than other minorities, although still not as well as whites. This change in the rank order reveals the limitations of such simple measures.

[61] Federal Register: "Federal Procurement; Proposed Reforms to Affirmative Action," 23 May 1996, 61(101): 26041-26063; "Federal Acquisition Regulation; Reform of Affirmative Action in Federal Procurement," 30 June 1998, 63(125): 35719-35726.

[62] The purpose and objective of the 8(a) program is to assist socially and economically

disadvantaged individuals participate fully and successfully in the business mainstream of the American economy. This goal is accomplished through the expansion of businesses owned by program participants, which, in turn, generates societal benefits through the creation of jobs and wealth. Program participants receive multi-year business development assistance. Because of the selection rules and the underlying composition of disadvantaged firms, the participants in the 8(a) program are predominantly minority, and this is particularly true in the early years.

[63] Tabulation by author of California Certification Information System (Calcert) 1999 database, California Department of Transportation.

[64] Stephen L. Klineberg, *Houston's Ethnic Communities, Third Edition* (Houston, TX: Rice University, 1996).

[65] Ron Nissimov, 28 June 1998: http://www.civilrights.org/aa/states/tx.html

[66] There is no equivalent exit poll on APAs for Houston's Proposition A or Washington State's Initiative 200, but there is some indirect information. An inspection of the votes by precinct in King County, which includes Seattle, reveals that most of the predominantly APA neighborhoods (by block groups) coincide with precincts where voters overwhelmingly (75 percent or more) voted against the initiative. www.seattletimes.com/news/local/charts/voted98/I200county.html, and

www.seattletimes.com/news/local/charts/voted98/I200race.html

[67] *Los Angeles Times*, 7 November 1996: A29.

[68] A part of the explanation might be that this group had been sensitized to the necessity to fight wedge issues sponsored by conservatives. In 1994, the state passed Proposition 187, an initiative designed to prevent undocumented aliens from public services but also had a strong anti-immigrant undercurrent. *Los Angeles Times*, 10 November 1994: B4.

[69] Kathy Feng and Bonnie Tang, *1996 Southern California Asian Pacific American Exit Poll Report: An Analysis of APA Voter Behavior and Opinions* (Los Angeles, CA. and Washington, DC: Asian Pacific American Legal Center and National Asian Pacific American Legal Consortium, 1997).

[70] Larry Shinagawa, *1996 San Francisco Bay Area Exit Poll Report: An Analysis of APA Demographics, Behavior and Political Participation* (San Francisco, CA. and Washington, DC: Asian Law Caucus and National Asian Pacific American Legal Consortium, 1997).

[71] Paul M. Ong and Suzanne Hee, "Economic Diversity, An Overview," in Paul M. Ong (Ed.), *The State of Asian Pacific America: Economic Diversity, Issues and Policies* (Los Angeles, CA: LEAP Asian Pacific American Public Policy Institute and UCLA Asian American Studies Center, 1994) 31-55; Robert M. Jiobu, "Recent Asian Pacific

Immigrants: The Demographic Background," in Bill O. Hing and Ronald Lee (Eds.), *Reframing the Immigration Debate* (Los Angeles, CA: LEAP Asian Pacific American Public Policy Institute and UCLA Asian American Studies Center, 1996) 35-57.

[72] Grant Din, "An Analysis of Asian/Pacific American Registration and Voting Patterns in San Francisco," master's thesis, Claremont Graduate School, 1984; Don T. Nakanishi, *The UCLA Asian Pacific American Voter Registration Study* (Los Angeles, CA: Asian Pacific American Legal Center, 1986); Paul M. Ong and Don T. Nakanishi, "Becoming Citizens, Becoming Voters: The Naturalization and Political Participation of Asian Pacific Immigrants," in Bill O. Hing and Ronald Lee (Eds.), *Reframing the Immigration Debate* (Los Angeles, CA: LEAP Asian Pacific American Public Policy Institute and UCLA Asian American Studies Center, 1996) 275-305.

[73] Paul M. Ong and David Lee, "Changing of the Guard? The Rise of an Immigrant Majority," paper presented at the Conference on Asian Americans and Politics, The Woodrow Wilson Center, Washington, DC, March 14, 1998.

[74] Post/Kaiser/Harvard Race Poll, 1995. Respondents were asked to choose which of the following two statement represents their opinion: "White Americans have benefited from past and present discrimination against African Americans, so they should be willing to make up for these wrongs" or "Most white Americans have not benefited from past and present discrimination against African Americans/Hispanic Americans/ Asian Americans, so they have no responsibility to make up for these wrongs." Forty-six percent of APA respondents selected the first statement when applied to Hispanics or APAs.

[75] "APA Agenda: Asian Americans on the Issues," *Asian Week*, 23-29 August 1996: 14-17. For questions on giving preferences to underrepresented minorities in employment and public contracts, 51 percent agree, 33 disagreed, and 16 percent had no opinion.

[76] Gabriel Chin, Sumi Cho, Jerry Kang, and Frank Wu, *Beyond Self-Interest: Asian Pacific Americans Toward a Community of Justice, A Policy Analysis of Affirmative Action* (Los Angeles, CA: LEAP Asian Pacific American Public Policy Institute and UCLA Asian American Studies Center, 1996) 25.

Asians and Race Relations in Britain

Shamit Saggar

Introduction

By European standards, Britain is frequently characterized as a country in which the social and political integration of ethnic minorities has advanced substantially. Starting from a limited base in the immediate post-war period, a substantial proportion of minorities emerged from the 1970s onwards as relatively active in the mainstream political process and able to harness tangible benefits in the employment, housing and educational markets. In large measure, Britain's transformation into a multiracial, multicultural society was driven by its particular immigration history.[1] Significant numbers of labor migrants were recruited from both colonial and post-colonial sources during the 1950s in order to fill often-specific shortfalls in the effort to reconstruct after war. Additionally, others from similar countries of origin responded to this labor shortage and joined often spontaneous migration chains to build new and, hopefully, better lives for themselves and their offspring in what at that time continued to be described as the mother country. Finally, putting aside the large numbers involved in family reunification (a theme that spawned major political rows over immigration policy in the 1970s), a third component of this transformation was made up by politically displaced refugees. Three successive nationality crises in Kenya (1968), Uganda (1972) and Malawi (1976) resulted in major inflows of British nationals of South Asian ethnic origin.

This chapter is concerned with charting the nature and effects of this transformation in British society and with examining the part played by Asians[2] in this process. The following section reviews both the historic context of post-war immigration as well as recent Census and other indicators on the components of multiracial Britain. A key theme in the historic background has been the question of race and racialization, a perspective that suggests that the post-war newcomers were systematically perceived through the prism of racial difference and distance. Indeed, the idea that British politics and society in some way became racialized in the 1950s is to suggest that a quasi-formal racial code became the basis for public debates over immigration from Asia, Africa and the Caribbean. This argument, as this chapter will argue, has become increasingly redundant in recent years precisely because of diminished predictive capacity of race in tracking and explaining the social circumstances of ethnic minorities in Britain. The third part of the chapter turns to consider specific aspects of the Asian presence in Britain. Attention focuses on participation patterns in employment, education and mainstream politics, again raising questions (taken up in following section) over the nature of the public policy framework as a whole. The primary underlying theme of the fourth part of the chapter is to shed light on the extent to which the Asian experience within multiracial Britain follows patterns that adequately describe other significant minorities. The purpose of exploring this theme is not merely to track different trajectories in their own right; rather, it is to assess the intellectual and practical relevance of the British liberal race relations paradigm. This liberal framework, as we shall see, has a long-standing pedigree in British approaches to social policy more generally. However, it is important to bring out its genesis in U.S. thinking and practice in race relations, influential both at home and abroad throughout the twentieth century. The chapter closes with a discussion of the Asian experience within a society whose norms have been largely driven by the development of ethnic group-based political rights. Such an outcome, it is suggested, has left the British case appearing increasingly anachronistic when measured by continental European standards.

Asian Demographics and Related Patterns

Britain's Asian population significantly outnumbers any other single composite group among the ethnic minority population. Based on now-dated evidence from the 1991 General Census, Asians constitute a little less than 3 percent of the general population. More recent estimates based on Labor Force Survey data released just before the last general election in 1997 indicated that Asians as a combined group might have swollen by a further 12-15 percent during the 1990s; moreover, the overall number of Asians, based on these LFS trends, was likely to expand by an additional fifth by the time of the next census (2001).[3] Therefore, at century's end, an Asian community hovering around the two million mark seems to be a credible estimate.[4]

While this population size may only be modest in absolute and proportional terms, it is important to emphasize that it is relatively concentrated geographically. In broad terms, around three-quarters of its members are found in urban areas of Britain, while its Bangladeshi-origin component is essentially a London-based subgroup (over nine in ten are found in the capital city, the great bulk of whom is concentrated in London's East End). It is not hard to see immediately the implications that such urban concentration might have on the salience of certain public policy issues rather than others. Moreover, in Britain's traditional first-past-the-post electoral arrangements, there are some very clear benefits that accrue from geographic density in a limited number of parliamentary constituencies and local government wards.[5]

TABLE 1. ETHNIC ORIGIN BREAKDOWN OF UK RESIDENT POPULATION, 1991

Ethnic group	Number (in thousands)	Percent of total population	Percent of nonwhite population
All	54,889	100.0	—
White	51,874	94.5	—
All others	3,015	5.5	100.0
Black Caribbean	500	0.9	16.6
Black African	212	0.4	7.0
Black other	178	0.3	5.9
Black total	891	1.6	29.5
Indian	840	1.5	27.9
Pakistani	477	0.9	15.8
Bangladeshi	163	0.3	5.4
South Asian total	1,480	2.7	49.1
Chinese	157	0.3	5.2
Other Asian	198	0.4	6.6
Other non-Asian	290	0.5	9.6
Total Asian *	1,835	3.4	60.0

Notes:

* Calculation based on total of all South Asian, Chinese and other Asian groups
Source: 1991 General Census

The composition of the Asian community is rather more revealing, however. As Table 1 above shows, Indians are by far the largest individual group, and very probably over a million in number in actual terms. As a group, Indians will, of course, comprise many different religious, linguistic, regional and even caste sub-groups, though in the British case Hindus from Gujerat and Hindus and Sikhs from Punjab are the largest and best-known components of the Indian-origin population. Ethnic Pakistanis' numbers are something over half the Indian size, while ethnic Bangladeshis amount to just over a tenth of the aggregate number (or a third of the size of the Pakistani group and a fifth of the Indian group). With a considerably younger age profile than the white population, the growth that is likely to take place among Asians will be considerable. Labor Force Survey findings from the mid-1990s reveal that more than two-thirds of Asians are below 35 years of age, as compared with less than one-half of their white counterparts. The former group then is heavily represented in the major child-bearing and rearing age cohorts with obvious knock-on effects in terms of growth patterns (taking no account for external sources through further primary or secondary migration, however restrictively regulated by policy). It is also worth adding that growth rates for Pakistani and Bangladeshi groups have tended to be larger than Indians, partially reflecting aspects of socioeconomic class and educational backgrounds, but also the possibility of cultural differences at work. Asian Indians, therefore, hold an important numerical grip for the time being, though the implication that this might be reflected in areas such as electoral strategy may turn out to be mistaken. Proportionately smaller, yet more tightly packed, these Asian groups might easily be capable of greater political leverage.

Policy Problems and Frameworks:
Patterns of Change and Continuity

British integration policy has broadly been geared to addressing direct and indirect discrimination in different aspects of British society.[6] It is a framework that largely has its origins in the 1960s, an era in which British governments began to develop fresh ideas and approaches to the longer term consequences of earlier immigration and settlement policies.[7] The nature and characteristics of the British approach is a topic that has been widely debated, and we shall return to consider certain elements of the model and its impact upon Asians in Britain in a later part of this chapter. For the time being, however, it is worth shedding some light on the form that Asian participation in public life has taken.

In very general terms, the British policy thinking and practice has operated under the assumption that forms of under-representation would normally characterize the participation of significant ethnic minorities such as Asians and blacks. Racial prejudice, it was thought, was the cause behind such under-representation and that this factor could and indeed should be countered through a combination of enforced social reforms (tentative anti-discrimination laws), and educational leadership (typically seen in early stabs at introducing cross-cultural awareness into the school curriculum as well as into professional hiring and training programs). For instance, the arena of electoral politics provided a good early illustration of the kinds of problems that social policy and wider reform efforts were aimed at addressing. In national parliamentary elections, the first ethnic minority, mainstream party candidate (a black doctor) emerged only as recently as the 1970 General Election. The first Asians in similar situations did not appear until the mid-1970s and no minority, black or Asian, was successful even at the level of winning a party nomination in a nationally winnable seat until 1983. It was not until as late as 1987 that the first batch of ethnic minorities was finally elected to Westminster

Transforming Race Relations

under the colors of one of the major parties (four were returned including a single Asian).[8] Later in 1992 an Asian Conservative MP was successfully returned by a west London constituency comprising a sizable number of Asian voters, though this breakthrough was something of a false dawn due to his emphatic defeat five years later. Finally, by 1997[9] the total Asian presence in the House of Commons stood at just five MPs (all of whom represented the Labor Party).[10] In the world of local elections the picture was slightly more promising, but certainly not substantially different. Writing in the mid-1990s, one respected commentator was able to paint a rather upbeat picture of Asian electoral progress at sub-national level:

> The broad picture is that Asian communities have been more successful in producing councillors than their black counterparts. The Asian community has achieved a position close to parity in 40 local authorities [in which the Asian population exceeded 10 percent]. The most remarkable fact is that in these 40 authorities the proportion of Labor councillors is 93.4 percent and that of the Conservatives 4.5 percent and Liberal Democrats 2.1 percent. The extent of this party-based imbalance is a fact that needs to be driven home in popular coverage of race-and-representation themes.[11]

Under-representation thus referred to a situation in which aggregate data pointed to either shortcomings in the supply of suitable participants or, more disturbingly, to worries over prejudice and discrimination in the recruitment and selection activities of political parties. Outside politics, in areas such as employment and education, the under-representation formula instead concerned job hopefuls and employers or students and teachers, respectively.

With this background in mind, it worth devoting some space in this chapter to examining the reality of Asian participation in British society. Three fairly specific areas are reviewed—employment, education and electoral politics—to try to gauge two interrelated questions. First, to what extent is it reasonable to point to under-representation generalizations? The question has meaning because it has been suspected for a long time that the Asian group is likely to contain important variations within its very broadly set parameters. Second, what signs, if any, are there to suggest that Asian participation, or at least the participation of segments of the Asian-origin population, is driven by ethnic commonness as opposed to other secular factors such as social class? This question stands out mainly because a great deal has been claimed about the notion of Asianness, a loose descriptive term that is frequently cited as if to highlight the salutary importance of ethnicity and ethnic kinship in shaping the position of an ethnic group. As the following discussion observes, such an argument has been somewhat over-emphasized in the three fields that are examined.

LABOR MARKET CHANGE AND CONSOLIDATION

The structure of the British labor market has changed dramatically over the past two decades and Asian participation in different forms of employment has also evolved to keep pace with these changes, while in some areas there are considerable signs of falling behind in labor market participation patterns.[12] It is worth beginning, however, with a brief overview of the types of manual and non-manual work in which Asians are involved, taking account of the underlying class structure in Britain. Table 2 below tells the story. It is immediately clear that Asian employment is slightly skewed towards participation at the lower end of the status scale. This is particularly pronounced among Pakistani and Bangladeshi origin Asians. Equally, these two groups contain large numbers in the middle-ranking, skilled manual employment category, partly reflecting the kind of labor migration patterns of which they were originally a part. Meanwhile, the start of a distinctive Indian pattern can be discerned with heavy concentration, comparable to whites, in the three categories at the upper end of the scale. Interestingly, a similar picture is also true of black Caribbeans (except in professional jobs) on the basis of 1991 Census figures, thereby dispelling the belief that few among this group could or had reached into a stable middle-class employment. The most noteworthy figure relates to the one-in-ten rate of Indian professional employment uncovered almost a decade ago, a finding that has presumably increased even farther in the intervening period.[13]

TABLE 2. SOCIOECONOMIC EMPLOYMENT STATUS OF SELECTED ETHNIC GROUPS, 1991

| Occupation | Ethnic group (%) | | | | |
	White	Indian	Pakistani	Bangladeshi	Black Caribbean
Unskilled	6	3	5	4	7
Semi-skilled manual	15	21	24	32	19
Skilled manual	21	16	25	26	22
Skilled non-manual	24	23	18	20	24
Managerial	29	28	22	13	26
Professional	5	9	6	5	2

Source: 1991 General Census

Census data, therefore, paints a picture of partial upward socioeconomic mobility among all members of the at-large Asian community.[14] This is true only to an extent, however, because there are clear signs of Asian Indians beginning to stretch away from the pack. Not surprisingly, this has led to talk of a new Indian middle-class by which it is hard to ignore this group's very high rate of participation in professional employment. Aspects of this Indian-led pattern are likely to be reflected in areas such as political identity and behavior (including voting preference). Additionally, forms of new middle-class identity are unlikely to be built on employment patterns alone, and we would expect some similar outcomes in areas such as housing (tenure type, mean equity value, neighborhood character, etc.) as well as education (selective entry, fee-paying, attainment levels, etc).

An interesting question concerns the origins and trajectory of Asian middle-class groups. For one thing, it has been suggested that straight comparison of the main Asian groups may risk masking the possibility that these groups' class structures were highly dissimilar at the point of entry as immigrants into Britain. Certainly, Asian Indians were over-represented among the East African refugees of the 1960s and 1970s.[15] East African Asians displayed a marked different employment and class background to their sub-continental counterparts. The former was mainly drawn from white-collar, public sector employment and also from independent business backgrounds. As such, most were already familiar with two key elements of British society following migration: the use of the English language as the *lingua franca* of the new home society, and urban residential experience in common with new settlement patterns after arrival. In contrast, Asian immigrants from South Asia directly had tended to settle in Britain at a much earlier period and had been drawn from mainly rural, agrarian backgrounds. Few held the linguistic background of their later East African counterparts and many were recruited directly into semi-skilled and routine manual work in manufacturing, transportation, the health services and textiles. The wide disparities uncovered within superficially similar ethnic groups are a factor that needs to be treated with caution.[16] In short, the burgeoning Indian middle-class in modern Britain may owe their upward socioeconomic mobility less to their ethnic origins than to a series of fairly specific factors such as language and previous employment that have in turn made important, though indirect, contributions to their social class status.

Finally, a word or two must be added on the question of

unemployment (conspicuously not scanned in the employment-based social status profile of the previous table) and average earnings (an indicator of position within social status scales). Labor Force Survey data from the mid-1990s revealed even greater reason to believe that a large schism had opened up between Asian Indians on one hand and all the other significant ethnic minority groups (including Pakistanis and Bangladeshi) on the other.[17] Male unemployment among whites stood at 9.9 percent, a figure not too dissimilar to that for Indian males (13 percent). Meanwhile, comparable rates for Pakistanis and Bangladeshis put together had reached a staggering 27 percent (within reach of the upper end rate seen among black males of 30 percent). This is fairly reliable reason to think that segmented labor markets are at work among different Asian ethnic groups. Furthermore, LFS data showed that average hourly earnings of Indian men stood only modestly below those of their white counterparts (the former amounted to 91 percent of the latter). The ratio of Pakistani and Bangladeshi males earnings to those of whites, meanwhile, was a paltry 68 percent, substantially below that of black males and ethnic minorities as a whole (88 and 89 percent respectively).

EDUCATIONAL PARTICIPATION AND PERFORMANCE

The pattern of excess among selected Asian groups in relation to other Asian communities is substantially reinforced in the area of educational take-up and mean attainment rates. Table 3 below notes that the one of the root ingredients of attainment involve the capacity—or perhaps opportunity—to participate in post-compulsory education beyond 16 years of age. The data relate to the mid-1990s period and demonstrate that, once again, it is exceedingly hard to lump together the profiles of all three main Asian groups. Furthermore, the data reveal that, in the case of educational participation, non-Indian Asians continue to outstrip the rates found among ethnic minorities at large, though it is striking that by 18 years of age considerable fall-off has occurred among Pakistanis and

Bangladeshis as well. This further drives home the earlier observation about Indian exceptionalism. This is important because it signals a rough age-driven indicator for potential recruitment into higher education and with it the main avenue into future possibilities for professional training and employment.

Interestingly, all minority groups exhibit participation rates considerably in excess of the white benchmark, probably suggesting that young members of these ethnic groups and their parents increasingly view education as a primary means for securing social mobility. At age 16, this generalization appears to apply to all minorities, Asian and black, but by age 18, this has become much more of an Asian-only phenomenon. Furthermore, in the case of other Asian groups, staying on in schools, colleges and universities has become something of an article of faith.

TABLE 3. PARTICIPATION IN POST-COMPULSORY FULL-TIME EDUCATION, 1994 *

	Aged 16 %	Aged 18 %
White	71	38
Indian	95	65
Pakistani/Bangladeshi	80	61
Other Asian **	89	72
Black	86	50

Notes:
* England and Wales only
** comprises Chinese, Japanese, Korean and SE Asian

Source: Youth Cohort Study, Department for Education and Employment, Spring 1994

In the area of attainment, once again Asian Indians scored highest when measuring the proportions succeeding in gaining five GCSE passes between grades A-C. Figures for the mid-1990s showed that 45 percent of this group reached this threshold, the same as among whites. Interestingly, the other Asian group (which includes Chinese) also matched this rate of success.[18] However, a significantly lower rate of achievement was recorded among Pakistanis and Bangladeshis (just 25 percent). Local surveys in 1997 of the picture in London relating to those holding degree-level qualifications showed a marked disparity between Pakistanis and Bangladeshis: 46 percent of the former (in London) held degrees against just 25 percent of the latter.[19] This implies that the standard method of collapsing together the performance of these two groups (in order usually to deliver sufficient sample group numbers) is probably likely to remit misleading results. The same survey also revealed that both Chinese and South Asians generally were substantially more likely to be studying for academic qualifications than other ethnic groups. Black and white students, meanwhile, were considerably over-represented on vocational course enrollments.[20]

In the early years of research on, and policy development of, ethnic minority educational participation it was generally assumed that lower levels of attainment were limited to black Afro-Caribbean groups. Certainly pockets of low achievement could be pointed to among Asians in comparison with whites at large, but these were generally thought to be isolated examples. However, more recent data has consistently pointed to marked variations in performance within the Asian population, and there has been little point in denying the very considerable records of over achievement by Indians in particular. These differences, of course, cannot be seen in isolation and it is likely that social class and attainment patterns are closely entwined with one another.[21]

Questions of educational outcomes, however important and fought over, only relate to one prominent aspect of debates over education policy. Another key dimension stems from the nature and content of the educational curriculum, in turn raising often-febrile arguments over the values and principles underpinning formal educational programs. This is an area in which only limited research has been carried out on the nature of ethnic group attitudes. One particular survey, now rather dated, indicated that distinctions could be made between different ethnic minority groups attitudes toward multicultural educational principles and even lesson content.[22] However, in pointing tentatively to some degree of reservation among Indian parents, it was not clear whether this tension was driven by their ethnic identity or rather by aspects of their social class. In any case, it masks the bigger division between minority parents on one hand and white parents on the other, many of whom exhibit attitudinal support for multicultural education, conditional on its targeting towards ethnic minority children or at the very least towards areas of high minority concentrations.[23] Further research is still needed to unlock the extent to which group perceptions of multicultural education are informed by frameworks that question, and possibly deny, its legitimacy in mainstream schooling.

ELECTORAL BEHAVIOR: PROSPECTS FOR VOTER DEALIGNMENT

If we now turn our attention to the third and final aspect of the discussion of Asian participation in contemporary Britain, it is clear that the arena of mainstream politics, centered on electoral choice, is one in which several important debates exist over the extent of Asian influence and leverage. Electoral politics holds the potential of rapid and observable change in the eyes of those eager to highlight the centrality of Asian participation. Critics have sometimes noted that such a preoccupation risks overplaying the actual impact that results from Asian electoral participation and, more troublesome, serves to overlook the dividends that might result from pressure group activity or protest politics.[24] These considerations aside, it is possible to identify the emergence of a core debate among analysts and commentators over the worth of mainstream Asian political participation. One side of this argument has tended to emphasize the idea that Asians specifically—and ethnic minorities more generally—have the potential to act collectively in order to maximize their returns from the political system.[25] A core element of this claim has rested on voter numbers and their strategic use in a concentrated and targeted manner.[26] For this school of thought, the ethnicity of Asians counts politically because it is the vital glue that binds together their political outlooks and behavior in what otherwise remains a political cold climate. Against this it is possible to identify a counter-school that sees little prospect in Asians using collective action to boost potential political rewards principally because, it is argued, the absence of convincing evidence to demonstrate high and enduring levels of ethnic-based political consciousness among this group.[27] The fact that they may share many, though not all, aspects of their ethnic background with one another, is not grounds for believing that Asians will adopt a similar position in terms of political participation. For one thing, it is doubtful whether they share a common issue agenda with one another, with little evidence to support the idea that a pattern exists within Asians' understanding of their political interests. For another, wide and not-easily-accountable variations exist in the actual rates of electoral involvement among different Asian groups, implying that generalizations about the wielding of electoral muscle are fraught with misdiagnosis.[28]

In order to flesh out this debate, let us consider three central elements of Asian electoral participation: the question of rates of involvement based on electoral registration and turnout; the extent to which the evidence points to a distinctive set of issues or interests that Asians share with one another; and finally, the ever-thorny puzzle over Asians party alignment. The third theme has arguably presented one of the greatest challenges for political analysts. The prime reason for this controversy has been the overwhelming allegiance of British ethnic minorities to Britain's traditional left-of-country political party, the Labor Party. At one level this has not only meant the rightist parties such as the Conservatives have missed out on an minority electoral dividend, but, moreover, have accepted that Labor's massive lead has been largely the product of the internal class composition of the Asian and black electorate. The difficulty has arisen from evidence that has shown that little or no propensity among the much smaller proportion of middle-class minorities to break with their traditional Labor mooring. Other considerations, notably the influence of group ethnicity upon political cohesion, are thus thought to be critical to understanding minority voting behavior generally and Asian participation in particular.

However, to start with the question of political involvement, evidence from the 1997 General Election indicates that, at the level of basic voter registration, all three main Asian groups that were studied exhibited impressive rates of participation. This participation is related to the second core element, that of turnout rates. Table 4 below summarizes the position in 1997 on both fronts and shows Asian groups in comparison with one another and also in relation to their white and black counterparts.

TABLE 4 - ELECTORAL REGISTRATION AND TURNOUT BY ETHNIC GROUP, 1997 *

Ethnic group (%)

	White	Indian	Pakistani	Bangladeshi	Black African	Black Caribbean	Misc.
Is your name on the electoral register?							
Yes	97.0	96.5	88.4	91.7	86.1	95.0	90.6
No	2.7	2.5	11.7	8.3	12.5	4.0	5.3
Don't know	0.2	1.1	0.0	0.0	1.4	1.0	4.2
Total N	2,480	284	120	60	72	100	95
Total %	100.0	100.0	100.0	100.0	100.0	100.0	100.0
Did you manage to vote in the General Election? **							
Yes	80.8	85.4	84.9	80.4	74.2	73.4	71.8
No	19.2	14.6	15.1	19.6	25.8	26.6	28.2
Total N	2,406	274	106	56	62	94	85
Total %	100.0	100.0	100.0	100.0	100.0	100.0	100.0

Notes:
* Excludes Scotland
** Excludes Don't knows

Source: British Election Study 1997 - merged file (weighted data)

The degree of variance among Asians is also of significance. The above evidence shows that an Asian pattern-of-sorts exists (registration and turnout rates that equal or exceed those of other minority groups). In addition, a regular Indian pattern is discernible. In all cases, Indians are shown to be the most participatory group with rates that appear to bring them somewhat closer to their white counterparts than other Asians: registration rates matched those of whites, while reported turnout in fact outstripped rates among white electors.

The upshot of this evidence is fairly clear. It would appear that a large segment of the Asian population is characterized by a form of political participation that is not immediately evident among other ethnic minorities. Secondly, this evidence suggests variations in Asian and minority political participation. In particular, the distribution of the Indian vote comes to mind and will be examined below. Thirdly, the evidence here tends to encourage the view that an underlying social class effect might be influencing patterns of Indian participation. The evidence on levels of participation, in other words, promotes as many questions as answers.

A second element of the discussion relates to the relative distinctiveness of Asian political interests and attitudes. In this respect it has been argued that in order that Asians can act collectively within the political arena, it is first necessary to show that they share sufficient similarities in their political outlook and even in their political thinking. The evidence is far from conclusive, however. Data from Gallup analyzed from as long ago as the 1987 General Election showed the startling fact that just 1 percent of Asian respondents ranked race as one of the two most important issues facing them (from a list of 10 issues).[29] Significantly, although this figure appears minuscule, it is entirely in line with that found among black voters (none) and whites (just 1 percent). Furthermore, survey data collected by National Opinion Poll in 1991 reported a revealing picture among whites, Asians and blacks in terms of the treatment all respondents perceived each group received from public institutions.[30] Interestingly, the proportions believing that the (public) schools provided worse treatment for whites and Asians differed very little (13 against 15 percent); the comparable figure for blacks was a colossal 38 percent. Likewise, at the hands of the courts, the notion that Asians and whites as groups received a raw deal attracted the support of 19 and 24 percent of respondents respectively, as against 57 percent in relation to blacks. In the area of policing the figures were 45, 48 and 75 percent, while in employment opportunities the findings were 42, 39 and 67 percent respectively. This particular survey appeared to paint a picture that, at the very least, distinguished Asians from their black counterparts in multiracial Britain. These data conspicuously failed to point to any degree of Asian-only distinctiveness as measured not by Asian attitudes and behavior but, rather, in terms of the views held by members of society as a whole.

Finally, more recent evidence from the 1997 General Election highlighted only modest grounds for a picture of Asian distinctiveness. One interesting variant on this theme has been to examine ethnic group attitudes toward political issues that do not normally tie in with debates over race or ethnicity.[31] The case of attitudes in relation to public spending as a means of tackling poverty is a good case in point since it may simultaneously represent something of an indirect link with the perceived political interests of discrete ethnic minority groups. Some 91 percent of whites probably or definitely agreed with the proposition that government spending ought to be raised to tackle poverty; however, this was also true of very high proportions of Indians and Pakistanis (89 and 86 percent respectively), with rather fewer Bangladeshis taking this position (72 percent). The complication is further reinforced by the supporters among those of black African origin (95 percent) and black Caribbean background (91 percent). Again, this does not point to any sign of Asian attitudinal distinctiveness. It is always possible that researchers are looking in the wrong places for the sort of evidence that could possibly support the hypothesis of Asian distinctiveness. Certainly, in fields such as cultural policy, opinions over the role of religion in politics and the role of women in public life have indicated that some groups of Asians hold different attitudes from those of other groups. However, this limitation is the rub in the thesis because such generalizations often do not apply to Asians as a bloc. The potential for Asians to develop collective positions and a strategy for political action is consequently diminished.

This effective roadblock is especially puzzling given that there is plentiful evidence for Asian (and ethnic minority) distinctiveness as measured by voting preference. Numerous studies have pointed to remarkably consistent partisanship across Asian voters of all different social classes, and the task, not surprisingly, has been to try to account for this stable pattern. Among Asian voters this need has been especially pressing given the growth in this group's middle-class numbers without any noticeable departure in its traditional patterns of party choice. According to Heath et al.[32] the deadlock, identified some years ago, points at least partly to the role of ethnicity as a separate political socialization agent and stimulant to attitude formation and political behavior:

> The political behavior of [Asians and blacks] is not to be explained by their class situation. They are much more inclined to the Labor Party than white voters in similar class situations. Perception of the group interests or processes of group identification are more plausible explanations.

A final area to consider is the matter of the partisan loyalties of Asian voters and the prospects, if any, for change. Voting studies going back over many years have shown that British ethnic minority voters have backed the Labor Party in quite staggering numbers: typically four in five minority voters have voted for Labor in a typical general or local election.[33] This pattern has applied historically as much to Asians as other minority groups. However, it has been Asian voters, more so than their black counterparts, who have been singled out by proponents of embourgeoisement-centered theories of voting behavior. These arguments have been built on the idea that changing social and economic relationships, chiefly rising social mobility, would drive similar changes in political outlook and behavior. In particular, evidence from the late 1980s and early 1990s showing clear signs of an emergent Asian—largely Indian— middle-class have been seized upon by this school as the raw material for future rightward drift in Asian political attitudes and beliefs.[34]

Two features of existing Asian voting patterns stand out. First, the overwhelming bias to Labor is self-evidently out of line with the varying (and usually weak) fortunes of Labor among white voters in this period. Second, this bias appears to be relatively insulated from short-term trends. For instance, the rout suffered by Labor in 1983 was not reflected among Asian voters. Minorities remained remarkably loyal to Labor in what then was a terribly cold climate. The upshot of this is that the Labor Party is probably enjoying saturation levels of Asian electoral support and has been doing so for many past elections. Table 5 below tells the story of Labor's quite staggering grip on Asian and black voters as compared with their white counterparts, and also summarizes a picture of continuity in the most recent election.

TABLE 5. ETHNIC MINORITY VOTING PREFERENCES, 1983-97

| | Ethnic group (%) | | | | | | | |
| | Asians | | | | Blacks | | | |
Party	1983	1987	1992	1997 *	1983	1987	1992	1997 *
Conservative	9	23	11	11	7	6	8	4
Labor	81	67	77	81	88	86	85	89
Centre parties	9	10	10	4	5	7	6	3
Other	-	-	3	4	-	-	1	4

Notes:
* Excludes those not intending to vote and undecideds

Source: S. Saggar and A. Heath, "Race: Towards a Multicultural Electorate?", in P. Norris and G. Evans, Critical Elections: British Parties and Voters in Long-term Perspective (London: Sage, 1999)

There is a long-standing interest among researchers, politicians, journalists and others in Asian voter alignment. The research points to three broad lessons for this varied audience. First, it is reasonably clear that a model ethnic minority beachhead does exist for Labor's rivals — principally the Conservatives — among the numerically large Indian electorate. This group contained around 18 percent who backed the Conservatives in 1997, an otherwise disastrous year for the Tories — around five times the rate found among black voters as a whole. The opportunity-cost of this development remains an open question from the perspective of Tory strategy, putting aside the question of how far, if at all, it is the product of conscious effort. Second, it is likely that Asian elites can and do have an influential role to play in advancing any potential for dealignment with the Labor Party. However, this is compromised first by the short-term success of Labor in winning (or retaining) a great deal of elite loyalty, and secondly, by the tendency to overstate the basic leverage capacity of elite activity. Certainly, this has been a continuing feature of Tory strategy, which has been lead, and often limited, by over-reliance on elite initiatives. Third, the cultural thesis, by which a supposed overlap between ethnic group values and party values was emphasized in campaigning, is probably a red herring in explaining, let alone predicting, the possibility for Asian dealignment.[35] For one thing, this school of thought pays virtually no interest in the rather more illuminating evidence for class-based factors in possible dealignment, an approach that recent research has devoted a lot of attention towards.[36] Additionally, the argument over Tory cultural campaign themes in 1997 was eclipsed by Labor's success in mobilizing basic bourgeois themes for its own partisan benefit.

Race Relations and Asian Public Policy Agendas:
Fits, Misfits and Recalibration Politics

At the start of this chapter mention was made of the nature of Britain's modern immigration debate that began in the 1950s as well as the ways in which governments started the ball rolling in tackling the scourge of discrimination and promoting integration policy. This, in other words, was the central historic legacy of the mid-Twentieth Century through which developments by the start of the next century have to be seen. And yet, it is reasonably plain that this legacy has provided an analytical and policy lens that at best allows only partial understanding of the position of Asians in contemporary Britain. For one thing, to speak of the great race-and-immigration question in modern British politics is to miss the point that such a debate has largely ceased to exist. There have been many factors behind this transformation but, as the essay highlighted, the continuing political instability that all parties experienced at the hands of the immigration issue was finally put to rest in the early 1980s. The 1981 British Nationality Act ensured that on-going rows over unknown numbers of immigrant dependents were ended quite conclusively. The upshot was that immigration effectively dropped off the edge of the political agenda and British immigration policy has been characterized thereafter by an era of firm but fair controls. Additionally, it cannot be forgotten that, with family reunification largely completed for the first waves of immigrants, by the 1980s and 1990s the issue has become progressively less salient for the minorities themselves. Lastly, Britain has been increasingly preoccupied with the impact of European integration upon its immigration regime and this has meant that a new pan-European dimension has eclipsed older narrow concerns with Asian sources.

If immigration as a political issue is no longer recognizable in modern Britain, what then of the path taken by political efforts to secure integration and curb discrimination? In this area there has been no comparable decline in salience for these concerns among minorities. However, the growing class diversity found among South Asians described previously has meant those old assumptions about the value and purpose of integration policy can no longer be taken for granted. In one area, education, limited evidence already exists to show that there is a growing polarization of opinion within the Asian communities towards the role of multiculturalism in the curriculum. These variations are possibly masks for class-driven interests, and it is likely that more widespread examples in areas such as housing and health will emerge in the near future. Attitudinal evidence from 1997 suggests that, while all groups of Asians believe that the incidence of prejudice and discrimination is fairly widespread, some clearly assign very different meaning to this reality than others. Indeed, the centrality of race as a long-term source of division appears to be doubtful when it comes to drawing generalizations about Asians as whole in Britain. Furthermore, while recognizing the extent of racial discrimination, some groups of Asians are undoubtedly more eager and willing than others to embrace direct, racially-based forms of social policy in response. To be sure, South Asians of Indian ethnic origin stand in sharp contrast to their Pakistani and Bangladeshi counterparts on questions as fundamental as government approaches to equal opportunities. That said and to be fair, all minorities, and all groups of Asians, are clearly united with the white counterparts in their emphatic opposition to doctrines of racial preference.[37]

Race Relations and Asians: Future Prospects

Race relations in Britain are a field of endeavor that have been closely modeled on the U.S. experience in the middle part of the twentieth century. Starting from a low base, British political, policy and other elites were successful in devising a policy framework for immigrant integration during the 1960s that ran parallel to the major influxes from South Asia and the Caribbean. Much has been written about this framework and its attendant strengths and weaknesses.[38] This context is important in order to understand how far public policy responses have gone in the intervening years to appropriately tackle the problems facing British Asians.[39] In this concluding section of the chapter, we shall discuss the role and fit of public policy and also consider the question of race as the central unit of analysis and interpretation facing the policy community. In addition, it is imperative to ask whether a single race relations framework can any longer encompass the position of such increasingly diverse ethnic groups, to say nothing of the diversity of experience among Asians themselves. Three central lessons can be drawn at this stage.

First, there is the matter of sheer population numbers and their patterns of expansion and potential reconfiguration. Substantially-dated Census returns from the early 1990s place the total Asian population, from south, east and south-east Asian sources, at a little under two million or 3.5 percent of the greater UK population. These numbers constitute almost two-thirds of all ethnic minorities, with South Asians alone making up one-in-two of all minorities. However, it is clear that some striking patterns of integration, socioeconomic mobility and partici-pation characterize the experience of some Asians as opposed to others.[40] At the risk of slight over-generalization, it is now permissible to speak of Indians as following a rather distinctive path from other South Asians. Certainly this perspective commands weight in areas such as employment and education, though, significantly rather less so in the area of party political choice. In general, it is likely that these are the beginnings of class differentiation taking hold from within the Asian communities, thus rendering the notion of collective Asian interests as ever more improbable, as well as, implausible. That is not to say that there is no further steam in the idea of Asian politics as a major feature of the political landscape.[41] Rather, it is likely that Asians will take a more selective approach to the relevance of their ethnic origins in matters of attitudes and behavior. Public policy-makers might therefore conclude that a form of a la carte Asian ethnicity is at play at that; more seriously, this framework represents the best hope in preparing for cross-Asian responses in some areas alongside more targeted efforts in others.

Secondly, policy-makers have already begun to make necessary allowance for the capacity for self-help and self-determination. This is not a trivial thing to speak of, not least because of the continuing criticisms of paternalism that have been leveled by many grassroots activists against liberal-inspired public policy programs. In this respect, policy-makers have been sensitive to the charge that possibly not all policy measures ought to be driven by the need to root out discrimination in the delivery of public services. The area of health care is a good case in point. While a wealth of evidence exists to show that Asians do not necessarily receive a full or even reasonable share of publicly funded health care services, it is also striking that many of these groups' demands have been focused on their particular health needs. Issues of ethnic genetics and epimediology have played a part in this agenda. At the same time there has been a growing chorus calling for the focus and parameters of established health and social services to be recalibrated to better meet the needs of some Asian groups who traditionally are reluctant to search for external forms of assistance. Plainly there is the possibility that certain traditional values contribute to this reluctance. However, it is far from clear as to how far public services can be redrawn in order to cope with assumptions about ethnic groups who, in reality, may not operate at a group level (or least not operate effectively).[42] The challenge for public policy is to anticipate this possibility while avoiding a position of relying on assumptions that will often fail or disappoint or both.[43]

Finally, we must consider what role, if any, is to be played by

Asian politics in shaping the political landscape of public policy. Casting an eye upon racial politics in Britain at the end of the 1990s, it would appear that Asian participation in political life has developed, from a slow start, to relative maturity and strength. Electoral data confirms that in 1997 the registration and turnout rate of this large and varied group ranked alongside or even exceeded their white (and black) counterparts. Five Asians were elected in that year's general election, all but one representing seats in which large numbers of Asian voters were concentrated.[44] In local government, estimates from the mid-1990s revealed a fairly astonishing rate of improvement: that over 100 Asians had been elected outside London, achieving a position very close to parity. A similar picture emerged in several inner London boroughs. Lastly, due to the strong electoral alignment between Asians and the Labor Party, many independent commentators had begun by the late 1980s speculating, perhaps naïvely, about the potential benefits that might accrue from this relationship.[45] A generation previously, Asians had been few in number in electoral politics, rarely successful as candidates, often confined to the terrain of single-issue homeland politics, and generally undervalued by mainstream parties.

Three central factors underlie the story of political maturation. First, Britain's electoral arrangements have placed weight on electoral strength derived from sheer numbers of voters. For Asians, this has been an opportunity in the sense that the combined size of the three largest Asian groups— Indians, Pakistanis and Bangladeshis— had reached 1.5 million (according to the General Census and thus clearly a gross understatement of the true size by the late 1990s). One Asian media outlet in 1997 boasted of the possibility of some 36 Asian marginals, where Asian voter numbers were greater than defending majorities, possibly of some 36 Asian districts, where Asian voters outnumber defending majorities. While they may have talked up the actual figure, a number of candidates saw the importance of this potential voting bloc.

Second, the constellation of issues and interests that comprise mainstream parties' interest in Asian affairs has gradually shifted away from immigrant matters and toward the aspirations of British-born younger Asians (now a majority within the community).[46] The upshot of this has been that interest has gravitated to mainstream educational, employment and related policies in which it is increasingly conceded there is a legitimate Asian dimension. For instance, distinctive, though complementary, arrangements aimed at boosting recruitment in areas such as policing, civil service employment and higher education are now commonplace.

Lastly, the face of Asian political involvement has not been divorced from the group's participation in British economic life. In this regard, recent Labor Force Survey evidence has show wide divergence in the patterns of some groups of Asians as compared with others. However, in education, employment and business start-ups decisive headway has been achieved among Indian Asians, in particular. As part of a wider picture of advancement, such economic progress has been described by many as heralding a new era of weakening partisanship with the Labor Party. One of the most conspicuous barkless dogs, therefore, has been the singular failure of Labor's opponents to build a sizable following among Asians. Evidence from the 1997 contest indicated that the problem has not stemmed from lack of effort (there has been plenty), but rather from a failure to exploit a growing social class division in the political outlook of middle-class Asians compared with their more numerous working-class peers. The secret of Asian politics may thus lie in first understanding traditional British class politics.

Endnotes

[1] See I. Spencer, British Immigration Since 1939: *The Making of Multiracial Britain* (London: Routledge, 1997) for a recent and reliable overview of the main immigration trends since 1945.

[2] While readers are probably familiar with the broad immigration context of British race relations, it may be that there is less awareness of possible obstacles created by nomenclature and political custom. That is, the term 'Asian' is widely ascribed in Britain to what is in fact South Asian-origin groups (the largest of whom are Indians, Pakistanis, Bangladeshis and Sri Lankans). Therefore, the term is used rather casually in public debate as a form of practical shorthand to encompass immigration waves that were largely connected to Britain's imperial legacy in British India and, to a lesser degree, in colonial East Africa. The term has little meaning in relation to East or South-East Asian groups (typically the focus of North American understanding of the term Asian, though, interestingly, Chinese and Japanese communities are clearly elements of the ethnic mosaic found across Britain). Even less purpose is accorded to the term in describing much smaller groups from central or western Asian sources. The chapter will follow this British convention, but will additionally aid the comprehension of readers by adapting it slightly through the incorporation of the term South Asian (and its variants). Where a departure from this convention is required (for instance, in order to allude to East Asians), this will be clearly highlighted and explained.

[3] Estimates by David Owen (Centre for Research in Ethnic Relation, University of Warwick), cited in *The Runnymede Bulletin* (March 1997).

[4] Estimates based on Labour Force Survey data, 1995-97.

[5] M. Le Lohé, "Ethnic Minority Participation and Representation in The British Electoral System," in S. Saggar (Ed.), *Race and British Electoral Politics* (London, UCL Press, 1998).

[6] An early and thoughtful attempt to reflect on British integration strategies alongside U.S. experience in this field can be found in N. Glazer and K. Young (Eds.), *Ethnic Pluralism and Public Policy: Achieving Equality in the United States and Britain* (London: Heinemann, 1983).

[7] S. Saggar, (1993) "Re-examining the 1964-70 Labour Government's race relations strategy," *Contemporary Record*, 7: 253-81.

[8] The single Asian MP was joined by a second following the by-election in November 1991 in Langbargh. Although Ashok Kumar lost his seat in the subsequent general election, his success in 1991 broke an important barrier because of the miniscule number of ethnic minorities in his constituency. After a spell outside Westminster, Kumar was elected again in 1997 in a largely similar seat containing very few minority voters.

[9] Out of a total of 659 MPs (or a bit over one per cent of the House of Commons). The

overall size of the Commons has tended to vary from parliament to parliament as a consequence of constituency boundaries reviews though changes are often marginal. Following the 1997 election, five of the nine ethnic minority MPs were of South Asian ethnic origin.

[10] At the time of writing (October 1999) another Asian, Shilesh Vara, has been selected to fight as the official Conservative candidate in a Labour marginal (Northamptonshire South). Given the slim Labour majority in this seat, his chances of becoming the second Asian Tory MP appear to be fairly attractive.

[11] M. Le Lohé, "Ethnic Minority Participation and Representation in The British Electoral System," in S. Saggar (Ed.), *Race and British Electoral Politics* (London: UCL Press, 1998).

[12] D. Owen & A. Green, "Labour Market Experience and Change Among Ethnic Groups in Great Britain," *New Community*, 19: 17-29, 1992.

[13] T. Modood and R. Berthoud, *Ethnic Minorities in Britain: Diversity and Disadvantage* (London: Policy Studies Institute, 1997).

[14] D. Coleman and J. Salt (Eds.), *Ethnicity in the 1991 Census: Demographic Characteristics of the Ethnic Minority Populations* Volume 1, (London: Office of Population, Censuses and Surveys, 1996).

[15] Y. Tandon, *The New Position of East Africa's Asians: Problems of a Displaced Minority*, Report No.16 (London: Minority Rights Group, 1973).

[16] A similar point might also be made in relation to aspects of the work of W.J. Wilson in the United States.

[17] Labour Force Survey, 1994.

[18] Labour Force Survey, 1994.

[19] London Training and Enterprise Council Survey, 1997.

[20] Quoted in *Social Focus on Ethnic Minorities*, Office for National Statistics, 1996.

[21] A. Heath and D. McMahon, "Education and Occupational Attainment: the Impact of Ethnic Origins," in V. Karn (Ed), *Ethnicity in the 1991 Census*, Volume 4 (London: HMSO, 1997).

[22] *Asian Poll 1991*, unpublished data set JN99245, (Richmond: The Harris Research Center, 1991).

[23] British Election Study, 1997.

[24] K. Hahlo, *Communities, Networks and Ethnic Politics* (Aldershot: Ashgate, 1998), pp.1-4.

[25] See especially P. Werbner, "Black and Ethnic Leaderships in Britain: a Theoretical Overview", in P. Werbner and M. Anwar (Eds.), *Black and Ethnic Leaderships: The Cultural Dimensions of Political Action* (London: Routledge, 1991).

[26] Although there is sometimes worrying confusion between group numbers on one hand and registered voters on the other, to say nothing of the need to qualify observations on the basis of differential turnout rates.

[27] For illustrations of this more skeptical position, see the following: D. Studlar, "Non-White Policy Preferences, Political Participation and the Political Agenda in Britain', in Z. Layton-Henry and P. Rich (Eds.), *Race, Government and Politics in Britain* (London, Macmillan, 1986); A. Messina, *Race and Party Competition in Britain* (Oxford: Clarendon Press, 1989); and D. Studlar and Z. Layton-Henry, "Non-white Access to the Political Agenda in Britain," *Policy Studies Review*, 9: 273-93, 1990.

[28] S. Saggar, *The General Election 1997: Ethnic Minorities and Electoral Politics* (London: Commission for Racial Equality, 1997).

[29] BBC/Gallup, General election exit poll, unpublished data set, ESRC data archive, 1987.

[30] Quoted in K. Amin and R. Richardson, *Politics for All: Equality, Culture and the General Election 1992*. (London, Runnymede Trust, 1992).

[31] S. Saggar and A. Geddes, "Positive and Negative Racialisation: Mapping the Institutional Context for Debates Over Ethnic Minority Political Representation, Candidate Selection and Performance," *The Journal of Migration and Ethnic Studies*, 2000-forthcoming.

[32] A. Heath et al, *Understanding Political Change: The British Voter 1964-87* (Oxford: Pergamon Press, 1991), p.113.

[33] See A. Messina, "Ethnic minorities and the British party system in the 1990s and beyond," in S. Saggar (Ed.), *Race and British Electoral Politics* (London, UCL Press, 1998).

[34] V. Robinson, "Roots to mobility: the social mobility of Britain's 'black' population 1971-87," *Ethnic and Racial Studies*, 13: 274-86, 1990.

[35] S. Saggar, "A Late, Though Not Lost, Opportunity: Ethnic Minority Electors, Party Strategy and the Conservative Party," *The Political Quarterly*, 69: 148-59.

[36] British Election Study, 1997.

[37] 1997 BES - merged file (weighted data). See also: S. Saggar, *Race and Representation* (Basingstoke, Macmillan Press: forthcoming-2000), esp. ch. 6.

[38] S. Saggar, *Race and Public Policy* (Aldershot: Avebury, 1991); EJB et al, *Color and Citizenship* (London: Oxford University Press/Institute of Race Relations, 1969); B.

Parekh et al (Eds.), *The Politics of Race Relations* (London: Routledge, 1998); Z. Layton-Henry, *The Politics of Immigration* (Oxford: Blackwell, 1992); and S. Saggar, "Re-examining the 1964-70 Labour Government's Race Relations Strategy," *Contemporary Record*, 7: 253-81, 1993.

[39] S. Saggar, "Civic Values, Participation and British South Asians," paper presented at a conference on *An Asian Agenda for Public Policy?* the King George VI & Queen Elizabeth Foundation at St Catharine's, Cumberland Lodge, Windsor, April 1997.

[40] J. Brown and R. Foot (Eds.), *Migration: The Asian Experience* (London: St Martins Press, 1994).

[41] S. Saggar, "Asian Politics in Britain," in J. Ramsden (Ed.), *The Oxford Companion to Twentieth Century British Politics* (Oxford: Oxford University Press, forthcoming).

[42] K. Atkin and R. Rollings, "Looking After Their Own: Family Care-Giving among Asians and Afro-Caribbean communities," in W. Ahmed and K. Atkin (Eds.), *'Race' and Community Care* (Birmingham: Open University Press, 1996).

[43] E. Anionwu, "Sickle Cell and Thalassaemia: Community Experiences and Official Response," in W. Ahmed and K. Atkin (Eds.), *'Race' and Community Care* (Birmingham: Open University Press, 1996).

[44] Kumar, mentioned previously, was successfully elected to the north east constituency of Middlesborough South and Cleveland East (containing less than 2 percent who were ethnic minorities).

[45] S. Bald, "The South Asian Presence in British Electoral Politics," *New Community*, 15: 537-48, 1989.

[46] R. Ballard (Ed.), Desh Pardesh, *The South Asian Presence in Britain* (London: Hurst, 1994).

Asians and Race Relations in Australia

Christine Inglis

More than either the United States or the United Kingdom, Australia's demography identifies it as a nation of immigrants. The continuing significance of immigration to Australia is indicated by the almost one quarter of its population who, in 1996, were born overseas. When the children of these immigrants are included, more than 40 percent of the population are of recent immigrant stock, a level equaled in few other nations. Although the vast majority of the contemporary Asian population has arrived in Australia since the 1970s and their numbers doubled between 1986 and 1996, they cannot be viewed simply as the latest wave of new immigrants. Asians have always been an important component in Australia's population and in the national psyche. This chapter begins by highlighting their central role in the nineteenth century development of the Australian national identity. A century later, substantial Asian immigration to Australia coincides with another watershed, as changes in Australia, Asia and beyond raises question about the nature of Australian identity and institutions. Without this historical background, it is difficult to appreciate the personal or institutional features of Australian race relations as they impinge on various groups of Asian origin[1]. The main areas of contemporary inter-group relations addressed in this chapter concern the economic participation of Asian groups and issues of discrimination and racism, intermarriage, citizenship and identity. The chapter then concludes with some reflections on how policy responses and options shifted from assimilation to multiculturalism.

Consolidation of Australian Identity

From the earliest days of British settlement in 1788, immigration has been central to the growth and economic development of Australia. After the end of convict transportation, alternative overseas sources of labor were sought. Despite plans to introduce contract-laborers from Asia, few arrived before the discovery of gold in the 1850s, making the Australian colonies a far more attractive destination to voluntary immigrants, including those from China. Like many other miners, the Chinese were predominantly single, male fortune hunters who viewed their stay in the Australian colonies as a temporary sojourn. Estimates of the numbers involved are imprecise, but at certain points the Chinese were recorded as being 10 percent of the population of the rich Victorian gold fields. Whereas prior to the gold rushes, the Chinese were viewed as a potentially valuable source of migrant labor by farmers, their presence on the gold fields soon generated hostility and even physical violence from other miners who felt their interests threatened by the Chinese presence. A range of administrative and legal measures directed against the Chinese or Asiatics were introduced to restrict entry to the colonies and access to the gold fields (Price 1974). The "New Gold Mountain" (the Chinese name for Australia) was kind to only a few Chinese, many of whom could not afford to return home.

After the gold rushes, these Chinese turned to employment in agriculture. In the cities, they played important roles in the agri-food industry, ranging from truck farmers to retailers and importers and financiers of bananas and other agricultural produce. Another niche was furniture making where they roused the ire of the trade union movement which, perceiving them as a threatening source of cheap labor, campaigned for further restrictive legislation. There were few Chinese women in Australia, so the Chinese who established families in Australia usually married European or Aboriginal women. The economic hostility to the Chinese took on moral overtones with their depiction in the popular press as opium-smoking degenerate destroyers of white women (Yu 1995).

In contrast to the Chinese, other groups of Asian immigrants attracted less hostility. They did not compete with the European population, being fewer in number and their economic niches often located in remote areas. By 1891, the Asian numbered 46,600 or 1.5 percent of the total population, and 4.6 percent of the foreign-born population, 80 percent of whom were born in the United Kingdom. The 36,000 Chinese were the second largest foreign-born group after the British. When the six British colonies federated in 1901 to form the new nation of Australia, the numbers in the Asian population had changed little, but the growth in the Australian-born population meant they were now only 1.2 percent of the total population. Although the Chinese comprised 5.4 percent of the foreign-born population, unlike many other sojourners, they had not left during the economic depression of the 1890s. Within the Asian population there were, however, substantial changes. While the 29,900 Chinese were still the largest group, there had been an increase in the population born in British India to 7,600. Many Indians were Muslims from the Northwest Frontier who had been brought to Australia to look after the camel trains, which provided the main means of transport in the desert interior. The Japanese population had also increased eight-fold from 420 to 3,593. This growth followed the 1898 establishment of a Japanese consulate in northern Queensland and Japanese involvement in the sugar cane plantations and the pearling industry (Meaney 1999). The other major "Asian" group identified in the census was the 1,500 Syrian born. The majority of the Syrians were Maronite Christians, who occupied a niche as travelling traders. Unlike other Asian groups, their more permanent pattern of settlement was signaled by the presence of families.

The emerging working-class nationalism, closely linked to the trade union movement, emphasized assimilation as necessary for the maintenance of the then highest standard of living internationally. Asia was, in this scenario, a threat to Australian survival and Asians were viewed as inherently inassimilable, unwanted cheap labor. During the latter part of the nineteenth century, the Australian colonies built the "Great White Walls" (Price 1974) designed to protect the settler communities from Asian incursions. Similar legislation was also enacted in both western Canada and the USA. What was distinctive in the Australian case was the difficulties of the colonies in coordinating the six sets of separate legislation which constituted the walls. This difficulty was an important impetus towards the federation of the colonies into a nation.

Upon federation in 1901, one of the first acts of the new Commonwealth parliament was to introduce the Immigration Restriction Act, which provided the legal basis for the White Australia Policy to ensure, as one prominent magazine puts it, "Australia for the White Man." The egalitarian workers' paradise was one where full citizenship rights were henceforth restricted to Europeans with access to naturalization denied to foreign-born non-Europeans. The obvious economic benefits to Europeans were hidden behind rhetoric depicting Asians as essentially incapable of attaining the cultural attributes necessary for full and proper participation in Australian society. International diplomatic pressures and economic considerations, nevertheless, played a major part in molding the precise form and operation of the Policy. Despite the intention of closing the door to non-European immigration, exemptions allowed temporary entrance to new Asian arrivals (Willard 1923; Yarwood 1964; Palfreeman 1967; London 1970; Price 1974). Chinese businesses were able to import Chinese staffs, and Japanese came to work in the pearling industry. As an ally in World War I, Japan successfully sought special treatment for its citizens while the British Indian colonial administration monitored the experiences of Indians.

Despite these opportunities for limited entry, the Asian population declined in numbers. The growth of locally born Asians did not compensate for the death and departures of the older men. The Japanese were very much a transitory group of employees, compared with the Chinese, Indians, and Syrians. The nadir for the Chinese community was 1947 when the 9,144 Chinese and 2,950 part-Chinese comprised less than 0.2 percent of the total population. The next most significant Asian groups were the Indians, 2,480 as well as 418 part-Indians, and the Syrians, who numbered 1,675 with a further 223 part-Syrians. In contrast to foreign-born Asians, the Australian-born of Asian ancestry were Australian citizens but, nevertheless, experienced a diverse set of discriminatory behavior affecting employment, schooling and other areas of social life.

Despite their small numbers, during the first half of the twentieth century, the Asians were an important element of Australian diversity. In 1933, Chinese was the third most common language, after English and Italian, while China was the third most important non-British or Australian birthplace, after Italy and Germany. With assimilation dominating policies and attitudes toward immigrants (as well as Aborigines), the locally born Asians actively sought to acculturate. Few of the younger Chinese were literate in Chinese. Many adopted Christianity and were entering middle-class professions and occupations. However, full social assimilation was largely beyond their reach, although the economic discrimination against them had declined. Even if the more bizarre stereotypes and images of mysterious and enigmatic orientals or "celestials" had lost their currency, the main contact which most families had with the Asian population was that with the Chinese truck farmers selling their produce from door to door.

Mass Migration, Australia's Changing Relationship with Asia and Multiculturalism

The Second World War was an important watershed in Australia's international relations. It confirmed many of the popular concerns about Australia's vulnerability to threats from Asian powers seeking to acquire Australia's riches. The need to build the population from a base of only 7 million became an important priority for future security and for the restructuring and growth of the economy towards industrial self-reliance. Mass immigration to increase the population by 1 percent annually was the ambitious strategy adopted to achieve these objectives. Australians were assured that this migration would not change Australian society since the emphasis would be on attracting British immigrants. When this proved impossible, the search for immigrants extended from East European refugees to include immigrants from northern Europe and then the Mediterranean countries and, by the late 1960s, also Middle Eastern countries such as Turkey and Lebanon.

At the same time, Asian decolonization was changing Australia's geo-political environment. A foreign policy based on defense was complemented by a more active engagement in regional political and economic developments. As important was Australia's participation in the Colombo Plan, which brought substantial numbers of Asian students to study in Australia. Many of these students remained in, or subsequently returned to, Australia to live. There were also gradual changes in the White Australia Policy, allowing the entry of the non-European spouses of Australian citizens, the highly skilled, and part Europeans, including Anglo-Indians, and Ceylonese Burghers. Barriers to the naturalization of non-European immigrants were also removed. These continued modifications to the White Australia Policy were driven by a desire to avoid foreign diplomatic criticism (London 1970; Meaney 1999).

In 1973, soon after it was elected as the national government, the Australian Labor Party, which previously strongly supported White Australia, announced its replacement by a new non-discriminatory immigration policy which did not exclude on the basis of race, ethnicity or religion. Instead, the government developed a selection system to accommodate those admitted for refugee or humanitarian reasons, those coming on the basis of family reunion and, finally, those with specific economic resources or skills. The relative weighting attached to each of these components have changed from time to time in response to inter-national, domestic, and socio-political considerations. Recently, the distinction between permanent and temporary immigrants has blurred as policies now allow longer temporary entry periods for the highly skilled managers and professional workers who are part of the changing labor force associated with globalization (Inglis 1999b).[2]

Existing Asian communities had little influence on these changes in immigration policy which have, however, resulted in substantial increases in the Asian population. From the 1950s, there was a slow but steady growth in the numbers of Asian immigrants, especially from Southeast Asian countries such as Malaysia and Singapore. After the formal ending of the White Australia Policy in 1973, the first major Asian groups to arrive were refugees from East Timor, followed by Indo-Chinese, after the end of the war in Vietnam. Subsequently, it was Asian groups who took most advantage of further changes in immigration policies which favored family reunions and which were initiated in response to pressure from European immigrant groups. However, economic developments in Europe meant few Europeans were interested in emigrating to Australia, even to join their relatives. By the middle of the 1980s, it was evident that those members of the new Asian middle-class were most interested in and able to take advantage of the opportunities for immigration by highly skilled and wealthy business entrepreneurs. Well-educated, often in English in institutions with qualifications recognized in Australia, they became a significant part of the

Table 1. Australian Settler Arrivals by Region and Selected Birthplaces 1985-86 to 1997-98

Birthplace	1985/86	1986/87	1987/88	1988/89	1989/90	1990/91
	%	%	%	%	%	%
Oceania	16.9	14.6	17.8	19.3	12.6	9.0
New Zealand	14.3	12.0	14.6	16.2	9.2	6.1
Europe & the Former USSR	30.3	32.2	30.4	29.2	31.7	26.6
United Kingdom	15.9	17.8	17.1	16.5	19.4	17.0
Middle East & North Africa	7.0	6.6	7.0	5.5	4.7	5.9
South East Asia	19.4	20.3	20.6	21.8	23.3	24.2
Brunei	0.1	0.1	0.2	0.2	0.1	0.1
Burma/Myanmar	0.2	0.2	0.2	0.2	0.1	0.1
Cambodia	0.9	1.2	0.9	1.0	0.3	0.2
Indonesia	1.2	1.2	0.9	1.0	1.0	0.9
Laos	0.6	0.5	0.5	0.3	0.2	0.3
Malaysia	2.5	3.5	4.4	5.3	5.3	4.7
Philippines	4.5	5.7	7.3	6.3	5.0	5.2
Singapore	0.9	1.3	1.4	1.3	1.3	1.0
Thailand	0.8	0.8	0.6	0.7	0.7	0.8
Vietnam	7.8	5.8	4.2	5.5	9.2	10.9
Other	0.6	0.5	0.0	0.0	0.0	0.0
North East Asia	8.9	7.9	8.8	10.9	13.5	18.2
China excl. HK & Taiwan	3.4	2.4	2.3	2.6	2.5	2.7
Hong Kong	3.4	3.0	3.9	5.0	6.6	11.1
Japan	0.3	0.3	0.5	0.6	0.5	0.5
Korea	1.3	1.4	1.3	1.1	1.1	0.8
Macau	0.1	0.1	0.1	0.1	0.2	0.2
Mongolia	0.0	0.0	0.0	0.0	0.0	0.0
Taiwan	0.4	0.7	0.8	1.4	2.5	2.9
Southern Asia	4.9	5.5	4.7	4.8	5.0	7.7
Afghanistan	0.4	0.5	0.2	0.2	0.2	0.3
Bangladesh	0.1	0.1	0.1	0.2	0.1	0.3
Bhutan	0.0	0.0	0.0	0.0	0.0	0.0
India	2.3	2.2	2.1	2.1	2.5	4.2
Maldives	0.0	0.0	0.0	0.0	0.0	0.0
Nepal	0.0	0.0	0.0	0.0	0.0	0.0
Pakistan	0.3	0.3	0.3	0.3	0.3	0.2
Sri Lanka	1.8	2.5	2.0	2.0	1.9	2.7
Northern America	2.9	2.5	2.1	2.1	2.5	2.3
S & Central Amer & Caribbean	4.4	3.8	3.2	3.0	3.4	3.1
Africa excl. North Africa	5.4	6.6	5.3	3.3	3.3	3.1
South Africa	3.4	4.1	2.6	2.1	2.0	1.7
Not Stated	0.0	0.0	0.0	0.0	0.0	0.0
Total All Countries	100.0	100.0	100.0	100.0	100.0	100.0

Source: DIMA 1998 *Settler Arrivals 1997-98*, DIMA 1997 *Settler Arrivals 1995-96*

1991/92	1992/93	1993/94	1994/95	1995/96	1996/97	1997/98	1985/86-1997/98
%	%	%	%	%	%	%	% Total Arrivals
9.6	12.5	14.6	15.5	16.4	19.5	23.0	15.4
6.7	8.8	11.1	12.0	12.4	15.2	19.0	12.1
25.0	29.1	29.3	29.2	26.7	25.9	25.2	28.7
13.5	12.4	12.8	12.2	11.4	11.3	11.9	15.0
6.5	7.1	6.9	8.2	7.7	7.3	7.5	6.6
20.8	18.1	20.4	17.0	13.3	13.2	12.5	19.3
0.1	0.1	0.1	0.0	0.0	0.1	0.0	0.1
0.2	0.2	0.7	0.7	0.5	0.5	0.2	0.3
0.3	0.4	1.3	1.6	1.4	0.9	0.7	0.8
1.1	1.6	0.9	1.2	1.8	2.0	2.5	1.3
0.2	0.1	0.1	0.1	0.1	0.1	0.0	0.3
2.9	2.0	1.8	1.3	1.1	1.2	1.2	3.2
5.5	4.9	6.0	4.7	3.3	3.3	3.6	5.2
0.8	0.6	0.7	0.7	0.8	1.1	0.9	1.1
0.8	0.9	1.1	0.9	0.7	0.7	0.4	0.8
8.9	7.4	7.8	5.8	3.6	3.5	3.0	6.5
0.0	0.0	0.0	0.0	0.0	0.0	0.0	0.1
20.0	16.4	11.5	11.3	18.8	17.6	13.2	13.4
3.2	4.0	3.9	4.2	11.3	9.1	5.6	4.1
12.0	8.5	4.8	4.7	4.4	4.5	4.1	5.9
0.5	0.6	0.6	0.6	0.6	0.6	0.7	0.5
1.1	1.2	1.0	0.8	0.7	0.8	0.8	1.1
0.2	0.2	0.2	0.1	0.1	0.1	0.1	0.1
0.0	0.0	0.0	0.0	0.0	0.0	0.0	0.0
3.0	1.9	1.1	0.9	1.7	2.5	2.0	1.7
9.9	8.7	7.9	8.7	7.8	6.5	6.9	6.6
0.9	1.0	0.9	0.4	0.6	0.4	0.7	0.5
0.6	0.5	0.4	0.8	0.8	0.6	0.4	0.3
0.0	0.0	0.0	0.0	0.0	0.0	0.0	0.0
5.2	4.7	3.8	4.5	3.7	3.1	3.6	3.3
0.0	0.0	0.0	0.0	0.0	0.0	0.0	0.0
0.1	0.1	0.0	0.1	0.1	0.1	0.0	0.0
0.6	0.5	0.6	0.7	0.6	0.7	0.6	0.4
2.6	2.1	2.1	2.2	2.0	1.7	1.6	2.1
2.4	2.6	2.9	2.9	2.5	2.8	2.6	2.5
3.1	2.0	1.7	1.5	1.3	1.2	0.9	2.7
2.6	3.4	4.7	5.6	5.5	5.8	8.1	4.7
1.2	1.3	2.4	3.2	3.2	3.7	5.5	2.7
0.0	0.1	0.1	0.0	0.1	0.1	0.0	0.0
100.0	100.0	100.0	100.0	100.0	100.0	100.0	100.0

flow of immigrants. As Table 1 shows, in the 12 years from 1985/86 to 1997/98, 40 percent of all immigrants entering Australia came from Southeast (19.3 percent), East (13.4 percent) and South (6.6 percent) Asia. Vietnam, Hong Kong, the Philippines, China, India and Malaysia have been especially important source countries (Inglis 1999a, p.87).

The numbers of Asians increased significantly since the 1960s, when the majority of immigrants were still from the United Kingdom and Europe. With the exception of many refugees, they are very different in class background as compared to the earlier nineteenth century Asian immigrants and the more recent European arrivals. The majority is now from middle-class backgrounds. In 1997-98, 58.1 percent of all immigrants who had been employed prior to arrival had worked in professional and highly skilled occupations. In these groups, over half of the managers and administrators were Asian-born and nearly 40 percent of the professionals were Asian-born (Inglis 1999b, pp.48-9). The motivation for many of these Asian immigrants to immigrate to Australia is more complex than simple economic gain. After recent major recessions, Australia no longer appears as the New Gold Mountain for Asians. Instead, other aspects of the "good life" attract these middle-class immigrants. For some, it is related to political uncertainties and the lack of freedom in their homelands. For others, it is the lure associated with the Australian physical environment such as the weather and the lower levels of pollution and overcrowding. The presence of relatives and educational opportunities for children are other important incentives for many middle-class immigrants.

This growth in Asian immigration coincides with the waning of assimilation as the guiding goal for immigrants. This policy change in the 1970s resulted from a recognition of the failure of assimilation to take place and a need for policies designed to address the disadvantages experienced by large numbers of non-English-speaking background (NESB) immigrants. Under assimilation, the onus was on the immigrant to adapt to the existing society and its institutions, thereby removing any responsibility from the receiving society to make special policy provisions for addressing immigrant disadvantages. Despite the brief adoption of a policy of integration in the 1960s which envisaged the coexistence of public assimilation with private cultural maintenance, a wide cross-section of the community, including teachers, health workers and others working with NESB immigrants as well as European community groups, demanded a more interventionist policy in addressing disadvantages and cultural diversity. This demand grew during the 1970s. The outcome of these demands was the adoption of multiculturalism as the guiding principle for future policies addressing inter-ethnic relations.

In Australia, multiculturalism has significantly different connotations than in the United States. Not only is it the official government policy, rather than simply a policy of "resistance," it also explicitly addresses the cultural and the economic dimensions of difference which, as Wieviorka noted (Wieviorka 1998), is a major departure from the United States' disjuncture between the economic and the cultural policies, evident in the debate between proponents of affirmative action and those of multiculturalism. From its origins in the early 1970s under the Labor government to its institutionalization in 1978 under the conservative Fraser government, multiculturalism has been an evolving policy which varies in the emphasis given to cultural maintenance or addressing disadvantage (to the extent that the two objectives can be separated). Its scope has also extended, from a policy to address the needs of NESB immigrants, to include their children and, since 1989, to be a policy benefiting all Australians through the promotion of diversity and the reduction of social disadvantage[3]. Under multiculturalism, social cohesion and harmony arise from an acceptance of a non-socially divisive diversity, in contrast to assimilation, where these outcomes are seen as resulting from a homogeneous population. Certainly, after two decades, the attempted blending of the two dimensions of social justice and cultural maintenance has been remarkably successful in ensuring the incorporation of diverse groups into a previously homogenous society in an equitable and surprisingly non-contentious manner.

The growth in Asian immigration coincides also with increases in Australian involvement in the Asian region. In 1997, after the onset of the Asian economic crisis, 50 percent of Australia's export market was still with Asia, which remains the major source of tourists and fee-paying international students for the highly lucrative tourism and educational industries. Australia's political and economic reorientation away from Europe and towards Asia coincides with government-initiated domestic-economic restructuring intending to allow the Australian economy to adapt better to the effects of globalization. The macro- and micro-economic changes began in the 1980s with the intention of replacing reliance on agriculture, mining, and a highly protected manufacturing industry with a shift to a service-oriented, knowledge-based economy employing a highly-skilled workforce. A departure from the historical commitment to egalitarianism through state intervention has been another especially significant change occurring over the same period. Since 1996, the conservative Liberal-National Party government has placed even greater emphasis on dismantling existing economic institutions, including those of the welfare state.

For many Australians, including British and European immigrants, economic and political transformations have been disconcerting, especially since, for nearly two decades until the mid 1990s, they were associated with levels of unemployment (up to 12 and 13 percent) unknown since the 1930s Depression. Economic restructuring has involved the collapse of many industries and jobs, while principles of economic rationality and "user pays" have had particularly negative effects on the poor and rural populations. Traditional government strategies, of reducing immigration in periods of recession, have been unable to prevent considerable opposition to immigration. Economic opponents have combined with environmental groups to argue that Australia's fragile eco-system cannot support a large population. Some of these groups have individuals who are concerned with extending physical conservation to "social and cultural conservation." They argue that multicultural policies threaten Australian society, especially when these policies involve non-British groups, particularly Asian groups. The most recent in a series of (anti-) "Asian Immigration Debates,"[4] which began in 1984 and recurred in 1988, was linked to the election of two "Independent" candidates in the 1996 Federal election. One of these Members of Parliament, Pauline Hanson, subsequently went on to found her own One Nation party, which won 10 seats in the 1998 Queensland state elections. This success for the party's extremely populist program did not continue in the 1998 federal elections nor in the 1999 NSW state elections. The emergence of One Nation and the earlier debates highlight how the contemporary increase in Asian immigration has again become a major political issue, because it coincides with an economic, political and social change, which vocal groups in the population correlate, not altogether inaccurately, with a realignment in the Anglo-Celtic institutions underpinning the foundation of Australian national identity. What distinguishes the present hostility from that of the last century is that now it serves not to unify the nation but, rather, to highlight major divisions within the society between the urban and rural, young and old, the more highly educated and those less skilled, the more cosmopolitan and internationally oriented and those with a narrow view of Australian society. The next section considers how the Asians, whose immigration has become so contentious, actually experience life in Australia.

Asians in Contemporary Australia

By 1996, almost 5 percent of the Australian population

(856,144), more than since the height of the nineteenth century gold rushes, had been born in Asia (2.6 percent in South East Asia, 1.4 percent in North East Asia and 0.8 percent in Southern Asia). The major Asian birthplaces were Vietnam, China, the Philippines, India, Malaysia, Hong Kong, Sri Lanka, Indonesia and Singapore (see Table 2). In only a decade, there had been a doubling of the Asian-born population. In 1986, the 413,158 Asian-born people made up only 2.65 percent while 2 percent of the population, including those born in Australia, actually described themselves as belonging to one of the four major Asian ancestry groups represented in Australia, including Chinese (1.1 percent) , Vietnamese (0.4 percent), Indian (0.3 percent) and Filipino (0.2 percent). The doubling of the Asian population, between 1986 and 1996, was not spread evenly across Australia. The majority were concentrated in New South Wales, and, in particular, Sydney, where they comprised 6.3 percent of the population, compared with 5.4 percent in Victoria and 5.0 percent in Western Australia. The latter's proximity to South East Asia attracted many settlers from there and South Asia. The concentration of the Asian born in Sydney reflects, not only the role of social networks, but also how Sydney's aspiration to global city status ensures that it is perceived as the center, with the strongest economy and the best opportunity of providing employment for newly arrived immigrants.

Within Australian cities, ethnic concentrations have never acquired the reputation of being closed and exclusive quarters, as sometimes occurs in North American or European cities. Ethnic concentrations in excess of 5 percent are sufficient to cause comments while concentrations in excess of 10 percent are extremely rare. Using these criteria as a guideline, there are few substantial Asian concentrations in Australian cities. In 1996, the only Asian-born groups, which accounted for more than 5 percent in any area, were either from China or Vietnam. The Chinese comprised 5 percent or more of the population in five Sydney local government areas, with the largest concentration being 8.5

TABLE 2. SELECTED BIRTHPLACES OF THE AUSTRALIAN POPULATION, 1996

	,000	%
Australia	13,227,776	73.9
New Zealand	291,388	1.6
Oceania	378,112	2.1
United Kingdom	1,072,562	6.0
Europe & the Former USSR	2,217,009	12.4
Middle East & North Africa	192,642	1.1
Indonesia	44,175	0.2
Malaysia	76,255	0.4
Philippines	92,949	0.5
Singapore	29,490	0.2
Vietnam	151,053	0.8
South East Asia	456,460	2.6
China excl. HK & Taiwan	111,009	0.6
Hong Kong	68,430	0.4
North East Asia	254,186	1.4
India	77,551	0.4
Sri Lanka	46,984	0.3
Southern Asia	145,498	0.8
Northern America	75,022	0.4
S. & Central Amer. & Caribbean	75,539	0.4
South Africa	55,755	0.3
Africa excl. N. Africa	107,417	0.6
Other	762,757	4.3
Total	17,892,418	100.0

Source: 1996 Census Tables B05 & B06

percent in an area with an extremely ethnically diverse population. Much greater concentration was evident among the Vietnamese, who constituted more than 5 percent of the population in 13 different suburbs and local government areas. The largest concentrations were 24.6 percent and 16.1 percent in adjacent Brisbane suburbs where the refugees first settled on their arrival in Brisbane. Not all concentrations of Asian groups are in economically disadvantaged areas. In contrast with earlier groups of non-English speaking immigrants, wealthier, more highly educated Asians from countries such as Hong Kong, Taiwan, Malaysia and Singapore now live in middle-class suburbs.

The presence of Asian immigrants in wealthier areas of the cities is indicative of the economic resources possessed by significant segments of the Asian population. This was already evident in the 1986 census data showing that certain Asian ancestry and birthplace groups were actually faring extremely well on various economic measures (Inglis and Wu 1992). In particular, Indian men and women were especially likely to be employed in professional and managerial positions, with incomes well above the average for other groups of immigrants. Among the Chinese, there were major variations related to their birthplace (Inglis and Wu 1992; Jones 1992). Success was far less evident among the Indo-Chinese and other Asian refugee groups, who experienced high levels of unemployment, low incomes and were also typically concentrated in less skilled positions (Inglis and Wu 1992).

This pattern, old overall success coupled with internal diversity, was still evident a decade later in 1996. As Table 3 shows, employed immigrants from many Asian countries were substantially overrepresented in prestigious managerial and professional occupations. This pattern was repeated, though to a lesser extent, in the occupations of women and those who had arrived within the previous five years. Those born in Indochinese countries were least likely to be employed in these occupations, in which their participation was similar to that of immigrants

rom southern European countries such as Italy, Greece and the former
Yugoslavia. Consistent with these occupational patterns are variations in
he income of Asians, which shows that those from Indochina report the
owest incomes while those from India, Sri Lanka and Malaysia have
ncomes exceeding those of the British and Australian-born (Jayasuriya
and Kee 1999, 62). The picture of relative economic disadvantage of the
Vietnamese and Cambodians is continued in their elevated levels of
unemployment (Jayasuriya and Kee 1999, 66). Commenting on the
economic experiences of Australian-Asians, two recent authors have
concluded that "compared with earlier migrants and despite their
diversity, Asian migrants are reasonably well integrated as members of
Australian society"(Jayasuriya and Kee 1999,69).

TABLE 3. PERCENTAGE OF MANAGERS, PROFESSIONALS AND PARA-PROFESSIONALS IN
THE WORKFORCE BY SELECTED BIRTHPLACES, AUSTRALIA 1996

Birthplace	Total	Recent Arrivals 1992-96	Females	Female Recent Arrivals 1992-96
	%	%	%	%
Malaysia	58.7	45.2	53.9	38.8
Hong Kong	53.9	53.5	35.5	41.8
Singapore	51.7	48.4	47.7	40.9
Taiwan	50.9	52.0	44.2	43.0
India	46.2	41.5	38.5	35.8
Sri Lanka	43.0	32.3	33.2	24.8
Korea	37.5	31.4	33.9	22.2
China	34.6	29.5	29.4	21.2
Indonesia	30.9	18.2	28.4	16.9
Philippines	24.3	16.6	24.1	16.2
Vietnam	22.9	8.8	21.4	7.4
Cambodia	18.4	7.9	17.7	5.1
South African	52.2	57.5	45.5	49.0
United Kingdom	42.6	49.6	39.3	45.5
N & W Europe	42.5	55.5	39.8	45.9
Australia	37.7	n.a.	36.3	n.a.
Southern Europe	26.0	19.8	23.6	20.2

Source: 1996 Census

The variations in occupation, income, and employment status among the Asians highlight the complexity of their labor market experiences. The inevitable question is whether this diversity can be explained by variations in their human resources or by the existence of discrimination in the labor market. Appropriate educational qualifications are necessary for many high status jobs in the growth sectors of the modern economy. As a longitudinal survey of recent migrant arrivals shows, many Asians do have tertiary qualifications although there are wide variations, ranging from Malaysians, 60.1 percent of whom have tertiary qualifications, to Vietnamese, only 2.4 percent of whom have tertiary degrees (Shu 1996). But educational levels alone cannot ensure economic success, since knowledge of English and the recognition of credentials obtained overseas are critical to occupational outcomes in Australia. While the vast majority of immigrants from India, Malaysia, the Philippines, Singapore and Sri Lanka have native speaker levels of competency, this applies somewhat less to those born in Hong Kong, Korea, Taiwan and, less still, to those from China, Cambodia, and Vietnam[5]. Except for those born in the Philippines, competency in English is highest amongst those from former British Commonwealth countries, whose educational qualifications are more likely to be recognized in Australia than qualifications from other countries. Similarly, it is these groups of Asian immigrants who have been particularly successful in gaining employment in professional and managerial occupations (see Table 3).

The recognition of qualifications gained overseas is an important determinant of the job outcomes of immigrants. For those Asian immigrants who have had their tertiary training and education in Australia, the recognition of their qualifications is not an issue. Nor is it an issue for immigrants trained in many British Commonwealth countries such as Singapore or Hong Kong, whose degrees and qualifications are recognized after little or no additional examination. Other immigrants, including many of those from Asian countries, experience considerable difficulties in gaining recognition for their qualifications, often requiring considerable retraining and testing to meet the demands of professional accreditation bodies. Whether these demands are appropriate, in view of existing Australian levels of training and qualifications, or are an attempt by regulatory bodies to discriminate against those with overseas training, is often a cause of considerable debate among skilled workers, such as doctors who cannot practice without Australian registration. Discrimination against the overseas trained can also extend to their experience in seeking employment and promotion. A longitudinal study, of immigrants who arrived between June and December 1991, concluded that the achievement of appropriate employment remains a major problem for immigrants in the early years of settlement. However, there was considerable variation among arrivals with the skilled immigrants having lower rates of unemployment than skilled workers despite the continuing problems of skill-recognition. The study also identified the importance of country of birth. Not only did those from English speaking countries, such as the United Kingdom, New Zealand, Canada, South Africa and the United States, do well in the job market but so did those from countries with high levels of competency in English and British educational traditions (e.g. Hong Kong, India, Malaysia, Sri Lanka). Both groups fared significantly better in terms of employment, occupational status and income than those from China, Germany, Lebanon, the former USSR, Taiwan and Vietnam(Iredale and Nivison-Smith 1995, 97). From the perspective of Asian immigrants, these findings, which point to the existence of significant differences between Asian groups based on the appropriateness of their human resources and capital, reinforce the variations evident in the 1986 and 1996 census data reported above. A similar conclusion, concerning the occupational outcomes for immigrant professionals, also emerged from an analysis of 1991 census data. It emphasized the importance of English skills and Australian training, regardless of country of birth. Although the authors cautioned that for professionals who arrived in the late 1980s and 1990s during the most serious recession since the 1930s, the potential for regaining their professional level of employment was less rosy (Birrell and Hawthorne

1997, 80-81)[6].

For the growing numbers of Australian-born or reared young people of Asian background, the Birrell and Hawthorne study concludes that there did not appear to be employer bias directed at Australian trained persons born outside Western Europe. This is obviously an encouraging indicator of a lack of discrimination (Birrell and Hawthorne 1997, 77). It is also important for the many achieving high levels of success at school and university. While the term model minority has not been adopted in Australia to describe the educational success of Asian students, their increasing numbers among the high achievers in the annual high school examinations, to determine entry to universities, frequently draws comments in newspaper reports pondering on a particular Asian valuation of education. While children of earlier groups of NESB immigrants, especially those of Greek background, have followed a similar route into the universities, the success of those of Asian background often attracts critical comment. This comment, which is the obverse of the media speculation about the existence of some particular Asian cultural valuation of education, involves an association of their examination success with a focus on study at the expense of participation in other areas of school life. This critique is especially common in boys' schools where team sports, such as football, cricket and basketball, are still viewed as an important part of the curriculum which cannot be replicated by participation in activities such as debating, music or art. Disinterest in sport, which plays an important part in life for many Australians, all too easily leads to comments concerning the "un-Australian" nature of individuals or groups.

The economic experiences of recent Asian immigrants and the educational successes of their children can be interpreted as evidence for a relatively positive integration into Australian society. However, the hostile comments often directed towards successful Asian students is a reminder that discrimination and prejudice towards Asians may be a major part of their daily experiences. During the first of the so-called Asian Immigration debates in 1984, much of the commentary noted not that this was a continuation, or re-emergence, of the older patterns of anti-Asian hostility from the nineteenth century, or even of the hostility felt towards Japanese in the aftermath of World War II. Instead, the point was made that it was a pattern of hostility also experienced by earlier waves of post-World War II immigrants, beginning with the East European refugees and then more recent Italian, Greek, Turkish and Lebanese arrivals. What this analysis overlooked was the resonance with earlier anti-Asian sentiments, which gave additional force, especially among Anglo-Celtic sections of the population, to anti-Asian practices and attitudes.

In 1989, a major national survey was undertaken on behalf of the government to determine the response to its multicultural policies. As part of this survey, respondents were asked to rank the "acceptability" of particular ethnic groups. Although a majority of the population were tolerant towards immigrants from all ethnic backgrounds, 32 percent expressed negative feelings towards Vietnamese, slightly lower negativity towards Muslims and Lebanese, and much lower levels of negativity towards the earlier immigrant groups such as Greeks, Italians and the British (Ip, Kawakami et al. 1992, 23). A more detailed analysis of the survey data reveals that attitudes towards immigrants are very closely related to respondents' views about multiculturalism. Those opposed to multiculturalism, who were more likely to be born in Australia or the United Kingdom than either Europe or Asia, were less likely to support migrants from regions other than the United Kingdom and were particularly opposed to more immigrants from Asia (Goot 1993, 249). The anti-multiculturalists were also more likely to consider immigrants better off than others in terms of receipt of government payments, access to university opportunities, job opportunities, renting accommodation, as well as income and wages (Goot 1993, 250). As Goot concludes, in a climate where questioning of Asian immigration can be seen as racist distancing oneself from multiculturalism can be another way of doing the same thing, but in code (Goot 1993 252). The existence of generally negative views towards Asians in Australia is supported by a survey undertaken in Brisbane and Sydney in the early 1990s, in which a number of respondents acknowledged that Australians, in general, were hostile to immigrants, as well as being racist (Ip, Kawakami et al. 1992, 56, 73).

The actual interpretation of such attitudinal data can be complex, especially with regard to how such attitudes translate into actual behavior. Some indication of this translation into actual behavior comes from a survey of 1,220 Asian immigrants from China, Hong Kong, Japan, the Philippines and Taiwan, who arrived in Australia in the five years prior to 1995 and settled in Sydney, Melbourne, Adelaide, Brisbane or Perth. The interviews took place shortly before the emergence of the Pauline Hanson One Nation party. What is interesting, in retrospect, is that just over one-third of the respondents (37.5 percent) reported experiencing actual discrimination. Four main types of discrimination were particularly notable: verbal abuse (reported by 33 percent), feelings of discrimination (26 percent), inequitable treatment in employment and in the workplace (16.2 percent), and condescending attitudes by service providers (12.7 percent). Importantly, personal attacks and violence, unfriendly behavior, and housing related issues were encountered by only a very small percentage of the respondents. There was considerable variation in the reporting of discrimination with the highest levels being reported by those from the Philippines (45.8 percent) and Taiwan (43 percent) and the lowest by those from Vietnam (29.4 percent) and China (34.5 percent). There was a close relationship between English ability and the reporting of discrimination, with those most competent in English also being more likely to report discrimination. One explanation for this may be that these are the individuals who are best able to discern the subtle nuances of verbal discrimination. They may also be individuals who find themselves in employment or social situations below their expectations which create frustration and unhappiness. This, in turn, sensitizes them to discrimination (Ip et al. 1995). One surprising aspect of these findings was the low level of discrimination reported by Vietnamese respondents since, as a group, the Vietnamese are widely viewed as amongst the most disadvantaged ethnic groups in Australia. A partial explanation for the limited reportage of discrimination may lie in their limited English fluency but it may also reflect a certain desensitization among the Vietnamese community to instances of discrimination or to their more limited encounters with non-Vietnamese.

After the March 1996 electoral success of Pauline Hanson and the founding of her One Nation party, there was an increase in expressions of anti-Asian attitudes in graffiti, on talk-back radio programs, and in public places where Asians often became the butt of hostile and stereotypical abuse[7]. The failure of the Prime Minister to criticize or seek to silence Hanson's often bizarre and inaccurate statements concerning Asians, Aborigines and other "non-Australians" was widely viewed as inflaming relations between Asians, Aborigines and "true" Australians. While the Prime Minister's excuse was Hanson's right to freedom of speech, the effect of his silence was to remove previously existing social and moral constraints against such discriminatory and prejudiced activities, since it was widely assumed that the Prime Minister himself shared many of her prejudices and views. Indeed, it was not until October 1996 that the Prime Minister led a joint resolution in Parliament condemning such behavior and endorsing racial tolerance. What seems to have finally convinced the Prime Minister to take this step, at the urging of his Cabinet Ministers and many prominent Australians, was concerned about the effect which the anti-Asian sentiments were having on Asian countries and leaders. His attention to these effects was related to the

Australian economy's extensive reliance on Asian trading partners, tourists, and international students. With the decline of the One Nation party, expressions of anti-Asian sentiment have declined as have what, at the height of One Nation's popularity, were still the relatively rare fights and physical attacks directed against Asians or Asian property

The complexity of Australian race relations is evident in the way anti-Asian hostility coexists with more positive signs of acceptance and social incorporation of Asians into Australian society. One example is the high level of Australian citizenship among Asian residents. The barriers to acquiring Australian citizenship are limited since only two years permanent residence is required. There are no Australian barriers to retaining dual nationality and the extensive formal tests of English and knowledge of the local society and institutions required in the United States are absent. Figures show that, with the exception of Malaysians and Chinese, there is a growth in eligible residents taking up Australian citizenship (Bureau of Immigration Multiculturalism and Population Research 1995). Still, it is clear that the decision to become a citizen is frequently a decision to facilitate entry to Australia or permanent employment in the government public service. For many, it does not immediately translate into a sense of belonging to Australia or Australian society despite the changes associated with the development of multiculturalism. This was evident in the survey of recent Asian immigrants undertaken in the early 1990s and referred to above. While the majority of the recent arrivals had either taken Australian citizenship or planned to do so as soon as they were eligible, less than 5 percent described their identity simply as Australian. Furthermore, some two-thirds said that they still considered themselves as "migrants," yet many of these replies came from individuals who were actually Australian citizens. This tendency was especially marked among recent Vietnamese arrivals, where 41.2 percent still considered themselves as "migrants". While there were variations among the Asian groups in the reasons given for the continuation of a 'migrant' identity, the most commonly stated reasons, apart from being overseas born and not a citizen, were English language problems, the perpetual nature of immigrant status, and difficulties adjusting to the Australian life style (Inglis et al. 1998, 378). Clearly the development of policies of multiculturalism in Australia has not progressed to a point where citizenship is an immediate key to a sense of psychological belonging in Australia even if, as among the majority of the Vietnamese and Philippines, there is the intention to remain living in Australia rather than return to their birthplaces.

Another, less ambiguous, indicator of a more positive aspect of ethnic relations in Australia is the extent of intermarriage between Asian and non-Asian Australians. From the 1950s, many of the Colombo Plan students who came to study in Australia married non-Asians as did the descendants of earlier Asian settlers. This trend continues in recent years despite the growth in Asian populations, creating greater opportunities for Asians to find a marriage partner within their own communities (Penny and Khoo 1996). In the nineteenth century, European women who married Chinese men were frequently reported to have become outcasts from the European community. The same patterns are rarely recreated in contemporary Australia, where intermarriages involving Asian partners may, for the non-Asian family, be an extension of other exogamous marriages involving spouses from diverse backgrounds. In contrast to earlier periods, public curiosity or hostility is rarely displayed towards couples where one of the partners is from an Asian background. There is a class dimension involved in intermarriages, with intermarried couples tending to be better educated and more likely to have both spouses in the work force and less likely to be unemployed than when compared with in-married couples (Penny and Khoo 1996, p.55). A major exception to this pattern involves the Filipinos, who are the Asian-born group most likely to have Australian-born spouses (Penny and Khoo 1996,32). Filipinas frequently marry Australian-born or resident men whom they have met only through correspondences or on short visits to the Philippines. After marriage, the women often find themselves living in isolated rural area of Australia with men often less educated than themselves and many years their senior. Lack of employment opportunities for the women frequently combine with their husbands' desire for a homemaker to ensure that they do not enter the workforce[8].

Contributing to the more positive contemporary assessment of intermarriage by the non-Asian population is the growing familiarity of the non-Asian-Australians with Asian society and individuals from Asian backgrounds. Survey findings show that younger, more educated Australians have a much more cosmopolitan view of the world and are less likely to adopt the nativistic view that people cannot be "truly Australians," unless they were born, or resided for most of their lives, in Australia and belong to a Christian religion (Jones 1999, 23). However, growing familiarity with Asia is not restricted to middle-class groups. The anti-Asian hostility of the last decade has been tempered by the contacts that non-Asian Australians have acquired with Asia. Many young Australians and their parents traveled extensively in Asia and, at home, they encounter many forms of Asian cultures. Chinese and other Asian cuisines are widely eaten at home as well as in restaurants. The popularity of Asian leisure and cultural activities, ranging from bonsai to martial arts, continues, while traditional Asian medical practices are gaining widespread acceptance. An important effect of these developments is that, for many Australians, the fear of an exotic Asia evident in the nineteenth century has been replaced by a much greater familiarity with the region and its diverse cultural practices. Giving support and legitimacy to these developments are changes in school languages and social studies curriculum designed to create an "Asian literate" population. A major motive for these curriculum changes is the perception that such knowledge is important as a basis for developing Australia's economic and political relations with the region. One result of these various developments in education and daily life is that stereotypes based on ideas about traditional Asian societies are increasingly displaced by awareness of the changes which have taken place in Asian countries in recent decades. The result is that the Asian "other' (whether located in Australia or Asia) is ceasing to be viewed as exotic or, indeed, inscrutable and, hence, cause for fear.

The Changing Role of Policy

Australian governments have traditionally played a dominant role in fostering and controlling immigration and settlement in a manner unequalled in the United States or Canada. The abandonment of the White Australia Policy, for primarily international rather than domestic reasons, has been associated with the renewed growth of Australia's Asian population. As the predominant immigrant group, their incorporation into Australian society has been directly affected by policies developed to cater, not to Asians, but to immigrants from non-English speaking backgrounds[9]. Two specific policy areas deserve special consideration, that relating to economic settlement and incorporation and that concerning discrimination and racism. Under the umbrella of multiculturalism are a suite of policies, ranging from free English language classes to programs catering to specific linguistic and ethnic groups on the basis of identified needs. Access to the latter programs depends very much on the extent to which ethnic community organizations and social welfare workers are able to demonstrate the need for assistance. Larger ethnic groups with more concentrated populations and resources are always better placed to access support, regardless of whether they are Asian or European. Certain Asian communities, such as Indo-Chinese refugee groups, are active participants in multicultural welfare programs. Other predominantly middle-class groups, such as those from Malaysia or Taiwan, are primarily involved in programs relating to support for ethnic language classes and cultural activities.

By the late 1980s programs were developed to facilitate the re-entry of skilled workers into the Australian labor force. The initiatives ranged from specialist English language training, to the provision of re-training and bridging courses for special occupations and the provision of financial allowances for those undertaking these courses. At the same time, the National Office of Overseas Skills Recognition was set up to facilitate the assessment of the equivalence of overseas to local qualifications (National Multicultural Advisory Council 1995, chapter 5; Birrell and Hawthorne 1997, 20-21; Iredale 1997, chapters 6-7). Although the limitations of these initiatives were frequently noted, they constituted an unprecedented effort to re-incorporate skilled immigrants into the workforce. In his comparative study of the United States, United Kingdom and Australia, Reitz identified these policies as being a significant factor contributing to the high level of success of immigrants in the Australian labor market (Reitz 1997). Reitz, however, warns that changes towards a more individualized institutional system and cuts in social welfare spending have the potential to undermine many of the immigrants achievements of equity (Reitz 1997, 225).

By the 1990s, the developments of which Reitz warned were occurring in Australia. Growing criticisms of multiculturalism and its alleged financial costs to the community while privileging ethnic groups at the expense of "Australian," although still resisted by governments, nevertheless coincided with quite specific policies designed to limit government welfare and community payments. These moves to limit government social welfare spending accelerated after the 1996 election of the conservative Howard government which was concerned with replacing state involvement in service delivery by leaving delivery to the market. Among the steps affecting recent immigrants were restrictions on access to various social welfare and unemployment benefits for the first two years after arrival in Australia. Another change was the requirement hat, except for refugees and humanitarian entrants, all immigrants without adequate levels of English would need to pay for access to English language courses. While not targeting a specific group of recent immigrants, the large numbers of Asian arrivals meant they were particularly affected by these punitive policies which, critics point out, have the potential to create an ethnic underclass. While this may be a somewhat alarmist assessment, it stands as a reminder that the retreat from active government policies is occurring not, as in the 1950s and 1960s, in a time of affluence, but rather in a time of considerable economic uncertainty and change. This is a time when the resources required for successful economic incorporation are more complex than a strong back and a pair of willing hands.

Although not initially part of multicultural policies, since the 1980s and the first of the Asian immigration debates which specifically targeted Asian groups in Australia, the issue of policies to address discriminatory practices and racism have gained increasing public attention. However, it was not until 1991 that the first National Report into Racist Violence was prepared. This examined the experiences of indigenous Australians and those of non-English speaking backgrounds. The preface to that report notes that

> The evidence presented to the Inquiry indicates that multiculturalism is working well in Australia. In spite of our racial, ethnic and cultural diversity, our society's experience of racist violence, intimidation and harassment is nowhere near the level experienced in many other countries (Moss 1993, .x).

However, it then notes that the situation for indigenous Australians was far worse than for those of non-English speaking background. In the case of those of non-English speaking background, the most prevalent form of racist violence was the existence of a threatening environment, which referred not to the existence of physical force but "verbal and non-verbal intimidation, harassment and incitement to racial hatred." Those most common targets of such activities were identified as those who are visibly different. Clearly Asians were a major target of such violence and the subsequent first *State of the Nation Report on non-English Speaking Background People* undertaken by the Federal Race Discrimination Commissioner in 1993 included a status report on Asian Australians where the diverse experiences of communities were noted:

> Communities which were well-resourced in any of the following areas—fluency in English, locally recognized qualifications, financial arrangements or strong community support—were able to settle successfully in spite of some discrimination. However, communities lacking these resources were at risk, even a relatively large community such as the Vietnamese (Moss 1993, 264).

In the light of the subsequent reductions in government funding for programs contributing to the acquisition of fluency in English, providing support for the up-grading and recognition of overseas qualifications, as well as community development and financial assistance, the ability of community organizations to assist new arrivals has been substantially reduced.

With regard to racism, the 1993 *State of the Nation* Report noted that racism was raised only in community discussion by young people of non-English speaking background. It went on to note that there was insufficient evidence to say categorically that racism was seriously affecting the young people, although there was a clear need for monitoring the situation (Moss 1993, 264-5). By 1996, after the commencement of the Hanson debate, the *State of the Nation* Report gave a very different picture of the situation and the emergence of public hatred targeted at Asian Australians, many of whom, the Commissioner noted, experienced racism on a daily basis (Federal Race Discrimination Commissioner 1996, xi).

The law provides only partial protection. Since 1975, Australia has a Racial Discrimination Act, designed to make racial discrimination unlawful in all areas of public life and to give rights to equality before the law to people of all races, color, national and ethnic origins. In 1995, the scope of the law was expanded to include offensive or abusive public acts of racial hatred. While the existence of such legislation may be an important deterrent, the complexity of the procedures involved ensures that only a small proportion of the cases ever come within the jurisdiction of the Act (Federal Race Discrimination Commissioner 1996, 21).

What became evident in 1996 was the need on the one hand for a clear signal from the government that racial vilification was unacceptable and not to be tolerated. The longer the Prime Minister failed to join other community leaders in speaking out against the Hanson populist statements and agenda, the more anti-Asian sections of the community gained confidence and support for the correctness of their views. It was also evident that there was a need to undertake a major education campaign to counter the many wild and scurrilous statements made in the name of freedom of expression. Although government funds were available for this purpose, they were not expended for many months and, ultimately, were allocated to an advertising agency to undertake a feasibility study of what should be done.

Further compounding concerns about the inertia in implementing national policies to address racism, were moves by the government to emasculate the Human Rights and Equal Opportunity Commission, the national tribunal with prime responsibility in the area. The decline of the One Nation Party, in large part because of its own internecine feuding and subsequent loss of electoral support rather than because of any concerted policy to more effectively address racism within Australia, while welcomed, is a matter of concern. This is because it leaves open the possibility that, should circumstances see the emergence of another populist debate, racist violence could again become prominent.

An inevitable effect of the Hanson debate is that many Asian-Australians now have an increased sense of insecurity about their place in Australia. This insecurity includes long-established families, whose Australian-born children were finding that their hitherto unquestioned Australian identity was being called into question as they were treated as recent immigrants.

Significantly, the most recent report of the National Multicultural Advisory Council, entitled *Australian Multiculturalism for a New Century: Towards Inclusiveness*, only indirectly addresses issues of racism and discrimination involving immigrant and indigenous groups. It does this in its calls for political leadership and political parties to demonstrate consensus and support for the future development of multi-culturalism (National Multicultural Advisory Council 1999, 82). At the same time, it argues for the need to communicate more effectively the aims of multiculturalism to its critics. The general thrust of the report is to refocus multiculturalism, more specifically, to highlight its links with the evolving value of Australian democracy and citizenship, including a balancing of the rights and obligations of all citizens. This aim is evident in the primacy given to civic duty ahead of cultural respect, social equity and productive diversity. At the same time, there is a specific reference to the need to acknowledge the contribution of those from Great Britain and Ireland and to achieve reconciliation between indigenous people and all other Australians (National Multicultural Advisory Council 1999, 83).

Whether such well-intentioned sentiments will be effective in achieving inclusiveness without the allocation of substantial public resources is a moot point in current policy debates. The economic and social diversity within the Asian population in Australia means that individuals and groups often have different needs in achieving social equity. What does unite them, however, is that, to the extent that they are viewed by other Australians as a homogeneous group which symbolically represents the undesirable face of Australian society at the end of the twentieth century, their full incorporation into that society remains problematic. However, it is dangerous to see the current relations between Asians and others as simply a replay of the negativity and hostility Asians faced in the nineteenth century. Today's hostility can be viewed as a desperate effort rather than as the clarion call to the development of a new national identity. Notwithstanding such an interpretation, there is a widespread perception that the current Prime Minister, John Howard, is himself sympathetic to many of the views associated with the Hansonites. This includes a view of Australian society as a new Britannia, characterized by values such as "mateship," which were at the core of the discourse surrounding Federation in 1901.[10] Such a worldview now has little resonance with many Australians, including the large percentage from non-British origins for whom the shift in policy from assimilation to multiculturalism has created a much valued extension of options and choices as to the form of their incorporation into Australian society. Despite a highly regrettable retreat from many of the state institutional supports for multiculturalism, there now exists a generation reared under the policy and a growing awareness of its international value for addressing the challenges of globalization, even among a significant segment of the Anglo-Celtic majority. This coalescence of support for multiculturalism can only be beneficial for the future development of race relations involving Asians in Australia.

Endnotes

[1] Space will not allow a broader review of race relations between indigenous and non-indigenous Australians which are part of a different paradigm reinforced by distinct administrative, institutional and social agendas which separate them from the pattern of relations involving minority immigrant groups.

[2] Reflecting the historical concerns about cheap labour Australian governments have always been extremely reluctant to provide entry for unskilled or semiskilled labour.

[3] Since the 1989 National Agenda for a Multicultural Australia, multicultural policies have specifically included the indigenous, Aboriginal population within their scope. Policy makers are well aware of the highly sensitive nature of this inclusiveness given that Aboriginal groups assert their distinctive position as the original inhabitants of Australia who have experienced more extensive and damaging disadvantage and discrimination than any of the recent immigrant groups.

[4] The popular labelling of such highly vitriolic public discussions, which became linked with extensive racist behavior as "Debates," may be viewed as an attempt to deny their social significance and/or to ignore their highly emotive and anti-rational dimension.

[5] Unpublished data from the Department of Immigration and Multicultural Affairs.

[6] Both studies identified professionals from the Philippines as being an exception to the general finding that English competency is related to success in regaining former employment status. Whether this can be accounted for by employers' concerns about Filipino educational standards, or whether it reflects an employment strategy among Filipinos which involves professionals being more ready to take lower level jobs rather than risk unemployment than are those from other countries, is unclear. Birrell, B. and L. Hawthorne (1997). *Immigrants and the Professions in Australia.* Melbourne: Centre for Urban and Population Research, Monash University..

[7] Pauline Hanson, and another independent, Graeme Campbell, were unusual in winning their seats in Federal parliament after their respective political parties, the Liberal and Labor parties withdrew their party endorsement because of concerns about their racist attitudes and views.

[8] Frequent reports of physical as well as psychological abuse experienced by these women have become a major concern to welfare and government authorities with Australian embassies developing special procedures to alert applicants for fiancee visas of potential difficulties in marriages contracted after only a brief acquaintance.

[9] The growth in the Asian population was largely the unintended result of changing emphases in government immigration policies as they favoured initially family reunions and then skilled workers and those with substantial capital. However, subsequent policies by government to accept refugees from specific Asian countries such as Vietnam (as well as Latin America and Eastern Europe) and to attract students and tourists from

Asian countries were consciously adopted in response to foreign and economic policy considerations. Domestically, policies to target specifically "Asian" matters have not, however, reappeared.

[10] The Prime Minister took personal responsibility for constructing a highly contentious preamble to the Australian constitution, which reflected such sentiments but which was rejected in the September 1999 referendum.

References

Birrell, B. and Hawthorne, L. (1997). *Immigrants and the Professions in Australia.* Melbourne: Centre for Urban and Population Research,Monash University.

Bureau of Immigration Multiculturalism and Population Research. (1995). *Citizenship Australian 1991 Census*: Statistical Report 15. Canberra: Australian Government Publishing Service.

Federal Race Discrimination Commissioner. (1996). *State of the Nation: A Report on People of Non-English Speaking Backgrounds.* Sydney: RaceDiscrimination Commissioner, HREOC.

Goot, M. (1993). "Multiculturalists, Monoculturalists and the Many in Between: Attitudes to Cultural Diversity and their Correlates." *The Australian and New Zealand Journal of Sociology,* 29(2): 226-253.

Inglis, C. (1999a). "The New Asian Immigration and its Impact in a Period of Globalization." In Y.F. Tseng, C. Bulbeck, N.L.H. Chiang and J.C. Hsu (Eds.), *Asian Migration: Pacific Rim Dynamics.* Taipei: Interdisciplinary Group for Australian Studies National Taiwan University.

_____ . (1999b). "Middle Class Migration: New Considerations inResearch and Policy." In Hage, G. and Couch, R. (Eds.), *The Future of Multiculturalism.* Sydney: Research Institute for Humanities and the Social Sciences, 45-64.

Inglis, C. and Wu, C.T. (1992). "The 'New' Migration of Asian Skills and Capital to Australia." In C. Inglis, S. Gunasekeran, G. Sullivan, and C.T. Wu (Eds.), *Asians in Australia: the Dynamics of Migration and Settlement.* Singapore: Institute of Southeast Asian Studies,193-230.

Inglis, C. et al. (1998]). "Concepts of Citizenship and Identity Among Recent Asian Immigrants in Australia." *Asian and Pacific Migration Journal,* 6(3-4): 363-384.

Ip, D. et al. (1992). *Images of Asians in Multicultural Australia..* Sydney: Multicultural Centre, University of Sydney.

Ip, D. et al. (1995). *Asian Impressions of Multicultural Australia.* Brisbane: University of Queensland.

Iredale, R. (1997). *Skills Transfer: International Migration and Accreditation Issues.* Wollongong, Australia: University of Wollongong Press.

Iredale, R. and Nivison-Smith, I. (1995). *Immigrants' Experiences of Qualifications Recognition and Employment: Results from the Prototype Longitudinal Survey of Immigrants to Australia (LSIA).* Canberra: Australian Government Publishing Service.

Jayasuriya, L. and Kee, P.K. (1999). *The Asianisation of Australia? Some !! Facts About the Myths.* Carlton: Melbourne University Press.

Jones, F. L. (1992). "Labor Market Outcomes Among the Chinese at the 1986 Census." In C. Inglis, S. Gunasekaran, G. Sullivan, and C.T. Wu (Eds.), *Asians in Australia: the Dynamics of Migration and Settlement.* Singapore: Institute of Southeast Asian Studies, 117-156.

_____. (1999). "The Sources and Limits of Popular Support for a Multicultural Australia." In G. Hage, and R. Couch (Eds.), *The Future of Australian Multiculturalism.* The Research Institute for Humanities and Social Sciences, 21-30.

London, H.I. (1970). *Non-White Immigration and the 'White Australia' Policy.* Sydney: Sydney University Press.

Meaney, N. (1999). *Towards a New Vision: Australia and Japan Through 100 Years.* Sydney: Kangaroo Press.

Moss, I. (1993). *State of the Nation: A Report on People of Non-English Speaking Backgrounds.* Sydney: Federal Race Discrimination Commissioner.

National Multicultural Advisory Council (1999). *Australian Multiculturalism for a New Century: Towards Inclusiveness.* Canberra:National Multiucultural Advisory Council.

National Multicultural Advisory Council (1995). *Multicultural Australia: The Next Steps: Towards and Beyond 2000 vol.2.* Canberra: National Multicultural Advisory Council.

Palfreeman, A. (1967). *The Administration of the White Australia Policy.* Melbourne: Melbourne University Press.

Penny, J. and Khoo, S.E. (1996). *Intermarriage: A Study of Migration and Integration.* Canberra: Australian Government Publishing Service.

Price, C. (1974). *The Great White Walls Are Built*. Canberra: Australian National University Press.

Reitz, J. (1997). *Warmth of the Welcome: the Social Causes of Economic Success for Immigrants in Different Nations and Cities*. Boulder, CO: Westview Press.

Shu, J. (1996). "Labour Force Status in Australia of Newly Arrived Immigrants from Asia." *Asian Migrant*, 9(2): 48-55.

Wieviorka, M. (1998). "Is Multiculturalism the Solution?" *Ethnic and Racial Studies*, 21(2): 880-910.

Willard, M. (1923). *History of the White Australia Policy*. Melbourne: Melbourne University Press.

Yarwood, A. (1964). *Asian Migration to Australia: The Background to Exclusion 1896-1913*. Melbourne: Melbourne University Press.

Yu, O. (1995). "All the Lower Orders: Representations of the Chinese Cooks, Market-Gardeners and Other Lower-Class People in Australian Literature, 1888-1988." In P. Macgregor (Ed.), *Histories of the Chinese in Australasia and the South Pacific*. Melbourne: Museum of Chinese Australian History, 100-112.

Part IV

New Possibilities

Multiracial Collaborations and Coalitions

**Leland T. Saito
and Edward J.W. Park**

Focusing primarily on Los Angeles, New York City, and Houston, this chapter examines contemporary grassroots efforts to establish multiracial coalitions among Asian Pacific Americans, Latinos, African Americans, and whites in communities across the United States. By studying a range of collaborative efforts, we examine race relations and politics in America's increasingly multiracial cities. These grassroots efforts provide a rich source of information and offer "lessons" on what may or may not work, facilitating policy formation and raising theoretical issues aimed at initiating and supporting cooperative relations among diverse racial groups and efforts to address urban problems.

Within the last two decades, the populations of New York City, Los Angeles, and Houston have undergone a remarkable shift. Driven by the massive growth in immigration from Asia, Mexico, Central America, and the Caribbean, these cities have made the transition from white majority to "majority-minority" cities. At the same time, the influx of Asian Pacific Americans and Latinos has injected American cities with multiracial diversity and has complicated the dominant black/white approach to urban race relations.

Asian Pacific Americans share neighborhoods, schools, local governments, and commercial districts with a range of minority groups. For example, the majority of residents in Los Angeles' Koreatown are Latinos, and New York City's Chinatown is rapidly expanding into the Latino and African American Lower East Side. These multiracial conditions are replicated with local variations throughout the U.S. in major metropolitan communities such as: Chicago, Philadelphia, and San Francisco, and in small cities such as Garden City, Kansas, and Wausau, Wisconsin. Clearly, the increasingly diverse and complex demographics of the U.S. demand that we examine and address the relations emerging from these changing racial dynamics.

Media attention and scholarly research have focused primarily on conflicts—such as Black-Korean struggles in New York, Chicago, and Los Angeles (Min 1996). Receiving less attention, however, is the long history of efforts to establish cooperative efforts, such as Filipino and Mexican workers in California who created the United Farm Workers Union in 1965; Mexican American Edward Roybal who utilized an alliance of Latinos, African Americans, Asian Pacific Americans, and whites to win a Los Angeles City Council seat in 1949; and the contemporary efforts of the organization Committee Against Anti-Asian Violence (CAAAV) in mobilizing Asian communities to build multiracial alliances to counter racist violence and police brutality in New York City.

Also, by selectively highlighting the educational and economic "success stories" of some Asian Pacific Americans, media accounts have depicted the entire group as a high achieving "model minority." The image suggests that they have overcome obstacles faced by other minorities, and this perception has hindered the development of alliances with other groups (Lee 1996). What the image overlooks are the serious issues affecting the Asian Pacific American community—such as extremely high levels of poverty, low levels of education, hate crimes, and employment discrimination—that can form the basis for alliances among minorities.

Contemporary grassroots efforts strive toward equitable policies and resource distribution within the current political framework at the local level—a departure from the social movements of the 1960s that attempted transformative social change on a national scale (Fainstein and Fainstein 1991; Omi and Winant 1994). Neighborhood groups are part of a long history of progressive efforts aimed at improving neighborhood conditions involving such issues as housing, transportation, education, crime, drugs, health care, day care, and jobs. While a focus on local community issues can be viewed as a conservative retreat from national concerns, as Robert Fisher and Peter Romanofsky (1981 xi) explain, "neighborhood organizing can also be a progressive response by city dwellers who want to control the institutions that affect their lives..." driven by the desire for "political and economic democracy." Furthermore, while our case studies of collaborative efforts occur at the local level, the conditions they address are framed by national circumstances and trends.

The New Urban Race Relations

Major economic and political trends which frame contemporary grassroots collaborations include increasing globalization of the economy and increasing competition for capital, renewed national discussion on race relations and inequality, and shifting racial policies at all levels of the government. A reversal of economic fortunes in the U.S.—from the rapidly expanding post-WWII economy and growing incomes at all levels, to the rise in international competition in the 1970s, demand for greater corporate profits, and the increasing gap between the poor and the rich—brought equally significant changes in the political climate and social policies. In the 1950s and 1960s, the U.S. government began to address practices and policies by private entities and the state itself that supported racial discrimination in such critical areas as home mortgages, voting rights, and access to public education. These legislative efforts marked a turning point in U.S. racial policies and generated positive changes, as demonstrated by the increasing numbers of minorities elected to public office and an overhaul of U.S. immigration policies (Davidson and Grofman 1994; Hing 1993; Omi and Winant 1994).

Since the 1970s, however, fiscal conservatism gained momentum and firmly established itself in the 1990s in major urban areas across the country, and the liberal economic policies of the New Deal and social reform of the Civil Rights Movement came under attack (Plotkin and

Scheuerman 1994). Major components of this transition include less state regulation of corporations in support of "free market" policies; attack on labor unions to meet the corporate demands for a more flexible work force; and continued massive public subsidies and tax cuts for corporations in exchange for uncertain benefits such as job growth, which *Time* has dubbed "corporate welfare" (Barlett and Steele 1998). In contrast to "corporation friendly" policies, "big government" is portrayed as wasteful and inefficient, resulting in cutbacks in social services and a withdrawal from government support for civil rights (Ong, Bonacich, and Cheng 1994). Major forms of discrimination embedded in society have remained untouched by government reform efforts with limited government resources allocated to enforce civil rights legislation (Massey and Denton 1993). Efforts to address discrimination have been curtailed, such as when California's voters passed Proposition 209 in 1996, ending government affirmative action programs, or attacked, such as in Houston, Texas, where a similar proposition was voted down.

These policies have had a disproportionate impact on urban ethnic communities that are more closely linked to government funding in critical areas such as housing, education, transportation, and health services. Even with an upturn in the economy in the late 1990s, the general trend in policies remains the same, as indicated by the welfare-to-work programs, which were implemented without in-depth evaluation of the long-range implications. The era of limited government and resources forms the context and conditions which frame urban problems and interracial relations as minorities experience and bear the costs of economic restructuring. These developments are too large and sweeping for single groups to address alone, underscoring the need for responses whose effectiveness hinges on multiracial collaboration.

Revisiting Coalition Politics

In many cities, Asian Pacific Americans are potentially an important part of multiracial collaborations; however, their incredible heterogeneity poses new challenges to coalition politics. While Asian Pacific Americans have always been characterized by the diversity of their population, since the 1965 Immigration Act, renewed and new immigration has significantly increased the complexity of the population in terms of ethnicity, class, generation in the U.S., political ideology, and country of origin (Hing 1993; Park 1998).

The heterogeneity of Asian Pacific Americans calls into question one of the most enduring assumptions since the Civil Rights Movement, that is, that the political incorporation of racial minorities is inextricably linked with their participation in liberal coalitions (Browning, Marshall, and Tabb 1984; Sonenshein 1993). This assumption has been fundamental and pervasive to studies of race and power in contemporary American cities for compelling reasons. For much of America's urban history, conservative coalitions have actively and uniformly sought to exclude all racial minorities from the political process. Faced with hostility and the recalcitrance of conservative coalitions, racial minorities found a measure of political unity among themselves and worked with allies among white liberals whose political commitment included individual and procedural rights and distributive and representative justice (see Boussard 1993 and Taylor 1994).

The recent immigrants bring new multiracial complexities and challenges to the urban political process and pose daunting challenges for liberals in maintaining their traditional claim on racial minority incorporation. At the same time, racial politics gradually moved from the simplicity of white over black discrimination to the more nuanced and complex dynamics of "post-Civil Rights" politics (Omi and Winant 1994; Marable 1995). Since the 1970s, the very same political changes that the

Civil Rights Movement unleashed has opened the way for rearticulating racial politics such that charges of "reverse discrimination" now permeate American political discourse. As liberals find themselves struggling with new challenges, some conservatives have reached out for minority votes and support (Omatsu 1994; Park 1998). Whether these attempts reflect their anxiety in the face of demographic change or genuine commitment to racial inclusion, conservatives are increasingly reluctant to politically write off racial minorities, especially in large cities and diverse states where racial minority voters can shift the electoral balance. These emerging trends signal the new realities that bring into question the traditional liberal assumptions of race, power, and coalition building.

These events and our case studies suggest that participation in community politics is promoted by strong local organizations which facilitate resource development, community mobilization, leadership training, political lobbying, and serve as a basis for communication and negotiation among groups. A major concern is negotiating and establishing common issues, while recognizing that differences exist but will be put aside temporarily as the groups work toward common goals. Clearly, this is not always possible. In Los Angeles, for example, extreme conflict between Korean shopkeepers and African American customers and residents prompted the Los Angeles County Human Relations Commission to initiate the Black Korean Alliance in 1986. While achieving some success in the mediation of conflict, the Los Angeles Civil Unrest of 1992 underscored the magnitude of the problems in urban centers and the limitations of efforts such as the Alliance, which was dissolved in 1992 (Chang 1993; Min 1996). Elections in multiracial communities, such as Monterey Park in Los Angeles County, demonstrate that Asian Pacific Americans, Latinos, and whites would cross-over and vote for candidates of other racial origins. At the same time, however, when offered a choice of strong candidates, and able to cast multiple votes in elections with a number of seats up for election, voters in Monterey Park demonstrated that race continued to be the major factor as voters overwhelmingly cast their ballots in the largest number for candidates of the same race and ethnicity (Fong 1994; Horton 1995).

The fact that the Black Korean Alliance disbanded, or that coalitions fail to elect their candidates, does not necessarily signify that all meaningful work toward mediating conflict and creating alliances cannot succeed. On the contrary, the individual relationships and networks that are nurtured and supported by such struggles often live beyond their initial contact. Such attempts should be seen as part of larger, long-term efforts to address community concerns. The fact that individuals and groups are able to begin the process of dialogue and negotiation, develop an agenda to pursue jointly, and at least temporarily, work together lays the groundwork for future collaborations.

The next section offers four case studies of multiracial relations, examining the successful Houston mayoral campaign of African American Lee Brown that utilized a multiracial grassroots strategy; New York City Council redistricting and elections in Chinatown that involved discussions of Asian Pacific American/white and Asian Pacific American/Latino alliances and that met with mixed results; an effective multiracial effort to address high school violence in the San Gabriel Valley of Los Angeles County; and a notable international and multiracial effort to support union jobs in Los Angeles involving Latino workers, a Korean corporation, and Korean labor unions. These case studies illustrate the importance of forging common goals that transcend narrow, parochial interests, the role of building and sustaining relations among individuals and organizations that can form the basis for communication and collaborative efforts, and the critical role that organizations play as vehicles for leadership training, resource building, community mobilization, and a basis for communication and negotiation among groups.

Case Studies

A. THE LEE BROWN CAMPAIGN IN HOUSTON

In 1997, as Los Angeles and New York elected conservative Republicans into the City Hall to replace liberal African American mayors and as affirmative action programs were under a nationwide attack, Houston's racial politics were undergoing a defining moment. In a city with a well-earned reputation for political conservatism and white-dominance, the mayoral race pitted Robert Mosbacher, a conservative Anglo and a member of the city's famed oil elite, against Lee P. Brown, a liberal African American and the city's former Chief of Police (American Political Network 1997). Sharpening the racial overtone of the mayoral race was the bitter campaign surrounding Proposition A—inspired by California's Proposition 209—that called for the elimination of affirmative action in the city's hiring and contracting policies. The two candidates stood on opposite sides of Proposition A, with Mosbacher supporting and Brown opposing the controversial measure (Sallee 1997). In a hotly contested and closely watched race, the nation was stunned when Houston voters elected their first African American mayor and decided to uphold the city's affirmative action policy. In his victory speech, Brown vowed to lead a "new" multiracial Houston, based on politics of inclusion and economic justice (Benjaminson 1997; Bernstein 1997c). Sharing the spotlight with the mayor was a contingent of Asian Pacific Americans, most of whom were members of Asian-Americans for Lee Brown. According to the newly-elected mayor, for the first time in Houston's mayoral politics Asian Pacific Americans played a visible and a defining role in the city's mayoral campaign.

This case study examines the relationship between Asian Pacific Americans and Lee Brown's campaign. First, the case study focuses on why Brown viewed Asian Pacific American support—along with the support of Latinos—as such an important element to his overall campaign.

Second, the case study goes behind the scenes to examine the politics within the Asian Pacific American community that ultimately resulted in the community's visible support of the mayor.

Since the 1970s, African American politicians have mounted a steady effort to win the mayor's seat in Houston. Motivating their effort was the profound sense of their exclusion from Houston's political and economic structure (Rodriguez 1998a). As documented in Joe Feagin's influential Free Enterprise City (1988), the pro-business elite that dominated the politics of the city consistently viewed the African American community with a combination of hostility and neglect. As the Civil Rights Movement spread throughout the nation and brought unprecedented inclusion of African Americans in other major U.S. cities, Houston remained largely unaffected. As Houston's economy boomed during the 1970s, the African American community—without much political voice—bore the brunt of massive urban renewal programs that left much of their community uprooted and destroyed (Feagin 1988). While the political will of the community was strong, African Americans, with only 35 percent of the votes, could not find a candidate that could "cross-over" and win the majority of the votes (Rodriguez 1998a; Feagin 1988).

From the mid-1970s, Houston—much like many of the major cities in the U.S.—underwent a profound demographic change that would alter the politics of the city (see Table 1). Even as white residents were leaving Houston en masse in the aftermath of the oil crash, Houston become one of the major centers of immigration (Rodriguez 1995). Houston's established Mexican American community saw a renewed and massive migration from Mexico. They were quickly joined by other immigrants from Central America who made the Latino community in Houston one of the largest in the nation. During the same time, Asians and Pacific Islanders came to Houston in massive numbers, the largest flow made up of Vietnamese refugees fleeing their war-torn country.

Other Asian immigrants flocked to Houston in search of economic opportunities (Rodriguez 1995). By 1990, Houston had the eighth largest Asian Pacific American population in the country (Shinagawa 1996). For both Latinos and Asians, their entry into Houston has not been smooth. Latinos have had to struggle with chronic occupational and residential segregation and have had a profoundly strained relationship with the city's Police Department (Rodriguez 1995). For some groups of Asian Pacific Americans, their demographic growth and economic visibility have been met with backlash, including incidents of anti-Asian violence. Nonetheless, as Houston was preparing for the 1997 election, African Americans, Latinos, and Asian Pacific Americans accounted for 60 percent of the city's population (Bernstein 1997a, 1997b).

TABLE 1. POPULATION OF HOUSTON 1998 (estimated)

Race/Ethnicity	Population	Percent
African American	558,783	27%
Asian Pacific American	165,633	8%
Latino	599,581	29%
White	736,657	35%
Other	27,402	1%
Total	2,088,056	100%

Source: Compiled by Philip Law, UCLA Lewis Center for Regional Policy Studies, from Current Population Survey.

Given the historical experiences and contemporary realities, Lee Brown sought to build his campaign on the theme of "diversity" as a way to resist being labeled a narrow "black candidate" and as a way to acknowledge the growing racial complexity in Houston (Bernstein 1997a). From the beginning of his campaign, Brown placed reaching out to Latinos and Asian Pacific Americans at the top of his political agenda. In this effort, Brown resisted both working through established Latino and Asian Pacific American elected leaders and appealing narrowly to well-organized business interests. Instead, he addressed the social service needs of the Asian Pacific American and the Latino communities and underscored their political exclusion from the city's political process (see Rodriguez 1998b). A close observer of the race comments:

> The major difference between Mosbacher and Brown was obvious when it came to Latinos and Asians. Mosbacher worked to win the support of elected leaders and the business groups. I guess he went after the big names and the money. By getting their support, he could also claim that he had the support of these communities. Brown went the other way. He actually talked about programs and issues that would impact these communities. Programs for social service agencies to meet the needs of the youth and the elderly was a main platform and a major winner for Asians and Latinos who felt they were shortchanged when it came to city's social services. Brown was also explicit about his plans for bringing Asians and Latinos into the political process. Using the theme of "neighborhood oriented government," he urged us to participate: not just through our leaders or with our money but with our votes and involvement (Author's interview 1998).

Another observer comments, "reaching out to Latinos and Asian Pacific Americans made Brown really stand out from previous African American candidates. When Sylvester Turner ran in 1991, Latinos and Asian Pacific Americans were completely invisible in his campaign. By reaching out to these two groups—as well as lobbying for white liberals—Brown was also sending a message to all of the Houston's voters: namely that he is not just a black candidate."(Author's interview 1998)

As the election heated up during the summer of 1997, Brown was dealt a powerful blow when two of the major Asian Pacific American and Latino political figures threw their political support behind Mosbacher. First, Martha Wong, the sole Asian Pacific American member of the City Council and an established member of the Republican Party, declared her support for Mosbacher, citing both his support for pro-business policies and his opposition to Proposition A. In making her support public, she argued that Asian Pacific Americans, as a predominantly entrepreneurial group, would stand to directly benefit from pro-business policies and that affirmative action had hurt Asian Pacific Americans access to public employment in Houston (see Mason 1998a, 1998b). In addition, Gracie Saenz, a Latina Councilwomen and a Democrat, declared her support for Mosbacher. Echoing a similar theme, Saenz cited Mosbacher's "extensive experience in business," his commitment to traditional family values, and his goal of expanding international trade with Latin America (Bernstein 1997b; Bernstein and Benjamison 1997).

Reflecting back on these two developments, a Chinese American professor at the University of Houston comments:

> If Brown did not establish his relationship to Asian Pacific Americans and Latinos from the beginning, he would have faced tremendous difficulties when these highly visible politicians turned against him. I mean, these were seen as leading spokespersons of these communities. However, by this time, Brown had built his own network of supporters—mostly with social service organizations and community organizations. This allowed him to shrug off what would have been a potentially devastating turn of events (Author's interview 1998).

While Saenz's support for Mosbacher was countered with declared support for Brown from various established Latino politicians and the influential Tejano Democrats, members of the Asian Pacific American community found themselves scrambling to organize and declare their support for Brown (Bernstein 1997b). To provide a public platform for declaring their support, Asian-Americans for Lee Brown was created in October, 1997. Made up of a cross-section of Asian Pacific American community activists, social service organizations, and business groups, Asian-Americans for Lee Brown directly opposed Martha Wong (Asian-Americans for Lee Brown 1997). A Korean American community activist comments:

> The creation of Asian-Americans for Lee Brown was a major turning point for the Asian Pacific American community in Houston. On the one hand, the community showed that there is considerable political diversity within the Asian Pacific American community—that we are not just all conservative or that our politics is simply based on the interest of small businesses. On the other hand, Asian Pacific Americans showed that we have matured politically. Even though Martha Wong was, by far, the most influential politician in our community, we showed that our politics can take us beyond just one person. Just as important, we showed that we would not use a single issue to test a candidate. While Martha tried to use the affirmative action issue to pit us against African Americans, those of us who supported Brown felt that his platform, overall, was much better for us (Author's interview 1998).

During the runoff campaign, Brown relied heavily on the endorsement from Latinos and Asian Pacific Americans to rally support from these two communities and to send an unequivocal message that his political appeal was not just limited to the African American community (Benjaminson 1997). In the end, Brown won the runoff by 16,000 votes out of 300,000 total cast, securing 95 percent of the African American vote, 26 percent of the White vote, and running even in both Latino and Asian Pacific American communities (Bernstein 1997c). Addressing the diversity of Brown's support, Alan Bernstein of The Houston Chronicle reported that Brown won this election with an "ethnic medley with black chorus" (Bernstein 1997d).

B. REDISTRICTING IN NEW YORK CITY

In 1989, prompted by lawsuits charging racial discrimination and violation of the U.S. Constitution, the New York City Charter was amended to increase the number of city council districts from 35 to 51, a change intended to improve the political representation of minorities. Working from 1990 to 1991, a Districting Commission held a series of public hearings and crafted new council districts.

In the 1991 city council elections following redistricting, Asian Pacific American candidates failed in their attempt to become the representative of the Chinatown district, which contained the city's largest concentration of Asian Pacific Americans. In contrast, the number of African Americans and Latinos on the council increased dramatically from 26 to 41 percent (from 9 to 21), raising the question of why the districting process apparently worked for those two groups, but failed for Asian Pacific Americans.

Asian Pacific Americans agreed that Chinatown should be kept intact within a district and criticized past redistricting efforts which fragmented the community and diluted their electoral strength (Chong 1990; Fung 1990; Lam, N. 1990). Developing criteria to define Chinatown, studies presented to the Districting Commission focused on population, housing, schools, social services, employment, industry, organizations, and commercial enterprises. The "core of Chinatown" was contained in 8 contiguous census tracts (6, 8, 16, 18, 25, 27, 29, 41), and Asian Pacific Americans constituted over 70 percent of the area's population (New York Chinatown History Project 1990; Fung 1991; Koo 1990a).

Chinatown, located in Lower Manhattan, occupies prime real estate, a few blocks north of City Hall, with Wall Street and the World Trade Center a short distance to the south. The increasingly popular residential and entertainment districts, Soho and Tribeca, lay to the west, inhabited primarily by whites, while the Lower East Side borders on the east with large numbers of Latinos and some African Americans.

Before the release of the 1990 Census data, community members estimated that Chinatown contained from 100,000 to 150,000 inhabitants based on the number of housing units and average occupancy, a population sufficient to create an Asian Pacific American majority district. However, the release of the official census data revealed the impossibility of that solution. With a city population of 7,322,564, each of the 51 districts would require a population of approximately 143,579 (as compared to 212,000 with 35 districts) and the census counted only 62,895 in the eight tracts containing Chinatown, falling far short of the district requirement. The Census undercount of Chinatown's population and the decision to increase the number of districts to 51, rather than to the minimum of 60 recommended by community groups (Fung 1991), perhaps had minimal individual effects, yet they added to the overall political barriers faced by Asian Pacific Americans.

Community activists agreed on the general boundaries of Chinatown and the goal of keeping it intact within one council district. The fundamental issue which divided community activists centered on the decision over what areas should be added to Chinatown to meet the minimum population requirement. Two competing plans emerged in the debate over the relationship between race and political representation, offering contrasting alternatives for Chinatown and its relation to the predominately Puerto Rican neighborhood to the north and east and the white areas to the west and south.

Members of Asian Americans For Equality (AAFE), a social service provider, led the effort for a district based on descriptive representation (Pitkin 1967) and the historic opportunity to elect an Asian Pacific American. They characterized redistricting and the upcoming election jointly as a pivotal moment when the history of political exclusion nationally and locally—at that time, an Asian Pacific American had never been elected to the city council or citywide office—could be reversed. As city council candidate and AAFE member Margaret Chin (1990) explained in a presentation to the Districting Commission, "It is the opportunity for real representation for communities that have too long been under represented." With this in mind, AAFE (Koo 1990b, 4) proposed that the core of Chinatown should be joined with areas to the west, stating that "Asian candidates have done better than white candidates in the area west of the core, where one would assume white candidates with a liberal agenda would traditionally be at their best." They ruled out the areas to the east of Chinatown because their data analysis showed that Asian Pacific American candidates did poorly in local elections.

A variety of community activists and organizations—such as the Asian American Legal Defense and Education Fund (AALDEF), Community Service Society, and the Puerto Rican Legal Defense and Education Fund (PRLDEF)—focused on the needs and interests of the low-income and working-class residents as compared to the middle-class district proposed by AAFE. Recognizing that no single ethnic or racial group in the area was large enough to constitute 50 percent or more of a district, residents formed an organization, Lower East Siders for a Multi-Racial District, which proposed a plan that would create a majority Latino, Asian Pacific American, and African American district (Chan 1991). The plan proposed a district with a "minority-majority" population, incorporated the bulk of their communities, and considered population growth trends. Elaine Chan (1991)—a member of the Multi-Racial District organization and coordinator for the Lower East Side Joint Planning Council, a housing advocacy group—stressed the long history of multiracial activism in the area and how that defined and reinforced a tightly knit political community. She argued that "Asians, Latinos, and African Americans have had a historic working relationship on issues of common concern: housing, health care, immigration, day care, bilingual education, affordable commercial space, job training, and general quality of life issues." Chan also refuted the assumption that Latinos would not vote for Asian Pacific Americans, noting that Latinos supported two Asian Pacific American candidates in the 1987 judicial race (Ohnuma 1991).

Alan Gartner (1993, 67), Districting Commission Executive Director, maintained that the commission members believed that the majority of the Asian Pacific American community favored separating Asian Pacific Americans and Latinos so that the two groups would not compete against one another. By joining Chinatown with areas to the west, Gartner (1993, 67-68) explained, "Ultimately, the Districting Commission opted to craft a district designed to offer the only opportunity in the city to the Asian-American community to elect a candidate of its choice." However, according to Judith Reed (1992, 777), General Counsel to the Districting Commission, others affiliated with the commission believed that public testimony clearly favored a multiracial district, contradicting Gartner's interpretation of events. The history of combining minority populations in the U.S. is mixed, with groups both voting as a bloc and against one another (Ancheta and Imahara 1993; Guinier 1991; Saito 1998).

The districting plans joined Chinatown with areas to the west and created District 1 in which Asian Pacific Americans were the largest group at 39.2 percent, slightly ahead of whites at 37.2 percent, as shown in Table 2. However, in terms of registered voters, whites clearly dominated the district with 61.5 percent as compared to 14.2 for Asian Pacific Americans. Lower voter registration rates for Asian Pacific Americans and Latinos may have offered a relative advantage for Chinatown if it were linked to the Lower East Side where Latinos also show a dropoff in registered voters as compared to population as shown in Table 2.

TABLE 2. New York City Council District 1 and 2

Race/Ethnicity	Percentage of: District Population	Voting Age Population	Registered Voters (estimated)
DISTRICT 1 (Population: 137,930)			
African American	5.8	5.8	8.8
Asian Pacific American	39.2	37.9	14.2
Latino	17.4	15.3	15.5
White	37.2	40.7	61.5
DISTRICT 2 (Population: 151,883)			
African American	8.0	7.3	8.1
Asian Pacific American	7.1	7.0	2.3
Latino	25.2	20.8	18.4
White	59.3	64.5	71.3

Source: New York Districting Commission (July 26, 1991) letter to the Department of Justice. Percentages are rounded.

From the perspective of many Asian Pacific Americans, District 1 was inextricably linked with Asian Americans For Equality (AAFE) and its council candidate, Margaret Chin. AAFE has provided a range of community services, such as building and renovating affordable housing, providing information and training to small business owners, and enforcing tenant rights. Despite its indisputable progressive and community roots, critics of AAFE charged that it had become a developer intent on following its own agenda, and unilaterally putting forth its redistricting plan reinforced that image (Jacobs 1997). AAFE's support in 1982 for Chinatown garment subcontractors against workers and charges that it used a subcontractor that paid below minimum wages reinforced the view that the organization had strayed from its original mission (Lagnado 1991). Kathryn Freed, Chin's main opponent and eventual winner, was an attorney with a history of working for tenants' rights and affordable housing. Freed adopted the platform of the Asian American Union for Political Action—whose members included supporters of the multiracial district—and its emphasis on jobs and housing and received the organization's endorsement.

While racial minorities have forged alliances with white liberals to gain political incorporation, the driving force of such coalitions—the convergence of interests—did not frame District 1 events. Chin was unable to gain crucial West Side support, and major Democratic clubs and representatives backed Freed. The influential Soho Alliance argued that "Problems on the West Side—overdevelopment, the waterfront, the West Side Highway, loft laws, historic districts...have little in common with Chinatown community's woes, such as the need for affordable housing, jobs and education programs" (Hester 1991, p. 10). The rapid growth of Chinatown received little campaign attention, although the preservation of Little Italy—currently surrounded by an expanding Chinatown—continues as a major dividing issue.

While Asian Pacific American descriptive representation was not served in District 1, Freed's efforts to gain Asian Pacific American backing and her support of working class issues transcended narrowly defined racial politics and demonstrated the importance of building a larger, more inclusive base and platform which included Chinatown concerns. In addition, Chinatown was kept intact and not fragmented among different districts, a major goal supported by AAFE and the multiracial district advocates. Chin's loss demonstrated the need to rebuild and reinforce political relations. While white voters had supported Asian Pacific American candidates in previous local elections, Chin's campaign had apparently not laid the groundwork necessary to gain the endorsement of key community leaders and failed to generate compelling issues to win the support of a majority of voters. However, Freed's election was not a complete victory for backers of the multiracial district since a major concern that drove their plans was the preservation and reinforcement of the political community generated from the history of alliances in the Chinatown/Lower East Side region. Those two areas were divided into Districts 1 and 2, fragmenting the community. Adding to the complexity of political representation, Puerto Rican Antonio Pagan was elected in District 2, serving descriptive representation. Pagan championed community safety, Puerto Rican empowerment, and his work promoting affordable housing, while his detractors argued that his efforts were intended to support the interests of real estate developers (Ferguson 1993; Morales 1991). The struggle over nationalist concerns versus multiracial alliances is also a key issue in the next case study on high school violence.

C. THE MULTI-CULTURAL COMMUNITY ASSOCIATION AND THE ALHAMBRA SCHOOL DISTRICT

The issue of high school violence in the San Gabriel Valley of Los Angeles County offers an illustration of how community members address the political, economic, and cultural implications of rapid growth among Latinos and Asian Pacific Americans. Located fifteen minutes by freeway east of downtown Los Angeles, the region is undergoing dramatic demographic changes due to international and domestic migration. Primarily white in the 1950s, the region now has Latinos as the largest group. Asian immigration, led by ethnic Chinese but also including significant numbers of Vietnamese, Koreans, and other groups, has led to a large and rapidly growing Asian Pacific American presence, adding to the native-born Japanese American and Chinese American population which began entering the region in the 1950s and 1960s. Latinos are the most powerful politically at the regional level, holding all higher elected offices in 1998. The San Gabriel Valley is the center of the largest Chinese ethnic economy in the nation in terms of the number of ethnically owned businesses.

The Alhambra School District draws the bulk of its students from a cluster of cities—Alhambra, Monterey Park, Rosemead, and San Gabriel—which, according to the 1990 Census, collectively was 1.2 percent African American, 41.4 percent Asian Pacific American, 36.6 percent Latino, 20.1 percent white. Ranging in size from 37,000 to 82,000, the four cities are characterized more by mixed rather than segregated neighborhoods. Reflecting the relative youth of Asian Pacific Americans and their higher school-age population as compared to whites, the 9,700 high school students in the district are 51 percent Asian Pacific American, 38 percent Latino, 1 percent African American, and about 10 percent white (Alhambra School District 1990). This complex economic and political mix frames race relations in the region.

By the early 1990s, racial violence in local high schools, growing conflict among parents along racial lines as they struggled to resolve student issues, and the unresponsiveness of the Alhambra School Board prompted concerned residents to reconcile their differences and join together to force the school board to act. The local chapter of the League of United Latin American Citizens (LULAC) and the Chinese American Parents and Teachers Association of Southern California (Chinese American PTA), which was based in the San Gabriel Valley, established the Multi-Cultural Community Association to end the fragmentation of parents' efforts along racial lines and persuade the school board to implement policies to alleviate racial conflict.

In the mid-1980s, a fight involving Asian Pacific Americans, Latinos, and whites resulted in a non-fatal stabbing of a Chinese student. In 1991, two more fights involving Latinos, whites, and Asian Pacific Americans were reported. When parents expressed their concerns before the school board, some white members of the board dismissed the fights with explanations of "youthful hormones" and "boys will be boys." The five-member board was comprised of one Mexican American, one Chinese American, and three whites, although support for issues did not necessarily follow racial lines in the long and complex deliberations that followed. Latino parents were also very concerned about the tracking of Latino students into non-college preparatory classes and the dismally low percentage of Latino, as compared to Asian Pacific American, students who completed courses required for college eligibility (Calderon 1995).

The members of the Chinese American PTA did not agree with the board members' explanation of the student problems. In a letter to the board they stated that "...racial conflicts led to the stabbing of a Chinese student at Alhambra High School" and in 1991 at San Gabriel High School, "Two Chinese students were victims of an unprovoked beating by a group of Latino students on campus" (CAPTASC 1991). After the 1991 fight, 225 Asian Pacific American students signed a letter describing some of the forms of harassment faced by Chinese students at San Gabriel High School—which was 42 percent Asian Pacific American, 44 percent Latino, with the remainder primarily white (Alhambra School District 1990)—and sent it to the Board of Education.

The Chinese American PTA was established in 1979. The group's history was explained during a discussion involving white, Latino, and Asian Pacific American residents who had gathered during the coalition building process around the issue of school violence. A member explained that Chinese American parents created the organization because the school-based PTAs did not meet the unique needs of the Chinese immigrant parents who included many who did not speak English and were unfamiliar with even the most basic practices of U.S. schools, such as report cards. The school district's refusal to use translators at the PTA meetings demonstrated an unwillingness to recognize the concerns of the new immigrants and created a need for an organization which could deal with crucial education issues and involve parents in matters dealing with the safety and well-being of their children. Asian Pacific American parent groups have also been created in other Southern California communities with large immigrant populations, such as a Chinese group in Arcadia, Korean and Chinese groups in Cerritos, and a Korean group in Fullerton (Seo 1996).

At the same time that the Chinese PTA was lobbying the Alhambra School Board, members of LULAC were also attending school board meetings, requesting that the school district address conflict in the schools. Tension between the Asian Pacific American and Latino parents was exacerbated by the school board's reluctance to deal with conflict on the school campuses and the attempts of some board members to shift responsibility from the schools to the parents and to pit Latinos and Asian Pacific Americans against one another. According to Jose Calderon (1995), one of the founders of the multiracial coalition that emerged from the struggle, the initially antagonistic relationship between Latinos and Asian Pacific Americans was primarily due to the misconceptions each group had about the other. Latinos wrongly assumed that the Chinese PTA could use the large amounts of capital controlled by Asian Pacific American entrepreneurs in the region, giving them much greater access to local politicians and attorneys. Although there was a strong Latino middle-class population, it was composed primarily of salaried professionals who believed that they did not have access to the same level of resources as Asian Pacific Americans. On the other hand, Asian Pacific Americans incorrectly believed that since most of the local politicians were Latino, Latinos had greater political influence over members of the school board.

Calderon, representing LULAC, and Marina Tse, a Chinese immigrant woman and the president of the Chinese PTA, worked with a number of other individuals to try to overcome the "narrow nationalist" aims of each group and combine the two to form one organization

(Calderon 1995). Rather than combatants on opposite sides of a "racial" issue, Calderon and Tse stressed that as parents with children in the same schools, they should be united by the larger goal of seeking quality education in the school system where complex problems based on economic and demographic restructuring, class differences, cultural misunderstanding, and race were grossly oversimplified as racial conflict.

Calderon and LULAC had a long history of coalition building, demonstrated by LULAC's numerous meetings with the West San Gabriel Valley Asian Pacific Democratic Club and Calderon's involvement in multiracial politics in Monterey Park. His credibility among Latinos, Asian Pacific Americans, and whites as a person who was genuinely concerned about the issues of all groups was crucial as members of the different organizations worked to look beyond the immediate issue concerning campus violence to the larger issues involving quality of education and conflict management. The Los Angeles Mexican American Legal Defense and Education Fund and the Asian Pacific American Legal Center also contributed legal aid for the students involved in the fights and mediation to help settle disputes among the parents. These individuals and organizations worked over a number of months and formed the Multi-Ethnic Task Force, later called the Multi-Cultural Community Association, and were successful in changing the school district's policy of handling conflict after the fact through containment and punishment, to instituting prevention programs which addressed the roots of the conflict.

D. Organizing Beyond Race and Nation: The Los Angeles Hilton Case

While the above three case studies have examined multiracial coalitions in traditional political settings, this case study examines a coalition building effort in an economic setting. On October 28, 1994, the employees of the Los Angeles Hilton and Towers—one of the largest hotels in Downtown Los Angeles catering to mainstream conventioneers and tourists—received a notification from the Hilton Hotel International that they would lose their union contracts on New Year's Day, 1995. The owner of the building, Hanjin International, failed to come to terms with Hilton Hotel Corporation over renewing the terms of the two-year old management contract and decided to manage the Los Angeles Hilton itself (Silverstein 1994; Los Angeles Hilton and Towers 1994). As the first order of business, Hanjin International decided to cut labor costs by terminating the union contract between Hilton and the 575 mostly Latino employees who were represented by Hotel Employees and Restaurant Employees Union (HERE) Local 11, one of the most visible and activist labor unions in the city. Coming only two-and-a-half years after the devastating Los Angeles Civil Unrest, this event had all of the trappings of yet another volatile racial conflict, this time pitting a large and powerful Korean corporation against a small but activist Latino labor union. Given the potential for a bitter and divisive fight, the incident received almost immediate media coverage and the city braced for another racially charged incident (Silverstein 1994; Kang 1994; Garcia-Irigoyen 1994).

Hanjin International's venture into Los Angeles' real estate market came at the tail end of a decade-long Asian buying spree of high-profile properties. The Japanese began the trend during the mid-1980s with high profile purchases, including the Rockefeller Center in New York and the Beverly Hills Hotel in Los Angeles. Even though the commercial real estate market was taking a steep downturn during this time, Asian investors, flush with cash from their booming economies, acquired numerous buildings throughout the country. As a late comer, Korean companies joined others from Hong Kong, Taiwan, and Indonesia and bought some of the major buildings in Los Angeles (Cho 1992).

In purchasing the Los Angeles Hilton, Hanjin Group—the fifth largest Korean conglomerate of which Hanjin International is a wholly owned subsidiary—sought to add American real estate to its massive multinational business interests that included shipping, construction, energy, and, its crown jewel, the Korean Air Lines. Hanjin Group's purchase also reflected its own sense of economic vulnerability in South Korea. With growing democratic changes and the ensuing labor militancy of South Korean workers, Hanjin Group was no longer protected by the pro-growth policies of the South Korean government that had previously banned independent labor unions (Kim 1997). Indeed, their purchase of Los Angeles Hilton coincided with one of the largest labor struggles in South Korean history when workers from Hanjin Shipping Company successfully formed an independent labor union in 1992. The Los Angeles Hilton and Towers seemed far removed from the politics of South Korean labor relations. Despite their high hopes, Hanjin Group saw its investment in Hilton drop precipitously as the Los Angeles tourist industry became devastated in the aftermath of the civil unrest of 1992. With its investment shrinking by the day, Hanjin Group, through Hanjin International, decided to take over the management of the hotel and cut costs by eliminating the unionized workers.

Most of the Latino workers in Hilton were represented by Local 11, led by Maria Elena Dorazo, who has a well-earned reputation for innovative and principled organizing in the city (Cho 1992). Fearing that the event could become a racially-charged incident in a city that saw too many racially divisive conflicts, she called on Roy Hong, the Executive Director of Korean Immigrant Workers Advocates (KIWA) and a former consultant for Local 11, to help with the case. She had called on KIWA a couple of years earlier when Local 11 and KIWA successfully worked together to iron out a new contract for the workers at the nearby Koreana Hotel (Cho 1992). With KIWA's involvement, Local 11 hoped to defuse the racial dimension of the Hilton campaign as well as utilize KIWA's two sets of ties—its connections to the Korean American community and to the labor movement in South Korea—that could directly bear on the success of the Hilton campaign. KIWA immediately signed on as a full and open partner in the organizing campaign.

Almost immediately, the coalition between the Latino Local 11 and the Korean American KIWA brought increased visibility to the campaign. To a city that was wracked with racial division, the coalition between the two organizations won political support from mainstream political institutions. In particular, the Los Angeles City Council, at the urging of four of its most progressive members—Rita Walters, Jackie Goldberg, Mike Hernandez and Mark Ridley-Thomas—used the Hilton campaign as a forum to discuss the city's race relations and to protest the loss of unionized jobs (Los Angeles City Council 1997). After celebrating this important example of multiracial coalition in a divided city, the City Council urged Hanjin International to renew the labor contract with the workers. The public and visible support of the City Council brought added attention from others, including the media (Kang 1994; Garcia-Irigoyen 1994). In this way, one very real resource for the campaign was the coalition itself: by crossing the racial line, the campaign won important political support and visibility.

In addition, KIWA used the Korean American ethnic media to rally support from the Korean American community. In particular, KIWA exploited the conglomerate nature of Hanjin Group as it went after the most visible and vulnerable part of the Hanjin Group's presence in Los Angeles—the Korean Air Lines that is dependent on the Korean American traveling public. In campaign flyers and in Korea Times editorials, KIWA implored Korean Americans to boycott Korean Air Lines to punish Hanjin Group for its bad corporate citizenship and signed on numerous social service and religious organizations, including the Korean Methodist Church and the Korean American Interagency Council (an umbrella organization of Korean American social service agencies), to commit to a boycott (Kang 1994; Local 11 1994a, 1994b). Indeed, one of the major actions that the campaign undertook was at the Thomas Bradley International Terminal at the Los Angeles Airport where members of KIWA and the supporters of Local 11 distributed a flyer that was addressed to the customers of Korean Air Line, asking the question "what will happen to 500 Hilton workers when the new year comes?" (Local 11 1994d). Coming at the height of the travel season, the campaign effectively put tremendous economic pressure on Korean Air Lines, and, in turn, the Hanjin Group.

It is critical to note that the involvement of KIWA was essential in applying this economic pressure. By going after Korean Air Lines, the campaign had effectively mounted a "secondary boycott"—an activity that Local 11 as a labor union is strictly forbidden to engage in under the Section 8 (b)(4)(i) of the National Labor Relations Act (NLRA). However, KIWA, as a nonprofit "worker's advocate organization",was able to mount a secondary boycott of the Hanjin Group (Wong 1992).

As the campaign reached a fever pitch with direct action in Los Angeles, including picketing and civil disobedience, KIWA relied on its international ties with South Korean labor unions to pressure Hanjin International to settle (Sierra 1994; McDonnell 1994). In November 1997 KIWA hosted a fact-finding visit by Nam Sang Oh—a reporter from The Korea Labor News, based in Seoul, Korea. With close consultation with KIWA and Local 11, The Korea Labor News published numerous stories regarding the Hilton campaign in Korea (Author's interview 1998). On the heels of this publicity, Committee for the Struggle to Reinstate Hanjin Dismissed Workers was formed in Korea under the leadership of Kyong Ho An, a veteran of Hanjin labor strikes. Citing both the class-based solidarity with Latino workers in Los Angeles and the long-term self-interest of preventing Hanjin Group from exporting unionized Korean jobs to unorganized workers abroad, the Committee threatened the Hanjin Group with sympathy strikes and actions in Korea (Author's interview 1998). In this sudden transnational move, Hanjin Group faced the real prospect of its multi-million dollar problem in Los Angeles growing into a multi-billion dollar problem in its own backyard.

With mounting pressures from all sides, Hanjin International decided to settle with Local 11 on January 6, 1995. In the settlement, Hanjin agreed to renew the labor contract with Local 11 and to rehire all of the workers with their seniority firmly in place (Kang 1995; Los Angeles Times 1995). At a time when labor unions had been in full retreat nationwide, Local 11 won an important victory for its 575 workers against what had initially appeared to be impossible odds. Moreover, the Hilton campaign provides important lessons and possibilities for muliracial coalition building, including coalition building beyond the nation.

CONCLUSION: Lessons from the Case Studies

Our analysis suggests a number of lessons regarding multiracial coalitions and collaborations. First, racial coalitions emerge most strongly when groups are able to set aside short-term, group-specific benefits to address more fundamental issues that can bring progressive social change. In the Alhambra School District, Asian Pacific Americans and Latinos transformed the initial issue of school violence into a broader discussion of inclusive participation, conflict resolution, and tracking of minority students. Most importantly, Asian Pacific Americans and Latinos mobilized collectively to bring accountability to the school district and to improve the quality of education for all students. Likewise, in the Los Angeles Hilton case, Local 11 and KIWA worked together under the common vision of maintaining union jobs that pay a living wage and provide basic benefits. The fact that Local 11 and KIWA was able to recruit Korean labor unions to their campaign stands as a hopeful sign that coalition building on the part of labor can cross national boundaries in this era of transnational capital.

Second, in an ironic twist, successful multiracial coalition building must resist narrow race-based politics, while clearly recognizing the importance of race in society. In the Houston case, Lee Brown consciously resisted the label of "the black candidate." Instead, from the very beginning of his candidacy, he consciously reached out to Asian Pacific Americans, Latinos, and liberal whites, consistently promising a more inclusive and responsive leadership. Members of the Asian Pacific American community had to also go beyond its narrow racial politics to support Lee Brown: a segment of the community broke ranks with City Councilwoman Martha Wong when she endorsed Robert Mosbacher. As a member of Asian-Americans for Lee Brown states, "it was more important for the community to be divided and be true to itself, than united just for the sake of unity" (Author's interview 1998). The New York City Chinatown case illustrates that voters work within a constantly changing set of conditions and suggests that AAFE—whose well-run campaign for establishing district boundaries was a success—may have counted too heavily on past electoral victories for their candidate, Margaret Chin, without sufficiently working to re-establish support in the heavily white community west of Chinatown for AAFE's redistricting plans and Chin's city council race. While the Multi-Racial District group did not succeed in their efforts to create a Chinatown/Lower East Side district, Kathryn Freed worked to establish a multiracial base and adopted their platform in District 1.

Third, building alliances also underscores the importance of building and sustaining relations among individuals and organizations that can promote collaborative efforts. Jose Calderon's history of supporting alliances among Asian Pacific Americans, Latinos, and whites in the San Gabriel Valley proved essential with the issue of school violence; and the previous efforts between KIWA and HERE, and Roy Hong and Maria Elena Durazo, paved the way for joint action on the Hilton labor issue. A history of working together, constructing networks, and building trust can help lay the foundation as new concerns emerge. Organizations play a key role in this process, forming an institutional base from which individuals can meet.

Fourth, ethnic specific organizations, rather than generating divisiveness in society (Schlesinger Jr. 1991) as the Alhambra School District case study demonstrated, serve as vehicles for community mobilization, leadership training, resource building, and an effective basis for communication and negotiation among various community groups. Funding for these groups is paramount, and such organizations as Asian Americans For Equality, Korean Immigrant Worker Advocates, Asian American Legal Defense and Education Fund, and the Chinese American Parents and Teachers Association of Southern California play crucial roles in fostering grassroots participation. Funding—including private foundations and from the various levels of government—can be problematic, however, if the allocation of funds is used to suppress critical views about government policy and/or social issues among community groups (Mollenkopf 1992). Local community groups—such as the Multi-Cultural Community Association in the San Gabriel Valley and the Multi-Racial District group in New York City—often arise to face particular issues, and disband once their goals are met. However, even though community organizations come and go, the working relationships that such organizations nurture and support are meaningful because the same individuals often play key leadership roles in different organizations over time in a particular region, maintaining relationships between diverse segments of the community.

Finally, there are important structural impediments—such as the accuracy of the census and number of districts—to political participation and coalition building. Broader participation is necessary for Asian Pacific Americans, especially in the area of electoral politics. As a way of electing representatives, single member districts have been very effective for large populations of hypersegregated African Americans and whites, but in the case of New York City and much of the U.S., the more dispersed populations—including large numbers of non-citizens—of Asian Pacific Americans make such districts problematical. Suggestions for alternative election systems need to be considered, such as cumulative voting, in which voters can cast as many votes as there are open seats and can strategically use those votes by spreading them among the candidates or using all of their votes on one candidate (Guinier 1994; Reed 1992).

The emerging theme of the new millennium is the complexity and heterogeneity of U.S. minorities in contrast to the broad overlap of class and racial positions of America's earlier history. This diversity is the challenge for coalitions as different class positions, unbalanced levels of resources and power, and dissimilar immediate material interests potentially impede coalition formation.

* * *

Edward J.W. Park would like to gratefully acknowledge Mary Ann Park (USC) and Noemi Garcia (Princeton University) for their research assistance. He also acknowledges the Southern California Studies Center (Director, Michael Dear) for supporting the Los Angeles Hilton case study.

Leland Saito would like to acknowledge the research assistance provided by Antonio T. Tiongson, Jr.

* * *

References

Alhambra School District. (1990, November 1). *Alhambra City School District 1990-1991 Ethnic Survey*. Alhambra, CA: Author.

American Political Network, Inc. (1997, November 6). "Houston Mayor: A Look at the Runoff." *The Hotline*.

Ancheta, A. and Imahara, K. (1993). "Multi-Ethnic Voting Rights: Redefining Vote Dilution in Communities of Color." *University of San Francisco Law Review*, 27(4): 815-872.

Arax, M. (1987, April 6). "Nations's 1st Suburban Chinatown." *Los Angeles Times*.

Asian-Americans for Lee Brown. (1997, October 12). "Asian-Americans Announce Endorsement of Lee Brown for Mayor." Press Release.

Barlett, D.L. and Steele, J.B. (1998, November 9). "Corporate Welfare." *Time*.

Benjaminson, W. (1997, December 7). "Brown Says His Mayoral Victory Sends Message." *Houston Chronicle*.

Berger, E. (1998, June 29). "Local Black Leaders Say Wong's Letter Is 'Appalling.'" *Houston Chronicle*.

Bernstein, A. (1997a, June 1). "Brown Cites City's Diversity as He Opens Mayoral Race." *Houston Chronicle*.

_____. (1997b, November 18). "Election 97: The Race for City Hall." *Houston Chronicle*.

_____. (1997c, December 7). "Brown Makes History in Victory." *Houston Chronicle*.

_____. (1997d, December 8). "For Brown, Ethnic Medley with Black Chorus." *Houston Chronicle*.

Bernstein, A. and Benjaminson, W. (1997, November 12). "Election 97: Campaign Notebook." *Houston Chronicle*.

Boussard, A.S. (1993). *Black San Francisco: The Struggle for Racial Equality in the West, 1900-1954.* Lawrence, KA: University Press of Kansas.

Browning, R.P., Marshall, D.R. and Tabb, D.H. (1984). *Protest Is Not Enough* Berkeley, CA: University of California Press.

Calderon, J.Z. (1995). "Multi-Ethnic Coalition Building in a Diverse School District." *Critical Sociologist*, 21: 101-111.

Carmichael, S. and Hamilton, C.V. (1967). *Black Power: The Politics of Liberation in America.* New York, NY: Random House.

Chan, E. (1991, March 21). Oral testimony delivered to the New York City Districting, Appendix 3(7).

Chang, E.T. (1993). "Jewish and Korean Merchants in African American Neighborhoods." *Amerasia Journal*, 19(2): 5-21.

Chin, M. (1990, November 1). Oral testimony delivered to the New York City Districting Commission. Appendix 3(2).

Chinese American Parents & Teachers Association of Southern California (CAPTASC). (1991, April 1). An open letter to Mrs. Rutherford and members of the Board of Education.

Cho, N. (1992). "Check Out, Not In: Koreana Wilshire/Hyatt Take-Over and the Los Angeles Korean American Community." *Amerasia Journal*, 18(1): 131-139.

Chong, B. (1990, November 1). Written testimony delivered to the New York City Districting Commission. Appendix 3(2).

Dahl, R. (1961). *Who Governs? Democracy and Power in an American City.* New Haven, CT: Yale University Press.

Davidson, C. and Grofman, B. (1994). *Quiet Revolution in the South.* Princeton, NJ: Princeton University Press.

Fainstein, S.S. and Fainstein, N.I. (1991). "The Changing Character of Community Politics in New York City: 1968-1988." In J.H. Mollenkopf and M. Castells (Eds.), *Dual City: Restructuring New York.* New York, NY: Russell Sage Foundation.

Feagin, J.R. (1988). *Free Enterprise City: Houston in Political Economic Perspective.* New Brunswick, NJ: Rutgers University Press.

Ferguson, S. (1993, September 14). "Bucking for Realtors." *Village Voice.*

Fisher, R. and Romanofsky, P. (1981). "Introduction." In R. Fisher and P. Romanofsky (Eds.), *Community Organization for Urban Social Change: A Historical Perspective.* Westport, CT: Greenwood Press.

Fong, T.P. (1994). *The First Suburban Chinatown.* Philadelphia, PA: Temple University Press.

Fung, M. (1990, November 1). Written testimony delivered to the New York City Districting Commission. Appendix 3(2).

_____. (1991, March 27). Written testimony delivered to the New York City Districting Commission. Appendix 3(7).

Garcia-Irigoyen, L. (1994, November 4). "Paro Momentaneo de Empleados de Hilton Que Temen al Despido." *La Opinion.*

Gartner, A. (1993). *Drawing the Lines: Redistricting and the Politics of Racial Succession in New York.* New York, NY: The Graduate School and University Center of CUNY.

Gottdiener, M. (1987). *The Decline of Urban Politics: Political Theory and the Crisis of the Local State.* Beverly Hills, CA: Sage.

Guinier, L. (1991, June 17). "Voting Rights Act Overview." Submission under Section 5 of the Voting Rights Act for Preclearance of 1991 Redistricting Plan for New York City Council. Appendix 1.

_____. (1994). *The Tyranny of the Majority.* New York, NY: Free Press.

Harrison, B. and Bluestone, B. (1988). *The Great U-Turn: Corporate Restructuring and the Polarizing of America.* New York, NY: Basic Books.

Hester, J. (1991, April 10). "Downtown on the Chopping Block: How Downtown's Political Future is Being Divided." *Downtown Express.*

Hing, B.O. (1993). *Making and Remaking Asian America Through Immigration Policy 1850-1990.* Stanford, CA: Stanford University Press.

Horton, J. (1995). *The Politics of Diversity: Immigration, Resistance, and Change in Monterey Park, California.* Philadelphia, PA: Temple University Press.

Hotel Employees and Restaurant Employees (HERE) Local 11. (1994a). "Will Korean Air Lines Ruin Our Holidays." Flyer.

Hotel Employees and Restaurant Employees (HERE) Local 11. (1994b). "Local 11 Struggle for Justice: Los Angeles Hilton, "Our Jobs, Our Lives!" Flyer.

Hotel Employees and Restaurant Employees (HERE) Local 11. (1994c). "Downtown Hotel Workers Take Jobs to the Streets: Civil Disobedience at Rush Hour Will Close Figueroa." Press Release.

Hotel Employees and Restaurant Employees (HERE) Local 11. (1994d). "Attention Korean Air Lines Patron: What Will Happen to the 500 Hilton Workers on New Year's Eve?" Flyer.

Jacobs, A. (1997, January 12). "What a Difference Two Decades Make: Asian Americans for Equality Is Attacked as the Establishment It Once Fought." *New York Times.*

Johnson, S. (1998, January 7). "Asian-American Heath Issues Takes Spotlight: Must Demand Better Care, Study Group Told." *Houston Chronicle.*

Kang, K.C. (1994, November 17). "Korean Groups Back Union Fight for Jobs." *Los Angeles Times.*

_____. (1995, January 10). "L.A. Hilton Owner Will Keep Service Workers." *Los Angeles Times.*

Kim, E.M. (1997). *Big Business, Strong State: Collusion and Conflict in South Korean Developments, 1960-1990.* Albany, NY: State University of New York Press.

Koo, D. (1990a, November 1). Written testimony delivered to the New York City Districting Commission. Appendix 3(2).

_____. (1990b, December 10). Written testimony delivered to the New York City Districting Commission. Appendix 3(4).

Lagnado, L. (1991, September 9). "Friends in High Places: Margaret Chin's Ties to the Chinatown Elite." *Village Voice.*

Lam, N. (1990, November 1). Written testimony delivered to the New York City Districting Commission. Appendix 3(2).

Lee, S.J. (1996). *Unraveling the "Model Minority" Stereotype: Listening to Asian American Youth.* New York, NY: Teachers College Press.

Lipsitz, G. (1998). *The Possessive Investment in Whiteness: How White People Profit from Identity Politics.* Philadelphia, PA: Temple University Press.

Logan, J. R. and Swanstrom, T. (1990). *Beyond the City Limits: Urban Policy and Economic Restructuring in Comparative Perspective.* Philadelphia, PA: Temple University Press.

Los Angeles City Council. (1997, November 2). City Council Resolution.

Los Angeles Hilton and Towers. (1994, October 28). Letter to All Employees.

Los Angeles Times. (1995, January 7). "Accord Reached in Hilton Labor Dispute."

Marable, M. (1995). *Beyond Black and White: Rethinking Race in American Politics and Society.* New York, NY: Verso.

Mason, J. (1998a, June 24). "Wong Says Health Department Lacks Diversity: Councilwoman Sees Too Few Asians and Hispanics, and Too Many Blacks." *Houston Chronicle.*

_____. (1998b, July 2). "Wong Says She's Sorry for Remarks: Official Apologizes to Black Leaders." *Houston Chronicle.*

Massey, D.S. and Denton, N. A. (1993). *American Apartheid: Segregation and the Making of the Underclass.* Cambridge, MA: Harvard University Press.

McDonnell, P.J. (1994, December 2). "37 Protestors Arrested in Hotel Labor Dispute." *Los Angeles Times.*

Min, P.G. (1996). *Caught in the Middle: Korean Merchants in America's Multiethnic Cities.* Berkeley, CA: University of California Press.

Mollenkopf, J. H. (1992). *A Phoenix in the Ashes: The Rise and Fall of the Koch Coalition in New York City Politics*. Princeton, NJ: Princeton University Press.

Morales, E. (1991, August 20). "East Side Story." *Village Voice.*

New York Chinatown History Project. (1990, November 1). Written testimony delivered to the New York City Districting Commission. Appendix 3(2).

New York City Districting Commission. (1991, July 26). Letter to Richard Jerome, Esq., Department of Justice. Re: Section 5 submission for preclearance of 1991 City Council Districts. Submitted by V.A. Kovner, J. Berger, and J. Reed.

Ohnuma, K. (1991, April 26). "Asian Camps Split on District Lines for Lower Manhattan." *Asian Week.*

Omatsu, G. (1994). "The 'Four Prisons' and the Movements of Liberation: Asian American Activism from the 1960s to the 1990s." In K. Aguilar-San Juan (Ed.), *The State of Asian America: Activism and Resistance in the 1990s.* Boston, MA: South End Press.

Omi, M. and Winant, H. (1994). *Racial Formation in the United States.* New York, NY: Routledge.

Ong, P.M., Bonacich E., and Cheng, L. (1994). "The Political Economy of Capitalist Restructuring and the New Asian Immigration." In P.M. Ong, E. Bonacich, and L. Cheng (Eds.), *The New Asian Immigration in Los Angeles and Global Restructuring.* Philadelphia, PA: Temple University Press.

Ong, P.M., Park, K.Y. and Tong, Y. (1994). "The Korean-Black Conflict and the State." In P.M. Ong, E. Bonacich, and L. Cheng (Eds.), *The New Asian Immigration in Los Angeles and Global Restructuring.* Philadelphia, PA: Temple University Press.

Park, E.J.W. (1998). "Competing Visions: Political Formation of Korean Americans in Los Angeles, 1992-1997." *Amerasia Journal*, 24(1).

Peterson, P. (1981). *City Limits.* Chicago, IL: University of Chicago Press.

Pitkin, H.F. (1967). *The Concept of Representation.* Berkeley, CA: University of California Press.

lotkin, S. and Scheuerman, W.E. (1994). *Private Interest, Public Spending: Balanced-Budget Conservatism and the Fiscal Crisis*. Boston, MA: South End Press.

ortes, A. and Rumbaut, R.G. (1990). *Immigrant America: A Portrait*. Berkeley, CA: University of California Press.

eed, J. (1992). "Of Boroughs, Boundaries and Bullwinkles: The Limitations of Single-Member Districts in a Multiracial Context." *Fordham Urban Law Journal*, 19.

lodriguez, L. (1998a, Febuary 1). "African-Americans Develop New Strategies to Gain Power: Houston's Black Leaders See Cooperation as Key to Improvements." *Houston Chronicle*.

_____. (1998b, May 31). "Local Hispanic Clout Can't Count on the Numbers: Latino Seats at Tables of Power Few in Comparison to Population." *Houston Chronicle*.

lodriguez, N. (1995). "The Real 'New World Order': The Globalization of Racial and Ethnic Relations in the Late Twentieth Century." In M.P. Smith and J. Feagin (Eds.), *The Bubbling Cauldron: Race, Ethnicity, and the Urban Crisis*. Minneapolis, MN: University of Minnesota Press.

aito, L.T. (1998). *Race and Politics: Asian Americans, Latinos and Whites in a Los Angeles Suburb*. Urbana and Chicago, IL: University of Illinois Press.

allee, R. (1997, November 5). "Election 97: Proposition A Key Issue to Most Voters Polled." *Houston Chronicle*.

chlesinger Jr., A.M. (1991). *The Disuniting of America*. Knoxville, TN: Whittle Direct Books.

eo, D. (1996, January 16). "New Voices in Education." *Los Angeles Times*.

hinagawa, L.H. (1996). "The Impact of Immigration on the Demography of Asian Americans." In B.O. Hing and R. Lee (Eds.), *The State of Asian American: Reframing the Immigration Debate*. Los Angeles, CA: LEAP.

ierra, J.L. (1994, December 2). "35 Arrestos en Protesta Laboral." *La Opinion*.

Silverstein, S. (1994, November 1). "Workers at Downtown Hilton Get Job Warning." *Los Angeles Times.*

Sonenshein, R.J. (1993). *Politics in Black and White: Race and Power in Los Angeles.* Princeton, NJ: Princeton University Press.

Taylor, Q. (1994). *The Forging of a Black Community: Seattle's Central District from 1870 through the Civil Rights Era.* Seattle, WA: University of Washington Press.

Wong, K. (1992). "Building Unions in Asian Pacific Communities." *Amerasia Journal,* 18(1): 149-154.

Reaching Toward Our Highest Aspirations:
The President's Initiative on Race

Angela E. Oh

The Start of America's Conversation on Race

In June 1997, President William J. Clinton introduced The President's Initiative on Race (PIR). The purpose of the Initiative was to examine race relations in America[1] by using the tools of constructive dialogue and study, and its one objective was to move our nation closer to the promise of building a more just society. His Advisory Board was comprised of individuals who had very different, but valuable, experiences with race in America. The seven-member Advisory Board was chaired by the distinguished historian John Hope Franklin, and it included former Governors Thomas Keane and William Winter, businessman Robert Thomas, organized labor representative Linda Chavez Thompson, the Reverend Susan Johnson-Cooke, and me.

When the President first announced the Initiative, hopes were high. Never before in the history of the nation had a President, during a time of relative peace and prosperity, placed at the center of attention the issue of race relations in America—from our past, through the present, and to the future. The scope of the effort was broadly defined, but a central theme was that every American should come to understand that improving race relations today, as we enter the twenty-first century, is of utmost importance for the generations of tomorrow. The Initiative was designed to examine current problems, understand our history, and focus on options for the future.[2]

Under the leadership of the White House, the nation had the chance to affirm and expand upon the work that had begun in local communities all across the country. In many places, the fact of America's diversity had already emerged, transforming programs and policies and local culture. Cities such as Los Angeles had already experienced the best and the worst that could come from such change. The President understood that the rest of the nation would face somewhat similar changes, although perhaps less dramatic, and that this transformation would inevitably have an enormous impact on shaping our future.

It was the end of a century, the end of a millennium, and the beginning of a new era. From my vantage point, the President's commitment to raise the question of race relations was visionary, courageous, and an assertion of true leadership. He had the foresight to expand his genuine personal interest in this matter, recognizing and acting upon the fact that his Administration had the opportunity to take the first steps to address a complicated challenge that this nation could no longer avoid.

The Idea of Moving Beyond Black and White

In July 1997, at one of the Advisory Board's first meetings in Washington, DC, each Board member was asked to make a brief comment as to what needed to be done during the course of the year. I introduced the notion that the dialogue about race in America should move toward the inclusion of voices from those who were neither black nor white. I urged that we make room in the conversations for examining the experiences of Americans who are of mixed-race backgrounds. I also urged that the Advisory Board consider the work of poets, musicians, performing artists, and others who have deepened our understanding about one another by using means that help us transcend the realms of talk and dialogue.

Not so surprisingly, the proposition of moving beyond black and white proved to be both significant and contentious. It brought out all the resentment, anxiety, anger, and distrust that has plagued race relations for so long. Despite the civil rights movement, the passage of anti-discrimination laws, the broad public education that has taken place since the 1960s, and the scores of advocacy efforts that have been started in the pursuit of racial justice, it was clear that the basic trust had still not been established, that wounds remained deep, and that a common language to discuss race in America had not yet been found.

Why should America be concerned and interested in race relations beyond the black and white divide? This question was asked over and over again throughout the year that the Advisory Board met, and the fundamental answer is that it is necessary for keeping democracy alive because it is time to stop running from the complexity of the vast heterogeneity of our population. And it is time for the complexity to be examined in our public discourse, with a full understanding that many divergent points of view will emerge and that many intense differences of opinion will be voiced.

The decision to move beyond black and white is a challenge to the dualistic approach that American society has become comfortable with when problems must be resolved in order to maintain our sense of stability and security. As a consequence, we often find ourselves in untenable public policy debates that repel, rather than inspire, innovative thinking to meet our needs. Rather than allow ourselves to clearly grasp the complexities of circumstances, there is a tendency to simplify to the point of absurdity. This simplification can be seen throughout society; the war on drugs serves as a good example. The "war" was declared at a time when the number of drug offenses in the legal system was in decline. Yet, inexplicably, panic-produced policies were adopted—policies that increased law enforcement resources, stiffened sentences, and reduced rehabilitation services and options for offenders—with the result that we now have prisons that are filled with first-time, nonviolent offenders who will remain in custody for decades,[3] their families destroyed in the process. Yes, we as Americans have grown comfortable with dualities no matter what their cost. We find it troublesome to think in terms of multiple dimensions when it comes to people, politics, public policy, and history. Thus, the suggestion that the dialogue on race move forward to include those who are neither black nor white seems to be asking too much—even as we are approaching the beginning of a new century.

Resentment about the broader inclusion of those who are neither black nor white arose because the legacy of slavery continues to manifest in the lives of African Americans today. Anxiety arose because the people of this nation know that the first public conversations about race in America should speak to the historic injustices of racial bigotry. Thus, the notion of building a more inclusive framework for race relations pushes people beyond familiar ground and into arenas in which there are few leaders, no preeminent organizations that embrace people of conscience, and no clear framework in which to discuss or develop policy initiatives.

There were numerous concerns by Board members who resisted the idea that the new century would demand a new framework for thinking about race. For example, there was concern that the unique hardships and sacrifices of African Americans would be diminished or ignored. In addition, there was concern about how public resources would be allocated if other minorities began to establish needs and make a strong case for those needs. And finally, there seemed to be disbelief about the contributions and sacrifices by non-African American minorities in shaping race relations and our nation's future. But it was apparent that the numerous concerns all reduced to one key issue: the discomfort with change. And this discomfort was brought about by the realization that such change will affect the life of each and every American.

The population of the nation is expected to experience a dramatic demographic shift over the next several decades. Non-Hispanic whites will comprise a bare majority of approximately 52 percent.[4] African Americans, who comprise about 12 percent of the population today, will grow to about 13 percent. It is also projected that immigration will continue to increase, bringing people of mostly Asian and Hispanic descent to our shores. The Asian Pacific American (APA) population is predicted to triple and the Hispanic population more than double.[5] Moreover, the information age economy is already upon us, and it is clear that the advances we have realized in telecommunications and technology will re-shape human relations and race relations in dramatic ways. The implications of this data speak clearly to the complexities of the future.

The reaction to the suggestion that it is time to include voices never before heard in broad public discourse revealed regional differences as well as interracial suspicion. The West and Southwest regions have had some experience incorporating different cultural practices and languages into their societies. For those in other large urban centers, however, the idea of emerging perspectives that are neither black nor white was hardly an issue worth mentioning. Conversely, in the non-urban East and South, the suggestion to move beyond the black and white duality seemed radical. Indeed, it prompted accusations of racism against the members of the Advisory Board itself. Thus, the first foray into forward thinking created a flashpoint.

Given this context there nonetheless still remains the fundamental question of how to move toward a new race relations framework without having first settled questions about our past. The nation continues to struggle with the legacy of slavery in both measurable and immeasurable terms. The objective data available from government and private sources confirm that opportunities for racial minorities (particularly African Americans) continue to be limited. This is best evidenced by facts that confirm racial disparities in housing, employment and economic opportunity, public education, and health status. The following facts were brought to the attention of the Advisory Board during the course of the year:

• Housing segregation continues to be a problem, with blind testing demonstrating that there continues to be discrimination by landlords who refuse to make housing available to non-whites.[6]

- The Council for Economic Advisors published findings based on U.S. Census Bureau data which revealed that median incomes for black and Hispanic families is almost half that for white and Asian Pacific American families. Despite higher median income than other racial minorities, the rate of poverty among APAs is 50 percent higher than among whites.[7] In a study focused on marginal sectors of the APA population of Los Angeles County, researchers found a high rate of poverty, with the highest rates among Southeast Asian refugees, followed by Pacific Islanders.[8]

- In June 1998, the federal government announced that a study of its procurement contracting in more than 70 industries helped to establish a benchmark for the utilization (versus capacity) of disadvantaged businesses. The data revealed that there were several industries in which minority-owned business enterprises were being underutilized. Accordingly, in its revision of policy on contracts for minorities, the White House urged the use of affirmative action programs to correct the underutilization rates.[9]

- The states of California and Washington now make it illegal to use affirmative action in connection with the use of public funds—whether for education, contracting, or employment. The passage of these laws has had a devastating impact on students seeking the opportunity to learn in public institutions.

- Working people are facing tremendous challenges, with the shift of employment opportunities moving from manufacturing jobs to the service industry and sales. This shift has hurt minority workers in particular. A recent study by the AFL-CIO revealed that African American and Latino workers are concentrated in low-wage occupations. In 1997, 22 percent of African American workers and 20 percent of Latino workers were in the service industry—the second lowest paid occupation after farm work.[10]

• The health status research reveals more of the story in that there has been an acknowledged problem collecting health data and accurate mortality information for APAs.[11] Thus, a comparative examination of mortality rates indicating that APAs have the lowest death rates across all age bands between 1-65 years[12] may not be as comforting as it seems, since there is reason to believe that the mortality rate calculations are based on flawed information. The available statistics have been limited to information from death certificates provided by coroners, funeral directors, and the census count—all arenas in which there is a strong suspicion of undercounting. This, combined with the lack of national health data for this group (due to their exclusion from major population health studies until only the last 20-30 years), suggests cautious optimism about the research published to date.[13]

The findings above are but a small part of the picture that emerged during the course of a year in which race relations in America were examined. The broad observations and impressions of the Advisory Board are contained in the report forwarded to the President.[14]

Working Relationships Between PIR Staff and Advisory Board Members

The infrastructure of the PIR was headed by Judith A. Winston, who had previously served as Acting Undersecretary and General Counsel of the U.S. Department of Education for the Clinton

Administration. Her main responsibility was to direct the talent of some two dozen staff members who were either detailed from other federal agencies to work with the PIR, or were hired specifically for the various tasks that were to be undertaken during the course of the year. For a variety of reasons, this proved to have its share of difficulties and obstacles that had to be met.

The staff included individuals with impressive academic and professional credentials related to virtually every aspect of the Advisory Board's inquiry. Several staff members had experience working on related policies and programs in various federal agencies. Some had advanced degrees in fields such as public policy, political science, sociology, and governmental affairs. Still others had exceptional skills in managing logistics for large public meetings or were brought to the Initiative to take advantage of their abilities to provide administrative guidance. Individuals were diverse in every respect—race, ethnicity, gender, talent, experience, and interest in the subject at hand. Although this broad range and depth of backgrounds and diversity represented a leadership challenge that would have been daunting for any executive, Ms. Winston succeeded in bringing the staff to a shared focus and to an understanding of the parameters of the Advisory Board's task within the first two months.

The Advisory Board decided to hold meetings throughout America, and, in retrospect, this may have been a mistake. The skills and talents of staff members were unwittingly diverted from substantive to logistical matters. Rather than taking full advantage of the opportunity to utilize the training and experience of the staff that had been recruited to the PIR, key individuals were forced to spend much of their time preparing for town hall and Advisory Board meetings throughout the nation. The amount of time invested in advance work (including outreach to local leadership, site reviews, and coordination of events related to the topics covered), not to mention review and preparation of materials for Advisory Board members prior to the public meetings, was enormous. Given the short time-frame of one year, it would have made more sense to keep the Advisory Board meetings in Washington, DC, and allow the staff to concentrate its attentions to the analysis of some of the more difficult topics and substantive issues related to race relations.

The relationships between staff and the Advisory Board were almost always positive. Each Advisory Board member had a staff person assigned to work with directly, and the Executive Director made every effort to make herself available for any purpose related to advancing the work of the PIR. Prior to every session, materials were delivered to Advisory Board members in sufficient time to permit an opportunity to preview the writings and publications that would form the foundation of the subjects to be covered during the public discussions. Staff members made certain that any questions, concerns, or modifications that Advisory Board members had would be answered or incorporated.

Although the Advisory Board encountered a fair share of criticism during its tenure, Dr. Franklin was able to lead the group through some of the most trying circumstances, bringing to bear his wisdom and dignity to the efforts of the Advisory Board. He extended the opportunity to voice concerns to those who wished to be heard, but never lost sight of the purpose of the meetings.[15] Without a doubt, the leadership of Dr. John Hope Franklin and Executive Director Judith Winston made it possible for the Advisory Board to continue its work during an otherwise difficult year.

What Should Be Done Next?

The dialogue stimulated by the PIR was only a beginning. One of the things that I learned as a member of the Advisory Board is that this is not a situation in which anyone is being called upon to make a judgment—either/or, right/wrong, worthy/unworthy. Nor are we to draw a conclusion about race in America. The story is still being told. The conversation and its many related activities are an integral part of the intergenerational work that requires all of us to take a step into the future. This is a challenge that urges America to recognize its stature in the world community as other nations look to us for leadership. It is a challenge that reflects the multi-faceted dimensions of America's experience with the concept of race. The conversation will move us toward answers about how America can provide leadership to ensure that society honors pluralism in a democracy, but this will be accomplished only if we confront the greatest obstacle to success—and that is indifference.

In my discussions across America, young people ask me why my generation is so focused on the message of injustice. They simply do not see the world in such terms and they are not moved to involvement when they hear speeches about it. In some ways I feel frustrated because on the one hand I fear that indifference will set in and the concept of "reasonable racism" will replace the overt bigotry of our past.[16] Yet, on the other hand, what I also hear is that hope has not been extinguished, that this next generation has been taught to look for attributes in people that go beyond color. They have been inspired to learn about the histories of their families and how those stories relate to America's story. They recognize where injustice and poor leadership have been asserted, and they see a society that is much improved over what their parents and grandparents lived through.[17] And it is the message of today's youth, in all its manifestations, that must be incorporated into the analysis by examining how these sentiments expressed can inform the decisions that we will make in the future.

Today's leaders must find ways to continue the conversation by understanding what the next generation sees. Our future leaders are searching. Many already have impressive credentials that reflect a capacity to work in settings that are as diverse as the imagination allows. They have had the advantage of studying in programs that were created out of the movements for self-definition, free speech, and civil rights and women's rights. They are the beneficiaries of the technological advances that allow the curious to explore all of the worlds that the Internet and cyberspace have to offer. But the opportunities to bring diverse young people together face-to-face, to learn, to discuss, and to work in the context of institutions that affect us all, are still limited. How their individual talents can inform and shape the whole is seldom explored. The fact that hard decisions are always part of living is not shared and examined with our youth. As a consequence, participation among high school and college students in political campaigns is down as compared to 30 years ago, and although volunteerism in community service activities and religious groups is up, indifference is too often the main theme for the majority. Realizing this fact is essential to answering the question, "What should be done next?"

There is a strong belief that bigotry and prejudice can be overcome with education. Access to quality public education in primary schools is essential and almost everyone agrees that our children deserve this, at the very least. For many, the pursuit of higher education is another path to hope. In today's economy, it is clear that a failure to grasp the information age concepts and skills means being left on the margins. In addition, there is the recognition that we need to utilize our technology and media to deepen insight into problems that may appear to be racial but in reality are far more complex. People are looking for the chance to come together in order for the messages and strategies to be developed. Creating opportunities to engage our communities in the important task of telling our stories, documenting our experiences, and analyzing what those experiences mean in the larger context must be a part of any strategy that is designed to strengthen the chances for creating a more just nation.

A Brief Response to the Critics

The wisdom of many cultures recognizes that the past informs the future. Thus, part of the work that lies ahead for America is the continuing effort to unearth the facts related to our past. Indeed, as that work is done, the opportunities to shape new options for the future will grow.

Though critics suggest that there is no value to continue the conversation about race in America, the circumstances we face in the next century suggest otherwise. The conversation must continue because there are many Americans who remain committed to the idea that this nation offers the promise of equality. It is the vehicle that offers the opportunity for all Americans to deepen their understanding of how their individual decisions and experiences affect our collective future. Some have had the chance to participate in conversations about race relations for generations; others are only beginning to find their way to the table. There are many more voices that must be heard to ensure the expansion of possibilities for positive participation in the domestic and international economy, for governance at all levels, and for planning and building the leadership in the next generation.

The conversation must continue in order to confront the contextual changes that are occurring all around us. Our connections to the rest of the world are growing through economic relationships, political negotiations, and international family relations. It was neither happenstance nor calculated decision-making that moved our society into this position; rather, it was the unavoidable consequence of our advancement in technology, the development of new markets, and the growth of our capacity in telecommunications. Yet, even with all of these advancements, what has been left unaddressed are the consequences of how people will respond once the successes of governments, businesses, and scientists are realized. The unfortunate fact that preliminary experiences have not always been positive—conflicts based upon troubled race and ethnic relations in Europe, Asia, the African continent, and America—illustrate that the challenges we face are enormous.

Concluding Remarks

If we are to be realistic about the future, we must accept the idea that complexities await for which there is no single best answer or resolution—only infinite possibilities exist. Thus, if we seek to be inventive and intentional in forging the possibilities that will shape our society, we have no choice but to continue the conversation. The conversation, however, need not be limited to verbal exchange. It can occur in a myriad of creative outlets, through the arts, through language acquisition programs, through child health and immunization efforts, and through self-assessment and candidate development programs in the private sector.

The richest sources of information are likely to be found in those places that are undergoing the most rapid change. Our most valuable tools in the future may not be based on what has been previously tried and tested. Instead, they may emerge from the segment of our population that has forged relationships during a time in which "the politics of protest" has been joined by "the politics of possibilities." In essence, the politics of possibilities allows people to see where the limitations lie, assess the alternatives in light of the limitations, set priorities, and work together to create new ways to meet needs.[18]

Those who called the President's Initiative on Race disingenuous, ineffective, and off-target are wrong. The PIR was not compelled by violence or crisis. It was not an initiative that would earn the politician who introduced it significant political capital. In fact, it was an effort that seemed designed to bring to light the conversations that were already taking place in local communities across the nation. While critics offered examples of inadequate progress made since the work of the 1960s by the McCone Commission and the Kerner Commission, their criticism did not give adequate attention to all the pertinent factors, including those that I have raised.

My experiences are those of an immigrant family growing up in a time when America was forced to confront the moral degradation of racial segregation and discrimination in the middle of the twentieth century. The world and society that I was born into are far different from the world and society in which I now function. At the beginning of a new century, my voice follows and precedes generations who have sought, and new generations who will seek, ways to bring our nation closer to its highest aspirations. And I, along with many others who are neither black nor white, have a voice and contribution to add to those who recognize that we still have a long way to go.

* * *

Angela E. Oh served on the Advisory Board to the President's Initiative on Race. She is currently a Commissioner on the Los Angeles City Human Relations Commission and a national lecturer on issues of race, diversity and the future of American society.

* * *

Endnotes

[1]The President's Initiative on Race was introduced on June 13, 1997 during the commencement ceremony at the University of California, San Diego. In the course of his remarks, President Clinton noted that the focus of his Initiative on Race was to help educate Americans about the facts surrounding issues of race, to promote dialogue in all communities, to recruit and encourage leadership, and to recommend concrete solutions to bridge the racial divides. See "Remarks by the President at UCSD Commencement," www.whitehouse.gov/Initiatives/OneAmerica.

[2]Recognition of the unique experiences of African Americans in this country was an explicit part of the President's Initiative on Race.

[3]For a discussion on the need for multi-disciplinary approaches to criminal justice and the complexities of race, class and economic factors see Robert F. Sampson and Janet L. Lauritsen, "Racial and Ethnic Disparities in Crime and Criminal Justice in the United States" in Michael Tonry (Ed.) *Ethnicity, Crime and Immigration* (Chicago, IL: University of Chicago Press, 1997).

[4]Council of Economic Advisors, *The Changing Face of America: Indicators of Social and Economic Well-Being by Race and Hispanic Origin.* For The President's Initiative on Race, September, 1998. This document can also be found at: http://www.white-house.gove/WH/EOP/CEA/html/publications.html.

[5]Presentations at the September 30, 1997 meeting of the Advisory Board, held in Washington, DC. Gary Sandefur, Molly Martin, Jennifer Eggerling, Susan Mannon, and Ann Meier, "An Overview of Racial and Ethnic Demographic Trends," unpublished paper presented to Advisory Board members.

[6]Testimony of Douglas Massey, University of Pennsylvania, at Advisory Board meeting on Race and Poverty held on February 11, 1998 in San Jose, California. Massey's remarks were about the problem of housing segregation. His studies document the persistent problem of racial discrimination. For blacks, he said poverty is linked to segregated housing and that discrimination is the cause of much of the segregation. He urged active government intervention to eliminate such discrimination.

[7]Council for Economic Affairs Research Conference on Racial Trends in the United States, National Research Council, October 15-16, 1998.

[8]Paul M. Ong (Ed.), *Beyond Asian American Poverty: Community Economic Development Policies and Strategies* (Los Angeles, CA: LEAP Asian Pacific American Public Policy

Institute, 1993).

[9]"White House Revises Policy on Contracts for Minorities," *The New York Times* (June 25, 1998), 1.

[10]The information prepared by the AFL-CIO Labor Research Division was presented during a meeting of the Advisory Board held on June 18, 1998 in Washington, DC A summary of findings was entitled, *The Continuance of Racial Disparity* (AFL-CIO, June 1998).

[11]Raynard Kington and Herbert Nickens, "Racial and Ethnic Differences in Health: Recent Trends, Current Patterns, Future Directions," unpublished manuscript presented during National Research Council Research Conference on Racial Trends in the United States, October 1998.

[12]Herbert W. Nickens, "Race and Ethnicity as a Factor in Health and Health Care," *Health Services Research*, 3:1 (April 1995).

[13]On June 7, 1999, President Clinton signed Executive Order 13125, directing all federal agencies to include Asian Pacific Americans in programs that address health and quality of life issues (including education, housing, labor, economic and community development). Many hope that the lack of information about Asian Pacific Americans will not persist in the future with the adoption of this new White House directive in place.

[14]The Advisory Board's report to the President is entitled, "One America in the 21st Century—Forging a New Future." In addition, the Advisory Board also produced a book entitled *Pathways to the Future*. This book provides a tool for those who want to know about promising practices that were identified by the President's Race Initiative during its cross-country travels. The programs, organizations and resource materials listed in the book were selected because they offer innovative approaches to expanding opportunities for involvement and change. The publications can be viewed at www.whitehouse.gov/Initiatives/OneAmerica. The publications can be obtained from the U.S. Government Printing Office, Superintendent of Documents, Mail Stop: SSOP, Washington, DC 20402-9328. ISBN 0-16-049944-5.

[15]During a session held on March 23, 1998 at the University of Colorado in Denver, various Native American Indian tribes staged a protest, voicing concern about the absence of a native person on the Advisory Board. As the meeting started, Dr. Franklin was repeatedly inter-rupted as he tried to explain his family's background, the special efforts that were being made to reach out to Native American Indians during the year, and the different points of view from other tribes that had met with members of the Advisory Board. In the end, the protests were made part of the record and the Advisory Board was able to receive information about stereo-typing of racial minorities.

[16]The concept of "reasonable racism" is one that speaks to the way in which we have become rational about our bigotry and prejudice. It says in essence, "My prejudice is rational (however regrettable), because all of the information I have about the other says I should hold this prejudice. It is not subtle, it is not embarrassed. It is simply a reasonable position for me to take, in light of what I know." For more on this concept, see Jody David Armour, *Negrophobia and Reasonable Racism: The Hidden Costs of Being Black in America (Critical America)* (New York, NY: New York University Press, 1997).

[17]The writings of people like Abigail and Stephen Thernstrom have documented facts that support the point of view held by these young people. The improvements in quality of life, the institutional changes in our courts and political systems, and the disapprobation of overt discriminatory practices are, in fact, positive changes.

[18]The politics of possibilities is a dynamic that is illustrated by what occurs in many immigrant populations. I first came upon this notion in a conversation with a veteran journalist who made the observation that in her day, the politics of protest served the civil rights movement well. Today, it is different and rarely are mass demonstrations viewed as effective or meaningful. Rather, it is the response of newcomers that is dramatically changing the dynamics of our country. These are people who are typically locked out of participation in society because of language barriers, differences in customs and social practices, and a sheer lack of informal networks that are often necessary to navigate the social, economic and political environs. As a consequence, immigrants will establish their own enclaves, create their own financial assistance programs through networks that are family-based, and in the first generation, invest time and effort in stabilizing the family so that the second generation can experience success.

Contributors

Contributors

Pauline Agbayani-Siewert has a joint appointment as an Assistant Professor with the Asian American Studies Center and the Department of Social Welfare at UCLA. She has focused much of her research on cross-cultural mental health practice and service delivery, with an emphasis on Asian and Filipino American populations and also does work on gender roles, program evaluation and community needs assessment. Her research includes secondary data analysis in studies of cross-cultural competence of mental health workers; Asian American gender roles and domestic violence; and minority mental health. Her list of publications includes "Identifying social support characteristics among African American and Filipino American parents with school-aged children," the chapter "Filipino Americans," in *Asian Americans: A Survey of Ethnic Groups*, and "Filipino American Culture and Family: Guidelines for the Practitioner."

Yen Le Espiritu is Professor of Ethnic Studies and Sociology at the University of California, San Diego. She has a Ph.D. in sociology from the University of California, Los Angeles. She has served on advisory committees for the Smithsonian Institution, the American College Testing, and the UC Office of the President's Asian Language Task Force. Professor Espiritu has done research on race relations, ethnic identities, gender, and immigration. Originally from Vietnam, she is the author of numerous journal articles and three books: *Asian American Panethnicity: Bridging Insitutions and Identities* (1992), *Filipino American Lives* (1994), and *Asian American Women and Men: Labor, Laws, and Love* (1997).

Tarry Hum is an Assistant Professor of Urban Studies at Queens College (New York) and an affiliated researcher with the Asian/Pacific/American Studies Program at New York University. She recently completed her dissertation on immigrant ethnic economies in Los Angeles at the Department of Urban Planning, School of Public Policy and Social Research in UCLA. She has a Masters in City Planning from MIT. Her degree research interests include urban inequality, immigrant labor markets, community planning, and workforce and economic development issues. Her publications include *Beyond Asian American Poverty: Community Economic Development Policies and Strategies* (1993)," The Economics of Ethnic Solidarity: Immigrant Ethnic Economies and Labor Market Segmentation in Los Angeles" (1996), "The Promises and Dilemmas of Immigrant Ethnic Economies," in *Asian and Latino Immigrants in a Restructuring Economy: The Metamorphosis of Los Angeles* (forthcoming), and "A `Protected Niche'?: Immigrant Ethnic Economies and Labor Market Segmentation" in *Fault Lines in a Multiracial Metropolis: Race, Economics, and Residential Space in Los Angeles* (forthcoming).

Christine Inglis is Director of the Multicultural Research Centre and Associate Dean (Research) in the Faculty of Education, University of Sydney where she is Associate Professor in the School of Social, Policy and Curriculum Studies and is also President of the International Sociological Association. She has a Ph.D. from the London School of Economics in Sociology and an M.A. from the Australian National University. She has undertaken research and policy evaluation in migration and ethnic relations in Australia with a particular focus on the Asia Pacific region. Current research interests include examining the impact of Asian immigration on Australian institutions and a comparison of the migration and settlement patterns of Chinese and British professionals. Recent publications include: "Middle Class Migration: New Considerations in Research and Policy" (1999) in *The Future of Australian Multiculturalism* edited by G. Hage and R. Couch; "Australia" and "Papua New Guinea" (1998) in L. Pan ed. *The Encyclopedia of the*

Chinese Overseas; *Multiculturalism: New Policy Responses to Diversity* (1996); and (with D. Ip and C.T. Wu) "Concepts of Citizenship and Identity Among Recent Asian Immigrants in Australia," *Asian and Pacific Migration Journal* (1997).

Robert George Lee is Associate Professor of American Civilization at Brown University. He previously served as Associate Director of the Brown University Center for the Study of Race and Ethnicity in America and has been chair of the Rhode Island State Advisory Committee to the United States Commission on Civil Rights. Professor Lee has written on a wide range of topics in Asian American history and literature. He is the editor of *Dear Miye, Letters Home From Japan 1939-47* (Stanford University Press 1996) and the author of *Orientals: Asian Americans in Popular Culture* (Temple University Press, 1999).

Taeku Lee is Assistant Professor of Public Policy at Harvard's John F Kennedy School of Government. A political scientist by training, he specializes in public opinion, racial politics, social movements, and social policy. His forthcoming book, *Two Nations, Separate Grooves*, examines the mobilization and activation of public beliefs on race during the Civil Rights Movement. Lee also writes on Asian Pacific American politics with a special focus on the racialization of Chinese Americans during the campaign finance controversy and the measurement and significance of anti-Asian attitudes. Lee holds degrees from the University of Michigan, Harvard University, and the University of Chicago. At Harvard, he is affiliated with the Malcolm Wiener Center for Social Policy, the Joan Shorenstein Center on the Press, Politics, and Public Policy, Harvard's Program in Health Policy, and its new Multi-disciplinary Program on Inequality and Social Policy. He is on leave during the 1999-2000 academic year as a Robert Wood Johnson Health Policy Scholar at Yale University.

Angela E. Oh is a trial attorney who is currently engaged in writing and public lectures on a wide spectrum of issues related to race, diversity, and American society. She serves as a Commissioner on the Los Angeles City Human Relations Commission and is a Trustee or Board Board Member for several organizations. Ms. Oh was a partner at the Los Angeles law firm of Beck, De Corso, Daly, Barrera & Oh until June 1997, when she was appointed by President Clinton to the President's Initiative on Race. At the conclusion of her appointment, she turned her focus from the law in order to expand the depth of the race dialogue across the nation. From January to June 1999, she was a Lecturer, Visiting Scholar, and Lawyer-in-Residence at UCLA. Ms. Oh continues to address audiences at universities, government agencies, professional and private organizations, and business enterprises. Her speeches and writings reflect the opportunities and challenges of America's diversity in the 21st century.

Michael Omi is associate professor of Ethnic Studies at the University of California, Berkeley. He received an A.B. in Sociology from the University of California, Berkeley and a Ph.D. in Sociology from the University of California, Santa Cruz. Along with Howard Winant, he is the author of *Racial Formation in the United States* (2nd edition, 1994) and numerous articles on racial theory and politics. He has also written about right-wing political movements ("Shifting the Blame: Ideology and Politics in the Post-Civil Rights Era, *Critical Sociology* (Fall 1992); Asian Americans and race relations ("Situating Asian Americans in the Political Discourse on Affirmative Action," *Representations,* Number 55 (Summer 1996), and the U.S. Census ("Racial Identity and the State: The Dilemmas of Classification," *Law & Inequality*, Volume XV, Number 1 (Winter 1997). He is currently completing a study of the emerging practices of anti-racist organizations in the United States. In 1990, he was the recipient of Berkeley's Distinguished Teaching Award.

Paul M. Ong is Professor of Social Welfare and Urban Planning at UCLA's School of Public Policy and Social Research and Director of the Lewis Center for Regional Policy Studies. He has a Master's degree in urban planning from the University of Washington and a Ph.D. in economics from the University of California, Berkeley. Professor Ong has done research on the labor market status of minorities and immigrants, displaced workers, and work and welfare. His publications include "Race and Employment Dislocation in California's Aerospace Industry" (with Lawerence, 1995), "Spatial Mismatch or Automobile Mismatch? An Examination of Race, Residence, and Commuting in the U.S. Metropolitan Areas" (with Taylor, 1995), "Work and Car Ownership Among Welfare Recipients" (1996), "The Labor Market: Immigrant Effects and Racial Disparities" (with Valenzula, 1996), "Income and Racial Inequality in Los Angeles" (with Blumenberg, 1997), "Subsidized Housing and Work Among Welfare Recipients" (1998), *The State of Asian Pacific America: Economic Diversity, Issues and Policies* (1994), *The New Asian Immigration in Los Angeles and Global Restructuring* (1994), and *The Impacts of Affirmative Action: Policies & Consequences for California* (1999).

Edward J.W. Park is the Director of Asian Pacific American Studies Program at the Loyola Marymount University in Los Angeles. He received his Ph.D. in Ethnic Studies and a Master's degree in City Planning, both at the University of California at Berkeley. His research topics include Asian American politics, ethnic economy, and race relations. He currently serves on the Program Committee of the Korean American Museum and the Advisory Panel of the L.A. as Subject Project of the Getty Research Institute. His publications include "Competing Visions: Political Formation of Korean Americans in Los Angeles, 1992-1997" (*Amerasia Journal*, 1998); "Friends or Enemies?:

Generational Politics in the Korean American Community in Los Angeles" (*Qualitative Sociology*, 1999); "Racial Ideology and Hiring Decisions in Silicon Valley" (*Qualitative Sociology*, 1999); "Asians Matter: Asian Americans and the High Technology Industry in Silicon Valley" (in *The State of Asian Pacific America: Reframing the Immigration Debate*, 1996); and "A New American Dilemma?: Asian Americans and Latinos in Race Relations Theorizing (with John S.W. Park, *Journal of Asian American Studies*, 1999).

Shamit Saggar is a Senior Lecturer in Government at Queen Mary & Westfield College, University of London. He was awarded his Ph.D. at the University of Essex in 1989. He has held faculty posts at the Universities of Essex and Liverpool. He is currently on leave from QMW and holds a John Adam Fellowship at the Institute of United States Studies of the School of Advanced Studies, University of London, where he is working on an intellectual history of Anglo-American race relations. His main research and applied interests are British politics, ethnic minority political participation, comparative immigration policies, think-tanks and advocacy groups, urban regeneration, and regulation policy. His next book, *Race and Representation*, will be published by Macmillan Press in 2000. Dr Saggar's previous books include: *Race and Public Policy* (Avebury, 1991), *Race and Politics in Britain* (Harvester Wheatsheaf, 1992), *The General Election 1997: Ethnic Minorities and Electoral Politics* (CRE, 1998), and *Race and British Electoral Politics* (ed) (UCL Press, 1998).

Leland T. Saito is Associate Professor of Ethnic Studies and Urban Studies and Planning at the University of California, San Diego. He received his Ph.D. in Sociology from the University of California, Los Angeles. His research and publications focus on urban politics, economic development, and race relations among Asian Americans,

Latinos, and Whites in multiracial communities, particularly in Los Angeles, New York City, and San Diego. He has written numerous articles on these topics and a book, *Race and Politics: Asian Americans, Latinos, and Whites in a Los Angeles Suburb* (1998). He has served on advisory committees on race relations and urban economic development, including committees established by the Lieutenant Governor of California and the city of San Diego.

Karen Umemoto, Ph.D., is an assistant professor in the Department of Urban and Regional Planning at the University of Hawai'i at Manoa. She received her Master's degree in Asian American Studies at the University of California at Los Angeles (1987) and her doctorate in Urban Studies from the Massachusetts Institute of Technology (1998). Her general area of interest is planning and governance in a multicultural society with a focus on race relations and racial conflict. Her publications include "A Profile of Race-bias Hate Crimes in Los Angeles County" (with Mikami, 1999), "Blacks and Koreans in Los Angeles: The Case of LaTasha Harlins and Soon Ja Du" (1994) and "Life and Work in the Inner City" and "Diversity Within a Common Agenda" (with Ong, 1994). Her areas of research include hate crimes, gang violence and community building. She is currently a consultant for the National Institutes Against Hate Crimes, a program of the Museum of Tolerance in Los Angeles.

Michela Zonta is a doctoral student at the Department of Urban Planning, UCLA, and a researcher at the Lewis Center for Regional Policy Studies, UCLA. She was previously a researcher at the Istituto Superiore di Sociologia (Institute of Sociological Research) in Milan, Italy, where she published a number of reports on Italian metropolitan development and governance, including the final demographic and socio-economic report for the New Master Plan of the City of Turin, and the analysis of Italian metropolitan areas for the Ministry of Urban Areas, in view of the administrative establishment of metropolitan areas in Italy. She holds a Master in Urban Planning from UCLA. Her research interests include residential segregation among ethnic and racial groups, the history of the built environment, federal housing policies, and Welfare Reform.

Leadership Education for Asian Pacifics, Inc. (LEAP)

Leadership Education for Asian Pacifics, Inc. (LEAP) is a national, non-profit, nonpartisan, community-based organization based in Los Angeles, California. Founded in 1982, LEAP's mission is to achieve full participation and equality for Asian Pacific Americans through leadership, empowerment and policy. With a wealth of information on Asian Pacific Americans and a national reputation as a leading Asian Pacific American organization, LEAP continues to raise the visibility and leadership effectiveness of Asian Pacific Americans.

Through its Leadership Management Institute, LEAP has trained tens of thousands of people nationwide — university and high school students as well as individuals in the community, public, and private sectors —and remains the only Asian Pacific American organization offering extensive leadership and cultural diversity training programs and services. LEAP is also the founder of the Asian Pacific American Public Policy Institute, the only national center devoted to analyzing policy issues impacting Asian Pacific Americans, and the Community Development Institute, a national effort to build the leadership capacity of Asian Pacific American communities.

BOARD OF DIRECTORS (1998–2000)

Alvenia Rhea Albright, American Express
Ghulam Bombaywala, Fivestar Restaurants
Ming Chang, MEC International, LLC
J.T. (Ted) Childs, Jr, IBM
Rockwell Chin, NYC Commission on Human Rights
Muzaffar Chishti, UNITE!
Vishakha Desai, The Asia Society
Erwin Furukawa, Pacific Bell
Harry Gee, Law Office of Harry Gee
Patrick Hayashi, University of California
Clinton Helenihi, Community Activist
Kenton Ho, TRW
Kenneth Kasamatsu, California Bank & Trust
David L. Kim, Anheuser-Busch Companies, Inc.
Janice Koyama, University of California, Los Angeles
Ngoan Thi Le, Illinois Dept. of Human Services
William H. "Mo" Marumoto, Boyden, Inc.
Cao O, Asian American Federation of New York
Frank Quevedo, Southern California Edison
Prany Sananikone, University of California, Irvine
Diana Sun, Capital One
William Tamayo, Attorney at Law
Tritia Toyota, KCBS-TV
Peter Wiersma, Asian Business Ventures
Sou Wong-Lee, Raytheon Systems Company
Helen Zia, Author & Community Activist

J.D. Hokoyama, President & Executive Director

STAFF

Linda Akutagawa, Director of External Relations
Christine Itano, Director of Training
Glenn Kawafuchi, Vice President for Leadership
Gena Lew, Director of Development
Dean Mimura, Information Technology Specialist
Grant Sunoo, Administrative Assistant
Melissa Szeto, Development Associate
Grace Toy, Director of Finance and Administration
Jill Tsutsui, Program Coordinator

CONSULTANTS

Fatima Bustos-Choy, Gaia Flow Consulting
Alan Kumamoto, Kumamoto Associates
John Y. Tateishi, Tateishi/Shinoda & Associates

LEAP

Leadership Education for Asian Pacifics, Inc.
327 East Second Street, Suite 226
Los Angeles, CA 90012-4210
Tel: 213-485-1422   **Fax:** 213-485-0050
Email: leap@leap.org   **Web:** www.leap.org

UCLA Asian American Studies Center

The UCLA Asian American Studies Center, founded in 1969, is the largest and most comprehensive program of its kind in the nation, focusing on the historical, contemporary, and future status and experiences of Asian and Pacific Islander Americans. The Center has active multi-disciplinary core programs in basic, applied, and policy research, undergraduate and graduate teaching, publications, video documentation and new media technology, archival and library acquisitions, student leadership development, joint university-community research projects, and public educational activities. Annually, it offers over 70 classes, which enroll over 3,000 students in its BA and MA programs. The Center's Press publishes Amerasia Journal, the leading interdisciplinary journal for the field of Asian American Studies, as well as other major reports, publications, CD-ROMs, videos in public policy, the arts and humanities, the professional disciplines, and the social sciences. The Center attracts scholars, writers, artists, decision-makers, and students from across the nation and world, who use its extensive library and archival holdings in Asian American Studies, and consultant with the Center's distinguished faculty and staff. It also maintains close working relationships with organizations, museums, media, and social services agencies in Southern California and throughout the country.

UCLA Asian American Studies Center, Faculty Advisory Committee, 2000

James Lubben, *Chair; Social Welfare*
Pauline Agbayani-Siewert, *Social Welfare*
Emil Berkanovic, *Public Health*
Mitchell Chang, *Education*
Lucie Cheng, *Sociology*
King-Kok Cheung, *English*
Clara Chu, *Library and Information Studies*
Cindy Fan, *Geography*
Gaurang Mitu Gulati, *Law*
Nancy Harada, *Medicine*
Wei-Yin Hu, *Economics*
Yuji Ichioka, *History*
Marjorie Kagawa-Singer, *Public Health*
Jerry Kang, *Law*
Snehendu Kar, *Public Health*
Harry Kitano, *Emeritus, Social Welfare*
Vinay Lal, *History*
Rachel Lee, *English*
Jinqi Ling, *English*
David Wong Louie, *English*
Mitchell Maki, *Social Welfare*
Takeshi Makinodan, *Medicine*
Valerie Matsumoto, *History*
Ailee Moon, *Social Welfare*
Robert Nakamura, *Film and Television*
Kazuo Nihira, *Psychiatry*
Paul Ong, *Urban Planning*
William Ouchi, *Management*
Geraldine Padilla, *Nursing*
Kyeyoung Park, *Anthropology*
Michael Salman, *History*

Shu-Mei Shih, *East Asian Studies*
David Takeuchi, *Psychiatry*
James Tong, *Political Science*
Cindy Yee-Bradbury, *Psychology*
Henry Yu, *History*
Min Zhou, *Sociology*
Don Nakanishi, *Director; Education*

UCLA Asian American Studies Center Staff, 2000
Don T. Nakanishi, *Director*
Robert A. Nakamura, *Associate Director/EthnoCommunications*
Enrique dela Cruz, *Assistant Director/Curriculum*
Christine Wang, *Center Management Coordinator*
Cathy Castor, *Center Office Manager*
Marjorie Lee, *Reading Room Coordinator*
Judy Soo Hoo, *RR Assistant Coordinator*
Jennifer Kim, *Assistant Director; Center for EthnoCommunications*
Russell C. Leong, *Publications/Amerasia Journal Editor*
Glenn Omatsu, *Amerasia Journal Associate Editor/Crosscurrents*
Mary Uyematsu Kao, *Publications Coordinator*
Charles Ku, *Publications Business Manager*
Meg Malpaya Thornton, *Student/Community Projects Coordinator*
Sefa Aina, *SCP Assistant/Coordinator*
Yuji Ichioka, *Associate Research and Adjunct Professor*
Irene Soriano, *Curriculum Assistant*

UCLA Asian American Studies Center
3230 Campbell Hall
405 Hilgard Avenue
Los Angeles, California 90095-1546
web site: http://www.sscnet.ucla.edu/aasc

TEL.: (310) 825-2974
FAX: (310) 206-9866
E-mail: dtn@ucla.edu

OTHER PUBLICATIONS BY THE
LEAP ASIAN PACIFIC AMERICAN PUBLIC POLICY INSTITUTE
AND UCLA ASIAN AMERICAN STUDIES CENTER

THE STATE OF ASIAN PACIFIC AMERICAN SERIES

REFRAMING THE IMMIGRATION DEBATE

This study examines the socioeconomic impact of Asian immigrants and formulates new ways of viewing immigration in a constantly-evolving global environment. Specific emphasis is placed on the participation of immigrants in the nation's education system, entrepreneurial sector, and political process. 1996/322 pp/$17

ECONOMIC DIVERSITY, ISSUES & POLICIES

A report that documents the labor, immigration and education patterns that shaped the diverse Asian Pacific American population. The study also examines key sectors of the economy heavily impacted by Asian Pacific Americans and shows how APAs can transform major public policy debates over economic restructuring. 1994/305 pp/$15

POLICY ISSUES TO THE YEAR 2020

This report forecasts a near tripling of the Asian Pacific American population by the year 2020 and examines the profound implications of these demographic changes for national public policy. APA experts offer policy analysis and recommendations in a range of areas, including race relations and civil rights, education, health, labor, media, and the arts. 1993/318 pp/$15

OTHER TITLES

BEYOND ASIAN AMERICAN POVERTY:
COMMUNITY ECONOMIC DEVELOPMENT POLICIES & STRATEGIES

This study examines the needs of low-income Asian Pacific communities in Los Angeles and offers community economic development strategies and recommendations in the areas of housing, job training, workers' rights, and small business development. 1993/171 pp/$12

COMMON GROUND:

PERSPECTIVES ON AFFIRMATIVE ACTION... AND ITS IMPACT ON APAS

A compilation of essays written by prominent Asian Pacific American business, government, and community leaders that examines the issues and far-reaching implications of affirmative action. 1995/44 pp/$3

COMING SOON IN 2000

POLICY ISSUES TO THE YEAR 2020, 2ND EDITION

Based on new demographic data, this report contains updates of the original policy monographs, as well as new chapters addressing current policy issues impacting APAs, such as the campaign finance reform debate, the Hawaiian sovereignty movement, high technology business development, and racial stereotyping in the media.

THE LESSONS OF PARCEL C: REFLECTIONS ON COMMUNITY LAWYERING

The first volume of a new series exploring the intersections between legal research and public policy, this report documents Boston Chinatown's organizing experience in its battle to wrangle Parcel C from institutional expansion and preserve it for community use.

For more information or to order, contact:

LEAP Asian Pacific American Public Policy Institute

c/o Leadership Education for Asian Pacifics, Inc. (LEAP)

327 East Second Street, Suite 226

Los Angeles, CA 90012-4210

Tel: 213-485-1422

Fax: 213-485-0050

Email: leap@leap.org

To better serve the needs of our readers, your answers to the following questions are greatly appreciated.

How did you learn of this publication?
❏ Friend/Colleague
❏ Teacher/Professor
❏ Internet/Web
❏ Newspaper:
❏ Magazine:
❏ Event (please specify): _____
❏ Other (please specify): _____

Did you purchase this book for:
❏ Work/business (if yes, please answer questions below)
❏ Personal interest
❏ School
❏ Other (please specify): _____

Which of the following best describes your work?
Check all that apply:
❏ Business/Professional
❏ Civil rights/social justice
❏ Cultural preservation
❏ Economic development
❏ Education
❏ Government/Politics
❏ Health
❏ Leadership/Training
❏ Social services
❏ Other (please specify): _____

What population(s) does your work most impact?
Check all that apply
❏ Asian Pacific American
❏ Cambodian
❏ Chinese
❏ Filipino
❏ Hmong
❏ Japanese
❏ Korean
❏ Laotian
❏ Pacific Islander
❏ South Asian
❏ Vietnamese
❏ Other: _____

❏ Black/African American
❏ Hispanic/Latino
❏ Native American
❏ White/Caucasian

❏ Immigrants/refugees
❏ Youth
❏ Elderly
❏ Low-income
❏ Small business/entrepreneur
❏ Other (please specify): _____

Please add me to LEAP's mailing list

Name _____
Title _____
Organization _____
Mailing Address _____
City _____
State _____
Zip _____
Phone _____
Fax _____
Email _____

Please return to LEAP: 327 E. Second St. Ste. 226, Los Angeles, CA 90012 4210